The Fire of Orhowyn

Table of Contents

The Fire of Orhowyn

Bounders, Volume 1
Saoirse Temple

Published by Saoirse Temple, 2025

THE FIRE OF ORHOWYN

First edition. September, 2025
Copyright ©2025 Saoirse Temple
ISBN: 978-1-0697505-4-9
Written by Saoirse Temple

Also by Saoirse Temple

<u>Bounders Series</u>

The Fire of Orhowyn (Book 1)

<u>Dear Diary Style Files</u>

Dear Diary; Punctuation Can't Save the World (But It Did Save Grandma)

Dear Diary; I have 99 Problems and All of Them Are Numbers

Dear Diary; I Think the Alphabet is Gaslighting Me

Dear Diary; I've Committed a Capital Offence

Dear Diary; I Don't Think That Word Means What I Think It Means

SAOIRSE TEMPLE

For Susan S.

Prologue

Sok followed the deer path through Braydon Wood to the Well of the Ancients. The velvety night sky was dusted with stars that glittered like flakes of gold between parting clouds. The trees, stirred by the chilly autumn breeze, whispered softly of the coming winter season. Sok breathed in the crisp night air, filling his entire being with the glorious scent of the rain-soaked earth. This was his favourite time of year. The world was cooling down. The days were growing shorter. The heavy work of summer was almost done and soon he could look forward to the Dragonfoil burnings. As a young elf, about to come of age, Sok still felt the thrill of seeing the Dragonfoil trees burst into flame and crumble to ash as they did every fall only to grow again in the spring.

He stepped out from the trees into the clearing where the Well of the Ancients stood. More of a pool than a well, the Well of the Ancients was fed by a natural spring and ringed by eleven small standing stones, each carved with symbols of elven magic. He was there that night to receive his guild assignment from the ancestors—a personal ritual that all young elves were required to participate in. That night, he would discover his destiny.

He paused before the well, uncertain of what to expect. He had no desire to enter any guild. To do so would mean being bound for life to one craft. He might never be able to travel the world or be free to explore his passions. Whatever the Ancients decided for him would become the only path he'd walk. But the Elders were waiting. Already, the guilds were preparing for his induction into whichever one the Ancients chose for him. As much as he longed to, he couldn't put it off any longer.

Typically, the elves brought trinkets, gems or small carvings that they would drop into the well. Sometimes, they brought wildflowers or offerings of food that they placed next to the standing stones. Occasionally, they offered moon wine, which they poured from a goblet onto the ground next to the well. But Sok had something different with him that night: eleven Dragonfoil leaves, one for each of the well's standing stones. And instead of placing them on the stones, as tradition dictated, he let the silvery, purple-blue leaves fall from his hands into the water.

There was no specific ritual to follow when making an offering to the Ancients; each elf was free to make the offering in any way that felt right. Aside from not putting food or plants into the water, there were no other rules. Sok had no idea what would happen when he broke that one. Being rather more curious and somewhat more rebellious than was cared for by the Elders, Sok tended to follow his heart. And his heart said to drop the Dragonfoil leaves into the water.

Thus, he was more than a little disappointed when nothing happened. The leaves simply did what leaves simply do when they land on water. They floated. Sok watched for a while, thinking that it might take a little time for a reaction to occur. But the Dragonfoil leaves merely drifted on the surface, pushed by the chilly autumn breeze toward the edge.

Sok sighed at the anticlimax. He had anticipated a spectacular alchemy to occur. The Dragonfoil leaves in the Well of Ancients should have... done something.

He knew the legend of the Dragonfoil, as it had been told to him, by heart. Many centuries before a knight named Orhowyn Bravvenshyn conquered the great dragon, Xzynthyrius Dreamfinder. As the dragon lay dying, his blood, and thus his magic, seeped into the earth and from it the first Dragonfoil tree grew. Every autumn the leaves took on the colour of Xzynthyrius Dreamfinder' scales and when the last leaf fell from the branches, the tree was consumed by dragon fire, serving as a reminder of the dragon's great power over the land.

Sok was sure that combining the Dragonfoil leaves and the water in the Well of the Ancients would invoke something. But it seemed, as he gazed into the crystalline waters, that he had been mistaken.

His disinterest in joining a guild had been a source of trouble for Sok. While his peers spent their time visiting the Guild Houses and learning all they could about the trades and crafts each house was expert in, he preferred to wander the streets of Colwygshire and sit in at Court while King Gnik presided over the petitions brought forward by his subjects. His fascination with the humans was frowned upon by the

Elders and he was constantly being reprimanded for it. Even that night, as he set out for the Well of the Ancients, he'd been warned not to tamper with the wishes of the Ancestors.

He kneeled down and rested his elbows on two of the standing stones, then rested his chin on his arms as he gazed at the Dragonfoil leaves. The stars reflected in the water along with the silvery shimmer of the leaves made the well look like a pool of jewels. Sok was tempted to reach in and drag his fingers through the water and he wondered what would happen if he did. No one had ever expressly forbidden him to touch the water. Maybe it wasn't the offerings that mattered. Maybe to get a message from the ancestors, he had to make contact with – possibly even drink? – the water. Sok slowly stretched out his hand toward the surface of the well.

His fingers were so close to the water that he could feel the coolness of it when one of the leaves burst into flames as it came into contact with a standing stone. Sok pulled his hand back, startled by the bright purple-blue flash next to him. He watched, half horrified, half excited as the ash from the leaf sunk in a silver spiral under the surface of the water. *Did I just pollute the well? Or did I summon an Ancestor?* Sok wondered. He continued to watch as, one-by-one, the Dragonfoil leaves were blown against the standing stones and ignited. He jumped back, ready to run and already wondering what he would tell the Elders when a phosphorescent green mist started to rise from the well.

As curious as he was scared, Sok stopped backing away and leaned forward to look at the mist. It rose higher, swirling and churning in an ever-quickening vortex. Sok gasped! In the center of the vortex, an ethereal figure was taking form.

Orhowyn's flaming armor! I have summoned an ancestor!

Sok wanted to flee. He backed further away from the well, wishing he'd never come. Hoping that whoever was rising from the well had nothing to tell him.

"Sok," said a soft voice. "Why do you run from your destiny?"

Sok stopped. And gulped. Slowly he looked up at the face of the most beautiful elf he'd ever seen. The mist had dissipated. Only wispy vaporous tendrils of it remained to dance around a regal elven queen.

She wore a simple, silver circlet of intertwining leaves. Her hair was the colour of a tropical lagoon and fell in gentle waves to her knees. Her eyes were sparkling aquamarine gems, a perfect match to her silken robe. She smiled at Sok and beckoned him to come closer.

Wide-eyed and hesitant, Sok approached. *Should I bow? Who is she? What do I do?*

"Be still, Young One," the elven queen said. "I am Reine, the Singing Queen of the Braydon Woods. You wish to know what fate awaits you."

Sok dared not speak. He nodded.

"You, Young One, will help to bring a lost child of Epoh home. You will travel far to find him and before he can return to take his place as king of this land, you will quest together to untangle the Truth of who he is. You will be one of many guides for him, but you must trust that no matter what happens, the path you travel together is the path to his birthright. You will be bound to him for a time, just as he is bound to the Dreamfinder forever by the fire that burns within him."

Sok's heart leaped with terrified joy. He had a purpose. But...

"Am I not to be inducted into a guild, then?" Sok hardly dared to believe this could be true.

Queen Reine laughed. "Do you wish to become an apprentice?"

"No, your majesty. I wish to Bound to other worlds or to serve the king of Epoh in the castle." Sok swallowed, afraid that he'd been too bold.

"Then that is what you shall do, young Sok." Reine's smile was radiant.

Sok couldn't quite believe what he was hearing. "But..."

"The Ancestors do not dictate the destiny of elves, Sok. We affirm what is in their hearts." Queen Reine paused. "And someone must bring the lost child home. Shouldn't it be an elf, like yourself, whose heart longs for the adventure?"

Sok was overcome with joy and awe and so many questions. "How will I know who this lost child of Epoh is?"

"When you see a man holding a silver fox, you must give him this." Reine held out a gold coin.

Sok reached up and took the coin. On one side was stamped the image of a dragon inside the fire of a burning Dragonfoil. Beneath it was the single word, Epoh. On the other side was the face of a human king, but there was no name, nothing to say who he was or when he may have reigned.

"So, I just give a man carrying a silver fox this coin and he becomes king of Epoh? Epoh already has a..." Sok looked back up, but Reine was gone. The mist was gone, too, and the Well of the Ancients was still again. "...king."

A gust of the chilly autumn breeze lifted Sok's long, silver-blond hair and tossed it over his shoulder. His emerald eyes were glued to the Well of the Ancients in hope that Reine would return. He had questions. So many questions.

Where did he have to travel to? Who was this lost child of Epoh? How did he get lost in the first place? What was going to happen to the king Epoh had now? What if this silver-fox-holding man didn't take the coin? What does it mean that they would be bound together for a time? And how could anyone be bound forever to the Dreamfinder? Xzynthyrius Dreamfinder – if that's who Reine meant – was long, long dead. And what would the Elders say?

When it became clear that Reine was not coming back, Sok looked at the coin again. It wasn't very well made. The edges were uneven and the surface was rough. Not a very good casting at all. "Well, you're not very impressive, are you?" he said aloud to the coin. "I hope that whoever this lost child is, he's more remarkable than you." He flipped the coin into the air and caught it before tucking it into his pocket for safe keeping.

As exciting as this was to him, Sok was not one to speculate too deeply. Mysteries had a way of resolving themselves and so he resolved to bide his time. Besides...

"I'm hungry," he said aloud and, with one last look at the Well of the Ancients, he turned away from it and returned to his tree house to look for something to eat.

Chapter 1

When Arthur Prentice woke up on that fateful Monday morning, he should have felt at least a small measure of excitement. He should have leapt out of his bed, greeted the glorious spring day with a smile and donned his new mantel with enthusiasm. He should have felt proud of his achievement. Instead, he groaned in misery.

With a heavy sigh, he tossed the covers back and swung his feet to the floor. Sitting on the edge of his bed, he rested his elbows on his knees and let his head hang forward in an air of despondency. He knew he would fake his way through the day, let everyone see how right he was for the job, show them what a great boss he was going to be... But he needed to take a few minutes to convince himself of that first.

Until ten hours earlier, he had all the confidence in the world. He had been looking forward to today, to donning that new mantel with pride and stepping enthusiastically into this next stage of his life. And then his cell phone had rung.

He had been ironing a clean shirt, preparing it for its first day wrapped around the body of a store manager, when his girlfriend's ringtone – the X-files theme – split his smile into an even bigger grin across his face.

"Babe!" Arthur answered the call expecting a personal cheerleader to be on the other end. He listened for a few moments. "What? Are you serious?... I don't understand... I thought you... What do you mean a lowly comic book store manager?... Cheryl, honey, please don't... Why don't I come over and we can..."?

And then, like his smile, his personal cheerleader was gone.

He stared at the cell phone in his hand like he'd never seen one before. The wallpaper on the home screen stared back. It was a photo of Arthur and Cheryl taken at a party shortly after they had started dating. They were smiling, happy to be together, looking forward to seeing what the future would bring. He put the phone down on the counter and stepped away from it as if it was now something dangerous. Poisonous.

A lowly comic book store?

Fox Comics was not a lowly comic book store...

Or did she mean lowly manager?

And Arthur was no lowly anything!

How dare she!

His ironing forgotten, Arthur snatched the phone off the counter and called Cheryl back. On the fourth ring an unfamiliar voice... an unfamiliar male voice... simply said, "It's over, Arthur."

He was stunned. He hadn't seen the breakup coming, but that unfamiliar male voice sent him straight into blindsided shock. The phone *was* dangerous. It was poisonous.

This promotion to store manager at Fox Comics was supposed to have launched a new chapter, not just in Arthur's professional life, but in his personal life too. He and Cheryl had been talking about moving in together and... possibly... maybe... getting married some day. Arthur was ready to settle down. And there was no one he would rather settle down with than Cheryl, who, by the way, was an assistant manager at a bead store. And then, on the eve of what should have been a great day, she pulled the plug on their plans and turned his reward for eight years of hard work into something... *Lowly?*

With another heavy sigh, Arthur forced himself to get up and get moving. He moved through his morning ablutions by rote, showering, shaving and getting dressed on autopilot. He tucked the half-ironed shirt into his jeans and reached for his new nametag. *A. P. Prentice, Store Manager.* The irony printed in black on the nametag was not lost on him as he fastened it to his shirt pocket. *Always gonna be an apprentice,* he thought, giving the magnetic nametag a small adjustment to straighten it out, then tucking his shoulder-length hair behind his ears. Looking in the mirror, he saw a stranger looking back.

The hair was dark brown, just like his. The eyes were gray, just like his. The nose was a little crooked, just like his. The lips were full, just like his. The shoulders were a little too narrow, just like his. To all intents and purposes, this was an accurate reflection of Arthur, a thirty-year-old, newly-promoted comic book store manager. With a nametag to prove it. But Arthur barely recognized him. It took a minute to realize what was so different. The man in the mirror was single. And, Arthur reflected, it didn't look good on him.

He turned away from the sadness in the mirror. He needed to make his bed. And this he did with the precision befitting a boot-camp private avoiding failed-inspection push-ups. A point of pride with him was keeping his apartment clean and tidy. His mother, Marian, had taught him the value of a neatly organized home. As a boy, making the bed had been a ritual that set the tone for the whole day ahead. Smoothing out the wrinkles in life was as easy as smoothing out the wrinkled sheets and blankets on a bed. "You can overcome anything," his mother said.

Well, there was a wrinkle in his life now, wasn't there? And what a huge, painful, confusing, gut-wrenching, terrifying, awful wrinkle it was.

Before leaving for work, Arthur stowed the iron and ironing board he had left out the previous night in the hall closet. He had been too upset after hearing that unfamiliar male voice telling him *it's over* to bother with it then. His world had shattered, those two tiny words falling on it like a bomb the way they had. It had been all he could do to stagger off to his room, undress and go to bed. Alone. And now he just had to get out of his apartment. Everywhere he looked, something reminded him of Cheryl. Her yellow sweater hanging on a peg next to the door. The spider plant she'd given him that hung by the patio door. The photo of the two of them at the Edmonton Comic and Entertainment Expo. A framed reproduction of a Daredevil comic cover from 1973 that she had given him for his birthday. The precious, ugly afghan she made for him when she was learning to crochet. How many nights had they spent snuggled under it watching sci-fi and fantasy movies together?

Arthur grabbed his dangerous, poisonous cell phone, his keys and a hoodie, and slammed his apartment door shut on the collection of agonizing mementos, each one a horrific relationship zombie, bent on devouring his heart.

He left his apartment and walked west on Whyte Avenue in the trendy arts district of Edmonton, Alberta. The eight-block walk to Fox Comics would do him good. The bright, spring morning was already infused with warmth at 7:45 a.m. and Arthur was determined to make his first day as store manager as good as it could be. He stopped at a bakery and bought a box of donuts for the staff. At the counter, he chatted with the pretty Customer Service Rep about the clement weather and how welcome it was after the long, cold prairie winter. He stopped again at a bus stop to help a middle-aged man in a tweed blazer figure out when the #4 was going to show up to take him to the university and discuss the warm weather for a few minutes. He stopped at Little's Books to pick up a copy of *a book he had ordered, and* there he exhausted his repertoire of arrival of spring in the city platitudes with the perky girl with the too-thick glasses who worked there. For the millionth time, he wondered what her name was and for the millionth time he refrained from asking her, though he couldn't say why. As always, it struck him odd that he knew her cats' names and that her brother was gay, but had no idea what to call her. By the time he finally arrived at work, he was only ten minutes early, but the *wrinkle* was far enough behind him then that he could put it away for a while. Tucking it under a sigh, he withdrew his keys from his pocket and unlocked the door to his kingdom.

"Okay, Arthur, you're the manager now," he said aloud as he disarmed the alarm and flicked on the overhead lights. "So, figure out how you're gonna manage!"

Fox Comics was more than just a comic book store. It was a sprawling labyrinth of aisles and islands, filled with graphic novels and sci-fi/fantasy memorabilia and merchandise from bobble-head superheroes to elaborate, licensed costumes from every major franchise in the genres. Need a Hobbit sword? Fox Comics had them. Looking for a first edition Spiderman comic? Fox Comics was the place to go. There was even a transporter room set up in one corner where customers could have their photos taken being *beamed up* next to life-size cardboard cut-outs of their favourite Star Trek characters.

Arthur loved this place. Every beep, buzz and whir, every flashing light, every tacky souvenir, every poster, every page in every book was a bit of magic. To him, Fox Comics was a gateway to other worlds.

He stood for a moment, surveying this haven of geekdom and delight. This was a place where whole universes existed side by side. There was nothing lowly about it. And, yes, he was proud to be the manager.

He was dragged from his contemplation by his cell phone vibrating in his hoodie pocket. He pulled it out and looked at the screen. It was his boss' assistant, Toby, calling.

"Hello, Arthur Prentice here," Arthur said, trying to sound like a confident and competent comic book store manager and not a broken-hearted sap.

"Toby Poppins, calling. Just want to remind you that Mr. Fox will be stopping by the store today around eleven." The effeminate inflection of Mr. Fox's assistant's voice, as it often did, made the statement sound more like a question.

"That will be perfect," Arthur said. "I'm looking forward to seeing him." Arthur was not looking forward to seeing Mr. Fox. Not on his first day. Not with the wrinkle threatening to fold in on him at any moment.

"Of course, you are," Toby crooned. "Tootles." He disconnected the call.

Arthur *tootled* off to a tiny room in the back of the store that served as his office. His office! That was weird. Until a few days ago, it had been Cliff's office and now Arthur was struggling to come to terms with the concept of it being his. The staff at Fox Comics referred to it as *Engineering*, because that's what comic geeks do; they indulge in making unobtainable personal goals such as science fiction space travel seem real. The room itself was barely bigger than a broom closet. There was no window and Arthur could touch opposite walls with his elbows still bent. There was a built-in desk to the right of the door. To the left of the door were two small filing cabinets and a double safe beneath built-in, wall-to-wall shelves that, appropriately, held office supplies. If anything about Fox Comics was lowly, it was the manager's office. The staff washroom was bigger.

Arthur draped his hoodie over the back of the chair and booted up the computer. He had to do the deposit from the previous day, count the cash in the safe, and put the cash drawers in the tills so they were ready when the staff arrived and the store opened at 10 a.m., a chore that would take all of fifteen minutes. As expected, the sales for Sunday were relatively low. He was neither alarmed nor surprised by the small numbers. He was surprised that everything balanced. To the penny. That never happened. Arthur wanted to take that as a good omen, but he was too raw, too hurt by being dumped that, at best, he could only dub it a small win for the day.

Once he was done with the deposit, he traded it for the cash drawers from the safe and took them to the tills. He booted up the computers and logged into the POS system. He had plenty of time before the store was to open to go through his emails and make some phone calls. Once Allen and Sherry arrived for work, he would get ready for Mr. Fox's visit. He wasn't sure why Fox was coming in, but he assumed it was a first-day-on-the-job courtesy and, probably, to approve Allen as assistant store manager, a position Arthur had recommended Cliff recommend Allen for before Cliff handed in his keys. He had a few ideas that he wanted to run past his boss and he needed to write them down so he wouldn't forget them. After that, it would be lunch time and after lunch he expected to be on the floor, helping customers and generally enjoying a relaxed afternoon. This manager stuff wasn't so hard.

Shortly before ten, Allen arrived. The six-foot, three-inch, ginger beanpole shook his new boss' hand and clapped Arthur on the back. He'd brought coffee and he handed one of the steaming take-out cups to the new captain. "So how does it feel?" Allen asked.

"Well, the first hour was uneventful." Arthur shrugged. He had a sudden urge to blurt out that Cheryl had dumped him, but he swallowed it and sipped his coffee instead.

"You'll be great!" Allen said.

"We'll be great," Arthur amended.

"So, it's official? I'm the new ASM?"

Arthur felt bad. That's not how he meant it to sound. "Not yet. Fox is coming in this morning. I'll find out for sure then." *I hope.*

Allen nodded and hid his disappointment by taking a sip of his own coffee.

A tap on the front door alerted them to Sherry's arrival. Not being a key-holder, she had to be let in and Allen granted her access.

Sherry, in high heels, bright pink skinny jeans, and a low-cut sweater blew a pale pink bubble between her neon pink lips as she waltzed past Allen into the store. Her hair was, incongruously, a poison green that morning and her eyelids were framed by sparkly fake lashes long enough to cause a breeze when she blinked. "Thanks, Al," she said in her nasally voice. Then turned to Arthur. "So, boss man, did ya bring donuts?"

"On the counter." Arthur watched her pick out a donut hole with two-inch-long, black and green nails. How she managed to do anything with those talons glued to her finger tips, Arthur didn't know. "It's showtime, people!" He announced.

Allen re-unlocked the door and Sherry flipped the switch for the open sign. Within minutes customers began trailing in, spreading out and browsing through the stacks and aisles. Arthur watched from the door to the back room, wishing Cheryl was there to enjoy this moment with him and wishing he understood why she wasn't.

At five minutes past eleven, the door opened and a silver-haired man in a dark-blue suit entered the store closely followed by blue-haired man in a silver suit and twenty feet of blue lame scarf looped around his neck and shoulders. A black, leather satchel hung from his shoulder. Mr. Fox and his infamous PA, Toby, had arrived.

"Where's Arnie?" Mr. Fox asked Allen.

"It's Arty," corrected Toby.

"Uh...*Arthur* is in his office," Allen said, correcting them both.

Mr. Fox and Toby headed for the back of the store. Allen and Sherry exchanged glances and the odd couple disappeared through the staff-only-beyond-this-point door.

"Ah, Arnie, there you are," Mr. Fox said as he approached Arthur's office.

"It's Arty," Toby said patiently.

"I prefer Arthur," Arthur said, coming out of his office and shaking his boss' hand.

"Son," Mr. Fox said, "You're doing a find job here. A really fine job."

"Uh... Thank you?" Arthur was confused. He looked to Toby for some sort of clarity. Was he talking about the last eight years or the last two hours? Toby tipped his head slightly and shrugged one blue-lame-draped shoulder.

"So, it pains me to tell you this," Mr. Fox continued, draping an avuncular arm around Arthur's shoulder. "I'm afraid that, effective immediately, Fox Comics is out of business."

What!? Arthur was paralyzed.

"I know, it's quite a shock. It was a shock to me too, believe me. But my accountants assure me that it's for the best. You and the staff will, of course, receive generous severances. Toby?" Mr. Fox snapped his fingers and Toby stepped forward to place a stack of envelopes he had retrieved from the black, leather satchel in his raised hand, which Mr. Fox then handed to Arthur. "We'll be liquidating the entire inventory and all of the store assets online over the next few weeks, but feel free to take anything you like. Anything at all. Toby will instruct the... my people to overlook any inconsistencies in the inventory." He touched the side of his nose, conspiratorially. "It's the least I can do. Right, Toby?"

"That is correct, sir," Toby agreed whole-heartily.

What is happening? Arthur stared stupidly at the stack of envelopes in his hand. The top one had his name printed on it.

Mr. Fox removed his arm from Arthur's shoulder. "I'll let you break the news to the staff. And if you could all be out of the store by two p.m., that would be great. The... my people will be in to start cataloging the inventory at that time."

When Arthur didn't lift his arm to shake Mr. Fox's outstretched hand, Toby lifted it for him. It was enough to loosen Arthur's incapacitated tongue. "But..."

But Mr. Fox was already half way to the door.

"I think you'll find that generous was a bit of an understatement." Toby patted Arthur on the cheek. "I did that." He winked and then followed his boss out of the store.

"But..."

But they were gone.

Arthur stood there. To say he was dumbfounded was yet another understatement. Nonplussed. Flummoxed. Discombobulated. All fit. None completely. This was bigger than any of them. In less than twenty-four hours, he'd lost his girlfriend and his job. In the category of shortest managerial careers, this had to be a world record. There was no reconciling any of it.

"So, did I get it? Did he say I am the new ASM?" Allen had waited until Mr. Fox and Toby had left the store to rush into the back room. "Arthur? Are you okay? What happened?"

Mouth agape, Arthur just stood there.

"Speak to me, dude." Allen waved his hand in front of Arthur's face.

"I... We... The..." The words wouldn't come. Saying them would make it real.

Allen took the stack of envelopes from Arthur's feeble grip. Seeing Arthur's name across the top one, he flipped through them to see who the others were for. When he came to the envelope bearing his own name, he tore open the flap and pulled out the contents. A record of employment, a letter of reference, a paystub and paycheque to the end of the week, a severance cheque – six week's pay - and another envelope with a card expressing Mr. Fox's sincerest regrets and best wishes for a bright future.

"Um... Arthur? What's going on?" He looked at his new and soon-to-be-ex boss for some kind of explanation. "Damnit, Arthur, talk to me!"

Arthur met his co-worker's troubled eyes with troubled eyes of his own. "Fox Comics is out of business."

"Why?"

"He didn't say. Just that his accountants said it was for the best."

The two men stood in silence, trying to come to terms with this strange and inexplicable turn of events. Then Sherry poked her head in the back room. "A little help out here, please."

"Go," Arthur told Allen. "And send Sherry back here when it's quiet again."

Allen's tall, slim frame slumped and Arthur watched a young man appear to age right before his eyes. He felt guilty about that, though he couldn't say why. He'd done nothing wrong. Though he felt like he was being punished nonetheless.

Arthur had to deal with the rest of the staff. These were phone calls he dreaded making, but he sucked it up and started dialing. Each of the four people he talked to took the news rather more calmly than he expected. There was disappointment, a little fear, some confusion. It didn't help that he had no real information to give them. He gave them each the option of coming to pick up their envelopes before two o'clock or have them mailed. Everyone opted to have them mailed. The only key-holder among them asked what he should do with the store keys and Arthur told him to just throw them away.

When he'd finished the last phone call, Sherry had still not come to the back. It was after noon already and Fox had said that they needed to be out by two o'clock. He had to get the customers out and close the store. Then he'd talk to Sherry.

Arthur opened the door leading from the back room to the main store and found it empty of customers. At the till, Sherry was sitting on a high stool, hunched over and sobbing into tissues that Allen was feeding into her hands every few seconds. Obviously, Allen had taken it upon himself to tell her that she was out of a job. Glaring at the helpless would-be assistant store manager, Arthur took advantage of the lack of customers and locked the doors. He signaled Allen to turn off the open sign and then, steeling himself to face the blubbering Sherry, approached the tills.

"Why?" Sherry wailed. "Why?"

"I don't really have an answer for you," Arthur said, quietly and calmly. "All I know is that the store is closed and we all have to be out of here by two."

"What?" Allen broke in. "I thought we had until the end of the week."

"Apparently, not," Arthur said.

"But I was paid until the end of the week."

"Bonus," Arthur shrugged. He still hadn't opened his envelope. "Look, I'm going to try to find out what's going on, but for now, let's just do as Fox says. When I know more, I'll let you both know."

"I need this job," Sherry wailed.

Arthur's fortes did not include crying females. He wanted to fix this, make it all go away, but there was nothing he could do. "Fox told me we could take whatever we want from the store." *Free stuff always cheers women up, right?*

Allen's eyes went straight to the replica Excalibur sword from the latest King Arthur movie and Arthur nodded his head toward it to let him know it was his if he wanted it. Allen didn't need to be told twice; he abandoned Arthur to deal with the snot and tears alone.

"Can I have the Zena costume?" Sniffle. Sniffle.

"Anything you want," Arthur said, handing Sherry a fresh handful of tissues.

While his distraught employees were occupied looting the store, Arthur dashed off a sign for the door: *Out of business. We apologize for any inconvenience*, and taped it to the glass. He didn't know what else he could do. Cash out? Why bother? So, he wandered over to the locked cabinet where the limited and first edition comics were kept, opened it and retrieved a rare copy of a Batman comic from the 1940s worth $15,000.00. He'd been longing to have it ever since it showed up in box of old comics that had been donated to the store almost a year earlier. While most of the comics in the box had ended up in the *FREE* bin, the value of this one was recognized and it was added to the inventory. Arthur had suggested that Cliff call the lady who had donated the box to let her know, but Cliff's sense of ethics was dubious at times. The only thing that had kept him from taking it himself was the fact that Arthur had been the one to recognize its rareness and knew it was there. A few people had looked at it, but after its value had been confirmed, it remained in the store under lock and key.

"You're mine, now," Arthur whispered. And then he headed back toward Engineering to delete it from the inventory software. *No point in taking any chances that Fox didn't include rare and valuable comic books in 'anything at all'.*

Just as he reached the back-room door, he heard a grunt coming from the Excalibur display. He turned to see Allen yanking on the replica with all his might. *Seriously?* He walked over and stood beside Allen at the display where Excalibur was sticking out of a molded resin stone. Allen had one foot braced against the stone and was pulling and pushing the blade back and forth, trying to wiggle it free.

"Need some help?" Arthur asked.

Allen continued to yank and wiggle the sword for a few more seconds. "Be my guest," he said, finally giving up.

Arthur rolled his eyes and stepped forward. He gripped the sword hilt and smoothly drew it out of the stone. Handing it to the open-mouthed Allen. Arthur patted him on the shoulder and left to complete his clandestine task of erasing the vintage comic from the system.

An hour later, Allen and Sherry, laden with bags full of merchandise, announced that they were ready to leave. Arthur nodded. He could feel the tears welling up in his eyes and blinked them away. He wasn't going to break down in front of them.

"Are you sure this is okay?" Allen asked, holding up the bags in his hands.

Arthur shrugged. "Fox said we could take anything at all."

"I'm taking Kirk and Spock too," Allen said, referring to the life-size cut-outs from the transporter room display.

"I'm sure you'll give them a good home," Arthur said with a small pang of regret for not having claimed them himself.

"You can come visit them anytime," Allen offered.

Arthur smiled and nodded. "I'll do that."

Sherry remained strangely quiet, standing back a bit and keeping her head down. Arthur wanted to say something witty and wise, but all that came out of his mouth was, "See ya around."

He let them out of the store and, taking one last look around, felt his heart break completely in two. It struck him hard that losing this was a hundred times worse than losing Cheryl and he realized that if he'd have had to make a choice between the two of them, he'd pick Fox Comics hands down. *I'm a terrible person.* Maybe he was just entering the anger stage of grief over the breakup. Or maybe this new breakup, for that's what it felt like, was just fresher.

He put the comic book and the envelopes for the staff into a bag with the store logo depicting a silver fox wearing a superhero cape, switched off the lights and, out of habit, started to set the alarm. He flipped the panel cover down and was just about to punch in the first number of his code when he stopped. It was a few minutes before two and Fox's *people* were supposed to be arriving on the hour. He didn't know who Fox's people were or if they had an alarm code. *Why should I make it easy for them?* His inner terrible person was having a field day. He patted his pocket to confirm his cell phone was there and finished punching in the code. Then he locked the door on another, even bigger wrinkle.

Arthur stood on the sidewalk wondering what he should do next. Eight blocks to his left was his apartment. But it was full of pesky relationship zombies and he didn't have the energy to face that apocalypse right then. To his right was O'Bryan's Pub, his favourite watering hole on Whyte Avenue. As if making the decision for him, Arthur's stomach growled. O'Bryan's Pub it was. Some food and some beer might just help smooth out the wrinkles. He turned to his right and walked a block to the pub.

Being early on a Monday, the pub was relatively quiet when Arthur walked in. A half-dozen people were dispersed throughout the Irish-style tavern at tables and booths, but there was no one at the bar itself. Arthur took a stool at the far end and waited for John, the bartender, to finish loading the beer cooler, getting ready for the busier hours ahead when folks would arrive after work looking to wash away one grind with a drink – or two or three – before going home to face another.

While he waited, Arthur nibbled on some pretzels from a bowl on the bar. He looked at himself in the mirror on the wall. *Who am I now?* he wondered. *A jobless, loveless nobody, that's who. Maybe it's all just a dream. Maybe I'll wake up and everything will be the way it was.*

"Oh, hey, there, Arthur. Sorry I didn't see you come in. What can I get for ya?" John put a coaster on the wood and was already reaching for a glass in anticipation of...

"Just a beer. Thanks."

While John pulled a draft for Arthur he continued to chat. "So, what's new? I haven't seen ya in a while."

"Well, Fox Comics is closed for good and Cheryl dumped me last night," Arthur said, pulling a ten-dollar bill out of his wallet and sliding it toward the bartender.

John traded the beer for the money and moved to the till to ring in the sale and pocket his portion. "Oh, wow! Sorry to hear that, man." He almost gave Arthur's tenner back. Almost.

Arthur sighed and lifted his beer to his lips. "Yeah, well, what are ya gonna do, right? Stuff happens." He tried to sound nonchalant.

"What *are* ya gonna do?" John asked.

"Find another job. I guess. I haven't really had any time to think about it." Arthur twirled his beer glass between his fingers. Then a thought struck him. "I haven't been on a vacation in a long time. Maybe I'll do that first."

"Oh, yeah? That sounds good. Where to?"

"Thinkin' maybe I'll throw a dart at a map."

John laughed, splitting his mustache and his goatee to reveal an unnaturally white set of unnaturally straight teeth. "Well, it's a big, bad ol' world out there, Arthur. Let's hope that dart lands somewhere where the women are hot and the drinks are cheap."

Arthur raised his glass to John and downed the rest of the beer. "Another, please," he said. "And a burger and fries," he added. Just then Arthur was thinking that hot women were not all they were cracked up to be. But cheap drinks? That he could go for. He drew two twenties out of his wallet to cover the burger and beer.

"Keep it, man," John said, wishing he'd known Arthur was going to order a meal. He'd have made that previous *almost* a for sure if he had. "Seems like you could use a break today." He handed Arthur his beer and told him the burger would be out in a few minutes.

This one he took to a table at the front of the pub. John was a great guy, but Arthur didn't want to chat anymore. He finished his beer and the burger, when it was served, and gave John another tenner.

"Thanks, man," John said, taking the tip. "Hey, if you're interested, one of my guys just quit. It's just part time, but the tips are good…" He held up the ten-dollar bill. "…and I'd be happy to have you if you want it."

"Oh! Thanks. Can I think about it?"

"Sure thing. Let me know soon, though. Guy's last day is Friday and I'll need to replace him right away."

"I will. Thanks, again."

Arthur hoped he didn't sound too ungrateful. After the last twenty hours, making a decision – any decision – felt like a huge risk. He needed time to think, to process things, to figure out what he should do. But the first thing he needed to do was mail the envelopes to the staff members. This felt like an easy, non-threatening step to take. All he needed to do was pay for a few stamps.

He left O'Bryan's and crossed to the south side of the street. From there, he walked to 104 Street and turned right. As he passed the alleyway that provided access to loading zones for the business on Whyte Avenue, a motion caught his eye and he turned to see what it was. A large man in a top hat was standing about forty feet away. He waved a cane of some sort, then appeared to fade and blur as he walked right into the wall of the building and vanished. Arthur did a double take.

What the… He shook his head and rubbed his eyes and looked again. Unable to quell his curiosity, Arthur walked down the alley to the spot where the man had been standing. There was no door, not even a window, anywhere close. Just a solid brick wall. Arthur touched it. It was, indeed, solid. He looked for a seam that might indicate a hidden entrance, but found nothing. *Great! Now I'm hallucinating.* Arthur left the alley, determined to get to the post office, mail off the envelopes and go home. Suddenly, the zombies waiting for him there didn't seem so bad.

The post office was in a drug store on the east side of 104 Street between 80 and 81 Avenues. There was a short lineup when he arrived at the counter. Two people, a man and a woman, ahead of him had packages to send. While the woman just paid for the fastest delivery time, the man had to question every detail of the transaction, eating up fifteen minutes before he took out is wallet and produced his debit card. Finally, Arthur was called forward and he handed the four envelopes over to the clerk, who weighed each of them separately before announcing the total. Arthur handed over his last ten-dollar bill, thanked her and left.

He returned to Whyte Avenue the way he had come, glancing up the alleyway as he passed it on the opposite side of the street. The only thing moving was a plastic shopping bag caught on spindly tree bobbing in the breeze. As he tried to recall what he thought he saw, he had the strangest feeling that there was something familiar about the man in the top hat. He'd only seen him for a split second, but still... *No. I'm just tired. My mind was playing tricks on me.* He continued to the corner to wait for the light to cross Whyte Avenue again.

As he approached the intersection, Arthur noticed an abrupt change to the rhythm of the traffic. Tires squealed. Horns blared. People shouted obscenities. A scream crescendo-ed above the commotion. He pushed through the crowd in time to see a tall, slender man leaping across the intersection between and over vehicles that were swerving to miss him. He was wearing brown leggings under a velvety green tunic and knee-high leather boots. His hair was a gleaming cascade of silver-blond that fell nearly to his waist. A bejewelled dagger hilt protruded from an ornately tooled, leather scabbard attached to his belt. His eyes were brilliant emerald and his sharply-pointed ears were adorned with golden dragon ear cuffs.

With a final and spectacular bound off the hood of a grey Ford Escort, the man landed on bent knees right in front of Arthur. He looked up and saw the bag with the silver fox logo in Arthur's hand and his eyes widened. "At last! This is for you, brother," he exclaimed as he pressed the coin he'd been carrying for eight long years into Arthur's hand. "Come! We must get to the Boundary before the Bounder Guard..."

It seemed impossible, but Sok's eyes widened even more when he saw a large man in a top hat pushing through the crowd toward him and Arthur. He grabbed Arthur's arm, pulling him into the street.

"Let go of me!" Arthur hollered. He yanked his arm free and turned into the throng of people that had gathered on the corner curious to see what all the tire-squealing and obscenity-shouting was all about. He didn't see the large man in the top hat, but he was relieved to see the slender man in the elf costume run off. The last thing he wanted was to get caught up in some street performance.

Rather miraculously, the congestion in the intersection caused by the strange man, had not resulted in any serious damage. A large, angry man on a motorcycle had wiped out and his loud, angry epithets could be heard over honking horns as the rush hour traffic was even further held up. Arthur wove his way, against the light, through the knot of cars to the north side of the street and resumed his own path to his own destination. Behind him, pedestrians and drivers suddenly lost interest in the fracas and worked to cooperatively untangle themselves from the mess they found themselves in. The traffic resumed its sluggish flow.

He looked at the coin he'd been given. It was about the size of twoonie. The image of a man wearing a crown was stamped on one side and the image of a dragon inside a burning tree was stamped on the other. There was nothing to indicate its value or its origin. At least nothing in English. There were four characters, possibly letters, stamped below the dragon, but Arthur didn't recognize the language. The coin itself was crudely cast, the edges uneven and the surface flawed. *Must be a home-made game piece,* Arthur concluded. *But who makes solid gold game pieces?* It was too heavy to be anything but real gold. He'd have to take it to the gaming shop and see if they could tell him what it was. *I wonder if there's a LARP happening on Whyte Ave.* Arthur pocketed the coin and carried on toward his apartment.

Chapter 2

Harpur Diggins had to make a decision quickly. Follow the elf. Or follow Arthur.

He decided to follow Arthur.

The elf, while certainly disruptive, wasn't much of a threat. Whyte Avenue, collectively speaking, was used to strange-looking characters running around and an elf would just be another arts district story that folks would tell at dinner. The kerfuffle at the intersection was easily remedied; a quick spell to realign a few memories and all was well again. It wouldn't do for people to remember seeing an elf jump from the roof of a three-story building and land unscathed on his feet, much less leap across an intersection afterward.

Stupid elf!

The priority now was to catch up to Arthur and set things straight with him. That coin in his pocket was a problem. A big problem. And Harpur needed to solve it fast.

He knew who Arthur was, of course. Arthur was the reason he'd set up permanent residence on Earth, the reason he lived in human form instead of in his natural state. Decisions have consequences and looking out for Arthur was the consequence of a decision Harpur had made eight years earlier. Knowing what he now knew, Harpur felt he had little choice but to stay here on Whyte Avenue and be ready... Well, for exactly what, he couldn't tell. Yet.

In the meantime, while he watched and waited, Harpur occupied himself as a Bounder Guard on Whyte Avenue, which was named after Sir William Whyte, superintendent of CPR's western division between

1886 and 1897. At the time, Whyte Avenue was the main street in the growing City of Strathcona. As the City of Strathcona became absorbed into the city of Edmonton, Whyte Avenue became a hub for arts and entertainment in what subsequently became known as Old Strathcona. Filled with shops, café's, restaurants and bars, and surrounded by theatre venues, it was a natural place for festivals of all kinds to take place. So, while ordinary folks worked and played every day on Whyte Avenue, a few extraordinary folks dropped by now and then. Generally, though, a guy dressed as an elf was just another Monday on Whyte Avenue. A potential photo op, but nothing to get overly excited about.

What no one on Earth was aware of was that on a Whyte Avenue roof top, a Boundary existed. These practically invisible - unless one knew what to look for - portals formed in places where the separation between universes is thin enough that a skilled being from either side could breakthrough, or Bound, as it were, from one world to another. They existed all over the world, with the highest concentration of them being in the UK, and were the reason that people believed, or disbelieved, in accordance with their personal inclinations, in aliens, fairies and other *mythical* creatures.

The Whyte Avenue Boundary led both to and from an Earth-like planet called Thraeh (pronounced Tree) and was geographically synchronized within an area known as Braydon Wood that stretched from north to south across the western side of the Kingdom of Epoh. Adjacent to the vast forest was the city of Colwygshire, from where the people of Epoh were ruled by a King Gnik. Because of its relatively secluded location, the Boundary was mostly unguarded, though patrols occasionally did apprehend unauthorized Bounders attempting to cross through. Also because of its isolation, coupled with the arts-oriented atmosphere on Whyte Avenue, it was a strong draw for young and adventurous Thraehlings wanting to make the attempt, a sometimes-dangerous undertaking requiring skill that could take years to perfect. Often, by the time the young and adventurous Thraehlings even came close to acquiring enough skill, they had long passed their adventurous youths and had lost interest. But some still tried. And some of them died. It was the natural Bounders that had the best chance of making it.

Petitions for authorization to Bound were typically denied, adventure not being one of the valid options on the 18-20/B, a twenty-seven-page application form that included a six-generation family history, a nineteen-point personal history and a sixty-two-day waiting period. Proof of natural bounding ability and/or a two-year bounding certification diploma from an accredited bounding school were listed as definite assets, but remained no guarantee of success in obtaining authorization. What the application process came down to, in the end and for the most part, was the mood of one Edlyngton Bloomregaard, Senior Bounding Officer, Braydon Wood Division, Colwygshire, in the Kingdom of Epoh and a checkmark in the box buried in small print on page twenty-two of the 18-20/B form stating: *I swear on my mother's grave, current or future, that I have read Section 56 in its entirety and agree to abide by all of the conditions thereto set in, including, and especially, 56.13 that neither I, nor any of my heirs, current or future, shall hold the Braydon Wood Bounding Office liable for any loss or damage incurred to my person or my personal effects in the attempt to Bound through the Braydon Wood Boundary and, further, I recognize and accept that the probability of my survival is minimal, at best.* The chances that Bloomregaard was in a good mood and the box was checked were about one in 10,000. And the Bounding Office, Braydon Wood Division only processed about 100 applications a year. Needless to say, Edlyngton Bloomregaard *never* authorized a Bounding application, save for those that were accompanied by a healthy bribe.

But that didn't stop some rejected applicants from trying. Approximately one-quarter of the annually denied applicants, along with about another dozen or so non-applicants journeyed to Braydon Wood each year to attempt to Bound to Whyte Avenue, Edmonton, Alberta, Canada, Earth. On average, only six made it unscathed. The rest were either squished as the Boundary pulsed closed or were bounced back. Hard. Into a tree. Or a rock. Either way, it wasn't pretty.

The Bounding Office did not see this culling of stupidity from the general population as being worthy of the expense of a permanent guard detail. A patrol was sent through periodically. And sometimes the fates aligned and they were able to stop a potential Bounder. Basically, however, the patrols just enjoyed a nice hike through the forest. Still, the ones that made it through had to be dealt with. That is where Harpur Diggins came in.

On Thraeh, Harpur Diggins existed in his natural form: a dragon. Like most dragons, he enjoyed eating livestock, burning crops, terrorizing villages and hoarding gold in his mountain lair, though he limited those activities within the borders of Epoh to occasions that required that he make an example of some rebellious group of individuals. As the Dragon Lord of Epoh, it was his duty to protect the citizenry as well as keep unruly dissenters in line. The trick was to do this without blatantly revealing his role as the official ruler of the kingdom.

Like all dragons, he had no interest in virgin sacrifices. That people would willingly hand over a lovely young maiden to be burned alive was beyond comprehension. What kind of person does that? But it is the nature of dragons to be big and scary, just as it was the nature of people to be afraid of dragons and try to appease them by giving them innocent, young women to roast. Sure, the occasional hero would attempt to slay him, which always ended badly for the hero and always left Harpur a little pissed off. So, he would eat a few cows, burn a few crops and terrorize a few villages. It was a vicious cycle.

Until a bored Harpur Diggins happened to be digging through his hoard one rainy afternoon and came across a small, nondescript, wooden chest. How such an innocuous thing had ended up among the shiny gold and bright gems he'd so lovingly collected over the centuries, Harpur did not know. He assumed that it was part of a larger haul and that he'd simply overlooked it while sorting through the valuables. Usually, he was more judicious about what he kept, but occasionally a worthless item such as this one failed to be thrown out.

It occurred to Harpur that the chest might hold something precious. Humans were wont to conceal expensive jewels in austere containers, believing that no one would be interested. So, he opened the chest and discovered, to his deep dissatisfaction, that it held nothing more than a bundle of lilac-scented love letters tied with a faded pink ribbon.

Sentimentality barely registered on Harpur's emotional scale and his first inclination was to burn the chest and its mushy contents. He was about to render the letters to ash when he noticed a familiar name across the top of one of them: Dearest Ylemnir.

Ylemnir had been a powerful wizard as well as the first king of Epoh. Harpur had assisted him in the brief, but bloody, war against invaders from across the Crysteel Sea some four hundred years previously, and the two of them had become rather good friends. The chest and the letters must have been in the small hoard that Harpur had inherited from Ylemnir upon his death. Harpur's dragon hands were too big to handle the delicate stationery, but he was curious, so he used his magic to unfold the topmost letter and read it. It was written by a woman named Beatrice Cooper and it advised Ylemnir that she was pregnant with his child. Beatrice Cooper was not a Thraehlian name and a little more investigation revealed that she was from Earth. Harpur was not the least bit surprised that his friend had kept this secret from him. He was, however, distressed. If Ylemnir had fathered a child on Earth, it was entirely possible that his descendants possessed magic.

Harpur was no longer bored. Earth was assumed to be devoid of magic. It wasn't that magic wouldn't eventually evolve on Earth. But if it had been introduced by Ylemnir, then someone needed to find it and put a stop to it. That someone was Harpur.

According to the letters, Ylemnir's clandestine affair took place in Edmonton about the time the Hudson Bay Company was establishing itself there in the late 18th century. The Braydon Wood Boundary would take him there. If Ylemnir and Beatrice's descendants were still around, and they possessed magic, Harpur would find them.

A few centuries had passed since he'd last Bounded to Earth through the Braydon Wood Boundary. He arrived on Whyte Avenue in a time and a place that was completely unfamiliar to him. The progress human civilization had made during the intervening millennia was astounding. And not merely a little worrying to Harpur. Technology had advanced considerably and this natural precursor to the development of magic had, it seemed, accelerated rapidly.

Harpur was fascinated as he explored the city in human form, constantly scanning for any sign of magic. Several days passed before his efforts were rewarded. He was walking along Whyte Avenue, two blocks from the Boundary when he noticed a young man leaving a comic book shop bump into a woman and knock her coffee cup out of her hand. Harpur was standing only a few feet away and couldn't help but see this seemingly innocent event unfold. People bumping into each other was not uncommon on this busy street. What was uncommon was the fact that the young man used magic to prevent the falling cup from hitting the ground. It was so obvious to Harpur as he watched the cup stop dropping for a split second before the young man took hold of it and returned it to its grateful owner. It was nothing spectacular in and of itself, but still, it was clearly magic.

In his eagerness to find out how the young man was able to do what he did, Harpur approached him. "Excuse me," Harpur said, "my name is Harpur Diggins."

"Arthur Prentice," Arthur said, shaking Harpur's hand and assuming he wanted something in the comic book store. "I'm afraid we're closed now. Was there something you needed?"

Harpur realized he was referring to the store, but he was pleased to have gotten the young man's name. "Actually, there is. Can you tell me about your magic?"

Arthur looked confused. "This is a comic book store, not a magic shop. I think there might be one on Jasper Avenue somewhere, but I'm not sure exactly where it is."

Harpur looked confused in turn. "I meant *your* magic."

Arthur's confusion turned to suspicion and he assigned a minor level of crazy to Harpur. "Sorry, man, I don't do magic," he said and walked quickly away.

Harpur didn't know what to do. He hadn't expected the young man to spurn him that way. *Perhaps he isn't aware of his powers.*

Harpur decided to follow Arthur, hoping to learn more, but in a bizarre twist of fate, Arthur was struck down and killed when a speeding car careened around a corner at an intersection Arthur was crossing. And that is when Harpur made his fateful decision. Amid shouts and mortified gasps, he scooped Arthur's lifeless body up, became invisible and spirited him away to a secluded spot in Elk Island National Park, where he brought Arthur back to life by giving him some of his own blood. It was not the habit of dragons to dabble in necromancy, but he had to know about this young man from Earth who possessed magic.

Unfortunately, Arthur was unable to provide any answers, but since dragon blood could have dire consequences for him, Harpur made another decision. He wiped Arthur's memory and decided to live on Whyte Avenue where he could keep an eye on the young man. When any of the myriad effects dragon blood might have on Arthur manifested, Harpur would do whatever he would have to do. And since the good folks of the Kingdom of Epoh were quite capable of looking after themselves for a while, Harpur came up with a plan.

He returned to Epoh and called a parlay between himself and Edlyngton Bloomregaard and both sides agreed on a meeting time and place. Due to Harpur's size, the meeting took place in an open field south of the city of Colwygshire and was scheduled for dawn on the Epohian equivalent to the Summer Solstice.

Bloomregaard and his entourage arrived the night before and camped on the edge of the field. Bets were made around the campfire as to whether and how many men would be roasted if things went bad. Almost everyone wanted to bet against surviving the parlay, reasoning that if they lost, they wouldn't have to pay. Except for Bloomregaard. He put a large amount down in favour of remaining alive, reasoning that if they did survive, he'd clean up and, if they didn't, he wouldn't have to pay anyway. In his eyes, he couldn't lose.

At dawn, Bloomregaard and two chosen champions walked to the middle of the field. And waited.

And waited.

And waited.

A stool was brought out to the field by a servant for Bloomregaard to sit on. The champions, in full armour, started to complain. Harpur remained un-present as the sun inched higher in the sky dragging the temperature up with it. Bloomregaard positioned his champions on the sunny side of the stool to provide shade with a warning to both of them that if either of them collapsed, they'd both gain first-hand knowledge of what an arrow piercing their visors felt like. To be fair, his gout was particularly disagreeable that day and, in spite of the confidence he conveyed, he harboured a healthy dose of fear for his own life at the hands, or fiery breath as was more likely, of the dragon who appeared to have forgotten the terms of the meeting. Cranky didn't even begin to describe the mood that was developing within him.

Not many people knew the full extent of a dragon's magical ability. They can do all kinds of things besides burn crops, terrorize villages, eat livestock, hoard gold and consume virgins. For example, they can become invisible. Which is what Harpur had done an hour or so before dawn that day.

It wasn't that he feared Bloomregaard. It was more a matter of preserving his secret magic that caused him to exercise extreme caution. He arrived early for the meeting, became invisible and waited far more patiently than the folks he was meeting with for things to unfold. It was not outside the realm of possibility that Bloomregaard was planning something other than a sensible parlay. Harpur wanted to know what he was coming to the table with before the table got turned to Harpur's disadvantage and would be forced to make another example of someone simply for choosing to take an unfortunate course of action. He also wanted to make sure that Bloomregaard, Bloomregaard's champions, as well as the rest of the pathetic entourage, were duly weakened by the heat and unable to mount any appreciable attack against him. Hot and tired, he reckoned, they would be more inclined to agree to his terms than if they were refreshed and energetic after a good night's sleep. Not that he couldn't take them. But, seriously. Why were people so determined to endorse the stereotype?

He waited, watched and listened. And when Bloomregaard was about to *throw in the stool*, in a fit of pique, Harpur launched himself into the sky. The gust of air his massive wings pushed toward Bloomregaard and the champions in doing so provided a brief respite from the heat, but no hint that it was caused by a dragon. At an altitude of about 1000 feet, where he was sure he was no more than a speck, he became visible again and swooped back down to land dramatically (let's face it, there are some stereotypes that are kind of cool, not to mention satisfactorily intimidating) about twenty feet away from the sweaty trio, whereupon, the two champions sealed their fates by collapsing in heat-weakened terror next to the severely pissed off Bloomregaard, who rolled his eyes in abject disgust.

"You're late!" Bloomregaard growled. His parched throat left him incapable of the authoritative and accusatory bellow he had intended.

"Actually, I was early," Harpur replied in his deep, but smooth and utterly unaffected-by-the-heat voice. "You just didn't notice me."

Puzzled by that statement, Bloomregaard wondered how he could possibly not have noticed a forty-foot dragon. But rather than challenge it—now that his champions were useless metal heaps on the ground—he elected to dismiss it and move on with the meeting. He wanted to get this over with. Instead, he unfurled a scroll he had concealed in his sweat-wilted robes and began to read from it.

"By order of King Gnik (pronounced Nick) of the Kingdom of Epoh, I, Edlyngton Bloomregaard, Senior Bounding Officer, Braydon Wood Division, Colwygshire, also in the Kingdom of Epoh, am hereby authorized to provide you, Harpur Diggins, Dragon of the Kingdom of Epoh, the title of Sir Harpur Diggins, Bounder Guard of Braydon Wood Boundary, in perpetuity, effective immediately and to be compensated annually with one hundred gold bars and one vir..."

"Stop right there!" Harpur roared.

Bloomregaard scrambled backward away from the huge, purplish beast, tripped over a clump of grass and landed about as unceremoniously as a man could on his backside on the ground. From there he crab-walked a few more feet before the advancing dragon left him paralyzed and in need of a fresh pair of underdrawers.

Harpur lowered his colossal head down to within a few feet of the trembling Senior Bounding Officer and whispered (in as much as a dragon can whisper), "If you say virgin, so help me, I will roast you alive right where you lay."

"N-n-n-no. O-o-of course, I wasn't going to say vir... that. I would never say vir... that." Bloomregaard stammered.

"Then what were you going to say? What could you possibly offer me that is not a virgin?"

"Well... Um... Well... I was going to say virrrrr..." He looked around for inspiration. *Ah-ha!* "...idian. Yes! I was going to say viridian gemstone. Very precious, they are. Very valuable viridian gemstones are. I'm sure you will love them. One viridian gemstone. That's what I was going to say." His confidence, though still badly shaken was returning.

Harpur inched his head even closer and looked hard and disapprovingly at Bloomregaard. "You lie," Harpur said. But instead of roasting the odorous civil servant, he raised his head and looked at the still unconscious champions. Then at the retreating entourage at the edge of the field. When his ferocious gaze returned to Bloomregaard, he sighed. A hot, plume of smoke escaped his mouth and washed over the prone and once again terrified man. "You were going to say virgin. Weren't you?"

Bloomregaard's mouth opened and closed several times before he could force any sound out of it. "Well, y-y-yes. B-b-but we can change that. W-w-w-we just thought dragons liked vir..." Thinking better of actually saying the word and further invoking Harpur's wrath, he amended his lexicon and said, "those," instead.

"What is wrong with you people? Are you insane? Why do you think that we like virgins? They are chewy and flavourless and they scream like banshees... And who sacrifices beautiful young women anyway? Who does that? Do you know what happens to the virgins you give us?" Harpur demanded.

"You eat them?" Bloomregaard suggested.

"No, we don't eat them! That's just cruel." Harpur corrected. "We take them to distant lands and drop them off at night outside affluent cities where they are found and taken in by local farmers or merchants and adopted and cared for. Many of them end up married to wealthy noblemen and live amazing lives in luxury. Eat them! Pfft!" Another contemptuous puff of smoke spurted out of Harpur's nose, and he made a mental note to wipe Bloomregaard's memory after they were done.

Bloomregaard processed this information. "So why do you take them in the first place?" he asked, his curiosity getting the better of him.

"To save them from idiots like you!" Harpur yelled.

"I didn't know that," Bloomregaard said. "Well, we do happen to have some nice viridian gemstones we can substitute..."

"Enough!" Harpur yelled again. The champions, who were beginning to stir, fainted again, and the entourage had all but abandoned the camp at the edge of the field. "Here's what's going to happen. I will guard the Braydon Wood Boundary for two hundred gold bars and... You said those viridian gemstones were valuable?" Harpur knew exactly how valuable viridian was. Not nearly as valuable as Bloomregaard claimed. But they were pretty and shiny and... Well, pretty and shiny was sometimes enough for a dragon.

Bloomregaard nodded. "Very valuable."

"I don't believe you," Harpur said, "but I'll take a dozen of those as well. Annually. To be delivered to Braydon Wood side of the Boundary on the Summer Solstice." He paused to think. "At dawn."

"Wait," Bloomregaard said. "What do you mean by the Braydon Wood side of the Boundary? Where will you be?"

"I, dear fellow, will be on the other side of the Boundary. On Earth."

"But that's impossible! You are to guard the Boundary from the Thraeh side. We can't agree to allow a dragon to go to Earth. There are no dragons on Earth."

"Not a problem," Harpur said. Then he looked around again. The champions were still out and the entourage had scarpered far enough away that they couldn't see what he was about to do.

In a flash, Harpur transformed into the form of a man. The same form that Arthur had met and subsequently forgotten he'd met.

Bloomregaard gasped. "Wow! Well, I'd have to talk to King Gnik. And then there's the 18-20B to be filed. And, of course, there's the sixty-two-day waiting period..."

Harpur turned back into his dragon-self. "Do we have an accord?"

Bloomregaard took in the red glow of the fire burning in Harpur's chest. "Yes. Yes, of course. We have an accord."

Suspecting that Bloomregaard would say anything to extract himself from the situation he found himself in, Harpur kept the red glow of the fire burning in his chest for effect. "Good. Now go and make it so."

Bloomregaard clambered to his feet and started to retreat toward the empty camp, delighted by his new-found knowledge about dragons and their ability to shapeshift.

"One more thing, Bloomregaard," Harpur called after him.

Bloomregaard stopped and turned back toward the dragon.

"Don't forget that's two hundred gold bars and twelve veridian gems." Then he lifted a front leg and waved his talons in an arc through the air, thus, erasing any memory of his magical ability from Bloomregaard's mind.

"Of course! It will be done."

Harpur watched the slightly confused Chief Bounding Officer walk away muttering under his breath about forgetting something important. Then he leapt into the air and flew back to Braydon Wood to return to Whyte Avenue.

Now, here he was, eight years later and the effects of his blood on Arthur had still not come to anything. Nor did Arthur seem to realize that he possessed magical powers. But that coin the elf had given to him was not going to be so subtle. Harpur couldn't believe that the elf was unaware of what giving an item from a magical world to someone from a non-magical world would do. He had to know that unless Arthur travelled to Thraeh and returned the coin to him they would become *Entangled*. The elf was up to something.

Why did he give it to Arthur, of all people? Would Arthur's magic be enough to quell the Entanglement? What were the odds that this was random?

Harpur would soon find out. But first he had to get Arthur to understand the predicament he was in. Doing so entailed the possibility of reviving Arthur's memory of their first encounter so long ago. He wasn't sure he wanted to do that. He wasn't sure he needed to do that. He'd have to talk to Arthur and see how things went.

To that end, he trailed Arthur to his apartment, staying a half-block behind. When Arthur reached the outer door to the building he lived in, Harpur quickened his gait and came up beside him. Arthur turned, expecting to see a fellow apartment-dweller arriving home at the same time. He eyes widened. He blinked. He shook his head and blinked again.

"It's you!"

"It is me," Harpur agreed, more than a little alarmed that Arthur seemed to know who he was. He'd never exactly been hiding from Arthur since coming to Whyte Avenue, but they had never actually met again after that fateful first day eight years earlier. "How is it you know me?"

"You're the guy in the alley. I saw you walk through a wall!"

Ah, yes. That had been a small lapse in vigilance. Usually, Harpur was more careful when he entered his lair, but he'd seen Arthur coming and rushed to get out of sight. But perhaps it was a fortuitous lapse. If Arthur had seen him walk through the wall, telling him about the Entanglement might not be as difficult as he expected.

"Harpur Diggins," Harpur said, extending his hand, neither confirming nor denying his ability to walk through walls.

Arthur looked at the man attached to the outstretched hand. In human form, Harpur Diggins stood six feet, four inches tall. With his top hat on, as it was that day, he was closer to seven feet even. His shoulder span was thirty inches measured across mountainous pectoral muscles that, even under the full-length, black leather duster he wore, were unmistakably apparent. In contrast to his bald pate, his jawline was adorned with an impeccably groomed, raven-black beard that ended in a point so sharp, Arthur thought he could stab someone with it. His skin was the colour of finely polished poisonwood and his eyes were deep electric violet. He carried an ornate walking stick with a large amethyst held in place by silver claws. Arthur's hand looked like a child's in Harpur's.

"Arthur Prentice," Arthur said. "So, how did you do that? That walk through the wall thing?"

"Well, if you've got a minute, I can explain. It has a little something to do with the coin the elf gave you."

"How do you know about that?" Arthur asked, alarmed. He had seen this Harpur Diggins fellow at the intersection—he was kind of hard to miss—but he hadn't realized that Harpur has witnessed the elf passing him the coin.

"The elf and I are... acquainted. I saw him hand it to you. Please, can we go inside to talk about this?" Harpur was growing weary of being so polite.

Arthur reached into his pocket and withdrew the coin. He held it out to Harpur. "You can have it back," Arthur said. "It's just a game piece." As curious as he was about it, this big guy was starting to creep him out. By giving it to him, Arthur hoped he would just go away.

Harpur looked at the coin. He wanted to take it. Taking it from Arthur would slow down the Entanglement, but he needed to get Arthur to let him into his apartment where they could talk privately. "That's very kind of you. Nothing would make me happier than seeing that coin put back where it belongs. But it's not as simple as me taking it from you."

"Look, man," Arthur said, thrusting the coin toward Harpur. "I kinda got a lot of stuff going on right now. I'm sure whatever LARP you and the elf are playing is super cool, but I really don't have time for this. Just take the coin and leave me alone."

Harpur smiled again. Then he tapped Arthur on the shoulder with is walking stick and zapped them both from outside to inside Arthur's apartment.

Arthur yelped when he found himself suddenly standing in this living room. He stood there, frozen and afraid to move, eyes as big as saucers and heart pounding like a drum.

"And I don't have time to argue with you about it," Harpur said.

"What just happened?" Arthur squeaked. It seemed to be the question of the day. "What are you?"

"Do you mind if I sit down?" Harpur asked, taking a seat on Arthur's sofa. "This might take a while."

Arthur forced himself to move. Slowly. Cautiously. Eventually, he ended up sitting in a wing chair, opposite Harpur. *Mom always says that trouble comes in threes. This is the third thing, so all I have to do is get through this and then I'll be okay,* Arthur thought, working hard to stay calm. Then he noticed that something was different about his apartment. Besides the enormous man in the top hat sitting on his sofa.

The precious, ugly afghan was gone. The spider plant was gone. The photo of him and Cheryl at Expo was gone. He turned to look at the peg beside the door. Cheryl's yellow sweater was gone. The only relationship zombie that remained was the reproduction Daredevil comic cover. Arthur stood up and walked over to the kitchen counter. In the dish he used to keep his keys in, he saw the set of keys to his apartment that he'd given to Cheryl on their six-month anniversary. She must have brought them over while he was at work. Next to the dish was a folded piece of paper with Arthur's name on it. He picked it up and read the note.

Then he started crying.

Seriously? Harpur stood up and walked over to Arthur. He took the note from Arthur's trembling hand and read:

I've taken all my stuff. Keys are in the dish.
Your things are in a box in your bedroom.
Sorry, Cheryl.

Harpur sighed. This was all he needed. Arthur's broken heart was not something he cared to have to deal with. He'd have to circle back to him later. He tapped Arthur's shoulder with his walking stick and caught him as he collapsed, unconscious from the spell. He carried Arthur to the bedroom, laid him down on the bed and removed his shoes. That would keep him until he could come back. *I should have dealt with the elf first.*

Harpur had no doubt that he would find the elf. That wasn't at all what concerned him as he marched all dragon-wizard-like up Whyte Avenue toward his quarry. What bothered him was the gold coin. He kept wondering why the elf had given it to Arthur in particular. It felt so calculated. In a weirdly random way. And Arthur didn't seem to know what it was. *What had he called it? A game piece?* Arthur didn't possess enough guile for subterfuge of this magnitude and Harpur couldn't imagine Arthur—or anyone—willingly becoming Entangled. Harpur's musings percolated at the back of his mind while his super dragon-vision scanned the street for the elf.

He knew the elf was still close because he had warded the area around the Boundary between 99 and 109 Streets with a barrier that no creature from Thraeh could penetrate, except himself, of course. This force field, for lack of a better term, would repel any Thraehlings and keep them safely contained. The elf couldn't enter any of the buildings, either. Every entrance—door, window and vent—was enchanted to keep Thraehlings out. Harpur was nothing, if not thorough. While there were still many places the elf could hide, he couldn't get far. It was only a matter of time before Harpur, who knew every inch of Whyte Avenue, apprehended the elf.

When Harpur didn't find the elf at street level, he went up onto one of the rooftops. And there, two roofs over, right next to the Boundary, Harpur spotted the elf. A couple of dragon-worthy leaps and Harpur was upon him.

"That was almost too easy," Harpur said as he seized the elf by the collar and lifted him to his feet.

Sok was almost as tall as Harpur. In fact, when he finished growing, in a decade or so, he'd be taller. Like all elves, he was light, slight and agile, but deceptively strong. Even when he was fully grown, though, it was unlikely he could have bested Harpur in a fight. Dragons, whether in human or dragon form, were heavier, but equally as agile. Plus, they had that fire thing going on. So Sok stayed calm and submissive.

"Sok. I thought it was you." Harpur was not surprised to find Bloomregaard's favourite assistant in his grip, though he was surprised to find him on Whyte Avenue. "Do you have any idea what you have just done?"

"Not exactly," Sok said.

Harpur let go of the elf, took up a menacing stance and glared at his prisoner. "What were you thinking?" he prompted.

The only way Sok could see himself getting out of this was to tell Harpur about the prophecy. He told Harpur how he'd gone to the Well of the Ancients to receive his destiny. He described Queen Reine and what she had said to him about giving the coin to a man holding a silver fox who was a lost child of Epoh and that it was Sok's destiny to help his man find his way home so he could become king.

"I didn't know I'd find him here, though." Sok ended his confession.

"So, what are you doing here, then?" Harpur's mind was racing with the implications of what Sok was telling him.

"I was curious to see what this place was like. Bloomregaard gave me some time off and... I think he's up to something bad... anyway, I was walking through Braydon Wood and came to the Boundary and no one was around, so... I Bounded."

"Bloomregaard is always up to something bad," Harpur dismissed the aside about the Senior Bounding Officer. "What exactly did this Queen Reine say about the man holding the silver fox?"

"Just that he was a lost child of Epoh and that we would be bound together for a time just as he was bound to the Dreamfinder by the fire that burns within him. Oh, and he is to be king. I don't understand any of that. Epoh has a king. And how could a human from Earth be the king of Epoh anyway? It's illegal for earthlings to even be on Thraeh."

Harpur looked at the elf. *Of all the elves in Epoh, why did this one have to be the one to fulfill such a prophecy?* Sok wasn't a bad elf. He was, however, young, ambitious, idealistic and somewhat rebellious. In the eight years that Harpur had known him, Sok had been something of an amusing mystery to him. It was virtually unheard of for an elf to work outside of the forest, but somehow Sok had managed to worm his way into being a clerk at the Bounding Office. Until then, Harpur had not been curious enough to find out more about that. His attention had been firmly focused on Arthur and what Harpur had done to him. Now he was not only curious, he was in the throes of a developing dilemma. Duty-bound to turn Sok in as an illegal Bounder, Harpur should toss the elf into a prison cell. But he also had a duty to Arthur. And that coin was a big problem.

"Tell me, Sok," Harpur said, "how did you become a clerk for Bloomregaard anyway?"

Sok wasn't expecting this. But talking about his clerkship was better than talking about going to prison, so he was happy to answer. "I was there at the negotiation between you and Bloomregaard when you were working out the terms for you to be here. I saw and heard everything."

"Everything?"

"Everything!" Sok said, hoping that knowing Harpur's secret would give him some leverage. "I was the only one who didn't run away when it looked like you were going to roast Bloomregaard. He fired his old clerk for running away and offered me the position. He must have been grateful that I stayed with him."

Harpur doubted that gratitude had anything to do with it. "Why were you there? How did you become part of the entourage?"

"I was out on the Colwygshire Road and saw them all come out of the gates, so I followed them to see where they were going." Sok shrugged. "I don't suppose you have anything to eat?"

Harpur snapped his fingers and handed Sok a chilli-cheese hotdog and a can of cola. The elf sniffed the hotdog. He'd never seen one before, but it smelled delicious. Then he examined the can. Having no idea what to do with it, he shook it.

"Don't do that!" Harpur snapped, snatching the can out of Sok's hand and putting it down on the roof ledge. "Eat your hotdog."

Sok had been just about to take a bite. "Dog!?" Repulsed, he held the gooey repast away from himself.

"That's just what they are called. It's not a real dog. Just eat it."

Sok looked dubious, but his stomach harboured not a single reservation. He took a tentative bite. "Oh, wow! That's hot!" He chewed and swallowed. "And good."

The spicy chilli was making Sok's eyes water. Harpur picked up the can of cola, pointed it away from himself and opened the pop top. Beige foam oozed out of the hole and dribbled down the side of the can. "Drink," he ordered handing it back to Sok.

Sok watched the foamy bubbles bursting on the can. This was the strangest goblet he'd ever seen. He tipped the can up to his lips and instantly spit the carbonated liquid it contained all over the front of Harpur's coat. "What is this?" Earth was proving to be an astonishing place, indeed.

"Just eat," Harpur said through gritted teeth as he wiped the cola off his coat with a wet cloth he conjured. There was no point hiding his magic from the elf any longer.

Sok was happy to oblige and devoured the chilli-cheese hotdog in a few more spice-induced eye-watering bites. "That was great. Thanks!" he wheezed. Then, better prepared for the bubbling cola, he guzzled the rest of it.

"Sok, you do realize that I'm supposed to arrest you, right?" Harpur asked when Sok was finished eating.

"I'm kind of hoping you won't, though," Sok said. "I mean, it's my destiny to bring that man back to Epoh and if I'm in prison, that's going to be hard to do. I don't suppose you know where I can find him?"

Harpur glared at Sok. "You really don't know what you've done, do you?"

"I found the future king of Epoh and I..."

Just then a crack sounded from the Boundary. Followed by a frantic yelp. Harpur and Sok looked up.

"Oh, for the love of Orhowyn!" Harpur growled. Then he turned back to Sok and ordered, "You stay here. Don't move a muscle. I'll be right back."

"What's happening?" Sok called after him as Harpur prepared to leap into the roiling, black mess above him.

"Some idiot is caught in the Boundary," Harpur snarled and then jumped into the middle of the shimmering vortex.

Sok had nowhere else to go. And he wasn't going to go anywhere near the Boundary. Whatever was going on inside, he wanted no part of it. Once it was clear, though, he would have to find the man he gave the coin to and persuade him to Bound to Epoh with him. Now that Harpur knew about the prophecy, he was almost sure that the dragon-wizard would help him fulfill his destiny. In hindsight, he should have enlisted Harpur's help in the first place. Then again, he hadn't known he would find the man holding the silver fox in this strange world. How could an heir to the throne of Epoh possibly be a man from Earth? It didn't make sense.

A few minutes passed before Sok noticed Harpur's walking stick lying on the roof. To pass the time he figured he'd take the rare opportunity to examine it. Expecting it to be enchanted with some sort of protection spell, he walked around it a couple of times looking for any signs of glamour. Seeing none, he poked it with his toe. It didn't move. It didn't zap him, sting him or kick back at him either. He squatted down next to it and reached out to give it a tentative touch. Still nothing. It just laid there. He repeated the tentative touch action three more times before feeling brave enough to wrap his hand around it. But when he tried to pick it up it still wouldn't move. It was as if it weighed a thousand pounds. *That bloody dragon thinks of everything.* He briefly entertained the notion of going down to street level and checking the place out. But quickly dismissed that idea. If Harpur returned to find him gone, he might not even make it to prison.

Instead, he settled for leaning against the roof ledge and watching the action from above. For the next half hour, Sok watched Monday night on Whyte Avenue come to life. The crowds had thinned and the vehicles moved faster, but with less urgency than they had when he'd first arrived. People entered and exited shops and cafes. There was more laughter and a busker with a strange, stringed instrument, similar to, but much bigger than a lute was singing songs on the far corner. People dropped silver and gold coins or what looked like blue or purple pieces of paper into the instrument's open case. *So, they have bards on Earth*, Sok

46

thought. *And it appears they are valued. Look at all that silver and gold that fellow's getting.*

Before he had leapt into the intersection and handed the coin to the man holding the silver fox, Sok had watched the activity below much as he was doing now. The scene was far more daunting than he had imagined. Hundreds of people walked back and forth. And the noise from the vehicles that moved magically on their own was really loud. A strange blaring noise, not unlike a battle horn, emitted from some of them periodically. Now and then people shouted odd and angry words out the vehicle windows as well. He noticed that the vehicles were controlled by glowing lights that hung from thick cords across the streets where they intersected and that the people walking were directed by illuminated orange hands and white ghosts enclosed in little boxes on each corner. Sok was fascinated.

As he had watched and waited, he scanned the crowds for Harpur. Having gotten to know him in his human form over the past couple of years, Sok was certain that Harpur would stand out, even among this throng of people. His certainty was rewarded when Harpur emerged from a shop holding a white vessel with a lid on it, from which he took short sips every so often. Sok had waited until Harpur disappeared around a corner behind the Boundary building and then he had made his move. With Harpur safely out of the way, Sok had jumped down and leaped over the traffic, hoping to put more distance between himself and the formidable Bounder Guard. He'd planned on exploring a while and then return to Epoh undetected and un-imprisoned. But then he'd spotted the man holding the silver fox and everything changed. All he could think of was giving the coin to the man and getting him to the Boundary. Harpur's sudden appearance, coupled with the man's resistance, put paid to that impromptu plan and he had run away. At the next corner, he turned and within a few steps was abruptly introduced to Harpur's warding of the area around the Boundary. When he realized that he couldn't escape Whyte Avenue, he made his way back to the Boundary building to try to figure out what he should do next. He was almost relieved when Harpur had shown up and caught him.

Harpur returned a short while later, covered in a bit of gore, grumbling about the level of stupidity it took to Bound without proper training. Sok had the good grace to look contrite, but otherwise did not bother to acknowledge Harpur's judgment. "How'd it go?" he asked.

"The idiot's head exploded, that's how!" Harpur barked.

He retrieved his walking stick, picking it up like it was a feather, and used it to zap away the brain matter, blood and offal that clung to his face and coat. "You didn't touch this, did you?" he asked holding the precious cane up for Sok to look at.

"No," Sok said, failing miserably to meet Harpur's gaze. "Didn't even notice it there."

Then, his curiosity trumping his dread, he asked, "So what does happen when a Bound goes wrong?"

"If they don't get bounced back, they get torn apart. Like that one did," he pointed toward the clear-again Boundary. "Or they get crushed into little balls of ooze. Usually the Boundary devours them, but sometimes they get stuck."

"Like that one did?" Sok asked, cringing a little at the realization of what could have happened to him.

"Yeah. Like that one did. And now you have some more explaining to do."

Sok gulped. But explaining was better than prison, so he figured it best to take full advantage of the gift. The problem he now faced was that he had already told Harpur everything.

"I already told you everything."

"You haven't told me how you intend to stop the Entanglement between you and Arthur. You do realize that you two are Entangled now?"

"Yes, I know. Queen Reine said we would be bound for a time. After I saw him and gave him the coin, I assumed she meant Entanglement. I figure we can just Bound to Epoh and I'll ask him to give the coin back to me. It's not a big deal. He's to be king there anyway..." Sok stopped. "Wait! His name is Arthur? He's already a king?" Sok was excited.

"Whatever gave you that idea?" Harpur was truly puzzled.

"There's a reference to a King Arthur in the archives at the Bounding Office. He was a pretty important guy on Earth."

Harpur rolled his eyes. "The King Arthur you are talking about was a king, but not here. A Bounder from Earth went to his world hundreds of years ago and documented his life. Here he is considered a legend. No one really believes he was real."

Sok thought about that for a minute. "So, Earthlings do know about the Boundaries? They Bound?"

"They used to. The knowledge of such things was lost as humans became more territorial and the chaos and violence grew. Occasionally, someone stumbles on one, but as long as their feet don't leave the ground, all they see is a shimmering mirage and pass through it without anything happening," Harpur explained.

"That's kind of sad," Sok said. "It must be awful not having magic and not knowing about other worlds."

"They seem to manage. Did it occur to you that Arthur might not be able to Bound? That Bounding might kill him?"

Sok looked up at the Boundary. "Why would he be part of the prophecy if he couldn't Bound? That's just dumb, Harpur."

Harpur dropped his head forward and rubbed his brow. "Do you really think it's going to be that simple? Arthur knows nothing about Thraeh. He's a human from Earth. He's not just going to accept that he's destined to be a king on a different world. He doesn't even believe that other worlds exist."

"I didn't pick him," Sok said. "I just did what Queen Reine told me I was supposed to do to fulfill my destiny. The way I see it, this Arthur has no choice. It's his destiny too. Let's just go talk to him and explain everything. You might be surprised. Maybe he wants to be a king and will be thrilled when we tell him."

Harpur had half a mind to drag Sok through the Boundary and throw him in the deepest, darkest dungeon in the castle. But it was odd that Sok had received the prophecy of his destiny involving a lost child of Epoh only shortly after Harpur had used his own blood to save the life of an Earthling who possessed magic and that Earthling was, apparently, the lost child of Epoh from Sok's prophecy.

"Think about it, Harpur," Sok stood up, feeling somewhat empowered by Harpur's silence. "People here have no idea what's out there. And people on Thraeh really want to come here and learn what life is like on Earth. Wouldn't it be amazing if this Arthur was the reason that Earth found out about Thraeh? Maybe we could open up trade between our worlds."

"Uh, no, it wouldn't be amazing. It would mess with the whole natural order of things."

"How bad could it be? Besides, you live here and everything is fine."

"I live here to protect our world from idiots like you. Have you seen what goes on here? Do you really want humans from this world bringing vehicles and cell phones and computers... and worse to our world? It would set us back centuries. It's bad enough that the humans on Thraeh are always trying to invent stuff we don't need. People wear shorts here, Sok! Do you want shorts on Thraeh?"

"What are shorts?"

Harpur led Sok to the ledge and scanned the crowds below until he spotted a guy in blue camo Bermuda shorts and flip-flops to whom he pointed. "Those are shorts!"

Sok's eyebrows elevated. "Good point," he said.

"So, tell me, Sok," Harpur rested a big hand on the elf's narrow shoulder, in part so Sok would feel that he wasn't angry and in part to be able to grab hold should an escape attempt be made. "Did you really think that it would be as easy as getting Arthur to just give the coin back to you?"

"Would you want to be Entangled with me forever?"

"Also a good point."

The other-worldly pair stood in silence for a while, taking in the wonder of the world around them, lost in their own thoughts. Sok was desperately hoping his destiny didn't include going to prison. Harpur was desperately trying to think of a way to save Sok's life. Only one of them was aware of what they were both thinking.

When a while had passed with neither of them seeing a way out of their predicament, Harpur spoke, "You know we have to fix this, right? The Entanglement could kill both you and Arthur."

"Kill us?" Sok said. "I thought we'd just end up having to stay close together, like good chums. How would it kill us?"

Harpur looked at Sok. *How gruesome should I make this?* "Oh, you'd be more than good chums, Sok. Eventually your bodies would absorb into each other and..."

"We have to fix this!"

"Any ideas?"

"Let's kidnap Arthur, take him back to Epoh and make him give me the coin. Then we can figure out the rest of it."

"There are also Bloomregaard's wraiths to consider." Harpur said.

The wraiths were three soul-sucking, spectral beings from the Black North, a region on Thraeh that was neither black, nor north, but grayer and north-easterly—chromatically and geographically speaking—that lay beyond the Chrysteel Sea. How Bloomregaard had acquired, much less maintained the fealty of these wraiths was unknown. All Harpur knew was that they roamed Colwygshire sniffing out and reporting any infringements on the law, particularly magical infringements, to Bloomregaard. They had no official or even recognized association with Bloomregaard's official and recognized duties as Senior Bounding Officer. This was a private deal between them. And one that struck fear into the hearts of the entire population of Epoh. Including King Gnik.

Many had tried to have them banished, but whatever the creatures had uncovered and reported to Bloomregaard about King Gnik created a strong enough hold over him to cause him to defend Bloomregaard's right to employ anyone he chose. He drew the line at enacting a law that made Bloomregaard's right to employ these creatures official and recognized, stating that in doing so they would open the doors for others to do the same. Bloomregaard saw much merit in this decision and supported it because it gave him a monopoly of sorts as no one else wanted more of these cold and terrifying beings in or around Colwygshire. Bloomregaard was nothing if not a slimeball. And Harpur was suddenly regretting not having stepped in to eliminate the threat the wraiths now posed upon him.

"I didn't think about that." Sok shuddered at the thought of the wraiths.

"You didn't think about a lot of things. Where does Bloomregaard think you are?" Harpur asked.

"He gave me some time off. I'm supposed to be visiting my grandmother in Pollybush."

"We have some time, then," Harpur said, calculating that it would take Sok two days to travel to Pollybush. With time to visit and the return trip... they had some time. For what, though, Harpur didn't know.

"Can they detect the Entanglement?"

"You, Arthur and the coin are on this side of the Boundary. No one can detect it from Thraeh."

"If we all just stay here, then no one will ever know."

"You *will*, oddly enough, be missed eventually. And if you and Arthur don't both Bound back to Braydon Wood and he doesn't give the coin back to you there, the Entanglement will consume you. Remember? And it's supposed to be excruciatingly painful. Arthur doesn't deserve that."

"*Arthur* doesn't deserve that? What about *me*?" Sok was offended.

"You caused this. If it were up to me, you'd be experiencing some excruciating pain right now."

Sok tried to move away from the big dragon-wizard, but Harpur's grip on his shoulder tightened just enough to let him know that he wasn't going anywhere. "I was just fulfilling my destiny!" he squeaked.

Harpur sighed. "You're a good elf. You're stupid and right now you're a bigger pain in my tail than you know, but for some strange reason, I like you, Sok. We'll figure this out."

"So, what are we going to do?" Sok asked.

"We are going to go back to my lair and get some sleep." Harpur guided Sok toward the back of the building they were standing on. When he was sure no one was around, he signalled Sok and they both jumped to the ground.

"I'm hungry," Sok announced.

Harpur just growled.

Chapter 3

Harpur's lair was, as would be expected, an enormous cavern, complete with stalactites dripping water and an impressive hoard of gold and jewels and other treasures he had collected over centuries and brought with him when he took up his post as Bounder Guard on Whyte Avenue. At first glance, upon entering it through the enchanted back-alley doorway, it appeared to be a regular, normal dragon lair. At second glance, however, the lair contained a few features that set it apart from a regular, normal dragon lair. There was a king size bed, a fully functioning kitchen and a conversation pit with plush, leather sofas and natural rock fireplace. A grand chandelier hung over the conversation pit and cast dazzling prismatic light throughout the cavern. A large hot tub filled a corner on the far side of the bed and was separated from a palatial bathroom outfitted with gold fixtures and amethyst embedded tiles by an arched entrance. Lavish wall sconces set into the rock walls cast soft, white light that reflected off the pile of gold and jewels, making it sparkle and glint with a golden aura.

Sok, never having been inside any dragon lair before this, was, as also would be expected, in awe. The cavern was enormous, but it felt cozy somehow; weirdly homey and inviting. It was as if...

"You have a girlfriend!" Sok blurted.

Harpur was in the kitchen pouring himself a glass of beer when Sok, after having completed a slow 360° turn to take in and fully appreciate the grandeur, made this blunt and astute, if not entirely accurate announcement.

"Not exactly," said a voice attached to a woman emerging from the bathroom wrapped in a thick, purple towel. She was tall and slender. Her auburn hair fell in dark, wet waves to her waist and her emerald eyes gleamed.

Sok spun to face her. "Who are you?" he asked in amazement tinted with the flush of awkward realization that she was severely underdressed.

"Sok, Anayah. Anayah, Sok." Harpur introduced them.

Anayah moved toward Sok with her hand extended. Sok took it, bowed in greeting and kissed it. "A pleasure, m' lady," he said.

"Well, aren't you just the cutest thing?" Anayah smiled. To retract her hand from Sok's grasp, she had to give it a little tug; so captivated was he by her stunning beauty. Then, to relieve the elf's obvious discomfiture with her current state of dress, she swept her hands down either side of her body causing a dense cloud of red smoke to envelop her. When the smoke cleared an instant later, Anayah was dressed in an orange, Mandarin-style sheath of body-hugging silk. Her hair was sculpted into a complicated cascade of braids and curls. Amethyst earrings dangled from her perfect lobes and a large, marquise-cut amethyst graced the ring finger on her right hand. "Harpur, why didn't you tell me we were expecting a guest tonight?"

Harpur snorted. "I wasn't expecting to need to."

"Who are you?" Sok asked again.

"Anayah is my..." Harpur began.

"I'm not *your* anything," Anayah corrected with a firm hint of long-suffering and assertive defiance tinged with a hint of flattered amusement. Then, turning back to Sok she explained, "I'm what you might call the tech support."

"*Tech* support?" Sok was duly and understandably confused. His first thought was that Techs were some sort of magical race that he'd never heard of before.

"Let me show you." Anayah slipped an arm through one of Sok's to guide him toward a small alcove that contained a large mirror in an ornately carved frame.

Anayah waved her hand and the surface began to ripple like a still pond that someone had tossed a pebble into. When the ripples dissipated, an image appeared. Sok was looking at scene from Whyte Avenue. A busker was singing about answers blowing in the wind in front of a restaurant. Anayah waved her hand again and the scene changed to a group of men smoking a shared joint on a small common green.

"I use this to monitor Whyte Avenue when Bounders come through from Thraeh. I help Harpur track them with this scrying mirror."

"You're a witch?" Sok asked, astonished. Witches on Thraeh didn't look like Anayah.

"I am. I'm from Mysturna," she confirmed.

"Mysturna?"

"That's the world where I was born."

Just then Sok's stomach growled.

"Oh, you poor thing," Anayah said. "Let's get you something to eat. How do a nice ham sandwich and some beer sound?"

Anayah guided Sok back to the conversation pit where Harpur had settled with his beer on one of the sofas. A fire roared in the fireplace and Harpur was pointing an elongated device at what looked like a moving picture mounted above it. Every time he touched a button, the picture changed. First, there were a bunch of men in uniforms holding bent sticks with wide blades on one end chasing a small, black disc that they hit with their sticks. It appeared to be some sort of contest, but Harpur pushed the button before Sok could figure out what it was all about and the picture changed to an excited man talking excitedly about a piece of cloth that he used to wipe up a red liquid that he spilled purposely on a table. Harpur pushed the button again. This time the picture showed a group of people with gray-green skin and tattered clothing who were walking in jerky motions down a street obscured in mist. Harpur seemed to approve of this one. He put the elongated device down on a low table beside the sofa and pushed another button, hidden on the side of the sofa. The whole section of sofa started to transform as the back reclined, the seat slid forward and the bottom lifted, thus elevating Harpur's feet. Sok leaned over the side of the sofa on which he was now sitting and found and pushed an identical button. It took a few tries, but he figured out that he had to hold the button until the seat had transformed into the position he wanted. A single tap returned the seat to its original arrangement.

As soon as he was settled, Anayah returned with a large tray laden with food. There were ham sandwiches—just as she promised—grapes, cheese cubes, a plate filled with small, flat, round cakes and three empty plates, three linen napkins and three large glasses of beer. Sok's stomach growled again in anticipation, but he was dismayed at having to right his seat in order to reach the welcome repast.

"You just ate a chilli-cheese hotdog," Harpur said as Sok heaped food onto his plate.

"That was nearly an hour ago," Sok said as if hourly meals were the norm.

The trio ate in silence as the gray-green skinned people continued to trudge across the TV screen. Even muted, their spectral presence made Sok a little uneasy, so he looked around the cavern to keep himself from having to look at them. And to keep himself from staring at the lovely Anayah. Once their hunger had been sated, Harpur announced that he had had enough for one day and asked Anayah to prepare a place for Sok to sleep. With a slight nod, he indicated that he needed to speak to Anayah privately.

"Are you his servant?" Sok asked after Anayah had conjured a soft bed and a nightshirt for him to sleep in, in yet another alcove opposite the one with the scrying mirror.

"Hardly!" Anayah said. But said no more. She just smiled at the smitten elf, bid him good night, snapped her fingers and disappeared.

"Good night, Anayah," he whispered to the empty space she had just occupied. Then, suddenly unable to keep his eyes open a moment longer, he fell deeply and soundly asleep.

Now that the surprise guest to the lair was settled under her magical influence, Anayah returned to the conversation pit. "Are you going tell me why there's an elf in the lair?" she asked. In all the time she'd been living in the lair with Harpur, not once had any other living being ever been there.

Harpur told her about the prophecy and how, apparently, it was Sok's destiny to help Arthur become the king of Epoh.

"Our Arthur?" Anayah said when Harpur finished. "That's interesting."

"It's not interesting at all," Harpur growled. "It's an Orhowyn-damned nuisance."

"How so? I would think that you would be relieved to have an excuse to get Arthur off of Earth and onto a world where his magic isn't a problem." Anayah said.

"I should have taken him to Thraeh as soon as I found him."

"It's not like you knew this was going to happen. You did the right thing allowing Arthur to live a normal life. I'd say the only real problem is the Entanglement." Anayah sipped from a steaming cup of tea.

"You think? What if he can't Bound? How do we get him to Thraeh safely?" Harpur ran his hand over his head. He needed time to think. "I'm going out for a while," he said. He stood up, retrieved his top hat and his walking stick and left the lair.

When Harpur was gone, Anayah zapped herself out of her dress and into a pair of soft, flannel lounge pants and a t-shirt. She traded the complicated arrangements of braids for a single, thick plait. To complete the ensemble, she added a pair of bunny slippers and then made herself comfortable on the king size bed. She had some thinking of her own to do.

She had always been adventurous and loved nothing better than exploring other worlds. At her home in Danaleedh, a community of witches on Mysturna, she studied Akashic Records to learn about other realms and, when she discovered something that interested her, she found a Boundary and went off to see it for herself. Akashic Records are, more or less, the compendium of memories stored by the collective consciousness and they tend to be jumbled together much like an unassembled jigsaw puzzle. It takes practice to sort through them and put them into their proper order. All the information is there; it just needs to be organized to be fully understood.

When Anayah had stumbled upon the record of a dragon living on a world where dragons don't exist, she couldn't resist poking around to find out how it had happened. As she had delved into Harpur's records, she learned that he was there to protect a human who possessed magic, which wasn't supposed to exist on that world. And a dragon living on a world where dragons don't exist so he could protect a human who possessed magic on a world where magic doesn't exist was about as interesting as anything could be. She had tried to learn more by studying the Akashic Records, but because Harpur had wiped Arthur's memory, there was a gap in the records and she hadn't been able to find the connecting records so she could fill it in. So, she had come to Earth to try to figure out what Harpur had done and why the Akashic Records were locked behind a veil of secrecy.

It had taken some time to win Harpur's trust. A witch from Mysturna was not as interesting to Harpur as a dragon from Thraeh watching over a human on Earth was to Anayah. But eventually he had come to appreciate having someone from another world around. Anayah's presence made him feel less alone, less isolated. He knew she knew that Arthur possessed magic, but he made it quite clear that he did not want her snooping through the Akashic Records to find an explanation for it. He was hiding something else. So far, she had honoured his wishes, but now that Sok's prophecy involving Arthur was part of the equation, she decided that she had to solve the mystery without Harpur's permission.

She closed her eyes and took a deep breath, emptying her mind as she drifted into a deep trance.

Anayah awoke early the next morning and took advantage of the quiet that only the early hours of the day possess to reflect on what she had learned from the Akashic Records. Arthur, it seemed, was the centre of three destinies. Four, if she counted herself. But Harpur, Sok and Arthur were deeply bound by a thread of fate that had woven their lives together and was leading them, she was sure, to a shared destiny.

There were pieces still missing. Try as Anayah might, she had been unable to unlock Harpur's secret. She knew his involvement in Arthur's life went beyond a mild curiosity about the magic he possessed, but no amount of rummaging through the Akashic Records had revealed what that might be. She did, however, discover a couple of other interesting tidbits. Now, she had to decide whether or not to confront Harpur with them. How angry would he be when he found out she'd tried to find more about Arthur's magic? She was just about to conjure a cup of tea to accompany her quiet morning contemplations, when this soft start to her day ended abruptly with an elf landing cross-legged on the end of her bed.

Goooood morning, Anayah!" Sok said, a huge grin splitting his elven features in two.

Almost as soon as Sok finished the salutation, Harpur approached out of nowhere and, in one swift move, lifted him by the back of his nightshirt and held him dangling a foot off the floor. "She's meditating!"

"Not anymore," Anayah said, not correcting Harpur's assumption. "Oh, put him down, Harpur. This is going to be a rough day as it is. We don't need any bloodshed before breakfast." With that, she disappeared in a puff of red smoke.

Harpur dropped Sok. "Idiot."

"Sorry," Sok apologized as he leapt both back up and away from Harpur.

There being no natural light in the lair, unnatural, but not unpleasant light magically paled and brightened in synchronistic harmony with the sun. From the level of illumination at the current time of year, it was about six in the morning. Harpur was already dressed in a long, black coat, black pants and black boots. His top hat was already perched on his bald head. A purple, silk cravat was tied expertly at his throat, held in place by a large, oval amethyst pin.

"There are some new clothes for you on your bed. Go put them on," he ordered.

Sok, obeying, retreated to his alcove to comply.

When he returned a few minutes later, Harpur was sitting at a table by the kitchen with Anayah, eating bacon and eggs. The scent of fresh coffee formed the top note of the appetizing aromas that beckoned Sok to join them, which, meeting no opposition, he did. He was wearing a pair of faded jeans, a black t-shirt and a pair of runners. Anayah gave him the once-over and nodded her approval. Like her own wardrobe of faded denim jeans, a royal blue, scooped-neck t-shirt with a matching light sweater and a pair of pointed-toe ankle boots, the outfit would allow the young elf to fit in on Whyte Avenue.

"Man-bun?" she asked Harpur, who just rolled his eyes. She snapped her fingers and the top half of Sok's long silver-gold tresses were coiled into a man-bun while the rest hung smoothly down his back. The effect was a modern look that also served to hide his pointed ears.

"Lose the ear cuffs," Harpur decreed.

"Oh, but I like the ear cuffs," Anayah cooed.

"So, do I," Sok objected.

"Lose them!"

Anayah snapped her fingers again and the ear cuffs were replaced by two small gold hoops. Harpur snorted, but held back any further protest.

When breakfast was done, Anayah waved her hand over the table and the remnants of the repast vanished. In its place, a polished black disc appeared and Anayah pulled it toward herself. She leaned over it and as she did, an image materialized on its surface. The image was of Arthur, still sleeping in his apartment. She slid the smaller version of a scrying mirror over so Harpur could see.

"I better get over there," Harpur said. "Before he wakes up."

"I'll come with you," Sok offered. "Then we can all go to Thraeh and get this Entanglement sorted out."

"No. You stay here with Anayah. I'll bring Arthur back here in a while." Harpur stood and left the lair.

Sok wasn't happy about not being able to go with Harpur. At least he had the lovely Anayah to keep him company. He wanted to know more about her. "So, why are you're here and how did you come to live with a dragon?" Sok asked.

"I'm a bit of an explorer," Anayah said. "When I discovered that there was a dragon and a magician here, I wanted to find out why. Harpur and I became friends, so I decided to stay for a while. Why are you here and how did you come to be staying in a dragon's lair?" She knew the answer, but she wanted to hear Sok's version.

Sok repeated what he had told Harpur about the prophecy and how he was now hoping Harpur would help him get Arthur to Thraeh. "He will bring Arthur back here, right?" Sok wanted to be assured that Harpur would not do anything to sabotage his destiny.

"If Harpur says he will bring Arthur here, he will bring Arthur here. Do you know anything about Arthur?" Anayah inquired.

"Not much. Just that he was holding a silver fox and now I have to get him back to Epoh so he can give the coin I gave him back to me so we don't end up..." Sok didn't want to talk about the possible results of the Entanglement.

"Yes, that would be awful," Anayah commiserated. "Did Harpur tell you anything about Arthur?"

"Like what?" Sok asked.

"Oh, I don't know. Like why Harpur feels the need to live here and keep an eye on him?" Anayah prompted.

"I didn't know Harpur did feel a need to live here so he could keep an eye on him. I thought he was here because he wanted to be a Bounder Guard. Is there something I should know about Arthur?" Sok was growing suspicious.

"I'm sure it's nothing. Just my over-active imagination." Anayah laughed.

Sok decided that if anyone needed to have an eye kept on them, it was Anayah. Suddenly, being alone with a pretty witch didn't seem so great. He hoped he was wrong about her. "Do you think that when Arthur becomes king, he will open up trade between Earth and Thraeh?"

"While Earth is rich in wonderful resources, it's lack of magic makes revealing the truth of the multi-verse impossible. In time, perhaps... When humans here evolve and are a more... open-minded about things like that." Anayah smiled. "But it's too soon to know what Arthur might do if he becomes king."

"You mean when he becomes king," Sok corrected her. "The prophecy says I will help him find his way home to Epoh where he will become king."

"Of course," Anayah agreed. *Home to Epoh? Curious turn of phrase.*

"What's it like on Mysturna?"

"It's beautiful. It's peaceful." She sounded a little wistful.

"You miss it, don't you?" Sok said.

"I do," Anayah confirmed. "But I'd rather be here with Harpur than anywhere else right now."

"So... Are you two...?" Sok made a gesture to indicate a relationship that was more than friends.

"Are you asking me if I love him?"

"Sure..."

"I do. Very much. And he loves me in his own way. But we are not in love... *that* way." Anayah said, gesturing back at Sok's gesture.

"I see," said Sok. What he saw was a clear case of unrequited love. Something he knew a little something about. He pushed that depressing thought aside.

"Besides, my dear elf friend," Anayah continued, "he's a dragon and I'm a witch. It's complicated."

Sok had to agree with that. It would be an unconventional match by any standards. Sok circled back to Arthur being king and what that meant for relations between Thraeh and Earth. "If Earth is so rich in resources, why would it be so bad if we traded with it?"

"You're not the first one to think about this," Anayah said.

"I'm not?"

"Not in the least. Many Thraehlings have attempted to form an alliance between your world and Earth."

"What happened to them?" Sok asked though he wasn't sure he wanted to know.

"They were killed."

Sok gulped. "Killed? Why?"

"Because it had to be done, Sok. If people from Earth went to Thraeh now, they would destroy it."

"How do you know that?" Sok wanted to retain his defiance, which was difficult once this new bit of information was factored in. *Prison is bad enough. But killed?*

"Let me show you something," Anayah said. She got up from the table and led the elf to the alcove with the large scrying mirror.

Anayah waved her hand and Sok found himself looking at scenes that shocked and horrified him. In one a large flying beast like nothing Sok had ever seen dropped a dozen or more egg-like objects out of its belly. When they landed, they exploded, killing people and destroying buildings. In another, a vehicle leading five others along a dirt road suddenly jumped into the air in a ball of fire. When the other vehicles stopped to avoid the same fate, a group of men holding strange sticks emerged from behind a hill and somehow caused the sticks to discharge tiny projectiles at the people in the vehicles who shook and shuddered violently when the projectiles hit them before falling dead where they were. A few of the people from the vehicles with similar sticks did the same to the men from behind the hill. In another, a man pulled the stem off of an object that looked like a metal fruit and threw it into a window of a building. A few seconds later the wall of the building blew out and through it came two bodies.

Sok watched for a few minutes before he turned away and looked at Anayah. "What is happening?"

"That's what war looks like on Earth." She waved her hand again and showed Sok scenes of drive-by shootings in city streets, stand-offs between police officers and criminals that ended in shoot-outs and an incident where a group of five men were beating another man to death with pipes.

All the colour had drained from Sok's face. He was sad and angry and frightened all at once. "I want to go home," he said. He didn't want to see any more. "When is Harpur coming back?"

"He will be here soon, I'm sure. Why don't we go have a nice cup of tea?"

Anayah led him back to the conversation pit where she made him comfortable.

She conjured up a blanket and a steaming cup of aromatic tea for the shaken elf. Then she proceeded to explain to him that not everyone on Earth was violent and that, while wars were almost always being waged somewhere, it didn't happen everywhere and that he was in no danger of being bombed on Whyte Avenue. Probably. She assured him that he wouldn't be shot either. Almost certainly. She told him about the politics on Earth and how dangerous it would be if they were to be introduced to a magical world like Thraeh.

"So, you see, Sok, we can't allow Earth to know about Thraeh – or any other world. We have to find a way to get Arthur back to Thraeh so he can return the coin to you. But I'm not sure that he can stay there."

"Why don't we just Bound back, get him to give me the coin, send him back here and wipe his memory? He's destined to be the king of Epoh. I don't understand why this is so difficult."

Anayah took a deep breath and let it out slowly. "Because, first, we don't know if he can Bound safely. As you well know, Bounding can be dangerous. And, second, there's a possibility that we won't be able to wipe his memory once he's been to Thraeh."

"Why not?"

"We're not entirely sure how it works, but in the two cases – that we know of – where a human from Earth has returned unharmed from Thraeh, neither of them ever forgot. No matter what was done to make them forget."

"What happened to them? No, don't tell me. I don't want to know."

Anayah ignored Sok's plea to remain ignorant. "One was deemed a lunatic and died in an insane asylum and the other one made a fortune after publishing a memoir. You remember the whole crazy ring thing that happened about a hundred years ago in Midd Thraehdamas?"

"It was before I was born, but, yes, I know of it. Who doesn't?"

"Well, a human from Earth was there and documented it all. When he got back to Earth, he wrote it all down and sold the book under the guise of a fantasy story. People here ate it up. Still do. He changed all the names, of course. You know, to protect the innocent. But essentially, he made known an important part of Thraehlian history here on Earth."

"He must have been there for a long time," Sok observed.

"Sort of. He was on Thraeh for many years, but there are different types of Boundaries, called *Veilrifts*, where time is somehow affected. We don't exactly how they work because they are so rare, but the usual rules of Boundaries don't seem to apply. Anyone can go through them at any time. And if they are thinking about a specific time and place, that's where they end up. Apparently, this guy was thinking of the time and place he Bounded from and so ended up back at that same time and place. He wasn't even missed. Anyway, we have a few witches studying Veilrifts and we are learning more about them all the time."

"What about the guy who wrote the story of King Arthur, then?"

"That happened on a different world altogether. We honestly don't know much about it other than what he wrote. We don't even know the name of the world that he Bounded to. What we do know is that whatever world that happened on, Bounding there doesn't seem to affect the Bounder the same way it does between here and Thraeh. Every world is different. Every Boundary to different worlds is different."

"Are there any... Veilrifts... near here?" Sok had never heard of Veilrifts before. In all the years he'd worked at the Bounding Office, he'd only ever come across information about conventional Boundaries.

"Not close. Why do you ask?" It was Anayah's turn to feel suspicious. She made a mental note to put a binding cuff on Sok as soon as he was distracted.

"I'm just curious. I've never heard of them before," Sok said. "I don't suppose you can conjure up some of that crispy bread with the jam we had for breakfast?"

Anayah snapped her fingers and handed Sok a stack of toast and a jar of jam.

Meanwhile, over at Arthur's apartment, he and Harpur were having a different conversation. It wasn't quite as amiable and was punctuated by accusations of insanity and threats of calling the police, but little-by-little Harpur was making headway, so to speak, through Arthur's incredulity and chipping away at his staunch opposition to the wild and wildly preposterous notion that he was somehow Entangled with a being from another world and that he could die trying to get to that other world, which was the only place the Entanglement could be un-entangled. Not to mention that the being from the other world was an elf—*the elf*—who had caused this Entanglement in the first place by giving him a coin, which, he was quick to point out, he had tried to give to Harpur, though that was moot because the Entanglement began when Arthur first touched the coin and it didn't matter who else touched it after that. It was just fortunate that Harpur noticed the exchange at all. Then there was the issue of the people from the other world not wanting the people from this world to know about the other world, because the people from this world were violent war-mongers with sketchy political practices who, in all likelihood—and Arthur did have to agree with this—would bring their unwanted war-mongering ways and sketchy political practices with them to the other world. Who on Earth would buy into a story like that?

All Arthur had wanted to do that day was to go to the library and borrow a few books. And try to forget about Cheryl and Fox Comics and seeing men disappear through walls and being zapped from one place to another, so he could just get on with his life. Instead, his day was being shanghaied by a guy claiming to be a dragon-wizard who was not offended by being called insane or in any way phased by the threat of the cops being summoned, but who was extending an invitation to his lair where he could prove to Arthur the veracity of his bizarre tale.

"Why don't you just kill me now and be done with it?" Arthur said. For the third time.

Harpur sighed. "I already told you. I don't want to kill you, Arthur. I just want to get you un-Entangled from Sok."

"Sok's the elf, right?"

"Exactly. Now you're getting it." Harpur tried to sound encouraging.

"Look, dude," Arthur said, sighing, "this is nuts. You're nuts! There are no other worlds or universes or dragons or elves. The guy with the coin was just some cosplayer. You're just a cosplayer... though, I have no idea what game you're from... and I'm just a guy who was in the wrong place at the wrong time. Please, just leave my apartment."

"No problem." Harpur stood and followed his host to the door.

When Arthur leaned forward to open the door to let Harpur out, Harpur grabbed him by the back of the neck, slammed his walking stick down hard on the floor and, in a bright flash of violet-white light, the two vanished from the apartment.

Arthur, eyes shut tight, was still screaming when they appeared a split second later in the lair. Anayah and Sok looked over from where they were sitting in the conversation pit and waited for the shrieking to abate.

It took several seconds for Arthur to run out of air. But at last, the lair was silent, except for the dripping water from the stalagmites, the crackle of the fire in the fireplace and the soothing sounds of a 1970's song about dreaming about California in the background. Arthur stood, cringing, in the silence for yet another several seconds before he opened one eye and began to take in his surroundings. It was clear that he found himself in a cave. Then that the cave was rather large. Then that there was a pile of gold against one wall. Then that there were living quarters set up across from the pile of gold. Then that there was a gorgeous red-head watching him. This last realization caused Arthur to pull himself together in the vain hope that she hadn't witnessed him screaming like a little girl.

"Tea?" the red-head asked, holding a steaming mug up for him.

Arthur stared at her in disbelief.

"Welcome to my lair, Arthur," Harpur said.

Arthur spun around to face him. "This is real? You were serious?"

"As a heart attack," Harpur concurred.

It took all of the effort Arthur could muster to stay calm. "I...I... I don't know w-w-what you d-d-did. B-b-but you need to undo it. Right now!" He was only marginally successful.

"I will," Harpur promised. "Eventually."

"Come, come, Arthur," the red-head said, placing a comforting arm around Arthur's shoulders and gently coaxing him toward the conversation pit. "A nice cup of tea will help calm you down."

Then Arthur noticed Sok leaning over the back of one of the sofas. "You!" Arthur shouted. After that words failed him and were replaced by a fit of seething anger. All Arthur could think about was that it was the elf who had started all this. He launched himself toward Sok, arms outstretched with the focused intent of strangling the cause of his current predicament.

"Should we stop him?" Anayah asked, turning toward Harpur.

"Nah. Let them wrestle it out," Harpur said.

"Tea?"

"Thanks."

Anayah handed the cup of tea meant for Arthur to Harpur. The two of them watched Sok and Arthur tussle in the conversation pit.

Stronger and more agile, it took Sok little time to pin the enraged Arthur to the floor and hold him until he'd exhausted himself trying to escape. Once Arthur had settled down, Sok lifted him up and deposited him onto a sofa where he sat panting and rubbing the ache in his shoulder, on which he had landed none too gracefully during the melee.

Not exactly the meeting I was hoping for, Anayah thought as she, Harpur and Sok congregated in the conversation pit with the blubbering human. She perched next to Arthur, intent on projecting a gentle and calming air and acting as a bit less threatening buffer between the confused man and the others. Directing Harpur and Sok to the other side of the conversation pit, Anayah took the lead in the discussion.

"Hi, Arthur," she began. "I'm Anayah. You've already met Harpur." Arthur looked up, but didn't say anything. "And this is Sok." She gestured toward the elf who smiled, only mildly annoyed by Arthur's attack. Arthur didn't bother to look back at him.

"I'm really glad you were able to join us, Arthur," Anayah said in a soothing voice.

"I wasn't *able* to join you," Arthur interjected. "I was abducted! That crazy dragon-wizard guy kidnapped me!"

"Right," Anayah chose not to dwell on the obvious, which would not have been necessary if Arthur had just cooperated. "Be that as it may, we really are here to help you, Arthur."

Arthur sighed. "I wouldn't need help if that stupid elf hadn't given me that stupid coin, would I?" He dug the coin out of his pocket and threw it at Sok.

"I know you're upset. I would be too," Anayah said, her tone still gentle, but beginning to take on a slight edge that indicated there was no time for petulance and his peevish attitude would not be tolerated for long. "But what's done is done. And now we have to work together to put it right again. Whether you like it or not, Arthur, you're part of this. You can cooperate and help us help you. Or you can sit in that cage over there while the rest of us figure this out."

Arthur followed Anayah's pointing finger to an iron cage suspended from the cavern ceiling and blanched. The medieval thing looked cruel and cramped and put Arthur in an instant mood of amenability. Though it was empty, he easily envisioned his rotting corpse inside of it.

"What do you need me to do?" he asked.

Anayah smiled. "I need you to relax, Arthur. Have you had breakfast?"

Arthur shook his head. He had been woken from an incredibly sound and restful sleep by Harpur shaking him. From there, his morning had gone straight to hell. Again! He hadn't even been able to make himself a cup of coffee. Let alone brush his teeth or change his clothes. He still couldn't figure out how he had gotten to his bed the night before. The last thing he remembered was reading Cheryl's note.

"Well, I've set up the kitchen to provide you with anything you want. Just go on over to the table and whatever you ask for will be brought to you." Anayah stood up and pointed Arthur in the direction of the dining table. "We'll just be around the corner working on our little problem. You can join us when you are done eating if you like."

Arthur nodded again. "Thank you," he said and proceeded toward the table while avoiding making eye contact with either Harpur or Sok, both of whom also stood to go with Anayah to the alcove with the scrying mirror. He didn't believe that breakfast would magically appear the way Anayah said it would, but he was glad for some time alone to figure out how to get out of this.

Arthur sat down and stared at the empty table. *Some bacon would be nice*, he thought. A plate filled with bacon appeared. Reluctantly, Arthur reached out and picked up one of the crispy slices and sniffed it. It smelled like bacon. He took a small bite. It tasted like bacon. Within minutes, Arthur found himself being delightedly surprised by dishes of food and cups of beverages appearing out of nowhere on the table before him. Hot, strong coffee. A flute of mimosa. A large stack of pancakes. Another rasher of bacon. Perfect over-easy eggs. A side of sausage. A stack of toast. Pan fries. Fruit salad. Quiche. A veritable smorgasbord of culinary pleasures materialized before him. He soon realized that he had to control his thoughts to control the food. When seven plates of pancakes appeared, he had to change his focus and think of something else. When all of the bacon vanished before he could eat it, he had to think about it again to bring it back. As food blinked in and out of existence, Arthur learned how to make only what he wanted to appear and then stay put long enough to be consumed. He soon forgot about trying to figure out how to get out of the lair.

"Is that safe?" Harpur asked Anayah as he watched Arthur's unpracticed efforts at feeding himself magically.

"Safe enough. I restricted the spell to only allow breakfast foods to appear for him."

While Arthur was busy conjuring his breakfast, Harpur, Sok and Anayah convened near the scrying mirror.

"I was doing a bit of research last night," Anayah said.

"What kind of research?" Harpur asked. He had a feeling he already knew what she was going to say.

"I looked into Arthur's Akashic Records and..."

"I told you not to do that." Harpur's tone was calm and even, but there was an edge to it that made Sok back up a step.

"I know. And I'm sorry, but I think you will be glad that I did." Anayah's tone was also calm and steady as she looked Harpur right in the eye while she spoke.

Sok saw the non-verbal communication between the witch and the dragon-wizard, but he couldn't interpret it. Clearly, a power struggle was happening and Sok wasn't sure how close he wanted to be to it.

"It seems that Arthur is in a state of paradox," Anayah announced.

"Paradox?" Sok ventured. "What does that mean?"

"It means that for some reason, about eight years ago, his Akashic Records end. Apparently, he was killed in a car accident." She kept her eyes directly on Harpur, whose eyes narrowed slightly, but otherwise showed no reaction.

Sok leaned back and looked around the corner at Arthur sitting at the table. He was eating a stack of pancakes. "He's got a pretty good appetite for a dead man."

"Your Akashic Records are wrong," Harpur said.

It was Anayah's turn to narrow her eyes. "They are not my Akashic Records. And they are not wrong. But this information does add a layer of difficulty to getting him to Thraeh."

"What kind of difficulty?" Sok asked, still watching Arthur eat and wishing he could try some of the pancakes.

"Essentially, he doesn't exist," Anayah said. "And someone who doesn't exist can't go through a Boundary."

"Why not?" Sok asked, tearing his gaze from the pancakes.

"Well, it varies, but if someone in a state of paradox were to attempt to Bound, there could be catastrophic consequences. In the worst case, the worlds the Boundary connects are completely destroyed. At best, Arthur would really cease to exist." Anayah watched Harpur closely as he absorbed this information.

Harpur considered confessing everything. Instead, he kept his expression neutral and asked, "What are the options?"

Anaya sighed. Clearly, he wasn't going to be goaded into telling her his secret. "I believe we can take Arthur through a Veilrift without killing him or blowing up any worlds. Probably."

"Probably?" Harpur asked.

"Hopefully, might be a better word," Anayah said.

"It doesn't sound better," Sok observed.

"Well, it's more accurate." Anayah said a little snappishly. "I was talking to my Aunt Analeetah on Mysturna last night and according to the latest information she has, Veilrifts differ from Boundaries in that they are actual tears, or holes, in the fabric of the multiverse, meaning that they are devoid of thought. Boundaries, however, are comprised, like virtually everything that is perceived to exist in the multiverse, of concepts that have manifested and possess a physical nature. The rules that apply to Boundaries are dependent on the way the thought from which they developed was compiled. For example, a Boundary between Earth and Thraeh is designed to pulse requiring skill in order for someone to get through safely. Because all of the Boundaries on Thraeh were conceived by beings from Thraeh, it has qualities that make it difficult for beings from many other worlds to go through easily. That is typical of all Boundaries on all worlds. The conception of them is influenced by the natural laws as they are understood by the beings that conceive them."

"So, I could think up a Boundary?" Sok asked.

"Not by yourself," Anayah explained. "The manifestation of something like a Boundary requires a great deal more thought than you could muster alone."

"Hey!" Sok was offended.

"I couldn't do it either," Anayah consoled. "Boundaries are the product of evolution. They need to be thought about a lot for a long time. The energy to create a Boundary has to be gathered in the collective consciousness until it is strong enough to become a belief. When it has become a belief, then it can become a fact."

"So why don't you just snap your fingers and conjure up a Boundary that we can all get through safely?" Sok suggested.

"Because I can't manipulate energy that way. I can only manipulate existing manifestations. I could make a Boundary appear to disappear. I could make a Boundary appear to appear. But because it is part of the natural world, I can't create one or change one. Like I can't magically make a being that does not exist already. I can make you think something is real, but I can't make a real thing that isn't already real."

"Are you saying my tea last night wasn't real?" Sok asked.

"Technically nothing is real, Sok. But I assure you that your tea was as real as you are."

"I don't get it." Sok was beginning to develop a headache.

"Let's just get on with the plan. We can philosophize over this existential crap later," Harpur interrupted. "Go on, Anayah."

"Thanks," Anayah said, gathering her thoughts again. "Where was I?'

"The difference between Boundaries and Veilrifts," Harpur said.

"Right. Suffice it to say that Veilrifts, being devoid of all thought, should allow us to get Arthur from here to Thraeh without anything blowing up."

"So, we can just hop through the one that guy who wrote about the crazy ring thing in Midd Thraehdamas went through," Sok said.

"That was the first thing I checked," Anayah replied. "But it's too small."

"Too small?" Harpur and Sok asked in unison.

"It shrunk." Anayah shrugged.

"How?" Harpur asked.

"The popular theory is that all the thinking about it since we started studying it has filled it in. At the moment it's barely big enough for a rabbit to pass through."

"But there are other Veilrifts, right?" Harpur asked.

"There are," Anayah said. "The thing is that they are very rare. That is the only Veilrift that leads directly from Earth to Thraeh that we know of. But there is one that leads from Earth to Mysturna."

"How is that helpful?" Harpur was growing skeptical.

Anayah took a deep breath and then continued, "We can go from Earth to Mysturna, then from Mysturna to Ychonol. From Ychonol we can go to Dyrl. From Dyrl to Terra Nine and from Terra Nine we can get to Thraeh."

"Sounds simple enough. Let's do it." Harpur said.

"It's not any kind of simple," Anayah said. "Mysturna is not a problem. But none of us will be able to breathe on Ychonol. There's no land on Dyrl – just two-hundred-degree water. And on Terra Nine not only will our magic not work, but it is populated by a race of giant reptiles and a race of highly advanced humanoids with big heads and eyes, tiny mouths and gray-green skin. And they are at constant war with each other. Also, while the Veilrifts leading from Dyrl to Terra Nine and from Terra Nine to Thraeh are only a few hundred feet apart, that area is currently the centre of the war zone. Sok, you thought war on Earth was horrific? It's like child's play compared to what happens on Terra Nine."

"Hopeful wasn't the right word either," Sok said.

As amused—and more than a little freaked out—as Arthur was with making the best breakfast he'd ever had appear and disappear, he was ready to wake up from this bizarre dream and get on with his life. Somewhere between the second rasher of bacon and the fifth slice of buttered toast, he had decided that playing it cool was the best way to go. Having no previous experience with dragon-wizards, elves and gorgeous, ginger witches, it was difficult to know the proper protocol. Be polite, of course. Don't get twitchy or yell or make any un-accomplishable threats. *Just go out there, say thank you for the amazing breakfast, bid them all a good day and leave.*

That was the plan.

Being a thoughtful and gracious guest, Arthur zapped the vestiges of his magical repast away, leaving the table clean and tidy. He would not be an inconvenience, even if his hosts were only figments of his imagination. He may have been an adult, but he could still hear his mother's voice reminding him of his duty as a visitor in someone else's home: *Leave it better than you arrived.*

To be sure that he was living up to his mother's standards, he inspected his surroundings. For a dreamscape, the lair was impressive. The living quarters were furnished with obviously high-end fixtures. From the soft leather sofas to the elegantly carved table and chairs, everything was immaculate to the point of perfection. It crossed Arthur's mind that he wasn't sure he had the capacity to dream up such opulence. But he pushed the thought aside because he felt the dangerous notion that this was not, in fact, a dream creeping into his consciousness. It was as imperative that he did not go there as it was imperative that he get home or wake up, in which case he would be home anyway. Either way, home was his goal and it was time to put his simple, but direct, plan to get there into motion.

He followed the sound of voices to where Harpur, Sok and Anayah were conferencing around the scrying mirror. To get there he had to pass the hoard of treasure and the dripping stalactites, both of which served to reassure him that this was a dream. He reminded himself that it was his dream and he was in control. There was no need to be afraid. Nothing could harm him here.

Anayah spotted him first. "Arthur! How was your breakfast? Did you get enough to eat?"

"Sure did," Arthur said, patting his stuffed belly. "Thanks, guys. It's been really great. But I gotta get going." He waved and backed further away from the trio toward where he hoped the exit was.

"Nonsense," Anayah cooed. "We've hardly had a chance to get to know each other." Faster than anybody should be able to move, she was by Arthur's side and taking him by the arm. "Come join us. We have some things we need to discuss with you."

"No, really," he said, trying to pry his arm free from her grasp. "I don't want to be a bother."

"You're no bother, silly," Anayah said. "Come." She pulled him toward the others.

"Look," Arthur said, attempting to sound assertive, "I don't know what you guys are doing here, but I'm pretty sure it has nothing to do with me. I really need to get home now."

Anayah took a deep breath. She hadn't wanted to do it, but it was clear that Arthur needed some persuasion. To make her point, she pointed to the iron cage, still suspended from the ceiling, and caused it to swing back and forth, just a little bit, on its creaking, rusty chain. Arthur gulped.

"Arthur, I know you don't want to believe any of this. But it is all real. I also know that Harpur has explained things to you. So, I'm going to insist that you suspend your disbelief and let us figure out how to help you." She gave him a look that was, at the same time, sweet and intimidating.

Several emotions passed over Arthur's face as he attempted to put everything into perspective. Like a wheel of fortune landing on a consolation prize, his expression stopped at resignation. There was simply no circuitry in his brain capable of connecting all the dots into a logical line that ended in a win for him. He looked at the three strange persons he found himself with and concluded that, for the time being, he had to go along to get along.

"Alright," he said softly. "What do you need me to do?"

"Well," said Anayah, "we'll start with you apologizing to Sok for attacking him. Then you can promise not to do that again. Keep in mind that if one of you dies, the Entanglement cannot be broken."

Arthur and Sok both let that sink in.

"Are you saying that if one of us dies, the other one does too?" Sok, the more adjusted to the situation of the two ventured.

"I'm saying that if one of you dies, the other one will be absorbed into the dead one's corpse." Anayah said.

"Ew!" Sok and Arthur said in unison.

The elf and the man adopted a reluctant, but acute, desire to ensure each other's safety.

"This ought to be interesting," Harpur observed with a shake of his head.

Anayah reminded Arthur of his first task. "I haven't heard you apologize to Sok yet, Arthur."

"I'll apologize to him if he apologizes to me." Arthur folded his arms across his chest and glared at the elf.

"Why should I apologize?" Sok asked defensively.

"Because you are the one that dragged me into this mess by giving me that stupid coin in the first place."

"I was just trying to fulfill my destiny. You're the one who was holding the silver fox. I'd think you'd be grateful to find out that other worlds exist and that you are the future king of Epoh."

"What makes you think I even wanted to know about Thraeh? What right do you have to mess around with my blissful ignorance? I was fine not knowing. Now I might die trying to give that dumb coin back to you." Arthur was beginning to accept the reality of the situation. And the acceptance of the reality of the situation was as frightening than the reality of the situation. The total discombobulation had him off balance. He felt like he was losing control of his sanity. "And what do you mean I am the future king of... What is Epoh?"

"Technically, you're already dead!" Sok took more pleasure in that rejoinder than a nice elf should have, but he wasn't feeling nice right then.

"Sok!" Anayah admonished. This was not how she wanted Arthur to find out about the state of paradox with all its own inherent dangers.

Arthur blanched. "What is he talking about?" The idea that this was the afterlife had not occurred to him.

Harpur stepped in and explained the bit about Arthur's Akashic Records ending and how that put him in a state of paradox that meant he couldn't just Bound, even if he was capable of just Bounding, to Thraeh. "We have a plan, though."

He felt his fists curling into tight balls at the end of his arms, but resisted the urge to accumulate another obligatory act of contrition. "This is insane. You're all insane. Whatever game this is and as impressive as all your special effects are, I don't want to play. I demand you send me home."

Anayah reached the point of enough. "I assure you, Arthur, this is not a game. And these..." She snapped her fingers and two finely engraved leather cuffs appeared on Sok and Arthur's right wrists. "...are not special effects."

"Hey!" Sok and Arthur both yelled as leather laces magically tightened the cuffs on their arms.

"Those will keep you both from wandering away from either Harpur or me. Now, apologize to Sok so we can get you to Thraeh and get you un-Entangled."

Even Harpur looked a little afraid.

"I'm sorry I attacked you," he said loud enough for Anayah to hear. Then he leaned closer to Sok and whispered, "When this is over..." He raised one fist in a silent threat.

Sok rolled his eyes.

"Now the rest," Anayah prompted.

"Fine!" Arthur griped. "And I promise I won't do it again."

Sok took the wise route and simply nodded his acknowledgement.

"Okay, boys," Anayah said," now that we're all friends, we need to get things rolling. Harpur, what are you going to do about keeping the Boundary guarded while we're gone?"

"I'll Bound back to Braydon Wood and get Bloomregaard to post a patrol. I'll tell him I have some personal business to attend to and need to be away for a while." Harpur said.

"Will he go for that?" Anayah was doubtful.

"Fire-breathing dragon," Harpur said, pointing at himself. "I don't think it will be a problem. But you will have to keep an eye on things here until I get back."

"Sok and I can handle things," Anayah said, then looked at Sok. "Right, Sok?"

"Right!" Sok consented, secretly thrilled to be wearing the mantle of Bounder Guard. Even if it was temporary and not likely to require any action on his part.

"Great," Harpur said without enthusiasm.

Not having a lot of choice in the matter, he decided to leave it at that and so he left the lair. He had total faith in Anayah, if not Sok.

"So, does this mean I can get this off?" Sok asked after Harpur had gone. He held out his arm with the wrist cuff.

"No." Anayah challenged him with a look daring him to argue with her about it.

Sok ignored the challenging look. "What if someone Bounds through? How am I going to take them back with this thing on my arm?"

Arthur stared in disbelief at the cuff on his own wrist. Not only was he magically Entangled with an elf, he was also magically handcuffed to a witch. *Talk about wrinkles!*

"I'll modify its limitations when, and if, necessary. But for now, they both stay where they are." Anayah assured him.

Sok groaned. But also having no choice in the matter, he elected to let it go. It was rather cool-looking.

"While Harpur is away, I'm going to get Arthur up to speed on the plan. Sok, I need you to sit here and watch the mirror. I doubt there will be any Bound attempts, but keep a close watch on the Boundary. If you see anything or anyone other than Harpur come through, call me. Understand?"

"Yes, ma'am!" Sok said, moving to stand in front of the scrying mirror.

"Arthur, let's go sit down. There's a lot to go over." As she led Arthur to the conversation pit, she called over her shoulder, "And don't touch anything!"

There was nothing to touch. Scrying mirrors were not all that exciting to him. He settled for amusing himself by watching the action on Whyte Avenue. He wanted to go out there and mingle. Maybe meet a few of the locals. He'd had enough of the lair, grand as it was, and longed to be outside. Elves weren't made to stay indoors for long. Even their homes had open-air spaces so they could soak up the sun or bask under the moon. They needed natural light and Sok was beginning to rankle at being cooped up underground. But he knew that Anayah and Harpur didn't fully trust him. As much as he yearned to go explore, he also knew he had to bide his time. So far, Anayah had only put the wrist cuff on him. There was still that iron cage hanging overhead. It would be way worse if Anayah decided to put him in that. So, he sat still, kept his hands to himself and watched the people and vehicles moving about freely above him.

By the time Harpur returned from Thraeh, having accomplished his task with a surprisingly minimal need for intimidation, Arthur was mostly done sobbing. Wrapping his head around what was happening to him was proving more difficult than one might expect. Or, perhaps, it was exactly as difficult as one might expect. In the movies, characters adjusted rather more easily to metaphysical and paranormal situations than Arthur seemed able to. But in real life, there were no time restraints and having lived for thirty years with the firm belief that none of this was other than the product of vivid imaginations, for Arthur even seeing was not tantamount to believing. His brain was working overtime trying to rationalize, with the objective of rejecting, all that had happened in the past mere thirty-something hours. Dragons, wizards, witches, elves, tears in the space/time continuum, other worlds and magic, in general, were the stuff of fantasy. They belonged in storybooks and video games, not in lairs under his beloved Whyte Avenue.

Then there was this whole Entanglement thing. Arthur could not begin to understand how a tiny chunk of gold passed randomly to him on the street could result in him being absorbed into another person. *Are elves even considered persons?* But the thought of his body and any other body, let alone Sok's, being absorbed into each other was the most repulsive thing he had ever heard of. He shivered every time he thought about it.

This whole paradox issue was even more baffling. What was an Akashic Record, anyway? And how could it have anything to do with whether or not he was alive? He was alive!

Aren't I?

And it bothered him that no one seemed to care that he had his own personal issues to deal with.

Arthur felt the panic rising again. The only thing that kept him from bolting toward what he was sure was the exit was the tap on the forehead Anayah had administered when he had broken down after she had explained what was going to happen. He wasn't sure if he was grateful for the calming spell or not. Maybe if he just closed his eyes and fell asleep, he would wake up and everything would be back to normal again. Arthur tried to relax. He took a few deep breaths and let his eyes close.

I am not going to be taken to another world. I am not going to be taken to another world.

Then Harpur arrived.

Anayah, who had been talking quietly with Sok by the scrying mirror, looked over and, putting a finger to her lips, gestured to Harpur to stay quiet. She pointed at the reclining Arthur, who she hoped was resting, if not coming around to what was happening. She knew he had a ton of questions. And she wanted to answer them all. But right then they had things to do and she would be happy with his cooperation.

"How's he doing?" Harpur asked in a low tone as he approached Anayah and Sok.

"Not sure," Anayah admitted. "But at least he's staying put. I tapped him when he started freaking out again, but he's a lot stronger willed than I expected. The faster we get this show on the road, the better. How'd it go on Thraeh?"

"With surprisingly minimal intimidation required on my part," Harpur said. "Bloomregaard suspects something is up, but he doesn't know that Sok Bounded here. His wraiths are all in the east doing Orhowyn knows what, so they haven't figured anything out. A patrol guard is setting up at the Boundary as we speak and will stay there until I release them. And I arranged for a letter from Sok to arrive at Bloomregaard's quarters in the morning saying his grandmother has fallen ill and he needs to stay in Pollybush for a while. I was vague, so hopefully Bloomregaard won't be too quick to investigate. I reckon we have about a week before things will start getting sticky. Do you know where the Veilrift to Mysturna is?"

"Wow! You thought of everything, didn't you?" Anayah was impressed. "The Veilrift is near Drumheller. We could easily zap ourselves and Sok and Arthur there, but I'm afraid if we do," she gestured toward the conversation pit, "our friend might lose it again."

"No problem," Harpur said. "We'll take the Lexus."

"The what?" Sok said, speaking for the first time since Harpur's return.

"You'll like it," Harpur assured him.

"But that will take four hours," Anayah complained. "What happened to the faster the better?"

"I'm a wizard, Anayah. It'll only take us an hour." Harpur turned and walked over to the conversation pit. "Come on, big guy, we're going on a road trip."

"Where we going?" Arthur asked.

"Drumheller."

"How long will we be gone?"

"Not long."

"Can we stop by my apartment so I can pack?"

"No need. We'll make sure you have everything you need while we're gone."

"Can I at least call my mother? She worries you know." Arthur patted his pocket and realized that his cell phone was not with him. "Crap!" he said. "I need my cell phone."

Harpur snapped his fingers and Arthur's cell phone appeared in his hand. He gave it to the disappointed young man whose nascent escape plan dissolved before it even had a chance to fully coagulate. "What should I tell her?" he asked in a surly voice.

"Tell her you're going on a road trip." To Harpur it was obvious.

Arthur glowered. He pressed the home button and was pleased to discover that he had no bars. His hopes soared once again. "I can't get a signal down here."

"You can call her from the car," Harpur said as he tucked the coin Arthur had thrown at Sok into Arthur's pocket.

Chapter 4

A few minutes later a dragon-wizard, a witch, an elf and a man entered Whyte Avenue from an alley between 104 and 105 Streets. With the exception of the extremely tall, dark-skinned man with the long black coat and elaborate top hat, the group appeared unremarkable. Passers-by couldn't help but notice Harpur, but even he garnered nothing more than a raised eyebrow or a second glance. Regulars on Whyte Avenue had seen him before. Newcomers expected to see something unusual. Thus, they walked unimpeded a short block north to 83 Avenue and a parking lot filled with vehicles belonging to the afternoon shoppers and daily workers in the arts district.

The crowds Arthur had hoped to escape into were somewhere else as they made their way to the parking lot. With Anayah on his left and Harpur on his right, it was unlikely he would have gotten far anyway. Then there was the leather cuff on his wrist. It felt as if it had been there all his life, so perfectly did it form to his arm, but what would it do if he did try to make a run for it?

As they approached an empty slot in the far back corner of the lot, Arthur assumed the vehicle they were intending to take on their road trip had been stolen. He was unable to suppress a snicker that snuck passed his lips to punctuate what turned out to be a short-lived delight. Ignoring him, Harpur waved his walking stick at the empty space and a sleek, black Lexus NX 300 materialized. Arthur groaned.

"Get in," Harpur commanded.

Sok, not familiar with this particular mode of transport, watched Anayah open the front passenger door and mimicked what she did to gain entry to the back seat. The immaculate interior smelled of leather and luxury. Even Arthur appeared to be impressed by it, though he did not display any of the uncertainty that Sok felt. He could only assume that Arthur's experience with cars was relatively more advanced than his own, being that they were so common on Earth. When Arthur reached for and pulled a strap from behind the door across his body and fastened it to a strange buckle sticking out of the seat beside him, Sok did the same thing. But when he felt the vibration from the engine and the Lexus began moving forward, he couldn't help but brace himself against the unexpected motion.

Arthur laughed. "Never been in an SUV before?" he asked the nervous elf.

"What's an SUV?" Sok asked.

"It stands for Sport Utility Vehicle," Arthur explained, though it did little in the way of providing clarity.

As Harpur maneuvered the SUV out of the parking lot and into the flow of traffic, Arthur tutored Sok on the different types of vehicles they passed. Sok was fascinated. And the lesson was the perfect distraction from the terrifying speed—about 30 kph on average—and frequent stops and turns Harpur skillfully completed on their way out of the city.

Arthur called his mother from the car once Sok had relaxed into taking in the scenery hurtling past them as they drove. He chose to keep things vague, giving her just enough information to keep her from worrying about him for a few days. She was disappointed that he wouldn't be at Sunday dinner, but accepted it with only a minor dollop of guilt before telling him to have a good time and disconnecting. Arthur felt a pang of anxiety shoot through him. He still didn't believe he was about to travel to another world, but at least he had his phone and, if things got any weirder, he could always call for help.

"I don't suppose you could zap my charge cord to me?" he asked Harpur, who glanced at him through the rearview mirror.

"You know your phone won't work where we're going, right?" Harpur replied.

"Still, I'd like to have it if you don't mind."

"I don't mind at all," Harpur said.

And the charge cord appeared.

"Thanks, man," Arthur said and tucked the precious piece of wire into his pocket.

The exchange drew Sok's attention and his curiosity about this phone thing. Arthur tutored him on cell phones and a few minutes later Sok was giggling over moving pictures of candy with his finger into lines and watching them disappear. "This is the strangest magic I've ever seen!" he repeated every time he lost or passed a level. Arthur showed him how to use the map app, the calculator, the compass, and some social media apps.

"People take pictures of themselves and you can see them on this thing?" Sok was amazed.

By the time they arrived in Drumheller a mere hour later, due to Harpur's magic, Arthur had about a hundred selfies of Sok on his phone.

To Arthur, though, the trip had seemed to take the normal amount of time. Thus, he suffered a bit of jet-lag-like discombobulation when they pulled into a rest stop and alighted from the Lexus. Still, it felt good to stretch his legs and the warm, spring evening breeze was refreshing.

Anayah and Harpur had gone off a little way to confer in private. Arthur tried to appear nonchalant as he ambled closer to them to listen, but as soon as he got within earshot, he found himself turned around and walking in the opposite direction. It was annoying, to say the least, to be so easily manipulated by their magic. It was equally annoying that he was not as taken aback by their magic as he had been only a few hours earlier. Starting to feel a little peckish, he thought he would ask Sok if he could conjure up some food.

"Sorry, Arthur," Sok said, "I can't do magic like that."

"I thought everyone from your world could do magic," Arthur said.

"Most can. Wizards... And dragons, apparently... can make things appear and disappear or change shape or location. Elves can do natural magic, like healing people and animals and plants. We're especially good at tree magic. Dwarves can manipulate the earth, minerals and metals. Humans have no magic at all. All they do is think up things that will do work for them. I guess it's their way of compensating for not having any magic." It was Sok's turn to tutor Arthur.

"Hmm," said Arthur. "I didn't realize that there were different kinds of magic. What do you mean apparently dragons can do magic?"

"It's not common knowledge that dragons can change shape and perform complex magic. Until a few years ago, I thought all they could do was breathe fire and wreak havoc in exchange for virgin sacrifices."

"They don't breathe fire and wreak havoc in exchange for virgin sacrifices?"

"Oh, they breathe fire and wreak havoc all the time. It's what they do. But they are not, as it turns out, appeased by virgin sacrifices. They just pretend to roast them. Then when it's safe they take them to other cities where they can, hopefully, live safely instead of being eaten. The thing is, only a few people know this and we are sworn not to tell because it's a point of pride with the dragons that they are able to save dozens of young women from the heartless men who are so willing to let them die such horrible deaths," Sok explained.

"Isn't it kind of obvious? How do people explain all these virgins showing up?" Arthur asked with an air of superiority at having poked a huge hole in Sok's story.

"Dragons are magical creatures. They erase the virgins' memories. They don't remember how they get to where they are dropped off or where they came from. It's kind of an accepted mystery. The appearance of a virgin is considered a good omen. They are celebrated and looked after well. For the most part."

"For the most part?" Arthur was concerned.

"Well, there are some unscrupulous men who take advantage. Once in a while, a virgin is enslaved. But even they are generally well cared for. To the dragons, it's better than leaving them with people who would sacrifice them so cruelly and if the occasional one falls through the cracks, at least they tried."

"So, you're telling me that dragons are noble creatures," Arthur mused.

"I guess. But they don't really want too many people to know that."

"Why not?"

"Because it is the way of things. Humans, elves, witches, dwarves, sprites, dragons, and even the Faefolk have existed together this way for ages untold. Dragons don't want anyone messing with it. And it's not advisable to mess with dragons. So, the handful of folks who know the truth have sworn to keep the secret. It works. No need to mess with it." Sok pointed over Arthur's shoulder. "Anayah and Harpur are coming back."

While Sok was educating Arthur about magic and life on Thraeh, Anayah and Harpur were discussing getting to Mysturna. Their plan was simple. They would tell Arthur that they were just stopping to stretch their legs and suggest a short hike before carrying on to the Veilrift, which was actually just over a rise about a two hundred feet from where they were parked. They would just walk through it and be on Mysturna before he realized what was happening. The Veilrift was wide enough for two people to walk through together. Harpur would position himself next to Arthur and go through first, moving Arthur as far away from the Veilrift as he could so that Arthur couldn't run back through. Anayah would follow with Sok. They would be met by Analeetah, Anayah's aunt and Doyenne of Danaleedh, who would escort them to Wildwood where they would prepare to go to Ychonol.

Harpur had never been through a Veilrift before, but Anayah assured him it was like walking through a door. "You will see a faint, translucent mist. Walk into the center of it. You won't see that you've crossed through until you pass the mist. On the other side, you will be in a small clearing. Move to your right. You'll see a large stone and Analeetah will be there. Get Arthur to the stone as fast as you can and keep him facing away from the Veilrift until Sok and I get through. He probably won't be able to tell exactly where it is after he goes through. Unless he notices the mist and then looks for it. But I'm guessing he will be disoriented enough that we can keep him from trying."

Harpur echoed Anayah's instructions. "He'll want to stay with us as we will be the only things he's familiar with. He'll be depending on us. It won't be a problem."

It was a problem.

"I'm hungry," Arthur said. I haven't eaten since breakfast and I really don't feel like hiking around the Badlands. Why can't we just go to a restaurant and get some food?"

"What do you want to eat?" Anayah asked, her pleasantry emitted through a forced smile.

"A burger and fries," Arthur announced, hoping to be brought to a restaurant and forgetting that Anayah was a witch.

Anayah snapped her fingers and a large cheeseburger with a side of fries appeared. She handed it to Arthur who mumbled his gratitude. "You can eat while we walk," she said.

"I can't eat this and walk around out here. I need two hands for this monster," he indicated the delicious smelling burger.

"Can I get one of those?" Sok's own stomach was prompted to growl in response to the savoury aroma wafting through the air.

Arthur plonked himself down on a cement barrier that divided the rest stop from the highway and began to eat.

"What's another twenty minutes?" he said, lifting the hamburger to his mouth and taking a big bite.

Anayah's annoyance was mirrored by Harpur's, but she decided that acquiescence was far less detrimental than knocking the insolent human out. She snapped her fingers and handed Sok an identical meal to Arthur's. While Sok took a seat next to Arthur on the barrier and dug in, she turned to Harpur. "I suppose you'll be wanting a steak?"

"Why not?" Harpur said. "Medium rare. With mashed potatoes and gravy."

Anayah zapped an enormous steak for Harpur and a plate of tortellini with Alfredo sauce and a side of Caesar salad for herself. Then they joined Sok and Arthur at the barrier to eat.

"This is incredible!" Sok said around a mouth full of hamburger. "Great idea, Arthur." He'd never seen a hamburger before and was already making plans to *invent* them on Thraeh when he got back. He decided that Earth food made everything they were going through worthwhile.

"Right?" Arthur said. But as much as he was enjoying what was an incredible burger—the best he'd ever tasted—he was also frantically trying to figure out how next to put off the inevitable. There was something suspicious about Anayah and Harpur wanting to go for a hike. The only thing he could think of to do, if the issue was forced, was to walk behind them all and watch what they did. If they disappeared suddenly, he would make a run for it, flag down a car on the highway and take his chances getting a ride into Drumheller. From there he would find a way home. But for now, relishing every bite of burger for as long as he could, would have to do. As if it knew what Arthur was planning, the cuff on his harm tightened slightly. Arthur looked at Anayah, who was looking meaningfully back at him. She shook her head.

Anayah's patience lasted exactly as long as it took her to eat her road-side dinner. Sok had devoured his burger and Harpur was swallowing the last bite of his steak, but Arthur was chewing every bite slowly and was only about half done. Eager to get back to her own world, Anayah saw right through the ruse. She zapped away the remnants of her own and the others' meals and informed Arthur that he would have to eat the rest as they walked.

"What's up with this hike you want to take, anyway?" Arthur challenged her. "I thought you were in a big hurry to get to Mysturnian."

"Mysturna," Anayah corrected. "I am. But there's something near here that I need to get before we go." *Not a bad improvisation*, she thought.

"So, go get it," Arthur said, waving his hand at the hills. "I'll just wait here for you." He took another bite of his rapidly cooling burger.

A few feet away, Harpur growled. His eyes glowed orange-purple and Arthur could have sworn he saw a puff of smoke come out of the wizard's nose. That was alarming, to say the least, but Arthur knew that they needed him. He was almost positive that Harpur had to be in dragon form to breathe fire, but even the small measure of doubt was enough to give him pause. The thing was, he really did not want to go traipsing about in the hills.

Sok stood up and rubbed his sated belly. "I'll go with you, Anayah," he volunteered. Any bit of exploration was an attractive proposition for the elf.

"We're all going," Harpur said towering over Arthur, who wasn't entirely sure the giant hadn't grown another foot taller.

"Fine," Arthur said, "I'll go. But I'm doing this under protest."

"Duly noted," Harpur declared. "Now move."

Anayah zapped away Arthur's dishes, but left him holding what remained of his burger. They formed a line and headed up a narrow trail to the top of the embankment next to the rest stop. When Arthur looked back, he was dismayed to see that the Lexus had disappeared. Thus, his suspicion that this was not just a hike to stretch their legs was confirmed. They weren't coming back. He wolfed back the rest of his burger and followed helplessly behind Anayah.

The trail they were on ran along the top of the embankment for about thirty feet, then veered off and downward into a small box canyon. When they reached the bottom, Harpur moved up beside Arthur and guided him toward the far end of the canyon. Anayah stopped and appeared to be looking at something on the ground until Sok was even with her, at which point she fell into step with him. Taking his arm, she whispered, "Let them get ahead a bit." Sok, ever eager to comply, slowed his gait and let the gap between them and the other two widen.

"It's straight ahead," Anayah called out when she glimpsed a fine spray of mist near the end of the canyon.

Harpur had seen it too. Arthur, peering into the shadows cast by the canyon walls saw nothing but the rock. "It's a dead-end," he observed. But before he could turn around, Harpur grabbed his arm and propelled him forward straight at the canyon wall.

"What the..." Arthur shouted as he prepared to slam into solid rock.

"...hell?" he finished as he stumbled, alarmed and unharmed, into a grassy glade surrounded by enormous trees with multi-coloured leaves. Barely hesitating and still holding his arm, Harpur pulled Arthur to their right toward a large standing stone on the other side of the clearing. Arthur scrambled to keep up, but was powerless to extract himself from the wizard's strong grip. When they finally stopped and Harpur released him, Arthur looked back in the direction they had come from. The canyon was gone.

Before he could say anything more, Harpur swung him around to face the standing stone. At just that moment, Sok and Anayah came through the Veilrift and jogged over to them.

"Bloody hell!" Arthur shouted. "Why didn't you just tell me we were at the wormhole?" He rubbed his arm where Harpur had held it.

"It's a Veilrift," Anayah amended. "And we thought it was better not to."

"So, is this it? Is this…. Whatever you call it?" Arthur didn't know whether he was relieved not to have been hurled into a rock face or more frightened by the strange landscape he found himself in.

The trees were incredible. Towering a good hundred feet above them and covered in jewel-toned leaves of blue and orange and red and purple, they looked like something out of a fairy tale. For all their beauty, Arthur found them eerie and he half expected to see malevolent, glowing eyes to be squinting at them from between the branches. Seeing none, he decided it was probably best not to look too closely.

"Welcome to Mysturna," a voice said from behind Arthur.

He turned to see a tall woman walk out from behind the standing stone. She was dressed in teal-coloured leggings with a matching vest embroidered with tiny, silver flowers. Soft, gray boots were laced snuggly around her calves and her bare arms were decorated with silvery tattoos. Her raven hair was long and straight with a streak of silver that was braided on the left side of her head. Her eyes were a dark blue, nearly matching the teal of her costume and while she bore a strong resemblance to Anayah, she had an air of age and wisdom about her that made Arthur think she was much older than she appeared. He was instantly mesmerized.

Anayah and the woman embraced. It was clear to everyone there that the pair shared a deep bond. Their happiness at being reunited was palpable. Harpur, Sok and Arthur all recognized the profound significance of their relationship and respectfully stepped back to give them space as aunt and niece renewed their connection.

Arthur could feel the reverence Anayah and Analeetah felt for each other. *This is Love*, the thought. *This is what real Love is*. And a part of him longed to know what it felt like to experience a love that deep, that pure. He thought he loved Cheryl, but this... This was something so big and so weighty, he thought that just by being this close to these two beings, it could crush him. And he welcomed it; he welcomed the oblivion he thought it could generate. For the first time since all this began, Arthur was at peace with where he was and what was happening. For the first time, he hoped it wasn't just a dream.

The embrace only lasted a few seconds, but it seemed to fill lifetimes. Arthur blinked away tears from his eyes as Analeetah turned her attention from Anayah to him.

"You must be Arthur," she said. "The cause of all this."

Arthur was taken aback. *Where did she get that idea from?* he wondered. "No, ma'am," he said. Then he pointed to Sok. "He's the cause. I'm just experiencing the effect."

"I see." She turned her attention from Arthur to Sok. "So, you're the one I need to thank for bringing my beautiful niece home again."

"Well," Arthur interjected, realizing his mistake, "I did accept the coin from him. So, yeah," he giggled, "I guess I am the reason Anayah is home."

Sok kicked Arthur's leg. "He just happened to be on the corner when I needed to hand off the coin. I'm the real reason we're *all* here."

Analeetah looked amused. "Speaking of the coin, where is it now?" she asked.

"I have it," Arthur spoke up. He pulled the coin from his pocket and held it up for the others to see.

"We believe that if neither one of you holds it. the Entanglement will be slowed down." Analeetah said. "Perhaps Harpur could keep it?"

"I could," Harpur said, "but if I have to transform, someone else will have to take it. My scales don't have pockets."

With her focus now on the dragon-wizard, Sok and Arthur were jostling for position in hopes of regaining it. Anayah kicked them both in the leg.

"Well, then, we'll leave it in Arthur's possession for now," Analeetah decreed.

"I could hold on to it," Anayah offered.

Analeetah considered her niece for a moment. There was something a little too eager in Anayah's offer. "No, I think it will be okay if Arthur keeps it for now. Anayah, dear, let's get these gentlemen back to Wildwood. I'm sure they all would like to get settled for the night." Ignoring the sour look on Anayah's face, she took her niece's arm and the two of them led the smitten males and the dragon-wizard out of the glade and into the forest.

The path, well-tended and free of obstacles, wound through the trees. Arthur noticed as they walked on that the leaves were constantly changing colour. The process took several minutes, but once he saw what they were doing, he could hardly take his eyes off them. Then he realized that not only were the leaves changing colour, but the trees themselves were changing shape. Branches would grow and recede. Trunks would expand and shrink. He became so engrossed in the constant modifications that he fell farther and farther behind the others. Stopping to watch the patterns in the bark on a tree swirl slowly into new ones, he failed to notice that the path had disappeared. By the time he realized that he was alone and there was no path to follow he was standing surrounded by the huge ever-shifting trees with no idea even of what direction he should be going.

Panicking, he turned around a few times, which only served to intensify his disorientation. "Harpur!" he called out. But his voice seemed to get swallowed by the forest around him. "Harpur! Where are you guys?" he yelled again. Only silence answered him.

"Oh, boy, what have I done?" he said aloud.

He tried to figure out which tree he had been staring at. If he could find the tree, he would know which direction he had been headed in. But all the trees had changed again. The one beside him that had been an arm span wide a moment before was now only the width of his body. The one next to it with the dark grey bark was now light brown. The trees, it seemed, were changing faster. The leaves were almost flashing. Yellow. Red. Purple. Blue. Orange.

And then, suddenly, a dull ache began to form in Arthur's solar plexus. At first, he thought it was just anxiety over being lost in this weird forest. But within minutes it became so intense he could hardly breathe.

Doubled over and scared out of his mind, Arthur tried to yell for help again. The effort caused him to fall to his knees and a few seconds later he passed out altogether.

The others had walked on unaware that Arthur had fallen behind. Anayah and Analeetah were chatting and laughing as they caught each other up with what was happening in their lives. Harpur and Sok were not talking at all. Sok was enjoying the view that was swaying seductively a few feet ahead of him. Harpur was trying to adjust to his new surroundings. He had a sudden urge to change to his dragon form and fly. But the trees were so close and he didn't want to damage any of them by expanding about a hundred times in size and trying to launch himself into the air. It took all of his concentration not to spontaneously transform.

They had been walking for a while when Harpur noticed Anayah lower her left hand and wave her fingers as if she was casting a spell. At the same moment, Sok abruptly stopped and clutched his stomach.

"You alright?" Harpur asked, looking at Anayah, who kept walking and talking as if nothing had happened.

"Yeah. I think so," Sok said. "That hamburger must not be agreeing with me."

The pain seemed to abate, so he started walking again. A few steps later, though, he fell writhing in pain to the ground. Anayah, Analeetah and Harpur all stopped walking and looked at the suffering elf in alarm.

"Sok! Are you alright?" Anayah asked.

"No," Sok grunted.

"What's wrong? What's happening?" Anayah asked, kneeling beside him.

Harpur thought her reaction was a bit forced. It was almost as if she had been expecting this to happen.

"Don't know," he wheezed. "Can't breathe."

"How is Arthur?" Anayah asked, keeping her head down and not making eye-contact with anyone.

Harpur turned around. "Where is Arthur? Where is the path?" Behind them the trees had closed in and Arthur was nowhere to be seen.

Analeetah gasped, but didn't say anything.

"What's going on here?" Harpur asked.

"It's the Entanglement," Anayah said. "It has to be. Arthur must have fallen behind. It's their separation that is causing Sok's pain."

"If Sok is this bad, Arthur must be in pain too." Harpur said. "Analeetah, can you open the path again? We have to get back to Arthur."

"I can ask the trees," she said, "but I've already bargained for passage and they may not be willing to allow us to go back."

"Ask them!" Harpur demanded.

On the ground, Sok started screaming in agony.

Analeetah started singing in a strange, lilting language to the trees. Her song was soft and chant-like and seemed to go on for ages.

"Can you do anything for him?" Harpur asked Anayah.

"Of course," she said, "But we need to find Arthur."

"I'm going to go and look for him," Harpur said.

"No!" Anayah said sharply. "The forest is constantly changing. And even if it allows us to go back to Arthur, it probably won't allow us to find you too. Stay put. We'll wait until Analeetah is done bargaining with the trees before we do anything rash."

"I can't just leave him back there." Harpur, not used to feeling so helpless, sounded desperate. The urge to transform grew stronger. "I can change into dragon form and fly over the trees. Maybe I can find him."

"No!" Anayah said again. "You'll hurt the trees. And then they will never let us go back. They might even kill Arthur."

"Anayah," Harpur said too quietly, "why did you deactivate the cuffs? What have you done?"

"Please," Anayah pleaded, ignoring his questions. "Just hold on a little longer. Analeetah is almost done."

"How do you know? She's been going on for ages."

"The cadence in her voice has changed. Please, Harpur! Don't do anything that will hurt the trees!"

"I'll try." It was the best he could promise.

Anayah bent over the squirming elf and laid her hands on his abdomen. A subtle, blue light started to emanate from her palms and flow over Sok's body. At first, nothing happened, but after several minutes, Sok's struggling began to subside and he stopped screaming. Anayah kept her hands on him until he grew completely still and fell unconscious.

Harpur clenched his fists and closed his eyes, willing himself not to change while Anayah worked on Sok. Analeetah's song finally ended and she turned back to her companions looking more sorrowful than Anayah would have liked.

"Well?" Anayah asked. "Will they let us get him?"

"They will not," Analeetah answered.

Anayah hung her head. Close by, Harpur moaned, in an agony of his own.

"But," she continued, "they will bring Arthur to us." She then turned to Harpur. "If the dragon will destroy the keetor that is killing trees in the south. They have been calling to you since you entered the forest. When you didn't answer, they trapped Arthur."

"Why the hell didn't you tell me?" Harpur demanded.

Analeetah's eyes flashed dangerously. "They were calling you!" she said.

Anayah quickly intervened. She could see the anger escalating in both her beloved aunt and her beloved friend. "Where can Harpur transform so he doesn't hurt the trees?" she asked her aunt.

"Up ahead is another clearing. It should be large enough for him to transform and take flight." Analeetah said.

Harpur started to run down the path.

"Stop!" Analeetah shouted. "We have to go together or the path will close behind Harpur and we'll be lost here too."

Harpur sighed and ran back to the prone elf. He picked Sok up and slung him over his own shoulder. "Let's go!"

The four of them ran together in the direction of the clearing.

"By the way," Harpur asked as they bolted down the path, "what's a Keetor?"

"You'll know it when you find it," Anayah said. "It'll be the big, scaly beast eating the trees."

"How big?"

"How big are you in dragon form?"

"Thirty feet or so."

"Yeah, about that big."

"So, I just burn it, then?"

"They are impervious to fire."

"That's not helpful."

"I suggest you drop a boulder on its head."

"Tell me keetors don't move fast."

"Fast enough," Anayah said. "But not as fast as a dragon."

When they reached the clearing, Harpur put Sok's limp body down under a tree. He sprinted to the centre of the dell and as he leaped into the air, transformed into his magnificent dragon-self. It felt good to stretch his wings and feel the wind beneath them again. As he rose into the sky, he realized that there were two suns and he didn't know which way south was. He circled back to the clearing and swooped low enough to call down to the two beautiful witches. "Which way is south?"

"That way," Anayah and Analeetah said together pointing to the right where the path that had already disappeared behind them used to be.

Harpur changed direction and sped away. The forest he flew over was vast indeed. Staying low, all Harpur could see in any direction was the multi-coloured canopy of trees. It looked like this world was carpeted in jewels. There was no sign at all of the path he and the others had been following, no break in the trees anywhere and, though he kept looking, no trace of Arthur. The undulating canopy was so dense and so thick, he almost believed he could land on top of it.

But his mission was not to find Arthur; it was to find the keetor and kill it. Not knowing anything about them, Harpur knew he'd have to form an attack strategy on the fly. Literally. Anayah had suggested dropping a boulder on its head. To do that and avoid harming any of the trees in the process, he would have to draw the beast out into the open. That was what concerned him the most. As he flew a little higher to get a broader view, he realized that there didn't seem to be any clearings. The one by the standing stone and the one that he transformed in must have been like the path—temporary. If he had to get on the ground to fight, he might not be able to avoid harming a few trees.

Eventually, the landscape began to change. The trees were less dense and he could see gentle, rolling hills in the distance guiding a meandering river between them. When he reached the edge of the forest, he veered to his right and glided along the treeline scanning for the tree-eating monster. Not finding it, he turned and flew back the other way. Still nothing. Growing frustrated by his uncertainty, Harpur climbed higher to get an even broader view. There was nothing but jewel-toned leaves for miles.

Then he saw what he was looking for and it was a matter of chance that he did. About a half-mile to the west and hundred feet from the edge of the forest, a tree suddenly shuddered violently and then disappeared as if it had been sucked into the earth. Almost instantly, the trees around it crowded in to fill the space, making it impossible for Harpur to be sure of the exact position of the keetor. He wondered how a beast as big as he was could possibly have gotten that deep into the forest.

As he drew closer, Harpur saw another tree shudder and vanish. Again, the nearby trees closed in to fill the brief gap it had left. He still couldn't see the keetor, though. Circling above the area, he kept a close watch on the canopy. When a third tree shuddered and was sucked down, he glimpsed the lumbering brute he had to kill. It was well camouflaged, but Harpur's keen eyes picked up the glint from the two suns off the creature's scaly back.

So now what do I do? Harpur thought.

He couldn't get near the thing without tearing through the trees. There was no way and nowhere to draw it out into the open. And if he left to go search for a boulder to drop on in, he might not find it again. Keeping his eyes on the spot where the last tree had vanished, Harpur swept down closer. He roared, hoping to get the beast's attention and as he did, the trees parted, drawing away from the keetor and giving Harpur his first good look at it.

The beast was big. Its elongated body tapered off on either end to a rounded point. Harpur couldn't tell which end was the head and which end was the tail. It was covered in multi-coloured scales that seemed to form rough circular patterns all over its body, but as Harpur studied his quarry, he saw the scales change from the jewel tones of the leaves to the green-brown colour of the ground so that it blended in almost perfectly. Only the dull reflection of light from the suns gave the keetor's position away. It remained perfectly still and made no attempt to get back into the trees.

Harpur circled and watched for a few minutes. The beast finally started to move, not deeper into the forest, but back toward the outer edge. It moved slowly, inching worm-like forward. Harpur got the impression that it was relieved, though he didn't know why that thought struck him. He continued to circle overhead, moving along with the beast. As they made their way to the edge of the forest, the trees continued to part, opening a path for the keetor. If he flew higher, the trees closed in on it. Harpur was puzzled. Why were the trees letting it escape? It was as if they were opening a clearing only so that he could attack.

When the Keetor drew close to the edge of the forest, Harpur heard a voice. A gruff whisper on the wind chanted: Kill it. Kill it. Kill it.

But Harpur's instincts told him that the beast did not deserve to be killed. There was something else, something he felt was more sinister, going on. The keetor, now free from the trees, seemed determined to get as far away as possible. As Harpur watched it make its escape toward the hills, the chant he was hearing changed.

"You have failed. Arthur will die. You have failed. Arthur will die."

Harpur roared again! It was clear to him that the forest could communicate with him. He did not know the language that Analeetah had chanted to it in, but he was almost positive that it would understand him anyway. He landed on a hilltop and faced the trees.

"Why do you want me to kill the Keetor?" he called.

There was silence for a few seconds and then a voice, the gruff whisper, said, "It has destroyed our kind."

"Because you trapped it," Harpur boomed.

"It had not bargained for passage. It is our way."

"But you could have just released it," Harpur said. "It was frightened and only destroyed your kind trying to escape."

"It had not bargained for passage!" the trees insisted.

"It didn't know it was supposed to bargain for passage." Harpur wasn't sure that was true, but from what he saw of the keetor, he felt it was a reasonable assumption.

"It is our way. If there is no bargain, there is no passage."

"Then let me bargain for it," Harpur offered.

"It is too late. The beast has destroyed our kind; therefore, it must also be destroyed. Our bargain, Harpur Diggins of Thraeh, was that you kill the beast in exchange for the release of your friend. You have failed. Arthur will die."

"No!" shouted Harpur. "Arthur has nothing to do with this. He was included in Analeetah's bargain for passage and you trapped him too. Killing him would be dishonourable."

"We are not dishonourable," the trees said. "It is our way."

"Well, your way is dishonourable! Let Arthur go."

"In exchange for what?"

"In exchange for me not burning all of you!" Harpur released a long stream of fire into the air to demonstrate his might.

This seemed to give the trees pause. "Why do you care about the keetor?"

"I don't care about the keetor. I care that you trapped it and forced it to destroy your kind just so you had an excuse to kill it."

"It is our way."

"It is my way to burn things."

The silence that followed stretched on. Harpur began to worry that he had gone too far.

"Your way and our way are not unalike," the trees finally said. "But we will free Arthur in exchange for a scale from your breast."

"Seriously?" Harpur hadn't seen that coming.

"Leave your heart exposed and your friend will live."

It has always been a point of pride for Harpur that his scales were all intact. Throughout his long life, he had never lost a single one. Not in battle. Not in illness. And certainly not because he plucked one out himself. No self-respecting dragon would ever do that. But he couldn't let Arthur die for the sake of vanity. Though it hurt, both physically and mentally, Harpur tore a scale from his breast and threw it into the trees.

"Now clear the way for me," he shouted and launched himself back into the air. A trickle of blood flowed from the new wound and dripped onto the trees.

Harpur saw the trees part ahead of him. On the ground, Arthur lay still and pale. Instead of landing, Harpur scooped up his motionless body and flew on to the clearing where Anayah and Analeetah waited with Sok. Not wanting to stay in the forest any longer, for fear that the trees would try something else, he ordered the witches to climb onto his back. He picked Sok up with his other talons and sprang back into the air.

"Which way?" he asked.

"Left," Analeetah shouted over the wind. "Toward the mountains. Danaleedh is at the base of the highest peak."

The malady that had struck Arthur and Sok eased almost as soon as they were back in close proximity and, within minutes of taking off, they both experienced a miraculous recovery. Their responses to finding themselves suspended under the colossal body of a dragon several hundred feet above the ground were polar opposite, though. Sok whooped with joy at flying for the first time. Arthur screamed in terror. Then he vomited. Even after expelling his burger and fries, the nausea persisted, so he kept his eyes shut tight and held on tighter to Harpur's large foot. Or hands. Or whatever they were. It occurred to neither of them that they might have just suffered the first effects of Entanglement. Sok just wanted to keep flying. Arthur just wanted to get back to the ground safely and find somewhere to curl up in the fetal position for the rest of his life.

After what seemed like hours to Arthur, but only fleeting minutes to Sok, Harpur deposited them, Anayah and Analeetah on the ground outside the walls of Danaleedh. The witches slid off Harpur's back and brushed their wind-tangled hair from their faces. Sok jumped up and down in delight while Arthur slumped on the ground and waited for the queasiness in his stomach to abate. Harpur swiftly transformed back to human form and immediately helped Arthur to his feet. He looked at Anayah, who looked away the second their eyes met. Neither of them spoke to one another.

Once everyone assured everyone else that they were all in relatively good shape, they set off through the gates to Danaleedh and on to Wildwood, Analeetah's palace. Needless to say, there was much to discuss. At the same time, the walk provided the opportunity to gather their thoughts and formulate their questions. Thus, they walked in silence through the streets of Danaleedh all the way to Wildwood.

Wildwood was, as its name conveyed, built of living wildwood that was woven together into intricate patterns. Faces and animals were carved into pillars and lintels. Branches with normal, green leaves, Arthur was relieved to see, formed natural awnings over windows and doorways none of which contained glass or doors, but were open so that people, birds and animals could come and go as they pleased. Arthur watched birds fly in and out of windows high above. A couple of squirrel-like creatures with bushy tails and a blue-green cast to their lustrous fur scampered up the wall next to the main, arched entrance and leapt onto a branch to chitter at the new-comers from a safe distance overhead.

Entering the palace, Sok gasped. The living wood grew to form natural stairs and ladders leading to the upper floors, but everything was open; there were no walls creating separate rooms. The floors were inlaid with complex designs depicting people and animals of all kinds. Even the furniture appeared to be made from living trees that had shaped themselves into chairs and sofas and tables. It was a giant treehouse that reminded Sok of his home in Braydon Wood.

Arthur gasped as well, but not because he was in awe of the beautiful environment. A rather large spider-like thing with a body the size of Arthur's head dropped on a web in front of him and said hello.

"Oh, shoo, Mezzi," Analeetah said to it. "Don't be bothering our guests now. Let's let them get settled before we start socializing."

Arthur was sure he had no desire to socialize with a giant spider, but he was glad to see it wave good-bye in a friendly manner and retreat back up into the branches it had descended from.

"Are there more of those around here?" Arthur asked his hostess.

"I'm pretty sure that Mezzi is the only one in permanent residence. But don't worry, koobars are completely harmless. Mezzi tends to be a little eager, but she just wants to be helpful. If she bothers you, just ask her to leave. She won't be offended." Analeetah smiled. Arthur shuddered.

There were other strange animals in Wildwood. A small bear-like creature was perched on a newel post at the bottom of a stairway. A cow-sized goat stood in a corner being groomed by a young girl with bright yellow hair. A pair of golden owls with long, fluffy, pink tail feathers rested on a branch over the entrance. Arthur wondered how much weirder things could possibly get and, once again, was dismayed to find that the weirdness was not as startling as it should be. He decided to sit down and made his way over to a chair randomly placed—or growing—in the middle of the open space. It was surprisingly comfortable and as he relaxed into it, it moulded itself to his body and gently reclined. His new view from the chair was of Sok, sitting on a branch chatting with Mezzi like they were old friends.

Harpur had also found a place to sit. His chest ached where he had torn out the scale and he found himself wrestling with the implication of it. He was flawed now. Only in human form would he ever be able to hide the fact that one of his scales was missing. As a dragon, he would forever be vulnerable to a well-spent arrow to his heart. In a moment of un-forgiveness, he cast a spiteful glance at Arthur. Their journey had only just begun and already he was scarred because of the human. He knew it wasn't Arthur's fault, but he needed to blame someone and Arthur was most handy. If only they had flown out of the clearing by the Veilrift. If only he had been more vigilant and kept an eye on Arthur. If only Arthur had kept up with them. If only Arthur hadn't taken the damned coin from Sok. If only Arthur hadn't been killed by that car. He should have been angrier with Sok. After all, it was Sok who had started all this. The soft spot he had for the elf was unexplainable and it was Sok, as much as Arthur, he was doing this for. The idea of seeing him and Arthur Entangled was unbearable. So Harpur blamed Arthur instead of Sok. And he hated himself for doing it.

Anayah, meanwhile, was getting re-acquainted with her friends at Wildwood. She was laughing with and hugging everyone in the building it seemed. Arthur watched her delight in every reunion and again he felt the immense love between her and each person she engaged with. It took a while before he realized that there were no other males, beside himself, Sok and Harpur, present and he looked around to confirm it. Wildwood was filled with beautiful women, all witches like Anayah, he suspected, but not a single man was in sight. It left him with an odd feeling and he wondered if the lack of men had anything to do with the fact, he also came to realize, that none of the women were paying attention to him, Sok or Harpur. It was as if they were invisible—to everyone except that creepy spider, Mezzi. He had the sudden urge to join Harpur and thank him for the rescue. He didn't know all the details, but he understood that something terrible had happened in the forest. When he looked over at Harpur, though, he saw the look on his face and, although confused by it, decided that the dragon-wizard did not want his company. Anayah was busy with her friends. Analeetah was talking to a couple of other witches. Sok was still with the spider. He suddenly felt very alone. He also had to pee.

For a while, he thought he could hold it. But like most people, once aware of the need, it quickly intensified and he couldn't ignore it any longer. Anayah and Analeetah had both seemed to disappear, so he extracted himself from his chair and approached a white-haired witch carrying a basket of humungous mushrooms.

"Excuse me," Arthur said. "Can you tell me where the bathroom is?"

"The bathroom?" The witch looked puzzled.

"The loo? The latrine? The head?" Arthur grasped for synonyms.

"I don't understand," she said.

"I need to... you know... pee." Arthur gestured to his nether regions.

"Pee?"

"Uh... urinate."

"Urinate?"

This was getting him nowhere but more uncomfortable. How else could he put it?

"I need to relieve my bladder." Arthur tried to keep the exasperation out of his voice.

The witch still looked confused.

"Make water? Take a leak? See a man about a horse?" Nothing. "Piss?"

"Oh! Of course!" The witch laughed. "Just through there." She pointed toward a doorway just beyond the staircase. As she walked away, Arthur heard her mutter something about bathrooms and leaks as she shook her head in wonder.

"Thank you," he said to her retreating back.

The doorway the witch had directed him to lead him into a large courtyard with a pond about six feet in diameter in the centre of it. Arthur, forgetting that there were no other males around, assumed he was supposed to pee in the pond. He had just released himself from his jeans and was about to relieve himself when Anayah shouted from the doorway.

"What are you doing?" she said, alarmed.

Arthur barely managed to stop the flow and tuck himself back in before Anayah was beside him.

"I asked that witch with the white hair where the bathroom is and she told me to come out here." Arthur's face was bright red.

Anayah giggled. "We call it a water closet. And it's just over here. Please don't pee in the well." She led him to the other side of the open area to a narrow path that led on to what Arthur could only term as an outhouse.

Avoiding looking at her, Arthur thanked Anayah and entered the water closet. It was, like the rest of Wildwood, constructed of living wood and, instead of the expected odours, smelled like fresh pine. It was clean and neat and could accommodate up to eight bottoms, which Arthur found somewhat disconcerting, considering that there was no door and anyone could come in anytime. But his bladder was complaining at the building pressure and Arthur had no choice but to take his chances. Already the whole no doors thing was getting old.

As it turned out, no one else felt the call of nature while Arthur was in the water closet. Both relieved and *relieved*, Arthur exited the facilities and found Anayah waiting for him next to the well he had come so close to polluting. She was staring at her reflection in the water, but when she heard him approach, she looked up and smiled.

"Feel better?" she asked.

"Much. But what's with no doors anywhere? Don't Mysturnians believe in privacy?"

Anayah shrugged. "I guess privacy is relative."

The answer was hardly satisfying, but Arthur chose to move on. "I noticed that there aren't any men here? Why is that?"

"On Mysturna, we choose how we wish to live. There are men-only communities, mixed communities and female-only communities. Danaleedh is female-only."

"So how do they," Arthur gestured to encompass the females of Danaleedh, "feel about Harpur, Sok and me being here?"

"We have men visiting all the time. They just don't live here."

"So how come no one talked to us? Except that weird spider thing?"

Anayah laughed. "Mezzi is a little precocious, isn't she? But here we expect visitors to talk to us first. We do not presume that they want interaction."

"That's kind of ru... uh, weird." Arthur corrected himself.

"It's neither weird nor rude," Anayah elbowed him playfully in the ribs to let him know she hadn't missed his near accusation. "It's just our way. If you lived on Mysturna, you would think it perfectly normal."

"I suppose," Arthur agreed.

"Analeetah wants us all to meet her inside. She's prepared supper for us. And we need to go over things for the trip to Ychonol."

"Are there any killer forests there?" Arthur asked.

"There is nothing there," Anayah said. "It's nothing but a vast desert. And the air is toxic."

"Great!" Arthur said. "So, do we hold our breath and run to the next Veilrift?"

"Don't worry, Arthur. We will keep you safe."

After the day he had on Mysturna, Arthur couldn't help but feel skeptical.

Anayah guided Arthur up a staircase to the second floor of Wildwood. Sok and Harpur were already there, seated with Analeetah at a large round table laden with food. Analeetah stood when Arthur and Anayah approached and welcomed them to the table. Harpur stood as well, showing respect. But Sok was already filling his plate with meat and bread and cheese from a huge platter. Harpur jabbed him in the shoulder and bade him to stand up. Analeetah chose not to comment on the breach of protocol, but nodded her appreciation to Harpur for paying attention.

Everyone sat down again and Analeetah announced she would say a short blessing of gratitude for the food before they started eating. Sok redeemed himself by looking contrite.

"Our thanks for the good food the world and our hard work have provided. May it sustain and nourish us."

Short and simple. Arthur, Harpur and Sok all expressed silent gratitude for that as well.

Analeetah was first to put food on her plate, signalling the others that it was time to dig in. Which they did with relish.

"Does anyone else think it's odd that Sok and Arthur were just now farther apart than they were in the forest and neither of them is suffering?" Harpur asked as he spooned gravy onto his meat. He looked directly at Anayah when as he spoke.

Anayah reached for a piece of bread, but did not return Harpur's gaze. "I suspect that what happened in the Forest of Dheersha today was because that was the first time Sok and Arthur have been so far apart since the Entanglement began." She took a bite of the bread.

"But they weren't together at all after Sok gave the coin to Arthur until we all met in the lair." Harpur kept staring at Anayah, his food as yet untouched.

"Maybe that's what triggered the Entanglement... them meeting in the lair. And then when they got separated in the forest, it kicked in." Another bite of bread disappeared into Anayah's mouth.

"So, why weren't they both writhing on the floor just now?" Harpur's eyes never left Anayah.

"I'm not entirely sure of all the details, but I would imagine that over time, the Entanglement will grow steadier and more severe." Anayah said. She still couldn't bring herself to look at Harpur.

"Is there something I should know?" Analeetah asked. She had been watching the odd exchange between her niece and Harpur closely.

"Is there something *we* should know?" Arthur interjected. "Sok and I are sitting right here."

Harpur didn't respond. He glared once more at Anayah and then started eating his dinner.

There was an awkward and prolonged silence until Analeetah decided to press on. She would be speaking to Anayah later, but there were other matters to attend to. One of which was what had happened in the forest. She felt it was her duty to her guests to help them understand this part of her world.

As they all continued to eat their meals, Analeetah explained that the Forest of Dheersha, as it was called, was considered a race of people more than a forest of trees. Collectively, it fiercely guarded its borders and rarely granted passage to anyone for fear of being cut down. Only by bargaining for something of value would they permit passage and that sometimes took several seasons to negotiate. Analeetah only bargained with them because the Veilrift was deep within Dheersha territory and she had no other option. When asked what she had given them, she declined to answer, saying only that it was worth the sacrifice if it helped dissolve the Entanglement.

"So, does this Entanglement thing happen every time someone from one world gives something to someone from another world?" Arthur asked, changing topics.

"Entanglement is a somewhat rare phenomenon," Analeetah explained. "It happens only when one world either has no magic or does not believe in magic."

"Well, I believe in it now," Arthur argued. "Doesn't that count?"

"You didn't when you received the coin," Anayah explained. "It was that first moment of contact that invoked the Entanglement."

"Which is my deepest concern," Analeetah said. "Arthur and Sok couldn't have been more and a few dozen meters apart when the pain struck. If that is happening so soon, you will need to get to Thraeh as quickly as possible. In the meantime," She looked pointedly at first Arthur and then Sok, "you two must stay close together at all times. On one hand, it may accelerate the Entanglement, but at least you won't have to experience the pain of being separated like you did today."

Arthur frowned. "Are you sure it was the separation that caused the pain?"

"What do you mean?" Analeetah asked.

Anayah and Harpur's forks both paused half way between their plates and their mouths.

"Well, it's only been a day since Sok gave it to me. Would the Entanglement really be that acute that fast? I don't know all the details either," he looked at Anayah, "but I don't think that the pain I experienced today had anything to do with it. From what Harpur told me, it takes time... weeks... for the Entanglement to get that bad. I think it was that creepy forest."

"Go on," Harpur urged. He found it intriguing that Arthur didn't think the Entanglement was responsible either.

"Well, maybe the forest was rejecting Sok and me. Like when a body attacks a foreign object It's just a theory."

"Then why didn't the forest attack Harpur?" Sok asked.

"Because it needed Harpur's help to kill the keetor," Analeetah said, seeing some merit in his theory.

"Makes sense to me," Arthur agreed.

"I'm sure it was the Entanglement. I've never heard of the forest doing anything like that." Anayah seemed determined to make it all the fault of the Entanglement.

"I have," Analeetah said. "But only to beings that trespass on their territory. Arthur and Sok were granted passage. I can't see how it could have been anything but the Entanglement." She reverted back to the Entanglement theory.

Anayah smiled a satisfied smile. And the group lapsed into silence once again.

"I have another question," Arthur said a few minutes later.

Everyone looked at him and waited for him to speak. When he didn't right away, Anayah encouraged him, albeit reluctantly. "What is it, Arthur?"

"If there are no other Veilrifts between Thraeh and Earth besides the shrinking one in England, how am I supposed to get home after I give Sok the coin? Or do we have to come all the way back the way we are going?"

Anayah, Harpur and Analeetah exchanged glances. It was the question they had all been dreading.

Finally, Anayah cleared her throat. "We're working on that, Arthur. None of us want to have to do that all again. It's quite possible that there is another Veilrift that we just haven't found yet. Let's cross that bridge when we come to it."

"Who knows," Harpur said, "you might like it on Thraeh."

"Harpur!" Anayah scolded.

"Well, let's be real here," Harpur said. "If he can't go through the Boundary in his state, he may have to stay on Thraeh for while. And I, for one, have no desire to go to Terra Nine once, let alone a second time. That's just insane." He deliberately avoided the topic of the prophecy.

Arthur still didn't know he possessed magic and Harpur wasn't ready to go there with him just yet.

"Well, you can't live with me," Sok said. Their truce was tentative at best and as far as Sok was concerned, his job would end with getting Arthur to Thraeh and accepting the coin back.

Arthur tried to imagine having Sok for a roommate. He couldn't see the appeal in it either.

"So, explain to me how this paradox thing works," Arthur changed the subject again.

"Well," said Anayah, "as I told you earlier, your Akashic Record ends with your death in a car accident when you were twenty-two. You claim that you were not in a car accident at that age, which is really, really strange. But the fact that the Akashic Record has that recorded basically means that you don't actually exist. Clearly, you do, or you wouldn't be sitting here. But there is no record of you for the past eight years. Thus, you're in a state of paradox." She noticed Harpur was focusing a little too intently on his food. *What are you not telling me, Harpur?*

"And an Akashic Record is...what exactly?" Arthur still didn't get this part.

"Think of it as a database of every thought that has ever been thought." Anayah used the only analogy she could come up with that Arthur would understand. "Thought—or consciousness—is the only thing that is real. Everything you think is real is just a projection of thought. And every thought that has ever been thought is recorded by the consciousness that thinks everything."

There was logic in what she said, but Arthur was still trying to wrap his head around it all. "So, what if, for example, I had a dream when I was twenty-two about being in a car accident? Would that be recorded in this thought database?"

"Of course, it would," Anayah agreed.

"So that could explain where the idea that I died in one came from, right?"

"Sure," Anayah agreed again.

"So, what if the rest of my thoughts after that point just got misfiled in the database? What if consciousness just made a mistake and recorded my dream as fact and then started putting the rest of my thoughts somewhere else in the Akashic Records?"

Anayah was speechless. She wasn't exactly an expert on Akashic Records, but this possibility hadn't occurred to her.

"How could consciousness make a mistake? That's absurd." Analeetah asked. But she was impressed with Arthur's ability to philosophise the way he was. "What is a data-base?"

Arthur tried to explain data-bases to his hostess, but with no experience with technology, everything he said only served to confuse her more. Then he remembered his cell phone. He pulled it out of his pocket and took it over to where Analeetah was sitting. Showing her his contacts app, he explained how information was stored electronically on Earth.

"This is fascinating!" Analeetah declared. "Anayah, dear, you must bring me one of these when you come home next time."

"Trust me, Aunt," Anayah said. "You don't want these here."

But Analeetah wasn't convinced. She returned the device to Arthur with something less than enthusiasm and got the discussion back on track. She would follow up on cell phones later, but for now, the priority had to be on getting Arthur and Sok safely to Thraeh and dissolving the Entanglement.

"Do you really think that Arthur's Akashic Record has merely been misplaced?" she asked Anayah.

"I suppose it's worth looking into," Anayah said. "I just never thought of consciousness as being that fallible."

"Neither have I," Analeetah said. "It seems impossible."

"Why?" asked Arthur.

"Because consciousness is what drives all of creation. If it can make mistakes like that, what prevents it from making bigger, worse ones?"

"Everybody makes mistakes," Arthur pointed out, "and if what you say about consciousness is true, then the mistakes that everybody makes have to be mistakes that consciousness makes. Maybe mistakes are just consciousness experimenting with things. Maybe misfiling someone's Akashic Record isn't that big of a deal."

"I'm not sure I even want to think about it." Analeetah found herself questioning everything she thought she knew.

"Well, I don't want to think about Ychonol, Dyrl or Terra Nine," Harpur interjected. "And yet, if I don't, I'm going to suffocate five minutes after I get to Ychonol. Or get boiled to death on Dyrl. Or be stomped or lasered to death on Terra Nine. So, I'd appreciate it if we could move on to how we are going to survive the next three worlds so I can get back to Earth and resume my relatively safer life as a Bounder Guard."

"Of course," Analeetah said. "Unfortunately, we have little time to prepare. A friend of mine will be arriving in Danaleedh in the morning who has had experience on each of the worlds you are going to. He is more than willing to help with equipment and contacts on Ychonol, Dyrl and Terra Nine and we should be able to get you on your way within a couple of days."

"Who is this friend?" Harpur asked.

"Kel Wyndrummer. He has experience on each of the worlds you are going to." A wistful smile crossed Analeetah's lips.

"Oh, I haven't seen Kel in ages! But back to the Akashic Records?" Anayah asked. "Do you think Anabettah can find out if it's possible that Arthur's have just been misplaced?"

"Who is Anabettah?" Arthur asked.

"Anabettah would be the best witch among us to ask," Analeetah said, ignoring Arthur. "But she is away at the moment and I don't know when she is due to return."

"Who is Anabettah?" Arthur repeated.

"Anabettah is the oldest witch in Danaleedh. She has studied the Akashic Records all her life." Anayah said to Arthur and then turned back to her aunt. "Away where?"

"She's gone to The Pole to meditate and renew. I don't think you have time to go there, but you can try scrying her." Analeetah suggested.

"How far away is this Pole place?" Harpur asked.

"It's a sacred place," Anayah explained without answering Harpur's question. "People from other worlds are not permitted there." She left out a key piece. Other-worlders were not permitted without an invitation.

"Of course, not!" Harpur grumbled under his breath.

"I will contact Anabettah tonight," Anayah said. Then she turned to Harpur, meeting his gaze for the first time since they'd arrived. "We really do need to get Arthur to Thraeh as fast as possible. Even if you could enter the Pole, the trip would just be an unnecessary delay."

Harpur squinted his eyes and rubbed his chin. *What are you not telling me, Anayah?*

Arthur thought a delay might actually be a good thing. These other worlds did not sound at all hospitable and, while there was an element of urgency in getting to Thraeh, an extra couple of days might give them time to find an alternative, less perilous, route. He was uncomfortable with how invested Anayah was in the current plan. One look at Harpur and he knew that the dragon-wizard felt the same way. *Trust me,* Harpur's eyes said, *I'll find a way out of this.*

Arthur didn't respond, but the large meal he had just consumed initiated its own protest. It felt like his guts were flipping over inside him and the nausea returned. Maybe he just wouldn't eat again until he got back to Earth. *If I get back to Earth!*

"It's getting late," Analeetah announced. "I think we should retire for the night. We can reconvene in the morning when Kel arrives and finalize everything then. Anayah, will you show Sok and Harpur to their beds? I'd like to chat with Arthur alone for a while."

As everyone stood up to disperse, Arthur had a thought, "Do you think that's a good idea?" He pointed at Sok, then to himself. "Aren't we supposed to stay close?"

"I forgot," Analeetah admitted. "Anayah, you go see if you can contact Anabettah. I'll escort these gentlemen myself."

Anayah kissed her aunt on the cheek and wished her companions a good night. She left them and retreated up a flight of stairs and out of sight.

"Follow me," Analeetah said, moving toward a different set of stairs. The trio followed her up the winding steps to a secluded space near the back of Wildwood. There they found three beds growing out of the structure of the palace, each with a soft blanket and a small pillow.

"I do hope you'll all be comfortable." The Doyenne waved her hand and three small lanterns lit up the room for them. Then she moved toward a doorway that led out onto a small balcony and beckoned Arthur to come with her.

When the two of them were outside, Analeetah whispered to the wood, which shifted to fill in the doorway. They had the privacy Analeetah wanted and she invited Arthur to join her at the railing.

A spectacular view spread out before them. They were several stories above the ground and Arthur felt the pangs of vertigo as he took in the city of Danaleedh extending out below them. To his left, in an open common lit by torches, a group of people were dancing to lively fiddle music. He could see animals roaming through the streets and people walking among them. Laughter and chat drifted up from below. Lights in windows blinked on and off as folks moved about in their homes. Beyond the city walls a vast plain spread out and he could see the edge of the Forest of Dheersha glittering in the distance. A range of purple mountains curved around from his right. The horizon beyond the Forest of Dheersha glowed with a violet and orange sunset. Stars were just beginning to twinkle in the velvety sky above.

"You've had quite a time these past couple of days," Analeetah said after giving Arthur a few minutes to take in the view.

"You could say that," Arthur agreed.

"What you suggested about the Akashic Records and the Entanglement earlier... Where did that come from?"

Arthur considered his hostess' question. "I'm not sure I understand what you're asking," he said cautiously.

"I guess I wonder how you reached those conclusions. Until a very short time ago, you weren't even aware of Entanglement or Akashic Records. You have no experience with either and yet you proposed ideas that never occurred to Anayah or me about them."

Again, Arthur took a little time to gather his thoughts. "I'm being directly affected by them," he said at last. "My perspective is different from yours. To you and Anayah Entanglement and states of paradox are only theoretical. But I could die, so I am looking for solutions. And, if not solutions, then at least ways to think about it that doesn't scare me to death."

It was Analeetah's turn to consider things. "You have an interesting way of expressing yourself, Arthur."

The two of them stared out at the city and watched it wind down for the night. The music in the commons slowed down then faded away into the gathering darkness and the dancers dispersed. More and more lights blinked out and a peaceful quiet descended.

"I have been Doyenne of Danaleedh for a very long time, Arthur. In all the many seasons that I have served this community, I have learned a great deal about a great many things. I have always thought of myself as being fairly intelligent. And I have always thought of myself as being empathetic, even when I do not have any direct experience with a situation someone is going through. Tonight, though, I realized that what I thought of as empathy has been mostly sympathy. I also realized that most of my knowledge has come to me not through experience, but through erudition. I am ready to believe what I am told by those who have been deemed experts without question. It's easier, I suppose, to rely on others this way. It frightened me when you suggested that the Akashic Records could have errors in them."

"Nothing is infallible," Arthur said. "I don't pretend to fully understand all this stuff about thoughts being all there is, but it does seem to me that any thought being thought, once it's out there, is subject to being interpreted in endless different ways. I am alive. I do exist. So, the thought of me exists. Otherwise, how could we be having this conversation?"

Analeetah smiled. "Thus, the paradox, Arthur."

"I disagree," Arthur said. "If what you believe is true, that the only thing that exists is thought and that anything physical is just the thought of sensory experience, how could Sok have given me that coin if I wasn't being projected as thought capable of experiencing that sensory event? The only answer that makes sense is that these Akashic Records of yours are incorrect."

"But there are records of beings being lost in this way."

"Are there?" Arthur challenged. "Or did someone just think that?"

"I don't understand what you're saying."

"Technically, what I think you guys are saying is that none of us exist the way we think we do. We are nothing but a piece of consciousness thinking we exist on a physical plain. Right?"

"I think that is correct."

"Then maybe whatever piece of consciousness was thinking me before I was supposed to have died might have stopped thinking about me and another piece of consciousness picked up where it left off. Nothing about me is being thought differently, only recorded differently. If your Akashic Records are real, it's only because you think they are. The fact that we are here together having this conversation is all the proof I need that I exist. Unless you don't exist either and we are not having this conversation. Why don't you check your own Akashic Record and see if this is happening? If it isn't, then what are you actually doing right now? And who are you doing it with?"

Analeetah frowned. She was enjoying this philosophical exchange very much, but Arthur's perspective was so different from the one she had adopted as truth for so long, she was having difficulty accepting it. At the same time, she couldn't help but admit her long-held belief was deeply flawed.

"You said yourself that you accept what you are told by others. Was it Anabettah who told you that my Akashic Record ended with my death in a car accident eight years ago?" Arthur continued.

"No," Analeetah said. "It was Anayah who looked into your record and discovered the paradox."

"What if Anabettah, or you, or I for that matter, looked at the records and saw something Anayah didn't?"

"Like what?"

"Like anything. What if what Anayah saw in my record was what something the piece of consciousness that thinks her into existence only thought?"

"Why would Anayah's consciousness choose to think something that wasn't accurate?"

"Why would any consciousness choose to think anything? Maybe it was just for the sake of the story."

"The story?" Now Analeetah was intrigued.

"Consciousness can think anything it wants, right? Isn't that what creation is according to you? Consciousness playing around with thoughts? This is a story being told. A good story needs drama and conflict. Making me a paradox forced the story to unfold in such a way that the problem of me being a paradox requires us all to face difficulties that we wouldn't have to face if I could simply hop through a wormhole and hand Sok back his stupid coin. The story wouldn't be nearly as exciting."

"So, you believe that Anayah's consciousness is driving all of this? That she created the concept of the paradox and all of the inherent obstacles it places in the way of a solution?"

"I don't know what I believe anymore," Arthur admitted. "I think, though, that we can all think our way out of this."

"Isn't that what we are doing?"

"I think that's exactly what we're doing. What I can't figure out yet is how to get all of us thinking together and just thinking that I am not in a state of paradox and that the coin is not causing Sok and me to Entangle and I am back on Earth planning a vacation with palm trees and margaritas instead of toxic atmospheres, boiling oceans and warring reptiles and aliens. What it all comes down to is belief. And the strongest belief is what ultimately drives experience."

"So, what is stopping you from believing all that and ending this right now?"

"Now, there's the real paradox," Arthur said. "On some level, I don't believe what I want to believe."

They fell silent. Looking out at the world beyond the landing, Arthur thought he should feel tired. Or at least more frightened than he did. His conversation with Analeetah, so far, had left him feeling a little unsettled and yet a little more at peace. His emotions being so at odds had seemed to become normal and he realized that these emotional crossroads were nothing more than points of choice. He could choose, right then, to be upset by things, or he could choose to be okay with them. He could, alternately, choose to be okay with some things and upset by others. But he didn't have to choose at that moment. He just needed to keep sifting through it all and make his choices as things unfolded. Piece by piece. The big picture was, he decided, too much for him to handle all at once. So, he chose to be okay with standing on the landing with the beautiful Analeetah beside him. That was enough.

A short time passed while Arthur contemplated all that had happened to him in the past two days. He was just about to suggest that he turn in when a spicy fragrance caught his attention and he turned to see Analeetah holding two goblets filled with steaming mulled wine. She offered one to her guest and Arthur took it.

"Cheers," he said, raising his cup toward her before taking a sip of the delicious beverage.

Analeetah looked puzzled.

"It's a toast," Arthur explained. "On Earth, when we share a meal or a drink, we often give a toast as a way of honouring our companions or expressing gratitude for something we are celebrating. Saying cheers is sort of like... Well, cheering for a successful venture."

"That's lovely," Analeetah said and responded in kind.

Appreciative of the excuse not to have to go to bed, Arthur asked, "So what exactly does a Doyenne do?"

"Whatever needs to be done." Analeetah looked speculative. "I am Doyenne here, but the title Doyenne, which is given in matriarchal communities like Danaleedh, is primarily just a title."

"Like a queen," Arthur surmised.

"Like a queen, but not a queen," Analeetah said. "I suppose I am considered the ruler, but traditionally, a Doyenne's rule is not absolute."

"Like a queen," Arthur concluded.

"Not exactly. What I mean is that I hold the title, but we rule together by consensus."

"What's the point? Of the title, I mean." Arthur was genuinely curious.

"I suppose I do have some measure of privilege as well as responsibility. I am, as Doyenne, the representative for Danaleedh on the High Council, which comprises all of the Heads of State throughout

Mysturna. We don't have countries or governments like you do on Earth, but each community of culture has an appointed representative to the High Council who shares the knowledge of their community."

"So how do you govern if you don't have a government?"

"Here we live communally. It's different in other regions, but in Danaleedh, everyone participates as part of the community, doing what they are best at in exchange for what they need. People who enjoy growing food, grow food. People who enjoy cooking food, cook the food. People who are good at weaving and sewing make clothes. Everyone takes part and everyone is cared for equally."

"That's very socialist of you," Arthur said. "But how do you make rules, enforce laws, deal with crime?"

"By consensus, as I said. Basically, the law here is that you do your part and, in exchange, the community ensures your safety and that your needs are met. No one is above, or below, anyone else."

"But you live in a palace."

"Sometimes. Anyone who wishes to may stay in Wildwood. It's not mine; it does not belong to me. It belongs to all of Danaleedh. When I am here, I help wherever I am needed, just like anyone else."

"Cool." Arthur nodded his approval. "But what happens when someone doesn't participate?"

"It does happen, of course. But it's rare. If someone tries to take advantage, they are quickly brought to account."

"How?" Arthur insisted.

"They are named by their accuser at Circle. It is a great offence to falsely accuse someone. We are all encouraged to assist first. But if it comes to making an open accusation, the accused is given the opportunity to fully justify their actions and, if it is deemed that they have indeed been in breach of the expectations, they are invited to propose their course of amendment. That is then recorded and three people step forward to assist the person in making amends according to their proposal. Once amends are made, we carry on as if it never happened."

"What if they can't justify their actions? Or they don't make proper amends?"

"They are banished from the community."

"You just, like, turn them out of the city?"

"Not at all. We care about each other. We would never leave anyone without a place to go. Usually, they are integrated into a different community that will have them."

"What if no other community will have them?"

"There is always somewhere for them to go." Analeetah's vague reply had a sinister ring.

"What if someone commits, say, murder? What happens to them?"

"In my entire life... a considerable length of time to be sure... there has been one murder related to Danaleedh." Analeetah was hesitant. She did not like talking about such things, but she felt it was only right to satisfy Arthur's curiosity. "It was a long time ago. A man from a community called Walfig killed another man in a conflict over a witch from here in Danaleedh. The witch had just earned her place in Danaleedh when the two men had stopped here on their way north. They had been life-long friends and they were going to seek their fortunes in the Korat Fields as minors."

"Mining for gold?"

"Gold is common on Mysturna. No, they were going to mine for something much more precious to us; salt."

"Salt is rare here?"

"Very rare! But ultimately not germane to this tale."

"Sorry. Go on," Arthur apologized.

"Like many guests in Danaleedh who are not visiting friends or relatives, the two men were given accommodation here in Wildwood. The young witch took it upon herself to see to their needs and was escorting them to the very space you and Harpur and Sok are sleeping in," she gestured to the wall that divided them from his companions. "It seems the men had both become quite taken by her and had made a bet as to which one of them would win her affections. Neither, it turned out, were aware of our customs and assumed that the young witch was available and willing to reward them that way."

"Your customs being... abstinence?" Arthur asked for clarification.

Analeetah laughed. "Not at all. Though some of us choose abstinence, we are all welcome to pursue physical relations. When it is appropriate. Servicing our guests is not generally deemed appropriate."

"I see," Arthur said. The mulled wine had inspired his amorous side a little and he found this information disappointing.

Analeetah cleared her throat and continued. "One of the men invited her to stay and talk with them for a while. She declined and attempted to leave, but the other man grabbed her by the arm and pulled her toward his bed."

"He raped her?" Arthur was shocked and angered.

"I'm sure he would have tried," Analeetah said. "But our young witch kept her wits and paralyzed him with a spell. When his friend saw what she had done, he threatened to hurt her if she didn't release the man. She assured him that he was not harmed and that as soon as she was safely away from them, she would reverse the paralysis."

"That was nice of her," Arthur said.

"Indeed. And so, she left. She released the man, but put a barrier around the space so that neither of them could get out until she released them both. She immediately came to me and reported the guests' misconduct."

"What did you do?"

"I had them escorted out of Danaleedh and warned them never to return. They were no longer welcome. I sent a dispatch to Walfig, to their Emperor, telling him what had happened and how I had dealt with it."

"And the Emperor of Walfig arrested them?"

"No. He sent a dispatch to the Korat Fields directing them to arrest the men upon arrival."

"What if they hadn't gone to the Korat Fields?"

"They had no reason to suspect that they were in any danger. They left thinking their banishment from Danaleedh was the end of it."

"Jerks!" Arthur declared.

Analeetah, unfamiliar with that particular epithet, immediately understood it and smiled at their shared insight. "They arrived at the Korat Fields several days later and were detained. As is customary on Mysturna, they were accused in Circle and given the opportunity to justify their actions. The man that had not grabbed the girl was adamant that he should not be included in the accusation and this started a rift between him and his friend."

"So, they fought and one of them killed the other?" Arthur summarized.

"On Mysturna, conflicts are settled on the playing field. When a crime has been committed, or when two parties cannot agree, they challenge each other to a game. The accused gets to choose the game and the terms are set out in advance. The man who had not grabbed the girl challenged his friend at Circle and his friend chose a game that he knew he was better at. They were to run an obstacle course. Knowing that he could never match, let alone beat him in an obstacle course, the man who had accused his friend, called for a second."

"Someone with enough skill to stand in for him?"

"You are familiar with the rules of conflict?"

"We call it duelling. But on Earth—when duels were actually fought—it was with pistols or swords. To the death."

"How barbaric!" It was Analeetah's turn to be shocked.

"That's why we don't do it anymore."

"I'm glad for that, at least."

"So, what happened? Did he find a second?"

"No one would stand in for him. He was so angry at his friend for getting them both into the mess, he took a stone and beat his friend to death with it."

"Bloody hell!" Arthur said. "Things like that happen all the time on Earth. People kill each other over stupid things like that. What happened to the guy?"

"The murderer? He was taken to the Forest of Aranpoor and left to the trees." Analeetah sounded sad as she ended her story.

"Is that anything like the Forest of Dheersha?" Arthur shuddered.

"It is a community of trees that is similar to the Forest of Dheersha," Analeetah confirmed.

"So, people on Mysturna are generally non-violent, but the forests are manipulative killers. Huh!" Arthur said. "Good to know."

"Arthur, we do not sanction violence of any kind. All of the communities are built on mutual support and trust. We value life. All life."

"Even the manipulative, killer trees?"

"Even the manipulative, killer trees."

"So, how did that goose we ate for supper come to be cooked for us?" Arthur thought he'd found a hole in Analeetah's values.

"The goose, as you call it, volunteered to sacrifice itself for our benefit."

"The goose... what do you call it?... volunteered to be eaten?"

"Yes. All life on Mysturna understands what need it is here to fill. We call upon the animals to provide us food and they are happy to fulfil their purpose. And we call it a galing."

"So, you say, 'Hey, galings, I want to eat one of you for supper. Who's it gonna be?' And one of them just flops over dead for you?"

"Something like that," Analeetah said with amusement. "The witch who is to do the cooking calls to the animals in their language and one of them steps forward. The witch then feeds it a potion that causes it to die peacefully. Then she butchers and cooks it. In the case of your goose, that witch was me."

"You cooked your own goose?" Arthur laughed at his joke, which was completely lost on Analeetah.

"I cooked a galing, but it wasn't mine," she confirmed, sounding a little defensive.

"I'm sorry. That was a bad joke. But you did, in fact, kill it. With the potion."

"Only by agreement."

"I'm just sayin'," Arthur said.

"Saying what?" Analeetah was confused.

"Nothing. Forget it. It really isn't important. Our worlds are very different. Earth could learn a thing or two from you witches."

"As could we from you."

"Like what?" Arthur was curious.

"Like databases and cell phones."

"I think Anayah was right about that. You really don't want those things here." But he touched the pocket where his cell phone was for reassurance.

"Why not? I think they are brilliant."

"They are. They are also big distractions."

"Distractions from what?"

"From everything. People get addicted to them and can't put them down. They text and snap selfies while they're driving, which causes accidents. They don't talk to each other anymore. Everyone is too busy staring at their phones. People even break up with each other by text. It's kinda crazy."

"If they are so bad, why do you have one?"

"Well, they are useful too. I can use it to check the weather."

"Check the weather?"

"Yeah. Here, I'll show you." Arthur retrieved his phone and moved next to Analeetah. He opened the weather app, then remembered there was no cell service and that he'd picked a bad example.

"Damn, no service," he said. "Never mind. That's not going to work here. But I can show you how to take photos."

Arthur opened the camera app and instructed Analeetah to lean in close to him. He held up the cell phone and laughed when she gasped at her image on the screen. "Smile," Arthur told her and snapped the picture.

With a tap and a swipe, he opened the photo he had just taken of the two of them and handed the phone to Analeetah.

"Is that what I look like?" she exclaimed.

Arthur laughed. "Everyone is surprised by their own image. But I assure you, Analeetah, you look beautiful."

The witch tore her eyes away from her image on the small screen and looked up at the young man who had just delighted her with his strange magic. For several long seconds, their eyes were locked onto each other's. And then, before he could stop himself, Arthur leaned in and kissed Analeetah.

It was chaste and tender, a brief connection. But in that fleeting moment, Arthur understood the energy he'd felt when Anayah had embraced Analeetah at the standing stone. His heart leapt and his mind melted away as the entire universe burst open around him. He wanted more, but he was afraid to move, afraid to breathe. Seconds passed and just when Arthur began to think that he'd made a terrible mistake, Analeetah reached up and pulled him to her, kissing him again. This time not so tenderly. Their lips met and parted and they both became lost in each other. As if on cue, the first rays of the first sun rising broke over the horizon and bathed them in its bright light. Arthur knew then exactly what he believed in. He believed that a miracle would happen and he would not be single for long.

Staying up all night, talking with Analeetah would eventually catch up with Arthur, but for the time being, he was riding the high from the kiss they shared on the balcony at Wildwood. Always a diplomat, Analeetah had ended the spectacular moment with a smooth segue toward the more mundane, but equally essential need to resolve the issues at hand, namely his state of paradox and the Entanglement, both of which took *It's complicated* to levels previously unheard of. Arthur, driven by his deeply embedded, male biological imperative, chose to interpret it, not as a turn-down, but as a clearing-the-way for more. Nothing... not even the unexpected and unwelcome appearance of Mezzi... could dampen Arthur's blissful condition. In his mind he had already become Consort to the Doyenne of Danaleedh. *Does a crown come with that?* he wondered.

"You must come quickly, Analeetah! Kel Wyndrummer has arrived!" The spider waved at Arthur again as she made the announcement.

Chapter 5

Kel Wyndrummer, from the moment Arthur first set eyes on him, represented the first crack in his new-found belief. Tall and powerfully built, Kel Wyndrummer stood on top of a large wagon, tossing bundles and boxes down to a variety of only slightly less-powerfully built, but equally wild-looking men. Their braided and beaded beards and hair shone in the morning sun. They were bare-chested, bare-footed and their buckskin pants looked more like body art than actual garments. Arthur saw himself as the 98-pound weakling to their, but especially Kel's, Charles Atlas beach-body physiques.

Somewhere between the balcony and the wagon Kel was standing on at the entrance to Wildwood, Analeetah had changed from the teal vest and leggings she had been wearing into a sleek, midnight blue gown that hugged and enhanced her curves. A green-eyed monster stirred in Arthur's chest and rather than join Harpur and Sok, who had joined the men catching and carrying the bundles and boxes into Wildwood, he sidled toward a pillar and watched Analeetah hike up her skirts and climb onto the wagon with his new nemesis.

If she kisses him...

Analeetah threw her arms around Kel Wyndrummer's neck and kissed him.

No!

"What have you brought us?" Analeetah asked as she extracted herself from the wild man's embrace.

"Silks and spices and other nice things," Kel said with a lustful grin and a more-than-friendly pat on Analeetah's bottom.

"Oh, you!" she scolded, giving Kel a playful and wholly insincere slap on the wrist.

The crack in Arthur's new-found belief widened.

Kel tossed the last bundle down and, scooping Analeetah up in his brawny arms, jumped off of the wagon. He carried the laughing Doyenne inside Wildwood. Behind them, the crowds that had gathered pushed their way in behind them. The early morning crackled with an air of celebration, but Arthur couldn't bring himself to join in. Instead, he pushed against the tide of bodies and sulked off down the street and away from the revellers. The farther he walked, the less he felt the sting of seeing Analeetah kiss Kel. Somehow the growing distance soothed the hurt.

He had no idea where he was or where he was going. He just walked and wondered more and more why he wasn't back at Wildwood with the others. Something in him kept tugging at his heart, wanting him to go back. But he stubbornly forced himself to foster the bitterness and keep going. He wanted to be hurt, but the hurt didn't want to happen. His emotions were playing strange with him and he convinced himself that he was only walking farther so he could understand why he wasn't harbouring murderous thoughts toward Kel and Analeetah. The Earth Arthur wanted to be angry and jealous. The Arthur on Mysturna wanted to celebrate the moment he'd shared with the beautiful witch and rejoice with her in her reunion with someone who clearly meant something to her. No matter how hard he tried, though, he could not maintain a single hateful thought for either of them. The crack in his new-found belief closed a little. Not all the way, but enough to keep the thick, sticky bitterness from seeping all the way in.

He arrived at a small green space just as this epiphany blossomed in his awareness. A cobblestone path led him into the green space toward an arbour laden with huge, blue roses. Their honey-rose scent filled the air and Arthur had to resist the urge to pluck one from the vine they grew on. He ducked under the hanging flowers and passed through the arbour into an enclosed space surrounded by lush trees and bushes. In the centre of the enclosure was a tree with pink-gold leaves. It was only a few yards tall and perfectly rounded. As he drew closer, he noticed small strips of cloth draped over the branches. They were all different colours, some even had embroidered patterns on them. They all contained words and symbols hand-written in ink. While Arthur didn't recognize the language, he seemed to understand the sentiments being expressed. These were wishes, blessings, prayers to a god Arthur didn't know, but intuited was present in this place. He knew he mustn't touch the strips, but he found himself bending and craning to look at each of them, wanting to feel them, drawn to their warmth and candour. Just being there close to them, Arthur felt content and at peace.

"Do you wish to ask for something?"

Arthur turned to see Anayah, who he had yet to see that morning, standing by the arbour.

"I don't know what I would ask for," Arthur said.

"You can ask for anything." Anayah approached the tree.

"Yesterday I would have asked to go home." Arthur paused. "This morning I would have asked to spend eternity right here. Now, I want both and neither of those things."

"There is potential in everything we ask for to be a blessing or a curse. The trick, I think, is not so much to ask to receive as it is to ask for guidance. You cannot go back, Arthur. You can only go forward."

Arthur stared up at the branches of the pink-gold tree with all its wishes and blessings and prayers. "Whether I asked to go home or I asked to stay here, I would still have to go to those other worlds, wouldn't I?"

"That I can't tell you," Anayah said. "I do know that when we ask for anything, we are already on the path to it."

"Then why ask at all?"

"Because even when we find ourselves on the path to what we seek, we can still go astray."

"You're talking about doubt and fear," Arthur surmised.

"Among other things," Anayah said cryptically.

Arthur smiled ruefully. "More Mysturnian wisdom?"

"Call it whatever you want," Anayah said. "But in my experience, it applies on all worlds."

Arthur simply nodded.

"Do you want to ask?" Anayah asked again.

"I think I'll pass," Arthur replied. *I wonder what I asked for that landed me in this mess.*

"Very well," Anayah said. "Then you are wanted at Wildwood. Analeetah is looking for you."

"Well, let's not keep her waiting," Arthur said, holding out his arm for Anayah to guide him back to the palace.

When they emerged from the arbour, Arthur was surprised to see Harpur and Sok standing next to it.

"What are you two doing here?" Arthur asked. But even as he formed the words, he knew the answer. "Oh! I forgot," he said by way of apology.

"We didn't," Harpur said.

"We didn't want to take any chances," Sok said, "so we followed you."

"Thanks," Arthur said. "I..." He didn't know what to say. It didn't feel right to tell them about his encounter with Analeetah.

"It's okay," Harpur said. "Saved me from having to be in the same room with that Wyndrummer guy."

The four of them started walking along the path out of the green space and back to the street.

"Wyndrummer does seem to be..." Arthur began.

"A wart on Orhowyn's backside?" Harpur finished.

"I was going to say larger than life," Arthur said, "but if a wart on Orhowyn's backside works for you..." *Who or what is Orhowyn?* Arthur wondered, but was too afraid to ask.

"It does."

"Now, now, boys. Kel isn't that bad. And he is the guy that's going to keep us alive on our way back to Thraeh."

Harpur grunted. Arthur sighed.

"Harpur, why are you so grouchy lately?" Sok asked.

"I'm not grouchy!"

"You kinda are," Arthur said. "Ever since the thing in the forest yesterday... What happened back there, anyway?"

"Nothing. I just don't like those trees," Harpur said, clenching his fist so he wouldn't touch the spot where he'd torn his scale off to save Arthur's life.

Anayah noticed the fist and made a note to keep an eye on Harpur. She was concerned, but not enough to push the issue just yet. Instead, she changed the subject. "There will be a feast tonight in the square. Music and dancing..."

"I love to dance!" Sok said and started demonstrating his skill, much to his companions' amusement. Sans Harpur, of course.

"Do all elves dance like that? Or are you the only one who looks like a spastic robot?" Arthur teased.

"What's a robot?" Sok stopped jerking around.

"Another time, my friend," Arthur said, putting his free arm around the elf's shoulder to keep him from taking out a passerby with his wild cavorting.

Harpur just scowled, but kept pace with them.

When they entered Wildwood, Arthur thought it looked like Christmas morning, but on a large scale. There were wrappings and strings and empty boxes all over the floor and up and down every staircase. Spice jars were stacked up on tables and steps and chairs. Some had been tipped, their fragrant contents spilling out across whatever surface they were on. Groups of witches were unfurling bolts of bright-coloured silk and chattering about what they would make with them. Mezzi was busy skittering from empty box to empty box like a cat, first hiding and then popping out to startle anyone passing by. There was music and laughter, and the smell of food being cooked filled the air.

"Orhowyn's shaggy beard!" Harpur growled. "I thought we were supposed to be preparing to go."

"Things have changed," Anayah said matter-of-factly. Then, seeing Harpur's growing disgust, she added, "I know. I'm a little frustrated too. But Analeetah and Kel are upstairs and they do want to talk with us about their plans to get us safely to Ychonol as soon as possible."

Harpur shook his head and started picking his way through the chaos to the stairs. When a pretty witch with orange hair tried to place a large hat that looked a lot like a sombrero on Harpur's head, Sok quickly intervened and accepted the gaudy accessory in his stead.

Getting to and up the stairs was like traversing an obstacle course. While Harpur just kicked stuff out of his way, Sok leapt and danced around it. Anayah and Arthur zig-zagged past the scattered detritus of Kel Wyndrummer's gifts. But eventually, they arrived at the same table they had met with Analeetah at the night before. Still half-naked and still with bulging pecks and biceps, Kel somehow managed to look like he was all business. He was leaning over a large map, studying it as if to memorize every topographic feature. Analeetah was examining a strange piece of apparatus she had lifted out of a large crate near the table.

"How does this work?" she asked, tipping it this way and that. Then she noticed Harpur, Sok, Anayah and Arthur approaching from the top of the stairs and put it back in the crate. "Oh, there you are! It's about time. Where did you get to?"

Kel looked up from the map, but said nothing and bent back over the table.

"Arthur was testing the Entanglement again," Harpur said, looking at Anayah. "Seems it's still dormant."

Anayah's face reddened, but she ignored Harpur's less than subtle probe. "Just went for a little walk," Anayah said. "Shall we get started?"

"Anayah, dear, what's the rush?" Analeetah asked.

"The rush, I thought," Harpur interjected, "is saving Sok and Arthur's lives. Aren't we supposed to do that as quickly as possible? Or does this," He pointed at Kel, "mean rushing isn't necessary anymore."

Kel stood up and crossed his arms over his chest. The *multi*-universal male intimidation stance was mirrored by the dragon-wizard who locked eyes with Kel. They were clearly sizing each other up, but while Harpur was looking for Kel's physical weakness, Kel was looking for Harpur's emotional tell. He noticed Harpur wince slightly when his arms touched his body and understood that whatever the physical wound was, it was minor in comparison to the wound Harpur's ego was suffering. Harpur saw Kel as a threat for some reason, but Kel wasn't interested in which of them was ultimately the alpha.

"Now, now," Analeetah consoled. "I realize that Kel's arrival has caused a little bit of a... disturbance. But he is here to help. Kel, why don't you show us what you brought?"

Kel removed the large map from the table and invited the group to sit down. As they did, he retrieved some odd items from different boxes and crates. These he arranged on the table.

What's with the medieval scuba gear? Arthur wondered, though he suspected he knew.

The first world they were going to, Ychonol, had no breathable air. But the crude apparatus that Arthur was looking at did not inspire much confidence. He doubted the rectangular tanks would pass a pressure test. They also looked incredibly heavy. The hoses were woven out of some sort of grass and the masks looked more suitable for a costume party than a life-threatening mission through a toxic wasteland.

Arthur looked at Harpur and was relieved to see his own skepticism mirrored in the dragon-wizard's expression. This stuff looked like stage props made by middle school drama students. There was no way he was putting his faith in it to keep him alive. Sok, on the other hand, was straining to get a better look at the strange equipment. His curiosity, always piqued, was barely contained and Arthur expected him to leap across the table at any moment just to touch the stuff.

"This, my friends," announced Kel, "is what is going to keep us alive on Ychonol."

"Us?" Harpur was first to pick up on the inclusive plural.

"I will be accompanying you as far as Dyrl," Kel said.

"The last thing I need is more bodies to worry about," Harpur said.

Kel actually chuckled. "You don't have to worry about me, dragon."

Anayah rolled her eyes. "Harpur, Kel has been to both Ychonol and Dyrl many times. He knows what he's doing and if anyone can get us through—at least that far—safely, it's Kel. Now cool your fire and listen to him."

"He could have led with that," Harpur mumbled.

"And this," Kel continued as he started to unfold what looked like a large canvas blanket, "will keep us alive on Dyrl."

"Dyrl is the hot ocean world, right?" Arthur asked.

"It is," Kel affirmed.

"How is that," Arthur pointed at the thin sheet, "going to keep us alive?"

"We're going to ride it."

Arthur was no expert, but he was pretty sure that floating on a blanket was not a real thing. "Does it inflate somehow?" he asked.

"Inflate?"

"Expand. Blow up. Fill with air. Become buoyant."

"Why would we need it to... *inflate*?"

"If we put that on the surface of the water and step onto it, it's just going to sink. A blanket isn't going to hold one of us up, let alone all five of us," Arthur argued.

"Of course not," Anayah said. "It's not a boat."

Arthur felt like the dumb kid. Everyone else seemed to understand its purpose except him.

"We're going to fly on it, Arthur," Sok said with far more excitement and enthusiasm than Arthur felt.

"Ah," Arthur said. "It's a magic carpet. I should have got that."

"We just call it a flying blanket," Kel said, "but I like magic carpet better. I think we need to start at the beginning, though, and go through this step-by-step." He pushed the flying blanket out of the way and picked up the mask.

Arthur listened, growing ever more horrified as Kel explained and demonstrated the use of the weird breathing apparatus and the precision timing that would be involved as they moved from this world to the next. And the next. And the next.

"Don't worry, Arthur," Kel said when he noticed how green Arthur had become. "We'll do a few practice runs so you can get used to putting this stuff on and taking it off. We will test everything and get our timing right before we go."

Thankfully, one of the witches of Wildwood appeared just then to announce that lunch was ready. Kel removed everything from the table just in time for great platters of food to appear on it. Arthur had no appetite, but at least he had a distraction from the insanity Kel had just proposed. While the others dug in and filled their bellies with bread and cheese and fruit and thick slices of what looked and smelled like ham, Arthur sat brooding. He accepted a mug of strong, dark ale, but did not drink it.

Instead, he thought about the kiss he had shared with Analeetah. When he looked over at her, she was looking back at him and she smiled when their eyes met. He wanted it to mean something, but when Kel spoke to her, she turned that same bright smile on him and Arthur let the disappointment wash over him. Again, he marvelled slightly at how his emotions seemed so at odds. Along with his personal disappointment there was also a sense of happiness for Analeetah and Kel. It was all just too weird.

Arthur, then focussed on Harpur. He was watching Kel too closely. There was nothing friendly in his gaze and it made Arthur uncomfortable. Would the dragon-wizard be able to keep his alpha male propensities in check and not let his need to be in charge jeopardize their safety? This was a concern.

Then there was Sok. Amiable, goofy and too eager for adventure, would the elf do something stupid and get them all killed in the process?

And what about Anayah? Why was she doing all this? Strictly speaking, she didn't need to be going with them. At least not past this point. It made sense that she had accompanied them to Mysturna, but why was she going on to Ychonol, Dyrl, Terra Nine and Thraeh with them? She could stay here with her aunt and her friends at Wildwood. Or go back to the lair and keep watch over Whyte Avenue. But risking her own life for an elf and a man she had only met a couple of days earlier didn't make much sense to Arthur. There was something else going on. *But what?*

All too soon, it was time for them to go with Kel to prepare for their journey. They followed Kel out of Wildwood and along a pathway leading from the back of the palace to a gate in the city wall that opened onto a wide meadow. Several of the men who had arrived with Kel that morning were in the meadow setting up the equipment for the trial run. Arthur saw three glowing circles of light near the ground and spaced a couple hundred meters apart. Between the farthest two, wisps of steam rose from the ground that looked like it was rippling like water. Arthur assumed this was a Mysturnian version of virtual reality, a simulator of sorts, designed to test their ability to move through the Veilrifts from one world to the next without dying.

As they approached the nearest glowing circle of light, it shifted and became the same size and shape as the actual Veilrift they would pass through to Ychonol. On the ground were five sets of the breathing apparatus and five sacks with long shoulder straps that Kel explained would contain water and food and other supplies they might need on their journey. These sacks were just weighted to mimic the real ones. Only two of the sets of supplies contained a flying blanket. Kel would carry one and Harpur would carry the other one. Just in case.

"Just in case of what?" Arthur couldn't help himself.

"In case I don't make it to the Dyrl Veilrift. We need a backup."

"And why wouldn't you make it to the Dyrl Veilrift?" Arthur couldn't help himself.

"Things could go wrong," Harpur said ominously. "Why do you think we're practicing?"

"What things? How wrong?" Arthur insisted. "I thought Ychonol was a desert world, that nothing lived there."

"Nothing does live there. It's going to be alright, Arthur. Let's just walk through this a couple of times so we all know what we're doing." Kel picked up his sack and flung the strap over his shoulder so that it settled low on his back.

"What things could go wrong?" Arthur demanded. "I want to know why Kel might not make it through the Veilrift with the rest of us."

"Ychonol is uninhabited by other life forms," Kel said, "but it is, like all worlds, a life form in its own right. The last time I was there, I may have offended it. Ychonol has been known to take vengeance on visitors who have offended it."

"How does one offend a planet?" Arthur was incredulous.

Kel, obviously a little uncomfortable, said, "I ate something before I got there that didn't agree with me."

Harpur burst out laughing, which, due to its rarity, only added to Arthur's growing alarm. "Proof, Arthur 'that you know what' happens."

Arthur was having trouble processing this. "So, you took a dump on Ychonol and now it wants to get revenge?"

The situation would be laughable to Arthur, too, if it weren't for the fact that Kel was displaying genuine apprehension about it. "Ychonol does not like to be offended."

"Okay," Arthur said. "Two things. First, how does it even know? Second, what is it going to do to you?" He paused for a moment. "And why are you coming with us if you're just going to make things difficult for us?"

"That's three things," Kel said. "It just knows. It may try to kill me. And I'm going with you because I'm the only one with any chance of keeping you from being shot on sight when you get to Terra Nine."

"Jesus, Mary and Joseph!" Arthur shouted. "It's not bad enough that I'm in danger of being soaked into a freaking elf, but now a planet is going to take revenge on a barbarian with digestive problems and even if we manage to sneak through, we're going to be shot at when we get to Terra Nine? Why don't you just kill me now? Just kill. Me. Now!" Arthur slumped to his knees and buried his face in his hands.

The others all stood there looking at the distraught man.

"Are all people from Earth this dramatic?" Kel asked.

"Honestly," Harpur said, "I think he's taking it rather well."

It took a while, but Analeetah eventually managed to calm Arthur down enough for things to move forward. The first run-through was a bit sloppy, to say the least. But by the ninth go, everyone seemed able to get their equipment on, get through the Veilrifts, get onto the flying blanket and off again without falling into the simulated boiling water.

They all had to get their packs on and then put on the breathing apparatus, which was not as heavy as it looked after all. Then Anayah had to activate the equipment to make it work. *So that's why Anayah is coming with us. We need her magic*, Arthur concluded. Arthur was certain that the apparatus itself was not even necessary, that she could have just enchanted the weird masks, but Kel was adamant that the awkward rectangular tanks and the grass hoses were essential. Once through the first simulated Veilrift, they ran to the second one where Kel spread the flying blanket out on the ground. They all got onto it, kneeling in a tight group in the middle and flew through the next Veilrift. As soon as they were through, they all had to loosen and dump the breathing equipment over the side without knocking each other off the blanket that was flying through the air about twenty feet above the simulated water. Only Kel would keep his equipment as he would need it when he returned after taking them through the third Veilrift. Arthur assumed that Anayah's magic would be sustained for Kel until he was safely back on Mysturna.

Arthur fell off the blanket twice. The first time, Sok knocked him off with his tank as he tried to fling it over the edge. The second time he lost his balance and toppled off nearly dragging Anayah with him as he grabbed onto her in desperation. Both times, Anayah magically prevented him from crashing into the ground just in time.

Once they all got the hang of flying, the trial runs went much smoother. Only the final landing on pretend Terra Nine after passing through the last pretend Veilrift remained a bit of a challenge. They had to all roll off the blanket, get to their feet and run in a crouch to a large bush, which, when they got to the real Terra Nine, may or may not be where it was supposed to be, and hide there until Kel could signal his contact. Packs got in the way, and Arthur kept getting tangled up and tripping over things. On the last practice run, Harpur deftly grabbed the scrambling man and tossed him over his shoulder for the final dash to the pretend safety of the pretend bush.

Tired, hungry and both more and less frightened than ever, Arthur was relieved when Kel called an end to the drills. They may not have reached military precision, but they had achieved a relative level of ease with the process. Although, being unceremoniously tossed over Harpur's shoulder had been a little embarrassing. All he wanted to do was find a bed and crawl into it, but all Anayah and Analeetah could talk about was the feast. Analeetah may have been un-phased by the all-nighter, but Arthur was fully and truly spent.

"Do witches not sleep?" he asked Harpur as they trekked back to Wildwood.

"Not much. A couple hours a night," Harpur answered.

"What about dragons?" Arthur's curiosity expanded.

"Oh, we love our sleep. I could sleep anywhere, anytime. Used to sleep for days sometimes."

"Huh!" Arthur wished he could sleep for a few days.

Sok, Harpur and Arthur were asked if they wanted to freshen up before the festivities began. They all said yes and were taken to a small bathhouse in the city reserved for visiting males. To Harpur's dismay, Sok's delight and Arthur's pointed disinterest, Kel was already there, already soaking in the steaming water, when they arrived. How he'd gotten that far ahead of them, Arthur neither knew nor cared. He stripped down and slipped into the pool, submerging himself in its soothing warmth.

Kel was reclining against the pool edge on Arthur's left. His eyes were closed and he seemed to be as interested in Arthur as Arthur was in him. Harpur and Sok took up their own positions along the other edges of the square pool from where they, too, ignored everyone else. The goal was to relax and unwind. Whatever tensions may have existed between any of them were neutralized in this space. Still, Arthur wanted to get cleaned up and get out of there as quickly as he could. His plan was to wait until the others looked really relaxed and then slip back out and away as quietly as possible.

All was going according to plan. Kel, Harpur and even Sok were all reclining with their eyes closed, looking peaceful, within a few minutes. Arthur climbed out of the pool and made his way to the wall where he had dropped his clothes only to discover that his clothes were no longer there. A large towel had taken their place and, as irritated as Arthur was by this turn of events, he accepted the towel in lieu and wrapped it around his body. He had no qualms about returning to Wildwood dressed in nothing but a towel. He figured his clothes would find him again eventually. They were getting a little ripe anyway. Maybe one of the witches had taken them to be cleaned. The only thing that bothered him was that his cell phone and the coin were in the pockets. He hoped that whoever did laundry checked them. He didn't have the energy to be angry about it right then, but he'd be mad if he lost the selfie he took of him and Analeetah.

The walk back to Wildwood was uneventful. A few of the witches he passed looked at him strangely, but no one said anything. Even inside the palace, people ignored Arthur. Everyone seemed too focused on preparing for the feast to pay any attention to a towel-clad human. Arthur couldn't find the space with the beds that had been made up for him, Harpur and Sok, but he did come across a quiet corner with a long bench wide enough for him to lie down on. Just as he was falling asleep, Arthur saw a group of fireflies hovering near the ceiling.

He dreamed that he was at home in his apartment getting ready to go to work at Fox Comics. The normalcy of the routine was comforting and he hummed as he pulled on a clean shirt. As he did up the buttons, he noticed something in his pocket. He reached in and pulled out a gold coin. Stamped on one side was a relief image of a man. As he looked at it, the image smiled at him and began to talk. At first, Arthur couldn't make out what the man on the coin was saying.

"What was that?" dream Arthur asked the coin.

The coin man repeated itself, this time a little louder, but dream Arthur still couldn't make out the words.

"Say that again," dream Arthur instructed.

Coin man obliged. This time dream Arthur recognized the cadence of a limerick. But he still couldn't hear it properly.

"Louder!" dream Arthur commanded.

"Entanglement started on Whyte, giving you, oh, such a fright. Soon after the join, you must give back a coin, to the mark of the Reaver at night!"

Arthur woke up startled and disoriented. It was completely dark, but he could hear strains of music and laughter wafting up from below. The party was in full swing. He sat up hoping his eyes would adjust. Repeating the limerick over and over, so he wouldn't forget it, he felt the weight of its significance bear down on him. It was not just a dream.

Of that, he felt certain. The more he thought about it, the more he convinced himself that the dream was prophetic and was the key to the miracle he so longed for.

Earlier he had begun to suspect that Anayah had a hidden agenda. Though that was just a feeling, an ephemeral notion without substance or evidence, he was certain that Harpur harboured the same suspicions. Anayah was up to something. Were the coin, the Entanglement, even the whole paradox thing all—somehow—Anayah's doing? He wasn't sure. And he didn't want to believe it. He had to find Anayah and confront her.

Forgetting he was wrapped in a towel, Arthur stood up and started marching through the darkness toward the sound of the party. The cloth, having loosened while he slept, slipped down over Arthur's hips forming a twisted snare around his knees. Mass met momentum with predictable effect. Arthur fell forward. But instead of hitting the floor, he found himself falling through space.

Arthur screamed as he plummeted, naked and flailing, toward the ground far below. His shriek caught the attention of a group of four witches who were just leaving the feast. Even with no time to confer, they stepped out of the way of his descending body and formed a circle under him. One of the witches drew the towel down to them. Each of them took hold of a corner and, just as he reached their level, caught him in it like a net. They set him gently on the ground and, shaking their heads, continued on their way.

Chest heaving and shaking with terror, Arthur couldn't even say thank you. He just laid there with his eyes closed, waiting for the shock to pass.

When he finally opened his eyes, the first thing he saw was Kel, staring down at him with amused concern. "Nice of you to drop in," Kel said, reaching out a hand to help Arthur up.

Arthur would have groaned at the cheesy action movie line, but he was too busy groaning about the near-miss. His legs were not ready to support him just yet and he leaned heavily on his over-sized rescuer, who half carried-half dragged him to a bench near the outer wall of Wildwood. Safely deposited on the bench, Arthur looked down and became aware again of his nude condition. He blushed all the way from his toes to the roots of his un-combed and dishevelled brown hair.

"Would you mind?" he asked, pointing at the abandoned towel a few feet away and was a little surprised that Kel retrieved it for him manually rather than magically. "Thanks," he mumbled, arranging the towel across his body.

"That was pretty spectacular," Kel observed of Arthur's short flight. "What were you trying to do?"

Arthur took a deep breath. *What was he trying to do?*

The dream came back to him in a flash. Along with the limerick the coin man had recited and his suspicion that Anayah was behind everything. But how safe was it to tell Kel?

"How well do you know Anayah?" Arthur asked instead of answering.

"Very well. I've known her since she was born. Why?"

"Do you trust her?" Arthur asked.

"With my life," Kel declared.

Arthur was silent.

"What's going on, Arthur?"

"I don't know," Arthur said. "But something is off."

"I'd have to agree," Kel said. "Most people don't jump out of windows at Wildwood."

"I didn't jump," Arthur defended himself. "I fell."

"I see. I guess that's not that difficult if you don't know your way around."

"Kel?" Arthur said. "If I ask you something, will you be honest with me?"

"Sure," Kel said, but with a slight hesitation.

"What is the Mark of the Reaver?"

"Never heart of it," Kell answered.

"It's not some symbol or something with... you know... super woo-woo powers?"

"Not to my knowledge. Why are you asking?"

"Just curious," Arthur said. "You're sure you don't know what it is?"

"Mark of the... What did you call it?"

"Reaver."

Kel shook his head. "Can't help you, Arthur. Ask Analeetah."

"I'll do that," Arthur said. *Maybe it was just a dream.* "How well do you know Analeetah?" Again, with the questions he didn't want to know the answer to.

"We grew up together," Kel said. "We were inseparable until she decided to come here. Broke my heart when she chose Danaleedh."

"As opposed to... you?" Arthur suggested.

Kel looked nostalgic. "There was a time I was certain that we were destined to be together. But Analeetah was meant for greater things." He put on a brave face and swept an arm across the vista of the city. "She's happy here. And I'm happy for her."

"So, you love her."

"Love her? Of course, I love her. I'd die for that witch!" Kel said.

"So, if she were to... say fall in love with someone else... How would you take that?"

Kel looked at the towel-clad man with amusement. "Are you talking about yourself, Arthur?"

"Would that be so strange?" Arthur tried to inch away from the big man, but his butt cheeks were stuck to the bench.

"I think you have a different idea about what love is than we do," Kel said.

"I think you're right," Arthur agreed. "So how does it work on Mysturna?"

"Here we love everyone. Equally. It isn't an emotion that is reserved for someone we are attracted to."

"But you just said that you thought you and Analeetah would be together and you were heart-broken when she chose something else."

"I felt the loss," Kel said. "But I did not let it consume me. Because I love Analeetah, I put her happiness ahead of my own."

"Why didn't you fight for her?" Arthur asked.

"Fight for her?"

"You know... do whatever it takes to win her."

"She's not a prize, Arthur. She's not something I can possess."

"So, people here don't fall madly in love with each other?"

"I don't know what that means. How can you love someone and be mad at them?"

Arthur thought that should be obvious. But he was finding it difficult to explain. "By mad I mean crazy. Be so crazy in love with them that they are your whole world."

Kel scratched his beard. "Arthur, I'm pretty sure that's not love." With that, Kel stood up and stretched. "We got a big day ahead of us. I'm going to turn in."

Instead of walking back into Wildwood, Kel wandered down the street and away from the palace, leaving Arthur to his thoughts and his towel on the bench.

Just as Kel disappeared into a street leading to the back of Wildwood, Mezzi dropped down on her web and waved shyly at a startled Arthur. "Jesus! Why do you do that?" Arthur's heart rate soared again.

"Do what?" the spider asked.

"Sneak up on people!" Arthur sounded annoyed.

"I do not sneak," Mezzi said. "I only come to tell you that Analeetah wishes to see you."

"Next time, warn me before you just drop down like that."

"Okay." Mezzi waved at him and scuttled back up her web.

"Where is Analeetah?" Arthur called after the retreating arachnid, but she was gone.

Arthur secured the towel around his waist and went in search of the Doyenne.

The party was winding down. A few people lingered in small groups throughout the palace, but the music and dancing had ended. Arthur grabbed some food from a table as he walked past. No one paid him much attention as he wandered around scanning for a familiar face. Eventually, he spotted Sok, sitting on a branch high above the main floor and talking to Mezzi. As soon as Sok saw Arthur, he excused himself and climbed down from his perch.

"Analeetah was looking for you," Sok said.

"So, I heard," Arthur said. "Do you know where she is?"

"Last time I saw her, she was heading out back."

"How long ago was that?"

"Not long. A few minutes, maybe."

Arthur thanked Sok and turned to go in the direction Sok had seen Analeetah go. Sok fell into step with him. "What happened to your clothes?"

"Long story." Arthur shuddered, remembering his fall from the window. "Say, Sok? Do you know what the Mark of the Reaver is?"

Sok shook his head. "Never heard of it. What is it?"

"Don't know," Arthur said.

"If you don't know, why are you asking about it?"

"To find out," Arthur said.

"I mean if you don't know what it is, how do you know you should be asking about it?"

"I'm just curious, Sok. I heard it mentioned and I just want to know what it is."

"Ah," Sok said philosophically. "I see. Where did you hear about it?"

"In a dream."

"In a dream? Like a dream you have when you're sleeping?"

"Yes, Sok. In a dream I had while I was sleeping."

Sok laughed. "That's crazy! Dreams are dreams. They aren't real."

"I know that," Arthur snapped.

"Then why would you ask me if I knew what something that you heard in a dream is?"

Arthur stopped walking. "Dragons, Sok! Dragons and witches and parallel universes and paradoxes and elves, Sok! Two days ago, none of those things were real either!" Spittle flew from his mouth as he shouted and the elf leaned away from the spray. Then Arthur froze. "Where's Harpur?" he asked.

"Are you going to shout at me again?" Sok asked.

"Not if you tell me where Harpur is."

Sok took a large step back from Arthur. "I haven't seen him since he left the bathhouse."

Arthur whipped around looking for the dragon-wizard. "Did you leave first?"

"No. He was gone when I got out of the bath. I thought he left with you."

"Sok, have you felt the Entanglement tonight?"

Sok's hand flew to his solar plexus. "No. Have you?"

"No, I haven't."

"That's good a good thing, right?"

"The bathhouse is farther away from here than we were from each other in the forest. If you and I have been separated farther than that tonight, why haven't we felt the Entanglement?"

"Does it matter?"

"I think it does. I think that the pain we felt when we got separated in the forest has nothing to do with the Entanglement. Where's Anayah?"

Sok looked confused. *What else could it have been?* "She was here when the feast began," Sok said trying to recall if he'd seen her after that.

"Something is wrong, Sok," Arthur said. "We have to find Analeetah. Right now!"

"Make up your mind, Arthur. Do you want to find Anayah, Harpur or Analeetah?

But Arthur was already leaving. Keeping a firm grip on his towel, he sprinted through the doorway leading to the garden where the well was. A couple of witches were drawing water from the well into small urns, but neither of them was Analeetah. Arthur asked if they had seen her pass and they pointed farther along a path that led to the gate to the meadow. Arthur thanked them and ran on. Sok followed, curious and confused.

Just as they were about to pass an enormous bush and go through the gate, they were yanked off their feet and pulled into the thick foliage. A large hand clamped itself over Arthur's mouth, keeping him from yelling, while a smaller hand covered Sok's mouth with the same result. They were dragged deeper undercover and held tightly until they both stopped struggling.

"It's just us." Arthur heard a hoarse whisper in his ear. "Analeetah and Harpur. I need you both to stay quiet."

Arthur nodded and the big hand came off his mouth. In the dim light, he could see Analeetah releasing Sok as well.

"Stay here," Analeetah ordered. Then she and Harpur turned to return to their position closer to the gate.

Harpur, in the lead and crouching, walked into a large piece of cloth that was caught in the branches. "What in Orhowyn's name is this?" he said. He balled the towel up and tossed it back over Analeetah's head.

"That's mine," Arthur murmured. He picked it up and quickly re-attached it to his waist. "Long story," he said by way of explanation to the irritated dragon-wizard.

Analeetah shushed them all and, hand on Harpur's back, continued to follow him forward.

Arthur and Sok sat down with their backs against the wall. Fully concealed by the shrubbery, they listened intently. They could hear two voices arguing just beyond the gate. Arthur surmised that it was Kel and Anayah, but he couldn't make out what they were saying. Every now and then a shouted word made its way through the leaves to his ears, but not enough of them to piece together what the argument was about. He wondered how Kel had gotten to this gate and reasoned that the road he'd turned onto must circle back this way. Did what he had told Kel about his dream have anything to do with it? Kel had seemed sincere in denying any knowledge of the Mark of the Reaver. Arthur strained to listen, but the argument ended after only a few minutes.

"I won't do it!" Kel shouted as he passed the bush going back to the palace.

Arthur could hear Kel's footsteps retreating up the path toward Wildwood. A few seconds later, lighter footsteps followed as Anayah, too, ran past in the same direction. Arthur, Sok, Analeetah and Harpur froze where they were until they were all sure it was safe to move again.

"What was that all about?" Arthur whispered as he crept closer to where Harpur and Analeetah were hiding.

"Let's get out of this damned bush," Harpur suggested. "I feel like I should be gathering nuts for winter."

Harpur crawled out onto the path with Analeetah, Arthur and Sok right behind him. They picked twigs and leaves out of their hair and worked the kinks out of their joints from being crouched over.

"Did that have anything to do with the Mark of the Reaver?" Arthur asked.

"The Mark of the what?" Harpur asked. "And where are your clothes?"

"Long story," Arthur said again in reference to his missing apparel. "But I'd appreciate it if someone could zap me up some jeans and a t-shirt."

Analeetah obliged. With a snap of her fingers Arthur's towel disappeared and he found himself dressed once again in his jeans and a t-shirt. He patted his back pocket and was relieved to find his cell phone there. The coin was in the front pocket where it belonged.

"What's a Reaver?" Analeetah asked. "And why is it marked?"

"He heard about it in a dream," Sok explained.

"What?" Harpur and Analeetah said in unison.

"A dream? Like when you were asleep?" Harpur asked.

"It was weird," Arthur said.

"All dreams are weird," Harpur said. "Why do you think something you heard in a dream could have anything to do with... anything?"

Arthur told them about his dream. "Don't you think that it might be prophetic?"

"I think you're over-thinking things, Arthur," Analeetah said. "Sounds to me like you're worried about getting safely to Thraeh and in your dream, you came up with a solution to the Entanglement so you wouldn't have to go to Ychonol, Dyrl and Terra Nine. It's totally understandable."

Arthur felt a little foolish. "Yeah," he said, "that's probably all it is. Forget I said anything." Just then a half dozen fireflies flew past and Arthur shook his head. *Fireflies and Reavers! I must be losing it.*

"Tell them what you told me about the Entanglement, Arthur," Sok said.

"What about the Entanglement?" Harpur asked.

"Well," Arthur began, "when I left the bathhouse and came back to Wildwood for a nap, Sok and I were farther apart than we were yesterday in the forest and neither of us felt the Entanglement."

"That proves it," Harpur said. He looked hurt and confused.

"Proves what?" Arthur asked.

"That Anayah is manipulating things." Analeetah looked as hurt and confused as Harpur.

"I knew it!" Arthur said, punching his left palm with his right fist. "What were she and Kel arguing about back there?"

Analeetah sighed. "She asked Kel to steal the coin."

"Why?" Arthur was alarmed.

"She said she needed a tiny piece of it for a spell," Analeetah explained.

"What kind of spell?" Arthur could think of nothing else to ask.

"She wouldn't say," said a new voice that made them all jump, "Anayah believes that the coin can help her in some way, but she wouldn't tell me what she needs it for. So, I refused to steal it for her."

They turned to find Kel standing a short distance away on the path. He, too, sounded hurt and confused.

"Do you think she might be trying to close off the Boundaries between Earth and other worlds?" Harpur theorized.

"Why would she do that?" Arthur asked. "And how would the coin help her?"

"She really does feel strongly about the way humans behave toward each other on Earth. And, if it's true that if a paradox were to Bound that it could be catastrophic, maybe she thinks she can use the coin somehow to control the Boundary and keep Earthlings from using it."

"We're not that bad!" Arthur said in defence of all humankind.

"I don't know," Sok said. "Anayah showed me some pretty messed up stuff that goes on, on Earth."

Arthur made an exasperated face at the elf. "There must be messed up stuff on every world! Earth can't have a monopoly on messed up stuff. I mean those trees they have here are pretty messed up."

"You have to remember, Arthur, Anayah comes from a world that is focused on compassion and empathy. Disputes on Mysturna are settled without killing each other, without killing innocent people. Anayah finds the violence on Earth very difficult to deal with and when Sok and you became Entangled, she realized just how easily humans from your world could find out about Thraeh or Mysturna. She's afraid of what could happen if humans from Earth did find their way other worlds," Kel told them.

"That seems a bit of a stretch," Analeetah said. "I know she feels strongly about it, but I can't see her conspiring to destroy an entire world."

Arthur was stunned. "She's going to kill me, isn't she?"

"I can't say definitively that's what her plan is," Kel said. "But if it is, I can see her killing you for the coin if she has to."

"Wait! If you don't believe in killing other people, why would Anayah kill anyone?" Arthur couldn't keep the desperation out of his voice.

"She's been off Mysturna for a long time," Kel said. "And desperate people do desperate things."

Arthur turned to Kel and yelled, "I thought you trusted her with your life."

"I do," Kel agreed. "That doesn't mean that I trust her with yours."

Arthur accepted that he was in for a second sleepless night when the conversation was moved inside Wildwood and up to a tower. Without beds. Analeetah cast a barrier spell that would, she assured everyone, keep Anayah from finding them.

"Won't she be suspicious?" Arthur asked. "What if she's looking for any of us?"

"We'll just have to hope she isn't." Analeetah seemed un-phased by the possibility. But Arthur was nervous nonetheless.

Conjecture fueled most of the discussion. They knew Anayah was planning on using the coin for something. They did not know what she was going to use the coin for. Or how she intended to use it. Analeetah and Kel, having known Anayah all her life, were reluctant to believe she intended any harm. Harpur, having known Anayah for nearly eight years, didn't want to believe she intended any harm, but his dragon nature came with suspicion and wariness built in. So, whenever anyone behaved oddly, his default was to assume harm was intended. They assumed that the plan to get Arthur safely to Thraeh through the Veilrifts was somehow intrinsic to whatever she was planning now and that the new plan was the reason she was pushing to move things along quickly. From what they knew about Entanglement, its macabre climax took weeks to reach. In theory, they had time to figure out a safer way to accomplish what they needed to accomplish.

The incident in Forest of Dheersha must have been an attempt to emphasise the urgency, make everyone think that there wasn't much time. Analeetah, was appalled by this. She couldn't believe that Anayah would allow Sok and Arthur to suffer they way they had, especially by Anayah's own hand. It didn't make sense.

Sok was not contributing much to the conversation. Something was tickling at the back of his mind, something he'd heard. But he couldn't quite put his finger on what it was or when or where he heard it. He knew it would come to him sooner or later. He hoped it was sooner than too late, if Anayah was intent upon hurting someone. Maybe, if he could remember what it was, he could save the day and redeem himself. *Next time*, he thought, *I will have to think things through more carefully.* Elves are, by nature, caring folk, but even with the weight of guilt that was building on Sok's shoulders, he knew that his curiosity would get him into trouble again someday.

"She seemed so concerned about me," Arthur said. He did not want to believe that Anayah was plotting against him in any way. But he knew in his bones that she was up to something.

"Get over yourself. It might not have anything to do with you, Arthur," Harpur said. "Not everything does."

This outburst caused everyone, including Sok, to stop and stare at the increasingly irritated dragon-wizard. His dark mood was becoming as much a cause for suspicion as Anayah's uncharacteristic behavior. Before anyone could say anything to smooth things over, Harpur continued, "What I want to know," Harpur said, "is what happened to tip her like that. In all the time I've known Anayah, she's never once said or done anything like this. She's always loathed the way humans treat each other, but she's always tried to see the good in them too. She's always telling me that Earth is worth saving."

"Earth maybe. Just not humans?" Kel proposed.

"We don't know that's what she's planning," Analeetah reminded them.

"We're getting off track," Kel said. "This is about the coin. Where is it, by the way?"

"Arthur has it," Harpur said.

"Can I see it?" Kel asked Arthur.

Arthur started to pull the coin out of his pocket to show Kel, but Harpur stopped him. His inner conspiracy theorist, aroused at it was by the conversation, suddenly threw Kel into the middle of whatever plot Anayah was cooking up. "How did you know we were all by the gate?"

Arthur and Sok both took a step away from Kel and closer to Harpur. They sensed that Harpur's distrust was widening and while they didn't see the connection, they both instinctively put their trust in the dragon wizard.

Analeetah took a step closer to her friend. "Don't be ridiculous! Kel would never betray me."

"Maybe not," Harpur said, "But how do I know you both wouldn't betray us?"

Harpur put his arms out in front of Arthur and Sok and pushed them back toward an open window. He kept his eyes on Analeetah, figuring she was the biggest threat to his improvised plan. He would have to time things just right to do what he intended to do. If she suspected, he might not be able to counter her magic. He had to move fast.

And pray that neither Arthur nor Sok would screw things up.

"Harpur, please," Analeetah pleaded.

And to her relief, he appeared to relax. "You're right," he said. "I'm being paranoid. Arthur, will you hold on to this?" Harpur handed his precious walking stick to Arthur, who took it cautiously. Then he suddenly spun around to face the window and, in one deft move, grabbed Sok and Arthur by their shirts and launched the three of them out the window.

Not again! Arthur thought as they began to plunge toward the ground.

They only fell a few feet before Harpur transformed into a dragon. It was sheer luck that Harpur's great talons closed around Arthur and prevented him from dropping the walking stick. Sok's initial astonishment was almost instantly replaced by glee as he wiggled around to face forward. Arthur just closed his eyes and concentrated on not being sick again.

Beating his powerful wings, Harpur lifted them up into the night sky and flew away from Wildwood.

Chapter 6

Harpur flew through the night, wishing two things. First, he wished he knew more about Mysturna. Second, he wished that one of his passengers would go to sleep and stop wiggling about. Sok kept pointing out landmarks, shouting, "Look over there!" or "Did you see that?" Anyone would think he'd never seen hills and rivers and forests before. In all fairness, Sok's experience of seeing them from this particular vantage point was limited.

It was fortunate that they did not pass over any villages or towns. Once the lights of Danaleedh had faded behind them, Harpur saw no signs of life at all. There were only two roads leading out of Danaleedh. Harpur chose not to follow either of them and set a course over the Forest of Dheersha, north-westward toward the mountains. Still, Sok's incessant hollering was annoying. Harpur tried to shut him up by squeezing Sok tightly. But that only worked until the next holler-worthy sight appeared.

Arthur, on—as well as in—the other hand, eventually relaxed enough to doze off. The problem with that for Harpur was that his grip on the walking stick also relaxed, so he had to squeeze Arthur to keep him from dropping it. It was exhausting to have to focus on where he was going and pay attention to his cargo at the same time. When the first rays of the first sun started to wash the darkness out of the sky, Harpur turned his attention to finding somewhere to land. He wanted to be out of the sky before they became visible to anyone on the ground.

Even though he had seen no signs of life, they would be more vulnerable in daylight. He didn't want anyone to see them and report their whereabouts back to Wildwood. And he had no idea what sort of communication Analeetah and Anayah had with other communities. He was sure, though, that if they could, they would be sending out word asking others to be on the alert for a dragon, and elf and a man. He had to find somewhere remote enough for Sok and Arthur to stay hidden and have access to shelter, water and food. He scanned the mountainside for caves and finally spotted one fronted by an open slope wide enough for him to land on. Animal trails along the treeline and running into the surrounding woodland told Harpur that there was game to be had and a waterfall nearby meant there was fresh water.

Harpur landed and set Sok and Arthur down on the ground. Sok bounced around, expelling residual glee. Arthur just looked terrible, in spite of the in-flight nap.

Before changing back to his human form, Harpur checked out the cave. The entrance was too small for him to go through, but he could stick his head in far enough to get a feel for the place. There were no signs that the cave was inhabited, no bones from prey, no indication of cook fires, no scent of animals or people. The cave itself was not very large. Three men could fit into it comfortably and there was enough protection from the elements, but there was nothing to stop a predator from entering either. It would have to do.

Harpur transformed and called Sok and Arthur to join him in their new, and hopefully temporary, abode. Arthur didn't even have the energy to complain. He found a flat spot on the ground to the left of the entrance, curled up and went back to sleep. Whatever was going to happen next, he figured, could happen after he got some more rest. He'd already had too much time to ponder the implications of what Harpur had done. Overwhelmed hardly even began to encompass how he was feeling. Best not to think about it for a while. Best just to go to sleep.

Arthur's fatigue was contagious. The adrenalin rush Sok had going on ended abruptly when he heard Arthur start to snore softly. Minutes later, he found himself drifting off near the back of the cave. Harpur, more worry-weary than physically tired at that point, felt the call to rest as well. Not being familiar with the area, he knew he needed to guard the entrance to the cave. Who knew what might come out of the trees, out of the sky or over the mountain? So, he leaned his walking stick against the cave wall and went outside where he assumed his dragon form again. Then, becoming invisible, he coiled his long tail around his body, tucked in his wings and went to sleep in front of the cave. Anyone, or anything, attempting to gain entrance would be in for a bit of a surprise. Thus, they spent the day.

Arthur was the first to awaken. Needing both to intake and release some water, he stretched to relieve his stiff muscles, stood up and staggered groggily to the cave entrance. The first sun was beginning to set, but the second sun was still casting shadows and would continue to do so for a couple more hours. Arthur squinted against the brightness as he moved into the opening and walked into Harpur's invisible body blocking his exit. Confused, Arthur reached out like a blind man and felt his way forward somewhat more cautiously. When his hands met the unseen obstruction, it felt like warm metal plates beneath his touch. And then he sensed a rhythmic movement as the barrier repeatedly expanded and contracted. Feeling slightly creeped out and strongly in need of walking off the stiffness from sleeping on the ground, Arthur moved to the edge of the entrance and felt his way up the barrier until he noticed a gap between it and the rock. If he could grab onto the plates and brace his feet against the side of the cave entrance, maybe he could climb up and wiggle through the gap. It still had not occurred to him that the barrier was alive, much less that it was Harpur in invisible dragon form.

Reaching as high as he could, Arthur hooked his fingers of his left hand over the edge of an invisible scale, braced his right foot on a bit of rock sticking out of the side of the cave entrance and started hopping on his left foot to gain momentum for the leap upward that he would need to get him to the gap. He had to trust that his right hand would find and grip another plate higher up and that he would be able to sustain his body weight while he flung himself through the gap and over the barrier. He didn't treasure the idea of falling back to the ground on the other side, but neither did he know that he was attempting to climb a dragon.

Arthur jumped and reached up with his right hand at the same time. Instead of the edge of a scale, his hand found a firm, but pliable spike and he was able to get a good enough grip on it to enable him to reach up with his left hand, which also found a firm, but pliable, spike to hold onto. Suspended several feet above the ground, he swung his left leg up toward where he assumed the top of the barrier should be while he pulled himself up with his arms. He had to be careful because he didn't know exactly how much room he had between the barrier and the top of the cave entrance. But it no longer mattered. Just as he managed to get his leg up high enough on the third try to hook his foot over another spike, the barrier shifted and Arthur found himself being dragged upward toward the solid rock above him. He had two choices: let go and drop back to the ground, or be crushed against the rock.

Arthur let go.

Though he fell only a few feet, his right arm buckled under his weight as he landed and he felt his forearm snap just above the wrist. He screamed in pain. Then he laid there, writhing and moaning and cradling his injured appendage.

"I think my arm is broken," he grunted as he watched the invisible barrier become visible and transform from an enormous dragon into an enormous man, who looked down at him with consternation.

"What in Orhowyn's fiery tomb are you doing, Arthur?" Harpur said. "Why were you climbing onto my back?"

Arthur managed to sit up. "I was trying to get out of the cave," he said through gritted teeth.

"You could have just woken me up. I would have moved," Harpur said.

"You were invisible!" Arthur defended himself. "How was I supposed to know it was you?"

"Who else would it be?"

"I don't know," Arthur said. "Some weird Mysturnian killer cave trap."

Harpur had to admit that carried the weight of plausibility. "Not a very good one, if you could climb over it." He couldn't help pointing out the flaw in the theory.

Sok, who had been woken up by the kerfuffle, noticed Arthur's arm and squatted next to him to look at. "You were very brave! Can I look at your arm?"

Arthur, still cradling it, was starting to go into shock. He nodded at the elf, who gently lifted it to feel the damage. He wanted to remove the leather cuff, but when he tugged on the lace, it just re-tied itself. The cuff did not appear to be tightening against the swelling; it seemed to adjust itself to the new size and shape of Arthur's arm. Sok would have to work around it. "I can help you with this, Arthur," Sok said. "First, I have to set the bones and that's going to hurt a bit. You okay with that?"

Arthur nodded.

Sok positioned himself so he had better leverage. "Ready, Arthur?" he asked, but did not wait for a reply. He gave Arthur's hand a sharp tug with a slight twist, which both put the bones back into alignment and caused Arthur to cry out. Once that was done, Arthur did feel some instant relief. Having managed to not pass out, Arthur tried to struggle to his feet, but Sok held him down. "I need to wrap this so it stays stable and can heal properly."

Arthur nodded again and watched quietly while Sok applied healing magic to his arm. A soft, blue glow from Sok's palms flowed over his arm and into his skin, relieving the pain and reducing the swellings a little. Then Sok bound a splint Harpur conjured for him over his wounded wrist and hand. "It will take a few days for this to mend completely. Let me know when it starts hurting again, and I will give you more healing energy."

"I don't mean to complain," he said, when Sok had finished administering to his wound, "but what are we going to do now?"

It was a fair question. Harpur had to admit that his impulsive and dramatic exodus from an unsubstantiated threat did leave them in a bit of a bind. His only defence was that his gut told him to get Arthur and Sok, away from Wildwood. Beyond that, he had no answer to Arthur's question. Survival was not the greatest issue. There was water and game nearby. The cave was not perfect, but it was serviceable in the interim. But they did need help. Finding it was going to be the tricky part.

Harpur did not want to be flying around as a dragon in the daylight in a world where dragons did not exist. That would only draw unwanted attention. At the same time, flying around was the best way to scout out the land. That way he might be able to find a town or city where they might be able to find someone who might be able to help them.

Harpur decided that a direct and authoritative, if not altogether accurate, approach was his best chance of at least postponing, if not avoiding, the inevitable accusations and subsequent argument his actions were almost certain to provoke. So, he started issuing directives, sending Sok, the most able-bodied of the two, to gather firewood and collect water in pots he conjured and sending Arthur to scramble farther up the slope above the cave to act as a lookout. In the meantime, he would catch dinner, start a fire and magically appropriate any other supplies they might need. By creating just enough distance between each of them to discourage conversation and still not trigger the effects of the Entanglement, Harpur felt that he could maintain some measure of control over the situation. Sok was his usual amiable and cooperative self and set upon his assigned tasks without reservation, such was his faith in Harpur. Arthur, however, ambled up the slope with that look on his face that told Harpur he had much reservation and was transmuting it into innumerable questions.

Harpur discovered the first flaw in his plan when he spotted a large, rabbit-like beast that looked like it would make a fine feast for them. On Thraeh, when he wanted to eat, he simply blasted the hapless beast of choice with a prolonged jet of fire, both denuding it of any fur and cooking it in a single step. But the animals on Mysturna, as it turned out, were impervious to his normally lethal breath. After a few failed attempts, that seemed to merely annoy the rabbit-like prey, Harpur remembered the goose. Not knowing the creature's language to ask it if it was willing to be eaten and not having whatever potion was required to euthanize it so they could eat it, Harpur had no way of procuring meat by hunting.

His next option was to conjure an already cooked galing, which he was loathe to do as it meant taking said already cooked galing from someone who had already cooked it with the intention of eating it themselves. Conjuring was, essentially, an exercise in theft. In order for Harpur to feed Arthur, Sok and himself, he had to steal a meal from somebody. It brought forward all sorts of ethical considerations and just then he didn't feel desperate enough to do that. He did feel like burning a few crops and wreaking a bit of havoc in some nearby village, though. That would have been an excellent way to work through his growing frustration, but since havoc-wreaking would only result in that unwanted attention he was determined to avoid, he settled for pulling some wild fruit from the surrounding hills and a couple of flagons of ale from an untapped barrel at a distant public house, hoping it wouldn't be noticed.

The repast was dismal and less than satisfying. The fruit wasn't all that tasty and the ale was flat and bitter. But it filled their bellies, which was the goal. It also meant that a fire was unnecessary, so Sok, rather than waste the effort he'd invested in collecting it, amused himself by stacking the firewood into an expertly balanced, abstract sculpture. With the elf focussed elsewhere, Arthur took the opportunity to confront Harpur.

"So, now what do we do?" Arthur asked.

"We wait for nightfall and then we fly that way," Harpur, having made a decision to leave right away, pointed over the mountains, "and look for a town."

"We?" Arthur winced. "And why that way?"

"Well, I can't leave you two behind," Harpur reasoned, "and I'm not walking. We're going that way because that's the way I want to go."

"We get to fly again?" Sok looked up from his firewood sculpture with a gleeful smile.

Arthur looked up at the mountain peaks high above them. "It looks cold up there," he observed. "I'm not dressed for an over-mountain night flight."

"You survived the last one. You'll survive this one," Harpur said with an edge of warning in his voice.

"I might," Arthur agreed. "But if it gets too cold, I might not be able to hold onto your walking stick."

Harpur looked at the clever man. Then he turned to the elf. "Sok, how would you like to hold on to my walking stick while we're flying this time?"

Arthur gave himself a mental head-slap.

"I'd be honoured!" Sok was thrilled.

"That's settled, then," Harpur said. He made a mental note to strap it to the elf's body before they took off.

"What if I refuse to go?" Arthur asked.

"Then I will pick you up and take you anyway," Harpur said. "Look, Arthur, we have to find a way to get you and Sok to Thraeh."

"We had a way!" Arthur shouted, startling Sok, causing him to knock over his sculpture and have to start again.

"We thought we had a way," Harpur corrected. "But that way wasn't the right way."

"What?" Arthur was incredulous. "It was the only way."

"If you wanted us all to die, maybe."

"Maybe being the operative word."

"Not maybe about the die part," Harpur said. "Maybe about the wanting to die part."

"You don't know that."

"Neither do you know that I don't know."

"How do you know?"

"I just know."

"You just think you know."

"Yeah, well, you know nothing."

"I know we had a way. And I know we don't have a way anymore."

"You don't know we don't have a way. You just don't know what the way is."

"No one knows!"

"I know we are flying over those mountains as soon as it gets dark."

Arthur knew that he had no choice but to let the dragon-wizard take the lead. Without any magic of his own, he had little chance of making any appreciable difference. There was no way he could outrun Harpur—in dragon or human form—and the sheer enormity of being lost in the wilderness in a world he knew nothing about did not bear thinking about. Harpur was his best bet for survival. He got that! But he couldn't help feeling a smidgeon of resentment toward Harpur for putting them in their current predicament.

The daylight was fading. The first sun had set and the second sun was waving goodbye with the last of its rays. Soon the wizard would become the dragon and would be holding Arthur's life—quite literally—in his hands. Dangling from a dragon's claws hundreds of feet above the ground was not a prospect he could bring himself to look forward to. There had to be a better way.

Without knowing why, Arthur walked into the cave. Sheltered as it was from the last of the light, it was hard to make out much detail. But Arthur felt compelled to explore anyway. He started on the left side of the entrance and, trailing his good hand along the cave wall, walked around the perimeter. The surface of the rock was rough, but every so often, Arthur's hand fell into a groove that was deeper than the rock surface around it. He moved to the back of the cave where there was more light and looked closely at the rock. There were definite signs that the rock had been chiselled.

Then he noticed an odd bit of stone protruding out of the wall. To Arthur, it looked rather like a doorknob, but as he examined the wall near it, he could detect no seam to indicate that a door accompanied the apparent latch. Still, he reached out and took hold of the jutting piece of rock. To his surprise, delight and, if truth be told, his chagrin, it turned easily in his grasp. But that's all it did. At first.

Arthur twisted and pulled, pushed and twisted without effect. It was obvious that the rock nob had some purpose, but it seemed like that purpose was to perplex, for what could be more perplexing than a door-knob-size chunk of rock sticking out of a cave wall that could spin easily, but otherwise do nothing? Maybe it was like a combination lock and he had to spin it in certain directions a certain number of times. Perhaps he had to match up a notch on the wall with a notch on the knob. The light was quickly fading and it was beginning to get difficult to even see the knob, let alone a notch on it.

Arthur looked outside and saw that Sok was still arranging the firewood into a sculpture. Harpur was off a little way pacing back and forth. He kept looking up at the mountains and then back in the direction they had come from. Arthur watched Harpur watch the sky for a few minutes, but was unable to discern what the apparent internal debate was about or which side was winning, so he turned his attention back to the perplexing chunk of rock. *What do you do?* he wondered. He twisted it back and forth slowly, like a safecracker in a movie, hoping to feel something happen. That didn't work so he just started spinning it idly, hoping for further inspiration. That hope was dashed when Harpur stopped pacing and called to him and Sok that it was time to go.

162

Sok, eager to be swept off his feet, abandoned his art project and ran toward Harpur who tied his walking stick to the elf's arm before transforming once again into the giant beast he had been born to be. Arthur, in frustration and dread, gave the chunk of rock one last aggravated twist. "Argh!"

From beyond the cave entrance, he heard Sok call out cheerfully, "Come on, Arthur! This is going to be fun."

"I doubt it," Arthur mumbled as he walked reluctantly out of the cave.

He had just cleared the cave entrance when he heard a noise behind him. The distinct sound of rock scraping against rock stopped him in his tracks and he turned around to see an orange-yellow light flowing out of an ever-widening crack in the cave wall. The noise and the light did not go unnoticed by Harpur and Sok either.

"Orhowyn's hairy arse, Arthur! What have you done now?" Harpur picked up Sok and moved toward Arthur to do the same to him before whatever was going to come out of the cave came out of the cave.

Arthur, still not sure whether he should be excited or terrified, opted for both. He was excited about the crack in the cave wall and terrified that Harpur would get to him before he found out what the crack in the cave wall meant. He ran back inside and to the right, reasoning that it would at least buy him some time. Harpur would have to transform again in order to come in and drag him out. From his position against the cave wall, he continued to watch as the crack continued to widen and the orange-yellow light continued to brighten. From inside the mountain, he heard an androgynous voice shouting something about being patient and coming as fast as I can while the echoing reverberations of a deep-toned gong faded away. From outside he heard Harpur swearing as he scrambled to release his walking stick from Sok's arm and get to the cave.

Just as Harpur reached the cave entrance the scraping stopped and a tiny chariot with no wheels flew through the crack. Harpur barely managed to push Sok to the ground and jump out of the way as it sped past them and out of the cave.

"Weeeee!" the androgynous voice squealed from inside the chariot as it skidded in mid-air, banked sharply to the left and turned back toward the cave entrance where it came to such a sudden stop that the owner of the androgynous voice was hurled over the front of the carriage and into Harpur's arms.

"Ooph!" Harpur absorbed the impact of a bundle of blue-gray robes containing the body of a small person of indeterminate gender as they crashed into his chest. He deposited the bundle on the ground and backed away. It may have been small, but Harpur tended to be cautious whenever he was faced with an unknown entity. He stood on widely spaced feet with his knees bent and his walking stick held like a staff ready to defend himself, Sok and Arthur either physically or magically—whatever was called for. He kept a close watch on both the bundled of robes and the hovering chariot that was twitching at the cave entrance. He did not like the fact that these two things were between him and escape. Another step back and to his right allowed him to keep the new opening in the back of the cave in his peripheral vision. Orhowyn only knew what else might come flying out of it.

The bundle brushed off and re-arranged its robes with an androgynous giggle. "Well, that was fun!" it announced. "New hover gilly! Not quite used to all the features," it continued by way of explanation for the high-speed arrival.

Sok was delighted, both by the little person and the hover gilly. "I'm Sok," he said holding out his hand to the new-comer.

"Pleased to meet you, Sok! I'm Hiro."

The little person who shook Sok's hand was about four feet tall and resembled a garden gnome dressed in monk's robes. A floppy hat with a bright red feather-like a medieval bard might wear was perched on its bald head. Its feet were clad in green flip-flop-style sandals. It looked up—way up—at Harpur, saying, "You must be Harpur. Thanks for catching me. That could have turned out much worse!" and winked.

Harpur took the tiny hand that was being proffered in his large one and muttered, "You're welcome?"

Hiro leaned to the right to look past Harpur. "And you have to be Arthur! Do you always ring doorbells so insistently?"

Arthur blushed. "I... uh... didn't realize..."

"That's okay," Hiro interrupted. "At least I know it still works. Don't get a lot of visitors coming to the back door. Can't remember the last time it rang. Anyway, shall we?"

He whistled and the hover gilly glided over to him. It lowered itself to the ground so Hiro could climb into it and then lifted up to hover again for a moment before moving toward the opening in the cave wall. Sok, all curious and unabashed, fell in behind the hover gilly to follow Hiro through, but Harpur stepped forward to block them.

"Who are you?" Harpur demanded.

"And how do you know who we are?" Arthur asked.

"Forgive me!" Hiro giggled. "I don't mean to be rude, but a spotted muskink has been seen in the area. Nasty creatures, they are! We'll be much safer inside."

The hover gilly inched forward again, but Harpur stood his ground. "I'm not going in there," he said. "Now who are you?"

"And how do you know who we are?" Arthur reiterated.

Hiro sighed. "I will be happy to answer all your questions. In there!" It pointed to the opening in the cave wall.

"Not a chance!" Harpur growled.

"Harpur, I think Hiro is here to help us," Arthur said, lowering his voice to a confidential whisper.

"You really need to stop thinking," Harpur whispered back.

"He... it... knows our names."

"Exactly! And who do you think told him... it... our names?"

"Well, I imagine it was Analeetah, but..."

"Actually," Hiro broke in, "it was Mezzi..."

"Mezzi?" Harpur and Arthur said together.

"I miss Mezzi." Sok sighed sadly.

"Yes, Mezzi," Hiro confirmed. "She's quite concerned about you three. Now if you don't mind, we really do need to get inside and get this door closed before..."

Before became impossible when the large head of a spotted muskink appeared behind Hiro. Attracted by the orange-yellow light that flooded the cave and spilled down the slope, the spotted muskink waddled boldly

165

toward the cave entrance, stopping every few feet to sniff the air. Its beady, black eyes reflected the orange-yellow light and the horror-stricken looks on both Harpur and Arthur's faces.

"Orhowyn's crusty crotch!" Harpur shouted.

"Run!" Arthur yelled.

"Hurry!" Hiro urged.

"Aw," Sok cooed as he was yanked off his feet and dragged through the opening in the back of the cave by Harpur.

The opening led to a long tunnel that wound down and to the right. As they sprinted through the doorway, Hiro twisted another chunk of rock sticking out of the wall and the crack started to close with the same grating noise it had made when it opened. A few more yards along the tunnel, Hiro stopped again and cast a spell that sealed off the tunnel with an invisible barrier just in time to stop a jet of black slime from splashing over them. Hiro backed up another couple of yards and repeated the spell. A few more yards on, he did it again.

"What are you doing?" Harpur asked.

"Muskink ink is extremely corrosive. It'll eat right through the first barrier in a few minutes. It's slowed the ink down, but I'll need at least six or seven of these to keep it from seeping all the way in. It will also stop the smell," Hiro explained.

Barrier after barrier went up. To be safe, Hiro put up a dozen of them. And then he touched another chunk of rock sticking out of a wall, which caused another doorway to close. Satisfied that all that could be done had been done, Hiro turned to his guests and giggled. "It will be years before that door can be used again! I will have to look into reopening the north corridor. Always like to have at least two ways out of here."

"What was that thing?" Harpur asked on behalf of himself and the others.

"I told you, a muskink. It's been hanging around out there for a while. Nasty beasts!" Hiro giggled again.

"It looked like a giant blue skunk. With tentacles!" Arthur's face reflected the degree of repulsion he felt, which was significant.

"I am not familiar with skunks," Hiro said, "but those tentacles are revolting. The muskink sprays that ink you saw, which begins to dissolve its prey. Then it uses the tentacles to mash up what's left so the muskink can eat it. And the smell is worse than offensive."

The monstrous creature, compared to any skunk or be-tentacled beast on Earth, had been attracted by the light from the cave. For Harpur, Sok, Arthur and Hiro, it was fortunate that muskinks don't move fast. It was also fortunate that this particular one was not particularly hungry. Otherwise, it might have sprayed first and sniffed later. Spotted muskinks, however, are apt to kill for the sake of killing and, in spite of their large size somewhere in the hippo range, they don't make much noise, which makes up for their slowness, which makes them rather more deadly than one would expect, being bright blue with large spots ranging from dark yellow to bright red in colour. Arthur wondered if twelve magical barriers and two solid rock doors were enough.

To take his mind off the muskink and yet another horrific near miss, Arthur began to explore their new surroundings. They were in a cave, not unlike, albeit somewhat smaller than, Harpur's Whyte Avenue lair. Missing were the hoard of gold and the opulent living quarters. In their stead were a collection of odd statues and pottery, stacks of books and scrolls and a tiny cot, a tiny, rickety table with two three-legged stools and a hearth carved into the stone on which a tiny cauldron bubbled away filling the space with the enticing aroma of a rich and succulent stew. The space was neither especially tidy nor exceptionally disorganized. While things looked all a-jumble, Arthur got a distinct impression that Hiro knew exactly where everything was.

Harpur, too, was taking in his new surroundings. The miniature and less-well-appointed version of his own lair was comforting and, he had to admit, in spite of the disarray, impressive. The orange-yellow light seemed to just be in the room rather than emitting from a specific source. He made a mental note to ask Hiro about it. But first, he had to be suspicious and cautious and protective. He still didn't know what Hiro's intentions were and that was distracting from the comforting sensation of being in this charming lair. He was also having difficulty determining where the exit was. Hiro had mentioned other ways out, but there were no visible openings. He wasn't even sure where the tunnel they had entered through was.

Sok, afraid of knocking something over, sat down on a stack of very large books and waited.

After dismounting from the hover gilly and sending it off to hover in a corner, Hiro got busy preparing drinks for the guests. Filling four chipped cups with dark burgundy wine, Hiro offered them to Harpur, Sok and Arthur. Sok sipped his. Arthur sniffed his. And Harpur declined his. Seeing Harpur decline his, Arthur put his down on another stack of large books and Sok spit his back into the cup. Hiro, unperturbed by the snub, guzzled his own. Sok and Arthur looked to Harpur for guidance and were dismayed when he didn't relax his vigilant caution. Thirst-quenching thus postponed, Arthur, who had also noticed that an exit wasn't obvious started scanning the walls for incongruent chunks of rocks sticking out of them. He didn't know how to convey this to Harpur, but he figured Harpur would either figure it out, or he wouldn't.

Arthur wanted to trust Hiro. He couldn't explain what had drawn him back into the cave earlier, but his gut told him that whatever had guided him to search for, and find, the opening to the tunnel did not have malicious intent. Hiro had saved them from the muskink and him from dangling high above the ground underneath a dragon. Then again, he was effectively trapped underground with a strange, possibly benevolent, little being who giggled a lot, seemed to enjoy flying around on a mind-controlled, wheel-less chariot and had a long-distance alliance with a super-friendly, head-size, talking spider. Nothing weird about that!

Arthur spotted what he was looking for a short way away from the hearth. Then he saw another one a few feet away from it. And then another one. And then another one. In total, he counted fourteen rock doorknobs scattered along the cavern walls at slightly varying, but still within doorknob-range, height. Hiro had mentioned three entrances to the cave: the one they came through, an exit that needed to be reactivated and the main one. Arthur had no way of telling which of the knobs led to which of the exits. He, like Harpur, wasn't even sure anymore exactly where they had come in. So that wasn't as helpful as he had hoped.

Hiro sat cross-legged atop a stack of books sipping a second cup of wine and being amused by the different energies Harpur, Sok and Arthur were projecting. By far, Sok was deemed the favourite. His relaxed and amiable attitude was precisely as Mezzi had described. Perhaps he was a little too trusting, but Hiro knew Sok had nothing to fear there. Arthur's humility was both a boon and a disadvantage. A little more confidence would serve him well. Harpur's self-assurance was, Hiro was convinced, attributable to his dragon nature. He couldn't help being that arrogant. It was time to move things along.

"The exit is over there," Hiro pointed to the one knob directly behind Arthur that Arthur had not yet spotted.

Both Arthur and Harpur dedicated the position of the knob to memory. They exchanged looks. Harpur wanted Arthur to entice Sok closer to the exit. Arthur's nod confirmed that the message had been received, but whether or not he understood what was expected of him was anybody's guess. Hiro suspected that the bond between Harpur and Arthur was not one of total, mutual trust. This trio was not a tight-knit unit capable of anticipating each other's needs. But there was potential. And that was enough for Hiro.

"Gentlemen," Hiro said, "I understand your discomfiture. I know this is all unexpected and that you are all unsure what to do. I assure you, though, that I am here to help. I can get you to the Veilrift to Ychonol... if that is what you wish."

"How do you know about that?" Harpur's suspicions were once again heightened.

"If you will allow me to continue," Hiro said, "I will explain everything." A pause followed while everyone got their manners in order. "Good. Now I will try to keep things brief as time, I believe, is of the essence. If you could hold your questions until the end, that will save time and prevent me from leaving out any important details. It's likely that, if you are patient and pay attention, most of your questions will be answered before you ask them. Nod if you understand."

Hiro paused again watching for the requested nods. Harpur opened his mouth to say something, but a thump in the arm from Arthur prevented the faux pas from transpiring. He nodded.

Hiro giggled and clapped his hands merrily. "As you know, Mezzi is a koobar that lives in Wildwood. She is one of dozens of koobars I have stationed in communities throughout Mysturna for the sole purpose of reporting back to me on the comings and goings in each community.

"She has been keeping me up to date on the situation you are currently involved in and, after your narrow escape from Wildwood, a daring and reckless feat, I might add, she contacted me to let me know you were heading in this direction. I know you all believe that you are being betrayed. I am also aware of the plan to get you through the Veilrifts to Thraeh so that you can thwart the Entanglement, which isn't nearly as urgent as Anayah has led you all to believe, by the way. There is a little-known alternative that I will share with you shortly, but for now I want to focus on the much bigger issue of Arthur being in a state of paradox, which wasn't, as you may have discerned, that big of an issue until he left Earth. He could have lived out the rest of his natural non-existence on Earth without much consequence, but now that he's left Earth the paradox, if that is indeed what it is, is in full force. Once off its home world, a paradox becomes forgotten and eventually fades away. That is where we need to focus our efforts. On determining his actual state of being, or non-being as the case may be.

"As for the Entanglement, all we need to do is cut the coin in half and have Sok and Arthur each keep half on their person at all times. It's counterintuitive, I know, but it will keep things in check for the time being. Once we figure out the paradox thing—and we will—we can address the Entanglement issue on a more permanent basis.

"For now, though, unless you insist on attempting to return to Thraeh through the Veilrifts, our priority is to get you all to the Pole and to Anabettah, who has more information for us on how to fix that problem. The faster we get there, the better, so I hope you are all good with teleporting, as I understand it is called on Earth. I really must go there someday. Sounds like a fascinating world, but I digress...

"Analeetah, Anayah and Kel are currently on their way to the Veilrift to Ychonol, believing that you three will be seeking assistance to complete your mission as Anayah had planned. They intend to head you off at the pass, as it were. We will take advantage of their lack of faith in you and correct this mess. Then I will take you to the Veilrift or anywhere else you may wish to go. I imagine that we can find a safer and more easily traversed path to Thraeh, if you are willing to give me time to do some more research. All clear?"

For a moment there was complete silence. And just when Hiro thought it was safe to go on, Harpur, Sok and Arthur all started speaking at once.

"Anayah did lie!"

"Is Mezzi okay?"

"What do you mean I'm being forgotten and will fade away?"

"What if Anabettah is in on it too?"

"Teleport?"

"Are they actually plotting to destroy Thraeh and Earth?"

"What happens if Arthur fades away and the Entanglement isn't taken care of?"

"I can't believe that she lied to me!"

"Are we going to see Mezzi again?"

"Who's forgetting me? Are my mom and dad forgetting me?"

"I thought Anayah was our friend."

"I can't believe she lied to me. About everything. She's been planning this all along, hasn't she?"

"This is insane! I don't want to be forgotten. I don't want to fade away."

"Can I have some of that wine now?"

Hiro's tiny hands waving in the air went largely unnoticed. This should have been expected, but Hiro had underestimated their emotional investment in the situation. The summary had not, in fact, answered all their questions and had, in fact, sent two-thirds of them spiralling into self-centred pools of unwanted self-awareness while the significance of it appeared to have been lost on the remaining one-third. There was no time for this nonsense. Hiro hopped down from his stack of books, walked over to Arthur and kicked him in the shin.

"Ouch! What was that for?"

"I would have kicked him," Hiro pointed at Harpur, who had missed the attack, but not the outcome, "but he's bigger than me."

"I'm bigger than you." Arthur rubbed the spot where Hiro's unpredictably hard foot had connected with his leg.

"But not as bigger than me than he is," Hiro returned to the stack of books and stood on it. "We don't have a lot of time. I need you all to focus."

Harpur, still seething at the depth of Anayah's betrayal, clenched his fists and snarled. Arthur stayed near the exit. Sok remained seated on his stack of books, Harpur's telepathic message to Arthur having gone completely unheeded.

"I know none of you have any reason to trust me," Hiro continued. "But I'm all you got, so it's up to you. You can do as I tell you or not. I really don't care one way or the other."

"Gee, thanks," Arthur mumbled.

"What I don't understand," Harpur said, "is why Anayah, a witch from Mysturna who was raised to be compassionate and abhors violence, is plotting against us. It doesn't make sense."

"We'll have to ask her, won't we?" Hiro said. "Perhaps her heart has been blackened by her time on other worlds. Perhaps she has convinced herself that whatever she is planning is for the greater good."

"I can totally see why she might want to demolish Earth..." Sok began.

"Hey!" Arthur interjected.

"Have you seen what people do to each other on your world?" Sok reasoned.

"Yeah, well, we're not all like that. Most people are good," Arthur said.

"Please," Hiro said, "We could debate Anayah's motives all night. But only she knows what's in her heart. I can try to help you avoid whatever fate she has designed for you, though. It's up to you."

Arthur and Harpur exchanged looks again. Arthur and Harpur nodded at each other again. They both looked back at Hiro again.

"We're in," Arthur said.

"We'll take our chances on our own," Harpur said.

"What?"

"What?"

Hiro's tiny head shook in disbelief. While the argument that ensued raged on, Hiro hopped down from the stack of books and dished up two servings of the savoury stew that was bubbling on the hearth. Beckoning Sok to join in the repast, Hiro sat down at the rickety table and ate.

Hiro, the seemingly genderless being, was, in fact, not genderless at all. As Sok discovered, Hiro was and continues to be, a male-dominant member of a race known as Krists. Where they originate from is anybody's guess, including, literally, all Kristkind. They are found living throughout the multiverse, usually singly, but sometimes in small groups. Hiro, had no idea where he, for that is the pronoun he had adopted, came from or how he ended up on Mysturna. "It's as if we are just... thought into existence," he told Sok, who, unlike Arthur and Harpur, had no qualms about delving into the personal lives of those he found himself stuck underground in lairs with.

Krists are learners. That's what they do. They study. They absorb information. They have no vested interest in outcomes, nor do they harbour any personal agendas. Always willing to help, Krists are big-picture beings who are adept at connecting the dots and, thus, predicting outcomes without being bothered by them. Heed their advice, or don't; it's all the same to them.

Like all Krists, Hiro had the ability to adapt almost instantly to any world. He could easily travel to Ychonol, for example, without fear of being suffocated by the toxic atmosphere. He would not cook to death in the near-boiling waters of Dyrl. And while he was not immune to the lethality of the weapons of war on Terra Nine, he could build laser-repelling armour and a crush-resistant shelter and probably survive quite well.

As Sok and Hiro filled up on stew and wine, they shared stories about themselves. Sok told Hiro how he had come to give Arthur the coin and why. Hiro reassured Sok that the Entanglement was not as dire as Anayah had led them to believe. Hiro told Sok how he had come to employ the koobars as spies. Sok's candour matched Hiro's frankness and by the time Arthur and Harpur had quarrelled themselves out, the elf and the Krist had become fast friends.

"Well," said Hiro to the cold-shoulder silence on the other side of the cave, "have you two decided what you want to do?"

Arthur was the first to speak. "I think we should put it to a vote."

"Sure," Harpur sneered, "let's leave it up to the idiot that got us into this mess. What do you say, Sok? Do you trust me? Or do you want to put your life in the hands of a... this guy?" He pointed at Hiro.

"Of course, I trust you, Harpur!" Sok said.

"Ha!" Harpur spat at Arthur.

"But," Sok continued, "Hiro knows a lot about Mysturna and the Entanglement and how to get us help with Arthur's paradox problem. I think you ought to at least listen to him before we go off and get ourselves into worse trouble."

"Ha!" Arthur spat back at Harpur.

"You know what?" Harpur said. "This doesn't have anything to do with me. I don't even need to be here. I just came along to help you two get untangled and back to your normal lives. But if you don't want my help..."

"We do want your help," Arthur said. "That's what I've been trying to tell you. But we don't know the land. We don't know where the Veilrifts are. And even if we did know, we don't have the equipment we need to survive. I don't understand why you are being such a jerk about this."

"I'm being a jerk? Me? What about you?"

And both sides came out verbally swinging for round two.

"Do you play Shookin?" Hiro asked Sok.

"Never heard of it."

"Oh, I think you'll like it." Hiro retrieved a game that resembled a chessboard, but with a hundred squares instead of sixty-four and twenty playing pieces for each side. There was also a deck of cards and a set of coins and a three-hundred-page rule book. Sok asked for more wine.

The night wore on, as did the two battles—one friendly and one not so much—until a loud knocking sound reverberated through the cave, interrupting the laughter and the shouting.

"That must be Mezzi!" Hiro exclaimed, jumping up from the rickety stool and trotting over to a scroll-strewn table from which he extracted a scrying mirror just like the one Anayah used. "She always calls late."

"Does she always make that much noise when she calls," Arthur asked with a voice hoarse from yelling.

Hiro ignored him and lifted the mirror. He tapped it twice, causing the surface to ripple like the surface of a wind-ruffled pond and Mezzi's spidery image appeared. "There you are!" she said. "I've been calling for ages. Why didn't you answer?"

Hiro giggled. "Does that answer *your* question, Arthur?" Then turning back to the mirror, he addressed Mezzi. "I couldn't hear you over all the shouting."

"Shouting?" the koobar asked.

"Nothing to worry about. What news do you have for us?"

Arthur, Sok and Harpur all gathered behind Hiro to see and hear the exchange. When Mezzi saw Arthur, she waved. Arthur waved back, thinking that she was much less creepy via Skype stone.

"I just wanted to be sure you found them," Mezzi said. "Anayah, Analeetah and Kel have all gone to the Veilrift. They will be waiting for them."

"So, they still plan on ambushing them there?" Hiro seemed oddly delighted.

"As far as I know, that's what they are planning to do. I even hid three of the packs they were supposed to take with them. Kel believes that Harpur stole them and is going to try to get Sok and Arthur to Thraeh through the Veilrifts without him."

"Excellent work!" Hiro clapped his hands and giggled. "How did they travel?"

"Overland. Kel insisted on going by cart. He won't let the witches zap him anywhere."

"That gives us a day. Though I'm surprised that Anayah didn't zap herself."

"She doesn't know that Analeetah knows that she's planning something. Kel might be playing both sides, but I'm not sure if he's helping Anayah or trying to stop her."

"He is loyal to Analeetah," Hiro said hopefully.

"But he owes Anayah for... that thing."

"What thing?" Harpur and Arthur asked at the same time.

"Nothing," Hiro said.

"You really do need to get to the Pole," Mezzi said. "Anabettah is still there. Though I'm not sure for how much longer. Bezzi might be able to tell you more."

"Yes, yes. I can call her. I was planning to anyway." Hiro said. "Then we'll teleport to the Pole tonight."

"I'm not teleporting anywhere!" Harpur declared.

"Not this again," Hiro sighed.

"What is teleporting?" Sok asked.

"You stand on a circle and then a guy named Scotty presses a button and a beam comes down from the ceiling and basically separates all your molecules, sucks them up and moves them through time and space to whatever location you are supposed to go to. Then it puts all your molecules back together." Harpur made it sound kind of awful.

"I'm impressed, Harpur," Arthur said. "Never took you for a Trekkie."

Harpur snarled.

"Is that how it works?" Hiro asked. "I thought it was the transmission of quantum information from one place to another contingent upon previously shared entanglement between the sending and receiving locations. Who's Scotty?"

"That sounds worse!" Sok said.

"Gotta go," Mezzi whispered loudly and disappeared.

"So, like Entanglement entanglement?" Sok was beginning to think he'd been too quick to trust Hiro.

"Sort of, yes!" Hiro seemed to be having a eureka moment.

"Then count me out. I'm already trying to get un-entangled from someone. I don't need to get more entangled with somewhere." Sok folded his arms in defiance.

"Think of it as zapping for non-magical people," Hiro said.

Arthur digested that for a moment. "So, witches are teleporters?"

"No. Witches are witches. Teleporters are teleporters," Hiro sounded impatient for the first time.

"But they do the same thing," Arthur said.

"They get the same result," Hiro said. "That's not the same as being the same thing."

"So, let's just call it zapping so everyone can be happy with it," Harpur suggested.

"I'm not happy with it!" Arthur said. "Magical zapping is weird enough. As much as I enjoy science-fiction, I don't think I'm ready to have my molecules disassembled."

"Do you people want my help or don't you? A simple yes or no will do." Hiro giggled, but his giggle sounded more mad than happy.

"Yes."

"Yes."

"A little."

"I'll take that as a yes," Hiro said. "Now before anyone asks anything else, here's what we are going to do. First, we have to split the coin." Hiro held up his hand to stop Arthur from pointing out whatever flaw in that action he was about to point out. "I know it sounds weird, but it will work. We have to cut the coin in half and each of you has to take a piece and keep it with you at all times. I have a couple of pouches you can wear around your necks so you won't lose the pieces."

Harpur was considering the magical implications of this tactic. "So, basically, what we're doing is confusing the coin."

"Yes!" Hiro agreed enthusiastically. "We have to make it think that it's with both of them so that it won't try to pull them together."

"Coins can think now?" Arthur was still skeptical.

"Everything can think!" Hiro said.

"Okey-dokey," Arthur decided that this magic stuff hurt his brain too much.

"The coin is still a whole coin, even if it's cut in half. It won't know that it's not entirely with one or the other object of the Entanglement."

"If you cut me in half, I'd know it," Arthur said.

"Not for long," Harpur said, holding his hand out for the coin.

Arthur looked around at his companions. Then he pulled the coin out of his pocket and handed it to Harpur, who magically dissected it with his walking stick. Hiro produced two pouches with drawstrings and gave them to Sok and Arthur.

Hiro finally felt like worthwhile progress was being made. He wondered briefly why Mezzi had ended the call so abruptly, but koobars were prone to being a little flighty. Right now, he had to keep things moving forward. And with Sok and Arthur each in possession of half of the coin, the next steps were to find a way they all agreed on to get them all to the Pole, find Anabettah and find out what happened to Arthur's Akashic Record.

Anayah had to believe that Arthur was in a state of paradox. Otherwise, she would have just had him Bound through a normal Boundary instead of creating this elaborate plan to use the Veilrifts. At the same time, Hiro had to wonder, was it even possible for someone in a state of paradox to become Entangled? If, indeed, Arthur did not exist, how could the coin Entangle him with Sok? And why had no one else thought of that? That in itself was something of a paradox. He needed more information. And Anabettah was very likely the best person to fill in all the gaps and complete the picture.

First, while Sok and Arthur were discussing whether or not they felt any different now that they both were in contact with the coin, Hiro had to make sure that Anabettah was where she was supposed to be. He picked up the scrying mirror and concentrated on Bezzi.

The koobar came into focus and Hiro could see she was dangling from a rafter over a shallow pool of crystal-clear water. He tapped the mirror six times, the code he used to let her know he needed to connect with her, and watched as Bezzi retreated up her web and scuttled along the rafter to a far corner of the structure enclosing the pool. Using her front two limbs, Bezzi held up her own mirror and tapped it twice to complete the connection. The surface of both mirrors rippled. They were able then to talk to one another.

"Hello," Bezzi chirped cheerfully.

"Hello, Bezzi," Hiro returned the greeting. "I don't have much time, but I wanted to check with you to see if Anabettah was still at the Pole."

"She is," Bezzi confirmed

"That's wonderful. Do you know how long she plans on staying there?"

"She mentioned earlier that she was thinking she needed to get back to Wildwood soon, but she didn't seem like she really meant it."

"Perfect. Now, you're sure she's going to be staying there for a while?" Hiro asked. He didn't want to insult the observant servant, but he needed to be absolutely certain himself.

"Oh, yes!" Bezzi was adamant. "She always gives me plenty of notice before she goes."

"When was the last time you saw her?"

"Only a few minutes ago. Ritual is about to start. That's where I was when I heard your knock. I like to watch from the rafters."

"There is no one else there, Bezzi?" Hiro asked.

"No. Anabettah is the only visitor at the moment. But Ritual time never changes. I like to stick to the routine."

"Ah," Hiro said. "Well, thank you, Bezzi. I must go now."

"Is it true that you are coming to the Pole? And that you're bringing other-worlders with you?" Bezzi asked.

"Yes. And we will be there shortly. But, Bezzi, please don't tell Anabettah that I'm bringing visitors. I would like to tell her myself."

"Okay," Bezzi was incapable of being truly disappointed, but Hiro sensed that her joy had dropped an octave. Hiro knew that she would have liked to be the one to tell Anabettah. Delivering news was a high point in any koobar's day.

They disconnected and Hiro put the scrying mirror into a large, relative to the small person who would carry it, satchel along with a few other odds and ends that he picked up and thought might come in handy.

Harpur had been leaning against the wall near where Hiro had indicated the exit was. He watched Hiro gather his belongings and eavesdropped on the banal conversation Sok and Arthur were having nearby. He could tell the elf was getting antsy about being underground. Sok kept looking around like the walls and ceiling were closing in on him. Harpur couldn't help but like Sok, but he was looking forward to this being over. Dragons are solitary creatures, even in human form. That he had shared his lair with Anayah for the past couple of years was testament to how much he had believed in her friendship and loyalty. To think that she was keeping secrets was more than he could stand. He had scarred himself to save her and the others. He probably would have died for her. Harpur touched the spot on his chest where he had torn out the scale. That physical pain, he realized, was nothing compared to the pain of her betrayal.

When Hiro drew close, Harpur asked, "What thing?" He was referring to *that thing* between Anayah and Kel that Mezzi had mentioned.

"It is not my place to tell you, Harpur." Hiro busied himself with his bag so he wouldn't have to look the wizard in the eye.

"But it's your koobar servants' place to tell you? What makes you so privileged?"

"It is the nature of my kind to collect information. It is not the nature of my kind to use that information against anyone. If you are meant to know, then the information will find you." Hiro turned his back on Harpur and went to douse the fire in the hearth. Then he whistled for his hover gilly and climbed into it.

Harpur snorted.

"Time to go!" Hiro called out as he turned one of the rock doorknobs. Not the one Arthur and Harpur had thought was the exit, but one close to it. The door, undiscernible until unlatched swung open and Hiro motioned for the others to exit through it.

"I thought that was the way out," Arthur said, pointing to the rock doorknob he thought they should be using.

"No," Hiro corrected. "It's this way. You must have misjudged where I was pointing. In you go!"

Arthur followed Sok and Harpur through the door. "In?" he asked. But before he—or any of them—could protest further, Hiro pulled the door shut behind them and plunged them all into absolute darkness.

"What the..." Harpur yelled.

"This isn't..." Sok began.

They had just enough time to register the fact that they had been shepherded into a small, circular chamber when a bright beam of light illuminated their surroundings. Instantly everything blurred and faded. They each experienced a not-unpleasant tingling sensation that lasted a second or two and then they found themselves standing on a rocky plain. The first sun had already risen and the second one was following it in a dazzling array of blue and purple light that was unique to sunrises in the region of the Pole.

Which is where they had been covertly teleported to by the wily Krist who urged his hover gilly forward and called, with a giggle, for the others to follow.

"How does it feel to be zapped somewhere unwillingly?" Arthur asked Harpur when he noticed the murderous look on the dragon-wizard's face.

"Teleported!" Hiro corrected over his shoulder. "I apologize for the subterfuge, but there was no time for further debate."

Harpur snarled again.

They walked for several minutes in silence. Harpur, Sok and Arthur were taking in and adjusting to their new environment, a vast reddish-brown plain strewn with reddish-brown rocks. Here and there, gnarly, leafless, little trees grew out of the dusty ground. In the distance, huge, twisted rock formations towered high above the earth. To Arthur, they resembled stone giants frozen in time and space. One formation, however, was different. An enormous obelisk loomed above the landscape, casting a shadow that, in the early morning light, stretched for hundreds of feet across the plain. In contrast to the reddishness of the surrounding scenery, it was jet black, so black that it felt like it could absorb everything, not just colour, that came near it. Formidable was the word that crossed Arthur's mind when he first saw it. Even at a distance, it commanded a deep sense of reverence and respect.

"You couldn't have zapped us a little closer?" Harpur complained.

"You have to stay beyond the shadow's reach," Hiro explained.

"But the shadow is pointing away from us," Arthur pointed out.

"Yes. For now. But if you get within its reach, it will find you and you don't want that to happen."

"Why do I not want that to happen?" Harpur asked.

"Because it will devour you."

Harpur, Sok and Arthur let that sink in.

"Then maybe we should just stop here," Harpur suggested. He stopped walking.

Sok and Arthur stopped walking as well. Hiro, in his hover gilly, continued on for a good minute before realizing that his companions were no longer with him. He turned around and sped back to the on-strike walkers. "What are you doing? We can get closer than this." Hiro giggled.

"I think I'll wait back here. Though I don't actually know what I'm waiting for," Harpur said.

"There aren't any muskinks out here, are there?" Sok asked looking around.

"Not that I'm aware of. They tend to stick to the hills." Hiro said.

"So, can you tell us what to expect? Why are we even here? Or is that information your kind doesn't share?" Harpur asked sarcastically.

"We are here, as you already very well know, to talk to Anabettah. And you can expect to be invited into the Pole grounds, once I explain to Anabettah why we're here. You just can't walk in without an invitation." Hiro turned the hover gilly back toward the Pole.

"I feel like a vampire," Arthur said.

"A what?" Sok asked.

Hiro turned the hover gilly back to face his difficult companions. He was beginning to feel like a top spinning around and around.

"A vampire. You know, fangs, sleeps in coffins, allergic to the sun. 'I vant to suck your blod!'" Arthur's accent was passable, but sadly, lost on Sok and Hiro. Harpur got it. He just didn't want it.

"What does any of that have to do with any of this?" Harpur scoffed.

"Vampires can't enter a building unless they are invited. Duh!"

"Are all Earthlings this unfocussed?" Hiro asked.

"Pretty much," Harpur confirmed. "But invitation or no invitation, I'm not getting within reach of a killer shadow. Why don't you go ahead, talk to Anabettah and come get us when it's safe to move on?"

"Very well!" Hiro agreed and, once again, pointed the hover gilly in the direction he wanted to go. "But don't just stand still out here. Either find a large rock to stand on or keep walking in circles." He moved away.

"Why is that?" Harpur called after the Krist.

"Sand wyvers!" Hiro shouted over his shoulder and kept flying on.

"What are sand wyvers?" Arthur asked.

"I'm not going to stand still and find out!" Harpur looked around and, seeing a decent-sized rock formation that they could all fit on not too far away, said, "This way!"

They started jogging toward the rock just as the sandy ground near Sok's feet shifted and pitched him forward into Arthur who pitched forward into Harpur who didn't even bother to stop and assess the situation. He turned, thrust his walking stick into Arthur's outstretched hand, transformed, grabbed Sok and Arthur and flew away just as a large hole opened up right where they had been standing.

From his vantage point—hanging upside down in dragon Harpur's precarious grip on his legs—Sok was the first to be versed on sand wyvers as a huge lizard crawled out of the ground flicking its sticky tongue in and out. Expecting its prey to be on the ground, the hideous beast didn't look up until, thankfully, it was too late. It sat there, blinking in confusion, for a minute before retreating back under the sand.

Harpur landed on the rock and deposited Sok and Arthur safely down upon it. "I hate this Orhowyn-forsaken world!" he snarled.

Arthur sat down and rested his elbows on his bent knees. "Are all the animals here huge and deadly?"

"I have decided that I don't like flying upside down," Sok announced.

"I'm going to take a quick look around to see where that shadow is and make sure we're not within its reach here," Harpur said, backing up as far as he could to make room to launch.

"Harpur?" Arthur was staring off into the distance.

"What?"

"Thanks."

Harpur launched up into the sky.

The Pole, Harpur estimated, was close to 1000 feet tall. It was surrounded by a large oasis of lush gardens and sparkling pools. A labyrinth wound its way from the outer edge of the oasis through gazebos placed along its path. There was only one fully enclosed building, a circular structure that contained sleeping quarters for visitors to the Pole. Its shadows, cast by the two suns, looked like the hands of a clock stretching across the plain. As the suns rose, they would shorten and their deadly reach would become less of an issue. Not knowing how long it would take Hiro to get the invitation they needed to enter the sacred space, Harpur decided that they would remain where they were. He also decided that they would fly to the Pole when the invitation arrived. Arthur would just have to deal with that.

He circled around, enjoying the leisurely flight. A couple of loops, a short dive just for the sport of it and a lazy spiralling glide lifted his spirits. Satisfied that the rock Sok and Arthur were on was well out of the way of the shadow, he turned to go back. On his way, he noticed a gazelle-like animal leaping across the plain. When it stopped to nibble at one of the scrubby trees, the ground underneath it opened up and a sand wyver pulled it, screaming, back into the earth. Realizing just how lucky they had been standing still for as long as they had, even Harpur had to shudder at the close call.

As he approached the rock, Harpur called out and Sok and Arthur moved to the far edge so he could land. Remaining in Dragon form, but positioning himself in such a way as to keep his missing scale from being noticeable, Harpur described the oasis, but left out the gazelle's demise. There was no need to relive that bit of horror. He positioned himself so that Sok and Arthur were shaded from the climbing suns and their accompanying heat, conjured up two water skins, some meat and bread and a couple of small pillows. He didn't care where it all came from anymore, but he suspected that the Pole was now short a few supplies. They were all tired after another sleepless night—a pattern was forming in that respect—so he encouraged Sok and Arthur to get some rest while he kept watch.

The day wore uneventfully on. Harpur allowed himself to doze off around midday. Wrapping his long tail and neck to form a protective circle around the sleeping elf and man, he closed his eyes and went to sleep. If they were attacked by anything, maybe it would be kind enough to kill them before they woke up. Harpur just didn't want to deal with any more Mysturnian creatures.

Sok was the first to wake up. The suns had set and it was quite dark on the rock in the plain. He sat up and stretched out the kinks his body had collected while he was asleep and reached for his water skin. As he took a long drink, he noticed a small spark of light rising into the sky from just beyond the edge of the rock. And then another. And then another.

He stood up and stepped carefully over Harpur's tail so he could get a better look at what was happening. The entire plain was awash with the soft light from millions of these tiny sparks rising up from the sand. Sok looked at the ground trying to see what was causing them. It seemed like individual grains of sand were spontaneously combusting and floating up into the air. When they reached a height of thirty feet or so, they faded out again. They didn't seem to be having any effect on the trees, so Sok put his hand out and let one rise into his open palm. He felt nothing and when he turned his hand over, the spark continued to float upward.

"Harpur! Arthur!" Sok called out. "Wake up! You have to see this."

Harpur opened his big, dragon eyes and looked sideways at Sok and then beyond him. Seeing the sparks floating up he became instantly alert. "Orhowyn's crooked toes! What is this now?"

Harpur's oath woke Arthur, who sat up in alarm. "What? What's happening?" Then he, too, saw the sparks. "Wow! It's so beautiful. What are they?"

"Probably some new deadly threat," Harpur growled. "Just don't touch them."

"No, it's fine. Look," Sok said and demonstrated catching and releasing another spark.

Arthur, mesmerized, joined Sok at the edge of the rock and started catching and releasing sparks. They were like two kids during a first snowfall, laughing and horsing around. Sok initiated a game to see which of them could catch the most before they had to turn their hand over to let the sparks go. Harpur was not amused. He sniffed the air, but detected nothing amiss. And while it was rather pretty, he refused to believe that there was no threat attached to it.

"Where in Orhowyn's world of wonders is that shrimp of a Krist?" he grumbled, but Sok and Arthur ignored him.

Harpur had a mind to fly to the Pole right then. What's the worst thing that could happen if he arrived without an invitation? Considering all that had happened since he got to Mysturna that did not bear thinking about. The consequences were likely to be unpleasant in the extreme. For all their talk about compassion and living non-violent lives, Mysturnians had some odd and unsettling protocols. And far too many deadly creatures.

He pondered his relationship with Anayah. He thought of her like a good friend and it bothered him that he had trusted her so completely and had not seen her hidden agenda. Granted the evidence against her was more circumstantial than concrete, but why else would she have asked Kel to steal the coin? If she had some way of helping Arthur and Sok with it, why didn't she just tell them about it? It didn't make sense.

Sok and Arthur eventually tired of their game and the two of them settled down to sit and watch the sparks. Arthur was particularly fond of the way the sparks that caught on the underside of tree branches made them glow like twinkling Christmas lights as they faded out and were replaced by new ones. He wondered if this would go on all night.

"I wonder if this will go on all night?" he asked aloud.

"I wonder if it happens every night," Sok mused. "What if this is a once-in-a-lifetime phenomenon and we are the only ones to see it in a thousand years."

"How long do elves live?" Arthur asked, suddenly curious about the life of the being he was supposed to be Entangled with.

"I'm eighty-eight years old," Sok said. "If all goes well, I'll live for another three or four hundred years."

"Bloody hell!" Arthur exclaimed. "That's crazy."

"How old are you?"

"Thirty."

"You seem much older. I'd have placed you somewhere between one-fifty and one-seventy-five."

"Humans only live about eighty years or so."

"Seriously? Now that's crazy."

"What about you, Harpur? How old are you?" Arthur asked.

"We don't keep track," the dragon answered.

"Approximately, then. Ballpark it for me," Arthur encouraged.

"Time is different on your world than on mine," Harpur said cryptically. "There is no accurate way of comparing. The time that Sok measures as three or four hundred years is probably very close to the same time that you measure as eighty years."

Arthur did the math. "Eighty would be closer to two hundred thirty-five years."

"Only if eight-eight and thirty were equivalent ages, which they are not. Sok is an adolescent in elven terms. By my calculations, his life expectancy is closer to three hundred fifty-two years. But as I said, time does not pass the same on Earth as it does on Thraeh."

"So, our ageing process is being affected by our being on a different world and going through time differently?" Arthur was growing alarmed.

"It's possible." Harpur was beginning to be amused.

"So, when I get back to Earth, I could be like a hundred? I could be dead!" The implications were terrifying.

Harpur decided to take pity on the young man. "Not to worry, Arthur. We will return you to Earth through a Veilrift. All you will have to do is think about the time and place where you left and you will be returned to the same time and place. You won't have aged and no one will know you've been gone."

"So, what was the point of calling my mother to tell I was going on a road trip then?"

"Just in case," Harpur said.

"Besides, Arthur," Sok chimed in, "technically you've been dead for eight years and it hasn't slowed you down." He clapped his mortified companion on the back and laughed. Even Harpur had to chuckle along.

"What's so funny?" A familiar voice called out with an accompanying giggle.

The dragon, the elf and the undead man turned to see a large hover gilly approach the rock. Hero's diminutive size was further accentuated by the large size of the vehicle, which, unlike the hover gilly he'd left in, could easily hold a half dozen grown men. The tiny Krist had to stand on a box to see over the front. He looked like a child who had stolen his parents' car.

"Hop on!" Hiro called, not waiting for an answer to his question. "Anabettah is nearly ready to retire for the night, but she wants to meet you all first."

"I think I will fly myself," Harpur said as Sok jumped merrily onto and Arthur stepped tenuously into the gilly.

"Suit yourself," Hiro said and reversed then turned the hover gilly toward the Pole.

"Anything I should know about?" Harpur asked.

"Not that I can think of," Hiro answered. "Just land outside the gate and transform before you enter. The Pole grounds won't accommodate a guest of your stature. Wait for us at the entrance."

"What?" Harpur called as he took to his wings. "You don't want to race?"

Hiro laughed and the hover gilly shot forward. Arthur clung to the side as best he could. There were no handholds or seats to grab onto. Sok placed one hand on the edge and leaned out like a dog with his head out the window of a speeding car.

They rode in silence over the dark sands and through the rising sparks. "What are these?" Sok asked.

"The sand absorbs the heat from the suns during the day and it reacts with certain elements in the sand. As the night cools, the elements release the heat in these tiny bursts of flame," Hiro explained.

"They don't burn when you touch them," Sok observed.

"No, the elements ignite spontaneously and burn at very low temperatures. They are harmless. I don't recommend that you eat them, though."

Sok gulped. "Is that bad?"

"Only in large quantities. One or two won't bother you." Hiro watched Sok expel a sigh of relief.

A few minutes later, they arrived at the gate to the Pole grounds. Harpur was standing just outside waiting for them in human form. He joined the others on the hover gilly that glided smoothly above the labyrinthine pathway through lush gardens and over small bridges spanning a sparkling creek that spiralled outward from the centre. Occasionally, the creek would widen into a deep and tranquil pool, or the path would lead through a gazebo, or widen itself into an open area paved with brightly coloured stones. A native to Mysturna would have stopped at each pool, structure and open space to observe a short ritual, but the other-worlders were whisked through or past each of them.

"How long is this going to take?" Harpur asked fifteen minutes in.

"About an hour," Hiro said.

"Why don't you just fly a little higher and go straight overtop to wherever we're going?" Harpur suggested.

Arthur seconded that motion. The hover gilly did not slow down for the switchback turns in the labyrinth and he was afraid of losing his grip and being flung out of the chariot.

"Not allowed," Hiro said. "Anabettah insisted that you complete the labyrinth before she meets you. It's part of the protocol. Be happy she didn't insist that you walk it. You'd be walking all night."

"I see," Harpur said. "So, tell me then, what took you so long to get back to us?"

"Anabettah likes to take her time with things. She said she would not contact Anayah until after she meets with you, but she was not happy when I suggested that Anayah was up to something with the coin. Anayah spoke to her the night before last, asking about Arthur's Akashic Records and she did tell me that she'd found some interesting information, but would prefer to share it with Anayah and Analeetah rather than with just you. It took some doing to convince her that we couldn't wait for them. Then she had to set the terms for your invitation. Then she had to meditate and perform the rituals that are required and... Well, you get the picture." Hiro piloted the hover gilly through another switchback.

"And what are the terms of our invitation?" Arthur asked, feeling like it might be a good thing to know the protocols beforehand.

"Basically, complete the labyrinth and don't touch anything. Don't go off exploring. Stay at the cabin you are assigned—you may touch the cabin and its furnishings, of course. Stay out of the pools. Behave yourselves, in other words. Anabettah will not tolerate any disrespect of the grounds. You will be banished, and none too gently, if you cause any harm to anything while you're here." Hiro spoke with authority Harpur suspected he did not possess.

While the wizard and the elf looked appropriately contrite, Arthur nodded as if there was no question. This was all just good manners. What could go wrong?

"You said Anabettah had information about Arthur's condition," Harpur said, to change the subject. "So, he is in a state of paradox?"

"I will let Anabettah tell you what she found." Hiro expertly navigated another switchback to the right.

They glided on in silence. Sok would have liked to slow down and enjoy the scenery that was passing by in a blur. Arthur just wanted to slow down. But presently they arrived at the centre of the labyrinth, which was occupied by the base of the Pole, which was not as large as Harpur thought it would have to be to support the incredible height to which it soared. The base was also open. Archways on all four sides of the obelisk opened onto a gallery with candle-lit altars occupying the centre and each corner. Hiro brought the hover gilly to a halt just outside the gallery.

"Aren't we going in?" Harpur asked.

"This is as far as you go," Hiro said.

"But if we don't go in, we will not have completed the labyrinth. That would be a breach of protocol, wouldn't it?"

"One would think!" Hiro said. "There are strict rules about the sacred spaces on Mysturna. As other-worlders, you are not permitted to observe the rituals and the center is a space for the witch's most holy rituals."

"So, we just sit here then?" Harpur sounded annoyed.

"No. We are going to go back to the last gazebo we passed. Anabettah is waiting for us there. I just wanted to look at the monument for a minute." Hiro giggled, but it didn't sound joyful.

He turned the hover gilly around and lifted it above the gardens. This time they did fly over the top and directly to the gazebo they needed to be at. And at a pace more suitable to Arthur's sensibilities. When they arrived, they alighted and entered the structure, a wooden pagoda with a thatched roof. Each pillar was a totem of animals with jewels embedded in the dark wood for eyes. Arthur found it creepy. He assigned it to the category of one of the things not to be touched. He wished he didn't have to enter it.

But enter it he did. And was shocked to find Anayah, Analeetah and Kel standing behind a seated witch who smiled at them, perhaps a little ruefully.

"Hiro! I thought you said that she wouldn't contact them yet?" Harpur shouted at Hiro as he turned to go after the Krist, who was flying away in the gilly, and slammed into an invisible barrier that effectively prevented him from giving chase.

He wheeled back to face the Mysturnians and stepped protectively in front of Arthur and Sok. "What is this?" he demanded.

Anabettah rose from her chair and stood in aristocratic dignity as protectively before her entourage as Harpur did before his. She was beautiful in a gracefully aged and infinitely wise sort of way. Not quite as tall as either Anayah or Analeetah, Anabettah, nonetheless, had a presence that commanded respect. Her silver hair fell in a simple braid over one shoulder. She was dressed in a simple, silver-blue gown, belted at the waist by a delicate silver chain. Her arms bore a complex network of designs tattooed in silver and dark blue. An array of silver and sapphire rings adorned her fingers and a large sapphire pendant hung from a silver chain around her neck. In the torchlight of the evening, she seemed to glow with awe-inspiring power.

"I apologize for any misunderstanding," Anabettah spoke with a deep and feminine resonance in her voice, the sound of which was soothing and sincere. "Please sit down. All of you."

The invitation came with a hint of a decree that Harpur chose to defy. "I'd prefer to stand."

Sok, who would have been happy to comply, heard the inference in Harpur's voice and remained where he was as well. Arthur just stared at Anayah, trying to read her expression and determine her intentions. She kept her own gaze straight ahead. As did Kel and Analeetah.

"Very well," Anabettah said. "I, however, will sit. There's no need for both of us to be uncomfortable."

That she had seemed to have dismissed the others was intriguing to Harpur. Was she acknowledging his authority? Or was she deflecting the superiority of the threat the four of them collectively had over him, Sok and Arthur? He wasn't stupid. He understood that they were prepared and that he would have far less chance of escape here as there had been back at Wildwood. Still, standing felt better. At least for the time being.

"What do you want?" Harpur asked.

"What do I want?" Anabettah parroted. "You came to me. You tell me what you want."

Having been thrown off as he was, Harpur needed time to regroup, to assess and reconnoitre. Improvisation was limited and he was still feeling the ego-punch he'd received from bouncing off the unexpected barrier. He had no choice but to go along with things for a while and see if a way out presented itself.

"I want answers," he said simply.

"Answers generally follow questions, Harpur Diggins."

Anabettah put a whole lot of meaning into the use of his whole name and it wholly disconcerted him. Harpur was certain that this witch had looked into his own Akashic Records. She probably knew more about him than he did about himself. This was going to be interesting. The dragon felt challenged in a way he had not felt in a long time. This was a witch to be admired, respected, feared. But that only meant that she was a potentially great ally as well.

"Fair enough. My first question is: What are they doing here? I thought the Krist had convinced you not to contact them." Harpur pointed to Anayah, Analeetah and Kel.

"They are here at my request. We can't sort anything out with half the equation missing. They need to be here. As for the Krist, as you call him, Hiro did ask me not to contact them until I had spoken to you and I had said that I would consider it. However, I believe that it is easier to get to the heart of the matter when all parties involved are involved. I find it less likely that someone will make false accusations when the person they are accusing is in front of them.

"I want you also to know that Hiro did not betray you. He did not know that I had invited Analeetah, Anayah and Kel to be here. I did ask him to give us privacy after he delivered you here, but he was not aware that anything had changed."

"I'll accept that. For now," Harpur said. "Would it do me any good to ask for a private audience with you?"

"None at all," Anabettah declared with finality. "As I said, there will be more transparency if we all discuss the matter together."

"But you have had time alone with them," Harpur countered. "Do we not deserve the same courtesy?"

"We have not discussed anything pertaining to Arthur's state of paradox, the Entanglement or any plot, perceived or real, against you."

"How do I know that's true?" Harpur challenged.

"You don't."

"Then why imprison us in here?"

"That was for Hiro's protection," Anabettah said. "Now that he is well away from here, you will find that you are free to enter and exit the gazebo as you wish."

Harpur half-turned and motioned for Sok to test this. When the elf had successfully exited and returned, Harpur continued. "Thank you."

"You are most welcome. Now, are we done with the posturing?" Anabettah asked.

Harpur sighed. "One more thing."

"Go on."

"Analeetah and Kel are not a part of this. I would like this discussion to continue without them."

Anabettah studied Harpur for a few moments. Was he just evening the odds? No, she decided. He was being sincere.

"As you wish," she agreed. "Analeetah, Kel, please go back to the commons."

Without a word, the two Mysturnians left and disappeared down the path leading away from the gazebo. Harpur, as was Arthur, was amazed that they had not protested. They were both kind of amazed that none of them had said a word at all so far. Sok was just getting bored. But oddly, he didn't say anything either. Harpur suspected a spell of some kind. And to test his theory he turned to Arthur.

"How you doing, Arthur?" he asked.

Arthur just smiled and gave him a thumbs-up.

"As much as I appreciate these two being struck dumb, I think they have some things to contribute," Harpur said.

"I am sure they do," Anabettah replied. "And when we convene in the morning, they shall have their chance." With that, she stood up, gave her arm to Anayah and walked regally out of the gazebo.

Duped again! "What about us?" Harpur called after them.

"I will take you to your room." Hiro had returned with the large hover gilly and was floating just outside the gazebo entrance.

Harpur, Sok and Arthur all turned and looked at the little Krist peeking at them over the edge of the chariot.

"I didn't know she would summon the others," he said.

"I know," Harpur said.

"Are you angry?" Hiro asked when they had all boarded.

"I'm confused," Harpur said. "And that makes me angry. But I'm not angry with you if that's what you're asking."

Chapter 7

Arthur was irate.

Getting the ability to speak back barely relieved his ire, but fully released a tirade fueled by indignation. He raged on in half-finished, profanity punctuated sentences all the way to the small cabin on the eastern edge of the Pole grounds where they were all to spend the night.

"How dare...! Did you see...? I don't believe it! The nerve of her! That makes me mad. ...all doughy eyed and... I'll talk when I feel like talking. Who does she think she is?"

No one else really understood what he was going on about. He was so incensed he even forgot to hold onto the side of the hover gilly while they flew. Nothing could shut him up, so everyone left him to his rant. It wasn't until they landed at the cabin and Arthur landed a bone-jarring punch on its door did his tirade abate. With both hands now out of commission, Arthur crumpled to the ground and sat there stunned. Stunned, but finally—blessedly—silent.

Harpur carried Arthur into the cabin and deposited him down on one of the seven cots that were lined up along the walls so Sok could tend to his latest wound. Besides the cots, the cabin contained a table and four chairs, a single shelf above each cot and a small, unlit fireplace. The furnishings were utilitarian but sturdy. There was some food on the table, left there, no doubt, by Hiro. Harpur wasn't particularly hungry, but he helped himself to a chunk of bread and some meat and chewed it thoughtfully.

"What were you thinking?" Sok asked as he wrapped Arthur's swollen and bleeding knuckles in a strip of clean cloth.

"I wasn't," Arthur mumbled. "I'm just so bloody tired of people manipulating and controlling me like that."

"Why don't you get some rest?" Sok suggested.

He gently pushed Arthur down onto his back and covered him with a blanket. Then he joined Harpur and Hiro at the table and helped himself to some of the food. The meal was not fancy, but it was tasty. He had hoped that Hiro would be up for a chat or a game, but the little Krist announced that, having had no opportunity to sleep during the day, he was tired and retired to one of the cots for the remainder of the night. So Sok turned to Harpur.

"What are you thinking about?" Sok asked.

Harpur looked at the elf. "Did you notice anything strange about Anayah and the others?"

Sok thought about it. "They were kind of quiet."

"Exactly!" Harpur said. "I don't think it was really them."

"Who was it, then?" Sok picked up a slice of meat.

"I think, they were mirages."

"Why would Anabettah do that?"

"To see how we would react to seeing them. But Kel doesn't like to be zapped, so if it was really them, how did they get here so fast? Hiro said it would take a day for them to get to the Veilrift. How long would it take them to get here? Wherever here is." Harpur, too helped himself to more food.

Sok didn't respond. Instead, he chose a particularly thick piece of meat from the tray and took a bite.

Harpur looked over at Arthur lying on the cot and frowned. "I'll be back in a while," he said to Sok and left the cabin.

Not wanting to be alone, Sok followed the dragon-wizard out of the cabin a few minutes later. He couldn't see Harpur in the immediate vicinity, so Sok ventured down the path leading away from it. Still no Harpur. He called out the dragon-wizard's name, but when he received no reply, he continued down the path, which joined the main labyrinth a short distance away.

Sok looked to his right. He looked to his left. Seeing and hearing no one nearby, he stepped onto the labyrinth and stood there. They had been told not to wander around. *Don't go exploring.* Hiro had been explicit about that. Maybe, Sok reasoned, Harpur had forgotten. Maybe, Sok reasoned, he should go look for Harpur and remind him. It seemed logical and so Sok set off reasonably sure that he would find his way back.

The gardens were lovely, lush and luxuriant. Trees, shrubs, flowers, ornamental grasses and vines filled in the spaces between the winding path of the labyrinth. As beautiful as it was, Sok felt an odd eeriness creep over him as he walked. There were no birds. No animals. Anywhere. Sok deduced that the Pole grounds were not natural and that left him feeling a little dismayed. He was missing his home in the forests of Braydon Wood. The birdsong, the animals foraging, the wind making the trees whisper. That was another thing; there was no wind. The air was completely still. Sok felt a shiver slither up his spine. Anayah had called this place sacred, but there was something unholy about it that made Sok want to return to the cabin and the company of his companions there, even if they were sleeping. Harpur would have to manage on his own.

It was a point of pride with elves that they could always find their way and never got lost. But as Sok ran back in the direction he had come from, he soon realized that he had to have overshot the path to the cabin. He turned around, made note of his surroundings and headed back again. The path to the cabin should have been on his right. Wide enough for three grown men to walk side-by-side, it should have been obvious. But it wasn't. Sok could not find it.

Counting his steps and increasing their number incrementally, Sok swept back and forth along the path until he came to a switchback. At that point, he conceded that he had lost his way and did not know how to get back to the cabin. It was disorienting and left him feeling frightened. To be so vulnerable was foreign to the elf. The only thing he could do was to sit down and wait to be found. Someone would find him sooner or later.

The irony of being lost in a labyrinth was not lost on Sok. It wasn't like he was in a maze; this was a single, unbroken path from the outside to the centre. It is impossible to get lost in a labyrinth. And yet Sok was lost and unable to find his way back to the cabin.

He had wandered too far. In spite of being told not to go exploring, Sok's elven nature had taken over and led him down a potentially dangerous path. He wasn't concerned about being attacked by wildlife. Or plant life, for that matter. He was somewhat worried about what Anabettah would say and do when she found out he had broken the rules. That witch scared him! Maybe Harpur or Hiro would find him first and she would never have to know.

Sok had no idea how much time had passed, but he was pretty much at the end of his tether. A whole night spent doing nothing, seeing nothing, hearing nothing was more than he could stand. Why hadn't Harpur come looking for him? Maybe Harpur was lost too. That was not likely. If he had gotten turned around, he'd just transform and fly back to the cabin. Sok wished he could fly. The longer he sat there, the more he worried about the consequences of breaking the rules. And the eerier the gardens felt. The stillness was so unnatural, so forbidding. Sok could not sit there for one more second. He jumped to his feet and started marching with purpose back along the path toward where he thought the cabin should be.

He hadn't gone far when he heard a tapping sound on the path ahead of him. He stopped and was just about to duck behind a bush when Bezzi came skittering along toward him. "Looking for me?" Sok called out. Relieved to be found, he ran toward the koobar.

Bezzi stopped skittering. "There you are! I've been looking everywhere for you."

"I'm so glad you found me!" Sok began.

"You need to get back to the cabin right away. So far, I've been able to keep Anabettah from realizing you are gone, but if she notices, you're in big trouble. Come on," Bezzi said. "I will lead you back."

"Thank you," Sok said sheepishly.

Sok had to jog to keep up with the koobar. It seemed to him that they were going a lot farther than he could possibly have gone earlier. But eventually, they came to an opening in the bushes and the path to the cabin. Bezzi escorted Sok to the cabin door and directed him to go inside and to stay there until he was called for.

"Don't do that again!" she admonished.

"I'm sorry. I was just looking for Harpur. He left, too, you know?" Sok was defensive.

"Don't blame Harpur for your choices. If it was necessary for you to know where Harpur went, someone would have told you. Honestly! I thought it was going to be fun and interesting to have guests from other worlds. But you all are nothing but a pain in my spinnerets!"

With that, the koobar skittered away, leaving Sok to wonder where Harpur *had* gone. And what he had done. Feeling slightly vindicated, he entered the cabin to find Arthur and Hiro both still abed and both snoring loudly. He couldn't imagine how Arthur could sleep again after sleeping all day.

He took a moment to check on Arthur's freshly wounded hand and do a little healing. He pulled the blanket back up and tucked the mouth-breathing man in again. Perhaps a nap would help relieve his boredom after all. He still wasn't especially tired, but lying down might inspire lassitude. Arthur snuffled and snorted and groaned as he turned over in his cot. Once settled again, his snoring resumed in a slow-waltz, three-four timing in contrast to Hiro's molto vivace wheeze. There would be no sleep for Sok inside that cabin. He decided to break the rules, but only slightly, and find somewhere outside to curl up and snooze. He would stay close this time.

As he stepped away from Arthur's cot, his foot came into contact with something on the floor. Sok bent over to retrieve it and discovered that Arthur's cell phone had fallen out of his pocket and off of the cot. *Ah! Something to play with.* He took the cell phone with him outside and found a spot next to the cabin where he hunkered down and tried to get comfortable. The ground, though, was oddly unforgiving. He had seen Arthur use his passcode while they were driving to the Veilrift and he entered it then. The home screen came to life and cast a soft glow on Sok's face.

There were six rows of what Arthur had called icons. In the upper-right corners of some of them were little red dots with numbers in them. He hadn't noticed those before. He touched a green one that had a white circle with a little spike sticking out of it and the screen changed to a list of names, some with pictures next to them, some with circles containing letters. There were words beside the pictures and circles and under the names. Sok did not understand them. He did not recognize any of the people in the pictures. Except one.

It was Anayah. And, unlike, the other people in the other pictures, she was moving. It looked like she was talking. There were no words or numbers next to her moving picture. Sok touched the screen. Suddenly Anayah's picture filled the whole screen and he could hear her voice.

"Arthur, I know you think I've betrayed you, but I assure you I haven't. I will explain everything to you. If you agree to meet me, I will arrange it. Just tap the screen two times for yes and one time for no." When she finished speaking, she glanced furtively to her left. Then the picture jerked and she started speaking again, repeating exactly the same thing she had just said. Sok watched and listened to it a few times. He didn't know how to turn it off and he was afraid to tap the screen for fear of sending the wrong message back to Anayah. If he tapped once for no and Arthur wanted to say yes, Arthur would be mad. If he tapped twice for yes and Arthur wanted to say no, Arthur would be mad. But Arthur hadn't taught him any other way to open and close apps and so he was at a loss as to what to do. All he could do was wake up Arthur.

"Arthur! Arthur!" Sok hollered as he ran into the cabin and over to Arthur's cot. "Wake up! You need to see this."

Sok shook the snoring man who batted him away and then turned away from him. "No, Arthur, listen. You need to listen. Wake up!"

"Go away," Arthur mumbled.

"No! You have to wake up. It's important!" Sok insisted and shook him again.

Anayah's recorded voice penetrated the thick fog of sleep and Arthur woke with a start. He pushed himself up with his newly injured hand. "Ouch!"

As he breathed—and swore—through the refreshed pain, Arthur struggled to put the sensory input that his unwelcome consciousness was now throwing at him into some cohesive order. Pulling the strange surroundings he found himself in—Sok's excited jabbering, the total, painful recall of his attempt to put his fist through the door and the sound of Anaya's voice right beside him, though he couldn't see her—apart was like un-mixing several colours of play dough that had been mashed together by a toddler. Yawning, blinking the sleep from his eyes and shaking his head to clear it, Arthur willed his eyes to focus on Sok's face. "Coffee," he groaned. "I need coffee."

"You need to wake up and listen to this!" Sok held the cell phone up so Arthur could see it.

The video, if that's what it was, was half-way through the loop. "...If you agree to meet me, I will arrange it. Just tap the screen two times for yes and one time for no." The image jerked and Anayah started speaking again.

"What is this?" Arthur asked. "Is this my cell phone?" He patted his pocket gingerly, answering his own question.

"I found it on the floor," Sok explained. "I was going to play that candy game, but I opened this up instead and I didn't know how to close it."

Arthur reached out to take the cell phone from the elf. Just as Anayah's message started to repeat again, the screen went blank.

"No!" Arthur said. "The battery is dead."

"What is a battery?" Sok asked confused. From experience, battery was not something he could easily relate to the device in Arthur's hand.

"It's the thing inside the phone that makes it work." Arthur didn't know how else to explain it without getting overly technical. And technical was somewhat beyond him just then. "I need to find a way to recharge it. Where's Harpur?"

"He left here right after you fell asleep and I haven't seen him since," Sok said.

"Great," Arthur sighed in frustration. He felt the useless charge cord in another pocket, but left it where it was. "Did you watch the whole video?"

"Yes. A few times."

"What did she say, exactly?"

"Just that she didn't betray you and that she would explain everything to you and to tap once for yes and twice for no... Or was it twice for yes and once for no..."

"We have to find Harpur." Arthur threw the blanket off and swung his legs to the floor.

With one arm in a sling and the other hand bandaged and in pain, Arthur was unable to grip the door handle to open it. He turned back to

Sok, held up the cell phone and then pointed to the door to indicate that he needed assistance.

Across the room, Hiro stirred. He had been pretending to be asleep and had heard everything. His first concern was to stop Arthur and Sok from wandering away from the cabin. But he had to be casual about it all. He sat up and stretched.

"Where are you going? It's still early." Hiro rubbed the sleep from his eyes and smiled at his cabin mates.

"Uh, we're just going outside to get Harpur," Arthur said.

Sok walked over to the door and turned the handle. Other than the handle turning, nothing happened. The door did not open. "The door's stuck," Sok announced.

Arthur rolled his eyes and then hung his head in consternation. "It's not stuck," he said quietly. Then much louder, "It's been magicked!" He kicked the door as hard as he could and commenced hopping around on his one remaining good limb, cursing and swearing and generally losing his mind. Again.

Sok and Hiro allowed the tirade to play itself out. When Arthur finally slumped down on one of the cots, Hiro approached the door and lifted the latch that had fallen into place after Sok had burst through to wake Arthur up. He opened the door and turned to the distraught young man. "It's all right now, Arthur. I've lifted the magic." He and Sok stood back to let Arthur limp past with the tattered remnants of his dignity propping up his chin. "It's been magicked?" Hiro whispered to Sok with an eyeroll when Arthur was clear of the doorway.

"I think Arthur is getting a little paranoid."

Dawn was still several hours away when they exited the cabin and there was an oppressive quality to the darkness they found themselves standing in. A faint glow from the rocks that lined the pathway lit the Pole grounds with a patina of dull and muted blandness. In spite of the lush foliage that should have been inspiring, there was a falseness about the place that made Arthur think of a movie set and made Sok feel like his very life essence was being sucked out of him. Neither of them felt the least bit welcome.

"Where is Harpur?" Hiro asked.

"He could be anywhere." Sok said.

"Well, we can't just go wandering about looking for him," Hiro said.

"Why not?" Arthur challenged. "Why can't we walk around a bit? We aren't going to hurt anything."

"It's the rules," Sok said, sounding like an elf who had broken the rules and been caught.

"Oh, so now you want to follow the rules!" Arthur spat the words. "If you'd done that back on Thraeh and not Bounded to Earth we wouldn't be here being magicked and manipulated and betrayed. I could have just gone on not existing and not knowing it. I wouldn't have to walk around with a half a coin tied around my neck..." He reached for the pouch that contained his half of the coin. "Oh-oh! It's gone!"

Arthur looked frantically around on the ground for the missing pouch.

"You lost your half of the coin?" Sok checked to see if his was still where it was supposed to be and was relieved to find it was.

Arthur patted his body, hoping the string had just come untied and it had fallen down inside his t-shirt. It hadn't. He hobbled back into the cabin to check the cot. He shook out the blanket. Not there. He got down on his hands and knees and scanned the floor under the cot. Not there. Hiro and Sok helped him search. But after several minutes of desperately combing every inch of the cabin, they admitted defeat.

"Where did you last have it?" Hiro asked rather more calmly than the situation warranted, in Arthur's opinion.

"I don't remember," Arthur wailed. "It probably flew off when you were whipping us around the labyrinth in that contraption of yours like a bloody maniac."

"It could be anywhere, then," Hiro posited most unhelpfully, "like our missing dragon-wizard."

"That's not helpful!" Arthur barked. "How are we going to find it?" He gave the blanket another shake.

Hiro, grateful for the distraction from the topic of leaving the cabin, grasped his chin and appeared to be thinking. The missing pouch with its precious half-coin cargo was not the distraction he would have hoped for, but it served the purpose rather nicely, he thought. He would dowse for it later, but he wasn't going to tell Arthur that it would not be that difficult to find. If it came to it, he'd ask Anabettah to conjure it back. "I'm sure it will turn up."

"We could look for it while we look for Harpur," Sok suggested.

Hiro disguised his groan as a giggle.

"I thought you didn't want to break the rules," Arthur replied sarcastically.

"I don't," Sok said with some measure of hesitation. "But we can't just sit here and do nothing."

"I agree," Hiro said. "May I suggest we have some breakfast? I'm sure Harpur will be back soon. And I know that Anabettah will call for us shortly. We might as well eat something while we wait."

"It's the middle of the night," Arthur said. His broken arm, grazed knuckles and stubbed toe were throbbing along with his panicked mind. *Harpur is missing, I've lost my half of the coin and Hiro wants to have breakfast?*

"Anabettah is an early riser. She'll call on you before dawn, I'm sure. If you like, I can ask Bezzi to look for your pouch."

Arthur was at a loss. Based more on his awareness of his empty stomach than on an enthusiastic appetite, he agreed to the food. "Pancakes?" he asked. *Somebody help me!* Arthur thought.

"Pancakes it is. I'll get them ready while you two wash up," Hiro waved them back out the door.

"And where do we do that?" Arthur asked.

"Behind the cabin is a washstand. You can't miss it."

"Are you sure we are allowed to go back there?" Arthur's sarcasm was on a roll.

"Yes, yes. Stop your sass. Just don't go anywhere else. And I'll ask Bezzi to look for the pouch." Hiro closed the door on them and set to his task of preparing the repast. Which he did by reaching into his satchel and pulling out steaming stacks of pancakes, dripping with melting butter and sweet syrup. For Arthur, he also produced a thermos of hot coffee.

Meanwhile, Sok and Arthur walked to the back of the cabin as instructed and, as promised, found a washstand of sorts. In the middle of an open area of blueish grass there was a hand pump. Next to the hand pump was a wooden pail. But it was neither the hand pump nor the pail that caught and held their attention. It was the nearly naked couple making love in the grass that drew their gazes. Arthur and Sok stopped. The nearly naked couple did not.

Lips and limbs locked in lust, the nearly naked couple was oblivious to the audience that had stumbled upon them. And yet they were giving an excellent performance. Complete with requisite sound effects. All that was missing was the cheesy dialogue and lousy sound-track.

"Whoa!" Arthur threw his hand up to shield his eyes from the scene he would never un-see.

Sok's eyebrows levitated as far as they could go and he tilted his head to make better sense of the tableau. "What are they doing?" he asked.

"Eighty-eight years old and you've never...?"

"Not yet. But I think I'm going to move it up to the top of the list. I didn't think that's how it worked."

"Unbelievable." Arthur shook his head and approached the writhing mass of passion on the grass. "Excuse me."

The writhing mass ignored him.

"Excuse me," he said a little louder.

The female turned her head just enough to look up at Arthur, but not enough to disengage her mouth entirely from her partner's. The presence of a man standing over them did not seem to be of great concern to her. She held up a finger to indicate that she needed a minute. Then she hooked one leg around the male, thrust her hips upward and rolled him onto his back, rolling with him so that she was on top. Clearly delighted, the male smiled up at her. Then he, too, noticed Arthur.

"Greetings, friend!" he said. "Care to join us?"

If ever he needed a good come-back it was then. But as is so often the case at times like these, his wit failed him. "I'll pass, thanks. But I don't suppose you could do that somewhere else?"

"We can!" said the male.

"And we do!" said the female.

They both laughed! They both continued their passionate writhing.

Arthur looked back as Sok, who was no longer looking at the couple on the ground. He was staring beyond them to the edge of the blueish grass. Arthur followed his gaze to the far edge of the grass and saw an even more disturbing sight.

"I think I found Harpur," Sok said.

Sok ran and Arthur limped quickly across the grass to where Harpur lay unconscious and bleeding near a bush that Arthur swore was looming over him. As they approached, it leaned away a little, but Arthur still felt slightly apprehensive about getting too close. From a few feet away, Arthur inspected the scene.

Harpur's top hat lay crushed by his head. His coat had a jagged diagonal tear from one shoulder down to his waist and one of his boots was missing. Arthur was surprised to see a neon green sock with blue and orange dragons on it enveloping the wizard's large foot. He held his walking stick in his right hand, but Arthur could see that it was bent and broken just below the wizard's grasp.

"Is he dead?" Sok asked, also not wanting to get too close to the bush, which was now leaning forward again.

"I don't think so." Arthur had no idea, but the idea of Harpur being dead was not one he wanted to entertain. "Go get Hiro. We're going to need help to get him back to the cabin."

Sok wasn't sure how much help the tiny Krist would be, but he did what he was asked and dashed back to the cabin. As he passed the nearly naked couple, they emitted simultaneous cries and collapsed in a sweaty, panting heap together. Sok did a double-take, but kept going. Somehow an intrusion at this juncture seemed unseemly. Besides, Harpur needed help!

He burst into the cabin to find Hiro sitting at the table indulging in a large stack of pancakes. The Krist looked up when the door opened. "There you are! What took you so long?"

"Come quick!" Sok shouted. "Harpur's been hurt!" He grabbed a pancake from another plate and stuffed it into this mouth. No point in wasting the opportunity!

Hiro abandoned his own meal and followed Sok outside. His short stride should have been no match for that of the long-legged elf, but he managed to keep up as they made their way to the back of the cabin.

The nearly naked couple were sitting up by this time. While Sok ran past them, Hiro stopped beside them. "What are you two doing here?" he demanded, angry and annoyed.

"What does it look like?" the female asked provocatively.

"Don't worry about them right now!" Arthur called over. "We need you over here!"

"Coming!" Hiro said. Then he scolded the nearly naked couple, "This is a sacred place. Get out of here before Anabettah finds you."

He jogged past them and, ignoring the looming bush, Hiro knelt down next to Harpur. The bush tried to push him away, but he just swatted at it and told it to behave itself. It pulled away again, but left one branch resting against Harpur's arm.

Arthur took a tentative step closer. "We need to get him back to the cabin."

"We need to figure out what happened to him first. I don't know how badly he's been injured and I don't want to move him if moving him is going to make things worse." Hiro said.

"Of course," Arthur agreed. Having no first aid experience, he felt both helpless and stupid for not realizing that himself. At the same time, he was a little agitated that Hiro seemed to be doing nothing at all; he just sat there looking at Harpur. "What are you doing?"

"Shhhh!" Hiro swatted Arthur away like he had the bush.

He may have not had any first aid training, but Arthur was sure that just looking at wounds was ineffective. Clearly, however, Hiro did not want him involved. So, he turned around to see why Sok wasn't helping Harpur with his healing.

The elf was engaged in an animated conversation with the nearly naked couple. Arthur briefly debated calling Sok over, but decided to wait for instructions from Hiro. He positioned himself about half-way between Hiro/Harpur and Sok/nearly naked couple so that he could keep an eye on the former and an ear on the latter.

It sounded like Sok was interviewing the nearly naked couple on their recent activities. As long as his education remained theoretical and not experiential, Arthur figured that at least the elf was occupied and out of the way. Arthur dialed his awareness down from specific dialogue to tonal nuances, keeping himself ready to step in if need be while allowing his own thoughts to wander a bit.

He didn't like this place. There was something off about it and it bothered him that he couldn't put his finger on what that something was. The sense of falseness was strong and, at the same time, indefinable. From the plants to the nearly naked couple, everything about the Pole grounds was not merely surreal; it was unreal.

That's it! Arthur thought. This is all an illusion.

Arthur looked around. His eyes settled on a particular flower. It was impossibly large for the plant it grew out of. Its large, orange petals overlapped perfectly and were exactly the same size and shape. Its perfection made it somehow imperfect, ugly. He began to see this hideous perfection in everything he looked at. The leaves on any given tree were exactly the same size, shape and colour. The stems of flowers were exactly the same height. The shingles on the cabin roof were precisely the same size and lay in precise rows with precision spacing. Every blade of grass was identical. Only the nearly naked couple, stereotypically beautiful, right down to their nearly nakedness, which, Arthur realized with a start, was made nearly by the use of artfully arranged garlands of fig leaves, appeared real. He looked around for an apple tree. And a snake.

Then something really strange happened.

Arthur looked at Hiro and Harpur. Hiro was not just sitting and staring at Harpur; he wasn't moving. At all. Not even blinking.

He whipped around to look at Sok. The animated conversation continued, but only between the components of the nearly naked couple. Sok was frozen still like Hiro was.

He waved his arms around wildly just to prove to himself that he was not in the same state. He looked down at his feet and was alarmed to see that he was standing on top of the grass. It was as if he, Hiro, Harpur and Sok were superimposed onto a backdrop.

A feeling of vertigo washed over Arthur as he took a tentative step forward. The grass didn't flatten under his weight. He took another step. And then another. Then he took a few steps backwards. The ground looked like it was passing underneath him as if he was on a treadmill not actually moving forward himself. He moved forward again toward Hiro and Harpur. They appeared to be coming toward him instead of him moving closer to them. He turned to his left and started walking. The same thing happened. The scenery rolled toward him.

Some strange things had happened to Arthur over the past few days, but this was weird to the nth degree. He felt like he was in a video game from the early 90s. It was the creepiest thing he'd ever experienced.

He wanted to panic, but that led to an injured limb seventy-five percent of the time. So, he turned to face the nearly naked couple and waited for the background to adjust to his perspective. "Excuse me," he called over them.

The nearly naked couple stopped talking and looked at him.

"I was wondering if you could help me out," he said, trying to sound nonchalant.

"Certainly, my friend," the male said. "What do you need?"

"Well, I'm not entirely sure. Could you tell me if this place is real?" Arthur asked.

"It's as real as you think it is," the male answered.

"I don't think it's real," Arthur said.

"Then it must come down to whether you believe it's real," the female said.

"I don't believe it's real."

"But you must, my friend!" the male said.

"Why is that?"

"Because you are experiencing it." the male said.

"Or maybe you're dreaming it!" the female said. And the nearly naked couple laughed and laughed and laughed.

"If only," Arthur murmured to himself.

But in an odd and inexplicable way, the dream theory left him with a small measure of uncomfortable comfort. If it was all just a dream... Well, no harm, no foul. He'd wake up eventually. Unless he was in a coma. No! Best not to go there just yet. If it was an hallucination, then it would end eventually. But that would mean that something was causing it. And he didn't want to go there either. However, either way provided a reasonable explanation for all that had happened and, therein, lay the comfort.

They say that a confirmed diagnosis, even a dire one, is a relief. It's the not knowing that causes stress. Arthur felt he was a step closer to relief. But without the confirmed diagnosis, he had no way of knowing what to do next. If he proceeded with the dream theory, he could at least feel safe. Nothing in a dream could hurt him. If he proceeded with the coma theory, his fate was in the hands of people he could not communicate with. And he must have suffered an injury of some kind.

Perhaps that's where the whole paradox thing came into play. He had been in an accident eight years ago that had left him in a coma. Maybe he was beginning to come out of the coma and this was just his brain trying to put the pieces together as he inched ever closer to consciousness.

How many people had come out of a coma after eight years? And if that's what was happening, what would he look like? Eight years in a bed being kept alive by machinery would have taken its toll. He'd be an emaciated sack of skin and bones. The recovery would be excruciating. Would he even want to wake up after that? Now there was a depressing thought.

The nearly naked couple laughed again at a joke that was not at Arthur's expense and, thus, released him from his increasingly disturbing ruminations. He approached them and noticed that the grass was not flattened underneath them either. This was a good thing, he decided. It meant that they were like him. As was Sok's immobile body. He reached out to touch Sok and was relieved to make contact with a solid object.

"Do you know what happened to him?" Arthur asked.

"The same thing that happened to your other friends, I suspect," the female said, pointing to Hiro and Harpur.

"Okay. Do you know what happened to them, then?" Arthur amended.

"There are a number of possibilities," the male said. "Could be they left the story."

"What does that mean?" Arthur asked, swallowing a wave of panic.

"This is your story, Arthur. You said so yourself. It's your journey. Perhaps these characters no longer serve a purpose in furthering you along your path." The female stood up and adjusted her fig-leaf garland in such a way as to be more modestly provocative.

"I don't understand," Arthur said as he deliberately diverted his gaze from the adjustment zones and focused on her eyes. Three times.

The female smiled. "You can have or be or do whatever you want, Arthur. Nothing that happens does so without your approval."

"Are you saying that I have imagined all this?"

"Imagination certainly is what all creation is built out of." The male stood up as well. His fig leaves required no adjustment.

"Could you just cut to the chase?" Arthur begged. "All this philosophical mumbo-jumbo is frustrating."

"We could," said the female, "but unless you come to the realization yourself, it will remain meaningless. You won't gain anything. We can point you in the right direction. You, however, must make the journey yourself."

"What happened just before you came back here?" the male asked.

Arthur took a deep breath and thought back. "I had just discovered that I had lost my half of the coin."

"And what significance does losing your half of the coin represent?" the female asked.

"Hiro said as long as Sok and I each had half of the coin, the Entanglement would be confused because it would think that the coin was still whole," Arthur said.

"Does that make sense to you?" the male asked.

"No." Arthur shook his head. "None of this makes any sense to me."

"And yet here you are!" the female said.

211

"And?" Arthur had no idea where this was all going.

"Has it occurred to you that the coin is merely symbolic?" the male prompted.

"Of what?"

"Of what you fear." the female contributed.

Right then Arthur feared that he feared everything. There was no rhyme nor reason to anything that was happening. He began to regret talking to the nearly naked couple. After the uncomfortable comfort of almost having a reasonable explanation, he now felt like he had been sling-shotted back to the beginning. And he couldn't quite wrap his head around the notion that he had imagined all of this. His imagination wasn't that vivid.

He pulled his cell phone out of his pocket and looked at it. The battery was indeed dead.

"I need to charge this," he said. "Can either of you like abracadabra it back to life for me?"

"Do you want us to be able to do that?" the male asked.

"I would," Arthur declared.

"Then we can."

And they did.

The home screen lit up and Arthur saw that the battery was fully charged, but there was, of course, no cell service available. He tapped the icon that opened up the text message app. All the messages he would normally expect to be there were there. Sherry and Allan from Fox Comics, his mom, Cheryl, various friends and a few other work contacts. But the strange video of Anayah was gone.

He opened up the camera app and was relieved that the selfies of Sok and the photo he'd taken with Analeetah were still there. He took a photo of the nearly naked couple and it appeared in the camera roll. He closed the app and reopened it. The nearly naked couple smiled at him from the screen. He took a few more shots of Sok and Hiro and Harpur and himself and repeated the experiment of closing and reopening the app. The new pictures were all there. Arthur decided that this wasn't getting him anywhere, but he was grateful that the phone was charged again in spite of the fact that it was pretty much useless. He tucked it back into his pocket.

"So, who are you guys?" he asked.

"Who do you want us to be?" the nearly naked couple asked together.

Arthur thought about that for a minute. He needed them to be the ones to fix everything, to return him to his normal life back on Whyte Avenue. And the only things he could think of for them to be were genies. The grant three wishes – or six since there were two of them – kind.

"I want you to be all-powerful magic genies."

The nearly naked couple looked at each other inquiringly. Then they shrugged and nodded. "Sure," said the male. "We can be all-powerful magic genies."

"Great!" Arthur said. "And thanks for charging my phone. That doesn't count as one of my wishes, does it?"

"We weren't all-powerful genies when we did that." The female flipped her hair.

"Right. Awesome." Arthur was starting to feel a little all-powerful himself. "Okay, now what are the rules?"

"The rules?" the male asked.

"For my wishes. How exactly does it work?"

"You don't know?" the female asked.

"I just want you two to tell me so that I know we're all on the same page here. I don't want to waste a wish or have you guys misinterpret what I wish for," Arthur said with growing excitement and confidence.

"Well," said the male, "you can ask for anything you want and we'll give it to you."

"That's too simple," Arthur said. "That's what all all-powerful genies say and then when the guy makes his wish, they screw it up."

"So, do the genies screw it up? Or does the guy making the wish screw it up?" the female asked.

"The genie screws it up. Every time."

"Maybe you don't really want us to be all-powerful genies. Maybe you want us to be all-powerful sorcerers instead," the male suggested.

"What's the difference?" Arthur asked.

"You don't seem to have much faith in all-powerful genies to give you what you want," the female said.

"And as all-powerful sorcerers, you can do better?"

"That's up to you," they both said.

"Oh, for crying out loud!" Arthur complained. "Can you help me or not?"

"We can," said the female, "but it would be so much better if you helped yourself."

Arthur clutched his head and bellowed in abject aggravation.

He slumped down on the ground, or rather he slumped down on top of the ground and stared off into the distance. The nearly naked couple held hands and walked over to the hand pump. The male started priming it and soon water streamed from the faucet. The female cupped her hands under the flow and then drank from her palms. She filled her hands a second time, but instead of drinking the water she tossed it playfully at the male, who yelped and jumped back laughing. The game was on and while Arthur sat contemplating this latest bizarre turn of events, the nearly naked couple frolicked in the early-morning sunshine(s).

"What am I supposed to do now, Sok?" Arthur asked the lifeless elf.

Not surprisingly, he got no answer.

Arthur sat on top of the blueish grass for a while. His thoughts were all a-jumble and filled with nightmarish notions followed by whining bouts of despair followed by anger-ridden internal screaming, but not one single coherent plan of action occurred to him. Until his stomach growled and he remembered that Hiro was supposed to have made breakfast. He stood up and limped toward the cabin.

"Where are you going?" the male called after him.

"To look for something to eat!" he called back.

"Do you wish us to come with you?" the female asked.

"Why not?" Arthur granted.

"No reason I can think of," said the male.

And so, the three of them entered the cabin to find that the stacks of pancakes that Hiro had pulled from his bag were still sitting on the table, still dripping with butter and syrup and still steaming with warmth. A couple of hours must have passed and yet, the food looked and smelled as if it had just come off the grill. Arthur sat down and reached for the thermos to investigate its contents and was delighted to discover hot coffee inside.

"Dig in!" he said to the nearly naked couple, who joined him at the table, but did not eat.

The food and coffee worked their own brand of magic on Arthur's general demeanour. With his belly full and some quality caffeine coursing through his veins, he felt somewhat better.

"I wonder why no one has come for us," Arthur wondered out loud.

"You don't really want anyone to come for you, do you?" the female asked.

"Not particularly," Arthur admitted.

"Then why wonder?" the male injected logically.

Arthur nodded. "Good point."

He rubbed his chin and was surprised to feel several days' growth of beard under his hand. The stiff whiskers felt odd and he suddenly wanted nothing more than to shower and shave and change his clothes. Not since the bathhouse in Danaleedh had he been able to wash. A covert sniff of his pits told him that he was well overdue for a bath and the awareness of how much his personal hygiene was suffering was most unwelcome. A single coherent plan of action finally occurred to him.

He excused himself from the table and grabbed a blanket from one of the cots. Then he walked to the door.

"Now where are you going?" the female asked.

"To find a pool and have a bath."

"Would you like us to come with you?" the male asked.

Arthur looked at the nearly naked couple with exasperation. "Why not?"

"No reason I can think of," the female said.

The trio left the cabin and wandered down the path to the labyrinth. Arthur took the lead and led them to the left. He had no idea how far away the nearest pool was, but he figured it couldn't be all that far. They had passed a couple dozen of them on their way in the day before.

One had to be close. With the blanket over one shoulder, Arthur limped along the path at a relatively decent speed. He didn't think his toe was broken, but every step served as a reminder of his foolish freak-out. He scanned the pathway as he walked, hoping to find the pouch with the missing coin half in it. The nearly naked couple walked hand in hand a few steps behind him and did not scan the path for the missing pouch.

They reached the first switchback in silence before Arthur decided to make a second attempt at finding out who the nearly naked couple was. "So, what are your names?"

"What would you like our names to be?"

Arthur groaned. He turned around to face his companions and, walking backwards, said, "I will call you Adam." He pointed to the male. "And I will call you Eve." He pointed to the female.

"I prefer Ralph," the male said.

"And I prefer Holly," the female said.

"Why didn't you just tell me those were your names?" Arthur was exasperated by the constant ambiguity.

"Because those aren't our names," the one who preferred Ralph said.

Arthur stopped walking altogether. "Then why did you say they were?"

"We didn't," the one who preferred Holly said. "We just said we prefer them to Adam and Eve."

"Do you have names?" Arthur asked.

"Of course!" the one who preferred Holly said.

"Can you tell me what they are?" Arthur couldn't keep the impatience from his tone.

The one who preferred Holly opened her mouth and emitted a high-pitched squeal. The one who preferred Ralph opened his mouth and emitted a low droning keen followed by a complicated series of clicks and grunts.

"What was that?"

"Our names," the one who preferred Ralph said.

An acute twitch developed under Arthur's right eye. "Is it okay with you if I just call you Ralph and Holly?"

"Of course," Holly said.

"Absolutely," Ralph said.

"Thank you," Arthur said.

He turned around and started limping forward again. They passed through a gazebo a short distance on and Arthur couldn't help but make an observation. "Ralph and Holly are common Earth names," he said. "How did you come to choose them? I would've expected something more... Mysturnian."

"We heard them and liked them," Holly said.

"Where did you hear them?" Arthur pushed.

"They were friends of yours in school." Ralph said.

Arthur stopped walking. It was really no stranger than anything else that was happening. Curious, odd and peculiar were the order of the day. While he was grateful for the pronounceable monikers because he just couldn't see himself screeching and grunting to get their attention—God forbid he should have to introduce them to anyone—that they knew friends of his from school was just a bit more than Arthur could handle. "Who are you?"

"We are your guardians," Holly said.

Arthur decided he needed that bath more than ever.

Just beyond the next switchback, they arrived at their destination. The pathway widened slightly, providing access to a crystal-clear pool spanned by an arched, wooden bridge and fed by a small waterfall at one end. Arthur stripped off his sling and his clothes and went to the edge of the pool. It was not deep enough to dive into. He considered cannon-balling, but opted instead to slide into the water from one of the large stones that encircled it. Expecting it to be cool and refreshing, Arthur was more startled by the fact that it didn't feel any different from the air. It wasn't even wet. No ripples formed from his body's displacement. He felt no resistance when he moved around. He couldn't scoop any water up or cause a splash. The pool didn't react in any way to his presence within it. When he submerged and exhaled, no bubbles formed.

Arthur looked up at Ralph and Holly, who were both standing on the bridge. "Did you know about this?"

"About what?" Ralph asked.

"About the water not being water."

"We expected you to realize it. Nothing else is real to you." Holly said.

Arthur sighed and hauled himself back up onto the bank. Holly was right. He should have realized it himself.

He looked down at his pile of smelly clothes and sighed again. "I don't suppose either of you could zap me up some clean clothes?"

Holly waved her hand and Arthur found himself dressed in a clean pair of jeans and a pink tank top with a butterfly on it.

"Uh... Could you make the t-shirt more masculine?"

Ralph snapped his fingers and the pink tank top was replaced by a black t-shirt with a flaming skeleton riding a flaming chopper across the chest. "A simple Batman logo would have sufficed," Arthur mumbled. With a sigh, he thanked Ralph and Holly and limped onto the bridge.

"Where are you going now?" Ralph enquired.

"I'm getting the hell out of here!" Arthur barked.

"Would you like us to come with you?" Holly asked.

"Why not?"

"No reason we can think of," Holly and Ralph said in unison.

Arthur had no idea where the entrance to the labyrinth was. He also had no idea whether he was moving toward the entrance or toward the centre. He could see the obelisk getting closer, but that didn't mean the direction he was walking was taking him to it. It was quite possible that the next turn would send them away from it. All he could do was keep walking.

So, that is what he did. Ralph and Holly kept walking also. They were holding hands again and speaking quietly to each other. Every now and then one or both of them would laugh at something one or the other of them said. Arthur caught bits and snatches of their conversation, but didn't pay close attention. It had occurred to him that they only seemed to speak to him when spoken to and he was content with that. Their enigmatic replies and the way they turned all his questions back on him with more questions were annoying. He'd have to figure things out for himself.

Arthur estimated that two hours had passed. His toe was throbbing painfully. He was thirsty and tired and had grown increasingly worried about what he was doing. They were on a long, sweeping curve in the path at that point and Arthur decided to stop and rest. He spread the blanket out on the ground and sat down on it. At least he could feel the blanket beneath him. It gave him a sense, false though it may be, of being in touch with reality. Ralph and Holly stopped and stood next to the blanket looking down at him.

"You can sit if you want to," Arthur invited them to share his blanket.

Ralph and Holly sat down and immediately started to kiss and pet each other.

When Ralph was about to get to second base, Arthur snarled, "If you don't mind."

"Oh, we don't mind," Holly giggled.

"Well, I do!" Arthur snapped. "Just keep it in your fig leaf."

Ralph and Holly disengaged and sat shoulder to shoulder, heads touching, fingers entwined.

Arthur turned away from them and faced the outside of the path. He pulled off his shoe and examined his toe. It was swollen, but he could still bend it a little. Probably just a bad sprain, he decided. The knuckles on his left hand were swollen too, as was his right wrist. It hurt to do anything and he wished Sok was there to do his healing thing, which eased the pain, even if it didn't mend the damage completely.

Thinking about Sok led to thinking about Harpur, which led to thinking about Hiro, which led to thinking about Anayah, Analeetah, Kel and Anabettah. Were they all frozen? Were they suffering? What had happened to Harpur? That was the most disturbing thought of all. He had been badly injured. But how? Who—or what—could have done that to him? Were he and the nearly naked couple in danger of being attacked? Arthur pushed that thought out of his mind. But the urgency to escape the Pole grounds doubled.

"I don't suppose either of you knows if we are going in the right direction?" Arthur braced himself for whatever stupid reply Ralph or Holly would offer.

"That depends on what direction you intended to go." It was Ralph who spoke.

"I intended to go to the entrance of the labyrinth," Arthur said trying hard not to sound as annoyed as he felt.

"Then you are going in the wrong direction." Holly's straightforward answer took Arthur by surprise.

"Great!" Arthur sighed. "We've just wasted about two hours. Why didn't you tell me we were going in the wrong direction?"

"You didn't ask," Ralph said.

"But I told you I wanted to get out of here. You could have said we were heading toward the centre of the labyrinth when we left the pool," Arthur argued.

"We thought you wanted to get out through the centre," Holly said.

"How do I get out of the labyrinth if I'm in the centre of it?"

"Through the tunnel," Ralph said.

"There's a tunnel leading out of the labyrinth from the centre?" Arthur's hopes soared just a little bit.

"There is," Holly confirmed.

"And where does this tunnel lead to?"

"The Underworld," Ralph said.

"The Underworld?"

"The Underworld." Holly and Ralph reiterated.

"As in Hell?"

"Oh, no!" Holly exclaimed. "Hell is off-world. The Underworld is just a network of cities underground. Under the world, if you will."

"So, there's no cloven-hoofed red guy with horns torturing lost souls down there, right?"

"You mean Max? Yes, he's there. But he's not that bad." Holly said dismissively.

"Max? The Devil is named Max here? Not Lucifer?"

"I don't know of any Lucifer being on Mysturna," Holly said.

"Neither do I," Ralph agreed. "And Max is certainly a devil, but I don't know if I'd go so far as to call him *The Devil*."

"Right," Arthur said, not wanting to know anymore. "So, our choices are to turn back and walk another two hours to where we started or keep going in this direction and risk being tortured by Max. What do you think, guys?"

"We think we should just walk through these trees and leave the labyrinth right here." Ralph pointed to the bushes next to the path.

Arthur looked at Ralph. Then at the trees next to the path. "What? We can just walk out of here through the trees?"

"We are on the outer edge of the labyrinth." Holly smiled.

Arthur forced his tender toe back into his shoe and stood up. "What are we waiting for?"

"You," Ralph said.

Arthur rolled his eyes, but said nothing. He folded the blanket and put it down on the edge of the path. Taking it felt more like stealing now, so he left it and gestured for Ralph and Holly to lead the way.

The bushes were thick, but entirely insubstantial. Arthur walked right through them and before long they emerged and stood looking out at the vast red plain. The holes in Arthur's vague and not-well-thought-out plan for escape were now unavoidable. He had no way of knowing which direction to take or even where he should be going. The prospect of crossing the desert-like flats with the sand wyvers underneath him was not a prospect he found in any way appealing. It would take hours to find his way back to Harpur, Hiro and Sok. Even if they were somehow okay again when, and if, he did find them, who knew what good being together would do? Then there was the issue of whatever had attacked and wounded Harpur during the night. Was it still there? He had just walked for two hours without incident. On top of all of that, the guilt he was now feeling at having abandoned his companions was beginning to weigh heavily on his conscience. Harpur had risked a lot to save him from the forest. Leaving the dragon-wizard hurt like that was kind of unconscionable.

"What do you suggest we do now?" Arthur asked. "And don't ask me what I would like you to suggest, or I swear to God, I'll smack you."

Ralph and Holly looked at each other.

"We can't tell you," Ralph said.

"You have to decide," Holly said.

"Argh!" Arthur bellowed. He sat down on the ground to think. "What would you do if you were me?"

"We would go back to the cabin," Ralph declared.

"Why would you go back to the cabin?" Arthur was beginning to think he had figured out how to communicate with Ralph and Holly effectively.

"Because that's where you can find everything you need," Holly said.

"It was not clever of you to have left there," Ralph said.

"Why don't you tell me these things when they can save me so much trouble?" Arthur felt his anger rising again.

"You don't ask us before you get in trouble," Holly said.

"Is there a shorter way back to the cabin, then?"

"The cabin is about a five-minute walk this way." Ralph pointed along the edge of the Pole ground garden.

Arthur scratched his head in consternation. "You said everything I need is back at the cabin, right?"

"Right."

"What exactly do I need?" Arthur looked up at Ralph and Holly and braced himself to be further vexed.

"Help."

Arthur squeezed his eyes shut and pursed his lips to keep himself from screaming.

Holly knelt down beside Arthur and placed her hand on his arm. Her touch was warm and soft and, much like when Harpur had touched him with the walking stick, instantly made him feel calm. He decided that he both hated and was grateful for this magic. It was good to have the anxiety recede. And it ticked him off that another person could control him so easily.

"We are here to guide you, Arthur," Holly spoke softly. "But we can't guide you if you don't know what you want."

"What I want is for all this to end," Arthur said.

"For something to end, something new must begin."

"That's not helpful," Arthur replied. "And isn't it the other way around? For something to begin, something else has to end."

"If you want to leave things up to fate, yes."

"What does that mean?"

"It means that if you don't like something, you have to change it. Wanting it to change is only the beginning."

Arthur sat in quiet contemplation for a minute. "Anayah said that when we ask for something, we are already on the path to it. Is that true?"

"It is."

"She also said that even though we know what we want, we can sometimes go astray."

"That is true as well. Do you feel like you have gone astray?"

"I think that's an understatement."

Holly smiled. "You can have anything you want, Arthur. You know that, right?"

"I want to go home!" Arthur professed. "I want things to be normal again."

Holly didn't say anything. Arthur looked at her. Was she waiting for him to realize something? Her expression was passive. A Mona Lisa smile tugged lightly at the corners of her pretty mouth, but he could not read what lay behind it. Ralph stood behind her, looking equally as calm. Arthur sighed.

"Let's go back to the cabin and see if we can help those guys." Arthur stood up and held out his hand to assist Holly to her feet.

The darkness was just beginning to concede to the light of the first sun. On the horizon a pale strip of yellow-gray had appeared like a jagged tear in the fabric of the night. The walk back to the cabin along the outer edge of the Pole grounds took, as Ralph had said, about five minutes. They pushed their way through the thick underbrush and arrived on the bluish lawn a few feet away from where Harpur still lay perfectly still next to the still perfectly still Hiro. Sok still sat perfectly still over by the hand pump. Everything was perfectly still, which was still perfectly disturbing to Arthur.

"Any suggestions?" Arthur asked.

"The hover gilly," Ralph said.

"What about it?" Arthur asked.

"You can put them in it."

"I can put them in it? You're not going to help me?"

"We can help you if you want us to." Holly smiled.

Then another thought occurred to Arthur. "Didn't you say that they had left the story and that is why they are like this?"

"We said they could have left the story. It was one possibility."

"Next time, give me all the possibilities." Arthur sighed.

"That would take forever," Holly said.

"Okay. So, how do I get the hover gilly over here?"

"I believe you just have to whistle for it," Holly said.

Arthur put his thumb and forefinger in his mouth and blew through the gap between them. A shrill whistle filled the air and a few seconds later the large hover gilly came floating around the corner of the cabin toward them. It stopped next to Harpur and Hiro, probably thinking that it had been Hiro who hailed it. Assuming hover gillies can think.

Arthur instructed Ralph to pick up Harpur's feet while he lifted the large wizard's shoulders. Expecting Harpur to weigh a ton, Arthur braced himself and heaved. There was almost no resistance and Arthur watched in horror as Harpur's stiff body flew up into the air above his head. It was like tossing an empty cardboard box. Arthur screamed in surprise and barely managed to catch the wizard on the way back down.

"Crap on a cracker!" Arthur yelled.

"I thought you knew they weren't the real Harpur, Hiro and Sok," Ralph said.

"What are they?" Arthur put the insubstantial shell of a body back down on the ground. "And what happened to the real Harpur, Hiro and Sok?"

"I suspect they are with Anabettah in her quarters," Holly offered.

"What? How did they get there?" Arthur demanded. "And why didn't you tell me?"

"These are just images that Anabettah must have left here so you wouldn't realize that she had taken them right away," Ralph explained.

"Okay, you guys. I need information. I don't know what's going on around here, so I need you to tell me stuff when you know it so I don't get caught off guard like that all the time. I need your help!"

"Of course," Holly said. "That's why we're here."

"Then help! Don't leave me to figure everything out for myself all the time." Arthur barked. "Bloody hell!"

Arthur climbed into the hover gilly. "Do either of you know how to drive this thing?"

Ralph and Holly joined him. "You just have to think about where you want to go and it will take you there."

"I don't know where we're going," Arthur said. It was like talking to two two-year-olds.

"We do," Ralph said.

"Then, by all means, think us there, please!"

The hover gilly lurched into the air causing Arthur to hold painfully onto the side. He thought of a few features he'd add if these things ever became popular on Earth. Like seats. With seat belts. And a stereo system. Maybe a windshield.

The way the hover gilly was jerking around, Arthur wondered if Ralph's mind was fully on the task of driving it. The nearly naked couple did seem to be practically perfect for each other and a pang of loneliness washed over him. But like everything else—at least at the Pole—there was a falseness about them that nagged at Arthur. He wondered if they ever argued.

"So where are you two from, exactly?" he asked.

"Everywhere and nowhere," Ralph said.

Arthur's brows furrowed and his lips pursed. "Okay. What are you?"

"We are Holly and Ralph." The hover gilly pitched upward slightly.

"Not who are you. What are you? Are you people? Are you gods?"

Holly laughed. "Gods! There's no such thing!"

"Angels, then?"

"Do we look like angels to you?" Holly asked and giggled.

"I have no idea what angels really look like." Arthur didn't even believe in angels. Then again... "Can you tell me what you're doing here then?"

"We are here to help you. We are your guardians," Holly said.

"Right. You said that. I guess I want to know why."

"Why we are here to help you?"

"Yes."

"Because you need help."

Arthur was spinning his wheels again. "How did you know I needed help? Who sent you?"

"No one sent us," Holly said. "You asked us to come."

"I did?" Arthur was surprised. "I don't remember that."

"You asked for help. We wouldn't have come if you hadn't."

Arthur cast a line into his memory banks searching for a request for two nearly-naked, horny people who were the masters of the redirect. And came up blank. He'd forgotten the passing thought he'd had at the cabin. "Where do you live?" It was worth a shot.

"Within you."

Within me? Arthur scrunched his eyes and tried to figure that one out. All that came to mind was some airy-fairy, personal guide stuff that he didn't subscribe to any more than angels. "What type of beings are you?"

Holly looked down at her body. "Today I believe we are humanoid."

"And when you're not humanoid?"

Holly suddenly vanished and was replaced by a shimmering opalescent blob with a vaguely human outline. Arthur had to shield his eyes from the bright light that flickered and danced like the northern lights. He could not look directly at it. When she just as suddenly reappeared a few seconds later, Arthur had to keep his eyes shut tight for several minutes.

"You could have warned me!" he shouted at her.

Arthur's retinas continued to protest as they flew on above the trees. They glided past the Pole and between the superimposed flashes of the blob that Holly had become he noticed that it was carved with faces. Many of them appeared to be locked in expressions of terror. Others seemed to be asleep. The blackness of the thing was so deep Arthur feared he would be absorbed into it if they got too close.

"Who are they?" Arthur asked. He'd meant it to be rhetorical, but Holly answered anyway.

"They are the faces of those who got lost in the shadow."

Arthur trembled with revulsion.

"We are nearly there," Ralph announced, taking the hover gilly into a wide, downward curve toward the ground.

Arthur looked down and saw they were approaching a round, windowless structure surrounded by a verge of pinkish grass. There were four large, stone spheres, presumably positioned at the compass points around it. Next to one of the spheres, a group of people were standing and looking up at the hover gilly. It was, of course, Anayah, Kel, Anabettah, Hiro, Analeetah, Harpur and Sok. Harpur looked no worse for wear and Arthur felt a pang of relief seeing him standing with his walking stick and looking just as relieved to see Arthur.

The hover gilly came to a shuddering halt several feet away from the group on the ground. Arthur alighted, but did not approach. Holly and Ralph remained onboard the floating chariot. Several awkward seconds passed as the group looked at them and they looked at the group.

Finally, Harpur spoke. "You dropped something," he said as he tossed the pouch containing Arthur's half of the coin to him.

Arthur caught it and quickly tied it around his neck. It bought him a couple of extra seconds to decide how welcome he was at this gathering. *Screw it,* he thought. He was just as intrinsic to all this as Sok was. He made up his mind to be somewhat indignant about being left behind at the cabin.

"So," he said, "thanks for leaving me alone back there. Way to make a guy feel special." Harpur and Anayah both shook their heads in warning, but Arthur ignored them. "You know, I'm part of all this too. And I don't particularly like being left out. Especially when my friggin' life is at stake. Now will someone please tell me what the...?" Without warning Arthur's voice failed him. He clutched his throat and tried to speak again, but no sound came out. It didn't stop the silent diatribe that followed. Arthur gesticulated wildly and demanded silently to be released from whatever spell had been cast on him.

Holly stepped gingerly off the hover gilly and touched his shoulder. His calm was instantly restored, but it didn't stop him from glaring at her.

"It will be okay," she mouthed and smiled with reassurance at him.

"Are we quite done?" Anabettah asked.

Arthur, unable to respond, turned his glare on the ancient witch and mouthed a choice four-letter word in her direction.

"Now," Anabettah continued, "that we are all here, I think we should all sit down and talk about this situation." She gestured to a ring of Adirondack-style chairs just beyond the stone spheres.

Everyone, including Ralph and Holly, moved to take a seat. Everyone except Arthur. He stood next to the hover gilly and waited for someone to notice his silent protest. Anabettah, looked at the empty chair and then over at Arthur. She considered zapping him into his seat, but decided to take pity on him. She rose again and approached the defiant young man. It took all the will-power Arthur could muster to stand his ground.

Anabettah stopped a few feet away from Arthur and cocked her head to one side as she took in the rebellious gleam in his eyes. "You have nothing to fear from me," she said quietly. "And I am not your enemy. If you will allow me to, I can help you."

Arthur stared at her. Then he pointed to his throat. When Anabettah nodded, he spoke. "I would appreciate it if you would stop deciding when I can or cannot speak."

"That seems reasonable," Anabettah agreed. "And I would appreciate it if you would speak more respectfully in my presence."

"Fair enough," Arthur said. "I apologize for my outburst. I'm having a hard time with... everything that's happened."

Anabettah cocked her head to the other side. "Will you allow me to heal your wounds?"

Arthur wasn't expecting that. He looked at his splinted arm and raw knuckles. He nodded.

Anabettah put her hands on his shoulders and a soft-blue light flowed from them, down his arms and through his body. He kept looking into Anabettah's eyes as a warm sensation surged through his body. In a few minutes, all the pain was gone. The skin on his knuckles healed. His wrist and toe stopped throbbing. "Thank you," he whispered.

"You are welcome. Now the reason I left you behind was because you summoned your Guardians."

Arthur frowned. "Ralph and Holly?

"If that is what they are calling themselves, yes. I had hoped that you would allow them to guide you. But you are a stubborn one, aren't you, Arthur?"

"I don't remember summoning anything. Least of all a horny, nearly naked couple. And, to be honest, they really aren't all that helpful."

"They are as helpful as you allow them to be."

"I don't suppose you have a user manual for them."

Anabettah laughed. "Trust yourself. You'll figure it out. Shall we join the others now? I've missed one ritual waiting for you. I'd like very much not to miss the next one."

Arthur's face reddened. "Sorry," he mumbled.

When they were all seated, Anabettah looked around at the nine faces of the nine beings that had gathered in this sacred space before her. They made quite the entourage. What she saw was that many mistakes had been made. And it fell to her to set them on a course that would undo those mistakes. She could easily fix most of the damage. She had the power to send Harpur, Sok and Arthur to a Veilrift to Thraeh with just a snap of her fingers. But there was more than just a simple Entanglement that needed to be healed. Harpur had lost trust in Anayah. Anayah was keeping a secret from him and, so his loss of faith was justified. But Harpur had secrets of his own. Some potentially hazardous to their mission. Others more perilous to himself. And then there was Arthur. He knew nothing of his own magic. She could sense it in him, even if he couldn't. She also sensed the dragon blood in him and the great power that remained latent within him because of it. While she could unravel it all, repair much of it and send them on their way with much less fear, much less uncertainty, to do so would be to deprive them of the experience, and thus, the wisdom they were entitled to by sorting it out for themselves. She had to decide which bones to toss them and which to let them find on their own.

"Anayah contacted me about Arthur's Akashic Records and I have looked into the matter in some depth. According to the records, Arthur apparently died in an accident eight Earth years ago. From that, Anayah assumed he had become a paradox because his records appear to have stopped at that point. He is not, in fact, a paradox at all. If he were, he would be soulless. If anything, he has more soul than most men of his kind." She looked directly at Harpur as she said this and had her suspicions about his involvement in this part of the story confirmed by the way he averted his eyes and squirmed in his chair.

Upon hearing that he was not, in fact, a paradox, Arthur's head snapped up. He punched the air with his newly-healed right arm. "Yes!"

Anabettah chose to ignore the expression of relief and continued. "He is, however, an anomaly."

"That's better than a paradox, right?" Arthur couldn't help himself.

"It is. To some degree." Anabettah held up a hand to stay any further questions from Arthur. "It means that you may Bound without causing a catastrophe. A true paradox, of the type Anayah assumed you were, is exceedingly rare. And, quite frankly, I'm more than a little disappointed in Anayah for jumping to that conclusion. A little research would have prevented you from the mental anguish I'm sure her premature diagnosis initiated."

Harpur whipped his head around to look at Anayah. He saw relief where he expected disappointment. Embarrassment where he expected guilt. *So, she's not trying to destroy Earth after all. What then?*

"As for the Entanglement..." Again, Anabettah turned her attention to Harpur. "That is both simpler and more complicated than Anayah has made it out to be." Eight heads turned toward Anayah. "Entanglement between any two beings is influenced by the type of beings they are. Two non-magical beings would not, of course, become Entangled at all. A magical and a non-magical being would become physically Entangled, a phenomenon that would culminate in their being absorbed into one another unless the Entanglement is reversed. Two magical beings, however, become Entangled in a somewhat different manner. Their physical bodies are not affected at all, but their souls seep into each other until their entire personalities are exchanged."

"So, like a Freaky Friday sort of thing?" Arthur said aloud and nine heads turned baffled looks on him.

"A what?" Sok asked.

"Nothing. Forget it. It's an Earth thing. You wouldn't understand." Arthur's face reddened again.

"But what has that got to do with Sok and Arthur's Entanglement?" Anayah asked. She knew she had gotten, something wrong, but she didn't know what.

"Arthur is far more special than all of you realize. I suspect that Arthur himself is unaware of who and what he really is."

Nine heads turned to Anabettah, then eight of them turned back to Arthur.

"I don't understand," Arthur said. "What's going on?"

"It is not my place to tell you, Arthur. But I will tell you this. Before you continue to Thraeh to stop the Entanglement, you will need to do one more thing here on Mysturna."

"What's that?" Arthur asked yet another question he feared he was not going to like the answer to.

Anabettah hesitated. "May I speak to you and Harpur privately?"

Arthur and Harpur exchanged looks. "Sure?" Arthur said with some hesitation of his own.

"Come with me." Anabettah rose and walked toward the circular building.

Harpur and Arthur fell in line behind her and followed. As did Ralph and Holly.

"She said she wanted to speak to me and Arthur privately," Harpur snapped at the nearly naked couple. "You two... whoever you are... wait here."

"It's okay, Harpur," Arthur said. "They're kinda part of me."

Harpur grimaced. He didn't want to know.

Inside, Anabettah, Harpur and Arthur each took a seat on benches in the middle of the building. Around them, doors opened on small sleeping chambers, not unlike cells found in a monastery. Ralph and Holly stood apart from them several feet behind Arthur and wrapped their arms around each other.

"Not now," Arthur hissed at them.

Anabettah ignored them. "Harpur, do you have something you want to tell Arthur?"

Harpur looked at the witch, trying to calculate how much she knew and how much she might be only guessing at. Her passive expression gave away nothing of use and he had to make a decision. He knew this moment was coming. He just wished it didn't have to be now. Adding another layer to Arthur's problems before any of them had been resolved was not at the top of Harpur's priority list. Then again, the witch obviously knew something he didn't and this was likely the best way to find out what that could be. It was time to come clean with Arthur.

Harpur told Arthur about Ylemnir and his affair with Beatrice Cooper. "You inherited Ylemnir's magic and when I found you, you didn't seem to be aware of it. I tried to talk to you about it, but you weren't ready and you walked away from me. I followed you, but you were struck by a car and killed."

Arthur stared at the dragon-wizard. When he didn't say anything, Harpur continued, "I saved you by giving you some of my own blood. Dragon blood has the power to resurrect the dead. It also changes people who have been resurrected with it. I tried to explain things to you, but you were not willing to accept it. I wiped your memory and came to Whyte Avenue to watch out for you. If my blood had caused you to change... physically, I would have had to either get you to Thraeh immediately or..."

"Really kill me?" Arthur filled in the blank.

"If necessary, yes," Harpur said. "But so far, there has been no manifestation of any of the usual effects that dragon blood has." Harpur braced himself for the expected tirade.

But Arthur just sat there, staring at the dragon-wizard for what felt to Harpur like an interminable amount of time.

"Why don't I remember any of this?" Arthur finally asked in a spookily calm voice.

"As I said, I wiped your memory," Harpur admitted.

"Uh-huh," Arthur nodded. "I see."

"I am sorry, Arthur. I just wanted to make sure that if there was a human with magic on Earth that he wasn't causing any trouble. I had nothing to do with the accident, I swear."

"Right. Mm-hmm. Well, that makes sense."

"It does?"

"No, Harpur. It doesn't make any sense at all..." And he was off on another tirade about being manipulated and having magic forced on him and how he just wished everyone would just leave him alone and let him live his own life.

Harpur looked at Anabettah. "It's best to just let him run out of steam."

While Arthur ranted on, and Ralph and Holly cuddled on, Anabettah explained to Harpur what he needed to do. "There's a small chance that the procedure won't be necessary, but it's worth having him checked out."

"The checking it out part won't be a problem. I'm not looking forward to telling him I have to kill him to save him if the test is positive, though." Harpur sighed.

"One step at a time," Anabettah said.

"Now," Anabettah said, once Arthur calmed down and they were gathered outside again, "Harpur will fill you all in on what you need to do next. Is there anything else anyone needs before you leave?" Nine heads shook no. "Good. Then go. And leave me in peace." She turned her back on the others and retreated back into the round building.

Analeetah, Anayah and Kel bowed in respect toward Anabettah. When the door to the building closed behind the witch, Hiro motioned for everyone to climb onto the hover gilly. Arthur, spent after his latest meltdown, climbed wearily onto the crowded chariot. With nine bodies aboard, it was standing room only, but it had no difficulty carrying them all. *At least*, Arthur thought as they cleared the Pole grounds, *the ride is much smoother this time.*

They flew on in silence for a while as everyone gathered their thoughts. Arthur's thoughts, though, didn't want to be gathered. They bounced around like pinballs crashing into posts and zinging away from him. Too many to keep track of, he let them all drop into gobble holes to be kicked back later. He was standing wedged between Harpur, Sok and Kel and could see little of the passing landscape and much of Kel's broad back. Kel's flawless fan of latissimus dorsi was only interesting in that it inspired a mental note to renew his gym membership. Beyond that, it was just an irritating reminder that his elapsed gym membership had been, more or less, a waste of money. He turned his attention to Harpur.

"What happened to you back at the cabin? Where did you go?" Arthur was genuinely concerned.

"I noticed that your pouch wasn't around your neck, so I went looking for it. I needed a break from you guys."

"So how did you end up bleeding on the ground? And how did you end up not bleeding anymore?"

"I wasn't bleeding on the ground." Harpur's tone was pregnant with insult. "What are you talking about?"

"Must have been Anabettah's idea of a joke." Arthur couldn't even imagine why she would have set up such a scene. He decided to dismiss it. "Huh. Well, I'm glad you're okay."

Harpur looked at Arthur, touched by the sentiment, but only grunted in reply.

"So, where did those two come from?" Harpur nodded toward Ralph and Holly.

"Apparently, I summoned them to help me. They're supposed to be my guides or guardians or something. But they aren't very helpful," Arthur said.

Analeetah jostled to face Arthur. "Guardians, when they are summoned, will always appear in a way that reflects your inner-most desire," she explained to Arthur.

"My inner-most desire is to relive Genesis?" Arthur scoffed. "I don't think so. My inner-most desire is to go home and forget any of this ever happened."

"Is it?" Analeetah asked, then turned back to continue the quiet conversation she was having with Anayah.

"Where are we going?" Arthur asked.

"To the Sphere. It's like the Pole, but round instead of tall," Harpur said with a measure of sarcasm.

"Great," Arthur said. "'Cause the Pole was just so much fun."

"Right?" Harpur agreed. "The good news is, this will all be over soon."

Arthur nodded. That was good news. But without details, he felt he had to reserve judgement. Plus, there was something in Harpur's tone that belied the implied goodness of the news. Arthur intuited quite correctly that this statement was the condensed version of something that possessed a whole lot more bad than good and that 'over soon' was nothing more than sugar-coating designed to give Arthur hope where, perhaps, none, or at least very little, actually existed. He'd watched enough movies and read enough books to know that it wasn't going to be that simple.

"Arthur, do you want the memories I wiped back?" Harpur asked.

He was, of course, referring to what Harpur had told him about his magic and the dragon blood. "I think I do," he said, "but not here. I'll let you know."

Harpur nodded. *There may be hope for this kid yet.*

Chapter 8

They flew on. And on. And on.

Arthur grew increasingly restless. He wanted to know what was going to happen at the Sphere and he didn't want to know. He wanted to know more about this magic he was supposed to possess and he didn't want to know. He wanted to know what Harpur's blood had done to him and he didn't want to know. He had to get off the hover gilly.

"Are we there yet?" he called out.

"It's a three-day journey by hover gilly," Hiro said. "We'll get to our first stop before nightfall."

It was barely midday.

"I really think I'm going to freak out again," Arthur said with a faked catch in his throat. "I need some space."

"Are you sure?"

"Pretty sure."

"Alright, then." Hiro banked the hover gilly to the left and landed on a grassy knoll near a copse of trees.

Everyone stepped off of the hover gilly and moved out of Arthur's way. His outbursts were understandable, albeit tedious at times, and they were all thankful for the warning. They watched as he walked up the hill a way and pulled his cell phone out of his pocket before sitting down on the grass. He didn't seem to be freaking out. He seemed to be talking to his phone. This was new.

From his vantage point on the hill, Arthur noticed that Harpur and Sok had positioned themselves apart from the others and close to the hover gilly. Anayah, Analeetah, Kel and Hiro stood grouped together, chatting amiably. Ralph and Holly were, as was usual, locked in an embrace that threatened to spiral into an even more amorous display and Arthur was dismayed by an inner outburst of jealousy. He grimaced. Was his deepest desire to be less inhibited? Or was he just still feeling the loss of Cheryl and longing to be reunited with her? He really hadn't had time to grieve the breakup. But then, the loss of his job had felt even worse. Shouldn't his guardians have appeared like comic book heroes? That would have made more sense.

He sat down on the grass, holding his cell phone. He could tell from their expressions that the others were expecting another verbal onslaught from him. And that was sort of what he was doing. It had occurred to him that he could record the events on his phone so he opened the recorder app and started recounting the events of the past few days. He knew the others would not let him sit there for long, so he kept this first recording as brief as possible. He would fill in the details later, but he wanted to make sure he had the main facts, names and places on record. When he was sure he had all the information he needed, he saved the recording. Then he opened another app for making notes and composed a list of things he needed to do or learn. He needed to keep track of things and by writing them down, he felt like he was a little more in control.

He finished his list, stood up and walked back down the hill, stopping a short distance away from the hover gilly. "So, instead of spending three days crammed in the hover gilly, why don't we just zap over to the Sphere so we can get... whatever we have to do there over with?"

Harpur had not, as of yet, provided any details about Anabettah's instructions. This, in itself felt ominous to Arthur, and a seventy-two-hour delay was just seventy-two hours in which he could imagine the worst.

"Kel prefers not to be zapped," Analeetah said.

"Then how did you all get to the Pole so quickly?" Arthur challenged.

Anayah, Analeetah and Kell all exchanged looks. "Hiro's contraption can bend time," Kel said. "It's not the same as being zapped."

Arthur nodded. "Well, no offense," he looked at Kel, "but why are you coming with us anyway? I mean do we really need nine people on this mission? Now that we don't need you to get us to... those other worlds, I'm sure you must have something else you could be doing. Hiro could take you and Analeetah back to Wildwood and then he could go back to his cave. Anayah, Harpur, Sok and I can probably finish this on our own."

Out of the corner of his eye, Arthur noticed that Harpur was noticing him. And he was smiling. Arthur diligently kept his gaze focused on Kel so that no one else would see the pleasure Harpur was taking in this.

"We all want to help you, Arthur," Analeetah said as if it should be obvious that what they were doing required nine people.

Kel took a protective step closer to Analeetah. "What about Ralph and Holly?" he asked.

Everyone looked at the nearly naked couple. They were still lip-locked and being handsy with each other. "Seriously, you two!" Arthur shouted at them. When their rating went down from R to PG, he returned his attention to Analeetah, Kel, Anayah and Hiro. "Believe me, as soon I figure out how to unsummon them, I will. In the meantime, I don't think we need this many people involved in all of this."

"I can go with you or not," Hiro said, climbing back onto the hover gilly and stepping up onto the box. "Makes no difference to me."

Without the hover gilly, Kel would have to be zapped to the Sphere. Arthur could relate to Kel's aversion to the magical mode of transportation and he was betting that Kel would not consent to it now. If he could just get Kel to give up, he was sure that Analeetah would as well. He would miss Hiro, but there were just too many cooks in the kitchen, as his mother would say.

"I'm not leaving Anayah," Analeetah said sternly.

Kel looked at the Doyenne. "And I'm not leaving Analeetah." Kel did his alpha male arm-crossing thing, daring Arthur to make them leave.

As amused as Harpur was with Arthur's attempt to cull the herd, he stepped forward and whispered in Arthur's ear. "Good try. But let's let them hang around a bit longer. I'd like to try to find out what Anayah is up to before we cut them loose."

Arthur frowned. "Why? The longer they are with us, the more likely it is that she'll be able to carry out her plan," Arthur whispered back.

"I know. But as you pointed out before we found Hiro's cave, we don't know our way around. Let's see if we can find out where the Sphere is and what Anayah has planned. Then we can decide what to do next."

"Promise me you won't tell them what's supposed to happen at the Sphere until you've told me. Privately."

"Deal." Harpur clapped Arthur on the shoulder and then turned to the group. "Come on, everybody. We're going to the Sphere!"

Anayah stared at Harpur. *What was that all about?* She was the last to climb aboard the hover gilly, but managed to worm her way to the front next to Hiro. "Where are we stopping for the night?" she asked the tiny pilot.

"There's an abandoned temple in the Metaloc Valley. It's only a few hours from here." Hiro said. "I think by then, we'll all be ready for a break."

Anayah nodded. "Sounds lovely."

She looked over her shoulder at Harpur. She had to win his trust back. She should never have done what she did to Sok and Arthur in the forest. She really hadn't meant them any harm; she only wanted to make it look like the Entanglement was advancing faster than it was. Anabettah had been right to scold her for not doing more research. It was stupid to think that she could get the coin away from Arthur and use it for her own ends. Asking Kel to help her had been even more stupid. She'd managed to convince him and Analeetah that she was not planning any harm, but she had been too embarrassed to admit her true intentions to them. Now everyone was suspicious of her. But she was suspicious of Harpur. She knew he was holding something back, something important. And not knowing what that was, was infuriating. She was tempted to try to force the issue while they were on the hover gilly, but a confrontation like that, especially when she didn't know what to expect, was not safe. She'd have to bide her time. Once she knew what they were going to the Sphere for, she'd have a better idea of what Harpur was keeping secret.

The passengers on the hover gilly passed the rest of the afternoon with a running commentary on the passing landscape provided by the well-informed Krist. From his box at the helm, Hiro pointed out landmarks like a tour guide. "On the right you will see the ancient ruins of Gwydinmoor Castle. More of a monastery than a castle, Gwydinmoor Castle was the home to a group of warrior monks called the Order of the Gool. They were wiped out by a plague over five hundred years ago. Gwydinmoor is said to be the most haunted place on Mysturna."

"Can we stop?" Sok asked. "I'd like to meet a ghost."

"No!" several voices around him said.

"We are now passing over the Bootenryd Moor. A great battle was fought here between the witches and the Puremen three hundred year ago."

"Who are the Puremen?" Sok asked.

"I am a Pureman," Kel answered, but offered nothing more.

"Oh!" Sok said. "I'm glad you and witches have made up since then. What were you fighting about?"

"The witches sought to enslave my people," Kell said.

Harpur, Sok and Arthur all looked at Anayah and Analeetah questioningly.

"It was a different time," Analeetah said without further explanation.

"Can we stop?" Sok asked. "Maybe we can find some artifacts from the battle."

"No!"

The first sun had set when the hover gilly descended and came to a stop next to a stone hut. "Our home for the night, ladies and gentlemen." Hiro announced as he ushered his passengers off of the chariot.

A creek ran a short distance away from the hut, which was nestled in a thicket of evergreen trees on a hill. The building didn't look much bigger than the hover gilly and as each of the passengers stepped down from it, they began to utter their protests. Hiro assured them there was plenty of room as he led them to the door.

Harpur had to duck to get through the low doorway and was not surprised to find himself huddled with the others in a space that was, indeed, only slightly larger than the hover gilly.

"Do we sleep standing up?" Harpur harped.

From the other side of the room, Hiro giggled. "Unless you'd rather join me down here," he said.

He released a hidden catch in the wall and a narrow section of it swung open to reveal an equally narrow, sloping passageway. Hiro clapped his hands and an ambient light illuminated the passageway. Hiro led the way in and Harpur pulled the outer door of the hut closed behind him before following the others, happy that, at least the passage was high enough for him to walk upright and not have to stoop.

The passageway led to a large underground cavern. After standing in the hover gilly all afternoon, the group was happy to take advantage of the rustic, but comfortable, benches that were arranged much like pews in a church would be. A dais on the far side housed a stone altar on which stood several unlit candles. The faint scent of incense filled the air. The space could easily accommodate a hundred people.

"I think we should all be comfortable here for the night," Hiro said. "If anyone needs to freshen up, there are facilities just through here." He opened another door to another passageway on the right side of the cavern.

Anayah and Analeetah went through after Holly declined their invitation to accompany them. She had no need to freshen up.

Kel gravitated to a bench near the door Anayah and Analeetah had disappeared through. Harpur, Sok and Arthur stayed close to the exit. Ralph and Holly sat down on a bench in front of Arthur and immediately started kissing. Arthur leaned over the back of the bench and ordered them to behave themselves. He waited until they settled for chaste hand-holding before returning to stand next to Harpur and Sok. Hiro, meanwhile, found neutral ground on one of the benches between the obvious factions and began to pull copious amounts of food out of his satchel.

"He's a regular Mary Poppins, isn't he?" Arthur observed.

"Who?" Sok asked.

"As long as he doesn't start singing, I don't care what he pulls out of that bag," Harpur said, ignoring Sok.

"Mary Poppins is a character in a popular kids' story on Earth," Arthur explained. "She carries a big bag that she pulls stuff out of like Hiro does."

"Why does a world that doesn't believe in magic have stories about it?" Sok asked.

"It makes for good entertainment," Arthur said. "We have stories about dragons and elves too."

"Stories all come from somewhere. How difficult is it to see the truth in them?" Sok detached himself from his faction and followed the succulent aroma of roasted galing to the bench Hiro had filled with a feast. He and the Krist, being the first ones to eat, each went for the drumsticks. The galing leg looked comically enormous in Hiro's tiny hand, but he was more than up for the challenge.

"Why don't you go eat something?" Harpur suggested to Arthur. He could see that Arthur was trying to extract the logic from what Sok had said and it amused him. *Earth is closer to realizing magic than it realizes,* he thought.

As tempting as the food smelled, Arthur's appetite was locked behind the need to know what was going to happen when they got to the Sphere. "I'd rather you filled me in on what Anabettah told you."

"Not here," Harpur said. "And Sok needs to hear it too. So, go and eat and then we'll go for a walk."

"Do you think they will let us leave?" Arthur nodded toward the other faction.

"I'd like to see them try to stop us," Harpur said. He was feeling surly and it showed.

Arthur joined Sok and Hiro and the galing at the bench.

"Come and eat, everyone," Hiro said when Anayah and Analeetah returned. "There's plenty for all of us."

The food lightened everybody's mood. Even Harpur, seemed a little more amiable once he'd accepted a plate from Arthur and started filling his empty stomach. But as the meal wound down, the factions reasserted themselves and Hiro was once again, left in the neutral zone between them. He cleared up the remnants of the meal and then, pulling a thick book out of his satchel, settled down to read. He sensed a confrontation was coming, but he wasn't going to start it.

That job fell to Anayah.

She stood up and walked toward Harpur.

"I have nothing to say to you," Harpur warned as she approached.

"Well, I have plenty to say to you!" Anayah stated. "And you're going to listen."

"I don't want to hear anything you have to say," Harpur said, crossing his arms and staring angrily back at the witch.

"Now, now. Let's not be that way." Analeetah cut in. "We all have things to discuss. Why don't we sit down and Harpur can tell us why we are going to the Sphere?"

"I promised Arthur that I would tell him privately first. If he wants the rest of you to know, he can tell you." Harpur kept his gaze on Anayah.

"We're all in this together. Tell us all," Anayah demanded.

"I'm just the hover gilly driver," Hiro said from behind his book.

"No one asked you to come," Harpur challenged. "You forced your way into it."

"Yes," Analeetah said. "And how did you get involved?"

Hiro lowered his book. He could not tell the witches about his network of koobars and Mezzi's involvement. He gave Harpur and Sok meaningful looks hoping they would not reveal his secret. "I found travellers in need of help and so I am helping," he lied. Then to deflect unwanted attention on the matter he added, "What I want to know is how those two," he pointed at Ralph and Holly, "got involved."

Everyone looked at the guardians on the dais.

"Arthur asked us for help," Holly said.

"Arthur asked you? How does Arthur even know to do that?" Anayah asked.

"He was in need and we responded," Holly said.

"Ah," Analeetah and Anayah said together.

"So, he has two guardians?" Sok interjected. "That doesn't seem very fair."

"I think Arthur, Sok and I should go alone to the Sphere," Harpur said. "If you tell me how to get there, I can fly the three of us and we can finish this." This abrupt change of subject drew all of the attention away from the guardians and placed it squarely back on the dragon-wizard.

"You will never be received at the Sphere without a Mysturnian to speak for you," Analeetah declared.

"I must go with you," Anayah said. "Please don't do this, Harpur."

"Why must you go with us?" Harpur demanded. "So, you can finish stabbing us in the back?"

"That's not what I was doing!" Anayah said. "I would never hurt you."

"Oh, really?" Harpur bellowed. "Then why did you ask Kel to steal the coin?"

Anayah took a deep breath. "Please, Harpur. Can I speak to you privately?"

"No! You're the one that insisted we speak openly," Harpur snapped. "So, speak openly. Or not at all."

"I love you!"

In the silence that flooded the cavern after her unexpected declaration, Anayah ran up the passageway to the hut.

While Harpur tried to process Anayah's words, Analeetah rose from her bench and started to follow her niece. "It all makes sense now," she said, stopping briefly beside Harpur.

Harpur dropped his head and exhaled a plume of smoke.

The last thing Harpur needed just then was to have to deal with an emotional female. The revelation was shocking enough, but to think that love had motivated her to conspire to steal the coin was something he could not wrap his head around. What the coin had to do with it was a mystery that he knew he needed to solve. Yet he couldn't quite bring himself to follow her. Sok's and Arthur's needs trumped that of a lovelorn witch whose feelings he had no capacity to reciprocate. He was a dragon first. And while he spent most of his time of late in human form, the idea of a relationship with a humanoid was not among any concepts he had given credence to. Ever.

He cared for Anayah. Their time together in the lair on Whyte Avenue had culminated in a deep bond of friendship and, on that level, he did suppose that he loved her. But love-love? That was just crazy talk.

Kel waited until Analeetah had left before speaking. "Didn't see that coming, did you?"

Harpur glared at him. "Did you know?"

"I suspected. She said she needed a small piece of the coin for a spell, but she refused to tell me what it was for. When she begged me not to tell you about it, it seemed obvious that it involved you. I figured that she would either let it go or tell someone eventually. Anayah is not prone to irrational acts. I admit that I am ashamed to have considered the alternate plot. And that is not how a Mysturnian witch typically approaches love, but what else could it be?"

Harpur didn't respond to Kel. Instead, he went over to Hiro, who was reading again, and asked, "Is there another way out of here?"

Hiro looked up and shook his head. "The builders of this temple tended to be quite minimalist. I doubt that they would have considered a need for a second exit."

Harpur looked over at Arthur and frowned. He was sure Arthur was hiding a smile behind the hand he had clamped over his mouth. "Is there another room, somewhere Sok, Arthur and I can talk privately?"

"In there," Hiro pointed to the *facilities*.

Harpur motioned for Arthur and Sok to join him and entered the small anteroom that contained a stone fountain that served as a wash basin and a cubicle that, he assumed, served as the reason a wash basin was needed. A constant trickle of water diverted from a ground spring fed into the basin and drained through a hole drilled into the stone. There was nowhere to sit, so the trio each leaned against a wall.

"Sorry about this," Harpur said, referring to the accommodations they found themselves in. "But there's no other way out of here and I am not walking past those two witches to get outside unless I absolutely have to."

Arthur bit his lip to keep from laughing. "No worries," he said. "We get that it's complicated."

Harpur growled. "Do you want to hear this or not?"

"You tell me," Arthur said. "How bad is it?"

"It's pretty bad."

"Well, as long as I don't end up dying, it can't be any worse than anything else that's happened." Arthur was determined to stay calm and not lose his mind no matter what Harpur told him.

Harpur screwed up his face. "About that..."

"What!? Are you serious? How is me dying going to save me from dying?" So much for staying calm.

"There's a chance that neither of you has to die, but..."

"What!?" Sok shouted. "Why do I have to die?"

Harpur sighed. "Relax. Both of you. Let me start at the beginning."

Arthur and Sok adjusted themselves against the walls they were leaning against. Arthur stared at the floor while Sok stared at Harpur.

"There's a lot of stuff at play here. Because you both are magical beings, the Entanglement is affecting your souls. Which is a good thing. When we get to the Sphere a man named Bon is going to see how far it's gone. If he has to, he can temporarily reverse the exchange, but you have to be dead for him to be able to capture your souls and separate them. It won't stop the Entanglement, but it will buy us some time. Neither of you seem to be taking on the personality of the other, so there's a good chance you won't have to... you know... die at all."

Arthur and Sok glanced at each other and then quickly looked away. Becoming someone else, was something they had both fantasized about, but the potential of it being a reality was overwhelming.

"If this soul transfer thing were to be completed, would that mean that I would actually be the lost child of Epoh and that I would become king?" Sok theorized with something of a sinister glee.

Harpur shook his head. "You are truly unbelievable sometimes."

"You would," Arthur said, "but you would be in my body."

"Oh! Well, that doesn't work for me." Sok shook the fantasy out of his head. "I say we get to the Sphere and get this Bon person to fix us right away."

Arthur concurred. But he had another question. "And just how are we going to die if it comes to that?"

"I will do the deed myself," Harpur said solemnly. "I will make sure you don't suffer."

Arthur was already suffering. He was on the verge of another meltdown. He'd never thought of himself as being an emotionally volatile person before. Then again, he'd never been to another world in the company of dragons and elves and witches, or faced having to be killed by one of them either. The panic was rising and he wasn't sure he could stop it. "Harpur?" he whispered through his fear. "Can you do that calming thing with your walking stick on me?"

Harpur didn't hesitate. Nor did he question or mock Arthur for asking. He tapped Arthur's shoulder with his walking stick and watched the anxiety drain away.

"Thank you," Arthur said. Then after a few seconds he continued. "I don't want the others there, Harpur. I don't want them to come with us."

"I understand," the dragon-wizard said.

Arthur looked at the man who was willing to kill him to save him and decided that dragons were incredibly noble creatures indeed. He wondered how he was ever going to repay Harpur for any of this. "What happens after we get to Thraeh and I give the coin back to Sok?"

Harpur took a deep breath and exhaled loudly. "Let's just get through this part first. We can figure the rest of it out later." *One step at a time.*

Arthur nodded.

When they entered the main sanctuary again, they were greeted by four sets of eyes staring at them. The other two sets of eyes in the room were staring at each other, apparently uninterested in the drama that was unfolding around them.

"Well?" Anayah asked. Her eyes were red-rimmed from crying, but she held her chin up and looked Harpur right in the eye.

"Well, what?" Harpur rejoined, keeping his voice even and his annoyance with her concealed.

"I assume you've told Arthur why we are going to the Sphere. Now you need to tell the rest of us." Her chin inched up a little higher.

"That is for Arthur to decide," Harpur said evenly.

The four Mysturnians turned to Arthur. "We have decided to go on without you," he said quietly.

"Why, Arthur?" Anayah asked.

"This whole thing has gotten out of hand," Harpur said. "We appreciate you wanting to help, but honestly, I think it's best if I take Sok and Arthur on to the Sphere alone. You two, Kel and Hiro are not needed from here on."

"That's ridiculous!" Analeetah exclaimed.

"No, it's not. It's my job to deal with Bounders. I'm going to do my job." Harpur crossed his big arms as if to make his point final, hoping to deflect from the topic at hand.

"You can't get into the Sphere without us," Analeetah argued. "You need us."

"I don't think so," Harpur said. "Look, Anayah, I'm sorry about what happened earlier. I don't know what you were planning to do with the coin. There will be plenty of time to discuss all that later. Right now, Arthur and Sok are in danger and there are just too many things getting in the way of dealing with that. I'm going to take them to the Sphere and I'm going to get them the help they need to sort this out. I can fly to wherever this place is faster than we can all get there in the hover gilly. Hell, I can zap us there if I have to. But Arthur needs this to be finished. Sok needs this to be finished. We are going to finish it."

"You can't get into the Sphere without us," Analeetah reiterated. "It's forbidden."

"I can and I will," Harpur said. "What's going to stop me?"

"Respect!" Anayah said.

Harpur looked at her. "Excuse me?"

"You will respect our ways," Anayah said.

"I do respect your ways. I get it that the Sphere is a sacred place. Just tell me what I need to do and I will do it."

"No!" Anayah shouted. "You are not of this world and I will not allow you to go without us."

"You have no right," Analeetah said.

"I have every right!" Harpur said angrily.

"You can't go without us," Anayah insisted.

Harpur turned away from the defiant witches angrily.

"What if I told you that it's me who doesn't want you there?" Arthur asked quietly.

Anayah and Analeetah looked at the doomed man. "Why do you want to go without us?" Analeetah asked.

"Because this is personal." Arthur wasn't sure where he was going with this, but it felt right to him. "And because you've made mistakes."

Anayah gasped. "But..."

"I know you didn't mean any harm. Per se. But the fact is that you had a hidden agenda. And that hidden agenda has cost us time and has put my and Sok's lives in even greater peril.

"A few days ago, I was just a guy working at a comic book store minding my own business. Then this doofus," Arthur pointed to Sok, "handed me a stupid coin and now I have to let a dragon... I have to go through something that I just don't want to share with you all so that, hopefully, I can go back to Whyte Avenue and maybe resume some kind of normal life.

"We came here because you said you could help us. And I want to believe that you do want to help us. But clearly, there is a distraction here that has put that intention in some jeopardy. I'm sorry, Anayah, but I don't trust you. The three of us need to go on alone and once this is done, if we survive, we can sort out our feelings about each other. It's not that I don't appreciate everything you three and Hiro have done, but I gotta say, this is all just too freaking weird and if I'm going to... I don't want to do what I have to do in front of an audience."

Tears were streaming down Anayah's cheeks, but she refused to turn away. She looked at Arthur, not with anger, not with hate, but with pity and sorrow that reached into Arthur's heart and squeezed it painfully.

"You are right. I did make mistakes. I did have a hidden agenda. I thought I could help you and Sok and myself. I was wrong. But I can't allow you to go to the Sphere without me. Whether you trust me or not, I am going with you." Anayah stared through her tears at Arthur.

"Well, this is getting us nowhere," Harpur observed.

"And you!" Analeetah rounded on Harpur. "You don't deserve Anayah's love! You big, stupid, dragon!"

"Enough!" shouted Kel. "It's late. Why don't we all get some sleep and we can discuss this in the morning."

Everyone knew that no one was going to sleep. Though Arthur would have happily curled up in a corner and fallen into oblivion. He wanted to rage, but he had no strength for it. Having to die to live seemed melodramatic and sensational to him. How had he become the centre of all this fuss? He wandered away from the others, sat on a bench near the exit and tried unsuccessfully to think about anything other than dying. *How will Harpur do it?* Every method that came to mind was worse than the one before. Knife to the heart. Snapped neck. Suffocation. Yet there was something noble in Harpur's offer. In a weird way, Harpur was being kind. If he was going to let anyone kill him, it would be Harpur. *Dragons are efficient killers. Aren't they?*

The standoff on the other side of the room ended with the factions regrouping. Kel, Anayah and Analeetah went into a huddle, shutting the others out. Hiro opened his book and continued reading. Ralph and Holly started kissing again. And Harpur and Sok joined Arthur on his bench.

"It will take another two days to reach the Sphere and find Bon. I don't know how long it will take him to prepare and execute—sorry, poor choice of words—complete the spell work required." Harpur said.

Arthur nodded. "Can't we just zap straight to this Sphere place and get things going?"

"I'm working on it," Harpur said.

Holly approached from the dais. "We have to accompany you, Arthur. You haven't released us."

"Then I release you," Arthur said.

"It doesn't work that way," Holly said.

"How does it work then?" Arthur asked.

"You have to decide."

"Didn't I just do that?"

"No."

Arthur looked helplessly at Harpur for guidance. Harpur shrugged.

"The thing is, Holly," Arthur said. "I don't know how I asked for your help and I don't know how to let you know that I don't need your help. Can you tell me how that works?"

"When you need us, we come. When you don't need us, we go."

"But I don't need you anymore," Arthur said. "I'm not sure I ever needed you."

"You must. We're still here." Holly smiled.

"Why do I bother?" Arthur asked rhetorically.

"Can you ride on my back?" Harpur asked much to Arthur's horror.

"We don't need to ride." Ralph had joined Holly next to the bench.

"You can fly?" Harpur asked.

"We can just be with you." Holly and Ralph joined hands and smiled in their enigmatic, yet benign way.

"Good enough," Harpur said.

"What are you planning?" Hiro interrupted. A tone of suspicion prominent in his query.

"I'm not planning anything," Harpur said. "I'm just curious."

No one believed him. But no one challenged him either. The company fell back into silence.

"Anyone got some bourbon?" Arthur asked. "I could really use some bourbon."

Harpur started to laugh. His deep, booming guffaws reverberated off the cavern walls and filled the space with infectious hilarity. Arthur was first to catch the bug and his snickers grew into a hysterical howl. Sok and Hiro giggled along until they were doubled over by their belly laughs. Ralph and Holly stopped kissing and looked bemused.

Kel and the two witches broke their huddle and looked at the others. The awkwardness Anayah was feeling was replaced by a deeper awkwardness. *Are they laughing at me?* Analeetah intuited her niece's trepidation and marched over to the source of the mirth.

"What's so funny?" she demanded to know.

The laughter did not abate. Harpur and Arthur were wiping tears from their eyes. Sok and Hiro were holding their stomachs. Holly and Ralph were still looking bemused.

"What's so funny?" Analeetah shouted.

Arthur and Harpur looked at the witch and were taken over by fresh waves of laughter. They were powerless to respond, powerless to control themselves.

Eventually, Holly approached the angry witch. "Arthur asked for some bourbon," she explained. "And they all started laughing."

Anayah approached hesitantly. "What is going on?" she asked her aunt.

"Do you know what bourbon is?" Analeetah asked.

"It's an alcoholic drink. A type of whiskey. Why?"

"Apparently it's hilarious," Analeetah said.

The two witches, along with Kel, Ralph and Holly stood off to the side and waited until the laughter ran its course. When it finally quieted again, Analeetah stepped forward.

"Are we good now?" she scoffed.

"Oh, we're better than good!" Harpur said, regaining his composure. "Come on, boys. We're going to the Sphere!"

Sok and Arthur stood up and followed Harpur out of the sanctuary and into the night.

"This is crazy!" Anayah said.

Then Kel, the witches, the Krist and the Guardians went after them.

Harpur expected the others to follow him, Sok and Arthur out of the cabin. There was no way they were going to just let the three of them fly away. But Harpur didn't care. He transformed into a dragon and directed Arthur to take charge of his walking stick. Instead of just grabbing the elf and the man, Harpur had them climb into his hands and position themselves as comfortably as they could. They all knew they had no idea where they were going, but they all knew that they had to go on alone. Whatever happened had to happen without the aid of the witches, the Krist and the Pureman. As for Holly and Ralph, they would either tag along or they wouldn't. As it turned out, they would. When Harpur launched into the air, two shimmering opalescent blobs appeared just below them and flew along, keeping perfect pace.

"Harpur, stop this!" Anayah shouted at the dragon. "Come back here!" She raised her hands to cast a spell, but Kel stopped her.

"Let them go," he said.

"But..."

"They won't find the Sphere on their own. They'll be back." *I wasn't looking forward to two more days stuck with them in the hover gilly anyway.*

From the ground, they watched the dragon and two glowing orbs recede into the night sky.

Why didn't I reactivate those cuffs? Anayah scolded herself.

Arthur tried to relax. He knew he should be used to this mode of transportation by now, but there was something about dangling from a dragon's claws that one did not adjust to easily. As long as he didn't look down, Arthur's air sickness remained at bay, so there was that to be grateful for. And there was enough warmth in the beast's hands to keep the cool night air from becoming too uncomfortable. Arthur had to admit to himself that he felt safer in Harpur's grasp than he did on the hover gilly. He settled in as best he could and kept his gaze on the distant horizon. Whatever dangers this world may hold were far below them now. Another thing to be thankful for.

"Does anyone know where this Sphere is?" Arthur yelled over the rushing wind.

"We'll find it eventually" Harpur boomed.

A little voice in Arthur's head that sounded remarkably like Holly's sounded. "Veer southward."

"Is that you, Holly?" Arthur asked aloud.

The voice sounded again. "Yes. But only you can hear us when we are in this form. You will have to share what we tell you with the others."

"Thanks," Arthur said aloud again. Then he called out to Harpur, "I can hear Holly and Ralph telepathically. Holly says to veer south."

Harpur banked to the right and continued on without comment.

"You don't have to speak out loud to us." Ralph's voice joined Holly's in Arthur's head.

"Great!" Arthur said aloud anyway. "I'll keep that in mind."

In his head, he heard a giggle. "We know."

Below and behind them, Anayah, Analeetah, Kel and Hiro returned to the sanctuary to get some sleep. If Harpur didn't come back they would track him in the morning. They had no intention of allowing the dragon to enter the Sphere without them. But for the time being, at least they didn't have to listen to his heroic posturing. Or concern themselves with Arthurian outbursts. Let the dragon deal with the human. They would intervene before Harpur could do anything stupid. Right then they needed to rest. While the dragon wore himself out, they would refresh themselves and be better prepared.

Little did they know that Harpur had no intention of flying all the way to the Sphere. With Arthur's ability to telepathically communicate with his Guardians, all he needed to do was extract the exact location of the Sphere from them and then zap all of them there. Which is what he did.

Shortly after midnight, Harpur, Sok and Arthur, along with two shimmering opalescent blobs materialized in the air above an enormous obsidian Sphere and circled it looking for an entrance. Unlike the Pole, the Sphere was not surrounded by gardens. There was no elaborate labyrinth leading to it. There were no pools or gazebos. It was surrounded by open grassland.

From high above, it looked benign enough. But Harpur was not willing to land until he was sure that there were no threats to their safety in the form of underground-dwelling people-eaters of any kind. It appeared as if there was no life at all in the vicinity. But appearances, as Harpur well knew, could be deceiving. He was not going to put himself or his living cargo in danger just because things looked safe.

"Are your guardians aware of any dangers to us on the ground?" Harpur asked Arthur.

"They say it's safe," Arthur relayed the message.

Harpur dutifully trailed the shimmering opalescent blobs to the ground, whereupon, the blobs reverted to a nearly naked couple and Harpur remained a very large dragon. He wanted to be able to scoop Sok and Arthur up again fast should the need arise. This made sense to everyone. While Arthur did not treasure the idea, he deemed it prudent and accepted the wisdom of it.

On the ground, their view of the Sphere was limited due to its sheer enormity. It looked like a humongous marble sitting on the ground. Arthur was terrified that it would start to roll and almost wished he was back in Harpur's grip above it rather than under it as they were. Instinctively, he backed further away from it. In spite of its size, Arthur had the feeling that it wouldn't take much—a mere sneeze in the wrong direction—to get the thing moving. He wondered how far and how fast he would have to run to outrun it if it did start rolling.

"So how do we get in?" Sok asked as he craned his neck looking up at the huge ball.

There was no obvious entrance. The Sphere looked like a solid, giant marble sitting on the grass. Its black surface was neither metallic nor stone-like. To Arthur it looked like plastic, which may have been wishful thinking as plastic, it seemed to him, was not as heavy as metal or stone and, thus, felt less threatening to him. He doubted it was plastic, but it was, without doubt, not natural.

"Be patient," Ralph said. "Bon will come to us."

"Eventually," Holly added.

"Might as well get comfortable," Holly advised and, taking Ralph's hand, walked a little way away where they sat down on the grass and started kissing.

"I swear," Harpur growled, "if they go any farther, I will fry them where they lay."

Chapter 9

A silent consensus caused Harpur, Sok and Arthur to turn their backs to Ralph and Holly, but with no notion of how long it would take for Bon to decide to come out of the Sphere, this hardly seemed like a complete solution.

The night sky was brilliant above them with stars and, for the first time since arriving on this bizarre world, a pale green moon floated just above the horizon to the right of the Sphere. From the angle the trio of other-worlders were viewing it, it appeared to be about half the size of the jet-black Sphere. Still, as moons go, Arthur was in awe of it. As the night progressed, the green glow deepened, causing the surrounding grasslands to take on an eerie phosphorescent luminescence. It might have been an extraordinary and humbling experience, if not for the grunting and moaning going on behind them.

Harpur sighed. "Like it's not bad enough that you have to have two guardians. Did you have to have two insatiable guardians?"

Arthur sighed. "Like I have any control over them."

Sok sighed. "When I get home, I'm going to ask Yna to marry me."

Arthur and Harpur looked at the elf, who was taking frequent peeks over his shoulder at the coupling guardians.

"Is Yna your girlfriend?" Arthur asked.

"She's a girl. And she's a friend. But I'm guessing that a girlfriend has something to do with what Ralph and Holly are doing. And we've never done *that*!"

Arthur chuckled. "Do you love her?"

"Not particularly."

"Then why would you ask her to marry you?"

"What does love have to do with getting married?"

"Pretty much everything."

"Not where I come from."

"You don't marry for love on Thraeh?"

"Marriage is a business contract." Sok tore his gaze away from the action and looked at Arthur, confused.

"I'm confused," Arthur said. "On Earth, people get married because they love each other."

"Elves see marriage as an alliance. Love is something that develops over time. Sometimes." Harpur explained.

Arthur nodded. "So, you find Yna attractive and want to..." he tossed his head in the general direction of the moaning.

"I find Yna rich and powerful."

"And in possession of five concubines," Harpur added.

Arthur considered the implications of this cultural phenomenon.

"Eleven," Sok corrected.

"Eleven? Since when?" Harpur interjected with no little amount of surprise.

"Since she killed her sister and inherited all of her concubines."

"Wait!" Arthur said. "This Yna killed her sister?"

"It was an accident."

"What happened?"

"They were practicing for the winter combat trials and Yna got carried away and accidentally cut off Yla's head." Sok's matter-of-fact account made Arthur wince.

"Are you saying you want to marry a woman who competes in combat trials and cut her own sister's head off during practice?"

"Yna's a champion. And she's rich. And... Well, eleven concubines!" Sok didn't understand Arthur's problem with the scenario. "Since my destiny means that I don't have to enter a guild, the alliance would work well for us, I think."

"Why don't you want to enter a guild?" Arthur was trying to keep up.

"Because once an elf is accepted into a guild, they are stuck there for the rest of their life. I have never wanted that."

"What do you want?" Arthur thought Sok would have his hands full with a wife and eleven concubines.

"I want to be free to do what I want."

"Okay, then! I hope you'll all be happy." Arthur shook his head.

"The chances of Sok surviving the proposal are slim to none," Harpur said.

"Yeah. There is that." Sok said.

Harpur snorted. A great puff of smoke filled the air. "I'd pay to see you try."

"How exactly does an elf propose to another elf?" Arthur was curious.

"Marriage is considered to be a guild of sorts. If an elf chooses to be married, they must be accepted into it. If a couple feels like this is the path they wish to follow, they seek acceptance together. If it is granted, they are married. For life. Most elves just... play the field, as you call it. But Yna is of the Warrior class and so Sok here has to best her in a fight. If he wins, she has to marry him. If she wins, she has the option of killing him." Harpur pared it down to the basics for Arthur.

"That's just insane!" Arthur declared. "Why would you want to fight a woman for the chance to marry her? And how would she kill you if you lose?"

"The same way she killed her sister!" Harpur said.

"Yna wouldn't kill me," Sok said defensively. "She likes me."

"She likes that you do whatever she wants you to do," Harpur said.

"That's not true!" Sok's defensiveness ratcheted up a notch. "Everybody likes me."

"I don't like you," Arthur said.

"You do!" Sok said. "You just don't like the situation we're in."

"Ya think?" Arthur said.

"Look, Arthur," Sok said. "I am really sorry about all of this." He gestured toward the huge Sphere. "I didn't know things would turn out like this. I've been trying to find a way to tell you how sorry I am, how bad I feel about all this. For what it's worth, I do like you."

The remorseful elf stood up and walked away from his companions. Arthur watched him retreat and felt a twinge of guilt for having been so blunt. He was tired. He was so, so very tired.

"You know, Arthur," Harpur said quietly, "if we're going to get through this, we're going to have to do it together. You might want to apologize."

"Yeah, I know," Arthur conceded. He stood up and went after Sok.

While Arthur and Sok worked out their most current differences, complete with apologies, a firm handshake and a comradely hug, Ralph and Holly wrapped up their amorous commingling and adjusted their fig-leaves. They joined Harpur who appeared to be staring at the Sphere, but was really eavesdropping on the male-bonding going on between Arthur and Sok. Satisfied that the two had reached an accord, he looked at the nearly naked couple and grimaced slightly when Holly playfully bit Ralph's ear. *Now*, he thought, *would be a good time for Bon to make an appearance.*

No such luck.

Holly looked over at Sok and Arthur and asked, "Everything okay over there?"

"Okay enough," Harpur said.

Laughter drifted across the landscape.

"He's taking all this better than we expected," Ralph observed.

"Don't kid yourself. He's a wreck." Harpur squinted in the direction of the man he was going to kill to save. "As his guardians, you should know that."

"He's not as much of a wreck as you think he is," Holly said.

"He's resigned to his fate," Ralph confirmed.

Harpur growled is disagreement. "How much longer do you think it will be?"

"Perhaps he needs some encouragement." Holly took Ralph's hand and the two of them walked toward the Sphere.

Harpur sighed. He wanted to get this over with and right then he was rapidly reaching the rare, almost unprecedented, point of second-guessing himself. This was more disconcerting than the idea of thrusting a knife into Arthur's heart, and that was already about as unappealing as roasting a virgin alive. This Bon guy needed to hurry up.

Ralph and Holly glowed in the shadow of the Sphere. Harpur thought they should have been more concerned for Arthur and wondered exactly what guardians were supposed to do. He looked at Sok and Arthur, still chatting amiably a short way away. Then he scanned the grassy plain for any sign of a threat. Seeing none, he moved forward toward the Sphere and the nearly naked couple. *How do I encourage a guy in a Sphere to come out?*

The nearly naked couple were sitting on the grass together, heads touching, fingers entwined, lips whispering sweet nothings.

"Ah-hem," Harpur announced his intrusion into their quiet rendezvous.

They turned to face the dragon. "Yes?" Holly asked.

Harpur paused to formulate his question. "Is there anything you two can do to get Arthur out of this mess?" He finally settled on that.

Ralph and Holly looked at each other, then back at the dragon. "What mess?" they asked in unison.

"What mess?" Harpur had to use every ounce of restraint not to engulf them in flames. "The Entanglement. The Anomaly. The having to be killed. By me!"

Holly detached herself from Ralph and stepped boldly closer to the furious dragon. "Arthur chose this path," she said as if that explained everything.

"There are an infinite number of possibilities in any given moment," Ralph expanded everything a little bit. "This mess, as you call it, is what he's asked for. It's what he's created."

"He asked to be Entangled with Sok? He asked to be an anomaly? He asked to be killed? By me?" Harpur wasn't buying it.

"Perhaps not specifically," Holly ventured. "But generally, yes."

Harpur's patience, already worn thin and beginning to fray, was moments away from snapping altogether.

"You, for example," said Holly, "are about to make a choice. That choice, whatever it is, is like asking for something to happen. Once you've made your choice, the thing you've asked for will happen. It may not happen precisely the way you imagine, but it might. It depends on how specific you are."

"Just so you know," Ralph interjected, "You can't burn us with your fire."

"Ralph!" Holly admonished. "You're not supposed to tell him that!"

"Just thought I'd save him from making a grave mistake."

"I can't burn you with my fire as in you won't burn? Or I can't burn you with my fire as in doing so will have consequences beyond merely eliminating an irksome element of an already exasperating situation?"

"That you see there are more possibilities than one is a good thing, Harpur," Holly said approvingly.

"You still haven't answered my question," Harpur said.

"What question?" Ralph asked.

"Can you do anything to help Arthur?"

"We are doing all we can," Holly said.

"So, no, then?"

"Arthur created this. It's his to do with as he chooses," Ralph said.

"What good are you, then?" Harpur snapped.

"What good are we not?" Holly replied.

"What I mean is, why don't you intervene? If you are his guardians, why aren't you guarding him?"

"We are!" Another unified announcement.

Harpur needed to burn something. Rather than continue this maddening dialogue with those two wackadoos, he launched into the sky and disappeared over the Sphere.

Arthur and Sok came running over to where Holly and Ralph were already giving each other the googly eyes.

"Where's he going?" Arthur asked.

"He didn't say," Holly answered without taking her ogling eyes off Ralph.

Arthur and Sok ran back out into the grassy plain to see if they could see Harpur. A silhouette of a dragon crossed the enormous green moon and then disappeared against the black sky. Then they returned to the guardians, who were kissing each other passionately.

Arthur tapped Ralph on the shoulder. "Excuse me," he said.

"Yesh?" Ralph said through lip-locked lips.

"What did you say to Harpur?"

"Many things," Holly managed to say between sloppy, tongue-tied kisses.

Rather than try to get a straight answer, Arthur and Sok ran back out onto the grassy plain once again.

"What if he doesn't come back?" Arthur asked.

"He'll come back," Sok assured him. "He won't abandon us."

"Are you sure?"

"I think so."

Arthur thought he kind of understood that. He figured that after a conversation with the nearly naked couple, Harpur just needed to blow off steam. But he kept an anxious eye on the sky, hoping to see the dragon returning to the Sphere. If Bon showed up and Harpur wasn't there... Well, he didn't want to think about that.

Just then, Sok grabbed Arthur's arm and pointed. Arthur spun around to see a copse of trees in the distance burst into flames. Harpur's huge body was momentarily visible in the light of the fire as it flew over the engulfed trees moving back in the direction of the Sphere.

"He's going to start a grass fire!" Arthur yelled.

But the fire was so hot that the trees burned up in a flash and collapsed in on themselves in a heap of ash. Within seconds, the fire extinguished itself and darkness reasserted itself on the plain. Almost before it did, Harpur landed about fifty yards away from them and approached with residual smoke billowing out of his nostrils.

"You could have started a grass fire!" Arthur repeated, prudently leaving out an accompanying derogatory epithet.

"Don't be ridiculous!" Harper snorted. "I know how to burn stuff."

Fair enough, thought Arthur. *But still!*

"What was that all about?" Arthur was concerned.

"Those two useless twits," Harpur tossed his big head in the direction of Ralph and Holly, "drove me to it."

Also, fair enough, thought Arthur. There had been many times since meeting them that he, too, felt the strong desire to wreck something.

"I don't think they are useless," Sok suggested. "I just think we don't know how to use them."

"They are your guardians, Arthur. Can't you control them or something?" Harpur said, releasing another pungent puff of smoke.

"If I knew how, I would," Arthur said. "But they are as big a mystery to me as they are to you."

"Oh, for the love of Orhowyn! They are at it again!" Harpur growled.

Sure enough, Ralph and Holly were once again rolling on the ground in the throes of passion. Even Sok was no longer impressed.

"Got anything to eat?" the elf asked.

Harpur transformed back into his human form and produced a platter of meat and cheese along with a couple of flagons of ale out of thin air. "Where's my walking stick?" he asked as he handed the heavy platter to Sok and then the ale to Arthur. It was a rhetorical question. He held his hand out and, like Thor's hammer, the stick rose up out of the grass and glided into Harpur's grip.

Sok and Arthur sat down in the grass and began to devour the meal.

"I wish we had some potato chips," Arthur said.

"I wish we had one of those hamburger things we had back on Earth," Sok said.

"Yeah. That would be great. I miss hamburgers." Arthur wrapped a slice of cheese in a slice of meat and bit into it.

Harpur stood a short distance away, doing his best to ignore both the nearly naked couple and the savoury aroma of the meat and cheese. Instead, he stared at the Sphere, willing it to give him some indication of how to *encourage* Bon to come out. He knew nothing about this Bon character and debated with himself as to whether human form was better than dragon form to meet him in. On one hand, he wanted to be intimidating enough to obtain swift compliance. On the other hand, he didn't want to appear overly threatening. Not knowing what kind of magic Bon possessed was a disadvantage and Harpur now internally scolded himself for not having obtained that information from Anabettah prior to coming to the Sphere. He lacked the proper intelligence he needed to strategize with any measure of confidence. He was not happy about this. Not happy at all.

"May Orhowyn give me strength," he muttered quietly to himself.

Chapter 10

Dawn, in a simultaneous maneuver, both lightened the sky and darkened Harpur's mood even further. Anayah, Analeetah and Kel—with or without Hiro—could show up anytime and Bon was still a no-show. He needed to move things along and end this nightmare. *What was the saying on Earth? Let's get this show on the road?*

The Sphere, Harpur accepted, was impenetrable. There was no obvious entrance and he wasn't sure he had either the might to break through or the firepower to burn his way in even if there had been one. He knew as much about the Sphere as he did about Bon; next to nothing. What he did know was that time was running out and he had to do something. But what?

Arthur and Sok were sleeping in the grass off to his right. Ralph and Holly were cooing at each other off to his left. Thankfully, they had gotten their libidinous tendencies under control and were keeping things rather more on a family-friendly level than they had been earlier. Harpur saw no reason to disturb either duo. They would only find a way to mess things up if he did.

What he decided to do was so simple, he gave himself a mental slap in the head for not having thought of it sooner. He walked up to the Sphere and knocked on it. To his surprise, delight and synchronized chagrin, an aperture opened up right in front of him. He jumped back and affected a combative stance, legs apart and bent at the knees, walking stick held like a quarterstaff, a fierce grimace with teeth bared, mind keenly focused on whatever might attack from the interior of the Sphere.

Harpur's default to fight-mode was met with a mirthful laugh. As the aperture expanded and settled at a fixed diameter of six feet, a figure appeared and smiled at him. The figure, which Harpur figured was Bon, was wearing soft, grey robes over a white tunic. His hands were tucked inside the sleeves of the opposite arms and a simple, silver chain draped across his chest. From beneath the hood of his robes silvery-grey curls, matching the neatly trimmed beard that was punctuated by full and smiling lips, sought to escape. His eyes were the same shade of grey as his robes and the toes of a pair of soft, leather boots—also grey—peeked out from under the ankle-length garment. He was a half a head shorter than Harpur in human form and his slender form belied his physical strength. As Harpur assessed the man before him, he intuited a formidable opponent. Should Bon's physical strength be put to the test, Harpur surmised that his own would be as well. He wasn't ready to relax just yet.

"Welcome, Harpur Diggins! I've been waiting for you."

"You're Bon?" Harpur inquired.

"That is what they call me, yes," Bon confirmed.

"What do you mean you've been waiting for me?"

"Well, I saw you arrive around midnight and so I have been waiting for you to knock."

Stupid guardians, Harpur thought. "Why didn't you let us know you knew we were here? You could have saved us from sitting out here all-night waiting for you."

"Protocol dictates that visitors seeking entry to the Sphere must request it. It is not my place to invite you in."

Harpur growled.

"Well, may we come in, then?" Harpur was still in combat stance. At this point, he was thinking he might have to fight his way in.

"I am afraid not." Bon smiled as he denied the request.

"May I ask why?"

"You may."

Another growl leaked out through Harpur's clenched teeth. "Why can't we come in?"

"Because protocol dictates that other-worlders are not permitted within this sacred space."

"I don't care about your protocol!" Harpur shouted. "We need your help!"

"Are you suggesting that I ignore protocol?"

"That's exactly what I'm suggesting," Harpur seethed.

"That is impossible. I am not programmed to ignore protocol." Again with the smile.

"You're not programmed to ignore protocol? You're an android?" Harpur hadn't expected that.

"That is correct."

Harpur adjusted his stance and leaned on his walking stick. *That's interesting,* he thought as he tried to think of a way around the protocol.

"If it pleases you to be ignored, I am pleased to oblige," Bon said. And with that, the aperture closed and Harpur was left feeling even more helpless and entirely speechless.

"Wait!" But it was too late.

Now, what was he supposed to do?

Unbeknownst to Harpur, Arthur had woken up and gone off a little way to relieve himself. When he had turned back toward the Sphere, Arthur noticed the opening and had seen Bon talking to Harpur through it. His excitement levels went through the roof and he began to run to get to them. The aperture closed just as he arrived at Harpur's side.

"Holy! Was that who I think it was?" Arthur panted.

Harpur looked at his excited, and probably doomed, companion.

"He looks just like Obi Wan!"

Harpur couldn't help himself, he cuffed Arthur lightly on the side of his head.

"Ouch!" Arthur winced and rubbed the spot where Harpur's heavy hand had connected with his skull.

"It wasn't Obi Wan, Arthur. This isn't Star Wars!" Harpur walked away, cursing under his breath.

"Well, he looked like Obi Wan," Arthur defended himself under his own breath.

Harpur stopped walking away and transformed back into dragon form. "Arthur," he roared, "take my walking stick. Everybody, we're leaving." He held out his hands for Arthur and Sok to climb into.

Sok, roused by Harpur's booming voice, sat up and looked toward the commotion. Holly and Ralph were staring at Harpur. Arthur was staring at the Sphere. And Harpur was staring at Sok. Which was far more disconcerting than anything else. He stood up and brushed bits of grass out of his hair.

"Did you say we are leaving?" he asked as he got closer to Harpur.

"Get on!" Harpur ordered.

"But why are we leaving?" he climbed into Harpur's hand and settled in for the ride. He was curious, but decided that now was not the best time to question the clearly pissed off dragon too intently.

"Arthur! Now!" Harpur bellowed.

Arthur took a deep breath and turned to face Harpur. "I'm not leaving until I talk to Bon."

Harpur's eyes narrowed and smoke rose from his nostrils. He swung his huge head around and down until his face was inches from Arthur's own.

"I said we're leaving," he said in a hoarse whisper.

"No!" Arthur shouted back. "I don't know what Bon said to you..."

"You talked to him?" Sok forgot his decision not to ask any questions. "Where is he?"

"...but I'm not leaving until I hear that he won't help us from him."

Harpur dropped Sok on the ground, reared up and howled at the sky. Purple-red flames shot upward nearly a hundred feet. Arthur closed his eyes and winced, waiting for the flames to be redirected at him.

Sok rolled away from the dragon's enormous feet and dashed over to where Arthur stood. "Are you insane? Don't you see how angry he is?"

"I'm not sure. And yes, I do," Arthur replied. "But this Bon dude is our last hope of getting out of this without having to go to all those other worlds—worlds that are weirder than this one from all accounts—and unless I hear it from Obi Wan himself, I'm not going anywhere. Capiche?"

"Who's Obi Wan? And what is capiche?"

"Bon is Obi Wan. And capiche is Italian for do you understand."

"I don't understand."

"I didn't think you would."

Harpur's roaring stopped. And he turned back into Harpur Diggins the man. Snatching his walking stick out of Arthur's hand, he went up to the Sphere and rapped on it. Arthur ran to the left. Sok ran to the right.

As it did earlier, the aperture opened up and Bon smiled out through it at the fuming dragon-wizard. "Welcome, Harpur Diggins. I have been waiting for you."

"Yeah, yeah. Will you tell this idiot what you told me earlier?"

"I am not familiar with idiot; can you clarify that for me?" Bon continued to smile.

Harpur marched over to Arthur and, dragging him by his arm, hauled him back to the aperture. "This is the idiot. Now tell him what you told me."

"I will correct my database. I was told your name was Arthur."

"What's going on?" Arthur asked.

"Bon is an android," Harpur explained. "And if you mention Commander Data, I will kill you right now."

"Okay! I get it. You're not a sci-fi fan. Jeez, Harpur, you're hurting my arm."

Harpur loosened his grip on Arthur's arm and shoved him closer to Bon.

"Actually," Arthur said, "my name is Arthur. Idiot is just Harpur's nickname for me."

"Nickname? An endearment, a diminutive or sobriquet bestowed on a friend or loved one as a means of expressing affection. May I call you idiot?" Bon asked politely.

"Um, I'd rather you just called me Arthur."

"Of course. We are not familiar enough with each other for nicknames yet. You may call me Bon."

"Okay. Listen, Bon, we really need your help. I'm an anomaly and I'm going through Entanglement with Sok," he pointed to the elf, "and the only way we can stop the Entanglement from progressing and stop us from switching personalities is for us to let Harpur kill us and for you to capture our souls, separate them and put them back into us. Then you have to revive us. Though, to be honest I don't exactly know why we have to die. I mean, maybe you could separate our souls without either of, but especially me, dying, so we can go to Thraeh and I can give him the coin back, which we first have to put back together and I can go home and never, ever, ever have to leave Earth again." He ran out of breath.

"I am very well aware of your predicament," Bon said. "That was an excellent summation, by the way. However, protocol forbids other worlders from entering the Sphere."

"Well, does protocol forbid you from leaving the Sphere?" Arthur asked.

"I am free to go wherever I wish."

"Do we have to be inside the Sphere for you to collect our souls and put them back where they belong?"

"Not at all. I can collect and separate souls anywhere."

Arthur shot an I-told-you-so look in Harpur's direction. "Great! That's great!" Arthur exclaimed. "Will you come out here and help us then?"

Bon tilted his head, processing the request. "There is nothing in the protocol preventing me from doing so. I will be glad to come out there and help you."

"Thank you, Bon. Thank you so very much!" Arthur turned and stuck his tongue out at Harpur. "Okay, Dragon! Kill me now!" *Before I change my freaking' mind.*

Now was not the time for Sok and Arthur to die. Bon first had to prepare and that took a while. The suns were both fully up by the time Bon emerged from the Sphere with a satchel over his shoulder and a large tray with folding legs that would transform it into a table that would be filled with beakers and vials and scalpels and, inexplicably, a large set of tongs. With a slight and practiced jerk of the tray, the legs unfolded and Bon put the table down on a flat piece of ground. He removed the satchel and rested it against one of the table legs. Then he returned to the Sphere. "Do not touch anything!" he called over his shoulder as the group assembled around the table to investigate, and speculate, on the tray's contents.

"I don't like the look of that," Arthur said pointing to, but not touching, the scalpels.

No one else commented.

"So how are you going to do it?" Sok asked Harpur.

"Do what?"

"Kill us."

"I haven't decided yet."

Arthur's Adam's apple bobbed in appreciable dread.

"How would you like him to do it, Arthur?" Sok asked calmly.

"I'm still clinging to an eleventh-hour reprieve," Arthur said in a voice far more unsteady than he intended. "But if I had my druthers, I'd choose lethal injection."

"What is that?" Sok was intrigued.

"It's how they execute people who are sentenced to death in some places on Earth." Arthur explained. "Essentially, they are euthanized. It's supposed to be painless. And quick."

"I see." Sok said, though he didn't really understand. "Harpur, can you do that? Can you euthanize us?"

"It's a possibility," Harpur said by way of giving them some measure of comfort. He could not, in fact, lethally inject them, but only because he didn't have the stuff to do it with. Privately, he was leaning toward a knife to the heart. Perhaps not entirely painless, but quick enough, especially in the absence of whatever drugs were used in lethal injections. Harpur's hand went, unconsciously, to the spot where his missing scale still ached.

"I think you should do that," Sok said. "I'd really not like us not to suffer any more than we need to."

Harpur and Arthur both looked at the elf, Arthur with gratitude and fondness, while Harpur's expression was openly suspicious.

"You two must have really bonded last night," Harpur prodded.

The man and the elf exchanged a glance. "We came to an understanding," Arthur said, but said no more.

"Hmmm..."

Just then, Bon returned carrying what appeared to be a folded plastic tarp of some kind. This, much like the scalpels had, gave Arthur great pause. "First we need to assess whether or not this operation is even necessary," Bon explained, though no one had asked.

He handed Arthur and Sok each a small, hard, black tube and told them to put the ends of them in their mouths. "Now blow into them as hard as you can, but do not remove them from your mouth. When you have finished blowing, you must keep your lips sealed around the ends of the tubes and not breath until I tell you."

Sok and Arthur each took a deep breath and then blew into the tubes, which expanded impossibly as if they were balloons. They resisted inhaling again while Bon stared intently at the misshapen pipes. Sok's eyes crossed as he tried to see what Bon was seeing. Arthur plugged his nose to keep himself from breathing in through his nostrils. And Bon kept staring at the tubes.

Finally, the android seemed satisfied. "Now suck all the air back in through your mouths."

With relief they did. "Well?" Arthur asked, looking at the tube and seeing just a tube.

"It's farther advanced than I would have expected after such a short time. We will have to proceed with the extraction and separation." Bon delivered this assessment with typical android passionless control and picked up the folded tarp.

"What's that for?" Arthur squeaked, imagining his lifeless body laying upon it in a spreading pool of his own blood.

"Containment," Bon said, "to prevent your souls from escaping. I do not know how feisty the souls of humans and elves are when they are released. This should keep them from getting away."

"Should?" Arthur, Harpur and Sok asked together.

Bon stopped unfolding what turned out to be some kind of transparent fabric tent. It felt silky and soft. So, not plastic at all.

"Will?" he corrected for their approval.

With a snap, the tent expanded and erected itself next to the table.

"It's not very big." Sok observed. "How are we all going to fit inside?"

"We are not all going to fit inside," Bon announced. "Only you, Arthur and myself are going to be inside. There is plenty of room for the three of us."

Ralph stepped forward. "We," he indicated himself and Holly, "are Arthur's guardians. We need to be there when he... expires."

"And I promised them that I would do the deed," Harpur said. "I have to be there too."

If Bon had the capability to sigh, he probably would have. But his programming included infinite patience. It was not his time they were wasting.

He tapped the tent, which collapsed to the ground, and began to fold it back up. When it was once again a neat and tidy bundle, Bon returned to the Sphere. A few minutes later he came back with another transparent fabric tent that, when snapped open, was twice as large as the first one.

"I am going to allow you all to come inside because I cannot determine any other course of action that will not initiate a time-consuming ruckus. However, I will require you all to stay out of my way. The operation is delicate and I will need to concentrate fully on each step. Even the slightest interruption could cause things to end... badly.

"Harpur Diggins, I'm afraid you are going to have to break your promise. I will administer a concoction of herbs that will painlessly end Sok and Arthur's lives and eliminate any lasting damage to their bodies, which must be pristine in order for them to first be revived and then to survive the revival process.

"Sok and Arthur, I will need you both to remove those cuffs from your arms."

Everyone, except Ralph and Holly looked at the cuffs. Anayah had put them there back in the lair to keep Sok and Arthur from wandering off. It seemed to Sok that, since they had indeed wandered off, the spell must be broken. He tugged at the leather tie that bound it in place. Nothing happened. The knot that held it didn't budge. Sok tugged harder, but the harder he pulled, the tighter the cuff felt around his wrist.

"I kind of forgot about this thing," Sok said. "It looks like it's not going to let me take it off. Arthur, you try."

Arthur looked at Sok's hand turning purple from the pressure. "I'd rather not," he said. "I don't need my hand to fall off due to gangrene." Then he turned to Harpur. "Why didn't my cuff tighten up like that when I broke my arm? It just seemed to naturally conform to the swelling."

"Probably because you didn't try to take it off. They're obviously not activated to keep you close to Anayah, but they're still enchanted with her wards. She's the only one who can take them off," Harpur said.

"That is a problem," Bon said. "Until those cuffs are off, we will not be able to proceed with the operation."

Silence.

Followed shortly by the ruckus Bon was trying to avoid.

"What's the cuff got to do with anything?"

"There's got to be some way to get it off?"

"Come off you stupid thing!"

"What are we going to do now?"

"Isn't there anything you can do, Bon?"

"Somebody, do something. It hurts!"

Finally, Harpur turned to Bon and took him aside. "What is the problem with the Orhowyn damned cuffs?"

"My apologies. I thought it was a leather cuff. I am not familiar with the properties of Orhowyn damned cuffs. Although, I am certain that enchanted leather cuffs are a problem. I will search my files for Orhowyn damned cuffs to see if they are an issue, whether enchanted or not." The android assumed a blank look as he scanned his internal files for the information he was looking for.

Harpur's face contorted into exasperation and he pinched the bridge of his nose. "Bon," he said with restraint, "it is a leather cuff. Just tell me what the problem is with it."

Bon straightened his head and looked at Harpur. "I'm afraid I do not understand. You called it an Orhowyn damned cuff. Is that a type of leather on your world?"

"Sure. Yes. Yes, Orhowyn damned is a type of leather on my world. Now, please tell me why it has to come off before we can... do what we have to do here?"

"It's leather."

"And why is leather a problem?" *Why can't anyone just give me a straight answer?*

"Leather is a problem because when animals die, their life forces can remain embedded in their bodies. If any of that life force releases and mixes with the souls of either Arthur or Sok, it could cause them to take on some of the personality of the animal. And it's enchanted."

"And the enchantment could interfere with the process?"

"It is possible."

"So, let me see if I understand this. Let's say that the leather in that cuff came from a donkey and some of that donkey's life force is still in the leather. At some point some if that life force is released and mixes with the already mixed souls of Arthur and Sok. Then, when you have separated Sok's soul from Arthur's soul and returned them to their respective bodies, Sok and Arthur might start acting like a donkey?"

"Yes."

"They are already a couple of asses. No one would even notice!" Harpur dead-panned this supposition perfectly.

Again, Bon took a moment to process what Harpur said. "I would hate to think what would happen if the leather was from a muskink."

"I assure you the leather is not from a muskink. But I get your point."

Sok's hand was darkening alarmingly. "Harpur. I need to do something soon," he begged.

"If I cut off their arms, can you put them back on later?" Harpur asked Bon.

"I can, indeed. I'm an excellent physician, fully programmed for such a surgery."

"Great!" Harpur turned back to Sok. "Come here, you two."

"No!" Sok clutched his hand even closer to his chest. He winced in pain.

"No!" Arthur moved closer to Sok.

Silence.

Harpur was at the end of his tether. He stood there looking from one person to the other. He needed to think. He needed to figure this out. And soon. The morning was advancing far more rapidly than he felt comfortable with. It was only a matter of time before Anayah and the others showed up. He had to get Arthur and Sok sorted out and find a Boundary back to Thraeh so he could get back to his Whyte Avenue lair, where he intended to count gold coins and sleep for about a month. If he never saw another elf or human... Well, he could live quite happily like that.

His gaze finally settled on Bon. The android, he reasoned, was the best route forward. He had resources that none of the rest of them had. But first he had to deal with the cuffs. Apparently, cutting arms off, even if they could be reattached later, was not a popular solution. He could, of course, force them to let him do it. But that was just mean. And it was Sok and Arthur. And, for the love of Orhowyn, he couldn't be that mean to them.

Orhowyn's four-inch fangs! I can't take much more.

He walked over to the spot where Sok was rocking back and forth in agony on the ground and knelt down beside him. Placing a gentle hand on the elf's shoulder, Harpur said, "Sok? I'm going to try something to help ease your hand. I don't know if it will work, but I want to try. Are you okay with that?"

Sok nodded.

"Okay. Can you hold your hand out for me?"

Sok reached a shaking hand toward the dragon-wizard, who tapped it gently with his walking stick. Sok felt a tingling sensation and then a sharp, but blessedly quick, jolt of pain. When he looked at the appendage it had shrunk to the size of one of Hiro's tiny hands. Sok screamed! Not in pain, but in shock and horror. The cuff, however remained its normal size, hovering around his shrunken wrist. Even Harpur had to wince at the weirdness of the result.

"How does that feel?"

"It hurts!" Sok was mortified.

"Yeah, but does it hurt because the circulation is coming back?"

"I think so?" Sok wasn't sure.

"Good. Let me know if it doesn't get better in a little while." With that Harpur stood up and beckoned Bon to follow him away from the group. To Arthur he said, "Stay with him."

Bon did a double take as he walked past Sok and saw the bizarre hand. He caught up to the dragon-wizard and waited for Harpur to tell him what he wanted.

As confident as he could be that they would be okay, Harpur turned his back on his companions and led Bon to the aperture in the Sphere. He stood as close as he could without letting any part of himself enter the sacred space. His view was discouragingly limited to what appeared to be a small vestibule devoid of decoration. The walls, ceiling and floor all looked as if they were constructed of the same material that the Sphere itself was made of. No information was to be gained from it. He turned his attention back to Bon.

"Any suggestions?" While Harpur had about a million questions, he chose to let Bon think he was in charge.

"I have compiled several possible solutions. I have also analysed each of them and rejected all with less than a fifty percent chance of bringing about the desired outcome as I understand it."

"Okay. So how many suggestions does that leave us with?"

"None."

"None? As in zero?" Harpur wasn't even surprised.

"That is correct. The only way we can move forward right away is if Sok and Arthur were to permit you to cut off their hands, but since they are opposed to that course of action, we are left without any other options."

Harpur looked over at the elf. "You're sure you can reattach them later?"

"I am positive."

"And it will work? They won't be crippled or in any way disfigured?"

"It will be as if it never happened."

Harpur looked over at the elf again. "Is there anything—anything at all—that would prevent you from reattaching their hands?"

"Not that I am aware of."

"They don't have to enter the Sphere? You can do it out here?"

"I can do it out here."

"Can you cut off their hands after you kill them and then do the operation?"

"I only have a few seconds to collect their souls after they die. Even if they are contained in the tent, any delay could mean losing portions of their souls."

"What if they were unconscious first? Can we knock them out, cut off their hands and then kill them?"

Bon considered Harpur's proposition. "I believe that would work."

"Alright. Get things ready. We're not going to tell them what we're doing. Just act as if you are doing the operation." He started to walk away from the android, then paused. "What do I do with the hands while you're performing the... uh, operation?"

"I will provide you with containers to put them into that will keep them preserved until I am ready to reattach them." Bon said. "But how are you going to convince them that I can perform the operation now that they know about the dangers of the cuffs?"

Harpur sighed and scratched the back of his head. "I'll tell them you found a way."

Bon nodded and disappeared inside the Sphere, presumably to retrieve the containers for the hands. He tried smiling as he approached Sok and Arthur, but decided that might scare them more than anything at this point. Better to act normal, don't raise any suspicion.

"Looks like we're good to go," he said. "Bon thought of a way to block any residual animal life force in your cuffs. Why don't you head over to the tent? Bon is getting one last thing he needs and then we'll get this done and over with."

Arthur stood up, but didn't move. "What is he going to do?"

Harpur looked Arthur in the eye and lied. "Bon remembered that he has shields he can put around the cuffs to contain any life force that might be released. He's gone into the Sphere to get them."

"He just remembered, did he?" Arthur made no attempt to hide his skepticism.

"Yep! Now, go. Bon will be right out."

Arthur stared at Harpur for several long seconds, looking for signs of deceit. If he found any, he opted not to confront it and turned away to go to the tent. He took five steps and collapsed, well and truly unconscious, on the ground. He didn't have time to register what was happening to him. Still, Harpur guessed he would hear about it later.

Now for Sok.

Sok was only slightly alarmed by Arthur passing out. He was, truth be told, more alarmed by the grim look on Harpur's face.

"What did you do to him?" Sok called out.

"Just helped him to relax," Harpur said, stopping by Arthur's inert body to make sure his face wasn't buried in the dirt and he could still breathe.

"That's pretty relaxed," Sok observed.

"How's your hand?" Harpur asked as he drew next to the elf.

Sok had tucked his odd appendage into his vest so he wouldn't have to look at it. "It feels okay," he conceded.

"That's good." He helped Sok to his feet and guided him past Arthur toward the tent.

Just then, Bon came out of the Sphere with the boxes. Harpur moved to block Sok's view of them. Sok might be an idiot, but he had moments of insight that Harpur didn't need to happen just then. A giggle from Holly was the distraction Harpur needed. When Sok looked in her direction, Harpur tapped him with the walking stick and caught him as he, too, fell unconscious. He carried the elf into the tent and laid him on the floor. Then he went back for Arthur.

Bon followed Harpur into the tent and Ralph and Holly followed Bon. When they were all assembled, Harpur knelt beside Sok and lifted the deformed hand. This was harder than it should have been, but Harpur was committed. He tapped Sok's hand with his walking stick. It shook for a second or two and then, with an audible and wince-inducing pop, returned to its normal size. Harpur gently stretched Sok's arm out away from his body and reached for Sok's dagger, but Bon interrupted him.

"Use this." Bon handed Harpur a long, thin wire that looked like a garrotte and instructed Harpur to wrap around Sok's arm at the point where he wanted to amputate the hand. "It will cauterize the arm as you amputate. Just pull the end sharply and it will cut cleanly through."

As Harpur wrapped the wire around Sok's arm, it began to glow blue. He realized that it had been infused with healing magic and that made him feel a little better about what he was going to do. He took a deep breath and pulled hard on the ends of the wire, which sliced through the flesh and bone with no resistance. Sok's hand fell away from his arm and landed next to Harpur's foot.

Bon immediately wrapped the stump in a cloth that glowed blue like the wire while Harpur lifted the severed hand and put it inside one of the boxes. "I'm so sorry. I will fix this," Harpur whispered to his unconscious friend.

Harpur repeated the procedure on Arthur with no less apprehension. He hated duping them this way, but he had no choice. When he was done, Holly took the box with Arthur's hand in it from him and cradled it like an infant. Harpur didn't question her. He stood up and moved out of Bon's way so he could get on with the operation.

This was not Mysturnian technology; magical or otherwise. "Where are you from?" Harpur asked, realizing that an android was not Mysturnian technology either.

"Not here," Bon replied.

Harpur, though curious, didn't see much point in pursuing this. "Sok's hand didn't look too good." The ugly, purple swelling was deeply concerning.

"The box will slow the effects of the cuff. The faster we get this done, the faster I can reattach his hand. Then you can shrink it again. That will have to do until you can find the witch that put the cuff on him and get it properly removed." Bon's matter-of-fact way of expressing things was appreciated by the dragon-wizard.

While Bon prepared the tent for the operation, Harpur watched his every move. He had no idea what he would do if Bon did anything remotely threatening. All he could do was stand by and hope this android was on their side. Holly and Ralph stood silently and oddly solemnly near Arthur's head. Harpur stood next to Sok and let Bon proceed.

Bon began by mixing a blood-red potion in two small vials, which he set aside on the table. Then he mixed a neon-pink potion in two other vials and handed them to Harpur. "When I tell you, pour that on their foreheads."

Harpur nodded.

Next, Bon poured the blood-red elixir first into Arthur's mouth and then into Sok's. He then returned to the table where he quickly mixed a dark green potion that he poured into two large glass vases. A few moments later, Sok and Arthur shuddered and then relaxed. They were both quite dead. Harpur couldn't help but feel a pang of grief.

Holly laid the box containing Arthur's severed hand on the ground. Then she and Ralph, at the moment of Arthur's expiry, each placed a hand on one of his shoulders and faded away. A bright, golden-pink mist spiraled up and away from Arthur. A similar mist rose from Sok's body. Bon held the large vases containing the dark green liquid up and the mists drifted into them. As soon as the last of the mist entered the vases, Bon covered the tops with what looked to Harpur like rubber stoppers. He held the vases firmly and started to shake them like a bartender mixing martinis. He shook the vases a few times, then looked at the contents. Some of the golden-pink mist was now dark green. He shook them some more. Some more of the mist was green. Bon repeated this a few more times until there was no change in the amount of dark green mist.

"The potion has sought out the souls that don't belong and dyed them green," he explained to Harpur. "Now I have to remove it from the vases without losing any of it."

He stood next to the table and placed the vases into stands with small candles underneath them, which he lit with a match. Harpur was intrigued by this mixture of magic and the mundane. He concluded that Bon possessed no magic of his own. Rather he utilized magical properties in ordinary ingredients and manipulated them... scientifically? It was all somewhat fascinating and he almost wished he had time to interview Bon about it.

Bon then placed two smaller vases in smaller stands next to the large vases and inserted a length of tube into a stopper covering their openings, pushing them down about half way into the vase. The dark green mist, prompted by the heat from the candle, rose to the top of the large vases, hovering above the golden-pink mist that had settled lower to the bottom. When Bon was satisfied that the souls were completely separated, he took a metal rod and punctured the stoppers with it. The green mist swirled and churned like a miniature, inverted tornado around the rod. It was seeking an escape from the heat in the vase. Bon slowly began to withdraw the rod from the vase and just when the rod was about to be fully removed, he pushed the hose into the holes in the stoppers. The green mist rushed into the hose and ran into the smaller vases at the other end.

As the green mist flowed out of the vases, the golden-pink mist rose as well. Just before it, too, started to flow into the hoses, Bon blew out the candle and pulled the hoses out. He placed his thumb over the open ends of the hoses and placed adhesive patches over the holes in the stoppers. He was fast, but not fast enough to prevent a tiny tendril of golden-pink mist to escape from Arthur's vase.

"Keep your eye on that," Bon calmly instructed Harpur. "Don't let it out of your sight."

Harpur was alarmed, but did as he was bid while Bon secured the dark green mist in the smaller vases. Once that was accomplished, he picked up an even smaller vase and a corresponding stopper and looked in the direction that Harpur's gaze was tracing the path of the escaped soul mist. He deftly scooped the runaway mist into the vase and trapped it with the stopper.

"Is that going to be a problem?" Harpur asked.

"I do not believe so," Bon said. It wasn't as reassuring as Harpur would have preferred, but it was better than a definite yes. "Now I am going to put their souls back into their bodies. To do that, I'm going to have to make a small incision in their foreheads. As soon as I do, you must pour that potion into the cuts I make. Then I will pour the souls into the cuts. That potion will attract the souls back into their bodies. It will also heal the cut so that the souls cannot leak back out. I will start with Sok. Are you ready?"

Harpur nodded.

Bon cut an X in the middle of Sok's forehead and Harpur poured the neon-pink liquid into it. The inner corners of the X appeared to retract and a hole opened up in Sok's head. Instead of bone and brain being exposed, the hole looked like an empty, black shaft running deep into his head. Bon held up the vase containing Sok's soul. It was no longer dark green; the dye had faded and it was once again the same golden-pink that it should be. He poured it into the hole, which sucked it in and closed back up as if it had never been there. As soon as they were done with Sok, they moved to Arthur's side and returned his soul to him the same way.

"Everything is going perfectly," Bon said to Harpur. "Though I have no explanation for how or why your other friends disappeared."

"Trust me," Harpur said, "I don't think they will be missed all that much. Can we get their hands reattached now?"

"I suggest that we revive them first. Though, you might want to render them unconscious again while I reattach their arms."

"I'm way ahead of you, Bon," Harpur said, agreeing whole-heartedly that unconscious was the way to go.

Bon was the epitome of efficiency as he administered yet another potion, this one a silvery-teal colour, by pouring it into Sok's and Arthur's mouths. Since they were dead and unable to swallow, he had Harpur sit Arthur up so gravity could do its thing while he did the same for Sok. An interminable minute later, their bodies began to tremble and shake. When the convulsions ended, they gasped for breath. Their eyes opened and they both tried to sit up on their own. Harpur tapped them with his walking stick and they slumped back into comas.

Bon removed the cloth from Sok's stump and the hand from the box. It was purple and swollen and Harpur wondered if Sok wouldn't be better off with a hook. But Bon assured him that once the cuff could be removed, there would no indication that Sok had ever been separated from his hand. He need not ever know it even happened.

"You can follow my lead to reattach Arthur's hand if you like," Bon said.

The dragon-wizard and the android worked together to complete the task at hand, so to speak.

Bon lined up the hand with the arm and then slipped a black sleeve over both. The sleeve immediately formed to fit Sok's arm and then it began to shimmer and undulate. Harpur was dubious.

"Won't the cuff interfere with... whatever is happening here?" he asked Bon.

"The sleeve will ignore any foreign material and simply work on the flesh and bones. But you will need to shrink his hand again when it's done. I will construct a glove of sorts that he can wear so it doesn't look so unnatural until you can find a way to reverse the spell and remove the cuff."

"Where did you say you were from?" Harpur hoped for some more information about this remarkable being.

"I did not say where I am from."

Harpur didn't understand the secrecy, but he decided to let the android have his privacy.

It took about twenty minutes or so for the sleeve to complete its work. When it stopped shimmering and undulating, Bon announced that they were done. The purple, swollen blob that was Sok's hand looked awful, but there was no sign of the fact that it had ever been parted from the rest of the elf. Harpur tapped it with his walking stick and they watched as it shrunk away from the cuff. This time, Harpur didn't shrink it quite as much as before; just enough to pull it away from the restricting cuff so the blood flow could return. Bon rummaged in his satchel and produced a jar of some foul-smelling salve that he gently rubbed into Sok's skin. Within seconds, the purple started to fade to blue and the swelling began to recede. Other than the obvious gap between the cuff and the arm, the hand itself looked almost normal. Together, Harpur and Bon elected to forego the glove.

"Can I wake them up now?" Harpur asked.

"You may," Bon said with emphasis on the may. "I will put everything away now."

This odd declaration, not to mention grammatical correction, only served to deepen Harpur's growing sense of trepidation. Rather than explore it further, he simply nodded. While Bon gathered, sorted and stored away all of the paraphernalia from the operation, Harpur tapped Sok and Arthur back to consciousness. They sat up and stretched as if they had just awoken from a peaceful night's sleep.

Arthur was first to notice the change in his location. The last thing he recalled was walking toward the tent to get ready to be killed.

"Um... What's happening?"

"Arthur, you're awake!" Sok said.

Arthur looked at Sok sitting beside him. "Am I not supposed to be?"

Harpur intervened before this got complicated. "Alright, then! We're all done. What do you think about us getting out of here?"

"What do you mean we're all done?" Arthur was suspicious.

"We're done. It's finished. You have your souls back and now I'm going to find out where the closest Boundary back to Thraeh is." Harpur turned away to go talk to Bon.

"Where're Ralph and Holly?" Sok asked. The absence of the nearly naked couple was both disconcerting and a relief.

"They are gone," Arthur said. He looked like he was trying to recall a dream. "They told me their work was finished and that I had done well."

Harpur raised his eyebrows. "When did they say that?"

"Must have been while we were..." Arthur didn't finish the thought.

Arthur looked at Sok, who was looking at his hand. Other than being only slightly smaller than it should have been, it felt normal. "Arthur, how long were we asleep?"

"No idea."

"Do you feel strange?"

"I feel strangely normal," Arthur replied.

Sok continued to stare at his hand. He flexed it and made a fist. The cuff looked somewhat worn and maybe even a little bit shriveled, but it continued to hover around his wrist. He dared not touch it for fear of it tightening again.

Arthur was staring at Harpur, who was talking to Bon, who was finished putting away all the paraphernalia from the operation. He ushered his guests out of the tent, and gratefully accepted Harpur's assistance in carrying out the table and the satchel. Then he tapped the tent to collapse it and began folding it up into its original neatly-folded state.

While Sok and Arthur speculated about what had happened while they were unconscious, Harpur asked Bon about the nearest Boundary. When Harpur was sure he understood Bon's directions, he shook the android's hand and thanked him for his help. Bon retreated back into the Sphere with his apparatus and the aperture closed behind him. And

Harpur beckoned to the man and the elf to follow him away from the Sphere so he could transform.

Arthur nudged Sok with his elbow. "I think we're booked on another Dragon Air flight," he said.

Sok finally looked away from his hand. "A what?"

"Come on, Sok. I think you're going home." Arthur walked over to Harpur and took his walking stick for safe keeping.

Harpur transformed into a dragon and held out his hands. Without questioning him, Arthur climbed into Harpur's outstretched hand, clutching the walking stick close so it wouldn't be able to fall during their flight. While Sok did the same thing, without the walking stick, Arthur looked up at the huge body that loomed over him and noticed the missing scale on Harpur's chest. *When did that happen?* he wondered. Then he tucked the information away for later and settled to wait for the air sickness to settle in to him.

Chapter 11

Arthur settled in with much more success than the expected air sickness did. Not even the stomach-dropping liftoff was enough to engage it and by the time the grassy plain was behind them, he relaxed enough to peek beyond Harpur's talons and take in a bit of the spectacular view. He was beginning to feel the pangs of hunger, not having eaten since the platter of meat and cheese... *When was that? Last night?* Arthur wasn't sure, so he focused on the panoramic hills and forests and rivers and lakes that rolled past beneath him.

One dragon hand over, Sok was not engaging in the view as he had on previous flights. There was no hollering or shouting or wiggling about going on. He seemed uncharacteristically withdrawn. Arthur had expected more enthusiasm for a return to the elf's home world, but Sok did not appear to relish the prospect at all.

"You okay over there?" Arthur called over the wind.

"I guess." Sok shrugged.

"I'll bet you're looking forward to being on Thraeh again, hey?"

"I guess." Sok didn't bother to shrug.

"Well, I'm looking forward to seeing where you come from? Do you think we'll meet any other elves while we're there?"

Sok didn't answer.

But Harpur did. "We aren't going to be there long enough for you to meet anyone. Right after we Bound, I'm going to melt the coin back together... You do both still have your halves, don't you?"

"I've got mine," Arthur affirmed.

"Yeah," Sok sulked.

"I'm going to melt the coin back together and Arthur is going to give it back to Sok. Then we are going straight to Braydon Wood and Arthur and I are going to Bound back to Whyte Ave. And that will be the end of all of this."

Sok said nothing.

Arthur digested the plan for a bit. "What about the prophecy?"

"What about it?" Harpur asked.

"Well, aren't I supposed to become a king or something?"

Harpur thought about what Arthur was asking. He knew that it wasn't going to be as simple as he wanted it to be, but he needed some time to himself. "I'm going to get Sok home, you home and then I'm going to spend some time in my lair. Alone!"

No details in that speech, but Arthur had confirmation about what had happened at the Sphere that morning. "Harpur?" he called out.

"Yes, Arthur."

"How long were we dead?"

"Not long. Ten minutes or so."

Ten minutes? "Shouldn't we have brain damage after that much time?"

That was about as loaded a question as Harpur had ever heard! But he couldn't come up with a clever retort, so he opted to ease Arthur's mind. "Bon took care of that part. You have nothing to worry about."

They flew on for about an hour or so in a silence for which Harpur was equally grateful for and perturbed by. He was worried about Sok's unusual stillness. At the same time, it was a relief not to have to concern himself with losing his grip and dropping the elf because he was squirming around all the time. Whatever was eating the elf was eating at Harpur, but there was nothing he could do about it just then. Besides, he still couldn't shake the sense of urgency that was driving him to get this last piece finished before disaster struck. The longer they remained on Mysturna, the greater the chance that they would cross paths with Anayah again. She was a matter he knew he would have to face at some point. But not now. Not here.

"I need to pee," Arthur said.

Harpur didn't respond, but that was because he was looking for a place to land. He'd been expecting this pretty much since they'd taken off and was thankful, they had managed to get this far without needing a pit stop.

"And I'm hungry!" Arthur couldn't ignore the pangs any longer.

"Give me a minute. I'm looking for a place to land." Harpur banked to the right, having spotted a clearing on a hillside that would accommodate him. He circled it twice to make sure it was safe before alighting in a flower-dappled meadow. He released his passengers and while one darted off toward a stand of trees, the other ambled over to a boulder and sat down with a heavy sigh.

Harpur couldn't decide if this was genuine melancholy or if Sok was being over-dramatic. He conjured up some meat and cheese and ale again. It wasn't the most exciting repast, but it would fill their bellies and keep their strength up. He would have rather fed on a fat cow or deer, but if he transformed back into human form and ate what was before him, it would tie him over in dragon form until he could indulge his dragon nature with something more satisfying. He transformed into a man and took some food to Sok, who accepted it with an exaggerated sigh and mumbled thanks.

Definitely manufacturing a bit of drama about something, Harpur concluded.

He was just about to ask the elf what was bothering him when Arthur returned from the bushes, making a beeline for the food.

"How come I'm the only one who ever has to pee?" He asked, then took a bite of meat and cheese.

"You're the only one who feels he has to announce it all the time," Harpur said, then also took a bite of meat and cheese.

"Seriously. What's up with that?" This time he took a long drink of ale.

"I don't want to go to prison!" Sok wailed.

"What's that got to do with anything?" Arthur was confused.

"You're not going to go to prison. You're in Pollybush. Remember?" Harpur reminded the elf of the ruse.

"Yeah, but I can't stay in Pollybush forever," Sok whined. "I wonder how my grandmother is doing."

Harpur rolled his eyes and took another bite of meat and cheese.

"Is that what all this moping is about?" Arthur asked. He'd clued in.

"I wasn't moping!" Sok returned to the defensive.

"You were so moping," Harpur stated. "But it did make for a pleasant flight this far. So, feel free to continue moping."

"I thought you were mad at me," Arthur said.

"I am mad at you," Sok said.

"What did I do?" It was Arthur's turn to be defensive.

"You know what you did."

"No, tell me."

"You nearly cost me my hand!" Sok snapped. Then paused. "Wait! Harpur, did you cut off our hands while we were unconscious?"

"Only for a few minutes," Harpur confirmed.

Sok gasped. "How could you?"

"I'm sorry, Sok, but I had no other choice. We had to get your souls sorted out and we couldn't do it with those cuffs on your arms. Which reminds me..."

Sok wanted to protest, but Harpur's digression sounded ominous. "Reminds you of what?"

"We better get going. The Entanglement is still happening and the longer it takes us to get to Thraeh, the greater the chance that your souls will leak back into each other. And I have no intention of going back to that Sphere to sort you out again."

With that, Harpur stood and waved away the remnants of their meal. He moved away to give himself room to transform back into a dragon.

"Hey!" Arthur did protest. "I wasn't finished my ale."

"Good!" Harpur quipped. "Maybe we can get to the Boundary without needing to make another pit stop. Now let's go!"

Arthur did his duty with Harpur's walking stick, tucking it securely in next to himself as Harpur's hand closed around him. Sok positioned himself in Harpur's other hand so he could see the view while they flew.

"Sok," Harpur said before he launched them into the air, "I wasn't joking about the moping. Sit still!" He launched them into the air.

"Look at that!" Sok yelled a few seconds later as he pointed at a muskink slithering its way to the spot they had just abandoned.

"And be quiet!" Harpur had seen it too. Which was the real reason he had hastened their departure. But he wasn't going to tell his passengers that.

Harpur did not like having to fly in the daylight. The best he could do was to stay low and hope that no one spotted them. Of course, that meant that he lost the advantage of the longer view flying higher would give him. At the same time, it reduced the likelihood of them being spotted from a distance. It was the lesser of two evils and Harpur resigned himself to hoping for the best.

They had quite a way to go. The Boundary they were headed toward was on the other side of the mountains that they were then only just beginning to climb over. He was looking for a split peak that looked, according to Bon, like a cloven hoof. The Boundary was directly below that in a valley formed millennia ago by a meteorite that had struck Mysturna and was responsible for wiping out a vicious race of giants that had once roamed this world.

"The crumbling ruins of a statue to an ancient god is right next to the Boundary," Bon had said. "You cannot miss it."

"Anything I need to know about this Boundary?" Harpur had asked.

"Yes. You need to start it spinning and you must all go through together. The Boundary never takes you to the same place on Thraeh twice in a row. If you do not go through together, you will all end up in different places."

"Good to know," Harpur had said. "What are the chances that we will end up near Braydon Wood?"

"Precisely one in three thousand five hundred nineteen. But there is a fifty-six percent chance you will end up in the Kingdom of Epoh."

"And how do we get it to spin?" Harpur had asked as he processed the possible difficulties they would need to deal with after they Bounded.

"Just pull on it. When it is spinning fast enough, it will glow the universal colour to go."

"Green," Harpur had confirmed.

"No! Orange," Bon would have been alarmed had he been capable of emotion. "Purple for stop, blue for slow down and orange for go."

Okay, Harpur thought to himself, thankful for this vital information. "Where are you from again?"

"Not here."

When he needed a wider view, he would rise up and scan ahead, then drop back down, but as the afternoon wore on and he still saw no sign of the split peak, he began to worry that he might have passed it. There was nothing left but to take a chance and fly higher. He rose up above the peaks, banking in a wide circle and searched the breath-taking vista that stretched out below him. Nothing as far as he could see, and that was a long way, looked like a cloven hoof. "You cannot miss it," Bon had said. Apparently, Bon was wrong.

He reversed his course and flew back in the direction he had come from on the other side of the mountain range. With the suns now on that side of the mountains, he knew he had several hours of daylight left, but that didn't stave his sense of urgency.

Arthur noticed the change in direction. "Why are we going back?" he called out.

"I might have overshot our destination," Harpur replied.

"What are we looking for?" Arthur asked.

"A split peak that looks like a cloven hoof." Harpur kept scanning the peaks.

"We passed that about a while ago," Sok said.

Harpur's large dragon eyes rolled upward in consternation. "Why didn't you say anything?"

"I did. I said, 'Look at that weird mountain.'"

To Sok's credit, he had been doing his best to keep still and follow the rules. And he didn't know that they were looking for a weird mountain, but Harpur was dubious. How could the elf have seen it when he missed it? He recalled Sok saying something about a weird mountain. He made a mental note not to completely ignore the elf from now on. A *while* suddenly seemed like a long time.

They had been on the south side of the mountain range when Sok had seen the weird mountain. It may not look the same from the north side, so Harper angled back in a south-westerly direction hoping that Sok would recognize it again. He flew on knowing that no matter what, he would have to land soon. While he could fly all night if he had to, Sok and Arthur—especially Arthur—were getting cold at this high altitude.

A short while later, Sok shouted that he could see the split peak they were looking for. "On the left!" he said. Harpur looked to his left, but saw nothing that resembled a cloven hoof.

"Where?"

"Right there," Sok pointed. "Right beside us." Then, "Right behind us."

Harpur had flown past the peak that Sok was so adamant was the one they wanted. He turned to the left and circled around to approach it from the other direction.

Arthur craned his neck to see what Sok was pointing at and there—right beside them—was a split peak that looked exactly like a giant cloven hoof.

"I see it!" Arthur shouted. "It's right there."

"You're both daft!" Harpur sounded frustrated. "I don't see a split peak."

"I'm telling you," Arthur shouted, "it's right there. You just flew past it again."

Harpur crossed the mountain tops and swung in again from his left. Then he finally saw it and when he looked down, he also saw a forested valley that looked like a deep bowl at the foot of the mountain. Amid the trees, he could see the top of an enormous statue poking through the canopy. The mountain above it was split, but it didn't really look like a cloven hoof to Harpur. He was just glad that the valley fit the description well enough that it made it worth checking out. The problem was that there was no place in the valley for him to land. The nearest clearing was a good mile to the north-west. It would have to do. He could land there, feed his passengers and then hike back with them to the valley. More time would be wasted, but he figured they could still get there and get through the Boundary—if it was the right valley—before dark. He looked again at the mountain. *Close enough,* he decided and landed in the clearing.

While Sok and Arthur stretched the kinks out, Harpur stretched up to his full height raising his head above the trees so he could look again at the mountain that was supposed to look like a cloven hoof. It was supposed to be an obvious landmark. *"You cannot miss it,"* rang in Harpur's mind. The only distinct feature he could see was that its peak had a slight indentation between two rounded mounds of blueish-black rock. Rather than dwell on it, Harpur transformed once again and retrieved his walking stick from Arthur. He wanted to find the valley and the Boundary as soon as possible. There was no time to tarry over this incongruity. Either they were in the right place or they weren't.

He conjured up some meat and cheese, adding some bread this time. Sok and Arthur accepted the food without complaint and were just about to sit down on a fallen tree to eat it when Harpur announced that they would have to eat while they walked.

"It will take us at least an hour to get to the valley," he explained, "and I want to get us through the Boundary before nightfall."

"No ale?" Sok asked.

"We're walking?" Arthur asked.

"Is that a problem?" Harpur asked.

"Yes," Sok said.

"Yes," Arthur said.

"Why?" Harpur asked.

"I'm thirsty," Sok said.

"I'm not keen on walking through a forest," Arthur said. "They tend not to be very friendly on this planet."

"Bon assured me that this particular forest was harmless," Harpur lied. He inwardly admonished himself for not clarifying this with the android and grudgingly had to acknowledge Arthur's legitimate concern. He hoped Bon had not left out anything important. Like murderous trees.

Arthur noticed him touch his chest where the wound from the missing scale still ached, but said nothing. Harpur seemed a little out of sorts and Arthur wondered if the wound was affecting him in some way other than just physical. The fact that Harpur hadn't seen the mountain was odd. *It's a huge hoof, for god's sake.* You really couldn't miss it.

He took a bite of the meat and cheese and bread that Harpur had conjured and was dismayed to find it tasted more like cardboard than meat and cheese and bread. It was pretty awful. Dots began to connect in Arthur's head. That wound—whatever it was—was doing something to Harpur. At least that is what made the most sense to Arthur under the circumstances. He, too, wanted to get off Mysturna as soon as possible.

"Let's go!" Arthur chirped as he tossed his food away and marched toward the edge of the clearing.

Harpur watched Arthur's purposeful leadership in action until he reached the treeline. "Arthur?" he called.

"What?" Arthur stopped and turned back to face his companions.

"It's this way." Harpur pointed in the opposite direction and waited for Arthur to jog back across the clearing to join him and Sok and head the right way.

"So, no ale?" Sok repeated as they entered the forest.

As their trek to the valley they were looking for began, Harpur kept up a brisk pace, clearing a path for them whenever the underbrush was too thick. He left fallen trees where they lay, trusting that Arthur could scramble over them. Sok was deftly hopping along, easily hurdling tree trunks. He was quite at home in the woods and though he longed to run ahead, he stayed close to Harpur and Arthur. He hadn't forgotten the Forest of Dheersha either. That was not an experience he was in any hurry to repeat.

They stopped after about fifteen minutes and Harpur had Sok climb a tree to make sure they were still headed in the right direction. While the elf expertly scaled the tree, Arthur took advantage of the brief respite to get his breath back. With hands on his knees, he inhaled deeply until his heartrate restored itself to normal.

"I'm not carrying you," Harpur said.

"I'm good," Arthur gasped between breaths.

Sok, when he returned to the ground, suggested that they veer slightly to the right. Harpur adjusted the course accordingly and set out again, albeit at a somewhat slower pace for Arthur's sake. The ground from this point began to slope upward and grew steeper as they moved closer to the mountains. Harpur had them stop again ten minutes later to have Sok climb another tree and report any need for further course corrections. Arthur rested and recovered from the exertion and then they carried on.

They stopped twice more so Arthur didn't have a heart attack and so Sok could ensure they were still on the right course before they came to the base of a ridge that jutted up from the forest floor. It was about twenty-five feet high, a steep bank of rock and earth that formed a wall around the valley. Harpur had expected this. His birds-eye view from above had prepared him for an obstacle. It had not prepared him for an obstacle as sheer and unclimbable as the one that was now barring their way forward.

A sweaty, red-faced Arthur slumped at the base of the ridge, panting freely and more than content to let Harpur and Sok figure out what to do next.

"There has to be a way in," Harpur reasoned aloud. "It's a monument to an ancient race of giants."

"Giants?" Sok asked.

"Don't worry. They are long-dead." Harpur studied the ridge for any sign of a nearby entrance. "Do you think you could climb this?" he asked the elf.

Sok, too, was studying the rockface. "Not without a rope of some kind. It's too steep and there aren't many places to grip."

There wasn't enough room between the rock and the trees for Harpur to transform and fly them over. The only other option was to walk the perimeter and hope to find an opening. But if Sok could get to the top, he could scout out the situation and, with luck, save them some time. Harpur looked around for some way to get Sok to the top of the ridge. Seventy feet to their left, the trees grew within a few feet of it.

"What if you climbed one of those trees," Harpur pointed, "and then jumped to the top of the ridge?"

Sok followed Harpur's finger and quickly calculated the risk. "I don't know if I could jump, but I might be able to swing over." He was already moving toward the trees.

While Sok chose the best tree to climb, an enormous deciduous with broad, green leaves, Harpur hoisted Arthur to his feet and dragged him over to where Sok was preparing for his ascent. He was not going to allow them to get separated on the ground. Once Sok was at the top and could tell them if there was an easy way in, he'd decide what to do next. If he had to, he'd piggy-back Arthur up the tree himself and swing them both over. Hopefully, it wouldn't come to that.

The pair on the ground watched the elf's graceful springs from one limb to the next until he was all but lost in the dense foliage. The only indication that he was in the tree and still climbing was the shaking of the leaves as Sok's weight, slight as it was, landed on a new branch. He continued to climb until he was a few feet above the ridgeline where the tree's branches were thinner. Choosing a conveniently longer bough that curved up and almost parallel to the ridge, Sok reached up and, hand-over-hand, worked his way away from the trunk until his weight caused it to bend lower and bring him closer to the top of the ridge.

He was now only a few feet above and away from the ridge, which was barely wide enough for one person to stand on before it dropped sharply down in a steep slope toward the valley floor. From his vantage point, Sok could see that the ridge was roughly the same all the way around, forming a bowl at least a half a mile in diameter. He couldn't be sure, but it did not appear that there were any openings. He would have to be on the ridge to get a proper view.

He started to swing his body back and forth, building momentum. The branch swayed with the motion of Sok's body, creaking loudly under the unnatural strain. Sok judged the progress of the widening arc his body made as he dangled from the branch. When he felt he was close enough, he put a little extra oomph into the final swing and released the branch. As he rose up and away from it, he tucked his head down, curled his body into a compact roll and summer-salted down onto the ridge, landing on his feet, but too close to the outer edge.

Below him, Arthur held his breath in horror, certain that the flailing elf was going to tumble backward and fall off the ridge. Harpur moved closer, ready to catch Sok and prevent him from splattering on the ground. But after an interminable ten seconds, Sok regained his balance and fell forward onto his knees. Before the forward momentum could send him sliding head-first down the slope, he threw his body to the side and grabbed the edge of the ridge. After another interminable ten seconds, while he steadied his nerves, Sok pulled himself up and peeked over the edge down at the relieved Harpur and Arthur.

"I'm okay!" Sok hollered from above.

"Can you see an entrance anywhere?" Harpur hollered back. His relief was palpable, but he had to focus on getting himself and Arthur into the valley and to the Boundary.

Sok stood up and, balancing on the narrow ridge top, turned to survey the valley. Trees obscured his view of most of the ridge. He had no idea if there was an entrance through the wall formed by the ridge or not. The relatively small expanse of it that was exposed to him from where he stood yielded nothing. He relayed this discouraging news back down to Harpur.

"I'm going to walk along the edge and look for an opening." Sok turned to his left and started walking. "Follow me," he instructed. Harpur and Arthur had no choice but to follow on the ground.

They walked the perimeter of the ridge wall for a while. The valley bowl within the ridge wall was situated right at the base of the mountain, blending into it and blocking them from going any further in that direction. The good news, though, was that they could walk up the base of the mountain and join Sok on the ridge. From there they could all hike to the centre of the valley and get off this planet. Harpur and Arthur scrambled up to the ridge top and then, with Sok, scrambled down the slope to the valley floor.

Within twenty minutes, they had reached the centre of the valley and the first sun had dipped down below the horizon. In the muted light, the valley took on an eerie and unwelcoming ambiance. The giant, ugly, crumbling statue that they then found themselves standing next to had a gaping mouth and a horned belly that was menacing enough in full daylight. Now it just made Arthur want to keep Harpur and Sok between him and it, which is what he did, casually moving behind them.

"Where's the Boundary?" Sok asked.

"It's supposed to be right next to the statue." Harpur scanned the gloom for a sign of the Boundary.

"Maybe it's on the other side," Sok suggested.

The trio moved around to the other side of the statue. And there, right where Bon had said it would be, was a shimmering, misty puddle on the ground. Harpur had never seen a Boundary like it. In his experience, they were vertical, like windows. This one was flat against the ground and it was small, barely four feet across. For the three of them to get through it at the same time, they would have to huddle together and step in at the same time.

Arthur stepped close to it and leaned over as if he could look through it to Thraeh. All he saw was shimmering mist.

"So, that's a Boundary, huh?" Arthur said. He was expecting something a little more dramatic, like a stargate or something.

"It is," Harpur confirmed.

"So, where are we going to end up when we go in?" Arthur asked.

"Hopefully not in the middle of a desert," Harpur said as he strategized the best way to get them all through together.

"And you're sure it's safe for me to go through it?" Arthur asked.

"Ninety-nine percent sure." Harpur said.

"What's it like?" Arthur asked.

"For Sok and me it's like passing through a wall of water. There's a bit of resistance and then we just pop out on the other side."

"And that's what it'll be like for me?" Arthur asked.

"I don't know. Anabettah said there would be no problem and at this point, that's about all I can tell you." Harpur refused to think about all the things that could go wrong.

"So, what do we do? Just jump in and hope for the best?"

"Pretty much," Harpur said. "But we have to go together. This Boundary is not static, meaning that every time someone goes through, they end up in a different place."

"It's kind of small," Sok observed.

"It kind of is," Harpur agreed.

"Well, lets get this over with," Arthur said, stepping even closer to the edge of the Boundary. "On three... One..."

"Hold on!" Harpur snapped. "First, we have to get it spinning. When it starts glowing orange, we can jump in."

He reached down and felt the edge of the Boundary. To his surprise, there was a well-defined lip that he could grasp. He tightened his hold on it and pulled. The disc started to spin, slowly. He grabbed it again and pulled harder. The disc began to spin faster. A few more pulls and Harpur saw the edges start to glow a dull yellow. He kept pulling, getting it to spin as fast as he could. In a few minutes, the dull yellow glow deepened to mustard, then to orange.

Harpur handed his walking stick to Arthur and told him and Sok to put their arms around his neck. He gathered them both by the waists, lifted them up and jumped into the centre of the Boundary.

Chapter 12

Arthur squeezed his eyes shut and clamped his mouth shut so he wouldn't scream. Not that he would have had time to scream. He barely had time to register the odd tingling sensation that rippled through him before he had the wind knocked out of him by Harpur's heavy largeness landing on top him on a tiled floor.

Sok had let go of Harpur and rolled safely away from them. He bounced up on his feet and looked around. He kicked Harpur in the back with the side of his foot. "Get up!" he whispered hoarsely.

Harpur stood up and pulled the gasping Arthur to his own feet. Arthur struggled for both breath and balance as Harpur extracted his walking stick from Arthur's feeble grip. When Sok thumped him on the back with his fist, Harpur spun around to yell at him to quit kicking and hitting him, but was stopped short by the scene before him.

Harpur, Sok and Arthur were standing in King Gnik's private chambers. King Gnik and a busty red-head were staring back at them from the royal bed where they had been busy... Well, doing what any handsome, single king would be doing in the royal bed with a busty red-head.

After a short, shocked silence, the red-head screamed. King Gnik slapped a hand over her mouth and covered her bustiness up with the royal quilt.

"How did you get in here?" the king demanded.

"Uh... Well... We..." Harpur stammered. Of all the places on Thraeh he had imagined landing, this particular place never occurred to him. He had no explanation prepared, plausible or otherwise, for this situation.

"Guards!" King Gnik shouted.

Harpur turned to his left. Sok turned to his right. Arthur doubled over with a coughing fit and was sandwiched between them as they smashed into each other. Harpur's size and weight sent the others flying backward and sideways, respectively, onto the floor and he was just barely able to leap over them and land next to an open doorway leading out onto an open balcony. He spun back around, grabbing the dazed and sputtering duo and dragged them out onto the balcony. Pushing them over the ornate, stone railing, Harpur leapt over it behind them and in a swooping dive transformed into dragon form and caught the screaming man and thrashing elf in midair. Having no time to otherwise ensure the safety of his walking stick, Harpur had put it in his mouth.

Behind them, Harpur could hear the shouts of the foiled guards who had had to break down the door to the king's chambers to gain entry. The door, locked to prevent any unauthorized entry during the royal romp with the busty red-head, gave little resistance to the armour-clad guards throwing their bulk against it. What had bought Harpur the time he needed for the narrow escape was the heap of armour-clad bulk that had formed approximately in the same spot Harpur, Sok and Arthur had originally landed after falling through the Boundary. Even for well-toned and fit guards, getting up off a floor in full armour was a bit of a feat. By the time they reached the balcony, Harpur and his precariously held passengers were out of arrow range. Not that the guards had bows to begin with. Swords were generally considered sufficient for standing outside the king's private chambers, whether or not they contained a busty red-head.

Harpur got his bearings and used them to bear north-west of the castle toward his lair on Thraeh. Situated as it was on a rocky mountainside above Braydon Wood, it would provide a measure of safety until Harpur could get the coin repaired and get Sok and Arthur to the Braydon Wood Boundary. It was only a matter of time until some knight with a death-wish was dispatched to attempt to exact justice for the king. The location of the lair was no big secret. But the time it was a matter of was three full days and Harpur had no intention of being there for more than a few minutes.

As the dragon flies, it took less than an hour to reach the lair. Harpur landed in an alpine meadow that stretched out in front of the cave entrance, dropped Sok and Arthur on the ground and transformed back into his human form.

"Orhowyn's withered windpipe, that was close!" he snapped.

Arthur was too dazed to respond, but Sok recovered almost instantly from the harrowing flight from the castle. "Indeed!" he said. "I had no idea there was a Boundary in Colwygshire."

"Neither did I!" Harpur growled. "Great! My walking stick has teeth marks in it now."

"Why don't you just use a wand, like other wizards?" Sok suggested.

"Wands are for wusses. Can you see me flipping a twig around in the air?" Harpur mimicked waving a wand with his pinky extended. "Besides, I'd still have to put it somewhere when I'm in dragon form."

"Then if I were you, I'd go with an amulet on a chain. When you transform back and forth you can adjust the length of the chain to suit whichever body you are in."

Sok had a point. A good point. But Harpur was in no mood to indulge him. Besides, he was somewhat attached to his walking stick, so instead, he harrumphed and walked toward the lair.

Arthur stood on shaky legs and followed Harpur and Sok inside. It was an exact replica of the lair on Whyte Avenue, except that there was no kitchen, conversation pit, hot tub or king size bed. Otherwise, though, it was identical.

Also missing was an enormous pile of treasure, though a few gold coins, a bejeweled circlet, a couple of silver goblets and several loose gems were scattered about on the floor like trash abandoned to a clean-up crew after a concert. Arthur found a stalagmite that the top had broken off of and sat down. He tried to figure out how long it had been since they had left Whyte Avenue in the Lexus and realized he had lost count of the days. It seemed like a long time. Days? Weeks? He wasn't sure. A wave of home-sickness washed over him. He wanted to go home. He wanted to have a shower and put on clean clothes. He wanted to shave! He didn't care about the prophecy anymore.

"Can I go home soon?" he asked.

"Soon," Harpur said. "Let's deal with the Entanglement. Give me your coin halves."

Sok and Arthur removed the pouches from around their necks and handed the two halves of the coin to Harpur, who set them down on another broken stalagmite. He pointed his tooth-marked walking stick at them and a fine arc of purplish-white lightening shot out of the top of the amethyst on its end and welded the coin back together.

"Arthur, I need you to come over here and give this back to Sok," Harpur ordered.

Arthur stood and walked wearily over to the coin. He reached out and picked it up. It was still warm from the lightening, but not too hot to handle. He looked at it in awe. This tiny little chunk of gold had caused so much trouble. He couldn't wait to put it Sok's hand. He was one more step closer to going home. Sok accepted the coin in his not-shrunken hand and tucked it into a pocket.

They stood there for a moment looking at each other as if they were waiting for something else to happen. When nothing did, Arthur spoke. "Is that it then?"

"I think it is," Harpur said.

"Well, that was rather anticlimactic, wasn't it?" Arthur noted aloud.

"It kind of was, wasn't it?" Sok agreed. "I don't feel any different. Do you?"

Arthur shook his head. "Let's go," he said wearily.

"First I have to get rid of the patrol at the Braydon Wood Boundary before the king sends word to them that we are here." Harpur ran his hand down the scarred shaft of his walking stick and made face.

"Why would he do that?" Arthur asked, alarmed.

"Because we just landed in his private chambers and being there uninvited—for any reason—is punishable by death. He's going to be quite pissed with us for interrupting his little assignation with the busty red-head and I have no doubt that even as we speak, he's issuing an order for our arrest and execution."

Arthur gulped. *So close!*

Harpur's plan was simple. He would take Sok and Arthur to a clearing near the Boundary and have them hide in a thicket while he went and dispatched the patrol. Then he and Arthur would Bound back to Whyte Avenue where he would deposit Arthur back at his apartment. Once Arthur was safe on Earth again, Harpur would Bound back, pick up Sok and fly him to Pollybush, from where Sok would make his way back to Colwygshire. Harpur, then, would return to Whyte Avenue and resume his duties as Bounder Guard as if nothing had ever happened.

"Why do I have to go all the way to Pollybush?" Sok protested. "Can't you just drop me on the road to Colwygshire so I don't have to travel all that way?"

"I don't want to risk being seen near the town," Harpur said. "Besides, you might as well check in on your grandmother and legitimize this fiasco by actually doing what Bloomregaard thinks you're doing."

Well, that made sense. Even if it was somewhat more elaborate than Sok thought was strictly necessary.

They exited the lair and set off to put the plan in motion.

Meanwhile, back at the castle, King Gnik was incensed.

The busty red-head had been dismissed and sent back to the kitchens where she worked as a scullery maid. Her Cinderella fantasy, having been dashed to pieces by two strange men and an elf falling through the ceiling and an empty promise by the king to call on her the next day, became a revenge fantasy as she was escorted, none too gently, back to her straw pallet in the servants' quarters. She offered to pleasure her escort, one of the two guards who had belatedly broken down the door to the king's private chambers and grumpy from having his on-duty nap both disturbed and very likely discovered, but he was too busy trying to formulate an excuse that would prevent him from being flogged for sleeping on the job to entertain the possibilities contained in such a proposal. Though he did file them away for future reference should he come out of this with his hard-earned rank—not to mention the flesh on his back—in tact.

With the busty red-head thus taken care of, King Gnik plonked his everyday crown on his head and donned a purple dressing gown. He dispatched the remaining guard, surly over not having been assigned to escort the busty red-head to the kitchens, to find Bloomregaard and bring him to his private chambers. Normally he would have met Bloomregaard in the council room, but he had run out of guards and was not about to walk un-guarded through the castle in his dressing gown.

"And send someone up here with some wine!" he shouted at the guard's back through the splintered remains of the door.

Edlyngton Bloomregaard was at his desk in his office at the Braydon Wood Boundary Office not approving two new applications to Bound through the Braydon Wood Boundary when a panting guard burst in and announced the summons from the king.

"What does that fool want now?" Bloomregaard snapped.

"There's been a breach of protocol, sir. Two men and an elf broke into the king's private chambers and then escaped off the balcony. The king wants to see you in his chambers right away." The guard drew in a deep breath, this being a long speech for him to have had to make.

"Two men and an elf?" Bloomregaard asked, trying to reconcile the information and what it had to do with him.

"That is correct, sir," replied the guard.

"And they escaped off the balcony from the king's private chambers? That's impossible! It's at the top of the tower." The Chief Bounding Officer doubted the veracity of the story.

"Well, sir," the guard said by way of explanation, "one of the men was actually a dragon. After they jumped off the balcony, he transformed in midair. It was quite spectacular, sir. I had no idea dragons could do that."

The pieces were beginning to fit. "Ah," said Bloomregaard. "Then we best not keep the king waiting."

Bloomregaard had correctly surmised the identity of the dragon and the elf. Sok was his clerk and though Harpur had initially wiped the Chief Bounding Officer's memory, Harpur had to eventually re-reveal his true abilities. Bloomregaard had kept the secret, waiting for just the right time to use it against the Dragon Lord, and he was dismayed by the fact that the secret was no longer much of a secret. But he had no clue as to who the other man might be.

He thought something was up when Harpur had spun that tale about needing a patrol stationed at the Boundary while he went after a Bounder that had escaped his containment ward on Earth. And when the letter from Sok stating that he had to rush off to Pollybush to see his sick grandmother arrived, his suspicions had been confirmed. Without his wraiths close by to investigate, he had elected to bide his time. His time, it seemed, had come.

"Did the king recognize the men and the elf?" Bloomregaard asked the guard as they made their way to the king's private chambers. He was hoping to get some hint as to who the man with Harpur and Sok might be.

"He didn't say, sir," the guard said. "Things happened rather fast."

"Indeed," Bloomregaard said. "Did you see these three interlopers?"

"Not up close, sir. By the time we broke down the door, they were already quite a way away."

"You broke down the door? To the king's chambers?"

"Yes, sir. It was locked."

"And why was it locked?"

"King Gnik was... uh... entertaining a young lady, sir."

"That tiny blond thing again?"

"Uh, no, sir. It was the busty red-head this time."

Well, at least it wasn't the kinky brunette. She was a world of trouble. "I see. Did the king say anything else?"

"No, sir. He just told me to fetch you." The guard paused. "Oh, yes. He also wanted me to get someone to bring him some wine."

"Then you better go do that. I can find my own way up there." *It's only a hundred twenty-eight steps to climb!*

Fifteen minutes later, including a brief rest about two-thirds of the way up, Bloomregaard stood at the door to the king's private chambers. He knocked on a broken plank still attached to a hinge and waited for the King Gnik to acknowledge his presence.

"What took you so long?" King Gnik barked. He was standing on the balcony, one hand on the railing and one hand on his purple-robed hip. His everyday crown was slightly askew on his head.

Bloomregaard interpreted this as sufficient acknowledgement and entered the room. On his right, the royal bed was a jumble of sheets and pillows and quilts. The floor was strewn with fractured pieces of planking that had only a short while ago been the only barrier between the king and anyone who sought to gain entry to these rooms.

"I understand there was a break-in, sire," Bloomregaard said as he approached the monarch and bowed deeply from the waist.

"That's right! There was. And it was your Bounder Guard and your elf who broke in!"

"They aren't my Bounder Guard and elf, sire," Bloomregaard deflected.

"Isn't the elf your clerk? And didn't you hire the Bounder Guard?"

Yes, and no, Bloomregaard thought to himself. "I shall terminate their positions immediately, sire."

"That's not good enough! I want them found! I want them arrested!" the irate king yelled. "And I want them burned at the stake!"

Capturing, let alone burning a dragon at the stake, was problematic at best. But Bloomregaard sensed that this was not the time to apprise King Gnik of Harpur's secret. As for burning an elf at the stake, while it was physically possible, there was a treaty with the elves that didn't allow it. Sok could be arrested. Sok could be tried. Sok could be convicted. But only his own kind could decide what his sentence should be. And, sadly—at least to Bloomregaard—that excluded executions of any kind. The harshest punishment that they would give him would be to keep him in a dark, enclosed cell away from any trees for a while. Elves had a peculiar sense of justice when it came to their own people, but if the treaty were ever broken... Well, while elves looked all cute and friendly, they were vicious warriors. Especially some of the women! A war with the elves would not end well for the good people of Colwygshire. He would have to find some other way of dealing with those two. Perhaps, though, the man that was with them could be sacrificed to the fire. It has been a while since there was a good public burning at the stake.

Bloomregaard, looked at his king. Normally, Gnik was a rather meek ruler, shunning violence and parcelling out mercy at every turn. He was more inclined to ask questions first and burn only if it was absolutely necessary. This outburst, Bloomregaard believed, had more to do with the busty red-head than it did with having his private chambers broken into. If Bloomregaard was correct, and he was, Gnik was worried about his reputation. Having been caught in the sack with a scullery maid, while not particularly interesting or even cared about by most folks, was a potential skeleton that needed to not just be put in a closet, but sealed behind bricks and mortar in a wall somewhere. It was one of those ridiculous things that the cowardly king believed could be twisted and used against him by his enemies. It was all nonsense, of course. The king was being over-dramatic. The only real problem that could come of his assignations with the servants was the possibility of a bastard being born. But after all these many years on the throne, no such claim had ever been made. Bloomregaard was ninety-nine percent certain that Gnik was incapable of producing progeny.

"How did they get in?" Bloomregaard ventured. He wasn't willing to agree outright to fulfilling the king's demand.

"How in Orhowyn's name should I know?" the king blurted.

"I'm just curious," Bloomregaard said. "Perhaps it was a mistake. Perhaps the guards are the ones that should be punished for not doing their jobs."

King Gnik frowned. This hadn't occurred to him. He'd had his back to the intruders when they landed. "But the door was shut and locked. The guards had to break it down. They couldn't have seen the break-in happening."

"Was it? Are you certain of that?" Bloomregaard's gaslighting was starting to work. "How else could they have gotten in?" He had no idea himself that there was a Boundary in the king's private chambers. The fact that there was and that it only opened when someone came through and then shifted somewhere else, was not a Boundary-related phenomenon that Bloomregaard or the king were aware of. Bloomregaard's only experience with Boundaries was the one in Braydon Wood, and that one went to one place and one place only. But he didn't need to know the particulars—yet—of how Harpur and the others got in. He just needed to get the king to think in terms other than taking down a dragon or executing an elf. And guards were a dime a dozen. What were the lives of two guards worth anyway? Not much as far as Bloomregaard was concerned.

King Gnik thought this over. From the look of doubt on his face, Bloomregaard could tell he wasn't as sure of the sequence of events as he thought. "Still," the king said, not wanting to concede too easily, "they should be questioned."

"Of course, sire. I will see to it."

Just then a servant arrived with the wine. It was not the tiny blonde, or the kinky brunette or the busty red-head; it was a short, pudgy, grey-haired, grandmotherly woman named Finch that delivered the sweet nectar to the king. Finch didn't bother to knock or even wait to be invited in. She marched past the broken door and deposited the tray with the wine on a table next to the royal bed.

"Look at this mess!" Finch shook a finger at the king. "If you'd just marry one of those wenches, things like this wouldn't happen." She spun on her heals and marched back out. Over her shoulder she called back, "I'll send someone to clean this up and I'll send for a carpenter to repair the door. But none of this is coming out of my budget! You can charge it to Repair and Maintenance! Housekeeping is under enough of a strain. Orhowyn's dusty balls, I shouldn't have to put up with stuff like this at my age. It's bad enough I had to climb all these..." Finch's voice faded away as she descended the stairs.

The king and the Chief Bounding Officer stared in contrite silence after the feisty housekeeper.

"You might want to consider pensioning that one off," Bloomregaard said before the silence got awkward.

"I tried," said the exasperated king. "Somehow, I ended up paying her double. That's why her budget is so strained." He poured himself a glass of wine and sipped it thoughtfully.

As Edlyngton Bloomregaard retreated from the king's private chambers, he pondered the events. Strictly speaking, none of this fell under his purview. He had no authority to order an arrest, unless it was related to a breach of Boundary law, which it was, though he didn't know that. With Harpur Diggins and Sok involved, Bloomregaard strongly suspected that an unsanctioned Bound had occurred, but from where? And how did they end up in the king's private chambers? It made no sense to him. Boundaries are big holes in the air. They were obvious. He saw no such thing in the king's bedroom. He would get to the bottom of it sooner or later. But to do so, he had to find Harpur. The only place he could think of to start was the Braydon Wood Boundary.

Below him on the stairs leading down through the tower, Bloomregaard could hear Finch muttering to herself about the inconvenience of having to deal with broken doors and stretched budgets and kings demanding wine at such a late hour. (It wasn't even dark out. Dinner wouldn't be served for some time yet.) There were a couple of scullery maids that were in for a talking to, apparently, and Finch's aching back was now further aggravated by all this stair-climbing nonsense. Bloomregaard slowed his pace so he would not catch up to the long-suffering housekeeper. But he would have to hurry once he was safely beyond her potential reach.

Once back in his office, Bloomregaard called for a junior clerk and ordered him to dispatch a dispatch that he had composed by rider to the Patrol Chief at the Braydon Wood Boundary. The short missive directed the Patrol Leader to detain the Bounder Guard, who was generally referred to as DH, and detain him at the Boundary until he, Bloomregaard, arrived to question him in regard to an incident that had taken place at the castle. If anyone else should accompany DH, they should also be detained. No further details were included.

The chances that the patrol would be able to detain Harpur were slim. They were no match for a dragon—in any form. Bloomregaard imagined the trepidation the Patrol Chief would experience upon reading the dispatch. *If he can read,* Bloomregaard thought. Guards in general, found DH to be highly intimidating. Being ordered to detain him would not be a welcome assignment. And if Harpur had already revealed his secret the way it had been told to him, Bloomregaard couldn't be certain that the dragon would not do again. He had to hurry!

It was not his preference to ride a horse, but a litter would be too slow and a carriage would not be able to get him all the way to the Boundary, situated as it was in the middle of the forest. No roads had been constructed in that area, making access to the Boundary troublesome, though not impossible. He ordered a horse and two guards to accompany him and set off to Braydon Wood to, hopefully, head off Harpur. More guards were ordered to follow with provisions—food, a tent, wine, etc. Who knew when Harpur would show up? If he had to be out in the middle of the Orhowyn-forsaken forest for any length of time, he was damned well going to be comfortable.

Something was definitely afoot. He just had to hope he was looking for it in the right place. Whatever Harpur and Sok were up to had to be stopped. He needed Harpur on the other side of the Boundary and he needed Sok where he could keep an eye on him. And he needed to find out why Harpur had transformed where anyone could see him. But he wasn't about to let eight long years of planning be interrupted by the dragon and the elf.

Harpur deposited Sok and Arthur in the clearing and commanded them to stay put and stay out of site. The clearing was close enough to the Boundary that the patrol could easily come upon them. That is if the patrol was patrolling as it was supposed to and not just camping out next to the Boundary, which was what Harpur was hoping for. The ten-man patrol was, in theory, was supposed to have four men at the Boundary, two on guard and two resting, while three other pairs patrolled a perimeter around the Boundary at intervals designed to reduce the chances of any would-be Bounders getting close enough to it to possibly get past the guards. It was not beyond the realm of possibility, however, for a Patrol Chief to decide that all ten men in the unit would have a better chance of stopping a potential Bounder at the Boundary. The problem was that this often led to distractions such as drinking, dice games and subsequent accusations of cheating that caused fights to break out, thus allowing patient Bounders to slip past the melee and make the Bound. Under the present circumstances, a lazy patrol unit would serve his purposes better than a diligent one. If all ten men were at the Boundary and if they gave him any flack, he'd deal with them and there would be no one left to sound the alert.

As it happened, all ten men in the patrol unit were at the Boundary. Harpur watched them from the cover of a bush as they passed flasks and dice back and forth. They were not yet too drunk to be belligerent, but they were sufficiently relaxed enough that their reflexes were sluggish. He would use this laxness against them, threatening to report them for not doing their duty. Once they were sufficiently cowed, he would tell them he was letting them off with a warning and issue the order to suspend the patrol, effective immediately.

Well, that was the plan. Just as he was about to step out from behind the bush, a rider arrived with a dispatch from Bloomregaard, which he handed to the Patrol Chief.

Harpur hunkered down behind the bush again.

The Patrol Chief took the dispatch, broke the seal and pretended to read the contents.

"What is it?" one of the patrolmen asked.

"It's a dispatch from Bloomregaard." The Patrol Chief had recognized Bloomregaard's seal. "Says we've been relieved of duty and are to return to the castle immediately."

Cheers all around!

Thank Orhowyn!

Harpur decided to wait for them to pack up and leave.

"It says nothing of the sort!" the rider disputed. "It says that you are to detain DH if he comes here until Bloomregaard arrives to question them about an incident at the castle."

Groans all around.

The last thing Harpur needed was a confrontation with that odious man.

The Patrol Chief guffawed. "Sorry, lads. I was just joking with ya." He turned to the rider. "How are we supposed to detain DH? And what was the incident at the castle all about?"

"Bloomregaard didn't say," the rider said, mounting his sweaty horse and turning it back toward the forest. "Just figure out a way to keep him here until Bloomregaard gets arrives."

The rider and his horse trotted off, leaving the patrol to figure out how to deal with the very large Bounder Guard, who also happened to be their superior. They had no idea how far behind the rider Bloomregaard was. The Patrol Chief guessed it would be a while; the Senior Bounding Officer was a lousy rider. A trot was the fastest pace Bloomregaard would be brave enough to attempt and, if he didn't get bounced out of the saddle, he'd be taxed to keep it up for very long. Harpur estimated that he had half an hour at least. It would take him ten minutes to get Arthur, come back and make the Bound. He wouldn't have time on the other side to get Arthur to his apartment, but he could get him to ground level and then Bound straight back. With luck, he would be well away from the Boundary before Bloomregaard arrived.

A lot could go wrong, but the only other choice Harpur could fathom was to wait for Bloomregaard to get there and then render him, the patrol and any guards he had with him unconscious before getting Arthur. If he waited for Bloomregaard, Bloomregaard would know without any doubt that it was Harpur who had zapped him. The consequences would be minor, but the less Bloomregaard knew for sure about any of this, the better. Harpur harboured no illusions about Edlyngton Bloomregaard and his penchant for revenge. Eventually, Harpur would pay. He decided to take his chances getting Arthur back to Earth before Bloomregaard got to the Boundary.

He stepped out from behind the bush. "Hey, fellas! How's it going?" he called out in a friendly manner.

The arguing that had ensued after the rider had left stopped. Ten pairs of surprised eyes turned in Harpur's direction.

"What...?" the Patrol Chief started to ask something, but Harpur quickly raised his walking stick and with a sweeping wave rendered him and his men unconscious.

One by one, they fell or slumped over on the ground. Harpur dragged one man, whose boots had landed too close to the small camp fire, away from harm. He dragged two others away from the base of the Boundary so that when he returned after taking Arthur home, he wouldn't land on them. Then he ran as fast as he could back to the clearing.

"Arthur! Sok! I'm back," he called as he neared the thicket where he had left them.

The elf and the man crawled out and ran toward the dragon-wizard.

"Is it safe?" Arthur asked.

"Yes," Harpur lied. "But we have to move fast. Hop on my back."

The light was fading and Harpur didn't want to lose a second getting back to the Boundary. Arthur couldn't run as fast as he could and Harpur didn't trust Arthur's night vision to keep him from tripping on a tree root. Or a leaf for that matter. He bent over and motioned for Arthur to just do as he was told. Arthur complied and with a little hitch to settle Arthur's legs comfortably at his waste, Harpur set off again. "Stay put, Sok! I'll be back as soon as I can."

Harpur stopped about thirty feet from the Boundary and knelt down so Arthur could dismount. He held a finger to his lips, letting Arthur know that he needed him to be quiet. Then they advanced toward the Boundary, staying low and using the cover of the underbrush to keep from being seen by Bloomregaard if he was already there. When he was certain that Bloomregaard was not yet at the Boundary, Harpur led Arthur to its base. Like he had when they jumped into the Boundary on Mysturna, Harpur lifted Arthur by the waist and sprang up and into the centre of the swirling portal back to Earth.

Unlike the odd tingling sensation he had felt when he had Bounded from Mysturna to Thraeh, this time Arthur felt like his body had been turned to rubber and he was being stretched like silly putty. Just as he was beginning to think that he would be torn apart, they landed on a rooftop and Harpur was setting him down.

Arthur was home. He ran over to the edge of the roof and looked down on his beloved Whyte Avenue.

"Oh, my god!" he said. "We did it! We're back on Whyte Avenue! Thank you, Harpur!"

"You're welcome," Harpur said, relieved that Arthur had survived. So many didn't. "Now let's get you off this roof. I need to get back to Sok."

"Right. Of course." Arthur looked pensive. "How do we get down?"

Harpur rolled his eyes. Without answering he picked Arthur up again. When he was sure there was no one below them in the alley at the back of the building they were on, he jumped off the roof. Arthur braced for the impact, but Harpur landed on his feet and, once again, set his passenger down. "You should have more faith in me by now, Arthur," he said.

"Will I ever see you again?" Arthur asked. Suddenly he was awash with mixed emotions.

"I don't have time for any melodrama right now. But I'm sure we'll see each other soon. I'm a regular here on the Avenue!" He nodded toward the bustling street.

"Right. Well, I guess I'll see you around," Arthur said.

"Yep," Harpur agreed. He felt like he was releasing a tamed animal back into the wild. "Go on! Get out of here," he said to the stricken-looking man.

Arthur walked away slowly. He reached the end of the alley and looked back. Harpur was gone.

Before he could return to Thraeh, Harpur made a quick detour to his lair a block away from the Boundary. The enchanted entrance appeared okay, but he went inside to be sure that Anayah had not returned. Satisfied that everything was in order in his beloved lair, Harpur changed the enchantment on the entrance so that she would not be able to get in if, for any reason, she came back there. She was a loose end, an unresolved problem that would have to be dealt with at some point. But first, he had to get Sok to Pollybush and make sure that things were good on Thraeh. Back he went to the Boundary.

Bounding didn't phase Harpur in the least. He'd done it so many times that he was immune to any deleterious effects. This time, though, he wished he could see through so he would know what was waiting for him in Braydon Wood. So far things had gone according to plan. *What do I do if Bloomregaard is waiting for me?* He didn't have time to formulate a strategy. So, he jumped.

When he landed, he was relieved to find everything as he had left it. The unconscious patrol unit still lay on the ground. Many of them were softly snoring. He was just about to wake them up again when he heard a rustle coming from the same bush he had concealed himself behind earlier. Then Bloomregaard appeared. Oddly, he also appeared to be alone, though, now that Harpur took a closer look, there were three horses tied up to a tree near the path that led away from the Boundary.

"Welcome back," Bloomregaard sneered.

"What are you doing here, Edlyngton?" Harpur used his first name to affect innocent camaraderie. "And what did you do to these men? They are supposed to be guarding the Boundary?"

"Oh, very good, Harpur." Bloomregaard wasn't buying any of it. "Like we don't both know that you put some sort of spell on the patrol. Now, tell me what is going on. I understand that you paid an unexpected visit to the king today."

"What are you talking about? I just came back to let these guys," he gestured toward the patrolmen, "know that my business with the Bounder was finished and to dismiss them. And then I find you here and them... are they dead?" Harpur reached down to check the pulse of the nearest patrolman.

Harpur's improvisation was impeccable. A shadow of doubt passed over Bloomregaard's face as he tried to find the flaw in what he knew had to be a ruse. *Had the king been mistaken? Surely not.* The guards had seen a dragon fly from the balcony carrying an elf and a man. And the king recognized Harpur and Sok before they escaped.

Harpur was desperately fishing for some kind of explanation to offer Bloomregaard. But he had to be careful not to give anything away. Bloomregaard had to tell him what had happened first.

"Come now, Harpur. The king recognized you and Sok when you burst into his private chambers with... Who else was with you?" Bloomregaard prompted.

"Sok?" Harpur stood up with a puzzled look on his face. "I haven't seen that pest of an elf in weeks. I have no idea what you're talking about."

Bloomregaard's resolve began to waiver even more. He was about to concede when the two guards came out of the forest dragging a protesting elf between them.

"Look what we found hiding in a thicket back there," said the taller-of-the-two guards as they pushed the elf forward toward Bloomregaard.

"He claims he was just out for a walk," the shorter-of-the-two guards added.

"Well, well, well," said Bloomregaard. "How do you explain this, Harpur?"

"Oh, hey, Harpur," Sok said as he regained his balance. "It's been a while."

"It sure has," Harpur played along with the elf who was playing along with him. "What's it been, a month or so?"

"At least," Sok agreed. "By the way, I filed that report you gave me. You know, to file."

"Good to know," Harpur said. "Seeing as that's your job."

Bloomregaard watched this flawlessly mundane exchange between the two people he was supposed to be questioning in regard to the crime of breaking into the king's private chambers and found himself seriously doubting the king's sanity.

"So, what *are* you doing out here in the forest?" Harpur prodded to further the deception.

"Well, I just got back from Pollybush and I missed the trees here, so I decided to..."

"Hide in a thicket?" the taller-of-the-two guards provided.

"What? No! I wasn't hiding. I was walking by the thicket and I noticed something shiny on the ground." Sok pulled the deformed coin that had started all this out of his pocket and held it up for everyone to see. "It's just a chunk of gold, but I thought I would take it to Toburn, the goldsmith, and see if he can make it into a ring. I'm going to ask Yna to marry me."

If Harpur had been the hugging type, he'd have hugged Sok. This was better than anything he could come up with.

"Well, good luck with that," Harpur said. "Yna's one... incredible elf. Now, what are we going to do with these patrolmen?" Harpur asked, hoping Sok would shut up before he made a mistake.

But Bloomregaard wasn't quite ready to concede after all. "So, how do you explain what happened in the king's private chambers?" he looked from Sok to Harpur.

"Something happened in the king's private chambers?" Sok asked sounding eager for some juicy gossip.

"It was broken into today," Bloomregaard said, "by an elf, a dragon and some man that nobody seems to know. According to the witnesses, including the king himself, the elf and the dragon looked exactly like you and Harpur."

"Could a dragon even fit in the king's private chambers?" Sok was incredulous. "I mean, I've never been in the king's private chambers, but that tower isn't very big."

As impressed as Harpur was with Sok, he needed to end this before it could go south. "Maybe they were just disguised like us. Maybe the king was drunk. I don't know, Bloomregaard," he reverted back to the Senior Bounding Officer's surname. "What I do know is that it's getting dark and I have things to do. Like deal with these patrolmen, for example."

Bloomregaard was not convinced, but he didn't have anything else to throw at them. "Leave them here," he said, walking to his horse and mounting it awkwardly. "They'll either wake up on their own or the wolves will get them." He turned pulled on the horse's reins to get it to turn, but it just dropped its head and started munching on grass.

The two guards took this as their cue to leave as well. They mounted up, much less awkwardly, and the taller-of-the-two took hold of

Bloomregaard's horse's reins. The beast obediently allowed itself to be led away. Bloomregaard swore. Then he swore he'd get to the truth of the matter.

Harpur and Sok waited until Bloomregaard and the guards were well out of earshot.

"Sok," Harpur said, "you're a genius."

Sok liked the sound of that. "You should have more faith in me by now, Harpur."

Chapter 13

Arthur was lost in a fog. He had stood at the end of the alley staring at the empty space where Harpur had been, unable to believe that the dragon-wizard would have just left him like that. He knew that Harpur had to go and get Sok to safety. But to have just vanished like that felt so final.

What am I supposed to do now? he wondered. *What if Harpur doesn't come back? And what about my memories? What about my magic? What about the dragon blood? What about the prophecy?*

So much was unresolved. This couldn't be all there was to it. The story couldn't just end there in an alley.

Arthur was yanked out of his reverie by laughter coming from the corner. A group of people were waiting for the light to cross Whyte Avenue. Among them was a man wearing a gold-foil crown and seemed to be the center of attention with his friends. A pretty woman in black capris and a sequined top, heavy makeup and an expensive, trendy haircut clung possessively to his arm as if the contact enabled her to claim at least some of the attention that was being showered on him. Arthur watched this interaction for a moment until he realized that the pretty woman was Cheryl. His first inclination was to duck back into the alley so she wouldn't see him, but the light changed and she walked away unaware that he was there.

He watched her cross the street still firmly attached to whom he could only assume was the unfamiliar male voice he'd heard on the phone the night she'd dumped him. He couldn't remember her ever being that clingy with him and as she disappeared into a restaurant on the other side of Whyte Avenue, Arthur had the overwhelming sense that he had dodged a bullet with her. The Cheryl in the black capris and sequined top was not the Cheryl he knew—or thought he knew. His Cheryl had been a makeup-less, pony-tailed, jeans and t-shirt girl. *Which one is the real Cheryl?* he wondered as he made his way to the corner to wait for the next light that would take him in the direction of his apartment.

Whyte Avenue was alive with an air of festivity. The warm spring evening was filled with the sounds of cars and people and buskers. Honking horns and running engines mixed with laughter and chatter and singing as Arthur made his way along the sidewalk. He'd walked two blocks when he suddenly remembered John's offer of a job at O'Bryan's Pub. *How long have I been gone? Is it too late to accept?*

He pulled out his phone and looked at the date. He'd been gone almost two weeks. That couldn't be right! *It was only four or five days. Wasn't it?*

"...time does not pass the same on Earth as it does on Thraeh." Arthur heard Harpur's voice in his head.

If only I'd been able to return through a Veilrift instead of a Boundary...

Arthur pushed the thought aside. He was on the most festive street in the city, surrounded by happy people having fun, and he was thinking about magical portals to other worlds. He'd never see Whyte Avenue the same way again.

His phone screen was awash with notifications. Emails, texts and voicemails by the dozens were waiting for his attention, but he didn't have the energy to deal with them. He tucked the phone back into his pocket and continued walking home.

When he first arrived at his apartment, he discovered that he didn't have his keys. He called the building manager, who, cheerfully enough, came down from his third-floor apartment and opened Arthur's door. Arthur thanked him and apologized for the inconvenience. The building manager assured him that it was no problem.

"But your rent is overdue, Arthur. If you could get it to me right away, that would be good."

"Right," Arthur said, shocked and embarrassed. "It totally slipped my mind. I'll get it to you in the morning."

The building manager again assured Arthur that it was not a problem and said good night.

Inside the apartment, Arthur felt an overwhelming sense of disconnection to it. It felt tiny and foreign and unwelcoming. Even without the relationship zombies there to haunt him, Arthur felt the presence of Cheryl lurking in the corners waiting to jump out at him.

But it was something else that was missing that bothered him more. The apartment was completely devoid of... magic. *This can't be my life*, Arthur thought.

Arthur plugged his phone in so it could recharge and left it on the kitchen counter. He opened the fridge, pulled out a bottle of beer and then closed the door again so he wouldn't have to look at the food that had transformed into science experiments during his absence. His mother would not be proud! As he took his first sip of the beer, he thought about the bourbon he'd wanted so badly at the sanctuary on Mysturna. For the life of him, he could not figure out why that had been so funny. Still, it made him smile.

Then he looked at the cuff on his arm. That made him frown. He had to get it off. He had no idea when—or even if—he'd ever see Anayah again and he wasn't about to go around in long-sleeved shirts all summer so he wouldn't have to explain it to anyone. He didn't dare try to unlace it for fear of having his hand swell up like Sok's had if it tightened. *Maybe I can cut it off.*

He opened a kitchen drawer and took out a pair of scissors. Holding them awkwardly in his left hand he slid the blade between his arm and the cuff. The scissors didn't explode or melt. He wasn't zapped by a magical electric shock. But he hadn't actually started cutting yet. Holding his breath and wincing in anticipation of enchanted backlash, he slowly squeezed the handles. When the blades met the leather, Arthur hesitated. Still nothing. He squeezed again and the leather gave way to the scissor blades, splitting in a smooth, even cut until the cuff fell away from his arm.

"Hmm," Arthur said aloud. "Wish we'd known that before Harpur had to cut our arms off."

Thusly reminded of that, Arthur inspected his appendage. There was no sign of the amputation. Still, he was glad that he had been unconscious at the time. Even if he had been enchanted against his will.

He finished his beer and then decided that a shower and a shave were in order. Arthur studied his face in the bathroom mirror and wondered who the person looking back him was. He seemed older. Wiser? Well, definitely older. Arthur noticed lines by his eyes that he was sure weren't there before. And was that a grey hair? He raked his fingers through his hair, longer than it should have been... *Is it possible for hair to grow that much in two weeks?* Nothing felt real to him. Not the trip to Mysturna and Thraeh. Not the apartment. Not the world outside his windows.

He paced. He thought. He finally decided to do something with the leather cuff. He hadn't thrown it away because it was part of what he'd been through. *Do I even want a souvenir?* He carried the ruined cuff into his bedroom and stuffed it into a drawer. When he turned around, he noticed the box of his stuff that Cheryl had returned and tried to imagine what was in it. Clothes he'd left at her apartment? Gifts he'd given to her? Photos? *Do I even want to know?* He picked up the box and carried to the storage room next to the kitchen where he shoved it into a corner. Those relationship zombies could stay in the box. For now. He had no idea what to do next. So, he drank another bottle of beer and went to bed.

The next day, Arthur sat on his sofa and systematically deleted e-mails and messages. There were eleven voice mails in his in-box and he listened to them. The voices of friends passed through his eardrums only to blend into the rest of his scrambled thoughts and disappear. Thankfully, none of the were from Cheryl. Disappointingly none of them were from Mr. Fox or Toby saying that the store was not closing after all and he could still be the manager. The only one he couldn't ignore was from his mother, asking if he would be joining her and his father for dinner on Sunday and hoping he'd had a good road trip. He mustered up enough courage to return her call.

"So, you're alive!" his mother chirped.

"Hello, Ma."

"When did you get back?"

"A while ago."

"How was your trip?"

"It was okay."

"Where did you go?"

"Uh... Drumheller."

"Drumheller? What on earth did you go there for?"

Arthur nearly laughed at the irony. What on *Earth* indeed! "That's where everyone else wanted to go."

"Honestly, Arthur, you'd jump off a bridge if your friends all did."

Gee, thanks, Ma. "Well, it's been a while since I was there."

"Did you take lots of pictures?"

Pictures. Arthur remembered the pictures. Sok had taken dozens of himself in the Lexus on the way to Drumheller. Then there was the selfie of him and Analeetah. "A few," Arthur said. "Look, Ma, I gotta go."

"Well, will you at least be here for dinner on Sunday?"

"Sure, Ma. I'll be there."

Arthur disconnected and opened the camera app on his phone. The pictures of Sok and, more importantly, the selfie of him and Analeetah were still there, along with shots of Hiro and the cabin at the Pole that he had taken. He scrolled through the cameral roll, wishing he'd taken more pictures to commemorate the fantastical adventure he'd been on with Sok and Harpur. At least there was something tangible to prove that it had happened. Though he couldn't imagine who he would ever be able to share them with. Then he remembered the recording he'd made. He opened the app and pressed play.

His account was brief and unencumbered by hyperbole of any kind. *Just the facts, ma'am.* He recorded the rest of the story in the same way and appended it to the first recording. Then he e-mailed it to himself and saved it to the cloud so that he couldn't possibly lose it. *Maybe I'll write a book someday*, he thought. Suddenly, he missed the irritating elf and the grumpy dragon.

He needed coffee.

Rather than make a cup in his single-cup coffee maker, he decided to venture out and treat himself to a double-double and a donut. Arthur retrieved his wallet from his dresser and was pleased to find forty dollars in it. He tucked the wallet into his back pocket, but before he could leave, he had to make his bed. It felt both odd and normal to do be doing this, but he couldn't help himself. *No wrinkles today.*

Feeling like he was ready to go, he returned to the kitchen and reached for his keys in the bowl on the counter.by the door. That's when he saw the bag with the silver fox on it and remembered the vintage comic he'd taken from the store and his final paycheque. He extracted the contents from the bag and opened the envelope from Mr. Fox. Like Allen's envelope, his contained a copy of his record of employment, a letter of reference, a card with a touching apology from Mr. Fox (obviously written by Toby), his final pay cheque and a severance cheque, which made Arthur's eyes nearly pop out of his head. Toby had said he'd been generous, but this was astounding. Instead of the eight-weeks pay he'd been expecting, Arthur was looking at a sum closer to five-year's pay. Forgetting the comic, he folded the cheques into his wallet, grabbed his keys and left his apartment.

Traffic was light as Arthur made his way on foot westward along Whyte Avenue. He stopped for his coffee and donut and then continued on to his bank to deposit his cheques and withdraw some extra cash. The windows at Fox Comics were papered over and there was a sign on the door that said *Prophecy Comics! Opening Soon.* Arthur stared at the sign. *How ironic!* he thought. Then he forced himself to keep walking and resisted the temptation to peek inside where some of the paper had come loose. He'd given eight years of his life to Fox Comics and now it was gone. As was Cheryl. As were Harpur and Sok. The absurdity of it all left Arthur reeling and disoriented. It spooked him. Badly.

"I'm on Whyte Avenue. I'm drinking a double-double and eating a donut. I'm a normal, sane, unemployed man who never left the planet and didn't nearly switch personalities with an elf. There are no such things as dragons. I have never kissed a witch. I got drunk when Fox Comics closed and dreamed everything," he mumbled to himself, thankful that there were not many people walking around on Whyte Avenue that early in the day.

Arthur caught his reflection in the bank window as he approached and winced again at the length of his hair. The barber shop was a couple blocks back. He'd deposit his cheques and then head over to see if he could get it trimmed. Jason, his barber, was a great guy. A half-hour in the chair with him would be just what the doctor ordered. Arthur took a deep breath, opened the door to the bank vestibule and went inside.

After he deposited his cheques, he transferred the overdue rent he owed and then crossed Whyte Avenue at the nearest corner to walk back to J.J.'s Barber Shop. A bell rang as the door opened and Jason Jackson, a stocky man with unnaturally black, slicked-back hair, looked up from a cell phone on which he had been tapping with his thumbs.

"Jesus, Arthur! Has it been that long? I coulda swore you were just here a couple weeks ago!" He finished tapping on the cell phone and stood up so Arthur could sit down.

Arthur ran a hand through his hair as he took a seat in the vinyl-covered chair. "It must have been longer than that," he said, hoping Jason wouldn't pursue the issue.

He placed his coffee cup on the shelf in front of the barber chair and lifted his chin so Jason could tie a dark blue cape around his neck. "The usual?" Jason asked.

"That would be great," Arthur affirmed.

"I was sorry to hear about Fox Comics closing down." Jason started off the banter with an appropriately sympathetic and covertly probing observation.

"Yeah. Me too," Arthur said.

"What will you do now?" Jason drew a black comb out of a jar of Barbicide and shook it dry.

"I haven't really given it much thought," Arthur said. *I'm supposed to become the ruler of a kingdom in another world, but I'm keeping my options open,* he thought to himself.

"Well, you're a smart guy. You'll find something."

"I'm not too worried about it," he said.

"Say," Jason caught something in Arthur's tone and changed the subject, "did you hear about that weird incident that happened a couple weeks back?"

"No. What happened?"

"Some jackass dressed like an elf jumped off a building on the corner at a Hundred and Four Street. Landed right in the middle of the intersection. Didn't even get hurt."

*Oh, **that** incident!* It hadn't occurred to Arthur that Sok's little stunt would be the topic of conversation. He froze beneath a sudden wave of panic. *Didn't Harpur do his memory-wiping thing when that happened?*

Jason didn't seem to notice. "Damnedest thing! The guy just got up and ran away. Cars were piled up all over the place, but there wasn't a single collision. No one got hurt."

Snip, snip, snip.

"Ashley Booker was telling me about it. You know Ashley, don't you?"

Snip, snip, snip.

"Uh, no. I don't think so." Arthur reached for his coffee. The snipping stopped.

"Oh, he's a regular of mine. Big biker guy. Comes in twice a week to get his head shaved. Said he nearly hit the side of a pick up. He was right in the middle of it all on his way to pick up his wife at the university. She's a professor there."

The snipping started again.

The large, angry man's name is Ashley? And his wife is a professor? Suddenly elves and dragons didn't seem all that strange.

"That is weird." It was all Arthur dared to contribute.

"I wouldn't a believed it. But Ashley is a straight shooter. He wouldn't a made that up. Plus, a bunch of other people told me about it."

Snip, snip, snip.

Arthur sipped his coffee. No one was supposed to have remembered. Harpur must have missed a few minds.

Twenty minutes and thirty dollars later, Arthur found himself back out on the sidewalk. He'd finished his coffee and his donut while Jason had rambled on about the current events and the weather. Arthur sipped and nodded his way through it all, not registering any of it. Though it was still early, traffic was picking up as more people found their way to Whyte Avenue to shop and meet friends for lunch. Arthur headed east again. He had the sudden impulse to look for the entrance to Harpur's lair.

The alleyways off Whyte Avenue were, for the most part, well maintained and free of unsavoury detritus. A few wayward plastic bags and a couple of discarded take-out cups clung to dumpsters here and there, but all things considered, it was not that bad. Arthur made his was into the first access to the alley that he came to and looked up the narrow lane hoping to spot something familiar. From behind, the buildings all looked alike; nothing stood out as an obvious entrance to a dragon's lair. What Arthur dimly recalled was a green door below street level and a half-dozen or so steps leading down to it. But he wasn't certain. He knew that the entrance had been enchanted, but he had seen it when they had exited to go to the Lexus. He was almost positive that it was in between 104 and 105 Streets. Then again, it was enchanted and who really knew what street they had come out on. He spent two fruitless hours searching the alley from 100 Street all the way to 109 Street before he gave up.

Defeated, tired and hungry, Arthur caught the bus at 109 Street and rode it back to the Bonnie Doon Shopping Centre where he indulged in a hamburger at a steakhouse in the mall. When he was done, he popped into the Safeway and picked up a few incidentals to have at home. All this normalness, however, did nothing to sooth his increasingly jangled nerves. Riding the bus was awkward. Ordering food in a restaurant after having meals appear out of thin air was awkward. Paying for things was awkward. Being around people was awkward. Everything was awkward. He began to dread dinner at his parents' the next day.

Keeping busy was vital. When he returned home, Arthur put his groceries away and then gave his apartment a thorough cleaning. Two weeks of accumulated dust vanished under his ministrations. He vacuumed. He sprayed and wiped. He tidied. Though there wasn't much to tidy. Then he removed the replica Daredevil comic cover from its frame and replaced it with the whole vintage Batman comic he'd taken from Fox Comics. This was not an ideal way of storing such a valuable piece of comic book history, but Arthur wanted to be able to look at and enjoy it. When he'd first taken it, he'd planned on selling it, but with the generous severance that Toby had somehow arranged for him, he wouldn't need the money. And with Daredevil off the wall, the last relationship zombie was no longer a threat. He slid the print into an envelope and filed it in his desk drawer. One day, he might be able to enjoy it again.

When he was done, he surveyed his little home. *Now what?*

Sitting alone in his apartment didn't appeal. Neither did socializing. Restless and frustrated, he decided to go for a walk. Saturday night on Whyte Avenue was bound to provide some kind of entertainment. Maybe he would see Harpur. Maybe Harpur was looking for him. Maybe they would run into each other and go to the lair where Harpur would tell him more about his magic and the prophecy. Maybe he would ask Harpur to restore his memories from the first time they met eight years ago. Harpur had offered to do that for him. *I should have taken him up on it then.*

He walked back and forth along Whyte Avenue amid the Saturday night crowds for hours and with each step he felt more alone. He considered going to O'Bryan's, but both times he made his way to the door, he turned around and walked away again. He spent some time listening to a busker playing a beat-up acoustic guitar, hoping that if he stayed in one place, Harpur would find him. But when the busker packed up at midnight and there was still no sign of Harpur, Arthur gave up and went home.

Just as he unlocked the door to his apartment, his cell phone buzzed in his pocket. He went inside and closed the door behind him before he looked at his phone. Expecting a text message from someone, he nearly dropped the device when he saw the face of Hiro filling the screen.

Arthur gawked in total disbelief at the image of the Krist. It took him a second to realize that it wasn't just a photo; it was a still shot from a video. Hiro's face was frozen with his eyes half closed and his mouth open as if he was talking. There was no play arrow visible, but Arthur tapped the screen as he would to play a video. And Hiro came to life much the same way Anayah had in the video at the Pole.

"Hi, Arthur. I hope you are able to receive this message. We went to the Sphere to stop you, but we were too late. Bon told us what happened while you were there. Anayah and Analeetah are not happy with Harpur at the moment and Analeetah has forbidden Anayah from going after you, Sok or Harpur. I was able to get a few minutes alone with Bon at the Sphere and he showed me how to send you messages like this. That android is an absolute marvel with scrying technology. I wonder where he's from..." Hiro giggled. "Anyway, I will do my best to keep in touch and when I have a chance, I will return to the Sphere to see if Bon can help me find a way to communicate with you better. If you see Harpur..."

The video flickered, ended and then looped back to the beginning and started again.

Arthur watched it several times. "If I see Harpur, what?" Arthur said aloud. "What do I do if I see Harpur?"

He frantically looked for some way to reply, but there was nothing on the screen to allow him to do that. He tapped the screen, hoping that an icon would appear, but all that happened was the video disappeared.

Arthur was beside himself with joy and frustration. Over the next hour, the frustration slowly overtook the joy as he tried and failed miserably to recover the message from Hiro. "How did you do that, Hiro?" he asked repeatedly. "What do I do if I see Harpur?"

He didn't sleep much that night. All he could think about was seeing Harpur again. *Am I supposed to avoid Harpur? Am I supposed to tell him something? Ask him something? Give him something? What? Why did the message end before Hiro could tell me what to do?* All he could do was hope that Hiro sent another message soon.

The next afternoon, Arthur prepared to go to his parent's home in Glennora for Sunday dinner. He'd spent the day glued to his cell phone, willing it to deliver another message from Hiro. He checked the cameral roll and the deleted-photos folder over and over again, hoping to find the video. It just wasn't there. By the time he had to leave, he was tired and anxious and vexed to the point of despair. He didn't know how he was going to get through dinner.

Taking the bus from his apartment to his parents' home was a forty-five-minute exercise in mental torture. All he could do was fret about being there and having to listen to them gossip about neighbours (his mother) and complain about work (his father). They would, of course, want to know how things were with Cheryl and remind him that they were not getting any younger and would like grandchildren before they got too old to enjoy them. He wasn't sure if he would tell them that he had broken up with Cheryl. If he did, his mother would start a quest to find a replacement as soon as possible. Subsequent Sunday dinners would be a parade of eligible young women his mother rounded up and pressed into service as potential future mothers of her grandchildren. Maybe he'd tell them that he and Cheryl were taking a break and that they would get back together soon. *It's complicated, Ma.*

When he arrived at his parents' house, sans hostess gift, for which he received a stern look of disapproval from his mother, he was relieved to discover that he was not the only guest. Uncle Pete was joining them and that meant that the topic of conversation would be limited to fishing.

Uncle Pete was one of those mystery relatives, a distant cousin of a great aunt by marriage or something who popped in every now and then to boast about his latest catch. This time it was a ten-foot sturgeon he'd landed in the Fraser River near Hope, BC and Arthur was happy to let him ramble on about it. Whenever Pete appeared to be running out of steam, Arthur asked him a question and then deflected the telepathic daggers his mother threw at him with a smile and a compliment on the fantastic meal.

Marian Prentice was a petit fifty-two-year-old homemaker who took great pride in keeping a spotless house, cooking good meals for her family and entertaining friends and family every chance she got. She budgeted the money her husband Earl earned as a city administrator to the penny, never spending above their means and always saving a little more than was strictly necessary. She had three savings accounts. One for vacations, which she and Earl took every three years because that was the amount of time it took to save enough to go somewhere special; one for emergencies and one for a rainy day. Arthur never did understand what the difference between an emergency and a rainy day was and Marian had long since grown tired of trying to explain it to him.

She had a degree in business management, but the only business she had ever managed was the business of her family, which she ran in a business-like fashion. Once she and Earl tied the knot, she quit working and focussed all of her attention on household matters. While Earl, who also had a degree in business management, worked his way up with the city, Marian worked her way up as a domestic diva, becoming, at least in her mind, the envy of all of her friends.

She had raised Arthur, her only child, to be a conscientious, caring and respectful man. It vexed her that he had reached the age of thirty without having "settled down" with a wife and a couple of kids. He didn't even own a car yet! This, she was determined, had to change. But any efforts she might have had lined up that night were neatly and conveniently thwarted by Uncle Pete. By the time dessert was served, she was resigned to defeat and didn't even protest when Arthur excused himself with a vague reference to an early day coming up and needing to get some sleep. He offered to help with the dishes, but Marian waved him off. Cleaning up would be her excuse not to have to listen to *Uncle Pete Slays a Sturgeon* for the nth time.

The moment he escaped his parents' house, Arthur checked his phone. It had taken all the willpower he possessed not to look at it during dinner. The no-phones-at-the-table rule was strictly enforced at Marian's house. Nothing made a grown man feel less like a grown man than having his cell phone confiscated by his mother. So, he'd turned off the ringer and kept it in his pocket while he ate. Out on the sidewalk, however, there was no sign of a missed message from anyone. But especially not one from Hiro.

Arthur's despair enveloped him like sack and tied itself closed at the top of his head. It was going to be another long sleepless night.

The days that followed stretched out and became a void in Arthur's life. Messages from Hiro were void. Harpur was void. His love life and his work life were void. All he did was wander up and down Whyte Avenue, looking for the dragon-wizard or sitting on the bus stop bench across from the Boundary trying not to look like he was looking up at it. From where he sat, he could just make out the faint shimmering of the top half of the Boundary, but he was sure that if Harpur were to come through from or try to Bound to Thraeh, he'd be able to tell.

He thought he had spotted Harpur one day in late May, but by the time he reached the store he saw him come out of, Harpur was gone. This made him feel desperate, so he went to JJ's Barber Shop and asked Jason for a pen and a piece of paper on which he wrote a note for Harpur. *Need to talk. Received a message from Hiro.* It was short and simple and he knew that Harpur would not ignore it.

"You wouldn't happen to have any duct tape, would you?" Arthur asked the friendly barber.

"Sure thing," Jason said. "It's in the back." He retrieved the duct tape and watched as Arthur cut two strips from the roll. "Is everything okay?"

"Yeah," Arthur said as he attached the strips to the note. "My friend isn't answering his phone. Probably lost it again," Arthur made a face to stress how often this imaginary event occurred. "And he's not at home, so I'm just going to leave this on his door."

"Oh, well, I hope you reach him okay." Jason picked up the duct tape to return it to the back of the shop. *Who tapes notes to doors anymore?*

"I'm sure I will. Thanks, Jason." Arthur thought that went pretty well. Seemed normal enough.

He walked to the alley where he thought the entrance to the lair was and attached the note to the brick wall. Confident that Harpur would find him easily enough, Arthur walked home.

The next day, he returned to the alley. The note was still on the wall.

The day after that, he returned to the alley again. The note was still on the wall, but it had rained overnight and the ink had run. The duct tape holding the top of the note had come loose and the note itself was flopped forward, hanging upside down by the bottom piece of tape.

The day after that, when Arthur went to the alley, the note was gone. He searched the ground to see if it had fallen off the wall, but didn't find it.

Again, the despair engulfed him. He went to the bus stop bench and sat down. *Damn you, Harpur! Where are you?*

He sat for a while, trying to convince himself to give up, to just forget about dragon-wizards and Krists and elves and prophecies and magic. He needed to do something to end the funk he was in. He knew that. He just didn't have a clue what that might be.

Arthur was about to leave the bus stop and go home when a bus pulled up and disgorged a dozen or so passengers onto the sidewalk around the bench. Arthur remained seated, waiting for them to disperse and the bus to pull away before he left. One of the passengers, however, did not disperse. Instead, she walked over to the bench and sat down next to Arthur.

"Why so glum?"

Arthur looked over to see a cute, hippie girl with a mane of unruly curls and enormous green eyes, though Arthur couldn't tell if her eyes were really big or just magnified by the round wire-frame glasses that perched on her cute, little button nose. She wore a short, brightly coloured shift over mid-calf leggings and she smelled of patchouli. Crystals and beads hung in several layers around her neck. Bangles jangled on her wrists and most of her fingers and toes sparkled with semi-precious stones set into pewter rings collected from festival booths over the past ten years. Arthur smiled outwardly and sighed inwardly.

"Me?" he asked.

"Yeah, you," the cute, hippie girl said. "You look like you lost your best friend." When she smiled, a tiny diamond screwed into her cheek sparkled in the sunlight.

Arthur didn't think of Harpur, Sok or Hiro as being in the BFF category, but he was a little disconcerted at the odd accuracy of her assessment. "Not lost, exactly," he confirmed. "Misplaced?"

"What's the difference?"

What indeed? "I kind of know where they are. I just can't get to them." Arthur unconsciously looked up at the Boundary.

The cute, hippie girl followed his gaze. "They're on the roof?"

"Sort of," Arthur said enigmatically. Then he looked at her and something inside him popped loose. She was really cute. Maybe she could help him with the funk. It was worth a try. "I don't suppose you'd like to join me for a cup of coffee?"

The cute, hippie girl smiled. "Why not?" she said. "You can tell me all about your misplaced friends. I'm Alex, by the way."

"Arthur," Arthur said, holding out his hand for her to shake.

But instead of shaking his hand, Alex gave Arthur a Vulcan salute and that thing that had popped inside of him a few minutes earlier burst wide open.

As they stood to walk to the corner, Arthur looked up at the Boundary once again.

"What is so fascinating about that roof top?" Alex asked.

Arthur looked at her. It was too soon to tell her everything, but he decided to see if he could pave the way to that eventuality. "Alex, look up at the sky above that building again," he said pointing to where the Boundary shimmered. "Do you see anything weird?"

Alex indulged him. "What am I looking for?"

"Does the air look like it's shimmering, kind of like a heat mirage?"

Alex studied the sky above the building and frowned. "I don't see any... Oh! Yes. I do see it. That cloud looks a little blurry on one side."

"Yes!" Arthur did an air punch.

"What is it?"

"Probably just a heat mirage. But it's always there."

"If you like, after we have coffee, we can go up and check it out." Alex offered.

"Uh... I'm sure it's just a heat mirage. Let's go get that coffee." Arthur hadn't expected that. He'd need to be a little less eager for a while.

They crossed the street and went into the Second Cup. Alex ordered an iced cappuccino. Arthur ordered a large double-double and got scowled at for using the competition's lingo.

Sitting at a table by the window Alex started things off. "Tell me about your friends."

Arthur grasped for something to say about Harpur and Sok that wasn't a lie, but didn't make him sound insane. "There's not much to tell, really. You'd have to meet them to understand them."

"I'd like that. I'll bet they are really interesting." Alex said with a smile that lit up the whole café.

"That they are," Arthur had to agree. "Say, what's your position on chocolate cake? There's a huge slice on the counter that keeps calling my name. Want to share it with me?"

"Food of the gods," Alex said

Arthur purchased the chocolate cake, asked for an extra plate and fork and returned to his seat. He divided the slice and pushed both plates to the middle of the table. "I sliced it, so you get to choose."

Alex pulled the plate with the slightly larger piece of cake on it to her side of the table and started eating it. Arthur smiled with approval and the funk shriveled a little more.

"And what about dragons?" Arthur slipped in. Just to test the waters.

"I've never eaten a dragon. But I hear they taste just like chicken."

Alex and Arthur both laughed. *It feels good to laugh*, Arthur thought. "I meant what's your position on dragons?"

Alex sat back in her chair and regarded Arthur with curious surprise as she twirled her fork in her hand. "I'd have to say I'm cautiously neutral."

"Cautiously neutral? How so?" Arthur took another bite of his cake.

"Well, I've never met one," Alex began, "but they don't sound like very nice creatures."

"What would you do if you did meet one?"

"Probably the same thing I'd do if I met Big Foot or a leprechaun, go get my head examined." Alex laughed.

Time to change the subject. "Sounds like a wise plan. So, what brings you to Whyte Avenue on this lovely spring day? Do you live around here?"

Alex and Arthur spent the next couple hours learning about each other. Alex, it turned out, was a high school English teacher who had recently moved into an apartment on the west end of Whyte Avenue near the University of Alberta. Like Arthur, she was an only child. Her parents raised goats on Vancouver Island and taught philosophy and art at Vancouver Island University. Arthur shared his woeful tale of being a comic book store manager for a whole six hours, spinning the woe out of it and rinsing it in a warm wash of opportunity.

"What would you like to do next?" Alex asked.

"Become the king of a magical land." Arthur said it before he could stop himself. He froze, looking at Alex and hoping she didn't hear the seriousness in his voice.

Alex just smiled. "And who would be your queen in this magical land?"

Whew! "I don't know. But I think she should have curly hair and love chocolate cake."

Arthur didn't think it was possible, but Alex's smile brightened even more. "I wonder if the way to this magical land is up there," she pointed out the window toward the roof tops, "through the heat mirage."

Arthur gasped. *No!* "I guess we'll never know. How about we go see a movie or something."

"Come on," Alex said. "Let's go see what's up there." She stood up and held out her hand to Arthur.

Chapter 14

About a million reasons not to Bound made instant appearances in Arthur's mind. But they were slippery and fast and he couldn't catch any of them. Alex pulled him out of the café and to the corner.

"Alex, stop!" Arthur said as the light changed and she started to cross the street. "I don't think this is a very good idea." His eyes darted around, looking for Harpur. *Please, don't show up now.*

"Where's your sense of adventure?" she called back over her shoulder.

Arthur had no choice. He dashed after Alex and caught up to her just as she was opening the door to a small restaurant called *Rice On Whyte* that occupied the bottom floor of the building on which the Boundary was located. She approached the counter where she was greeted by a short, Oriental man with an enormous grin and grease stains on his white shirt. "Alex!" he shouted. "Welcome, welcome! What I get for you?"

"Nothing right now, Cho. We need to get up on the roof." She waved her hand back and forth between herself and Arthur. "Can you let us up there?"

"Why you want on roof?" he yelled.

Arthur cringed.

"I can't tell you. It's a secret," Alex whispered conspiratorially.

"Oh! Okay," Cho shouted. "I get keys. You follow."

Arthur was stunned. *It can't be this easy.*

"Cho's a sweetheart," Alex said. "He'll do anything for me."

Cho shouted something at an even shorter Oriental lady in Mandarin and beckoned for Alex and Arthur to follow him. The even shorter Oriental lady shouted something back at Cho, then smiled at Alex as she passed two fortune cookies over the counter to her. "You read," she shouted. "Bring good luck."

"Thanks, Mei," Alex said. She passed one of the cookies to Arthur.

Cho led them through the kitchen where more various-sized Oriental people were yelling at each other. One of them yelled at Cho.

Cho yelled back. When they came to a locked door at the back of the kitchen, Cho unlocked it and waved them through. "Third step from top broken. Watch your step."

"Thank you, Cho," Alex said. "What about the door at the top?"

"Not locked. No need."

She and Arthur entered a narrow stairwell and began their ascent. The building was only three stories high, and at each floor a boarded-up door explained why the door to the roof was unlocked.

"Is that legal?" Arthur asked.

"It's an old building. I'm guessing that this stairwell isn't used anymore."

"There must be a fire escape on the outside then," Arthur reasoned. "Why didn't we just use that?"

"If there is a fire escape, and I'm not sure there is, it would only go to a top floor window. We'd still have to get from there to the roof."

"Good point. But, really, Alex, this is not a good idea."

"Why? We're just going to see what's causing the heat mirage. It will be fine."

Arthur was desperate. "I just remembered; I have a thing..." *That was lame.*

Alex stopped a few stairs above him and turned around. "What thing?"

Arthur sighed. "Fine. We'll just take a quick look and then we're getting out of here."

"That's the spirit!" Alex continued climbing the stairs.

As promised, the door to the roof was unlocked. The doorknob turned easily, but the door itself was stuck. Arthur had to throw his shoulder into it several times before it budged enough for them to squeeze through.

They stepped out onto the roof and saw the shimmering Boundary looming above them. "Whoa!" Alex exclaimed. "I don't think that's a heat mirage."

Arthur knew it wasn't a heat mirage. *Why did I open my big mouth?* "Neither do I. I think we should probably just leave. It could be dangerous."

"How dangerous?" Alex moved to the front of the Boundary and reached to touch it.

"Don't touch it!" Arthur yelled.

But it was too late. Alex's hand when through the Boundary. Nothing happened. "It's okay. See?" She held up her hand to show Arthur that she was unscathed. Then she did the unthinkable and walked through it.

Arthur watched in horror, expecting Alex to disappear. But she didn't. She turned around when she got to the other side and to Arthur it looked like he was seeing her through a wall of water. She walked back to the front and stared up at the shimmering disk. The bottom was about two feet above the roof top; a short hop even for a petit woman like Alex.

"Okay, we've seen it. Let's get out of here," Arthur said, backing away from the Boundary. He was relieved when Alex backed away with him.

She took two more steps farther than Arthur and then sprinted forward, taking a running leap into the centre of the Boundary. "Right after I..." she called back. And then she disappeared.

"Alex! No!" Arthur shouted. He stood there in shock for several seconds building up the nerve to follow her. "Crazy hippie!" he snapped as he, too, ran forward and jumped through.

Harpur had felt pretty bad about leaving Arthur in the alley the way he had. He had needed to get back to Sok and make sure the elf was not detected. That hadn't worked out quite the way he'd planned, but they had managed to avert a complete disaster and Bloomregaard had let them go. As soon as the Senior Bounding Officer had been led away on his horse from the Boundary, Harpur and Sok both agreed that they needed to avoid drawing any further attention to themselves for a while.

"That was close," Sok said.

"Bloomregaard gave up too easy. If King Gnik recognized us, he'll want us punished. And I can't see Bloomregaard not wanting to indulge that. He's up to something." Harpur said.

"I told you he was!"

"When?"

"When you first found me at the Boundary on Whyte Avenue. I said, 'I think he's up to something bad.'"

"I had other things on my mind." Harpur only vaguely recalled Sok saying something to that effect.

"Why don't you just alter everyone's memories so they'll forget we ever Bounded into the king's private chambers?"

"I could, but I don't know who all who knows. If I miss someone and they say anything, Bloomregaard will just be suspicious about that. He's not stupid. He'd start wondering about what he can't remember. Wiping memories only disables the ability to recall what happened and I'm betting that Bloomregaard didn't push the issue tonight because he wants to find out who Arthur is first. Arthur is safe on Earth. We'll just leave him there and let this play out. You go back to work and keep an eye on our Senior Bounding Officer. Find out what he is planning if you can and let me know."

"I'll just Bound to Whyte Avenue if I learn anything." Sok was looking forward to learning anything just so he could do this.

"No!" Harpur said. "I'll check in with you here. Do not Bound to Whyte Avenue again."

"Fine," Sok said sulkily and headed back to Colwygshire.

Harpur burned the note the Patrol Chief had received from Bloomregaard. Then he woke up the patrolmen and convinced them there had been a slight change in plans and he was no longer to be detained. A little stereotypical dragon intimidation goes a long way with the likes of underpaid patrolmen. Once all that was settled, Harpur returned to his lair to lay low for a while.

Harpur had hoped that Arthur would get on with his life and not obsess about what had happened. He wasn't surprised when Arthur tried to find the entrance to the lair that first time. He wasn't even surprised when he found the note Arthur had taped to the wall outside the lair. There was no way that Arthur could possibly have received a message from Hiro and he'd put it down as a desperate ploy for attention. But the more he thought about it, the more curious he became. While Arthur did have his clever moments, Harpur didn't think he had enough guile to make something like that up. And if the Krist was Bounding to Earth, Harpur needed to know. More time to allow things in Epoh to cool down would be good. It was time to go and visit the would-be king of Epoh.

Harpur had detected a Bounding attempt right after he had found Arthur's note on the wall in the alley. He had just finished dealing with that and was just about to Bound back to Whyte Avenue to go find Arthur, when a cute hippie girl came flying through the Boundary right toward him. He barely had enough time to shift his stance and catch her.

"...I do this?" Alex finished what she had been saying to Arthur as she jumped into the shimmering air above the rooftop.

Expecting to land on a rooftop a few feet from where she had jumped, finding herself in the arms of a giant man with violet eyes and a top hat standing in a forest was altogether the most shocking experience of Alex's life. The involuntary scream she was about to emit was still forming in her larynx when Harpur suddenly leaped backward as a flailing Arthur sailed past them both. They watched as he literally hit the ground running. He took three huge, clumsy steps before losing his balance, falling to the side and rolling under bush where he lay groaning on his back.

"What in the flaming name of Orhowyn is going on here?" Harpur shouted.

He put the cute hippie girl down, but held onto her arm so she couldn't attempt to Bound away and dragged her with him to the bush where Arthur lay spitting dirt and leaves out of his mouth.

"Are you out of your mind?" Harpur railed at Arthur as he loomed over the dishevelled man. "What do you think you are doing coming here? And why is she here?" He pointed at Alex.

Not having had time to consider this particular scenario, much less prepare for it, Arthur opened and closed his mouth several times, but all that came out was, "I... We... That is... Um..."

Harpur looked back at Alex, hoping the cute, hippie girl would be less tongue-tied and able to produce a more coherent explanation. Alex's face was running through a series of contortions that dashed that hope in a tide of abject hopelessness. Harpur sighed.

"Okay, you two. You are both going back to Whyte Avenue and you are never to Bound here on your own again. Do you understand?"

Arthur scrambled to his feet and brushed more dirt and leaves off his clothes and out of his hair.

"Oh, for the love of Orhowyn! Are you *crying*?"

Arthur sniffled. "No," he whined in denial. He used his dirt-smudged wrist to wipe his nose. The dirt transferred from wrist to upper lip and, if he wasn't so mad, Harpur would have laughed.

"Unbelievable," Harpur muttered.

"Please don't be mad at Arthur," Alex said softly. "It was my idea to come here. I made him do it."

As embarrassed as she was for Arthur, Alex felt terrible. This was not how she imagined things would go. What she had imagined was that they would find a furnace or an air-conditioning unit on the roof top causing a heat mirage. She was just being playful. When Arthur had said he wanted to become king of a magical land, she had thought of the heat mirage and thought they could pretend it was a portal that would take them there. When she saw the Boundary shimmering away with no obvious origin, she didn't for a second believe that jumping through it was going to result in... this! Whatever this was.

It was taking all the self-control she possessed not to freak out. One minute she was on a roof top; the next she was in a forest talking to an enormous man in a top hat. *Maybe Arthur roofied my coffee with something.* No. This was real. It was fantastical, but it was real. Alex didn't know whether to regret sitting down on that bus bench or be thrilled to death that every fantasy she'd ever had about magical kingdoms and fairy tale worlds might be coming true.

Stay calm.

Harpur ignored Alex and pinched the bridge of his nose with his free hand. He took a deep breath and when he exhaled, a puff of smoke erupted from his mouth. Alex became very still.

"Arthur, do you remember what I said when we were in the alley after we got back from here?" Harpur asked.

Arthur sniffled again. The tears had stopped, but he felt devastated. The funk was back in full force. "You said that I should have more faith in you."

"That's right. Did it not occur to you that there might be a reason I was staying away from you?"

Several reasons had occurred to Arthur, but he hadn't liked any of them. "Not really," he said.

"You weren't supposed to ever have known about Thraeh. Or about me. Or about Sok. Or about any of this." He gestured to encompass the whole crazy adventure they had been on.

"So why didn't you wipe my memory again, then?" Arthur said angrily. "Why did you just leave me there with no one to talk about it with? And what about the prophecy? And my magic? I thought we were...friends."

Harpur looked at the distraught man. "I wanted you to remember, Arthur. I also needed to deal with Gnik and his wanting to burn us all at the stake for Bounding into his private chambers. And Bloomregaard is up to something and we can't figure out what it is. So, there's that to take care of. On top of that there's Anayah. As for the prophecy, I have no idea what to make of that. Epoh has a king. But once things got sorted out, I would have come to see you."

"How was I supposed to know that?" Arthur whined.

"I thought you were smarter than that, Arthur. I took a big risk in letting you remember everything. Humans on Earth have to stay on Earth. You know that."

Alex was trying to follow this very confusing exchange. *Prophecy? Magic? Anayah? Memory wiping?* It was all intriguing—in a terrifying way—but it was an injustice that her hippie-Spidey senses honed in on. "Why do humans have to stay on Earth?" Alex asked. "I'll bet there are tons of people who would love to know about this."

Arthur and Harpur both looked at the cute, hippie girl like she had two heads.

"No!" they said in unison.

"But why? Don't we have the right to know that we can go to other worlds?" Alex was insulted on behalf of all humanity.

"Alex, humans are advanced and our technology would upset the natural evolution of worlds like Thraeh and Mysturna." Arthur said. "It's kind of like the Prime Directive."

"Like in Star Trek?" Alex asked. "What are Thraeh and Mysturna?"

"Advanced?" Harpur barked with laughter, ignoring Alex. "Advanced? You think humans are advanced? Oh, Arthur, you really aren't as smart as I gave you credit for."

Arthur looked at Harpur. He was as insulted and confused as Alex, but he was determined to win this argument. "We are advanced. There are no cars or cell phones or computers on Thraeh or Mysturna."

"That's right, Arthur. There are no cars or cell phones or computers on Thraeh or Mysturna. But there used to be."

"What!" Arthur exclaimed. "When?"

"A long time ago." Harpur said. "Think about it, Arthur. What is there on Thraeh and Mysturna that there isn't on Earth?

Arthur thought about it. "Magic?" he suggested.

"And what is magic?"

Arthur thought some more. "I don't know," he conceded.

"It is the product of evolution. It's what happens after cars and computers and cell phones," Harpur said. "It's the next logical step."

"I don't get it," Alex said.

"Me either," Arthur said.

"And that's why humans from Earth have to stay on Earth," Harpur said to the great dissatisfaction of both humans. "For the time being at least. Either you will collectively get there. Or you won't. But unless and until you do, we can't have you dragging us back into the dark ages."

Arthur was confused.

Alex was confused.

Harpur was just frustrated.

"We need to get you out of here before anyone discovers you." Harpur stood up and gestured toward the Boundary.

"But I want to look around," Alex said.

"Ain't gonna happen," Harpur said.

"What if you disguised us as elves or something?" Alex looked hopefully at Harpur.

"Elves! You're both too short to be elves." Harpur dismissed the preposterous proposition.

"Maybe we're human-elf hybrids," Alex said.

"That's ridiculous!" Harpur dismissed the even more preposterous proposition.

"Make us invisible!" Arthur rallied to support Alex. "Or fly us around. No one will be able to tell who we are from up there." He pointed at the sky.

It has been a while since I've stretched my wings, Harpur thought. Then he came back to his sense. "No! Now drop it."

"But..." Alex started to plead with Harpur.

"Both of you! Just drop it. You're going back and that's all there is to it."

Defeated, Alex and Arthur moved closer to the Boundary.

"It's higher up of the ground here than it is on the roof top," Alex said. "I don't know if I can jump that high."

This was a legitimate, but not insurmountable concern. "I'll carry you," Harpur said. "Arthur, do you think you can make it on your own?"

"Maybe." Arthur wasn't sure at all. The bottom of the Boundary was chest height on him. High jumping was never his forte.

Harpur rolled his eyes. "I'll carry both of you."

Familiar with the routine, Arthur took Harpur's walking stick and then positioned himself to be picked up by the dragon-wizard.

"Still using this thing, eh?" Arthur said.

Harpur ignored the tone and the question. He gathered Arthur and Alex up by their waists and jumped through the Boundary to Earth.

Back on the roof top, rather than put them down, Harpur walked straight to the edge of the roof and, once he was sure no one was around, jumped off. Then he put them down. He took the walking stick from Arthur and pointed to the end of the alley, which is where he wanted them to go.

"You know," said Alex, "there's nothing stopping us from just Bounding back whenever we want."

Arthur was shaking his head at Alex trying to get her to shut up. The same thought had crossed his mind, but he at least was smart enough to know not to remind Harpur.

"By the time you get to the end of the alley, you'll have forgotten all about it," Harpur said sadly.

"No! Please, Harpur! Don't make me... us forget!" Arthur was on the verge of panic.

Harpur looked at the two problems standing before him. "Tell you what," he said. "If you promise that you will never—EVER—Bound again, I'll take you both back to my lair. I'll answer all your questions and then you, Arthur, will get on with your life. Deal?"

"Deal," said Arthur. "As long as you promise to find me when things get sorted out on Thraeh."

Harpur narrowed his eyes. "I already told you..."

"I promise," said Alex, not wanting things to deteriorate. She wanted to see this lair the big man spoke of. "I'm Alex, by the way."

Harpur grunted. It was all the introduction she was going to get.

Harpur led Arthur and Alex out of the alley, across Whyte Avenue and into another alley on the south side of the busy street. They stopped behind a squat, brick building where, with a wave of Harpur's walking stick, a green door a few steps below street level appeared before them. They descended and Harpur opened the door to let them in.

"You don't lock your door?" Alex asked a little alarmed by what she thought of as an odd lack of security.

Harpur looked at her in disbelief. "Why would I lock it? No one can even see it."

Alex blushed.

Then she gasped! The lair was an enormous cavern under the city. She stood there with her mouth open taking in the state-of-the-art, gourmet kitchen and the opulent conversation pit. Then she saw the huge pile of treasure. If this was all the result of being drugged, it was sure interesting.

"You just leave all this sitting out here like this?"

"It's a dragon hoard. That's what dragons do with their hoards." Harpur explained as if millions of dollars worth of gold and jewels was completely normal.

Alex stepped closer to the edge of the mountain of gold and reached out for a jeweled goblet that was sticking out of it.

"Uh, uh, uh!" Harpur said. "Do not touch it."

He said it gently enough, but Alex felt the warning edge of a threat like a dagger against her throat. She withdrew her hand and stepped away from hoard.

"So, how can this be here?" she gestured at the cavernous cavern. "Where are all the sewer and water pipes?

"We are much farther below the street than you think," Harpur said.

"But...?"

"It's magic." He smiled. "Pretty advanced, hey?" Harpur shot a mocking glance in Arthur direction.

It was Arthur's turn to blush.

While Alex and Arthur settled on a lush, leather sofa in the conversation pit, Harpur lit a fire in the fire place with a wave of his walking stick. The instant blaze delighted Alex so much, she clapped her hands in applause. She was no less frightened, but she wasn't going to let that diminish the experience.

"And for my next trick..." Harpur said, reaching into a glass-fronted refrigerator and pulling out three bottles of beer. He poured the beer into three tall, crystal glasses and handed one to Alex and one to Arthur, whose frown indicated that the bottle would have sufficed, before settling himself into his favourite spot opposite his visitors.

"Okay, Arthur, you have the floor. What do you want to know?" Harpur sipped the crisp ale and smiled at his guest.

Arthur didn't know where to begin. It took a while to sift through the supposition that had accumulated since he'd returned from his adventure to find the most burning question. He believed that if he started with the right question, the rest of the story would flow naturally. Suddenly, it was obvious.

"What happened to Sok?"

"Sok is fine. He's still working for Bloomregaard."

Okay! I guess I will have to prod harder, Arthur thought. "So, he didn't go to prison, then?"

"Nope! Bloomregaard was—still is, actually—suspicious, but he never gathered enough proof to convict Sok of anything. He does keep him on a short leash, which is a bit of a bummer for the elf, but you know Sok. Ever the optimist."

Arthur felt sad for Sok. "What about Yna? What about his hand? Did he ever get the cuff off?"

Harpur laughed. "Yna? She's still single. Let's just leave that one alone." Harpur continued to chuckle at some private amusement surrounding Sok's unrequited love for the warrior woman of his dreams. "As for the cuff, it just dissolved and fell off. Magic is never permanent; it was bound to happen eventually. His hand is returning to normal. I've opted not to intervene. What happened to your cuff?"

"I just cut it off. It's in a drawer in my apartment. I think." He hadn't looked at it since he'd put it there, but if Sok's cuff dissolved, maybe his had too. "So, what happened to Anayah? Where is she?" The fact that she didn't intentionally reverse the magic of the cuff was disturbing.

"I assume she's still on Mysturna. I haven't seen her since we left her at the temple to go to the Sphere." Harpur shrugged.

"Doesn't that bother you?"

"A little," Harpur conceded. "But if she wants to find me, she knows where I am."

"But she loves you!"

"I'm a dragon, Arthur. Remember? I don't feel love the same way that other beings do. I cared about her. Deeply. But I'm not capable of the kind of relationship that Anayah had in mind. That's not how things work for me. Anayah knows that. I don't know why she thought she could change it."

To Arthur, this matter-of-fact summary sounded more like Harpur was trying to convince himself of the way things were, than a revelation about true dragon nature. He felt bad for Anayah. He also noted the past tense Harpur had used. *Cared? Does that mean he doesn't care anymore?*

"Do you think she's okay?" Arthur asked, not daring to poke that bear too hard, but unable to resist asking.

"I think she's fine," Harpur said. His tone suggested the bear was losing his patience.

Alex, who had remained quiet through this wildly bizarre exchange spoke up. "What's next?"

"What do you mean?" Harpur asked.

"What happens now?" To Alex it seemed like a logical question.

"Arthur keeps his promise and gets his life here back on track." Harpur answered Alex's question, but he looked at Arthur as he did, driving his point firmly home.

"It just seems so... final," Alex said.

"Not final." Harpur templed his fingers under his chin. "The story will pick up again when it is meant to."

"Can you do me one favour?" Alex asked.

"What's that?" Harpur replied, curious.

"Can you change into a dragon for me?" She braced for an emphatic, if not irate, rejection.

Harpur took a deep breath, about to deny her request. *Oh, what the hell?*

He walked over to his treasure hoard where there was enough room to accommodate his dragon form. The transformation lasted only a few seconds and Alex watched in awe as the man, big as he already was, grew bigger right before her eyes. Harpur's hat dissolved and was replaced by opalescent purple spikes. His clothing seemed to melt and then convert into scales. A tail and wings grew out of his body. His neck stretched and his head changed shape. And suddenly, an enormous, reptilian giant filled the lair with majestic splendour.

And Alex fainted.

"Well, that's disappointing," Harpur said.

Arthur looked down at Alex. "At least I never fainted." He bent down and lifted Alex's limp body onto the nearest sofa.

"Actually, the first time you saw this, you did faint. A couple of times." Harpur watched Arthur closely. Will he take the bait?

"I'm not ready to get those memories back," Arthur knew that they involved him dying after being struck by a car. He wasn't sure if he wanted to remember that.

"Very well. When you are ready." Harpur said. Then he decided to take advantage of Alex's unconscious state. "Tell me about the message from Hiro."

"Oh, right!" Arthur said. "I almost forgot about that. It was the weirdest thing. He sent me a video message on my phone. Said Bon showed him how to do it."

Harpur saw no deceit in what Arthur said. "What exactly did this video message say? Can you show it to me?"

Arthur screwed up his face as if to wring the memory of the video out of his head. "It disappeared after I watched it. All he said was that they had missed us at the Sphere and that Bon had shown him how to send a message to me. He said he was going to go back when he had a chance to see if he could figure out a way for us to communicate better. And then he started to tell me something about you, but the video ended before he could finish."

"About me?"

"His exact words were, 'If you see Harpur...' Any idea what he meant?"

Harpur shook his dragon head. "I do not. Nothing since?"

"Not a thing." They lapsed into silence. "I have one more question, though."

"Shoot," Harpur said and then transformed back into his human form.

"What happened to your scale? The one that is missing from your chest."

Harpur hosted an internal debate to decide how to answer that. Telling the truth won. "I pulled it out and gave it to the trees in the Forest of Dheersha in exchange for your life."

"You did that for me?" That was not the answer Arthur had been expecting. He didn't know what he had been expecting, but it wasn't that.

"I did that for you."

Alex started to come around. She groaned and opened her eyes. When she saw Arthur and Harpur's human faces staring down at her, she pushed herself up and smiled. "That was awesome!"

"You okay?" Arthur asked.

"I think so."

"Good," Harpur said. "Now it's time you two went home. I've got work to do."

Harpur escorted his guests back out to the alley and, with a firm reminder of their promise to him, sent them on their way.

"Good night, Harpur," Arthur said over his shoulder as he linked arms with Alex and walked away feeling better than he had in weeks.

"Good night, Arthur," Harpur said quietly and then waved his walking stick in a sweeping arc toward his friend and the cute hippie girl.

Chapter 15

Arthur and Alex, arm in arm, exited the alley and turned left on 104 Street heading to Whyte Avenue. The smile Arthur had been sporting vanished as they joined the foot traffic on the sidewalk and he stopped walking.

"Wow! I must have blanked out there for a minute. What were we doing in the alley?" he said.

Alex thought about it for a moment. "I don't know. That's so weird. What were we doing back there?"

Arthur started walking again. Slowly. Trying to get his mental and emotional bearings. Alex, still attached to him at the elbow had no choice but to walk along with him. Not wanting to reveal the depth of his discomfiture, Arthur pasted his smile back on and said, "Well, I know what I was doing."

"What's that?"

"Enjoying the company."

"Aw," Alex cooed. "Me too."

"Should we get something to eat? I'm really hungry."

"Can I get a rain cheque? It's been a long day and I'm kinda bushed."

"Of course," Arthur agreed, smiling on through his disappointment.

Arthur walked Alex to her car. Miraculously, there was no ticket on the windshield in spite of the fact that it had been parked in the lot far longer than the allotted four hours. She offered to drive him to his apartment, but Arthur declined, saying he wanted to walk and clear his mind. Had he realized that his mind had already been *cleared*, he might not have been so calm. They exchanged cell phone numbers and Arthur promised to call Alex. Though neither one of them could remember what they had been doing together all day, they both declared that they had had a good time and that it would be great to get together again. Soon.

Arthur stood in the parking lot and watched Alex drive away in her lemon-yellow VW Beetle. When it disappeared around the corner, he suddenly felt very alone. Instead of going home and being more alone, he decided to appease his hunger at O'Bryan's. A burger and a beer sounded good and it had been a long time since he'd been there.

He walked up Whyte Avenue thinking about his day. He remembered Alex joining him on the bench at the bus stop. *But why was I at the bus stop?* He remembered getting coffee and talking for hours. *What did we talk about?* He remembered going to Rice on Whyte. *But what did we do there?* And finally, he remembered talking to a very large man wearing a top hat. *But who was he and what did we talk about?* He couldn't fill in the gaps between these bits and snatches of memory. Something big, something important was missing. *Maybe I'm losing my mind.*

Arthur had, indeed, lost part of his mind. And for that Harpur, back in his lair under Whyte Avenue, was feeling a small measure of guilt. It was a very small measure; dragons are not generally inclined to feel guilt in measures other than very small. What was done, was done, and Harpur knew that it was for the best. He probably should have done it when he first brought Arthur back to Earth through the Boundary. All he could do now was hope that Arthur's affections for Alex would develop into enough of a distraction to keep him from dwelling on any gaps in his memory. The real reason Harpur had wiped Arthur's memory was not because he was so concerned that he might Bound again; it was because he had Bounded with Alex. And now that Alex had been to the lair and had seen him, he had a new layer of vulnerability to deal with. He didn't know her and he didn't trust her. *There was no other option,* he told himself. The worst part was that Harpur knew that he'd have to deal with Arthur again at some point. He'd have to restore Arthur's memories and then he'd have to win Arthur's trust again. For now, though, this was how things had to be. At least he'd been able to get some information about the message Arthur had received from Hiro. Not much information, but it did not appear that the Krist had Bounded to Earth.

Arthur entered the pub and took a seat at the bar. The place was busy, but not over-crowded. Groups of people sat at tables, eating buffalo wings and drinking drinks. Laughter mingled with the music that was playing just loud enough to keep conversation from drifting too far away from the tables where it originated. In the upstairs lounge, shouts of triumph and groans of defeat from a live trivia game competed with the mingling music and laughter. Arthur heard the emcee ask what a dragon with only two legs and arms incorporated into its wings was called. This piqued his interest, but he didn't know why he would care.

John, the bartender, plonked a pint of draft in front of Arthur, who reached for his wallet to pay for it. "This is from the lady over there," he pointed to the far end of the bar and then drifted away from Arthur to tend to other customers.

Arthur looked toward the far end of the bar. A gorgeous red-head smiled back at him. He was uber flattered, but he did not move from his seat to join her. Instead, he just smiled back and raised his glass in a silent toast of gratitude. He had no desire to socialize. Not even with a gorgeous red-head, who looked oddly familiar to him. He had a distinct feeling that he had seen her somewhere before, but he couldn't place her. She didn't seem to be offended by his lack of interest. She finished the glass of red wine she was holding and left the pub.

"Are you not feeling well?" John asked when he saw this exchange.

"I'm a little out of sorts," Arthur admitted.

"You must be more than a little out of sorts to have passed up an opportunity like that." John was concerned. "What's up?"

"I spent the day with a girl I met and I can't remember what we did."

"That's weird," John said. "How do you forget a whole day? How do you forget a whole day with a girl? Was she that boring?"

"No," Arthur said. "She's pretty cool. I'm going to see her again."

"You know what you need, Arthur?" John leaned on his elbows on the bar.

"A burger? With fries and gravy?" Arthur's stomach growled as if to second that idea.

"Coming up. But what you need is a job." John scribbled the order for a burger with fries and gravy onto a slip and passed it into the kitchen.

"Yeah. I'm sorry I didn't get back to you before. Some other... stuff came up." Arthur said. He took a handful of pretzels from a bowl on the bar and put one in his mouth and tried to figure out what other stuff had come up.

"The offer's still open," John said. "The other guy didn't work out."

"Seriously?"

"Yeah. I'd love to give you a try. You'll have to work weekends, but at least you wouldn't be sitting here wondering what you did all day."

Arthur let this offer roll around in the gaps in his memory where it had lots of room to expand. "What the hell? I'll have to update my ProServe certification."

"You do that. I'll reimburse you for the fee. You can start next Wednesday. Day shift. Be here at nine thirty."

"Thanks, man. I will."

John moved down the bar to fill another order, leaving Arthur to his thoughts and his beer. He ate his burger with fries and gravy after John delivered it to him a short while later. By then his pint was empty and he held the glass stein up as he stuffed the first crispy French fry smothered in gravy into his mouth to let John know he was ready for another one. John was already on it and swapped the empty glass for a full one.

All things considered, Arthur felt pretty good about things. A full belly could do that for him. He had a job. He had a potential girlfriend. (His mother would be so happy!) A gorgeous red-head had bought him a beer. He decided to put the weird memory lapses down to a lack of focus due to the aimless lifestyle he had adopted since Mr. Fox had so arbitrarily shut down the store. The intervening weeks had taken their toll. Now, though, as he wandered not so aimlessly home, he resolved to stop dwelling on the past and start looking to the future. Arthur slept well for the first time in weeks that night.

When Anayah had left O'Bryan's Pub after buying Arthur a pint of beer, she made her way to the alley where the entrance to Harpur's lair should have been. She wasn't surprised, but she was nonetheless dismayed, that it was no longer visible to her. Harpur had been quite thorough in concealing it, but she refused to be daunted by his apparent deletion of her from his life.

She studied the wall where the entrance to the lair used to be, looking for any tale-tell signs of glamour. It was possible that he had moved it, but dragons are creatures of habit and even if he had moved the entrance, he wouldn't have moved it vary far, Anayah reasoned. It had to be close to where it had been originally and so she swept detection magic back and forth over the area, not knowing that every time she did an alarm sounded inside the lair. Well, not an alarm exactly. It was more like a doorbell, and a half hour of *ding-dong, ding-dong* was all that Harpur could take. He removed the concealment and flung open the door.

"Oh, for the peaceful snores of Orhowyn, will you stop already?" he shouted from the bottom of the steps. "Get in here!"

Anayah stopped mid-sweep and looked at Harpur standing there with his hands on his hips and a grimace on his lips. She nearly wept with joy at the sight of him. But her dignity kicked in before her tears betrayed her. "Still full of menacing bluster, I see," she said, brushing past him with her chin at a haughty elevation.

"Took you long enough," Harpur sneered to mask his own dragon-like joy at seeing the pretty witch again.

Once inside, though, Anayah could hardly keep her emotions in check. She looked around the lair and all the wonderful memories of the wonderful years she had spent there came flooding back. Mysturna may be where she was from, but this was home.

"I've missed you," Anayah said quietly. "And I'm so, so sorry. About everything. Please forgive me."

Harpur grunted. It could have meant he accepted the apology, or it could have meant that he didn't. Harpur wasn't sure himself. "Why are you here, Anayah?"

Anayah thought the awkwardness would wear off faster if she just acted like everything was normal. Like Harpur hadn't flown off and left her behind to save Sok and Arthur on his own. Like Analeetah hadn't decided to leave him to whatever fate was waiting for him and forbidden her to ever see him again. Like she hadn't declared her love for him. Like all that had passed was just a hiccup, a silly little misunderstanding...

"I'd like some tea," she said.

"Help yourself," Harpur sat in his favourite spot on a sofa in the conversation pit and drank from a glass of beer he'd been nursing since Anayah started ringing the doorbell.

Anayah conjured a steaming cup of tea and seated herself on the sofa opposite Harpur. "I see you've wiped Arthur's memory."

"There were... complications," Harpur said.

"What kind of complications?" Anayah sipped her tea.

"He Bounded back to Thraeh. With a girl."

"He what?" Anayah was alarmed.

"He Bounded back to Thraeh with a girl," Harpur repeated.

"When?"

"Today."

"Why?"

"To impress her, maybe. To prove to himself it was all real by showing someone else, maybe. It doesn't matter. The fact that he did it left me with no choice." Harpur took a long pull on his beer.

"I see," Anayah said, sipping and thinking.

"Why are you here, Anayah?" Harpur asked again.

"It was time to put things right. And I needed to apologize to you. I overstepped..."

"You did that. Let's move on." Harpur was not interested in a long, mushy apology. "Why are you really here?"

That was about as close as she was going to get to a declaration of forgiveness. Anayah lifted the steaming tea cup to her lips and sipped from it again, buying time to gather her thoughts. "I wanted to check on Arthur; make sure he was okay."

"He's fine."

This sounded like a dismissal to Anayah and she didn't want to be dismissed. She wanted to get back into Harpur's good graces. She wanted to come back to the lair. She had no solid plan for achieving this, though. Anayah knew that Harpur would not make it easy for her, but she had to try. "But you're not."

"I'm not what?" Harpur asked. There was a warning to tread carefully in his tone.

But Anayah assembled her courage and pushed the warning aside. She was ninety-five percent certain he wouldn't hurt her. "Fine," she said. "You're not fine. Wiping Arthur's memory weighs on you."

This was true. Harpur couldn't deny that wiping Arthur's memory weighed on him, but he wasn't going to show any weakness. "It had to be done." He downed the last of his beer.

"Did it?" Anayah challenged the dragon-wizard.

"Yes, Anayah, it did. He Bounded. And he took another human to Thraeh. That is unacceptable and you know it." Harpur paused. "I trusted him."

Ah! And there it was. Harpur felt betrayed. Again.

"Do you really believe that Arthur did it to hurt you?"

"I believe that wiping his memory was the best thing to do."

"What about the prophecy?"

Harpur stared into the flames crackling in the fireplace. "As of now, there does not appear to be an imminent vacancy on the throne. King Gnik is alive and well and still firmly attached to his crown."

"And Arthur's magic?"

"What about it? He doesn't need it here and unless and until he needs it there, there's no need to untie that twisted witch's knot."

Anayah's eyebrows lifted and she gave him a stern look of disapproval.

"Oh, don't look at me like that. A witch's knot is just a secret." Harpur stood up and poured himself another glass of beer.

"Tell me what happened eight years ago."

Harpur looked at Anayah. From the look on her face, he could tell that she knew something. "First you tell me what happened after I took Sok and Arthur to the Sphere."

"We went to the Sphere and you were already gone. Analeetah decided that you weren't worth chasing and we returned to Wildwood. I was forbidden to return here or to ever see you again. You're banned from Mysturna, by the way." Anayah sipped her tea. She left out the part that now that she had disobeyed her aunt, she was probably banned as well. Having defied Analeetah she knew there would be consequences if she ever returned to Wildwood.

Harpur laughed. "What is Analeetah going to do to me? Feed me to the trees?"

Anayah didn't respond.

"Why did it take you so long to get to the Sphere?" Harpur continued. "We were there until late in the morning. You should have been there before us."

Anayah sighed. "Kel wouldn't let us zap him there and we really didn't think you would find it as fast as you did. We weren't in any hurry. How did you find it?"

"Ralph and Holly proved useful after all," Harpur said sarcastically.

"They were an odd pair of guardians, weren't they? What happened to them?"

"They vanished while Bon was doing his thing to sort out Sok and Arthur's souls. After it was done, Arthur said they had told him he had done well and that their work was finished."

"Hmm. Interesting." Anayah put her tea cup down. "So... Eight years ago?"

"Right, that," Harpur stroked his beard as he tried to decide how much to tell her. "I learned that a wizard named Ylemnir had Bounded here in the early days of the city and had an affair with a local woman. She had a baby by him." Harpur watched Anayah as that sunk in. "I came here to see if his magic had been passed on to any descendants and I found Arthur. I followed him, hoping to learn more, but he was hit by a car and killed. I stole his body and revived him with my blood to find out how much he knew of his abilities, but he didn't know anything. I wiped his memory and set up shop here to keep an eye on him. That's it."

"Harpur, that's not even kind of it!" Anayah was more than alarmed. "Don't you know what giving your blood to a human could do to him?"

"Yes, Anayah, I know perfectly well what my blood could do to him. But, so far, it hasn't done anything to him. He hasn't sprouted wings or grown scales or started breathing fire or..."

Anayah stood up and walked into the kitchen to get Harpur another beer. "What about you?"

Harpur was beginning to feel the relief of sharing his burden, but the concern in her tone made him wince. "You mean what about me spending so much time in human form?"

"You could lose your power, your magic!"

"Don't you think I know that? If you knew what could happen to me, why are you only now so concerned about it?"

"If Arthur is affected by your blood, you might not be able to contain him." Anayah had always suspected that Arthur's magic was not the sole reason Harpur was there. "You need to take him to Thraeh and go back to living like a dragon again before something terrible happens."

"I will not force him to go," Harpur said, taking the glass Anayah held out for him.

"Why not? For someone who's so bent on keeping magic from this world, letting two dragons walk around here seems a little reckless, don't you think"?

"Arthur is not a dragon!"

"He's not not a dragon!"

Anayah wanted to yell at the stupid dragon-wizard for being such a stupid dragon-wizard, but she knew that doing so would not help her own cause, namely to be allowed to return to the lair. "Is there anything I can do to help?" *It would be better if the invitation to stay came from Harpur.*

Harpur laughed. "You're so transparent, Anayah. If you want to stay, you can stay." *It will be easier to keep an eye on her if she's here*, Harpur thought.

Well, that was too easy! Anayah thought. But she'd take it.

"Thank you, Harpur. I think I will." She wasn't fooling anyone, but she needed to assert her confident, witchy self if she was to have any chance of truly gaining Harpur's trust again. "Now, what did you do with my bed?"

The big bed that had dominated a corner next to the kitchen had been zapped out of the lair right after Harpur and Arthur had returned to Earth. "I think it ended up on the showroom floor at The Brick."

"Harpur, that bed is magical. What if someone tries to buy it? Get it back!"

"Oh, relax, Anayah. No one would know how to use it." But he waved his walking stick and returned the bed to the corner where it belonged.

At the same moment the bed appeared in the lair under Whyte Avenue, a middle-aged man in a house in Bonnie Doon and the much-younger woman he was having an affair with, suddenly found themselves tangled in a heap of bed clothes on the floor. The messy aftermath, while not chronicled in detail here, included several hours of hysterics, a complicated and amusing police report and a divorce.

But Anayah had her bed and she was back in the lair.

Chapter 16

May melted into June. Literally. A heatwave overtook the city and pushed people indoors seeking air-conditioned venues in which to socialize. O'Bryan's Pub was one of the more popular of these on Whyte Avenue and Arthur had to learn his new trade fast. He didn't mind being thrown in the deep end; it distracted him from thinking too much about the joint memory loss he and Alex had experienced on the day they met. Between shifts at the pub, and when he wasn't with Alex, Arthur watched videos on mixing drinks. He mastered Cosmos and Mojitos and other cocktails, but his passion was beer. Nothing was better than pulling a perfect draft. He even came to appreciate the subtle benefits of drinking beer from a glass instead of a can or a bottle. Every time he did, though, something tugged at his memory and the image of the man in the top hat he vaguely recalled speaking to in the alley popped into his head.

Once in a while, Arthur would see the man in the top hat standing on a corner or coming out of a coffee shop. He seemed to be a fixture on Whyte Avenue, as did the gorgeous red-head who had bought the beer for him. Occasionally, Arthur saw the two of them together and that, he thought, was strange. After the second time he had spotted them chatting animatedly on the corner of Whyte Ave. and 104 Street, Arthur's curiosity could no longer be contained. He crossed the street against the light, causing car horns to blare and fists to shoot out of windows, but by the time he reached the sidewalk and made his way to the corner where they had been standing, they were gone. He looked around for them, but they were nowhere to be seen. After that, he didn't see either of them for several weeks.

He tried to put it out of his mind. And Alex tried to help him. She made plans for every waking moment Arthur wasn't working at O'Bryan's. They went to Hawrelak Park and rented paddle boats. They picnicked in the river valley. They went to the museum and the art gallery. They went to the Ukrainian Village and pigged out on perogies. They attended performances at the Fringe Festival. They saw iMax movies at Telus World of Science and regular movies at the Cineplex.

And once a week, they went to Arthur's parents' place for supper. Since Arthur now worked on Sundays, the family dinner was held on Tuesdays.

Arthur's mother, Marian, couldn't have been more thrilled about her son's new relationship. She had never really approved of Cheryl. As soon as she found out that Arthur and Alex were seeing each other, she got out her knitting needles and began making baby booties and blankets.

"A little premature, don't you think?" Earl had said.

"Best to be prepared," Marian had said. "And don't you say a word to either of them!"

Earl was just happy that she was not complaining about Arthur being single.

While Arthur and Alex progressed nicely toward their futures, Harpur and Anayah were enjoying a rather relaxing summer patrolling Whyte Avenue and monitoring the Boundary, which was not exactly taxing their skills. No one, it appeared, was breaking the rules these days and so Anayah spent her free time studying the Akashic Records and occasionally popping back to Mysturna to confer with Anabettah on points of perplexity that came up. She had to meet with the old witch at the Pole to avoid any confrontation with Analeetah. The Akashic Records were complex and full of paradoxical twists. Her sessions with Anabettah didn't always help untangle the twists; there were things that even she couldn't explain. "Only experience will lead to understanding," Anabettah would say with a consoling pat on her arm.

Eventually, Anayah had to accept the impossibility of experiencing everything encompassed in the Akashic Records. But it was fun to snoop into the unbiased conceptualized records of beings and follow the trails from one to another as their consciousnesses expanded. The ripple effect of experience and the subsequent reaction to it was fascinating.

Harpur was happy to let Anayah do her own thing. He got really good at tuning out her ramblings on about the amazing things she discovered. Though, once in a while some snippet would catch his interest and he would end up getting drawn in to a saga of some creature's emergence into consciousness and its influence on the expansion of the Universe. Crazy stuff happened out there!

It wasn't until the early autumn when their peace was finally disturbed by a Bounder from Thraeh. Harpur and Anayah were just getting back from a late-night stroll down Whyte Avenue when they heard a startled shout from the Boundary. They immediately zapped themselves to the roof top.

At first, they saw no one. Then Anayah pointed toward the ledge across from the Boundary where a set of long fingers had a precarious grip on it. Harpur, in two long strides, approached the ledge and looked over. There, dangling three stories above the sidewalk was—surprise, surprise—Sok. He reached down, grabbed the squirming criminal by the back of his vest and hauled him up. None too gently, Harpur dropped Sok on the roof top and stood glaring down at him.

Sok, not expecting the abrupt and instantaneous rescue, recovered almost instantly from his bemusement. He jumped to his feet and looked at his rescuer with delight. "Oh, good!" he said. "You're here. I thought I would have to go looking for you. Thanks for the help, but I would have been fine."

"Sok, what are you doing here?" Anayah asked.

"Anayah! I didn't expect you to be here!" Sok embraced the witch, startling her with his enthusiastic greeting. "This is great!"

"It's not so great, Sok," Harpur growled. "I told you what would happen if you ever Bounded here again."

"I know," Sok said, brushing off the threat of prison so succinctly implied by Harpur. "But I had to see you."

"You had to see me," Harpur huffed. "Let me guess, you missed me?

Well, yes. But that's not why I *had* to see you."

Why did you come, Sok?" Anayah prompted. She sensed that Sok's unlawful Bound was not a matter that he had undertaken lightly.

"King Gnik is dead!"

In a million years, neither Harpur nor Anayah would not have guessed that.

"What?" they both said in shocked unison.

"Gnik is dead," Sok repeated. "And Bloomregaard is staging a coup to take the crown."

From the look on Harpur's face, Sok was confident that that was his get-out-of-jail-free card.

"The hell he is!" Harpur snarled as he turned to leap through the Boundary.

"Wait!" Anayah shouted.

Harpur was in a crouched position, ready to Bound. "What? I have to get back there and do something about this."

Anayah put a hand on Harpur's arm. "I think we need more information before you go storming back there into the middle of a mess you know nothing about. Let's all go back to the lair and listen to what Sok has to tell us first."

"Good idea," Sok said. "I'm starving. Anayah, could you whip me up one of those hamburgers?"

Harpur relented. "Fine," he said, allowing his bunched muscles to un-bunch. "But I'm warning you, Sok, if this is some kind of joke..."

"It's not a joke!" Sok was offended at Harpur's lack of faith.

They joined hands and Anayah zapped them all to the lair where she promised Sok a hamburger after he told them everything he knew. Sok opted for the condensed version, hoping to speed up the hamburger.

"King Gnik passed a law a few days ago, banishing Bloomregaard's wraiths from Colwygshire. Bloomregaard was using them to sniff out all sorts of things and dozens and dozens of folks were sent to jail. Most of it was untrue, but Bloomregaard manufactured evidence against them. Then the executions started. People were scared, but they went to the King and basically threatened to revolt if he didn't do something. So, he made a public proclamation without consulting Bloomregaard. The next day Gnik was dead and everyone assumes that Bloomregaard either poisoned him or had his wraiths bump him off somehow. Then, because Gnik has no heirs, he announced that he was taking over the throne. He had papers—forged, of course—proving his right to the crown. The people revolted and basically have the castle under siege, but Bloomregaard is planning his own coronation ten days from now. And he's ordered the guards to kill anyone who attempts to interfere." Sok looked hopefully at Anayah.

"That's insane!" Anayah said, not producing the promised hamburger.

"Why did you wait so long to come and tell me this?" Harpur glared at the elf.

"Because you threatened to put me in prison if I ever Bounded here again," Sok blamed Harpur. "And I figured you'd show up with a Bounder long before now. I couldn't wait any longer."

Fair enough, Harpur thought. The elf certainly had good reason to break the rules. But there had been no Bounders lately, which also now made sense. Everyone was focused on what was happening with Bloomregaard, not to mention grieving their beloved, if not-so-wise king. He could hardly hold that against Sok. Even though he wanted to want to.

"Harpur, this is unbelievable!" Anayah said.

Sok, still hamburger-less looked at them. "You know what's even more unbelievable?

"What?" Harpur asked as he braced himself for the answer.

"The prophecy! Arthur gets to be king now!"

The rest of the night was spent sifting through the debris left by Sok's little bomb. Questions got asked. Some got answered. Eventually, hamburgers manifested, giving the dragon and the witch some time to process Sok's story while giving Sok a bit of respite from the dragon and the witch. With their mouths full of 100 % grass-fed Alberta beef, they couldn't say things like, "That's insane!" or "Unbelievable!", which was starting to drive Sok unbelievably insane.

The popular theory among the occupants of the lair was that Bloomregaard had been planning this for some time. Neither Sok, nor Harpur could put their fingers on exactly why they had thought the

Senior Bounding Officer was up to something; the man simply oozed treasonous potential. It was likely that he had been biding his time, waiting for a situation that could not be connected to him to arise so that he could sweep in with his forged pedigree and take the crown. Either he'd gotten tired of waiting and used the wraiths to cause the uprising, or the uprising against the wraiths had forced his hand. Either way, he had to be stopped. And once he was, Arthur had to be accepted as the rightful heir to the throne. They couldn't just waltz him into the castle and expect everyone to bow down to him.

"What exactly does the prophecy say?" Anayah asked as she conjured up her fifth cup of tea.

Sok recited the prophecy from memory. "'You, Young One, will help to bring a lost child of Epoh home. You will travel far to find him and before he can return to take his place as king of this land, you will quest together to untangle the Truth of who he is. You will be one of many guides for him, but you must trust that no matter what happens, the path you travel together is the path to his birthright. You will be bound to him for a time, just as he is bound to the Dreamfinder forever by the fire that burns within him.'"

Anayah enchanted a pen to record Sok's exact words. "You being bound to him for a time must refer to the Entanglement. Arthur's magic must make him a lost child of Epoh. But what is this Dreamfinder?"

"Xzynthyrius Dreamfinder was a dragon that was slayed by the great knight Orhowyn Bravvenshyn a long time ago," Sok explained. "That part makes no sense."

Harpur shifted uncomfortably in his seat on the sofa. An idea was beginning to take shape in his mind, but he kept it to himself.

"What is it, Harpur? Do you understand what this means?" Anayah had noticed the dragon-wizard's uncomfortable shift.

"Huh? No. None of that legend makes any sense to me," he said. "It's all a bunch of hooey."

"Hooey? Really?" Anayah tried to make light of it, but she sensed that there was more than just hooey involved. *More twisted witch's knots, Harpur?*

"We need to go find Arthur and get him to Thraeh right away," Sok announced.

"I had to wipe his memory," Harpur said.

"Well, un-wipe it!" Sok said. "We need him!"

"It's not that simple," Anayah said. "Arthur Bounded to Thraeh with a girl he met. And we can't just give him his memories back and expect him to willingly go to Epoh and fight for the crown." She looked at Harpur. "Can we?"

Harpur was running through all the possible scenarios. Throwing Arthur into the middle of a war held no appeal whatsoever. Would he even be willing to go to Thraeh now that he had Alex in his life? Although Alex might be persuaded to persuade him; she had been quite keen to learn more about Thraeh. Then there was the issue of Arthur's friends and family. They would either have to have their memories of him wiped or be left to deal with him mysteriously going missing. Humans rarely handled that sort of thing well. The ethics of either of those actions were dubious at best. He'd hoped he wouldn't have to deal with all of this so soon, but there he was, standing on a bridge he didn't want to cross.

"I think," Harpur said, "we need to deal with Bloomregaard first. Get him out of the way and then come back for Arthur."

"But if Arthur isn't there and he doesn't gain the trust of the people, getting rid of Bloomregaard is just going to leave us open to having to deal with all the other pretenders who crawl out of the woodwork. Epoh will be no farther ahead." Anayah presented a huge flaw in Harpur's vague plan.

"We'll figure that out. Gnik has no known heirs, we'll just have to find a way to stall for time. Tell the people that there is an heir, we just have to find him. We'll come up with something." Harpur said. "Sok, what is the situation with the Guards? How did Bloomregaard manage to take over the castle?"

"The Guards are divided. He must have turned some of them before Gnik died."

"Is there anyone you know of that we can trust?"

"There is," Sok said. "There's a guard named Davynn Willhart. He hates Bloomregaard for executing his brother on some trumped up charge a moon cycle ago. He deserted and is standing with the people."

"Good. We'll need to talk to him. Once we've gotten Bloomregaard out of the way, we'll come back here and see if Arthur still wants to be a king."

"Who doesn't want to be king?" Sok asked.

"I don't want to be king," Harpur said.

"Yeah, but you're a dragon."

"What's that supposed to mean?" Harpur knew he'd be a great king. He was already a great ruler!

Anayah jumped in to stop the diversion from developing any further. "Before we do anything, I think we need to figure out what the prophecy actually means," she said, circling back to a place she was sure Harpur didn't want to circle back to.

"You're right," Harpur said to Anayah's amazement. "Anayah, you stay here and see if you can find anything that will tell us about how my blood has affected Arthur. That is the key to all of this. I'm sure of it."

"I will see what I can do." Anayah sounded dubious. "But unless someone is or has been conscious of it, it won't be in the Akashic Records."

"Try anyway," Harpur said. "Then come to Colwygshire and find us."

"Where will you be?" Anayah was taken aback by this change of direction.

Harpur looked to Sok for the answer. "Skull's Keep," the elf said. "It's a tavern near the North Gate. Anyone can give you directions. We can check in there regularly. They have the best ale in the kingdom."

"How's the venison?" Harpur asked.

"Almost as good as the ale."

Chapter 17

Arthur was spending less time thinking about the man in the top hat and the gorgeous red-head and more time thinking about his future with Alex. Classes had started and she had returned to work. With him working on the weekends at O'Bryan's Pub and Alex working during the week, they had little time for each other. He didn't want to quit working for John. He was enjoying his job. He could always fall back on the severance from Fox Comics, which was now Prophecy Comics and was being managed by the ginger beanpole, Allen, his once would-be assistant. It had crossed his mind to ask Allen for a job, but the store wasn't the same. It didn't feel right. The transporter room was gone. The costumes were gone. Excalibur was gone. On the few occasions he'd forced himself to go into Prophecy Comics, it felt too different. *Unwelcoming?* Reluctantly, he started applying for jobs that would allow him to spend time with Alex and keep him from getting bored.

Arthur had picked up an ancient copy of The Legend of King Arthur at Little's Books and was reading it to pass the time in the evenings when Alex had to prepare for her classes and couldn't be with him. It had been a childhood favourite of his and he was delighted to find that it was just as good twenty years later.

If only I was a king.

This thought passed through Arthur's mind on the same night that Harpur, Anayah and Sok were planning how to take down Bloomregaard. It was a passing notion inspired by another day of having no luck finding a new job and the emptiness of the pillow next to his own. He let it go, turned out the light and went to sleep.

While Arthur slept and dreamt of being a king in some fairy tale land, Harpur and Sok were, preparing to return to their own world. Harpur had relinquished his top hat and leather duster for something more appropriate in Colwygshire. Anayah fairly swooned when he appeared in a pair of leather pants and not much else. His feet were clad in soft leather boots. His wrists were adorned by two ornately tooled leather cuffs. A wide strap crossed his chest from shoulder to hip, serving the dual purpose of holding his walking stick and a broad sword in twin scabbards firmly on his back as well as covering the scar on his chest where he had ripped out the scale. Even if Anayah had seen the scar, she was too distracted by the muscles that bulged... everywhere! Sok, of course, had his dagger strapped to his waist and his ear-cuffs clipped to his ears. His long, silvery locks were loose and shimmering against a golden-brown vest. His dark brown pants were tucked into knee-high boots that matched the vest. An embossed leather strap encircled his left bicep. Together, they made a striking pair, but rather than attract attention on Whyte Avenue, Harpur zapped them to the Boundary and seconds later, they landed in Braydon Wood.

Harpur felt a chill that was incongruous with the warmth of the day. He wordlessly, motioned Sok toward the path leading to the main road to Colwygshire. Instead of transforming into a dragon and flying them to the city, Harpur zapped them there instead. He wasn't sure, but he suspected one of Bloomregaard's wraiths was the source of the chill he felt. If they had flown, the creature might have followed them. It was bad enough that the thing would report their arrival, there was no need to make it easy for it to find them.

They reappeared in a small copse of trees near a small gate in the city wall. From their hiding spot, they could see a group of three men and a woman just inside the gate. They looked like they were waiting for someone. In turn, each poked his or her head out the gate and looked from side to side and then retreated back inside, shaking his or her head. If they were merely guarding the gate, they were not doing it very well. This was Harpur's first inkling of how woefully unprepared the people were for a revolution. Still, they had managed to take the castle and hold it under siege. Harpur assumed this was due to the defecting guards and hoped that they had established some sort of training regime.

"Do you recognize any of them?" Harpur whispered.

"One of them is Toburn, the goldsmith. I know him. I don't recognise the others."

"And he's definitely on our side?"

"Of course, he is," Sok snapped.

"No need to get testy. I'm just making sure," Harpur snapped back.

They waited until none of the four amateur guards were poking a head out of the gate before emerging from the copse of trees. Sok lead the way across the short distance between the copse and the gate. They were about half way when the head-poking resumed.

A woman with a cherubic face and chubby body stepped to the edge of the wall and leaned forward looking to her right. As she pivoted her head to the left, she caught site of Harpur and Sok coming straight toward her and yelped in surprise. Her three companions rushed to see what had caused the alarm-raising cry and all but pushed the woman out into the open in the process. Harpur rolled his eyes and sighed at the ineptitude.

"Uh... Halt!" one of the men, not Toburn, called. "Who goes there?"

"It's just me." Sok said. "Sok."

"Seize them!" another of the men said, pushing the woman even farther away from the safety of the gate.

Toburn clouted the coward on the arm and pulled the woman back inside the gate. "Don't be an ass!" He stepped forward to shake Sok's hand and welcome him back to Colwygshire. "You've brought help. I hope."

"Toburn, this is Jerry. He's from... Pollybush." It was the first place he could think of.

Harpur's eyebrows shot up at his unexpected identity change, but he went along as hands were shaken and names revealed. The chubby cherub's name was Doria, the man who had ordered them to halt was named Iain and the coward's name was Boss. As soon as the social graces had been completed, Harpur nudged Sok to get him to move things along. He wanted to get inside before that wraith showed up. If one had indeed been near the Boundary, it might be able to follow his magic signature.

The six of them moved through the narrow gate and into a small, courtyard of sorts. Nets and branches had been strung across the tops of the courtyard walls to conceal the gate from the castle towers that loomed a short way away. Harpur examined this make-shift camouflage and realized its purpose. Rather than keep the gate closed and post guards on the ramparts, the branches and netting prevented archers from picking off the guards from the castle towers above. The trade off was that the gate was left open and the guards had to poke their heads out to check for anyone approaching. It was, in its own way, quite clever, but Harpur decided to refrain from pointing out what a single flaming arrow could do to this strategy, not to mention the guards underneath the netting. He also wondered why Bloomregaard hadn't already done it. *What is he waiting for?*

"We're looking for Davynn Willhart." Sok said to the guards. "Do you know where we can find him?"

Toburn spoke for the ragtag group of guards. "He's probably at the Bounding Office. We've taken it over and set up our headquarters there. If he's not there, he'll be at Skull's Keep."

Sok thanked Toburn and the others and led Harpur out of the courtyard into the streets of Colwygshire. As soon as they were out of earshot, Harpur turned to Sok. "Jerry?"

"It's the first name I thought of."

"Why didn't you just call me HD?"

"Everyone who knows you as HD, expects a top hat and fancy clothes. I thought you were in disguise. Jerry seemed the simplest way to avoid problems."

Harpur had to agree with Sok's logic. "You really do never cease to amaze me."

"I told you, Harpur, you need to have more faith in me."

Staying close to the walls on the castle side of the streets to avoid being seen from above, they made their way to the Bounding Office, which was located within an adjunct to the castle proper. Separated from the main gates to the castle at the top of the main road from the main gates to the city by a wide garden, this office complex was home to guilds and bureaus and agencies of all kinds; a convenient one-stop-shop for all of the citizens of Colwygshire to file applications, obtain licenses and pay fees to ensure their legitimacy and compliance with all the rules and regulations that kept things in order within the kingdom. Usually a bustling hive of harried administrative agents and often distraught clients arguing points of policy and procedure, Harpur and Sok entered a seemingly deserted warren of hallways and locked doors. There wasn't even a guard at the entry.

While Harpur was uncomfortable with this arrangement, Sok assured them that there was no need for guards and entered without hesitation as if this was a normal day and he was arriving for work. Harpur hesitated long enough to ready his magic. Just in case.

But there really was no need. No one challenged them and they made their way to the Bounding Office, which was located near the heavily barricaded passage leading to the main castle in an interior corridor. When they got to their destination, they found a few small groups of people, mostly ex-guardsmen, milling about and talking quietly amongst themselves. Some of them looked up at the new arrivals and nodded or muttered to acknowledge them, but none tried to stop Sok and Harpur from entering the offices.

Harpur took in every detail. He memorized the position of every person he saw, noting weapons or the absence thereof. He examined the barricade at the end of the hall and deemed it solid enough. Whoever was in charge seemed to have things well in hand.

They entered the commandeered Bounding Offices and were greeted by a handsome, young soldier sporting a full beard and mustache. His muscular frame was covered by a loose, homespun shirt and a pair of tailored, leather trousers, but this casual attire did not conceal his authority or the weight of responsibility that authority forced him to carry. He had been seated at Bloomregaard's old desk, making notes on a piece of parchment from Bloomregaard's personal stock of stationery with a green-feathered quill pen, but abandoned them and stood when he saw Sok enter.

"Sok!" He reached across the desk to shake hands with the elf. "You're back. Any luck?"

Sok stood aside to let Harpur enter the office. Introductions, this time with correct names, were followed by hand shakes. The ritual of transforming strangers into acquaintances complete, Davynn reseated himself and got right down to business. Harpur assumed that Sok had broken his oath to keep Harpur's identity a secret from Davynn already and that was confirmed when the young soldier spoke.

"Harpur, I'm glad you're here. We've been hoping you'd show up. I was relieved when Sok finally agreed to fetch you. He was a little concerned for his life when the subject first came up." Davynn smiled at Harpur.

"Well, I guess I can let it slide." Harpur shot a sideways glance in Sok's direction. "This time." *No point in letting Sok forget who he was dealing with.* He decided not to question Davynn's acceptance of who he really was.

"So, there were no problems getting through the Boundary?" Davynn asked.

"Should there have been?" Harpur heard the implication in the question.

"We believe that Bloomregaard has one of his wraiths stationed at the Boundary. We think he's waiting for you." Davynn wasn't mincing words, so much as couching them carefully, feeling Harpur out. His experience with the Dragon Lord's true abilities was limited to hearsay, primarily from Sok. He liked the elf, but Sok was Sok.

Harpur admired his wisdom. He decided to throw Davynn a bone. "It's possible that one of the wraiths was nearby. I didn't see anything, but I felt a chill. Why would Bloomregaard be waiting for me?"

"As Dragon Lord of Epoh, you are the biggest threat to him."

Davynn and Harpur studied each other across the desk. It was not in either of their natures to trust blindly and this blunt statement was not meant as a simple clarification. He was asking Harpur if he could trust him.

As far as Harpur was concerned, Davynn had the upper hand. Confined in this tiny office space there was no way for him to transform into a dragon. At least not without killing everyone else in the room in the process. He leaned back in his chair and studied the man he was likely to be going into battle with.

"Are you saying Bloomregaard wants me dead?" Harpur asked.

"I'm saying Bloomregaard wants you under his control."

With his wraiths and a dragon doing his bidding, Bloomregaard could do whatever he wanted.

"Well, that's not going to happen," Harpur said. "We need to kill that worm. Now!"

"How do you propose we do that?" Davynn wasn't being condescending; he was genuinely hoping Harpur had a plan.

"March into the castle and burn him out." It seemed fairly straightforward to Harpur.

"Believe me, I'd like nothing better. But those wraiths are a problem. We don't know how to kill them. Marching into the castle with them in there protecting Bloomregaard might be a suicide mission," Davynn said. "We think that our best chance will be at the coronation, but we don't have any details and so we don't have a plan."

Harpur thought about this. No wonder Davynn looked strained and worn out. "We need to lure the wraiths away somehow. If we could get them away from Bloomregaard, we could take the castle. Maybe killing Bloomregaard is the key to getting rid of the wraiths."

"Yes," Davynn said. "But what if it isn't? I've been watching them. They do seem to be bound to him somehow. Yet they also appear to act independently. A while ago, before all this happened, they left the city of their own accord and Bloomregaard was not happy about it. I overheard him talking to one of the captains and he was saying he was running out of something he needed to control them. I couldn't hear what he called it, though. I tried getting some information from the captain, but he pretended he didn't know anything. I've had people looking into it, but so far no one has come up with the answer."

"Have you asked the elves?" Harpur suggested. He and Davynn both looked at Sok.

"I don't know anything about wraiths," Sok said. "Except that they are dangerous and creepy and it's best to stay as far away from them as possible."

"I wasn't thinking about you, Sok," Harpur said. "I was thinking about Elder Dhonna. Could you go talk to her and ask if she knows of anything that we could use against the wraiths?"

Dread took over Sok's face. "I could," he said, "if I have to."

Davynn and Harpur exchanged glances, but it was Harpur who took the bait. "What do you mean, if you have to?"

"It's just that whenever I go there, the Elders remind me that I haven't applied to any of the guilds yet."

"I thought they gave you their blessing to work at the Bounding Office."

"Oh, they did. They had no choice. But they didn't expect me to stay. They thought if I was here for a while, I'd be eager to go back."

"And you're not," Davynn said.

"Not at all!" The very idea was horrifying to the young elf. "If I do, I will have to enter whichever guild chooses me. What if I got stuck behind a pottery wheel for the rest of my life? It's not that I'm not proud to be an elf. I just don't want to live like that. Every time I go there, I feel guilty for wanting something different."

"I'm not sure how working for Bloomregaard is better than living in Braydon Wood," Davynn said. He had often wished he was an elf. He saw the elven culture as one of freedom and wonder.

"It's not better," Sok said. "But I got to choose it and I have the blessing of the Ancestors."

Harpur could relate. He would hate it if someone else had the power to choose what he did with his life. "Ironically, the choice is no longer yours. The Bounding Office is closed." Harpur laughed at Sok's current circumstances. Then he took pity on the elf. "Would you like me to go with you?"

"Yes!" Sok said emphatically. "I would like that very much."

Davynn covered his mouth to hide his amusement. "Well, while you two go discover a way to deal with the wraiths, I'm going to go check on the troops. Some of them are getting restless. We've lived in peace for so long, there are a few who want to get this over with. Bloomregaard is not the only enemy we're facing. Fear is proving to be an equal foe."

Sok and Harpur made their way back to the gate where the head-poking foursome were still poking their heads out in turn. Toburn asked them where they were going and when they thought they would be returning to Colwygshire.

"We're going to Braydon Wood to talk to the elves," Sok said.

"They won't get involved in our problems," said Boss. "Why are you wasting your time with them?" There was an edge of bigotry against the elves in his tone.

"We aren't going to ask them to get involved in our problems," Harpur said with a different edge in his tone. "And if we were, I wouldn't blame them for not wanting to help us if this is the attitude they would have to contend with." Harpur's violet eyes flashed orange and Boss backed away.

Toburn stepped forward rather bravely to diffuse things. "We'll be off duty soon," he said to Harpur. "I'll be sure to let the guards who take over know to expect you. Good luck with the elves."

Harpur flashed his eyes one last time at the cringing Boss and then followed Sok through the gate. As they made their way to the copse of trees, they heard Toburn berate his patrol partner. "Are you a complete imbecile? Don't you know who that is?"

Harpur looked sideways at Sok, who kept his eyes straight ahead. "Seems like there isn't much need to keep calling me Jerry," Harpur said.

"Well, I might have had a bit too much ale and let a few things slip one night at Skull's Keep," Sok confessed as a large dragon-wizard hand came down on his shoulder.

"Times are changing, Sok," Harpur said. "Now let's go find us a way to kill some wraiths."

As soon as they were concealed within the copse, Harpur zapped them to the gates of the elven city. The city itself had no name. It was simply a portion of Braydon Wood where the trees grew and formed into living buildings similarly to the way the trees in Danaleedh on Mysturna grew to form Wildwood. Only the network of trunks and branches there fashioned hundreds of separate dwellings and shops that were connected by a web of walkways that threaded through the canopy high above the ground.

None of the elves they met as the made their way to the Healer's Guild were anything but friendly toward them. They were greeted in both the elven and the common language and several even stopped to ask Sok how he was and if he had any stories to share. Each time, Sok promised that when he did, he would return to entertain them at a Moon Ring gathering.

The Healer's Guild was housed in a relatively small tree building surrounded by herb gardens that were being tended by a group of singing elves. Their voices harmonized perfectly and Harpur could feel the melody as much as hear it. He stopped at the arched gate leading into the grounds beside Sok where they waited for one of the singers to acknowledge them. When the song ended a few minutes later, a young female elf approached the arch.

"Welcome, Sok!" she said. "Do you seek healing?"

"We wish to speak to Elder Dhonna if she's available." Sok replied.

"Of course." The elf stood to the side to let Sok and Harpur enter. "She's inside. You can go right in."

Sok thanked the elf and took a deep breath to steel himself for their meeting with the Guild Master. They found her at a table, arranging a spectacular bouquet of enormous flowers. The petals were a deep purple-black speckled with silver star-like dots. To Harpur they looked like reflections of the cosmos.

Elder Dhonna had her back to Sok and Harpur, but as they approached the table where she was working, she said, "Sok, my dear boy! Have you come at last to apply to the Guild?"

Sok took another deep breath. "No, Elder Dhonna. We have come to ask for your help with some wraiths that are terrorizing Colwygshire."

Elder Dhonna stopped arranging the flowers and turned to look at them. She was a remarkably beautiful elf who, unlike most elves, wore her brilliant red hair cut short. The back and sides of her head were shaved close to her skull, but the top was a fiery mass of crimson waves. She wore a simple cream-coloured caftan with gold leaves embroidered along the edges. Her feet were bare.

"Why Harpur Diggins! It's so very good to see you."

Harpur bowed his head slightly in deference to her Elder status. "It's good to see you as well, Bella Dhonna."

Sok watched this unexpected exchange with curiosity. "Who's not keeping secrets now?" he whispered to the dragon-wizard.

Neither Harpur nor Elder Dhonna elaborated on their obvious acquaintance.

"What can I do for you two?" she asked.

"We are hoping you can help us with a wraith problem in the city," Harpur said.

"I am a healer, Harpur Diggins, not a killer," Elder Dhonna said.

"I understand that," Harpur said, "but do you not rid the forest of pests that would harm it? These wraiths are pests that are harming the people of the city. If you do not want to help us kill them, do you at least know of a way we can incapacitate them so we can stop them from causing more harm?"

Oh, that's good! Sok thought. He was happy to let Harpur do all the talking. The less attention on him, the better.

The Guild Master smiled. "You're very clever, my friend. What will you give me in return?"

"What do you want?"

"I believe you are in possession of the Amber Chalice..."

"That's a high price to pay for the lives of three measly wraiths." Harpur kept his voice even.

The Amber Chalice is a myth. Sok was so confused. *What is going on here?*

"I doubt they are measly at all!" Elder Dhonna exclaimed. "You've come here to ask me to help you kill them. As I said, I am a healer, not a killer. If I am to do this for you, I expect a high price."

"Don't think of it as killing wraiths," Harpur said. "Think of it as healing Colwygshire."

The Guild Master laughed. She was enjoying this cerebral chess match very much. Sok got the distinct impression this was not the first time that Harpur and Elder Dhonna had engaged in such a negotiation. He was deeply impressed by Harpur's wit.

"Well done, Harpur Diggins!" Elder Dhonna said. "You've bested me again. Promise to bring me some stalagmite from your lair next time you come and you may have what you ask for."

"Thank you, Bella Dhonna," Harpur said with another slight bow and a wink.

Sok's mouth dropped open. *What just happened?*

Elder Dhonna walked to a cabinet on the far side of the room and withdrew a jar containing shriveled, black leaves. She opened a drawer under the cabinet, took out a finely woven net bag and returned to the table. "There are three wraiths?" she asked as she shook some of the leaves from the jar into the bag.

"Unfortunately," Harpur said. "What is that?"

"Wraithbane! What else would it be?" She handed the bag to Harpur.

"What do I do with it?" he tucked the bag into his pocket.

"Well, that is the tricky part," she said. "Wraiths are what are known as corrupted beings."

"Meaning...?"

"Meaning that they are neither dead, nor alive. They were once living people, humans, elves, dwarves, whose souls were damaged at the time of their deaths. The truth of how they became corrupted is lost in legend, but the story goes that a wizard, looking for ways to become immortal created a spell that was meant to harvest souls, which he would store and recycle in order to keep himself alive forever. Something went wrong and in the execution of the spell, the souls were corrupted and became anchored to the bodies of the people they belonged to on the outside. Being exposed, they blackened and tore as the bodies rotted."

Sok grimaced in revulsion.

"Indeed, Sok, it does make for a gruesome existence. The good news is that there are only a few dozen of them in the world." She agreed. Then she continued, "The wraithbane won't kill them. It will only paralyse them."

"How do I kill them?" Harpur said, thinking that he was probably doing the wraiths more of a favour than a disservice.

"They cannot go through a Boundary. It tears their souls apart. But it will also trap the pieces and if anyone else Bounds through, the pieces could attach to them and corrupt them too. But if the wraithbane is inside the boundary when the wraiths go through, it will destroy them." She smiled at Harpur who frowned back.

"How?"

"There are theories only. Perhaps the wraithbane acts as a catalyst for some other reaction to take place. No one has ever been inside a Boundary when it happened to see it." Elder Dhonna shrugged.

"But it will work?" Harpur didn't like loose ends.

"It will work. I guarantee it."

"So, I just toss the leaves into the Boundary and hope for the best?" He really didn't like loose ends.

"Yes. Leave them in the bag. It will be easier to throw them if they are contained. The wraiths need only be in the vicinity of the leaves for them to work. I've given you enough to paralyse at least three wraiths, but be careful, Harpur Diggins. It's never been done with more than one wraith at a time. I do not know what will happen with three wraiths in the Boundary together."

Sok and Harpur decided to walk back to Colwygshire. With that warning kicking around in their heads, they felt they could use some time to let it work the worst of its calamitous implications out of its system. Harpur was trying to figure out how to lure the wraiths into a Boundary and get the wraithbane into it with them. It would be tricky, indeed!

It took much less time for the calamitous implications to abate in Sok's mind. "So, are you going to explain what happened back there?" he asked.

Harpur, gave Sok a sideways glance. "You mean with Elder Dhonna?"

"You know her. How?"

"She used to come and play at my lair when she was a child," Harpur reminisced.

"Elder Dhonna? Used to play with you at your lair?"

"Yes. Before she joined the Healer's Guild, she would come to the lair and we would play games like that together. The idea was to find a way to get the other one to agree to something that they wouldn't normally agree to. We would tempt each other with imaginary gifts or try to get the highest price we could for what we wanted. Bella Dhonna was something of a delight to pass the time with." A wistful expression passed over Harpur's face.

"Like the Amber Chalice."

"She's been trying to get me to give that up for decades." Harpur actually chuckled.

"But it's a myth. It isn't real."

Harpur didn't reply.

"It is real?" Sok interpreted Harpur's silence as confirmation of the existence of the legendary chalice that the great knight, Orhowyn Bravvenshyn was supposed to have filled with the blood of Xzynthyrius Dreamfinder and consumed to assume the power of the dead dragon.

"Legends are better with some colourful embellishment," Harpur said enigmatically.

"You're not going to tell me, are you?" Sok was disappointed.

Harpur just kept walking.

"So, what are we going to do now?" Sok asked to take his mind off legendary chalices.

"We're going to Skull's Keep to wait for Anayah. I suspect she will be along soon," Harpur said.

Sok's stomach thought that was an excellent suggestion. "I could eat something."

"When can't you?"

Skull's Keep, before it was a public house, was the entrance to a warren of catacombs that snaked beneath the city and beyond the city wall. The tunnels had been sealed off during some long-ago, less-peaceful time and the entry converted into the bustling tavern it was then. Skulls, rescued from their resting places within the catacombs, grinned from niches cut into the walls above the tables. It was not uncommon for patrons to leave offerings of coins or small icons carved from wood or bone in the niches to appease these long-forgotten dead souls. When the niches were filled, the offerings were gathered and dispersed among the poor. Occasionally, rather than turn away the less fortunate, the offerings were used to pay for their meals. Skull's Keep was a haven for all who found themselves in need.

Sok found himself in need of a hardy bowl of venison stew and a large flagon of ale. He didn't require the dead to pay for his repast; he was happy to place a coin in the niche above his and Harpur's table for someone who did, though. This was one of the things he liked best about coming to Skull's Keep. He was well-fed and he could do a good deed at the same time.

Harpur looked at the small hoard surrounding the skull in the niche. It reminded him of his own, much larger hoard a world away. Collected over centuries and so carefully guarded, it represented his status as a dragon. The idea of giving it away for any reason was so foreign to Harpur, that it startled him when he found himself making an offering of his own. As he placed a coin in the niche, he had to willfully restrain himself from taking all of the coins to add to his own cache when he returned to Whyte Avenue.

I need to stretch my wings, he thought. *I've been too long in human form.*

Sok finished his stew and was thinking that a steaming bowl of cobbler was in order when the pub door opened and Anayah entered. Harpur saw her first, seated as he was, with a clear view of the entire room, and stood to get her attention. When she saw the dragon-wizard across the crowded pub, Anayah looked relieved. She ignored the other ogling, catcalling patrons and made her way to their table where she removed her midnight-blue cloak only to illicit more ogling and catcalling. Harpur's glare quickly quelled the unwelcome attention and the patrons returned to their own business of eating, drinking and socializing with their peers.

"This city could benefit from some street signs," Anayah said. "I've been searching for this place for over an hour."

"What's an hour?" Sok asked. The concept of time on Thraeh was not nearly as structured as it was on Earth.

Harpur looked at the pretty witch and smiled. Colwygshire was not the easiest place to get around, but Sok had chosen Skull's Keep for its proximity to the north gate. If she had asked the guards there for directions, it would have taken only a few minutes for her to find it. "You entered by the main gate, didn't you?"

"Well, the guards at the north gate are not the most hospitable in the realm. It was either make my way to the main gate or turn them both into toads." Clearly, she was uncharacteristically irritated.

"Only two guards?" Harpur was surprised.

"Two too many, if you ask me," Anayah grumbled. "What is the situation here?"

Sok, having decided on the cobbler, was too busy savouring the piquant sweetness of the thickened fruit and fluffy crust to contribute to the discussion. He moaned with each bite as the flavour exploded on his tongue. Harpur reached across the table and grabbed his wrist before the next forkful made it to his mouth. "Make one more sound and you will be wearing the rest of that pudding."

Sok looked over his fork at the dragon-wizard unsure if compliance was possible. He picked up his plate and moved to another table where Harpur couldn't hear him.

Once the elf and his cobbler had vacated the table, Harpur told Anayah about the wraithbane. "I just don't know how we can lure the wraiths through a Boundary and get the wraithbane into it without getting killed along with them in the process."

Anayah thought about it for few minutes. "What if you could get them to follow you through and someone on the other side threw the wraithbane in as soon as you passed?"

"I thought of that. But who? And where?" Harpur said. "The Boundary would have to be out in the open on both sides and we'd have to get the wraithbane to whoever is going to throw it in before hand."

"There's a Boundary to the south of here that leads to an open area near a lake on Mysturna. It's not too far from Danaleedh." Anayah was strategizing as she spoke.

"And Analeetah will help?" Harpur felt hopeful.

"Analeetah would feed me to the trees before she raised a finger to help either of us," Anayah said sadly. "But Anabettah might be able to help us."

"Anayah, you can't ask her to do this. She's old and this could be dangerous." Harpur wanted to give the witch a way out of what she was proposing.

"Anabettah will outlive all of us. Don't worry about her," Anayah assured the dragon-wizard. "Leave it to me. Do you have this wraithbane?"

Harpur retrieved the bag of blackened leaves from his pocket and handed it to Anayah, who examined the contents. "This is powerful stuff!" she said. "I can feel it's potency."

"Let's just hope that Elder Dhonna didn't give me witchbane by mistake." He smiled at the witch's eye roll.

Anayah laughed. "Not to worry. It's not affecting me. I can just feel its strength. It wants to fulfill its purpose." She tucked it into her satchel.

Harpur accepted that. "Did you find anything about how my blood is affecting Arthur?"

Sok rejoined them, rubbing his stomach and smiling. "That is the best cobbler in the universe! You guys should have some."

"Another time, perhaps," Anayah said, though she was tempted. "You're just in time to hear what I found out about dragon blood. Sit down, Sok."

Sok made himself comfortable next to Anayah and waved at the barmaid for more ale for the table.

"Unfortunately, I did not learn the specific way your blood is affecting Arthur," Anayah began. "What I did discover, though, is that when dragon blood is administered to a magical being, such as Arthur, a physical transformation isn't likely to occur. Instead, his magic is somehow enhanced. He'll have some power that is typical to dragons, but not other beings."

That could be any number of things," Harpur mused. "But unless we can figure out what it is, it doesn't help us with the prophecy."

"There's more," Anayah said. "Gnik was also a direct descendant of Ylemnir. Without any other known relatives, that makes Arthur the heir to the throne."

While Harpur digested that information, the barmaid arrived with the ale and Sok reached into his pocket for coins to pay for it. He was a coin short. When his eyes darted toward the niche, Harpur growled. "This round's on me," he said, handing over enough coins to cover the cost of the ale.

Sok, looking repentant, thanked Harpur.

"I'd have rather had tea," Anayah said and took a sip of her ale. "Oh! This isn't bad at all."

Sok retired to the little Council house that he lived in on the south side of the city. He was disappointed that Harpur and Anayah both said they had things they needed to do. When he opened the door to the cozy little cottage, it suddenly felt rather lonely. To the right of the door was a coat rack with a variety of elven cloaks and coats hanging from the branches. Next to it, on the floor, was a jumble of boots and shoes, an impressive collection for an elf. To the left of the door, under a shuttered window was a small table and three backless chairs. The table was strewn with plates and cups and other detritus from meals not cleaned up after. Opposite the table was a single cot with a single blanket and a single pillow. Next to the cot was a large trunk, that held the rest of Sok's wardrobe. Beside that was a small open fireplace and on the other side of the fireplace was a small counter with a water basin. Above the counter were two empty shelves meant to hold the plates and cups that were left unwashed on the table. Directly across from the coat rack was a narrow door that led to a water closet. Sok had all the amenities a single elf could want. They just weren't very tidy.

He changed into a nightshirt and then made his way outside and to the back of the cottage where a hammock hung between a sturdy tree and the Council house. He rarely slept inside. There were just some things that an elf would not easily give up and one of them was sleeping in the trees.

While Sok had made his way through the maze of streets to his home, Harpur flew Anayah to the Boundary she had mentioned at Skull's Keep. It was an opportunity to stretch his wings in dragon from and check it out. It would work well as a place to lure the wraiths to and destroy them. Providing Anayah could get the help they needed on the Mysturna side. After the brief reconnaissance of the Boundary, Anayah returned to her world with a promise to do her best. Everything depended on having someone on Mysturna ready with the wraithbane.

Once Anayah was through the Boundary, Harpur flew leisurely back north and to the west to his lair in the mountains. He needed to spend time in dragon form and, though devoid of most of his hoard, the lair would at least accommodate him comfortably. The offering he'd made had disturbed him more than he wanted to admit, but alone in his lair, he could be the dragon he had been born to be.

The following morning, Harpur, Sok and Anayah met at the main gates of Colwygshire and walked together to the former Bounding Offices in the castle adjunct to meet with Davynn Willhart. When they entered, Davynn was seated at the desk with his head down, focused on an array of paperwork that fanned out in a complicated exhibit of needs and demands he was somehow supposed to prioritize and delegate to whoever he could find who would get them done.

Without looking up, Davynn asked, "Any luck with the elves?"

"Some," Harpur answered, forcing the over-taxed young captain to reprioritize his priorities.

Davynn moved one more piece of paper from a pile on his left to a pile at the far edge of the desk and looked up. When he saw the beautiful red-head standing between the elf and the dragon-wizard, the needs and demands were all but forgotten. He stood and apologized for his rudeness.

Anayah didn't always enjoy the attention she garnered from men, but Davynn Willhart was one of the rare exceptions. She smiled and held out her hand. "Anayah." She introduced herself. "And you must be Davynn."

"Ah! The witch from Mysturna!" Davynn said, taking her hand and bowing. "Sok has told me a lot about you, but he failed to mention how beautiful you are."

Anayah withdrew her hand. "Thank you." Her coy smile sent a wave of delight through the young captain.

Next to her a low growl rumbled deep in Harpur's throat and Davynn quickly reverted to his usual business-like manner. He cleared his throat and invited his guests to sit down. There were only two chairs, so he called for someone to bring in a third. While they waited for the chair, Davynn gathered the papers into a single pile and pushed them to the side of the desk.

"Now, then," Davynn said, trying not to stare at Anayah, "what did the elves have to say?"

Harpur told Davynn about the wraithbane and laid out their plan to lure the wraiths to a Boundary. "Once Anayah and I lead them away from the castle, you and your men can take Bloomregaard."

Davynn listened to the plan. "Who will throw this wraithbane into the Boundary when you get them into it?"

"I have arranged for someone to be there," Anayah said. "She will be waiting for us and will be ready when the time comes. I've already given her the wraithbane."

Davynn heard the undertones and decided not to question her further.

"I think Sok should be the one to do it," Harpur said.

Sok sat up straight and looked at Harpur. "Me?" He felt a surge of pride for the confidence Harpur had in him. "I'd be honoured to do it!"

"Anabettah can handle it," Anayah said without looking at Harpur.

"I'm sure she can," Harpur agreed, "but I think Sok should be there as well."

Davynn studied the three people sitting across from him. There was tension between the witch and the dragon that made him feel uneasy. The elf was exuding his typical enthusiasm for the job and as much as he hated to oppose Anayah, he knew he had to assert his unwanted authority and make a decision.

"Sok will go to Mysturna and *assist* your friend," Davynn said. "I will feel better having someone I know there to assist." He looked at Sok when he stressed the word assist. It was as much of an appeasement as he could offer Anayah.

To everyone's surprise, Anayah acquiesced. "Very well."

"Good," Davynn said, feeling a twinge of guilt. "Now that that's settled, we have other problems. My people are getting restless. I've been able to keep them from doing anything rash so far, but we are running out of time. They want this done. And they want to know who will be king when it is."

"We've got that covered," Sok blurted. "Arthur is going to be king."

"Who's Arthur?" Davynn asked.

"He's the king in the prophecy," Sok said.

"What prophecy?" Davynn felt a headache start to develop behind his eyes.

"Well, a few years ago, I went to the Well of the Ancients and made an offering of Dragonfoil leaves and an ancestor named Reine appeared and told me to give a coin she gave me to a man holding a silver fox and I did and now that Gnik is dead, Arthur is going to be our king." Sok felt triumphant.

Davynn looked at Harpur and Anayah for help with this bewildering twist and Anayah elected to rescue him.

"The prophecy appears to be true," she said. "But you need to know that Arthur is not from here."

"Where is he from?" Davynn asked.

392

"Earth," Harpur said.

The headache intensified and Davynn was rendered speechless. He'd been expecting to hear that this Arthur chap was from some distant kingdom on Thraeh not some other world altogether. *This is what I get for getting involved with a dragon, an elf and a witch*, he thought.

Anayah filled in the gaps, explaining Arthur's relationship to Gnik through their shared ancestor, Ylemnir and how Harpur had met Arthur eight years earlier and had been keeping an eye on him through is role as Bounder Guard. She explained how Sok had illegally Bounded to Whyte Avenue and had recognized Arthur as the man from the prophecy and how the coin had caused them to become Entangled. She assured Davynn that the Entanglement had been dealt with and now all they had to do was get rid of Bloomregaard and the wraiths so that Arthur could come to Thraeh and take his place as king of Epoh.

Davynn leaned back in his own chair and stared at them. His eyes settled on Sok. "And you never thought to tell me any of this?"

"Well, we haven't quite figured out how that part is going to work yet," Sok said.

"Okay, so how in Orhowyn's name are we supposed to convince the people of Epoh to accept some man from another world... a world we don't want to know about us... as their king? Does this Arthur know all this?" Davynn asked, rubbing his temples.

"He does and he doesn't," Harpur said.

"What does that mean?" Davynn wasn't sure he wanted to know.

"I had to wipe his memory. He Bounded here with a girl just before Bloomregaard staged his coup and I couldn't let them both remember" Harpur said, realizing how difficult this was for the accidental leader. "But when the time is right, I will deal with him. Let's focus on Bloomregaard and the wraiths right now. We can figure out what to do with Arthur later."

"In the meantime, the people still want to know who is going to wear the crown once Bloomregaard is dealt with. There are rumours that there is a group who is going to propose me for the job. That can't happen!" Davynn was losing his poise and becoming distraught.

"Don't worry," Sok chirped. "Arthur is the king."

"We are going to have to find a way to stall for time, Davynn," Anayah said as soothingly as possible. "We can just tell them that there is an heir, we just have to find him and bring him to Epoh. Trust us; we will figure that part of it out. And we will help you with all of this until we do." She pointed to the pile of papers that represented the burden of responsibility that had been thrust on Davynn since Gnik's death.

The only thing Davynn could do was nod his head. Bloomregaard was the immediate problem. Whoever this Arthur was, Davynn would have to worry about him later.

When Harpur had made the bold and enigmatic play to become a Bounder Guard on Earth, Edlyngton Bloomregaard saw an opportunity to rid himself of the greatest threat to his life-long plan to become king of Epoh. Once Harpur was established safely on Earth, he had hoped to find a way to destroy the Boundary, thus keeping him from interfering, at least until it was too late. But the Boundary had proven to be indestructible. Frustrated and impatient, he had finally decided to push things forward and had the wraiths start to truly terrorize Colwygshire. He had expected a reaction, but he had not anticipated King Gnik to decree their banishment from Epoh. *Upon pain of death, Bloomregaard, get those vile creatures out of my kingdom!*

Upon pain of death, indeed! It had been almost too easy to slip the poison into Gnik's drink and watch him writhe in agony until, at last he had succumbed to its lethal effects. An unscrupulous forger was all too eager to create the documents Bloomregaard needed naming him Gnik's chosen heir. And the wraiths had saved him the steep fee the forger had demanded for his work by sucking his life force from his body and leaving the resulting dust to blow away in the wind.

He was sure that the horror of false accusations and public executions would draw the dragon back to Thraeh. But, so far, Harpur had not shown any interest in the prospect of having the kingdom fall under Bloomregaard's rule. There had only been the dashing Davynn Willhart and his ragtag bunch of deserters to contend with. Not that they were much of a threat. He had allowed them to take the castle under siege, believing that Harpur would eventually come to their rescue and he could put the final piece into place. If the wraiths couldn't kill the dragon, they could—and would—be able to enslave him with their soul-sucking magic. Which, if Bloomregaard had to admit, would be the better outcome. Between the wraiths and a dragon doing his bidding, his rule would be absolute. No one would dare to challenge him.

The announcement of a date and time for the coronation was his last ploy to draw out the dragon. But Harpur hadn't taken the bait. He knew that Harpur was in Colwygshire; the wraith had reported his arrival with that infernally annoying elf. Since then, however, Harpur had made no effort to challenge him. And that would never do! He made a point of spending time in plain view on the balcony outside of the throne room with the wraiths hidden nearby. If he appeared vulnerable, sooner or later, the dragon would show.

While Davynn felt like any control he might have had over the situation was spinning away from him, Harpur, Sok and Anayah felt like they were making great progress. They had a plan. All Davynn needed to do was get his men ready to storm the castle as soon as Harpur drew the wraiths away.

The first step was to get Sok to Mysturna. Anayah wanted it on record that she opposed this part of the plan, but did not say why. Neither did she refuse to take Sok to the Boundary, though she did not

Bound with him. "Just tell Anabettah that you are there to help if you're needed. If anyone else is with her... Well, just stay with Anabettah. She will protect you."

"Protect me from what?" Sok asked.

"There's a slim chance that Analeetah might be with Anabettah. If she is, I don't think she will try to thwart us, but she isn't pleased with any of us and I dare say she won't be happy to see you." Anayah looked concerned.

"What if they think the wraiths are following me and throw the wraithbane into the Boundary?"

"Anabettah knows not to do that until Harpur Bounds through. And we don't know when that will be. Hopefully, not long. Stay alert, Sok. And be careful."

Sok studied Anayah's troubled eyes. "It will be okay," he said. Then he Bounded to Mysturna.

Anayah returned to Colwygshire to find a cloaked and hooded Harpur sitting in the gardens outside the castle. He was watching Bloomregaard pacing back and forth on the balcony that overlooked the gardens while pretending not to be watching the sky for a dragon.

"You don't actually think he won't recognize you in that get up?" Anayah said as she took a seat on the stone bench next to Harpur.

"He's expecting me to come from the sky." Harpur said. "As are all the archers he has posted on the ramparts."

Anayah looked up. There were at least two dozen guards armed with bows and arrows along the walls on either side of the balcony. "As long as you stay out of range, they shouldn't be a problem. Any sign of the wraiths?"

Harpur thought about his missing scale. Staying out of range would not be an issue. "None. I don't think they are in there with him."

"Where are they, then?" Anayah was searching for them in the shadows of the balcony.

Harpur had no answer. "Sok get to Mysturna okay?" he asked instead.

"I believe so." She kept searching for the wraiths.

"Something I should know?"

"I'm sure Anabettah will keep him safe."

"You're afraid of Analeetah, aren't you?"

Anayah weighed her response. "Not afraid exactly. She's hurt and she's angry. She won't harm Sok, if that's what you're thinking. But she might take it out on me later. I promised her that I would keep you all away from Mysturna. I've broken that promise."

"I'm sorry," Harpur said. "Why did you agree to let us do this, then?"

"Because it's the right thing to do."

Harpur stood up. "Let's go find us some wraiths to kill, shall we?"

"Right now?"

"I'm thinking we might need to get Sok back here as soon as possible," Harpur said.

Anayah smiled ruefully. "How are going to do this?"

Harpur looked around. There were too many people in and around the gardens for him to risk transforming where they were. In spite of the standoff happening at the castle, it was business as usual for many folks. "I'll transform outside the city and we'll fly in over the walls. I want to give people time to find shelter."

"What do you intend to do?" Anayah was alarmed.

"Just talk to Bloomregaard. And see if we can get him to sick his creatures on us." Harpur assured her. "But it's best to be prepared. I don't know what he's planning."

"Right. Let's do this."

Davynn had sent his men to their posts, telling them to be ready. He had warned them that the action might start at any moment, but they were not to move until they saw the wraiths follow the dragon away from the city. He dispatched runners to covertly warn citizens near the castle to clear the area. Some had complied. Others had not. This was the problem with prolonged peace; people had no fear. But he had done his due diligence and, as frustrating as it was, he could not risk making a scene by trying to force onlookers to find shelter. He could not tip Bloomregaard off.

He had been standing at the top of the steps leading into the castle adjunct watching Harpur watching Bloomregaard. It was from there that he would lead the charge into the castle when and if Harpur successfully lured the wraiths away. When he saw Harpur stand up and guide Anayah out of the garden, he knew the time had come. He signaled the other men stationed around the gardens to be ready. Then he waited.

Above the city, Harpur, with Anayah securely held in his big hand, made several invisible passes past the castle. Neither of them saw any sign of the wraiths, but Bloomregaard was relaxing on a divan while servants served his every whim. They spotted Davynn and his men scattered, but close to the castle steps doing their best to look casual and not stare up at the sky. A few citizens loitered in groups throughout the gardens looking as if they were waiting for a parade to start. They had not been told about the dragon, so they remained focused on the guards. Harpur didn't know why they were still there, but, like Davynn, there was nothing he could do. He suspected that once he became visible, they would leave. It was time to make the appearance that Bloomregaard was waiting for.

Harpur circled around to the back of the castle and became visible again. As he banked to come in over the wall, his shadow fell over the gardens and everyone on the ground variously ran for cover or stood paralyzed looking up at the sky. Davynn followed their gaze. There, just above the roof tops and dangerously within arrow shot was Harpur Diggins, the dragon, hovering magically in the air. In his left front hand, perched Anayah, holding a broad sword and a walking stick. Davynn looked back at the archers assembled along the ramparts already nocking arrows and waiting for the order to shoot.

One of the archers spotted the missing scale on Harpur's chest and saw an opportunity. It was common knowledge that a normal arrow, such as the ones that he and his fellow archers were armed with would not penetrate dragon scales. They were taught, when facing a dragon to always aim for the eyes or the open mouth. The problem with these strategies was that the eyes were relatively small targets and if the mouth was open, it was probably emitting flames that would burn up an arrow long before it could do any significant damage. Without waiting for the order and driven by fear of the formidable beast, the guard shifted his general aim and took specific aim at the spot where the scale was missing.

Harpur saw the small movement. At the last minute, he rose above the oncoming missile and it flew harmlessly past the dragon and his startled passenger. He was tempted to burn the over-eager archer on the spot. Instead, he memorized the pitiful archer's face. He would pay for drawing attention to Harpur's vulnerability.

While the archer was being berated for his impetuous action by his commanding officer, Bloomregaard rose from the divan and stepped to the balcony railing to see what the fuss was. He took in the scene below and around him, noted the archer's self-created predicament and then allowed his eyes to settle on Harpur. He leaned arrogantly on the balcony railing and smiled at the dragon.

"Welcome back!" Bloomregaard called. "I've been expecting you."

It would be so easy, Harpur thought, noting that Bloomregaard was all alone on the balcony. No guards, no collateral damage, just a breath of fire sustained for less than a minute, and Edlyngton Bloomregaard would be no more. But that was not his mission. His mission was to lure the wraiths away so Davynn could storm the castle and take care of the usurper.

Pumping his wings to remain still, Harpur fought the temptation to burn Bloomregaard where he stood. "This has to end," he said calmly. "Surrender now and I will let you live."

Bloomregaard laughed. "Oh, it will end, Harpur. I'm going to be crowned king of Epoh soon. Haven't you heard?"

"I'm pretty sure you are not going to be crowned king. You have no right to the throne." Harpur was trusting that Anayah was watching for the wraiths and would alert him. Three taps on his hand was the signal they had agreed on. He kept his focus squarely on Bloomregaard.

"Oh, but I do! I may not have royal blood flowing through my veins, but Gnik, the poor man, not having any heirs, named me his successor should any... misfortune fall on him. I have the proclamation, signed and sealed by the king himself." Bloomregaard boasted.

"That's all rather convenient, isn't it?" Harpur said. He had to get Bloomregaard to call out the wraiths. This friendly banter was not going to work.

"I thought so," Bloomregaard said. "It would be to your advantage to accept it. I will reward you handsomely if you do."

"What do you want from me?"

"Your fealty. Swear an oath of loyalty to me as King of Epoh and *you* will live."

"Ha!" Harpur spat. "And who is going to kill me?"

Bloomregaard looked around at the archers lined up on the ramparts on either side of him. "Oh, I don't know. Any one of these fine men with bows could stick the killing shot. It seems you are presenting them with a perfect target." He was talking about the missing scale. "What happened, Harpur? Who took your scale?"

There was still no sign of the wraiths. The archers, to a man, adjusted their stance and took aim at Harpur's heart. Rather than reply, Harpur let the fire build in his chest. An orange-red glow spread out from his heart. He took a deep breath, preparing to let loose the flames that would end the egotistic ambitions of this repulsive little man.

Bloomregaard backed quickly away from the railing. "Kill him," he ordered as he dodged behind a pillar to avoid the flames.

Twenty-four arrows, aimed at Harpur's heart, were let loose. Harpur didn't move this time. At the moment the arrows left the bows, Anayah threw up a magical shield in front of Harpur and the lethal darts bounced harmlessly off it.

Below them, what few people still remained, scattered for shelter. A few more cries floated up; all cries of fear. Harpur heard none that sounded like injury and he was relieved. He didn't want anyone to have any excuse to attach a loss of any kind to him. He was still holding his fire. Still waiting for the wraiths.

Bloomregaard's order had not been directed at the archers, though it had pleased him that they were so willing to take on a beast like Harpur. The fools!

It had, in fact, been meant for the wraiths. But where were they? Even Bloomregaard, peeking out from behind the pillar, was getting nervous.

Anayah was frantically looking around for any sign of them. Harpur was tempted to look as well, but he had to keep Bloomregaard thinking that he was about to be fried. He shifted to his right to a position that would allow the flames to at least heat things up for Bloomregaard, if not kill him. Everyone had to think that the threat was to Bloomregaard. Surely, the wraiths would come to the aide of their master.

Then Harpur heard a cry from the bush Davynn had dived into for protection from the falling arrows. "Harpur! Behind you!"

The archers had new arrows ready to let loose. At the moment they did, Harpur rose up and swung around to see what Davynn's warning was about. Anayah did her best to magically shield herself and Harpur, but one arrow went wide and, on a down stroke, pierced his left wing. It was a minor tear, but Harpur had to will himself not to react to the pain.

"Aim for the wings!"

Harpur heard the order and rose higher. He couldn't keep an eye on the archers and deal with what appeared before him. Anayah would have to keep her shields up and keep them both safe from the arrows.

And there they were. The wraiths had been behind him the whole time. Now one was directly in front of him and the other two were flanking him, one on either side. They were too far apart for a single flame to get them all. If he breathed his fire at one, he was sure the other two would attack from the other directions. They were advancing slowly. Too slowly. He had to get them together. All he could do was rise higher and hope that they drew together to follow him.

Bloomregaard took advantage of the distraction to retreat back inside the castle. He was content to let the wraiths deal with the dragon and his passenger. He assumed the beautiful red-head Harpur was carrying was a witch. He didn't really care who she was. The wraiths would dispatch her when they took control of the dragon. His plan was coming together nicely. Harpur was the only living dragon with ties to Epoh. Even though he spent most of his time on Earth, Bloomregaard knew that Harpur would not stand by and let him just become come king on a whim.

Bloomregaard would rather Harpur join him. A dragon in his pocket would be a coup, indeed. But the wraiths were sufficient. As long as they didn't turn on him. They were unpredictable beings, but Bloomregaard knew how to deal with them if they did. And he was the only one who knew what he knew. That he knew of. He kept a good supply of wraithbane handy at all times.

Meanwhile, Harpur was soaring nearly straight up over Colwygshire. He had to draw the wraiths away and get them close enough together to burn them. He had no idea if they could be burned. If it worked, he and Anayah would return to the city and help Davynn take the castle. If it didn't, then he would lure them to the Boundary and trap them in it. This slight alteration to the plan was a concession to Anayah to try to avoid any potential of the wraiths running amok on Mysturna. It was worth a try.

The wraiths took the bait. They converged and followed Harpur up into the sky. When Anayah yelled over the wind that they were right behind and gaining on them, Harpur banked to his left, picked up speed and flew south toward the Boundary. They had to be close enough to him for his fire to reach them, but not so close that he couldn't get to the Boundary in time if his fire had no effect. There were too many unknowns. Harpur told Anayah to let him know when the wraiths were about one hundred feet behind.

"Three taps," he told her.

Harpur could see the Boundary a few hundred yards ahead. They were running out of time. The closer they got to the Boundary, the less room Harpur would have to maneuver.

"Are they close enough?"

"Almost!" Anayah yelled.

Harpur watched the Boundary getting closer. They had chosen it because it was the biggest Boundary they could find that lead to Mysturna and was out in the open away from any villages. Harpur would have to Bound in dragon form and most Boundaries would not accommodate his enormous size. As they drew closer to it, Harpur began to wonder if this one was big enough. But another problem was vying for his attention. The faster and farther he flew, the bigger the tear in his wing was getting. Soon it would affect his flying.

"Anayah?"

"Almost," she repeated.

I can't wait any longer! Between the looming Boundary and his ripping wing, Harpur had to make a move.

He cupped his wings and drew his lower body forward to slow his speed. Then, in a swooping forward, twisting dive, he turned and flew back upward, straight at the wraiths. He expected them to stop, but they adjusted their course and moved faster toward him, right into the searing column of fire that Harpur blew out in front of himself. At the last second, he pulled up to avoid colliding with the shrieking wraiths within the aerial conflagration. He banked to his right, hoping that the ear-piercing shrieks meant they were dying, but as the fuel-less flames died out, Harpur saw the wraiths were undamaged. If anything, they looked bigger and more menacing than before.

Anayah's screams, were lost amid the screeches from the wraiths. She had managed to hold on to the sword and the walking stick through the unexpected reversal in their direction, but when the wraiths started screaming and she tried to cover her ears, the walking stick had tumbled out of her grasp and fell to the ground below them. Harpur's hand had shielded her from the worst of the heat, but as she had scrambled to save the walking stick, the sleeve of her shirt caught fire. To smother it, she pushed her arm against Harpur's hand. He was impervious, but the heat left her arm severely burned from her wrist to her elbow. She knew it could be easily healed, but this was not the place or the time to worry about it. She gritted her teeth against the horrific pain and tried to focus on what was going on with the wraiths. They were still right behind them.

Harpur couldn't afford to think about his passenger. He had to get to and through the Boundary. The wraiths were closing in and he needed to maintain enough distance between him and them to get all the way through before they followed. If they followed. Harpur forced that particular unknown out of his mind and focussed on the Boundary. It was only a couple hundred yards away. Harpur suddenly knew one thing for sure. He wasn't going to fit.

But he was committed. He stretched out his neck and legs and flattened his wings as tightly around his body as he dared. He knew that he could easily crush Anayah, but all he cared about right then was getting through the Boundary. He pointed his nose at the center of the Boundary, closed his eyes and dove in to it. He felt his wings and left thigh touch the edges of the Boundary as he passed through. A burning cold shot through him and just as his head and neck emerged on the Mysturna side of the Boundary, he passed out.

On the Mysturna side of the Boundary Sok and Anabettah watched as the dragon burst through and, carried by the momentum, flew another five hundred feet before crashing to the ground and sliding to a crumpled stop next to a small lake. Knowing that Anayah was somewhere in the heap of ice-encrusted dragon, was more than Anabettah could bear. She stood staring in horror at the still form of the dragon.

Sok, too, was terrified, but he kept his head and snatched the bag of wraithbane out of the stricken witch's hand. With as much force as he had, he threw the bag into the center of the Boundary. At the moment of contact, the Boundary altered from its normal shimmering transparency into a bulging, writhing black mass that hung in the air above the ground. A fierce cold emanated from it, numbing Sok to his core. He barely had the strength to grab Anabettah's hand so they could run from the killing cold. They stumbled forward on frozen feet no more than fifty feet when they were blown forward by an icy shockwave.

The Boundary exploded in a spectacular blast of black ice that sent shards flying in all directions. The downward force of the blast, opened a large crater in the earth below the Boundary, adding dirt and rocks to the shrapnel. Anabettah, who had been a half-step behind, was flung forward onto Sok's back, protecting him from the worst of the razor-sharp shards of ice. She was dead before she hit the ground.

Sok laid, winded but mostly unhurt beneath the body of the old witch until he could gather his wits and roll out from under her. He sat up slowly, taking in the scene around him. The black ice shards were already beginning to melt into a thick, slimy goo that made the landscape appear as if a giant Jackson Pollock had visited. The Boundary was gone. The only indication it was ever present was the crater that had been blown out in the explosion.

He looked at the body of Anabettah lying on the ground next to him. She was covered with the black goo and her silvery hair was matted with clumps of dirt and small stones from the blast. In his shock, all he wanted to do was clean her up. It was wrong for her to have to lie on the ground like that, covered in sludge and blood. At the same time, he couldn't bring himself to touch her.

The shriek of a moorhawk drilled through his traumatized mind and he remembered Anayah. Circling over the huge body of the dragon, the moorhawk was letting others of its kind know that a there was food for the taking. Sok stood up, his feet slipping in the slime. He had never seen a moorhawk before, but he recognized it for what it was, a carrion bird. "No!" he screamed at it as it began to circle closer to its next meal.

He carefully made his way toward Harpur's body. He couldn't run. The greasy slime was being slowly absorbed into the ground, but the grass was slick and he would stumble if he didn't place each step he took with the greatest of care. It finally started to peter out about half way to where Harpur's body lay and he was able to walk faster. By the time he reached Harpur, he was beginning to feel dizzy from the effort.

Sok could see the dragon's wing rise and fall with each ragged breath he took. He was alive! The moorhawk kept circling above, but didn't land. Either Sok's approach or Harpur's ragged breathing was giving it pause. It stopped shrieking.

He walked to Harpur's head. His eyes were closed and he was clearly unconscious. This wasn't a good thing, but it did allow Sok to access the extent of his injuries. And look for Anayah. She had to be somewhere in the wreckage.

Harpur was on his side. The wing underneath him was clearly broken and the webbing was torn in several places. His other wing was stretched out forming a tent over his front legs and hands. It, too, was torn in places. The only blood Sok could see was from the tears in Harpur's wings. That was a good sign. Water from melting ice on his back leg and the exposed wing dripped, forming puddles on the ground. Sok didn't know what to make of that, if Anayah was anywhere, she had to be under the wing. He crouched down and crawled under, looking for the witch.

A broken sword lay next to Harpur's hand. And the hand was curled around Anayah. Sok steeled himself for the worst and reached out to check for any sign of life. With a sigh of relief, Sok felt a faint pulse on Anayah's neck. He checked Anayah for injuries as best he could. Harpur's grip on Anayah was too tight for him to be able to pull her free. It was as if Harpur was continuing, even in unconsciousness, to protect her. Sok needed to get help.

Then he noticed Anayah's bag tucked between her body and Harpur' talons. He pulled it out and reached inside, hoping Anayah's scrying mirror was in the bag and in tact. The mirror had cracked in two, but looked like it was still serviceable. Sok had seen Hiro activate his scrying mirror by tapping on it. Using his knuckles he began knocking on the broken mirror, hoping a friendly face would appear. Each time he knocked, the surface rippled, but no one answered. Frantically, Sok knocked harder.

"Come on!" he begged, willing something to happen. When nothing did, he tossed the mirror down and reached out to shake Anayah. Maybe he could wake her up. But just like the mirror, Anayah did not respond. He sat back on his heels and put his head on his knees in despair. *What am I going to do? How am I going help my friends now?*

"Anayah?" a whispered voice cut through Sok's anguish. "Is that you?"

Sok lifted his head and looked at the broken scrying mirror on the ground beside him. Half of Mezzi's face was looking up from it. "Mezzi! Thank Orhowyn it's you. I need some help?"

"Sok?" Mezzi exclaimed, then dropped her voice back to a whisper. "What are you doing with Anayah's mirror? Where are you?"

"Mezzi, listen to me. Something terrible has happened. Anabettah is dead and Harpur and Anayah are hurt really bad."

For the first time in her chatty life, the koobar was dumbstruck. She stared back at Sok unable to respond.

"Mezzi, did you hear me?" Sok pleaded. "I need help here."

The koobar disappeared and the scrying mirror went black.

Sok was not prone to crying, but as he rapped on the blank mirror, tears poured from his eyes. "Mezzi!" he yelled. "Mezzi, come back!"

The moorhawk, having abandoned the dragon, was now circling above Anabettah's lifeless body. Sok heard its screeching call and crawled out from under Harpur's wing to investigate. When he saw the bird land on Anabettah's back, he started to run. Waving his arms and shouting to scare the moorhawk away, Sok slipped and slid back to Anabettah. He couldn't leave her there for the birds to pick at, so he picked her up and carried her to a tree closer to the lake shore and laid her back down on the ground in a depression between the tree's roots. Then he started gathering rocks to build a cairn.

As he worked, he kept looking at Harpur, hoping the dragon would come to and tell him what to do. But as the hours passed, the dragon remained still. He finished the cairn and whispered an elven blessing for the dead. Then he went to the water to wash his hands and get a drink. He had no idea which direction Danaleedh was and he knew better than to wander away. Who knew what dreadful wildlife was out there waiting to pull him under the ground or spray him with bone-dissolving ink? *Maybe I can reach Mezzi again and get her to listen.*

In the shade Harpur's wing provided, Sok sat next to Anayah and tried tapping the scrying mirror again. It remained stubbornly blank. Not knowing what else to do, Sok performed some gentle healing on Anayah. He kept the healing general because he didn't know the full extent of her injuries. His emotions made the healing he was offering difficult. He knew he should stop, so that his fear and sorrow didn't mix with the energy and make things worse for Anayah, but he couldn't make himself give up. *Please! Please, Anayah, wake up.*

Anayah stirred.

The soft groan she emitted was like music to Sok's ears. He leaned closer.

"Anayah," he whispered. "Anayah, are you okay?"

Anayah groaned again. "What happened?" she croaked. She struggled to sit up.

Sok pushed her back down. "Shh," he said to soothe Anayah. "Are you hurt?"

Anayah assessed herself through the fog that was her mind. Sok's healing had soothed her burn. Other than being stuck in Harpur's hand, she seemed to be okay.

"Harpur!" she cried. "Is Harpur okay?" She struggled harder to extract herself from his grip.

"He's alive," Sok said. "He's unconscious, but he's breathing."

Anayah wiggled and wriggled against Sok's protestations until she was free. She crawled past the elf and out from under Harpur's wing. She tried to take it all in. The tears in his left wing. The obvious damage to his right wing. The water that had pooled next to him. She walked to his head and knelt down beside it. She could hear his ragged breath as she placed a hand on his jaw.

"We have to help him," she said, tears of her own spilling out and running down her cheeks.

Sok stood behind her. "I don't know if we should do any healing with him like this." Sok indicated the broken wing. He was afraid that if they used their healing powers, Harpur's wing might mend as it was—broken and bent.

Anayah looked up at Sok. "I don't either. But we have to figure it out. Can you find my scrying mirror? It should be in my satchel."

"I tried that. I got hold of Mezzi, and told her I needed help, but she disconnected and I haven't been able to reach her again."

"Sok, where is Anabettah?" Anayah asked, remembering that she should be there too.

Sok didn't know what else to say. "I'm sorry, Anayah," he croaked as he pointed at the cairn under the tree.

Anayah shook her head in disbelief. "No," she said. "No, Sok. Please, tell me she's not..."

"I'm so sorry."

Anayah ran to the cairn and dropped to her knees beside it. "Nooooo!" she wailed. "No. No. No!"

Sok stayed where he was next to Harpur's head and gave his friend the space she needed to grieve for Anabettah. "Now would be a really good time for you to wake up too, dragon," he said aloud to Harpur. "We need to get out of here. If Analeetah was mad at us before, she's going to be furious with us now."

An eternity seemed to pass before Anayah finally composed herself and returned to Sok and Harpur. "Thank you," she said, nodding toward the cairn. "That was kind."

"There was a bird... I couldn't... You're welcome," Sok said.

"I need to tell Analeetah." She started walking toward Harpur's wing to look for her scrying mirror.

Sok understood this, but he didn't think it was the wisest course of action. With Harpur so vulnerable, he didn't want to even think about what Analeetah could do to him. The witches claimed to be peaceful beings, but Sok didn't think that Analeetah's peacefulness would withstand what had happened. He had to stop her.

"Anayah!" Sok called, trying to sound excited. "I think Harpur is waking up."

Anayah was just about to crawl back under Harpur's wing when Sok's lie reached her ears. She stood back up. "Are you sure?"

"He just twitched." Sok hated himself, but he stepped back as Anayah approached the dragon's head again and knelt down beside it.

"Harpur! Harpur, I need you to wake up." She tried to shake him, but he was too big. "Harpur! Wake up. Please wake up!"

Getting no response, she stood up and fired every ounce of healing power she could muster through the palms of her hands into Harpur's head and body. She'd never healed a dragon before. Any healing she had performed on Harpur in his human form had been minor and probably redundant. She'd always believed that he had allowed it just to shut her up, so this fell squarely into the realm of experimentation. For both of them.

"I really don't think we should do this." Sok grabbed Anayah's arm to stop her. "We don't know how bad things are and if his wing mends without being properly set, Harpur might never fly again."

Anayah sighed. Sok was right. A fresh wave of tears flooded her eyes. "We have to do something."

"I know." Sok knelt down and put his arms around Anayah. "Let's focus our efforts on waking him up. Once he's conscious again, we can see to his other injuries."

Anayah nodded. Her eyes drifted to the cairn again and she had to force herself to keep her mind on Harpur. Together, they sustained the beams of blue-white light for over a minute. The intensity of concentrating to keep the magic energy flowing soon took its toll and Anayah had to pause to revive her strength. She did this a few times, shouting at the dragon to wake up between each attempt. Sok let her do what she had to do while he maintained his healing without a break.

She was about to begin her fourth attempt when Harpur opened his eyes. "Enough," he said. "I'm awake. Just stop doing that."

Anayah dropped to her knees and hugged the dragon's neck, weeping with relief and grief and about a dozen other emotions that Harpur was sure to mock her for. That thought made her laugh, perhaps a bit hysterically. But he was awake. That was all that mattered.

Sok sighed in relief.

Harpur lifted his head. Then rested it back on the ground. Then lifted it again. Anayah and Sok moved away from him to give him room to roll over and get up. He was thrashing about like the giant, wounded animal he was and Anayah knew he would find this humiliating. She got a little closer. "Can you transform?"

Harpur stopped his thrashing. He turned his head to look at her. "Good idea."

A few moments later the giant, thrashing dragon was replaced by a large, woozy man, with barely enough strength to stand. The witch and the elf ran to support him.

"Can you tell me what's wrong with you?" she asked.

Harpur focused on his injuries. "I'm pretty sure my shoulder blade is broken. And my left leg feels like it's been flayed. But other than that, I think I'm okay."

With Anayah's help, he hobbled over to a nearby boulder and sat down. He would heal. Probably. He just needed a minute or two.

Anayah conjured up a water skin and handed it to Harpur, who took a long drink. He then took some time to survey his surroundings.

His keen dragon vision swept over the landscape, noting the missing Boundary, the crater and the black goo that still covered the ground in spots. That did not bode well. For the time being, he was taking advantage of Anayah's healing ministrations to go over what he remembered. He knew there were going to be gaps to fill, but he needed to have what he did know straight before anything new got pushed into those gaps and ended up in the wrong places.

"Where's my walking stick?" he asked.

Anayah stopped her healing magic. "Uh... I... uh... dropped it," she confessed.

Harpur hung his head in frustration and sighed. "How?"

"When the wraiths started screeching, I tried to cover my ears and it slipped out of my hand. I'm sorry."

"No worries," Harpur said. He knew where it was; he'd deal with it later

"Really?" Anayah was skeptical.

Harpur raised his hand and held his thumb and index finger apart about a half an inch. "Maybe just a little worry."

Anayah realized that Harpur was trying to be stoic about it. But she'd take it. It was better than him yelling at her.

"What happened?" he asked, taking another long pull from the water skin.

Anayah's eyes strayed to the cairn "Anabettah is dead," she said and braced herself for the blame she knew she deserved.

"I'm sorry," he said. That was one gap partially filled. "We have to get back to Colwygshire. Does anyone know if the wraiths...?"

Anayah wanted to punch him. And hug him. *At least he didn't say I told you so.*

Sok saw Anayah's clenched fists and knew he had to keep her and Harpur from getting into a fight. "I think the wraiths were destroyed when the Boundary exploded," he said, hoping that this new problem of having no immediate way of getting home again would distract them from their personal issues.

A couple more gaps filled in. Elder Dhonna's warning about the possible dangers of destroying three wraiths in the Boundary had proven valid, if entirely too vague. He'd be sure to tell her when he took the stalagmite to her. But first he had to get to Thraeh and his best hope of doing that was a grief and guilt-ridden witch who he couldn't afford to alienate. He had to tread carefully.

"What do you want to do?" he asked Anayah.

Anayah was wary. She was putting Harpur's calmness down to his injuries, but it wasn't like him to just hand over the reigns like this. "I *want* to help you get back to Colwygshire," she said cautiously. "But I *need* to tell Analeetah what happened here."

Harpur stood up and winced with pain. His leg supported him, but it hurt and he had to work hard not to let it show. "Sok and I can't go to Wildwood with you."

"What if I call Hiro to take you to another Boundary? I'm not sure you should be zapping yourself around in your condition." she said. "I will wait here until you are safely away and then I will go to Analeetah."

Harpur nodded. He noticed the cairn a short distance away for the first time. "Will you be okay?"

"Eventually." Anayah's remorseful smile crumpled under a fresh wave of tears and to her amazement, Harpur pulled her gently into his arms and held her while she cried.

Chapter 18

"Um, Harpur?" Sok's voice cut through Harpur and Anayah's embrace and they pulled apart to see the elf pointing across the lake.

Harpur and Anayah exchanged puzzled looks. "When did you call him?" Harpur asked.

"I didn't," Anayah said, wiping tears from her face.

Even before his hover gilly crossed the lake and came to a stop close by, the little Krist was talking. "Sorry it took so long to get here. I accidentally transported to the wrong lake." Hiro giggled. "It took me a while to find you."

"How did you know we needed your help?" Anayah asked.

"Mezzi called me." Hiro dismounted from the wheel-less chariot and looked around. "I was led to believe there were some injuries and..." He continued to crane his neck. "Anabettah?"

Anayah couldn't speak. She and Harpur and Sok all looked toward the cairn.

Hiro turned and saw the stones piled at the base of the tree. His gaze lingered for a moment while he thought about what the loss of Anabettah's would mean to the witches of Danaleedh. Her wisdom. Her skill. Her leadership. Her magic. All of it entombed with her under the cairn. "How did this happen?" he whispered.

"Hiro, we need you to take me and Sok to the closest Boundary to Thraeh?" Harpur said.

Hiro's gaze left the cairn and passed over the devastated landscape. The crater where the Boundary used to be gaped like an open mouth ready to devour what remained of the beauty and serenity surrounding the lake. His eyes widened in shock and he looked at Harpur with a mixture of accusation and fear. He was torn between outrage and curiosity.

After Harpur had flown away with Sok and Arthur, Analeetah had forbidden Anayah to have anything to do with the dragon. She had deemed the dragon, the elf and even Arthur as unwelcome, if not on all of Mysturna, in Danaleedh without question. That Anayah had defied the Doyenne would be seen as a betrayal. That it had led to Anabettah's death would be unforgiveable.

"Can you fly?" Hiro asked Harpur.

"I doubt it. Broken wing." Harpur said. He wondered if he would ever fly again.

"Climb aboard, then," Hiro said, following his own directive. "We'll time bend to the nearest Boundary and get you two out of here. Anayah, will you be joining us?" The Krist was all giggle-less business.

"I must return to Wildwood," she whispered. Then she turned to Harpur. "I will come to Colwygshire as soon as I can." *If I can.*

"Are you sure you will be okay?" Harpur was both eager and reluctant to go.

"I will be fine. Go take care of Bloomregaard." She didn't wait for a reply. Anayah raised her arms and disappeared in a red puff of smoke.

Harpur stood and stared at the spot where Anayah had been standing. *Will I ever see you again?* Then he limped over to the hover gilly and climbed aboard. "Let's go."

The hover gilly lifted up and Hiro directed it back over the lake. Below the surface of the water, Sok saw a flash of brilliant blue and leaned over the side to get a better look at what it was. His eyes grew wide with surprise when the face of a woman with blue and gold hair smiled up at him. "What is that?"

Hiro looked over the front of the hover gilly to see the creature swimming on her back just ahead of them. "I didn't know Nyrids lived in this lake," Hiro said with a bit of surprise in his voice. He directed the gilly to rise higher above the lake just as the mermaid-like being breached the surface and reached for the edge of the hover gilly. It screeched in frustration when it missed and fell back into the water. "That was close!"

Harpur shook his head. *I really hate this world.*

"What are they?" Sok watched as the screeching Nyrid bobbed in the water below them.

"They are a nuisance is what they are," Hiro said. "They don't mean any harm, but they don't realize that we can't breathe under water like they can. She probably just wanted to play with us."

The hover gilly began to pick up speed until the scenery became a blur around them. Then, for a split second the world went black and suddenly they were approaching a Boundary next to a waterfall in a rocky ravine. When Harpur saw it, a wave of trepidation washed over him.

Now that they stood before another Boundary, Harpur discovered any enthusiasm he may have had for Bounding had waned considerably. The shocking cold that he had experienced as he and Anayah burst through the Boundary to Mysturna had very nearly killed him. Dragons were creatures of heat and if he hadn't ignited his fire as the first sensation of cold hit him, he was sure he would not be alive now. It had to have been caused by his body coming into contact with the edges of the Boundary, though that was just a theory. And it terrified him because it had never occurred to him before. He knew, from accidental experience, that passing through a Boundary while still in contact with the ground beneath it had no effect at all. It was as if the Boundary didn't exist. But breaching a Boundary's border while Bounding was, apparently, not a good idea. Duly noted!

"Where is this going to land us?" Harpur asked, buying for time while he mined his soul for the courage to make the Bound. He was not accustomed to feeling this way.

"Are you familiar with the Sands of Sancheera?" Hiro asked.

At least it's not cold there, Harpur thought. "I was born there."

"We'll come out near the northern border of the desert, close to Andon. You will have to zap us out as soon as we are through. Sok and I won't last long in the desert heat."

Harpur hadn't expected the Krist to be expecting to go with them. "You're coming with us?"

"Unless it's forbidden," Hiro said. "I should like to learn about your world."

"That's fantastic," Sok exclaimed. "You'll like it. At least you will once we get rid of Bloomregaard and get Arthur crowned."

Harpur didn't have the energy to argue. He couldn't stop Hiro and while, he was almost positive he could zap them out of the dessert, he wasn't sure if he was strong enough to zap them all the way to

Colwygshire from Andon. The hover gilly would be useful. "Can this thing bend time on Thraeh?" he asked, indicating the gilly.

"Let's find out!" Hiro giggled with glee and shot the hover gilly into the centre of the Boundary before Harpur could warn his companions to take a deep breath and hold it.

The Sands of Sancheera was a vast desert, the hottest place on Thraeh. For dragons, it was a playground. For pretty much any other living being, it was about five minutes of agony before they were reduced to crispy bits of bone and ash. The plan was for Harpur to zap them to the well in the village of Andon on the outskirts of the desert where they could rehydrate. Harpur, in human form, would feel the effects of the desert, but not to the extent that Sok and Hiro would. From there they would take the hover gilly to Colwygshire. They only had a few seconds after they Bounded.

Compared to the Bound to Mysturna, the Bound to the Sands of Sancheera was a relative walk in the park. The searing heat of the desert began to burn Sok and Hiro's lungs the instant they came through. Harpur, more prepared and knowing what to expect, summoned his magic and took them to the well at Andon, where Harpur dipped a bucket in the cool water and dumped it over first Hiro's, then Sok's heads and bodies. Then he handed them cups to drink from. Even after only a few seconds in the desert, both the elf and the Krist were drenched in sweat and parched by thirst.

A few of the locals stopped what they were doing to look at the newcomers to their well. People appearing there by magic was not uncommon, but a large man and a thirsty elf were not interesting enough to keep them from almost instantly returning to what they were doing. The tiny person and the hover gilly were what drew their attention and a few began to wander toward them to investigate. Harpur urged Hiro to get them moving again. Still panting, Hiro asked which way. Harpur pointed north.

Once they were on their way, Harpur glared at Hiro. "You could have killed yourself and Sok."

"You could have warned me," Hiro giggled. They had survived; he didn't see the problem.

"You could have given me a chance," Harpur growled.

Sok had never experienced heat like that. He looked at his hands. They were red from a sunburn and he wondered what his face must look like. If it was anything like Hiro's he wasn't sure he wanted to be seen by anyone in Colwygshire. He invoked his healing and let it sooth the soreness. In a few minutes the burning subsided and the redness had dulled to a soft pink. "Would you like me to heal you?" he offered.

Hiro waved the kind gesture aside. "Thank you, but all I need is a bit of this." He pulled a vial of clear liquid out of his ever-present satchel and took a swig. In seconds, his burned skin returned to normal and he handed the vial to Sok.

"What is it?" Sok held the vial up and looked at it with his usual curiosity.

"Just some herbs with a bit of koobar web mixed in. It will perk you right up. Harpur, you should take some too. It will do wonders for you." Krist giggles filled the air.

"I'll pass, thanks," Harpur said.

Sok tipped the vial up to his lips and drank a mouthful. It tasted like licorice and cinnamon. "Not bad," he said. Then a cooling jolt burst through him and his pink skin was back to normal. "That's amazing!"

Harpur grunted to hide how impressed he was, but he resisted the temptation to try it. His pride was unwilling to be set aside.

The hover gilly delivered them to the same spot near the gate they had entered before. This time the gate was closed and there were no heads poking out to see if anyone was approaching. Instead, as was customary, two guards stood on the ramparts above the gate in the shade of the guard tower. They were not royal guards, just two men from the city, probably members of the resistance led by Davynn Willhart. Harpur didn't know if this was a good sign or a bad one. What he did know was a bad sign was the black smoke that he could see rising up in a thin tendril from where the main castle tower used to be.

"That's a bad sign," Sok said.

"The king's private chambers were up there," Harpur said.

"They aren't anymore." Sok watched the smoke rise for a moment. "Shall we?"

"I suppose so," Harpur said and started to limp toward the gate.

"I don't suppose either of you would be willing to fill me in now?" Hiro asked, remaining where he was "What happened on Mysturna? How did Anabettah die?"

Harpur stopped and looked at the intrepid little Krist. "First tell me why you came with us? Why didn't you stay on Mysturna and help Anayah?"

Hiro smiled, but it was remorseful. "The witches have their own ways. I cannot interfere," he said. "Anayah knows her fate."

"Her fate?" Harpur didn't like the sound of that.

"She will likely be accused in Circle of betraying her community. She defied the Doyenne and Anabettah is dead because of it. I may not know the particulars of how that came about, but the fact that you two were involved does not bode well for our friend." Hiro urged the hover gilly forward.

"What will happen to her?" Sok was alarmed.

"That I do not know," Hiro said sadly, "but I would not expect to see her again for quite some time."

Harpur and Sok exchanged repentant glances. "Is there anything we can do to help her?" Sok asked.

"Let's deal with whatever lies before us here," Hiro gestured toward the billowing smoke. "I will find out what I can about Anayah. Then we can decide what to do for her."

Uncertain of what they would find inside the walls of Colwygshire, they elected to attempt to gain entry through the gate first. If they were denied, they still might be able to glean what was going on inside and determine where it would be best to zap themselves to. Sok stepped off the hover gilly and walked with Harpur toward the gate while Hiro floated along beside them. Harpur filled Hiro in about Bloomregaard on the way.

The guards watched them without speaking until they were directly below the guard tower. "Who are you and what is your business here?" the older of the two guards called down.

"I'm..." Harpur paused. "Harpur Diggins. And this is Sok and Hiro. We've come to see Davynn Willhart. Will you let us in?" In that moment, he had decided that there was little point in keeping his identity secret any longer.

The two guards conferred in whispers of their own. "If you are indeed Harpur Diggins, tell us what the colour of the avenue you live on is."

Harpur looked at Sok. It seemed that they already knew the truth about their Dragon Lord anyway. "Davynn is just being cautious," the elf shrugged.

"White!" Harpur called up to the guards.

It seemed that he had answered correctly. The younger guard called down for the gate to be opened and a few seconds later the damp elf and Krist and the dry dragon-wizard entered Colwygshire.

The guard on the ground, manning the gate, informed Harpur that Davynn could be found inside the castle and asked if they needed directions. He was staring at the hover gilly with suspicion, but did not want to challenge the dragon-wizard.

"We know the way," Harpur assured him. "What happened here?"

"The tower exploded, sir."

"I can see that," Harpur said. "Why did it explode?"

"I don't know, sir. It just exploded a few hours ago."

Harpur and Sok exchanged looks. Sok shrugged. He had no clue as to what might have taken place.

"Thank you," Sok said to the guard, who was closing and barring the gate again.

They made their way out of the camouflaged courtyard and into the rubble-strewn streets. Here and there, they saw people with carts picking up chunks of castle tower. Some of the stones were spattered with a greasy, black substance. Another look, even more puzzled this time, was exchanged. The trio hurried to the castle.

As they got closer, they saw more carts. Some of them were picking up bodies killed by the flying debris when the tower had mysteriously blown apart. As Harpur took in the carnage, he noted that most of the dead appeared to be guards, probably Bloomregaard's men. But a few were citizens, collateral damage in an event that Harpur needed an explanation for. Towers do not simply explode for no reason.

They climbed over and stepped around the wreckage on the steps leading into the castle proper and were not challenged as they passed through the open castle doors. More people, including guards that Harpur was sure were Bloomregaard's men, moved about, cleaning up, giving orders, following orders. An air of bewilderment had settled upon the city, erasing a division between the men and women that were now focussed on repairing their city. Working together, they would repair the ruined tower and, Harpur hoped, the deeper wound their previously divided loyalties had inflicted upon them.

Harpur saw the archer who had shot his wing seated on the ruined steps that had once led up into the tower. He had shucked his guard uniform and was wearing only a loose tunic over his breaches. A woman was bent over him, tending to a gash on his forehead. With each dab of the salve she applied, he winced and jerked his head away. He watched as the woman finally grabbed the archer by the hair to hold his head still. A wave of satisfaction rose up in Harpur. *Serves you right,* he thought.

They were heading to the council chambers when Finch, the housekeeper, appeared carrying a tray laden with food as if nothing at all was wrong. When she saw Sok and Harpur, she changed directions and waddled over to them.

Thrusting the tray into Sok's hands she prattled away. "You can save me the trip to the Council room," she said. "Like I don't have enough to do, I'm supposed to deliver food to Willhart now? Look at this mess." She threw her free hands up in the air. "Bits of tower everywhere..." Her voice trailed off as she waddled back toward the kitchens. The gray bun on her head clung precariously to one side. Every few steps, she pushed it back up to the top where it belonged, only to have it flop down and sit askew beside her ear.

Hiro leaned over the side of the hover gilly and plucked a small bunch of grapes off the tray as he watched the housekeeper's vocal retreat. "Friend of yours?" He popped one of the grapes into this mouth.

"Castle icon," Harpur said, taking a piece of cheese and a chunk of bread from the tray.

A guard with a bandage on his left arm passed by them.

"What happened to the tower?" Harpur asked, stepping into the guard's path to stop him.

"It exploded."

"That is obvious," Harpur said, impatience unchecked. "How? Why?"

"Dunno." The guard shrugged. "We were getting ready to storm the castle and take Bloomregaard and it just blew up."

"What happened to Bloomregaard?"

"Dead, I guess." The guard shrugged again. He was looking longingly at the food on the tray.

Sok handed the tray to the guard and helped himself to a piece of bread to go with the meat.

"You guess?" Harpur reached over and took some meat. He hadn't realized how hungry he was until he saw the tray full of food.

"Well, it would be a miracle if he survived," the guard said and passed the tray to Hiro so he could eat a tart. "He was on his way up to the king's private chambers when the tower blew up."

Harpur couldn't make any sense of it. He looked at Sok for any insight he might have on the matter. "Thoughts?"

"Yes," Sok said reaching for a tart. "I think you should take the tray before Hiro collapses."

Harpur took the tray. Hiro, relieved, grabbed some meat and cheese.

"When did the explosion happen?" Harpur asked.

"Oh, earlier this afternoon, not long after Bloomregaard's wraiths chased our Dragon Lord away." The guard wiped some filling from the tart off his chin and licked his fingers.

"About the same time the Boundary exploded," Sok observed. He popped a grape into his mouth.

Harpur had connected the same two dots. As Sok reached for a tart, he shoved the tray into the elf's hand and began to assemble a sandwich layered with meat and cheese. "So Bloomregaard must have been... What? Entangled somehow with the wraiths?"

"Why do you say that?" Sok tried to pass the tray back to the guard, but, inspired by Harpur, he was also assembling a sandwich.

"Right after we went through the Boundary, it exploded too. If the wraiths didn't come back here, I think it's safe to assume that they must have caused the Boundary to blow up the way it did. The same black slime that is on the debris from the tower was all over the ground there. There has to be a connection." Harpur took a bite of his sandwich.

"No one has seen the wraiths since they followed Harpur Diggins away from the city." The guard pushed the tray toward Harpur. This time he took it while Sok made his own sandwich. "I wonder happened with that?"

"Bad things," Harpur said. "Some very bad things."

"Sok!" a voice called from behind them. "Harpur!"

Sok and Harpur turned to see Davynn standing in the open doors of the council chamber.

The young captain in a torn and blood-stained shirt waved them over to him. Harpur pushed the tray back into the guard's hands. "Take this into the Council chambers."

Harpur, Sok and Hiro moved toward Davynn who was staring at the Krist in the hover gilly. He looked up at Harpur. "What is this now?"

"Davynn Willhart, meet Hiro. He's a Krist from Mysturna." Harpur made the introductions as the guard moved past them and set the tray down on a long table in the centre of the chambers.

"Pleased to meet you." Hiro giggled and shook the perplexed captain's hand.

They all entered the room and sat down on one of the dozen or so chairs that surrounded it, except for Hiro. Due to his diminutive size, he chose to stay in the hover gilly. The council chamber was a small anteroom joined to the throne room by a set of stairs where the king and his advisers met before court. And after court. And, whenever the king needed to be advised. Which had been often. Gnik was not the most decisive of kings. He liked to have on record, any advice he followed in case anything went wrong, so he would know who to blame. The role of adviser to the king was not a highly sought-after position under Gnik's rule, except by those who were ambitious enough and confident enough in their ability to manipulate the king to their advantage. Basically, Epoh was a typical kingdom with a typical king typically embroiled in typical political intrigue. For all that, however, Epoh had known peace the entire time Gnik had ruled. For that, the people had loved him. For his guards, his knights and the royal army, it had been an easy gig. Harpur now wondered if that had been a good thing.

As he studied Davynn, Harpur wondered if he could be persuaded to stay on as adviser once Arthur was crowned. He was bright and had stood up well under the strain Bloomregaard's failed coup had put him under. Not many men would have stepped up the way Davynn had. The kingdom needed him. Arthur needed him.

The next few hours were spent stitching together the pieces of day's events. Through the exchange of accounts and much debate, the foursome pared it all down to the facts and then filled in the many gaps with supposition embroidered with imaginative and whimsical fantasy, primarily contributed by Sok. In those chambers, on that day a new legend was born. A legend that, in time, would be embroiled with a prophecy about a man from Earth. Hiro absorbed every word, consigning it all to memory.

Their discussion was interrupted by various guards and citizens coming in to report and ask for guidance. Davynn listened to each of them and then sent them on their way with instructions. That virtually the whole city had opted to defer to the young man, who had only a few weeks earlier been a lowly guard with no authority, was nothing short of impressive. Harpur saw his leadership acumen in these interruptions. *This man is a true knight.*

Eventually, the topic turned to the prophecy.

"Everyone is in shock," Davynn stated. "But it won't last and I don't know what to tell them."

"Tell them what Anayah told you to tell them. There is a true heir to the throne, but we need time to track him down and bring him here." Harpur believed that was the best course of action for the time being.

Hiro had been listening to the exchange with great interest. In the short time he'd been on Thraeh, he'd gathered a great deal of information. "Prophecies have a way of unfolding as they need to," he contributed. "When the time it right, the right way forward will reveal itself. May I suggest that you bring Arthur here and start teaching him all you can about this world. I have a feeling that young man will astonish you all."

It was decided that Sok and Hiro would stay in Colwygshire and help Davynn with the clean up of the fallen tower. Harpur would go to Earth and deal with Arthur. Whatever was to come next was in the hands of fate.

As the meeting adjourned, Davynn thanked Harpur for luring the wraiths away. He saw the flash of guilt pass over the dragon-wizard's face. "No one could have possibly known this would happen, Harpur. We should be thankful that whatever tied Bloomregaard to the wraiths was his undoing. It could have been much worse."

It could have been much better too.

Harpur shook Davynn's hand in appreciation for his gratitude in light of what had happened. With a nod, he left the captain, the elf and the Krist who quickly became engrossed in a discussion about hover gillies and the potential for their development in Epoh.

Men and their toys! Harpur thought with a bemused smile. *Orhowyn save us!*

Chapter 19

Harpur made his way out of the city on foot. Before he went to see Arthur, there were a couple of things he needed to do. First, he needed to know how bad his injuries were. He followed the road away from Colwygshire until he was far enough away that he could shift into his dragon form. Until he transformed, he wouldn't know how well his injuries were healing. Anayah and Sok had certainly done their best for him and while dragons do tend to heal quickly, his wing had been badly damaged when he crashed on Mysturna. He could still feel it in his shoulder blade. His leg, too, still didn't feel quite right and he feared that he might never be the dragon he once was. A dragon that couldn't fly was no dragon at all.

When he made the transformation, Harpur felt the pain in his leg and his wing so sharply that he couldn't help but roar. There was no issue with his leg bearing his weight, but several of the scales were blackened and brittle from the frostbite he had sustained when his leg had come into contact with the edge of the Boundary. With every movement, pieces of scale flaked off and fell like ash to the ground. Harpur's heart was no longer his only vulnerability. He couldn't tell how deep the frostbite had penetrated and could only hope it had not gone into the flesh. He took the pain as a good sign. Maybe it meant that his scales had protected him from the cold.

He stretched out his wings to inspect them. The tear from the arrow had sealed, leaving a long, ragged scar across the webbing that throbbed with pain. But it was his right wing that was the biggest problem. It was bent backward at a slight angle about two-thirds of the way down. The once sweeping curve of bone was interrupted by a jog that twisted the wing tip back and downward. Harpur stretched it out to test its strength and with a second agonized roar abandoned the notion of testing its ability to keep him in the air. There was no way he was going to fly that day. With a third, deafening roar, he let loose a column of white-hot flame into the sky. His time in human form had begun to take its toll.

He was losing his regenerative power and he had no one to blame but himself. He regretted not taking Hiro's healing potion.

Harpur returned to human form and felt an instant relief from the intensity of the pain. His leg and shoulder blade continued to ache, but not so badly that he couldn't function. He had always been proud of the human form he had adopted, believing it to be strong and as majestic as his dragon form was. Now, standing on the road from Colwygshire, he felt small and weak. He was tempted to add defeated to that short, but overwhelming list. Instead, he steeled himself to move on. He had set powerful things in motion when he saved Arthur's life by giving him his blood and now he had no option other than to see them through. *Did the prophecy lead me to Arthur? Or did my actions create the prophecy?* These were questions that would haunt Harpur for the rest of his life.

He had hoped to fly to the Boundary he and Anayah had lured the wraiths into to look for his walking stick and to check out what things looked like on this side. That was not going to happen. He could call the walking stick to him, but that would take too much time. As it was, the walk to the Boundary to Whyte Avenue was going to take an hour. *I should have switched to the talisman,* the thought.

It wasn't that he needed the walking stick to perform magic. It was more that he had grown used to directing his magic through it. He liked how it made him feel classy and distinguished. The walking stick was a vanity piece and Harpur's vanity could have used a boost just then. In the mood he was in, he didn't know if he should even be facing Arthur. Maybe the walk would cool him down before that happened.

Arthur was sitting in a stuffy little office across a desk from a stuffy little man. He was being interviewed for a job at a national electronics store chain.

The stuffy little man was wearing a pink, short-sleeved shirt under a brown, olive-green and mustard argyle sweater vest. The fact that he was bald, did not negate a serious dandruff problem. The dandruff had simply migrated from his scalp to the uneven mustache that bristled under his glob of a nose. The mustache curved around thin, dry lips and pointed at the spot on his face where a chin should have been. He squinted at a printed list of questions through tiny eyes set so close together they fully explained the unibrow that sprawled across his enormous forehead. Not once since Arthur had entered the stuffy little office did those tiny eyes look directly at him. For this, Arthur was thankful.

They were at the most dreaded interview question in the history of employment interviews.

"What is your greatest weakness?" the stuffy little man droned in an androgynous pitch that grated on Arthur's nerves.

He never knew what to say to this. Alex had suggested formulating his answer as a strength. "I'm too organized," Arthur answered without embellishing.

The stuffy little man made a note on the blank line below that question on the printed list and squinted at the next one.

"What is your greatest strength?"

"I'm super organized."

Another note was made. Another squint was aimed.

"Tell me about a time when you provided excellent service to someone."

"Well, just a few months ago I taught a witch on Mysturna how to use a cell phone." *Where did that come from?*

The stuffy little man made a note. Arthur was certain that there was a pause before he went on to squint at the next question. He braced himself for a request for clarification, but the stuffy little man had apparently decided that he was better off without it. "Why did you apply for this position?"

Arthur heard the question, but his mind was no longer on the interview. It was being flooded with memories of elves and dragons and wizards and witches and walking sticks and androids and Krists and Boundaries and Spheres and Poles and muskinks and keetors and coins...

"Ho... Ly... Crap!" Arthur whispered loudly.

"Excuse me?" The stuffy little man was compelled to look up and squint at Arthur.

Arthur stood up. "Holy, crap!" he repeated.

"I'm afraid I don't understand." The stuffy little man was noticeably uncomfortable at having his interview go so awry.

At least his discomfort would have been noticeable if someone had bothered to notice. Arthur was too caught up in the refreshed memories to notice anything. "Dragons are real," Arthur said, a growing excitement filling him with awe. He continued to stand in the stuffy little office not noticing the stuffy little man.

"Mr. Prentice, thank you for coming in. We'll be in touch." The stuffy little man jumped to the conclusion of the interview, hoping that Arthur would leave. This was beyond what his stuffy littleness could bear.

Arthur looked at the stuffy little man and a maniacal laugh burst out of his mouth. He leaned over the desk, looking the stuffy little man in his tiny eyes. "Dragons are real!" he said. "Magic is real!"

He stood back upright and announced to the relief of the stuffy little man, "I gotta go!"

As Arthur exited the stuffy little office, the stuffy little man drew a large X on the printed list of interview questions. Through the open door, he could hear Arthur echoing is bizarre interview-ending assertions of the realness of dragons and magic, punctuating them with more maniacal laughter as he left the national electronics store chain store at which he was never—ever—going to work.

Getting back his memories of Harpur, Sok, Anayah and the others he shared such wild adventures with was overwhelming for Arthur. In a good way. It hadn't occurred to him yet, as he left the national electronics store chain store that these memories had been purposely hidden from him. He was just so happy that the niggling feeling that something was missing was gone and that the missing something was as fantastic as this was. Magic. Dragons. Elves. Witches. Lairs... *Ooh! Lairs! I have to go find Harpur.*

Neither did it occur to him that Alex shared some of these memories and might also be remembering them. They had talked about the sensation of missing memories, but with Alex's part in the real events having been so small in comparison to Arthur's, she was more inclined to brush it off. Then they'd have sex, so it was easy for Arthur to be distracted from the mental disturbance the missing something sometimes raised.

All he could think about when he stepped out onto the sidewalk was getting back to Whyte Avenue and finding Harpur. There was no need to concern himself with finding Harpur, though. Harpur was standing right outside the national electronics store chain store waiting for him. In his excitement, Arthur nearly collided with the super-sized dragon-wizard, who side-stepped out of the way and put an arm out to stop Arthur from charging past.

"Oh, my god!" Arthur gasped in surprise. "Harpur! You're here!" He threw his arms around Harpur and hugged him. "I missed you!" He paused. "I think."

Harpur cleared his throat to remind Arthur of the no-hugging rule.

Arthur released his friend and stepped back to proffer a more dragon-acceptable hand. "It's so good to see you. I have so much to tell you."

Harpur shook his animated friend's hand. "Not as much as I have to tell you," Harpur said.

At the curb, right behind Harpur, sat the sleek, black Lexus they had driven to Drumheller in back in the spring. Arthur climbed into the passenger seat. "So, why are you here?"

"I came to pick you up." Harpur pulled the Lexus away from the curb and joined the northbound traffic to take them to Whyte Avenue.

"How did you know where I was?"

Harpur just looked at Arthur.

"Right. Never mind. Where are we going? Can we go to your lair? I really want to see it again. Hey, where's your walking stick?" Arthur was clearly pumped.

"The lair is as good a place as any," Harpur acquiesced. "And I lost it."

"You lost your walking stick? How?" Arthur didn't know how touchy that subject might prove to be, but he had to ask.

"Long story," Harpur said, cueing a need for a change of subject.

"So, how is Sok? And Anayah? Did you ever make up with her? Any word from Analeetah?" *Ah, Analeetah!* Arthur stopped firing off questions to savour the memory of their kiss on the landing.

"Sok's fine. Anayah's fine. Analeetah is still pissed off at me." Harpur stopped for a red light.

"That's it? That's all I get? They're fine? Why is Analeetah pissed off at you?"

"Arthur," Harpur said as he eased the Lexus through an intersection after magically making the light change to green, "I will tell you everything, answer all your questions, when we get back to the lair. Okay?"

"Okay."

They drove in silence for almost half a block. "Alex is going to crap herself. We keep feeling like we've forgotten something and now when I tell her that I remember, maybe she'll remember too." He paused. "Oh, my god! What if she already remembers? I need to call her." Arthur pulled his cell phone out of his jacket pocket.

"She doesn't remember," Harpur said.

"How do you know? She might."

"She doesn't. Put your phone away."

Arthur looked across at Harpur as he dug through the memories. "You bastard!"

There it is! Harpur thought.

"You wiped our memories. Why did you do that? You promised me you wouldn't do that."

"Actually, I didn't promise that I wouldn't wipe your memory. If you recall—and I know that you do—you promised never to Bound to Thraeh again if I took you and Alex back to the lair and answered all your questions."

Arthur thought about that. "Well, you implied that you wouldn't wipe our memories." Arthur leaned back in his seat. Resting his elbow on the door, he rubbed his chin and looked at the cell phone he held in his other hand. "At least now I know who the hot chick I took the selfie with is."

Arthur had kept the selfie he had taken with Analeetah the night they had kissed. He'd deleted most of the photos of Sok in the Lexus, but those weird pictures had seemed so precious. Even if he couldn't figure out who the people were or where they had been taken. In the driver's seat, Harpur silently chided himself for not having dealt with the photos when he had wiped Arthur and Alex's memories.

The once-again familiar frustration at having been magically manipulated had magically dampened Arthur's mood. The remaining ten-minute drive to Whyte Avenue passed in silence. By minute eight, Arthur had settled back into being happy that his memory was once again in tact. He spent the last two minutes trying to come up with a good enough reason to convince Harpur to let him Bound to Thraeh again. He'd been thinking about proposing to Alex. How cool would it be to get married on a different world? Talk about your destination wedding! *Nah. Harpur has no sense of romance. He'd never go for it.*

The lair was as incredible as Arthur remembered. He stood for several minutes before the mound of treasure and wondered at its worth. There had to be hundreds of millions of dollars worth of gold and jewels sitting there. While Harpur poured beer for them both, Arthur tried to imagine what a dragon's life must really be like. Hunted and hated, these creatures must be constantly on guard. But Harpur seemed pretty relaxed. Or poised was maybe a better word. In control? Arthur tossed a few more adjectives for the dragon-wizard around and decided that Harpur was none of them and all of them at the same time. It didn't matter, really. Arthur felt like Harpur was the person... dragon... he could rely on more than anyone else. Are we friends? Arthur wondered. *Would a friend wipe out the coolest memories I ever had?* Then he chuckled to himself. The only fitting way to describe a relationship with a dragon was: It's complicated.

"What's so funny?" Harpur said, startling Arthur out of his reverie.

"Oh, nothing. Just thinking about some of the things that happened on Mysturna and Thraeh." Arthur grasped for an amusing memory. "The look on King Gnik's face when we Bounded into his private chambers." He laughed again because that really had been amusing.

Yes, the look on his face was priceless. But before this conversation degraded into a recollection of their slapstick escape in said private chambers, Harpur used it to segue into the reason he'd given Arthur his memories back. "Speaking of King Gnik..."

Harpur started with Bloomregaard's attempt to take the crown. He stressed that the ultimate fate of the usurper and his wraiths was left to pure speculation. It was assumed that when the wraiths went through the Boundary, the wraithbane had somehow caused a reaction that destroyed the Boundary along with them. There must have been some magical connection between them and Bloomregaard that caused the tower and, presumably, Bloomregaard to be destroyed as well. The truth was that no one knew exactly what Bloomregaard had been up to or in what way he was connected to the wraiths. All the years that he had these creatures doing his bidding must have had a greater purpose to it than anyone cared to find out. His explosive demise because of his connection to the wraiths did preclude the need for a battle between Bloomregaard and the citizens of Colwygshire.

"So, no one but Bloomregaard and his wraiths were killed?" Arthur asked.

"There were some casualties beyond them. But, all things considered, the death toll was much lower than it would have been if it had come to a battle." Harpur was touched, as much as a dragon could be touched, by Arthur's concern for the people. It was a good sign.

"Wow. I'm sure glad it wasn't worse for everyone. But poor Gnik. I wish I could have met him."

It seemed that Harpur had evoked Arthur's sympathies. Another good sign. It was a good place to start with what came next. "It appears that the prophecy is coming true." He let that sink in.

Arthur sipped his beer as it did. "What if I don't want to be the king?"

"I'm not going to force you to go to Epoh." *Unless I have to.*

"I have a girlfriend now," Arthur said. "I want to marry her."

The cute hippie girl was a snag Harpur knew he'd have to deal with. He hoped he wouldn't have to deal with it harshly. "We know that the prophecy has something to do with your magic and the dragon blood." He'd circle back to Alex later, but for now he needed to get Arthur's attention focussed on the prophecy.

"Yeah, I still don't get that part. I don't know any magic." Arthur's memories of his first encounter with Harpur had not been restored along with the others.

"You many not know how to use it, but you do possess it. You inherited it from a Thraehlian wizard named Ylemnir, who also happens to be a direct ancestor of Gnik. We will teach you how to use it." Harpur dangled what he hoped would be the right carrot.

"I still don't remember how we met." Arthur was curious about the magic he was supposed to possess, but those memories included his violent death and he didn't know if he wanted to remember that.

"I will give those memories back to you any time you want me to."

Arthur took another drink of his beer. Then he shook his head. "No. I don't think I want to remember dying."

"I can leave that part out," Harpur offered.

"How about just the part where you saw me do this magic you say I have?"

"Very well." Harpur waved his hand.

Arthur's eyes widened in surprise as the memory came back to him. He was leaving work one evening shortly after he'd started working at Fox Comics. He had just locked the door and was turning to start walking down the sidewalk when he bumped into a lady. The coffee cup she had been holding was knocked out of her hand when their bodies collided and he had reached out to catch it. But it had stopped falling and had hung in midair for a second or two until he took hold of it and handed it back to the lady.

"I remember," Arthur said in awe. "And you were there too. I remember you asking me where I came from."

"It got all kinds of weird after that. You died less than two minutes later and then..."

Arthur stood up. Other memories were coming back to him. "That happens all the time. Once when I was seven, I was playing soccer in the living room and I knocked my mother's lamp over with the ball. I was across the room. There's no way I could have gotten to it to stop it falling unless..."

"Unless you possessed magic that made it stop falling." Harpur finished Arthur's sentence. "

"I want you to teach me! I want to know how I do that!" Arthur looked at Harpur like he was ready for his first lesson right there, right then.

"I will teach you," Harpur agreed, "but not as long as you are living on Earth."

"That's blackmail!" Arthur barked.

"It's more of an ultimatum," Harpur rationalized.

"What's the difference?"

"I prefer the word ultimatum," Harpur answered. "Call it what you want, but I will not allow you to live on Earth and practice magic."

"What if I just teach myself?" Arthur sneered.

"Don't be naïve; you know I can't let that happen."

Arthur did know. But that didn't mean he had to like it. "So, what am I supposed to do? Just leave everything behind and move to Thraeh? Leave Alex? Leave my parents?"

"Pretty much," Harpur said.

Arthur started pacing back and forth across the conversation pit. He scratched the back of his head as if what he was hearing physically itched his mind. *I could be King Arthur if I went to Thraeh,* he thought. *I could learn magic.* "If I were to go to Thraeh, how exactly would I become king of Epoh?" He wasn't going to go; he was just being curious.

"The prophecy is pretty vague about that. I would think that you would need to pass some sort of test to prove your worthiness. As I said, we know that it has something to do with your power. We just don't know what yet."

"So, this test I'd have to pass," Arthur probed. "What would I have to do? Kill a dragon?"

"Don't be stupid, Arthur!" Harpur admonished. "We don't have nearly enough time to train you for that."

Arthur made a sardonic face at the dragon-wizard. "You don't think I could do it?"

"I know you couldn't do it. Besides, I'm the only dragon in Epoh and as much as you can drive me crazy, I have no desire to burn you alive. That would completely defeat the purpose. No, the test would be something else. We'll have to figure that out."

"So, something like pulling a sword from a stone, then? I'd be King Arthur after all."

Harpur wanted to say that that had been done before, but it did have some merit. Easy to set up. Relatively safe for Arthur. As long as he didn't cut off his foot or run himself through with the sword. Reasonably dramatic, without being too cheesy... "We'll think about it," Harpur said. He was tempted to lure Arthur with the glamour of being king, to play to his fantasies, but this was not a fantasy. And being a king was not always glamourous. Arthur needed to know what he was getting himself into. Harpur refused to make promises he might not be able to keep. Arthur had to do this because he wanted to.

Suddenly, Arthur stopped pacing and faced Harpur. "I'm sorry, I can't do it," he said. "I can't leave my parents. And I love Alex. I want to marry her."

"We can alter your memories of them too, Arthur. Once you were on Thraeh, you wouldn't even know they existed."

"No!" Arthur snapped. "No more screwing with my head. No more magic puppeteering! I hate that!" He waved his arms in the air, miming a puppet on strings.

"Okay. I promise," Harpur said. "I won't screw with your head."

Arthur looked at Harpur with suspicion. Was he just saying that? Or was this an olive branch? A gesture of faith. Arthur decided to trust Harpur. "Thank you," he said.

"Are you sure you don't want to be King Arthur of Epoh?" Harpur asked.

"Yes. I'm... sure."

The hesitation told Harpur a different story. He had never expected Arthur to simply jump at the chance to live on Thraeh and be king of Epoh. The seed, however, had been planted. There was no need to push. Yet. Harpur had to believe that the prophecy would find a way to fulfill itself.

"Alright. As you wish," Harpur said. "We'll just have to find another king." He drained the last of his beer from his glass.

"I'm sure you will," Arthur felt a stab of umbrage in his heart. He, too, drained the last of his beer from his own glass.

"You're probably wanting to go see Alex now. And I have to get back to Thraeh to tell the others you aren't coming." Harpur stood and moved toward the exit from the lair.

"Alex!" Arthur pulled out his cell phone to check the time. "Damn! I was supposed to meet her an hour ago."

"Well, you better hurry, then," Harpur said.

Arthur walked to the door. He stopped and turned back toward his host. "Are you going to give Alex back her memories?"

"You know I can't do that, Arthur." Harpur stood fast against the cruel guilt he felt in saying this.

Again, Arthur did know. He didn't like it, though. "Fuck you, Harpur." He left the lair.

Harpur didn't take any offence at Arthur's parting shot. He'd dumped a lot on the poor guy; he was entitled to his feelings. Nor did he return to Thraeh to tell the others that Arthur had declined the offer to leave his life and his world behind and become king. As a dragon-wizard, he still had a couple of tricks under his scales. He'd promised not to manipulate Arthur with magic, but he hadn't promised not to manipulate anyone else.

Alex, for instance.

While Arthur was rushing to the flower shop to buy a colourful apology for being late, Harpur calmly made his way to Alex's apartment near the university. Invisible, he let himself in and found the cute hippie girl sitting on a futon leaving a third message in Arthur's voice mail.

"Where are you? I've left two messages. This is the last one I'm going to leave. Call me!" She disconnected and plunked her phone down in frustration beside herself. Then she snatched it up again and started texting furiously. Literally.

My work is going to be easier than I thought, thought Harpur.

His plan was to make Alex break up with Arthur. It was mean and Harpur knew that. But Epoh needed a king and Arthur was, as far as he knew, not only the rightful heir to the throne, but the prophesied heir. A good heartbreak was just what Arthur needed to make him change his mind. In the throes of sorrow, it would be far easier to persuade the heir apparent to abandon the life he'd always known for a new life on new world where he could rule a kingdom he'd spent about an hour in to date. Once Alex dumped Arthur, Harpur would be there to help him pick up the pieces. That was the plan.

As Harpur knew well, plans have a way of not working out exactly as planned. Like all of the plans that he'd been part of since that fateful day when Sok had Bounded to Whyte Avenue and given Arthur a coin, this one was fraught with potential pitfalls. He could have given Alex's memories back and let her convince Arthur to go to Thraeh. He was almost positive that she would. But if he did restore her memory and Arthur still didn't agree to become king, he would just have to wipe it again so she couldn't convince Arthur to Bound again and that would just make Arthur even more mad. *Why are humans so complicated?*

Harpur waved his invisible hand toward Alex who had once again plunked her phone down on the futon next to herself. She crossed her cute hippie girl arms and then uncrossed them to pick up the phone and look at it. Then she plonked it down again.

Arthur burst through the door. "I'm sorry! I'm sorry," he called out before Alex had a chance to speak. He rushed in and handed Alex an enormous bouquet of flowers.

The look she gave the bouquet should have withered the blooms on the spot. She stood up and with all the force her cute hippie girl arms had, slammed them down on a coffee table strewn with crystals and candles. Thankfully, none of the candles were lit. Within minutes, the lovebirds were yelling at each other loudly and Harpur smiled an invisible smile and took his leave. He went to O'Bryan's Pub to wait for Arthur to arrive to drown the sorrows that were sure to follow such a screaming match.

It took just under three hours. Harpur was sitting alone at a table close to the entrance to the pub, nursing a beer when the door opened. He looked up hoping to see Arthur and was stupefied to see Alex instead. She stood just inside the entrance looking around the pub for someone. When her eyes found Harpur, she made a beeline to his table and sat down.

"Harpur Diggins, I presume?" she said as she stowed her hobo bag and coat on the chair next to hers.

"And you are...?" Harpur tried to look like he didn't know exactly who she was.

"Oh, cut the crap, Harpur!" Alex hissed. "Arthur told me everything. We know what you did."

Harpur had three choices. He could keep pretending that he didn't know who Alex was and not find out what she knew. Or he could wipe her memory again and still not know what she knew. Or he could give up the feeble ruse and find out what she knew. Really, there was no choice. He had to find out what she knew.

"What is it that you think I did?"

A server approached their table and Harpur ordered another beer. "And bring the lady whatever she wants," he added. Alex asked for the same.

"You cast a spell on me to make me mad at Arthur. You were hoping to break us up, weren't you?"

Harpur was beginning to like the plucky little cute hippie girl. "Only for a while," he said. "Eventually, I would have brought you both back together." This had only just occurred to Harpur as a possible future option, but he needed Alex to trust him now and this was about the most plausible thing he could offer that would not turn her further against him.

"So, what?" Alex sneered. "You were going to use Arthur's broken heart to get him to agree to be king of... "

"Epoh," Harpur filled in the blank for her.

"... Of Epoh and then later surprise him by bringing me over there after he's crowned?"

"Sure." Harpur nodded. *Not unless I absolutely had to.* "How much did Arthur tell you?"

"He told me everything."

"And you believe him?"

"Of course, I believe him!"

The server returned and deposited their beer on the table. Harpur handed her a fifty-dollar bill and told her to keep the change. That put a smile on the server's face and she flounced away almost forgetting how sore her feet were.

"Come on!" Harpur said. "You want me to believe that you believe that kingdoms on other worlds are real just because Arthur says they do?"

"Yes." Alex said. "And do you want to know why I believe him?"

"Do tell."

"Because I can't remember something that I know I should remember."

Ah! "So, what do you want? Why are you here instead of Arthur?"

"Arthur is still mad at you. He's gone back to his apartment to cool down. And I'm here because we have a proposal for you." She took a drink of her beer and waited for Harpur to say something. When he remained silent, she continued. "Arthur agrees to go to Thraeh and become the King of Epoh. But there are conditions."

"Of course, there are," Harpur smirked.

Alex rubbed the palms of her hands on her thighs and took a deep breath. "First, I get to go with him."

"Not a chance!" Harpur cut her off. "It's bad enough that he's from Earth. There is no way I'm going to agree to two humans from this world going over there."

"I go with him, or he doesn't go."

Harpur studied the young woman across from him. *Arthur would never be happy without her.* "What are the other conditions?"

Another deep breath. "You also have to make sure our families are looked after. Financially as well as making sure they don't remember us. And you can never use magic to manipulate either of us ever again."

"So, it's okay for me to manipulate your families, but not you? That sounds like a double standard."

"We just want to know that they are okay. We don't want them to be hurt by us leaving."

"Alex, I have never used magic on Arthur with the intention of hurting him."

"But you did hurt him," Alex said.

"How?"

"By taking away the memories of an experience that helped him grow as a person. By making him feel unworthy and stupid and less than you. Harpur, Arthur adores you. You're a freaking dragon, for god's sake. You made his childhood dreams come true and then you took it all away. That's not very nice."

"But I didn't do any of it to hurt him. I did it out of loyalty to my world and its customs and laws. I did it to right a wrong that was set in motion a long time ago."

"And now you want him to be king. That's not just a double standard, Harpur. That's outright hypocrisy."

"No. No it is not!" Harpur said. "It is adapting to changes that are beyond my control. It's making the best of a complicated situation. But it's not hypocrisy, Alex. If it were up to me, Arthur would not be part of this. And if he didn't possess magic, and there was no prophecy I would never have asked him to become King of Epoh."

"Arthur possesses magic?"

"He didn't tell you that?"

"No, he didn't. Does he know he possess magic?"

"He knows."

"I'm not sure I believe you. If Arthur is magical, the way you're magical, he needs to step up his game."

"What do you mean?"

"Well, just think. He could eliminate plastic and fossil fuel consumption and pollution..."

"Right! Well, you'll be pleased to know that plastic and fossil fuels are not used on Thraeh."

"Does that mean you accept our proposal?"

"That means that I am going to take your proposal back to Colwygshire and let the others decide." *It also means I am never going to make another plan again!*

Chapter 20

Arthur was pacing again. This time in his own apartment. Alex went there after her meeting with Harpur and told him that the dragon-wizard would return with a decision as soon as he could.

While Arthur paced, Alex sat on his sofa watching him. She was looking for any sign that he possessed any kind of magic. She didn't know what she was looking for, though, so her staring just got weird.

"Why are you staring at me like that?" Arthur frowned at his girlfriend.

"No reason." She shrugged. She wasn't sure if she should bring it up. Arthur was a bit stressed out at the moment and she didn't think that piling something else on top of everything else was a good idea. If Arthur knew that he was magical, though, she wanted to know why he never told her. If she possessed magic, you could be sure she would use it. She certainly wouldn't be teaching English to a bunch of teenagers who didn't care whether or not they could write a proper sentence.

"Well, stop it, it's weird." Arthur snapped and recommenced his pacing.

"Sorry," she mumbled. "It's really late. Let's go to bed. Harpur probably won't be back tonight and I do have to get up for work."

"What? Work? Why are you going to work? You're never going to have to work again once we get to Thraeh."

"I doubt it's going to be that simple," Alex said. "It's not as if the second we get there, someone's going to plonk a crown on your head and you'll be king. And who knows how long it will be before Harpur comes back. He might never come back. In the meantime, I have a job and I need to sleep."

"You go to bed, then. I don't think I'll be able to sleep." Arthur kept pacing. "If he shows up, I'll wake you."

Alex got up from the sofa and left Arthur to his pacing. She managed to get a good-night peck on the cheek from her boyfriend. As she left the living room, Arthur stopped pacing. "Are we doing the right thing?"

Alex turned back to him. "I don't know," she shrugged again. "Maybe we should have negotiated a satisfaction guarantee. If within ninety days we're not completely satisfied being king and queen, we can come back no questions asked and resume our lives here."

Arthur laughed. "Thank you," he said.

"For what?"

"For believing me."

"Well, if this turns out to be a joke and I don't get my happily ever after in a magical kingdom, you're gonna be in big trouble, buster." She blew him a kiss and turned away again.

"Love you!" Arthur called after her.

"Love you too!" Alex called back.

Harpur did not return that night. Nor did he return the next day, or the day after that. The Tuesday night dinner at Arthur's parents' place was an exercise in reminiscing about Arthur's childhood. He even got his mother to get out the old photo albums. Much to Marian's delight and Earl's chagrin, this prompted all sort of hilarious and embarrassing stories as they meandered down memory lane together. The requisite photo of Arthur as a baby laying bare-bottomed on a blanket, elicited the equally requisite "oohs" and "aws" from Alex. She snapped a photo of the photo with her cell phone and saved it as the lock-screen wallpaper. Arthur just smiled. He couldn't bring himself to remind her that she would have to leave the cell phone behind when they went to Thraeh.

Work was agonizing for both of them. Each encounter with a student, a customer or a co-worker had them wondering if this was the last time they would see them. In a few cases they found themselves hoping this was the last time they would have to see them, but even the challenging interactions were softly patinaed in a melancholic sense of loss. Would this be the last assignment Alex would ever mark? Would this be the last draft Arthur would ever pull? They both realized that they would grieve for this life and as the days and hours passed, their agitation grew. If they were going to do this, they wanted to get it done.

When they were together, they speculated on what life was going to be like without video games and movies, and art galleries and concerts and cars and electricity. Was there coffee on Thraeh? Every time they thought of something else, they would be sacrificing their awareness of how much they took for granted grew. Their emotions were taxed as they roller-coastered upward on excitement and expectation only to plummet into fear and doubt. On the third day they made a pact that if Harpur did not show up by the following Sunday, they would give it up and just get on with their lives on Earth. The pact was a release valve; a defined margin between not knowing and knowing. They had the power to turn off the accumulating emotional stress on their terms. Secretly, they both hoped Harpur would show up before Sunday.

When Sunday morning dawned and Harpur had still not returned, Arthur and Alex started the countdown. They planned a plug-pulling ceremony of sorts for after Arthur's shift at O'Bryan's Pub in which they would crown each other as king and queen of their own lives on Earth and they would each proclaim three things that they would do together over the next year. Harpur had until six o'clock to come for them.

Alex spent the day fashioning crowns for them from scraps of gold-foil wrapping paper left over from some past special occasion. She went to the thrift store and bought a couple of old sheets for them to wear as their royal robes. She decorated two wooden spoons to be their scepters. When everything was ready, she packed them into a reusable shopping bag, got into her lemon-yellow Beetle and drove to O'Bryan's to pick up Arthur from work.

She entered the pub, still hopeful, but resigned to have fun that evening no matter what happened. Arthur was sitting at the bar, waiting for her. He looked up at her hopeful face and his heart broke. He shook his head. Harpur was not there. Alex sighed. She pasted a smile onto her face and strode over to the man she loved. They hugged. All the release valve had done was release their profound disappointment.

"Well, m' lady," Arthur said, pulling away from Alex. "Let's go home and have us a coronation."

"Indeed, m' lord," she said. "Let's."

Arm in arm, they walked out of the pub, both doing their best to be brave and not let the betrayal they felt show. They'd made a pact after all.

Alex's car was parked on the street a few doors down from O'Bryan's. She had just unlocked the doors so they could get in when a familiar voice called out to them from a short way further down the block.

"Where're you going? The Boundary is this way!"

Arthur and Alex whipped around to face the voice. There was Harpur in all his top-hatted and leather-dustered glory looking at them like it had been them who had kept him waiting for nearly a week. Next to him stood a grinning Sok.

"Who's the blonde?" Alex asked over the top of the lemon-yellow Beetle.

"That, my love, is Sok!"

"They're late," Alex said and felt her resolve waver. The sight of Harpur and an elf standing on the sidewalk was too real. Too terrifyingly actual.

"Yeah, but only by a few minutes."

Alex smiled at Arthur. *I trust you.*

Two lemon-yellow Beetle doors slammed shut. Two soon-to-be monarchs ran to greet a dragon-wizard and an elf who would take them to another world. Forever.

"So, when do we go?" Alex asked after formal introductions confirmed her and Sok as official acquaintances.

"Right now," Harpur said.

"I'm already packed," Alex said. "We just need to zip over to our apartments and get our things." She turned to Arthur. "You're packed, right?"

"We won't be going back to your apartments. They aren't your apartments anymore." Harpur said.

Alex gasped. "What do you mean?"

"I mean that your apartments are not your apartments anymore. They are someone else's apartments."

"You've already erased our lives?"

"Pretty much," Harpur said.

"What if we've changed our minds? What if we don't want to go now?"

"Did you change your minds?"

"Well... No. I don't know." Alex was suddenly completely unsure. Again.

"Arthur?"

"I'm in if she's in," Arthur said, this being the most neutral thing he could think to say that wouldn't upset Alex or Harpur.

Alex started to cry.

"You two need a minute?" Harpur asked.

"Yeah," Arthur said.

He led Alex a short way away. "If you really don't want to go, we won't go," he said, holding her close to himself. "I'm pretty sure that Harpur can put everything back if we say we don't want to go. But if he does, we will never see him again. He'll wipe our memories and that will be the absolute end of it. Alex, I know this is hard. I know it's hard to leave our friends and our families, but that's a real elf standing over there. We'll be living in a world where elves and dragons and magic are real. And we'll be the king and queen of a real magical kingdom."

Alex started crying harder. Her sobs left streaks of tears and snot all over the front of Arthur's jacket. He was slightly repulsed, but more afraid about what was coming next than grossed out by what was on his jacket.

"I can't do it," Alex sobbed. "I can't go."

"Okay." Arthur sighed. "I'll go tell Harpur and Sok that we've changed our minds." He tried to disengage himself from the embrace.

"No," Alex said. "You have to go."

"What?" This was what Arthur was afraid of. "No, Alex. We agreed we'd both go, or neither of us would go. I don't want to go without you."

"You have to. You're King Arthur!"

"I'm not leaving without you!" Arthur declared.

"Yes, you are," Alex pulled herself away. With one hand she swiped at the tears on her face. With the other hand she pointed toward Harpur and Sok. "You are going to go and you are going to forget all about me. I'm sure Harpur can arrange that. Now go!"

"Alex, please," Arthur pleaded.

"Just go, Arthur." She turned and walked to her lemon-yellow Beetle. Then she got in and drove away.

Too shocked to comprehend what had happened, he stood there watching the love of his life drive away. Finally, he looked at Harpur and Sok. "Did you do that? What am I supposed to do now?"

"I did not do that," Harpur said.

"I think you should come with us." Sok said, not without sympathy.

"It's up to you, Arthur," Harpur said. "I'm not going to force you to go. But if you stay, this will be the end of it. There will no second chances." Alex's change of heart was a problem.

"The prophecy must be fulfilled," Sok interjected, giving Harpur a scathing look.

Arthur started to vibrate with hurt and anger. "Have you wiped her memory yet?"

"Nope."

"Then wipe it and let's get going."

Twenty minutes after Alex abandoned Arthur and the dream they had together on the sidewalk outside O'Bryan's pub, Arthur was standing in a forest on another world. Behind him was the Boundary he had just leaped through and everything he had held dear his entire life, except for the clothes on his back and the cell phone in his pocket. Before him was the stuff of fairy tales; a kingdom where elves and dragons and wizards and knights and kings lived magical lives.

He had been a little surprised when Harpur had not even asked about the cell phone. Ever since he'd gotten his memories back, he been checking it for messages from Hiro. He was beginning to think he'd hallucinated the video he'd received from the Krist so many weeks before. So, he was more than a little surprised when he found Hiro waiting for them in the woods.

"Welcome," Hiro giggled. Then he looked past Harpur, Sok and Arthur. "Where is your lady love?"

Arthur was torn between his excitement at seeing Hiro and the painful reminder of what Alex had just done to him. "She's not coming," he said.

Hiro looked to Harpur, who shook his head slightly to let Hiro know that now was not the time to pursue this.

"Well, we're all very glad that you are here. Let's get back to the city and get you settled." Hiro turned his hover gilly around and offered to give Arthur a lift. "It's a long walk," he said.

"That's okay, Hiro." Arthur remembered the harrowing hover gilly rides on Mysturna. "I'll walk."

"Suit yourself!" Hiro chirped as the chariot shot forward. "Let me know if you change your mind."

Arthur followed Hiro, happy to have his feet on the ground.

As they reached the road to Colwygshire Arthur felt the first spasm of doubt squeeze his heart.

"My parents?" he asked Harpur.

"Right now, your mother is wondering why she crocheted seven pairs of baby booties, two layette sets and four blankets."

Arthur wondered the same thing.

"She's also wondering why she bought a rack of lamb that she and your dad couldn't possibly eat by themselves. Your father is trying to remember when and where he bought the big-screen TV he's watching."

"You gave them a TV?"

"With a surround sound system. And I programmed the universal remote for them."

"Thanks, Harpur. That was nice. But why?"

"They were on sale," Harpur said with an enigmatic smile. The complexity of rearranging all the lives that were affected by Arthur leaving Earth had resulted in a leftover TV and surround sound system. Harpur decided to weave it into Marian and Earl's new existence. "Don't worry, Arthur. Everyone is fine."

"Why are we walking?" Arthur asked, partially relieved and partially disappointed.

THE FIRE OF ORHOWYN

"Harpur has developed an aversion to flying recently," Sok said.

"The walk will do us good," Harpur prevaricated as he glowered at the elf. "It will give us a chance to bring you up to speed on things over here."

Arthur knew next to nothing about the culture there. He had no idea what daily life was like for the subjects he was supposed to rule over. He imagined a medieval setting with a stone fortress and a walled city, idyllic on the outside and driven by intrigue and betrayal on the inside. He wasn't sure he was cut out for all that, nor was he sure when or if he'd be *cut out* of it. Suddenly, swords were no longer cool decorations one purchased at a FanCon. They were real weapons with sharp edges and he thought his first proclamation should be an outright ban of them. Along with bows and cross bows and catapults and barrels of oil. Anything sharp and pointy or flammable or capable of propelling heavy, wall-shattering projectiles through the air. Anything, really, that could kill him.

He knew he had to focus on what was before him. What was behind him was the source of a raw pain that he wasn't able to process right then. Another wrinkle that needed to be ironed out. *I wonder if they have irons here,* the weird thought popped up and Arthur rolled his eyes at himself.

It was early evening and the stars were just beginning to twinkle on in the velvety azure sky. On their left was Braydon Wood, an expanse of deciduous trees that covered thousands of acres and, as Arthur would soon learn, was managed by the Wood Elves. It provided all the fuel for Colwygshire hearths and smithies. The northern-most portion of it wrapped around Colwygshire and was, a city in itself, home to the Wood Elves. Humans were welcome to hunt, camp, hike and explore anywhere in the forest except where the Wood Elves lived, but they were forbidden to cut down or damage the trees in any way.

To their right, rolling hills and broad valleys extended to a range of mountains that formed the eastern border of the kingdom. Between Colwygshire and the mountains, farm villages dotted the land. A broad river dissected the kingdom, running south-west from the mountains and disappearing into the forest. It was all quite picturesque, but in the fading twilight, Arthur felt he wasn't getting the full benefit of the landscape. Besides, Sok was chattering away about what had happened with Bloomregaard and the wraiths and what they were going to do in the coming weeks. Harpur had allowed Sok to provide the commentary while they walked and he was relishing his authority in the matter. Arthur was only getting about a third of it, his mind preferring to plague him with visions of a crying Alex driving away alternating with rather graphic images of his demise at the hands of some wicked person bent on betraying him. It was all too much.

"Sok," he said, "would you mind if we went through all this in the morning. I'm a little tired and I won't be able to remember much of it."

"I think I've covered just about everything anyway, but sure, Arthur, we can go over it again later." Sok was not offended in the least. "I am after all going to be your senior adviser. We'll be together a lot from now on."

Arthur thought about that. "No offense, Sok, but I kind of thought that Harpur would... you know... be one of my advisers."

"I thought that too," Sok said, "but he has declined that appointment."

"Harpur?" Arthur wanted an explanation.

"I'll be around for a while," Harpur said. "But once you are trained up and crowned king, Sok here will be a much more appropriate adviser than me."

"What do you mean you'll be around for a while? Where are you going?" The doubt turned to fear and squeezed harder.

"At some point, Arthur, I will have to attend to the business of being a dragon again," he said. "Right now, we just need to get you to Colwygshire and let you rest." *You're going to need it.*

They arrived at Colwygshire at dark. Guided to the main gate by torches on either side, they entered the city and followed a narrow lane that ran along the wall to the right through what was essentially a residential district. After a series of jogs and turns through a complicated maze of streets and lanes they came, at last, to a small cottage at the end of what appeared to Arthur to be a back alley. Sok referred to it as a Council House and informed Arthur that it would be his home for the next while.

"Aren't kings supposed to live in the castle?" Arthur asked when they entered the spartan confines of the tiny house.

"You aren't king yet," Harpur answered.

"Weren't you listening?" Sok seemed annoyed. "I said you would be staying here while we teach you everything you need to know. If you're going to be king, you're going to have to pay attention." Sok busied himself laying a fire in the small hearth and lighting it so Arthur would have some warmth and light.

"Don't worry about the details right now," Harpur said. "Get some sleep and we'll be back in the morning to start your training."

"You're not going to leave me here alone, are you?" Arthur was slightly terrified.

"You'll be fine. Just stay in the cottage and don't go wandering around by yourself." Harpur opened the door to leave.

"Why? Is it not safe out there?" Visions of cutthroats danced through Arthur's head.

"No one is going to harm you, Arthur. It's just easy to get lost in the streets."

"There's a water closet through the door in the corner. You can wash up in there." Sok said. "And we've left some ale and bread and cheese in the larder for you."

"What am I supposed to do here all by myself all night?" Arthur really didn't want to be alone on his first night.

"Sleep!" Harpur said, like that should be obvious.

"I'm a little nervous," Arthur admitted. "It would help if I had a book to read so something."

"What would you like to read?" Harpur felt indulgent.

"Oh, I don't know. The latest Tom Clancy?"

Harpur shook his head in mild irritation. "Here, read this." He conjured a thick, leather-bound tome the size of a small table and handed it to Arthur. "Consider it the start of your training."

The book must have weighed twenty pounds and Arthur grunted with the unexpected strain required to hold onto it. He schlepped it over to a table that sat under the only window in the single-room cottage where he dropped it with a thud. "Gee, thanks," he said sarcastically.

"Good night, Arthur," Harpur said, suppressing his amusement.

"Good night, Arthur," Sok said.

"Good night," Arthur mumbled.

Hiro parked the hover gilly in the corner next to the door and dismounted. "I will stay with you, if you like," he offered.

Arthur gratefully accepted. He could ask Hiro about the video. "Thank you, Hiro. I'd like that very much."

Sok and Harpur left the would-be king and the Krist to get reacquainted. Harpur, now only able to fly short distances, zapped himself to a clearing in Braydon Wood where he transformed and slept as a dragon. Sok navigated the labyrinth of streets to his own nearly identical Council house a few streets away. Both were concerned about how Arthur would cope without Alex. A long debate had preceded the decision to allow her to come to Thraeh with Arthur and her sudden change of heart was yet another glitch in yet another plan. Harpur had returned her life to her, but he had not wiped her memory. He would let her stew for a while. In time, perhaps, something could be done.

Arthur surveyed his surroundings. A cot stood in the corner next to a large trunk, presumably for storing clothing. Save for a battered tricorn hat with an ominous hole through it, the trunk was empty. Arthur tested the cot and found it firm, but not unwelcomingly hard. The pillow was down-filled and covered in a surprisingly soft fabric. The larder—Arthur would have to get used to the local argot—consisted of a small cupboard mounted on the wall above a wooden counter. Shelves containing a random selection of mismatched plates, bowls and cups ran beneath the counter. A large ceramic pot sat on top of it. Arthur assumed this was the kitchen sink. *Probably the bathtub too.* There were pegs on the wall next to the door to hang coats or cloaks or whatever folks wore in Colwygshire. Arthur suddenly remembered that he was still dressed for modern-day Whyte Avenue and wondered where he was going to get clothes that would help him blend in better. He made a mental note to bring this up with Sok and Harpur in the morning. Above the hearth was a box filled with candles. Arthur had no idea how he was supposed to light them. There were no matches that he could see. *Advanced civilization, my foot!*

He braced himself for the worst as he opened the door to the water closet. Expecting to have his olfactory senses assaulted by unpleasant privy odors, he was surprised to find a clean, fresh-smelling room with all the amenities of a proper bathroom. Sort of. To the left of the door was a toilet that was indeed a hole in a bench over a cylindrical stone pit. On the wall next to it was a lever, which, when turned sent a jet of water into the pit that flushed whatever was deposited into it away. *Cool,* thought Arthur. Across from the door there was a small vanity on top of which sat another large ceramic vessel with a hole in the bottom. *A sink!* But Arthur could not tell how it was filled. Above the vanity was an oval mirror and below the mirror was a shelf that contained a lethal looking straight razor, a bar of soap and hair brush. *No toothbrush.* To the right of the vanity was what appeared to be a shower stall. Arthur drew back a plain, beige curtain to reveal a space about one-yard square. A pipe stuck out of the wall ending roughly in the middle of the space. On the end of it was a ring of metal tubing with small holes punctured through the bottom. Another lever just below the pipe allowed cold water to flow through the pipe and out of the holes. There seemed to be no temperature control. It looked as if cold showers were the only option.

Arthur returned to the main room of the cottage to look for anything he could write on. In a small cabinet next to the table, he discovered a bottle of ink, a quill pen and a stack of vellum. He pushed the enormous book he'd been assigned to read as far out of the way as he could and sat down on one of two stools tucked under the table to compose a list of things he'd be needing. Toothbrush, shampoo, a proper razor, towels, clothes, coffee maker, toaster, something to cook on and food. Under this basic outline of basic needs, he added a note for instruction on how to heat the shower and run water to the sinks. The list, by the time he finished it, was spattered with drips from the pen. It was barely legible and his hand was streaked with ink. He went back to the water closet to attempt to wash the ink off his hands with the soap using the shower and managed only to fade it a little. Having no towels, he dried his hands on his pant legs and went back to the larder to get something to eat.

Hiro watched Arthur explore his new home silently. He was sitting on the floor next to the fireplace, enjoying the warmth of the flames. When Arthur approached the larder, he stood up to see if he could assist. "Can I help you with anything?"

Hard cheese and flat bread were all that Sok had left for him. He dearly wished he knew how to conjure up a bag of potato chips. A flask of ale to quench his thirst accompanied the humble repast. Arthur stared at the unappealing contents of the cupboard. "I don't suppose you have anything better than this in your satchel?"

"What do you want?" Hiro was already walking over to the hover gilly to retrieve his bag.

"Anything but hard cheese and flat bread," Arthur said.

Hiro produced a bowl of fruit and a plate of tarts. He placed them on the table and invited Arthur to join him. Arthur sat down on one of the stools and reached for a tart. Then he pulled his cell phone out of his pocket.

Hiro gasped. "You're not supposed to have that here!"

"Harpur didn't take it from me. And I'm not going to remind him that I have it." Arthur said. "Neither are you!"

The Krist giggled conspiratorially. "I sent you a message once," he said.

"I know," Arthur said. "How did you do that? And why did you only send the one?"

"Essentially, I sent the message to you through a Boundary. First, I had to harness an electrical charge. Electricity is powerful and dangerous magic, but Bon showed me how to collect it safely. That android is a wealth of wonderful knowledge, by the way." Hiro was vibrating with enthusiasm for his subject.

"I'm familiar with electricity," Arthur said. "How did you send the message, though?"

"As I understand it, the electrical charge causes a scrying mirror to transmit the message through the Boundary to your device." Hiro simplified the complexity of broadcasting a video signal to its most basic elements.

"But you'd have to know the exact frequency of my cell phone to get it to me," Arthur was intrigued.

"All I had to do was connect telepathically with you through the Boundary. Magic does the rest," Hiro said. "If you did not possess magic, I would not have been able to send the message to you."

Arthur didn't even pretend to understand it, but he did think it was cool. "So, why did the message get cut off?"

"The electrical charge wasn't big enough."

"I see." That made some sense to Arthur. "So, what you're saying is if I have enough electricity to power my phone, I can use it like a scrying mirror?"

"I believe so, yes." Hiro nodded.

"Can I use it to send a message to Alex?" Arthur was excited about the possibility.

"Only if she possesses magic," Hiro said, dampening Arthur's excitement. "And only if you're near a Boundary."

"Figures." Arthur sighed. "Can I use it to direct other kinds of magic? Like a magic wand?"

"I don't know. But the principle is likely very similar." Hiro was warming to the concept.

"Do you have your scrying mirror? Can you show me how it works?"

"Harpur will not be pleased," Hiro cautioned.

"Harpur doesn't need to know. Can you do it?"

Hiro was intrigued. He wanted nothing more than to experiment with this new way of directing magic. For a minute or so his fear of the dragon battled with his curiosity. His curiosity won. "Okay. But just once. If it works, we'll find a way to test it more. But it's getting late. Sok and Harpur will be back early in the morning and there's a lot for you to do tomorrow."

"Agreed," Arthur said. He took another tart from the plate.

Hiro retrieved his scrying mirror and a copper plate from his bag and brought them to the table. "Our mirrors work through pure magic," he began, "but since your device isn't magic, I'll be connecting to you like I did when I sent the first message."

He placed his mirror on top of the copper plate and tapped it eight times. Arthur looked at his cell phone. Nothing happened.

"It's not working," he said, disappointed.

"Hmm..." Hiro tapped his scrying mirror again. "What did you do when you received my message the last time?"

"Nothing," Arthur said. "It vibrated like it would if I was getting a normal call or a text message and you were just there on the screen talking to me."

Hiro tapped the mirror again eight times. "Maybe we are too close..."

"It's working!" Arthur shouted as the cell phone started vibrating in his hand.

Hiro looked at the cell phone and saw his face on the screen.

"Say something to me," Arthur directed the Krist.

Hiro started to talk, but instead of his voice coming through the speakers, they heard a loud, sharp squeal. Then the screen went blank and the cell phone was dead.

"No!" Arthur yelled. He tapped the screen, but the phone did not respond.

"What was that awful noise?" Hiro asked.

"It's called feedback. You were right; we were too close. And now the battery is dead." Arthur pushed the useless device away from him and put his head down on the table, frustrated. With no way to recharge the phone, Arthur's hopes of using it to perform magic were dead too.

Hiro placed his hand on Arthur's elbow. "Let's get some sleep. We'll find a way to put more electricity back into it. I will go back to Mysturna and see if Bon can help us as soon as I can."

Arthur grunted. "I never should have come here," he moaned.

Hiro patted his elbow a few times and hopped down from his stool. He reached up and picked out a small bunch of grapes and two more tarts. Without another word to Arthur, he sat down in the hover gilly and ate his snack. The possibilities Arthur's cell phone presented were a source of delightful inspiration. He was sure he could figure out how to make it work for Arthur, but that was for another time. He curled up and went to sleep.

THE FIRE OF ORHOWYN

Arthur stayed sitting at the table with his chin resting on his hands, staring at the enormous book that Harpur had given him. He was tired, but he didn't think that sleep would come easily. *Maybe some reading will lull me to sleep.*

There was not enough light in the room to read by, though. He had squinted through the process of writing his list in the dim glow from the fire, which was keeping the room pleasantly warm, but he did not relish straining his eyes to read the miniscule text that filled the massive pages. Remembering the candles, he retrieved one from the box, lit it with the flames from the fire and attached it to one of the plates by gluing it in place in a puddle of melted wax. Thus, illuminated, he was then able to see the words. Reading them, however, was a different story and two paragraphs into the exercise, Arthur gave up. It was like reading Shakespeare and his brain hurt from having to interpret all the thys and thous and arts and forthwiths that peppered the calligraphic text. He turned a few pages to see if the entire book was like that and found that it was illustrated throughout with diagrams of plants and animals and several maps.

The diagrams of plants and animals were captioned with their names and their magical or medicinal attributes. Arthur was surprised to learn that many of the animals on Thraeh were the same as on Earth. There were wolves and deer and bears, only on Thraeh they had specific magical abilities. The plants were similar, though some had different names. A rose, for example, was called an elovium and a sunflower was called a sedbaria. Arthur hoped he would not be required to learn all this stuff and flipped on.

He spent some time with a map of Epoh. The names of the villages, rivers, mountain ranges and forests were all neatly printed in block letters that were incongruous with the calligraphy used elsewhere in the book. But it did make it easier for him to get a sense of where he was and what lay beyond the walls of Colwygshire. He was amazed to see how vast Braydon Wood was. The only place that was not named was an area inside Braydon Wood north of Colwygshire that appeared to be another city. He found it odd, but Arthur was growing tired and details were blurring in his mind as well as his vision. He was just about ready to turn in when he turned a final page and was stunned to see a portrait of Harpur glaring at him from the book.

It was the only illustration that was in colour and looking at it, Arthur knew he was not mistaken in assuming this was Harpur in dragon form. The portrait covered both of the open pages and Arthur chuckled at the thought of Harpur being a centerfold. The caption in the bottom right-hand corner of the page was puzzling though. It simply read:

Xzynthyrius (Amethyst) Dreamfinder inherited Epoh from Orhowyn Bravvenshyn, first Dragon Lord of the Kingdom.

Too tired to decipher the text that might explain what this meant, Arthur tucked a piece of the vellum into the book to mark the page and closed it. He would definitely be asking about it, but for now, he needed to get some sleep. He blew out the candle, stripped down to his underwear and crawled under the blanket on the cot. He wondered if he should have added more wood to the fire, but the crackling of the logs as they burned had an immediate lulling effect on him and within minutes he drifted off into unconsciousness.

He hadn't expected to sleep so well. He had stayed up partially to avoid dreaming about Alex. That he hadn't done so was a bit troubling. He wondered if Harpur had done something to him. He knew the tenuous nature of promises; like secrets they were not often kept. Harpur was not above doing anything for Arthur's own good, a habit that Arthur wished he would break. He hated having things fixed for him without his input.

He sat up and tossed the blanket aside. The chill in the air informed him that the fire had gone out, so he dressed quickly in the only clothes he had and went into the water closet to freshen up. Still unable to figure out the sink, he washed his hands and face with the shower and used his jacket to dry off.

The closest thing to a weather report was the view from the window. The day, his first full day in his new world, had dawned overcast with clouds that threatened rain. The ground outside the cottage was dry, but Arthur didn't think that was going to last. Of course, he knew nothing of weather patterns on Thraeh. His assessment was based on experience in a world far, far away.

I could really use some coffee.

Hiro was still snoring peacefully in the hover gilly. Arthur felt bad that the little guy had neither a pillow nor a blanket. If they were going to continue to be roommates, he would have to add those amenities to his list. He opened the cottage door and looked out. The alley was deserted, but he could hear voices and the clatter of cart wheels coming from beyond the houses that flanked it. He was tempted to go in search of something at least caffeine-like, but he didn't dare go out dressed the way he was. While not, strictly speaking, a magical manipulation, Arthur wondered if Harpur had left him without proper garb on purpose to keep him in the cottage. He closed the door again and decided to be a good boy. For now.

The flat bread and hard cheese were still in the larder. Arthur took them to the table and prepared himself a breakfast adding some of the leftover fruit and tarts from the night before. While he ate, he stared at the portrait of *Xzynthyrius Dreamfinder.* He wondered if the X or the Z was silent. Then again, it could be some guttural digraph of the native dialect. For all he knew xz sounded like the letter b. He flipped the page back to scan the calligraphy for Xzynthyrius and found it about half way down the left-hand page. Punctuation was limited to short dashes, which Arthur took to equal periods. There were no commas, or colons or semi-colons. No exclamation or question marks. No apostrophes. No parentheses. And the language was so thick with archaic idioms that all Arthur gleaned from it was that Xzynthyrius Dreamfinder was a dragon. *A dragon who, for some reason, went by the name of Harpur Diggins?* Arthur shut the book, thinking about the legend that Sok had told him about Orhowyn Bravvenshyn and Xzynthyrius Dreamfinder.

It didn't make sense. Orhowyn was supposed to be a knight who killed Xzynthyrius who was supposed to be a dragon. *But if Harpur is Xzynthyrius, then Orhowyn couldn't have killed him.* What did make sense, suddenly, was the bit in the prophecy about the fire of Dreamfinder burning forever within Arthur. That had to be a reference to the dragon blood that Harpur had used to revive him after he'd been killed on Whyte Avenue. *Does that mean I can breathe fire?*

Arthur looked over at the hover gilly in the corner. Hiro appeared to still be asleep. He took a deep breath and tried to imagine a fire burning in his chest, but when he exhaled forcefully, all that came out was hot air!

"What are you doing?" Hiro's voice startled Arthur who snapped the big book closed and pushed it away.

"Nothing," he said, hoping to sound relaxed and casual. "Just some breathing exercises Alex taught me that are supposed to help relieve anxiety."

"And did they work?" Hiro asked, hopping off the hover gilly and coming to the table. He climbed onto a stool and helped himself to a large chunk of bread and some hard cheese.

"Not really," Arthur said.

"Well, you better hide your device," the Krist said around a mouthful of food. "Harpur and Sok are coming."

Arthur looked out the window. The dragon-wizard and the elf were at the end of the alley. He grabbed the dead cell phone, shoved it into his back pocket and pulled his t-shirt down to hide it. Then he chose a piece of fruit and opened the book to a random page. He wanted Harpur to think that he was taking some initiative with his education.

Harpur opened the door and held it for Sok who entered with arms laden with bags and bundles and books, which he began to disperse throughout the cottage.

"We've brought you a few things we thought you might need." He deposited one of the bundles on the unmade cot.

"Is one of them coffee?" Arthur snapped.

"Not as such," Sok replied. "There is no coffee on Thraeh, but I'm sure you will find the wine we brought to be an effective alternative."

"Wine?" Arthur said. "First thing in the morning."

"You're not in Kansas anymore," Harpur quipped. "Things here are a little different. You'll get used to it."

"There are clothes in that package." Sok pointed to the bundle he'd dropped on the cot. "Go put them on. I'll start getting things organized out here."

Arthur picked up the bundle and went into the water closet to change. A few minutes later, he opened the door and poked his head out. "There's no underwear."

Sok stopped preparing the fire and looked at Arthur. "Underwear?"

Harpur wanted to see how this played out, but they didn't have time to argue about tighty-whities. "Just go commando," he instructed Arthur.

"Commando?" Sok asked, but got no answer.

Arthur emerged looking a little less foreign and a little more like a typical man from Colwygshire in a simple tunic over a pair of pants not unlike jeans. They were comfortable enough, but Arthur was not used to not wearing underwear and it showed in his lurching gait as he tried to adjust to the odd sensations. Harpur rolled his eyes.

"Seriously," Arthur whined, "this is uncomfortable. I demand you get me some underwear."

"Petulance is not a good quality for a king," Harpur pointed out. "Give it time."

Sok got the fire blazing again in the hearth. He poured a cup of the wine that was supposed to replace Arthur's morning coffee. Arthur took a tentative sip and was surprised to find that he liked it. It was sweet and dark and tasted a lot like coffee. "Mmm..." He held up the cup. "It's good. What's it called."

"Jamba," Sok said as he placed a pot on a hook over the fire. "Anyone else want some porridge?"

"Oh, yes!" Hiro said, popping the last tart into his mouth.

Arthur went over to the table and picked up his list of needs. He handed it to Harpur.

"A toaster?" Harpur said, shaking his head. "Where are you going to plug it in?"

Arthur's face reddened. "There must be a way to toast bread here."

Sok took the list from Harpur and read it. "What's shampoo?"

Arthur explained.

Sok just looked at him blankly. "There's a toothbrush and towels in the package by the water closet door. The rest of this stuff we'll figure out as we go."

Thus, Arthur's first day of training began. There was a great deal of questioning and answering and arguing about the differences between life on Thraeh and life on Earth. Harpur's standard answer to things Arthur found lacking was to say the he'd just have to get used to it.

After breakfast, Sok showed him how to use the sinks and shower. "Just tap the bowl once to fill it and twice to empty it. To get hot water in the shower, just tap the ring until it's as warm as you want it."

"This is magic." Arthur was impressed.

"Of course, it's magic," Sok said. Like sinks could be filled or emptied any other way!

After lunch—more bread and cheese—they took a tour of the city. Sok gave Arthur a chunk of blue chalk and pointed out black strips on the sides of buildings where he could leave marks to guide him through the streets. This was how new-comers got around until they learned the layout. It was a grave offence to remove any mark but one's own and Sok cautioned Arthur never to do that, but to always remove his own mark on his return to the cottage so that others had space for theirs. It was an ingenious system and Arthur felt an instant confidence.

They went first to the market. Arthur was dazzled by the stalls full of food and spices and clothing and pottery and jewelry and leather goods. Buskers filled the air with music and people danced and clapped and sang along with the lively tunes. Harpur paid for a leather pouch on a belt that Arthur found at one of the stalls. He'd seen other men wearing them and wanted one for himself. It functioned as a wallet for the coins that people used in trade and would make a better hiding place for his cell phone than his back pocket. Harpur gave Arthur twenty coins to put in his pouch.

At another stall, Arthur traded one of his coins for a sweet, sticky bun that all but melted in his mouth. Sok purchased flasks filled with a light, fruity wine for each of them. When the flasks were empty, they dropped them into a bin. They would later be collected, washed and refilled for sale at the next market. Recycling was alive and well in Colwygshire.

Arthur was continually amazed by the systems that were in place. Some magical. Others a matter of cooperation and compliance on the part of the citizenry. Crime, Arthur learned, was minimal. And justice was swift. In the absence of a king, an elected tribunal of magistrates sat in Council to uphold the law. In the weeks that followed this first day, Arthur would sit in on these court sessions and discover just how swift the justice was in Colwygshire. But for now, Sok had determined that an experiential education was the best way for Arthur to become integrated into the culture.

Overwhelmed by it all, Arthur finally announced that he was tired. Harpur insisted that they dine at the Skull's Keep and Sok reminded Arthur at every corner to leave his mark as they made their way from the market to the pub. There they were served huge flagons of crisp ale and platters of what looked and tasted like pulled pork swimming in a rich gravy. They shared a loaf of fresh bread and a plate of sweet corn on the cob. Arthur was relieved to know that bread was bread, corn was corn and pork was pork on Thraeh. He had crossed the information overload threshold and was not up to memorizing any new names for normal things.

After their meal, Arthur was instructed to guide them back to the cottage by finding and following his marks. They got lost twice before Arthur realized that he needed to include a directional indicator to his mark. When they eventually found their way back to the cottage, the sun was setting and Arthur was ready to collapse into bed. Hiro volunteered to stay with him again and Arthur asked Harpur to conjure a pillow and blanket for the Krist.

"I have everything I need in my satchel," Hiro said, "but thank you for the consideration."

It wasn't until Sok and Harpur had left that thoughts of Alex began to surface. Arthur had been so entranced by the sights and sounds of the city that Alex had not been able to worm her way into his mind. Once Hiro had fallen asleep, though, he found her drifting back into his heart and wrenching it with guilt and anger and sorrow. She should have been there. She should have been dancing to the buskers' music at the market. She should have been sharing his awe and his delight. But she wasn't. She was a world away and he was alone. Arthur cried himself to sleep.

For the next several weeks, Sok tutored Arthur on the history and laws of Thraeh in general and the Kingdom of Epoh specifically. Every day, they explored a different part of the city and Arthur was charged with the task of using his marks to find their way back to the cottage. Harpur showed up sporadically, sometimes just to check in. Other times he accompanied them, adding his own take on things he thought Arthur should know.

Hiro left Thraeh on Arthur's third day in Colwygshire, saying he needed to return to Mysturna to check on his cave and gather some more things he though he could use. "I will return soon," he said, giving Arthur a collusive wink before zipping away on the hover gilly. Arthur missed him as soon as he was out of sight.

When Arthur felt comfortable enough to make his own way through Colwygshire, Sok began meeting him in different places within the city rather than escorting him. At first Arthur made his own way to the market to meet Sok. Then he had to find his own way to Skull's Keep. Often, they would have lunch in the castle gardens and watch the reparation to the tower as it progressed. As Arthur got to know some of the vendors from the market and a few of his neighbours near the cottage, he began to feel more settled in Colwygshire, if not at home there. He missed coffee and technology. It was weird and disorienting not to know what day of the week or what time of day it was. Not being able to text or call people was inconvenient. He had to rely on making plans face-to-face, which meant, more often than not, finding people, or being found in order for plans to be made. He met people at sundown or mid-morning and soon discovered that these vague indications of appointments were interpreted in the loosest of terms.

His first foray outside of the Colwygshire walls took place a few weeks after he had arrived. Harpur appeared at the cottage and announced that he was to begin learning how to use a sword. Sok had negotiated the use of the training grounds in the Elven city and the great Yna, herself, would be the one to teach him.

"We'll use wooden practice swords, right?"

"Probably," Harpur said.

"Do I have to learn how to use a sword?"

"What if you ever have to lead troops into battle?"

"That's not going to happen, is it? I thought Epoh was in a state of peace."

"It is," Harpur assured him. "But things can change, Arthur."

This was not comforting in the least. "Is there something I should know?"

"You should know many things, but I'm not aware of any pending invasions or wars."

Harpur and Arthur left the city through one of the side gates and turned north. They followed the main road for about twenty minutes until they came to a fork veering to the left and leading into the forest.

"How much farther?" Arthur asked.

"Not far. The gates are just up ahead."

The closer they got, the less Arthur wanted to think about what he was going to do. "Sok told me that Anayah had returned to Mysturna. Is she coming back?"

"She might."

"Why didn't she come back with you?"

"She had business at Wildwood."

That's what Sok said. Arthur decided not to pursue it. "The new tower is coming along nicely."

"It is."

Arthur was growing frustrated. He'd been bombarded with information about so many things, but when he asked about Anayah or what was happening with him being made king, Sok and Harpur both deflected. He'd heard rumours, of course. People were getting uncomfortable without a king and while Davynn, whom Arthur had not met yet, was doing an admirable job of leading the council, the subjects of Epoh wanted a king on the throne.

"So, when do I become the king?"

Harpur stopped walking. He looked at Arthur. "Much has been sacrificed for you, Arthur."

"What does that mean?" Arthur felt the ominous undertone in Harpur's words.

Harpur weighed what he would say next carefully. Arthur had done admirably in learning the history of his new world and had demonstrated remarkable restraint by not pestering Harpur or Sok too much about the details of how and when he would prove himself worthy of wearing the crown. It was vital that Arthur maintain the backstory he'd been taught—he was a drifter, come to Colwygshire for the winter. Period. Arthur was to be vague about his personal history and, with the help of Sok, had done that by not lingering long anywhere or with anyone. His interactions with the locals were friendly, but short at all times. Still, Harpur felt he owed Arthur some explanation.

"Arthur, I can't tell you with any certainty how this will play out. We have set things in motion that we hope will culminate in your being crowned king. But you have to understand that sometimes things have a way of becoming what they need to in the way they need to, in spite of what we do."

"Are you telling me that I might not become king?"

"I'm telling you that whatever happens in the coming days, it is what is meant to happen."

"You know that I've sacrificed a lot, too, right? You know that I only agreed to come here because you said I was heir to the throne. I left my family... I left the love of my life behind for this." Arthur flung his arm out, pointing toward where the Boundary to Whyte Avenue stood behind them.

"I know," Harpur said. "This will be over soon. You have to trust me and Sok for a little while longer. There are still some things you need to learn and once you have at least some idea how to wield a sword and can present yourself to the people as someone who can lead them, we'll take the next step."

"What is the next step?"

"Whatever it is, it has to be to appear to happen naturally."

"Oh, for gods... Orhowyn's sake," Arthur corrected himself, "That's supposed to make me feel better?"

"No, I suppose not," Harpur said. "But since I can't break my promise not to use magic on you, all I have left is the truth."

"The truth?" Arthur threw his hand up in the air. "Chance would be a fine thing! All you and Sok do is put me off."

Harpur sighed. "Tell you what," he said. "If you do well in there today," he pointed toward the forest, "I'll treat you and Sok to a hamburger. And then I will tell you a story."

"A hamburger?" Arthur was intrigued.

"With all the trimmings."

"And what is this story you're going to tell me?"

"First you have to get through your lesson with Yna."

With that Harpur walked toward the gate to the elven city. And Arthur followed.

They were met at the gate by an elven woman who shook Harpur's hand and then looked Arthur up and down as if he was about to step onto an auction block. She was as tall as Harpur. Her powerful body was deceptively slender under an ornate, carved leather bustier and tunic. A thick, silvery-blue braid snaked across one shoulder and ended at her waist. Her wide-set, cobalt eyes distracted from a thin scar that ran diagonally from the bridge of her nose to her jaw across her right cheek.

"This is the drifter you want me to train?" The elven woman's voice was deep and melodious at the same time.

"Yna, this is Arthur. Arthur, Yna." Harpur introduced them.

Arthur reached out to shake Yna's hand and was ignored. Instead, she turned an annoyed gaze on the dragon-wizard. "He's too small."

Arthur couldn't help but take umbrage. "Excuse me?"

Harpur put a hand on Arthur's arm to quiet him. "Be that as it may, you agreed to do this. Just teach him a few basic moves. He's tougher than he looks."

Yna shrugged. "Very well. Come."

The warrior elf turned her back on them and walked through the gates.

"She's going to hurt me, isn't she?" Arthur asked as he fell in step with Harpur to follow Yna.

"You'll be fine," Harpur said.

Arthur doubted that.

Under different circumstances, Arthur would have found the elven city an awe-inspiring sight. But all he could look at as they wound their way to the practice grounds was the enormous sword strapped to Yna's back. The blade was four inches wide and at least four feet long. The two-handed hilt, wrapped in leather, fanned out into a silver pommel of three carved leaves. Arthur estimated that it gave Yna a reach of over seven feet. No wonder she was a champion; no one could get close to her. He felt sick.

The training began with a series of drills. Arthur thrust and jabbed and parried with a wooden practice sword while Yna corrected his stance and arm position. He drew his sword from its scabbard about a million times. That alone was harder than Arthur thought it would be. Clearing the scabbard with the long blade required holding onto it with his left hand and pulling it down as he pulled the sword up and out with his right hand. Eventually, he got it and he moved on to hacking, which was how Yna described his technique, at dummies. Just when Arthur thought he would keel over from thirst and the exertion of the drills, Yna called in another elf named Borak and ordered him to spar with Arthur.

Though not as tall as Yna, this young elf was nonetheless formidable. An hour later, battered, bruised and wholly humiliated, Arthur called, "Enough!" He lay, panting on the ground drenched in sweat with his eyes closed. The sight of a grimacing elf holding the point of a sword, even a wooden practice sword, at his throat had become all too familiar. His sparring partner helped him to his feet, bowed slightly and left him standing alone and in pain.

Harpur, who had been sitting in the shade and chatting with some of the elves who had come to watch, brought Arthur a flask of water and led him out of the practice grounds. Yna, Arthur noticed had disappeared, probably in disgust.

"Not bad for your first day," Harpur said as Arthur drank deeply from the flask and then emptied what was left of the water over his head.

"And last," Arthur gasped. "I don't think sword fighting is my thing."

"Nonsense!" Harpur dismissed Arthur's dismissal of the crucial skill-building lessons. "You'll be battle-ready in no time. Now let's get back to Colwygshire and have Sok see to those bruises. Tomorrow you'll put that elf on his back."

Arthur forced his fingers to let go of the practice sword and let it fall to the ground. Rubbing his aching wrist, he willed his feet to move and followed Harpur out of the training area and out of the elven city.

"I don't suppose you could fly us back to the city?" Arthur whined.

"No," Harpur said, slowing his pace in sympathy for Arthur's post-training pace. He did not elaborate.

"Don't you fly anymore?"

"I think you should go straight to the cottage and get cleaned up. I'll I will send Sok to tend to your bruises." Harpur ignored Arthur's question.

"Harpur, what's going on with you? You haven't been yourself since I've been here and it's starting to concern me."

"It's nothing you need to worry about," Harpur said, not denying there was a problem. "You need to focus on keeping on your feet with a sword in your hand."

"I'm not going back there unless you tell me what's wrong with you!" Arthur said.

Harpur stopped walking and spun to face Arthur. "You will go back there until I tell you you no longer need to. Is that clear?"

Arthur stood his ground. "No, Harpur, it's not clear. I'm worried about you and that worry is going to affect how well I am able to learn anything else. So, why don't you just tell me what's wrong? Maybe I can help."

Harpur laughed. "You, help me? Arthur, I admire your noble idealism, but there is nothing you can do to help me." He started walking again.

Arthur didn't follow. He stood there with his hands on his hips and refused to take another step. "I'm not moving until you tell me what's going on," he shouted at Harpur's back.

"Suit yourself." Harpur kept walking. "Sok and I will share your hamburger."

As if on cue, Arthur's stomach growled. *Crafty, stubborn dragon!*

He ran, or rather shuffled awkwardly, until he caught up to the hamburger-providing dragon-wizard.

Back at the cottage, Arthur showered and put on clean pants. He couldn't bring himself to lift his arms to pull a tunic over his head. Angry bruises, like purple clouds tattooed on his skin, adorned his arms, ribs and jaw where Borak had landed brutal blows with the practice sword. He supposed that bruises were better than gashes, but there wasn't an inch of his body that didn't hurt. There was no way he was going to be able to do that again the next day. He'd be surprised if he'd be able to get out of bed in the morning, let alone pick up a sword and defend himself.

Sok entered the cottage just as Arthur emerged, shirtless, from the water closet. "I see Yna took it easy on you," he said as he assessed the contusions on Arthur's body.

Arthur grimaced. "Yna didn't do this," Arthur explained. "It was Borak."

"Ah."

"He'd be dead if Yna had sparred with him," Harpur quipped from the doorway. Arthur was disappointed at not seeing any hamburgers in his hands. All he had was a bag with some pastries.

Sok had Arthur sit down on one of the stools and began to run his hands gently over the bruises. Arthur watched as a pale blue glow from the elf's hands seemed to sink into his skin. A feeling of warmth soothed the aches as Sok moved his hands over the bruises. Arthur closed his eyes and surrendered to the healing. When he opened his eyes again, he found himself lying on the cot being stared down at by a concerned elf and an amused dragon-wizard.

"Nice nap?" Harpur jibed.

"What happened?" Arthur asked, sitting up and staring at his pain-free, un-bruised arms and torso. He flexed his hands and stretched out his arms to test for any residual aching.

"You fell asleep," Sok said. "How do you feel?"

"Great!" Arthur said standing up and reaching for his shirt. "And hungry!"

"And what about you?" Sok asked Harpur. "How are you feeling today?"

Harpur shook his head at Sok to signal that he was not to continue this conversation. "I'm fine," he said.

Arthur was too busy not feeling any pain to notice this exchange. "When are those hamburgers getting here?" he asked as if they were expecting fast-food delivery to show up.

Harpur waved his hand and a feast of deluxe double cheese burgers with fries, onion rings and gravy appeared on the table. Arthur laughed out loud when he spotted a can of Pepsi among the plates of food.

"Don't get used to it," Harpur cautioned. "You did well today. You deserve a small reward."

"Yes," Sok said, stuffing an onion ring into his mouth. "How did it go this morning?" He wanted Harpur's take on the training.

"Arthur wasn't disarmed once," Harpur said.

Sok looked at Arthur with astonished pride. "Wow! That's amazing. Good for you, Arthur."

"Was I supposed to be disarmed?" Arthur asked around a bite of burger. Table manners had been tabled for the duration of this meal.

"That was the goal," Harpur said.

"Are you sure Arthur didn't have some help?" Sok probed, suspicious of such prowess in a beginner.

"If you're asking if I used magic to assist him, I did not." Harpur was emphatic. "He got the hell beat out of him all on his own."

They all laughed, though Arthur's contribution to the gaiety was more scornful than amused.

With their hunger sated, Sok announced it was time to hit the books. Arthur groaned with a different kind of pain. "Do we have to?" he moaned.

"Actually," Harpur intervened, "I will be giving the lesson today, if you don't mind, Sok.

Sok simply nodded.

Arthur didn't know whether he should be relieved or worried.

The trio got comfortable. Sok sat cross-legged on the cot while Harpur and Arthur each remained on a stool. Sok had offered to go do some recon to see what the mood was in regard to finding a king, but Harpur asked him to stay.

"Arthur, I would never have brought you here if it wasn't for the prophecy," the dragon-wizard began.

"I know that," Arthur said.

"But we don't know what it means precisely. Nothing in it explains how you are to become the king. We do know, thanks to Anayah, that you have a right to the throne because you and Gnik are both descendants of Ylemnir. But no one else does and we can't prove it."

"It's all in the Akashic Records, isn't it?" Arthur asked.

"Yes, but that doesn't help us. Only those who know how to access them can interpret them and we can't just make an announcement that your pedigree is filed in the cosmic-consciousness. There are records of Gnik's lineage, of course, but not of yours. For obvious reasons." Harpur paused. "We have shared the prophecy with the Council and we've made sure that it has become common knowledge. Sok has had some of his minstrel friends compose songs about it and it's given the people some measure of hope. But they need proof before they will accept you as the king in the prophecy."

"So how do we give them the proof they need?"

"That's the problem. We don't know." Harpur rubbed his hands on his thighs. "We have figured out that it has something to do with the dragon blood I used to revive you, but we don't know how my blood has affected you, so we don't know how to utilize it to our advantage."

"I think so too." Arthur pulled the huge book closer and opened it to the page with the portrait of Harpur.

Sok stood up and came to the table. "That's you!" he exclaimed.

Harpur didn't deny it.

Sok read the inscription under the portrait of the dragon. "Xzynthyrius (Amethyst) Dreamfinder inherited Epoh from Orhowyn Bravvenshyn, first Dragon Lord of the Kingdom. That makes no sense. The knight Orhowyn Bravvenshyn killed Xzynthyrius Dreamfinder."

"Not exactly," Harpur said. "It's all in the book."

"Yeah, well, that book might as well be written in Greek! I can't understand any of it." Arthur said.

"Really?" Sok said, still not quite able to wrap his head around this new information.

"Really, Sok." Arthur thought Sok was referring to the book. "The language in it is impossible."

Sok looked confused for a moment. "No. I meant really as in Harpur is really Xzynthyrius Dreamfinder. I know that book is impossible to read. Why do you think I haven't bothered going through it with you?"

"Yes, Sok, I am really Xzynthyrius Dreamfinder."

Sok clamped his mouth shut and stared at the dragon-wizard. "How?" Sok was more than amazed at this revelation, he was stunned. The legend of Xzynthyrius Dreamfinder had always, until that very moment been just a story. A story that had been changed, obviously, over the centuries. Sok, too, wanted to hear the rest of it. "I'd like to hear this."

"The legend as you know it is just that, a legend. Orhowyn Bravvenshyn was the dragon whom I defeated to inherit Epoh. Over time the true story took on a life of its own and Orhowyn became the one who conquered a mighty dragon. He was transformed into a knight who became a god by drinking the blood of the dying Xzynthyrius from the Amber Chalice—a total fabrication, no doubt the product of some minstrel's imagination. As Orhowyn gained in popularity, I was all but forgotten. The only accurate account of what really happened all those centuries ago is in here." Harpur placed a hand on the book.

"And you left me the book so I could figure it out?" Arthur surmised.

"Whether you knew or not makes no difference, but I hoped you would figure it out."

"Why?"

"I just thought it would be nice if someone knew who I am." Harpur shrugged.

"But why did you change your name?" Arthur asked.

"I was challenged by a young dragon who wanted Epoh for himself. I retuned from a Bound to Earth and found him at my lair. It was close. He was strong and he caught me by surprise. But I won."

"Who was this other dragon? Where did he come from?" Arthur was curious.

"And what does that have to do with your name?" Sok was trying to keep up.

"The young dragon's name died with him, but I assume he came from the Sands of Sancheera like most dragons do. Not that it matters. What matters is, I was badly wounded in the fight and a wizard named Harpur Diggins healed me before another challenger sensed my weakness and came along to finish what the first dragon had started. When I learned that Harpur Diggins had died, I honoured him for saving me by taking his name. It seemed more suited to my human form when I Bounded."

"That's so sad," Arthur said. "You should be immortalized in songs by bards, not forgotten."

"I'm okay with it, Arthur."

"Xzynthyrius is such a cool name..." Arthur paused. "...not that Harpur isn't cool, but... So, how did the portrait of you get in the book if the true story has been changed so much?"

"It is a very old book, Arthur. It's my life book. Every dragon has one." Harpur turned to look at Arthur. "I hope you will take very good care of it."

Arthur just nodded. He understood that a profound honour had been bestowed upon him and he didn't have the words to express how he felt. Which was inadequate and unsure he deserved the trust Harpur was giving him. The events of the afternoon had taken them all into strange and, Arthur sensed, forbidden territory. He changed the subject again. "What I don't understand is what you mean when you say you inherited Epoh. Don't the people own the land?"

"No one owns the land," Harpur said. "People rule the kingdoms and dragons rule the land."

"What's the difference?"

"Perception, mostly," Harpur said. "Kingdoms are made up of people. People do occupy the land and use the resources of the land, but the land itself does not depend on the people."

"It depends on dragons?"

"Yes."

Arthur tossed that around in his head for a while. Harpur's monosyllabic response seemed to signify that he was not going to elaborate any further. He looked at the book. "Will you interpret for me?" he asked. He suddenly wanted to know how the story of Xzynthyrius was supposed to be told.

"I will," Harpur said, "but I want to show you something."

"What is it?" Arthur expected Harpur to conjure something or take something out of his pocket.

"Come with me." Harpur stood up and went to the door.

He led them out of the city and through Braydon Wood to the clearing where Harpur had set Sok and Arthur down after they had been un-Entangled in his lair and Harpur walked out into the middle. The night sky was clear and a bright moon illuminated the dell with a soft white light. The elf and the man stayed near the trees. Arthur assumed that Harpur was about to transform and fly them somewhere else.

"Where are we going?" he called to Harpur.

"Here." Then he transformed into his dragon form.

"Whoa!" Arthur exclaimed as he took in the deformed right wing, the blackened scales on Harpur's left leg and the missing scale at his heart.

Harpur remained in dragon form for only a few minutes and then transformed back into a human.

"That explains your aversion to flying," Arthur said while Harpur walked back to where he and Sok stood. "What happened to you?"

Harpur explained how he had been injured luring the wraiths through the Boundary to Mysturna.

"Is there no one who can heal you? Sok, can't you do anything?" Arthur was deeply troubled.

"Anayah and Sok did their best when it first happened. I'm fairly certain that there is not much more that can be done."

"So, you can't fly?" Arthur asked.

"Oh, I can," Harpur said. "Just not very far or very fast."

"If he stays in human form, he could lose his dragon powers," Sok added.

"And if I stay in dragon form, some other dragon will sense my weakness and will come to challenge me for Epoh. I'm afraid that my days as a dragon are numbered either way."

Arthur felt the full weight of what Harpur was telling them. "I need you, Harpur," he said. Not out of greed for his own ends, but because he suddenly realized how much Harpur had sacrificed for him. And how much he loved the irascible old dragon.

"Is that how you lost your walking stick?" Arthur asked, the thought just occurring to him.

"It is," Harpur confirmed.

"I offered to get it for him, but..." Sok began.

"But there's no need. I have tried to call it back to me, but it must have been damaged when Anayah dropped it. I will get along with out it." They stood in silence until Harpur could no longer stand watching Arthur's helplessness. "Enough of this. I'll not have you pitying me. I'm not dead yet and we have much to do."

Arthur stood still while Sok and Harpur headed out of the clearing. "We have to find out what your blood has done to me, don't we?"

Harpur stopped walking and turned back to the heir to the throne. "Yes, we do."

They walked out of the clearing back toward the Boundary. As they passed it, Arthur looked at it with contempt, like it was the one that had caused such dire harm to Harpur. None of them would look at Boundaries quite the same way again.

Stomachs were growling again by the time they reached the road and Harpur conjured some pastries to keep them going until they got back to the city. He felt more and more guilty about doing things like that, but he figured he was going to run out of peaceful silence soon and he hoped that some food would keep Sok and Arthur's mouths busy for a while longer. He was wrong.

"What kind of trees are those?" Arthur pointed to a bushy tree with silvery, purple-blue leaves growing at the edge of the forest.

"Dragonfoil," Sok said. "According to the legend of Xzynthyrius and Orhowyn, the first dragonfoil grew on the spot where the dragon was killed. Is that part true, Harpur?"

"That part is true," Harpur confirmed. "Orhowyn's magic lives in the trees and is what makes the leaves turn the colour of his scales in the autumn. When the last leaf falls, the dragonfoil is consumed by fire."

"Cool!" Arthur said. "I'd like to see that."

"It will be another few weeks before the burnings begin," Sok said. "But I'll take you to some when they are ready."

They walked a while in silence. Arthur kept thinking about the effects of Harpur's blood. "Am I going to turn into a dragon or something?"

"No," Harpur said. "But it's possible that your magic could be enhanced. Or you could age much, much more slowly than a normal human. Some people grow scales..."

"Bloody hell, Harpur! Why didn't you tell me before? Scales! Scales?" Arthur started checking his body for signs that he was growing scales.

"Calm down. It's been eight years. If you were going to grow scales, you'd probably have done so by now."

"So, what did your blood do to me?"

"So far, I haven't seen any sign of anything that usually happens. But I do know that now that you have my blood, we are connected," Harpur said.

"Like we're Entangled?" Arthur was appalled. "Am I going to be absorbed into you?"

"No. Not Entanglement. Not like you were with Sok through the coin. That's an entirely different sort of magic."

"Well, what sort of magic is this?"

"The effects vary from person to person. And, as I said, I have not yet seen any of the usual effects in you."

Arthur stared at Harpur.

"This isn't a bad thing," Sok said. "Arthur, you could develop amazing powers because of this."

"What? Like Spiderman can spin webs because he got bitten by a radioactive spider, I can sprout wings and fly because Harpur dribbled his blood into my mouth?" He already knew he couldn't breathe fire like a dragon.

"That's one possibility," Harpur said casually. "Do you ever feel pressure around your shoulder blades?"

Arthur's mouth gaped. "No, Harpur! I do not feel pressure around my shoulder blades."

"Well, that's probably not it, then," Sok said. "I wonder what it is." He was actually wondering what Spiderman was, but wasn't sure he should ask.

Arthur looked from Sok to Harpur. "What are the other options?"

"In the absence of any physical manifestations, I suspect that it has affected your magic," Harpur said. "Ylemnir was a very powerful wizard. Half his talent mixed with dragon blood could make you extraordinarily formidable."

Sok waved a dismissive hand. "Arthur is about as magical as an old boot."

"It's latent in him," Harpur said, "but it's there."

Sok looked dubious. "Shouldn't we be training him to use his magic, then?"

"Not until we know what my blood had done to him. I'm not about to unleash something when I don't know what I'm unleashing," Harpur said.

"But maybe we could use his magic to make sure the crown does end up on his head," Sok suggested. "Maybe that's how the prophecy gets fulfilled."

Arthur stopped walking to digest this. He really wasn't up to any more training. Of any kind. Then again, if it got him out of another session with Yna... *How bad could doing magic be?* No. He'd lived without magic for thirty years and he couldn't see how it would make him a better king. If anything, magic would probably be a bad quality for a king to possess. Think of how he could manipulate people into doing everything his way. If he had magic, there would soon be coffee shops and burger joints all over Epoh, whether they were wanted or not. "I don't know, guys..."

"There's no way Arthur is going to get accepted to the Wizard's guild. Not at his age." Sok began working out the details aloud. "We'd need to engage a proper wizard to work with him. I wish Anayah was here. She'd be perfect."

"Hello!" Harpur said, pointing at himself. "Wizard."

"Oh, right!" Sok had the good grace to look apologetic.

"Do I get a say in this?" Arthur chimed in.

Sok and Harpur stopped walking as well and turned to the would-be king.

"I've played your Pygmalion for weeks now. And it's been great." Arthur said sarcastically.

"What's a Pygmalion?" Sok interrupted, he couldn't help himself this time.

"A sort of guinea pig," Arthur said.

"What's a guinea pig?"

Harpur glared at the curious elf. "Go on, Arthur."

"I've played your Pygmalion for weeks now," Arthur started again. "And I'm no closer to being a king than I was when I got here. The people are getting restless and even I can see that they aren't going to be patient much longer.

"If we don't move things along soon, I'm afraid that all of this is going to be pointless. I'll have given up the love of my life for nothing. I don't care about whether or not I possess magic right now. I'd rather know what Harpur's blood is doing to me. I think we need to figure that out. If... when I do become king, I don't want to have to worry about sprouting wings or accidentally setting someone on fire when I burp.

"And I want to get this done. No more sword fighting. No more history lessons. No more putzing around. Or you can send me back to Earth."

Harpur and Sok stared at Arthur. That last statement felt like the slap in the face it was meant to be.

"Fair enough." Harpur crossed his arms. "I do appreciate how difficult this is for you."

It was Arthur's turn to stare back. He had not expected his ultimatum to be accepted so easily. Harpur was far too shrewd to just give in like that. And Sok's silence wasn't helping

"I'm tired, Harpur," Arthur offered by way of explanation. "I'm lonely and I'm scared." There! He'd admitted it.

Harpur sighed. As Arthurian hissy-fits went, this had been a mild one. "I can't just snap my fingers and make you the king. If I could, I would have done it already. Give it a little more time. If the prophecy doesn't reveal the next step by the time the last dragonfoil burnings are done, I will send you back to Earth."

"And you'll give me my life back? You'll bring Alex back to me?" Arthur asked.

"I will make sure you and the cute hippie girl live happily ever-after."

Chapter 21

Arthur had yet to see much of the kingdom he was supposed to rule beyond the walls of Colwygshire. His one visit to the elven city had not gone well and Sok was tasked with letting Yna know that her services were no longer needed. She wasn't surprised. But she did give Sok the practice sword Arthur had used to give to him, which did surprise Sok. Yna was not known for her sentimentality and this gesture was out of character for her. She had even had a name carved into the blade—Drifter's Curse—in Elven.

"Are you mocking him?" Sok asked.

"I admire his courage. It's not usual for a man of his age to take up the sword for the first time. And to not have been disarmed... Let's just say that Borak is the one carrying the shame."

Poor Borak, Sok thought. Yna would never let him live this down.

A tour of the kingdom was something that Harpur had hoped to give Arthur before the winter set in. Flying was not an option in his current condition and it would take weeks to see it all by horse. They studied maps instead and this helped to enhance Arthur's working knowledge of Epoh.

The matter of Arthur being accepted as king was a bigger problem. The people were growing increasingly restless and to stave off their growing concern over the empty throne, Davynn had issued a public announcement reminding the people of the prophecy and asking them to be patient a while longer. *Pray Orhowyn delivers our new king soon.*

Harpur, Sok and Arthur were sitting in the cottage on a cold, rainy day about a week after Davynn's announcement, brainstorming ideas for some sort of trial that would prove Arthur was meant to be the king. They all agreed that it had to be simple with enough drama to invoke a sense of awe in those who witnessed it and safe enough that Arthur would survive unscathed.

"There must be some way to prove Arthur's worthiness," Sok said.

"There is," Harpur said. "We just don't know what it is. That Orhowyn forsaken prophecy is too vague."

"But we know it has something to do with how your blood has affected him. It has to." Sok was growing frustrated by the lack of dragon traits in his friend.

"I don't see why I can't just pull a sword from a stone," Arthur said. For the umpteenth time.

"I told you, Arthur," Harpur tried to keep the exasperation out of his voice, "it has to be authentic. This is not something we can fake with magic."

"So, we're back to me killing a dragon," Arthur sneered.

"Ha-ha!" Harpur rolled his eyes.

A knock on the cottage door prevented round umpteen of the circular argument they'd been having from starting over. They all looked at the door as if they'd never heard anyone knock on one before. Finally, Harpur stood up and opened it.

Hiro floated in on his hover gilly and parked it in the corner. "I see Arthur is still a peasant," he said with his signature giggle.

He stepped off the hover gilly and went to the fireplace to warm up and dry off.

"I don't suppose you were doing anything helpful to the cause on Mysturna?" Harpur said to the dripping Krist.

"Mostly harbouring a fugitive," Hiro said.

"Anayah?" Harpur surmised. He hoped the concern he felt for the witch wasn't obvious in his voice.

"She's not doing well," Hiro confirmed. "Analeetah will not forgive her for what happened to Anabettah."

"Anayah should just come here and be with us," Sok announced.

Hiro turned from the fire and faced his friends. The expression on his face was grim and sad. "After Anayah returned to Wildwood to tell them that Anabettah was dead, Analeetah accused her of betraying her world and her community."

Arthur swallowed a lump of fear. He remembered what Analeetah had told him about justice on Mysturna. "What happened?"

"Anayah told them the truth and the consensus was that she should not have involved Anabettah in the plan to lure the wraiths into the Boundary. Analeetah refused to accept any of the proposals Anayah submitted to make amends and forced Anayah to give up her magic and remain in Wildwood until such time as Analeetah says she may be released. Essentially, Anayah was Analeetah's prisoner."

"You said was." Harpur noticed the use of the past tense. "Where is she now?"

"She's safe. Some of the other witches came to realize that Analeetah is quite mad with grief. Her cruelty toward Anayah was beyond what they were willing to tolerate and so they helped Anayah to escape. She's with Bon at the Sphere. It is a sacred place and so Anayah has been granted asylum there. Analeetah cannot touch her. But without her magic, Anayah is as much a prisoner there as she was at Wildwood. Until she can find a way to get her magic back..." Hiro left that thought hanging.

"And the only way she can get her magic back is if Analeetah were to die." Harpur stood up, fuming with rage. "I can arrange that!"

Arthur thought about the deep love he witnessed between aunt and niece when they had arrived on Mysturna for the first time. The bond they shared seemed unbreakable. His own troubles suddenly felt petty in comparison to what Anayah must be going through. Analeetah's actions were beyond the pale. "We should do something to help her!"

Everyone looked at Arthur. But only Harpur noticed the faint purple-red flush of dragon fire glowing at the base of Arthur's throat. Harpur knew that he was not just about to throw another fit of pique. Arthur was vibrating with rage and if he lost control... Harpur didn't want to think about the damage Arthur could do. He had to distract him.

"Cookies?" Harpur all but shouted as he conjured a plate piled high with spicy biscuits and banged it loudly down on the table next to Arthur.

Arthur, Sok and Hiro all jumped in flabbergasted shock at Harpur's bizarre behavior. Harpur released an audible sigh of relief when the glow of dragon fire extinguished itself and Arthur's throat ceased to glow. *That's new.*

"Cookies?" Arthur looked up at the dragon-wizard, utterly baffled.

Harpur cleared his own throat. "I thought we could all use a snack," he said, picking up one of the tasty confections and taking a bite.

Sok and Hiro, came forward and helped themselves to the cookies. As weird as Harpur was acting, they both understood there was a purpose to it, even if they didn't know what that purpose was. Besides... Cookies!

"How can you think of cookies at a time like this?" Arthur was looking at his companions like they had all lost their minds.

Harpur sat down and looked Arthur directly in the eye. "Arthur, I need you to stay very, very calm, okay?"

Harpur's request was even more alarming than the sudden appearance of the cookies. Arthur nodded and slowly reached for a cookie, hoping that was what the intense dragon-wizard wanted him to do. "Is there like a giant spider on my shoulder or something?" he asked, keeping his own eyes locked on Harpur's.

Harpur ignored the odd question. "I need you to listen to me carefully." Harpur waited for another nod from Arthur. "I'm in no condition at the moment to fight a whole city of witches. Anayah is safe for now and I promise you that we will help her. But first we're going to figure out how to get that crown on your head. You let me and Hiro worry about Anayah. You just focus on you and if you feel anything strange or abnormal, you tell me right away. Okay?"

Arthur felt like a three-year-old who had just done something wrong and was being reprimanded by a long-suffering parent. "I will," he said. Just to be safe, he surreptitiously glanced at his shoulders to be sure there wasn't a big, hairy arachnid perched on one of them.

"Good!" Harpur said, patting Arthur on his spider-free shoulder.

Sok and Hiro had been mesmerized by this peculiar exchange. They both knew that Harpur had thwarted some potential disaster, but neither of them could fathom what it was. "What just happened?" Sok asked, his cookie forgotten.

Harpur just grinned at them. "Any other news from beyond the Boundary?" he asked Hiro.

"Nothing important," the Krist said. "But I did pass Davynn on my way here and he said the dragonfoil burnings have begun. He was heading out to do crowd control at one on the east side of the city."

"There's a burning today?" Sok asked. He'd been wanting to show Arthur what happens when the last leaf of a dragonfoil tree falls off.

"One is expected at the big dragonfoil in the copse on the east side of the city. People have been gathering there for days waiting for it to burn. Davynn said he was going to make sure no one gets too close and sets themselves on fire. After last year..." Hiro let that hang.

"What happened last year?" Arthur asked.

"A bunch of kids dared another kid to see how close he could get to one of the burnings and... Well, it didn't turn out so well. The kid died," Sok explained.

"So, when these dragonfoil trees burn up, they set everything around them on fire? How are there any forests left here? How often do people get killed?" Arthur was horrified at the thought of a child burning to death.

"Not often. But every now and then some idiot tries to see how close he can get. The dragonfoil fire doesn't harm other plants," Harpur explained.

"Would you like to see a burning, Arthur?" Sok asked.

"Sure," Arthur said. He was intrigued. A little disturbed, but curious nonetheless. And after the weird cookie thing, he thought he could use a bit of fresh air.

"Good idea," Harpur said. He couldn't have cared less about a dragonfoil burning, but after what he'd seen happen with Arthur, he thought it might be interesting to see how he reacted to one.

Cloaked against the late-autumn cold and drizzling rain, the foursome made their way to the east gate and out of the city. They could see a group of about one hundred people, also cloaked, huddling near a small thicket no more than a hundred meters from the wall. They were standing a good twenty-five yards away from the thicket looking at a large tree almost entirely denuded of foliage. Only three leaves remained on the branches.

Just as Harpur, Sok, Arthur and Hiro took their places among the crowd one of the leaves fluttered and fell to join its fellows piled around the trunk on the ground. The crowd cheered as, in unison, they all took a step farther back away from the dragonfoil. When neither of the other two leaves fell, they all started inching forward again. Two drenched guards and a soaking Davynn Willhart stepped forward to keep the crowd from passing the invisible twenty-five-yard mark.

"Isn't the rain going to keep the tree from burning up?" Arthur asked.

Sok shook his head. "Just watch."

Arthur watched. A gust of wind tugged at the last two leaves on the dragonfoil. They trembled on their branches, but held on. The crowd booed and tried to inch even closer. Davynn and the guards herded them back again.

Arthur felt like he was at a sporting event and didn't know the rules of the game. Wagers were being made around him. Two to one the highest leaf falls first. Five to one that they fall at the same time.

"Look!" a young boy shouted from the opposite end of the crowd.

Everyone turned in the direction the boy was pointing. In a thicket about a hundred yards south of where they were standing, a tree was glowing bright orange as if on fire from the inside. The glow intensified over several seconds and then the tree burst into flame, burning yellow at first and then turning blue-white. While the crowd's eyes were on the distant dragonfoil, another leaf dropped from the tree they had come to watch burn.

When they turned their attention back to it, a series of groans and moans accompanied by cheers rippled through the small throng. Coins began to change hands as wagers were grudgingly covered and gleefully collected.

The rain and wind picked up, causing the last leaf on the dragonfoil to twist and spin on its branch. Arthur pulled his cloak tighter against the inclement weather and began to regret his curiosity. He was tempted to march over to the tree and pluck the damned thing off himself just so he could get out of the weather and back into his warm cottage. Freezing his butt off to watch a tree burst into flame was quickly losing its appeal.

And then the crowd gasped. Arthur looked up at the tree to see the last leaf float slowly down through the branches until a gust of wind caught it and carried it back up into the air. It seemed to hang there for endless seconds before it flipped in a graceful loop and sunk straight down to the ground.

Davynn and the guards urged the crowd farther away and Arthur allowed himself to be herded with them. But he couldn't tear his eyes away from the tree. He backed up watching the strange phenomenon as it unfolded before him.

Like the first dragonfoil to burn, this one started to glow orange. It started in the trunk and spread upward and out through the branches. This close to it, Arthur could see the flame under the bark undulating in waves of red and black that streaked through the deepening orange glow. When it reached the outside of the bark, the tree became a silhouette of black ash suspended in the air. On the ground, tiny sparks drifted up from the purple-blue leaves in serpentine paths through the ashen silhouette that suddenly collapsed as a huge, purple conflagration surged upward to engulf the air where the dragonfoil had stood.

The crowd screeched in thrilled response to the burning. Arms and cloaks were lifted to protect them from a powerful current of heat that pushed them even further back and away. Only Arthur remained where he was, mesmerized by the sight of a dragon in the flames that seemed to be beckoning him forward into the fire.

Harpur had been watching Arthur closely and when he saw that the heat had no effect on him, rushed over to pull him away. "Pretend you feel the heat," Harpur hissed in Arthur's ear and he pulled him into the crowd.

"No!" Arthur struggled against Harpur. "Let me go!" But he was no match for Harpur's strength and by the time he was able to free himself from the dragon-wizard's grasp, the flames had dwindled to a soft blue and the dragon was gone.

"Did you see it?" Arthur was referring to the dragon in the flames. A few people close to him wondered how anyone could have missed a big tree going up in flames. No one other than Harpur and Arthur had seen the dragon.

"Not now," Harpur cautioned and when Arthur opened his mouth to protest, he repeated the warning, "Not now!"

As soon as the burning had ended, the crowd dispersed, running back to the gate to get out of the rain and wind. The guards, who would normally have remained stationed close to the thicket to keep away anyone foolish enough to try to collect ashes before they fully cooled, were permitted to retreat back to the gate and keep watch from there. Davynn didn't expect anyone to return that day. But one never knew! People do strange things.

Harpur, Sok, Arthur, Hiro and Davynn were the last through the gates. "We need to talk," Harpur said. "Davynn, can you come back to the cottage with us?"

"My office is closer," Davynn suggested. Rather than cross the entire city in the deluge, they took the closer option and followed Davynn back to his office in the castle annex where the Bounding Offices had once been. Bounding had somehow become Davynn's responsibility on top of everything else he was doing to keep the kingdom running.

Once inside the annex, they all shed their soaked cloaks and handed them to a young guard who hung them on a rack that had been set up next to a fireplace so they could dry. Sok went so far as to remove his boots and place them on the hearth. In spite of how damp he was, the cold, stone floor felt good on his bare feet. The others remained shodden, though Arthur did feel a pang of envy. His squelching boots felt wetter and colder now that they were inside.

Davynn led them through the warren of corridors to his office and ordered yet another guard to find extra chairs. When they were delivered, he instructed the guard to also bring something hot for them to drink. They got as comfortable as they could on the stiff, wooden chairs and Davynn invited Harpur to elaborate on whatever he needed so urgently to talk to them about. Rather than just saying what was on his mind, Harpur turned to Arthur.

"Tell them what you saw in the flames during the burning."

"So, now I can talk about it?" Arthur said snidely.

"Yes, now!"

"Okay." Arthur suddenly felt foolish, but he realized that Harpur had seen it, too, and he must have a reason for getting Arthur to say it instead saying it himself. "I saw a dragon."

Sok, who was stretching his feet out toward the little brazier next to Davynn's desk, turned to Arthur. "A dragon?"

Davynn simply raised his eyebrows.

Arthur took a deep breath, wishing that Harpur would help him out. "Yes. There was a dragon in the fire."

"You mean the flames looked like an image of a dragon. Like a face in the clouds." Davynn rationalized.

"No. There was a dragon in the fire. You saw it, didn't you, Harpur?"

"I did. But it wasn't a dragon so much as it was the essence of a dragon."

Arthur thought he was being thrown under a bus, but he couldn't quite reconcile how. "Define essence."

"Spirit. Soul. Ghost. Whatever. It doesn't matter. What matters is that you saw it."

"I'm lost," Davynn said with impatience. He had work to do. He always had work to do.

"I'm lost too," Arthur said, hoping no one thought he was crazy.

Harpur briefly brought Davynn up to speed on the dragon blood and how they didn't know how it was affecting Arthur. Davynn nodded. He still didn't know what any of this had to do with anything else.

"He also didn't feel the heat from the fire." Harpur added.

"There was heat?" Arthur asked. "All I felt was a bit of warmth in the wind for a second."

Sok, Arthur, Hiro and Davynn all looked blankly at Harpur. Dots were not connecting for any of them.

"Don't you see, Arthur? You're impervious to fire."

"Well, I don't know about that..."

Before he could finish, Harpur grabbed his arm and shoved his hand into the hot coals in the brazier.

Arthur started to scream. And then he stopped. His hand was on the red-hot coals, but it wasn't burning. All he felt was a comfortable warmth. Harpur let go of his arm and he pulled his hand away. He held it up and looked at it with astonishment.

"That's a neat trick," Davynn said, "but what has it got to do with our present situation?

"Everything!" Harpur said with more enthusiasm than either Sok or Arthur had ever seen. "I know what his trial is going to be."

Harpur explained the plan that started formulating in his head when he first saw the purple glow of dragon fire in Arthur's throat. When he had realized that Arthur could see Orhowyn in the flames and was not repelled by the heat from the burning dragonfoil, he understood the prophecy and knew what Arthur had to do.

"Oh, no!" Arthur objected, when Harpur had finished. "I'm not doing that!"

Harpur just smiled.

"So that's what your blood did to Arthur?" Sok asked. "That's what the prophecy meant by the fire that burns within him?"

No one answered Sok.

Davynn leaned back in his chair and crossed his arms. "Are you sure, Harpur?"

"I'm positive."

"Only fools are positive!" Arthur yelled.

"You'll be fine, Arthur," Harpur dismissed the slur. "Trust me." He winked at the mortified man.

Harpur asked Davynn to have a patrol keep an eye on the dragonfoils nearby and to let him know when a few medium sized trees were getting close to being ready to burn. "We'll need a few days, so none that are too close." Harpur qualified his request.

Then he took Sok aside and explained what he needed the elf to do. "Sure, Harpur, I'll do it right away."

"Traitor!" Arthur shouted at Sok's back as he left the office to do Harpur's bidding.

"You'll be fine!" Sok called back.

Davynn stood up and came out from behind his desk. "You're doing a brave thing," he said to Harpur.

"He's not doing anything!" Arthur squealed.

"You'll be fine." Davynn and Harpur said at the same time.

Davynn excused himself, leaving Harpur to deal with a seething Arthur. "If you want, we can find some dragonfoil and practice a few times."

Arthur just glared. "I'm not doing it. There's no way in hell I'm going to go through with this."

"You'll be fine. Now let's go to Skull's Keep and celebrate."

"Celebrate? What exactly are we celebrating? My pending death?"

Harpur ignored the sarcasm. "We figured out how my dragon blood is affecting you, for starters."

"And for after starters?"

"We have found the perfect trial for you. People will love it!"

"You're insane!" Arthur growled. He marched out of Davynn's office and down the hall oozing righteous indignation. Guards moved out of his way as he passed, so fierce was his aspect. At the first junction, he turned to his left.

Harpur followed Arthur to the junction where he had turned and called after him. "Arthur! The exit is this way."

Arthur stopped and took a deep breath before he did a one-eighty and marched back in the right direction. "Seriously, Harpur," he snarled as he past the grinning dragon-wizard, "you're nuts!"

Harpur laughed. "When it's done, I'll get you another hamburger!"

The young guard at the entrance handed them their cloaks, still damp from the rain and warm from the fire. Arthur was in too much of a mood to employ his manners, so it was left up to Harpur to be polite and say thank you for both of them. The guard remained un-thanked. All Arthur could do was storm out of the annex, storm across the castle gardens and keep storming through the maze of streets and lanes until, at last, he stormed into the cottage and slammed the door shut behind him. By that time, of course, his cloak was wet again and the rain had caused the warmth of the fire to bleed out of it completely. He threw the soggy garment on the floor and flopped down miserably onto the cot. Harpur, undeterred by the slamming of the cottage door, opened it and entered as well.

"Go away," Arthur commanded.

"No."

Harpur removed his own cloak and hung it on a peg next to the door. He picked up Arthur's cloak and hung it up too. Then he stoked the fire and settled himself on one of the stools, resting his elbow on his knees and clasping his hands between them.

"What are you so afraid of?" Harpur asked as gently as he could.

"I'm not afraid," Arthur mumbled into his pillow.

"Then what's with all this drama?" Harpur poked the bear to see how sharp its claws were.

Arthur's body stiffened on cot. He was acting like a petulant teenager and he knew it. If he didn't swallow his pride and reclaim his dignity right away, what kind of king would he be? He pushed himself up and sat on the edge of the cot facing Harpur.

"The dragon was calling me into the fire," he said quietly.

Hiro, who had accompanied them back to the cottage, was warming his hands by the fire. He remained quiet as Harpur continued.

"And you nearly went. If I hadn't noticed what was happening, you'd have walked into that fire. Wouldn't you?"

"I couldn't help myself."

"And that is what scared you, isn't it?" Harpur thought he'd figured it out.

"No." Arthur denied it. "Well, yes. That was pretty freaky. But what scared me was when you shoved my hand into the brazier and nothing happened." He subconsciously rubbed the hand as to make sure it was unharmed.

"I don't understand," Harpur said. "Why is that frightening?" Being a creature of fire, he couldn't see how Arthur could possibly see how being impervious to fire was a bad thing.

"It defies everything I thought I was. I don't know who I am now."

Ah! "You're Arthur Prentice," Harpur said. "You're just an enhanced version of him now. You have a superpower. You should be proud."

"But I don't want a superpower, Harpur. I don't want to be some... freak who can walk through fire and not get hurt. That's just... bizarre."

"Arthur, I've seen your comic book collection. Don't tell me you've never fantasized about having a superpower." Harpur cajoled.

Arthur rolled his eyes. "I'm not a twelve-year-old boy anymore. Those things aren't real!"

"They aren't?" Harpur was incredulous. "Arthur, you're living on a different world in a different universe. You're this close to becoming the king of a magical kingdom." He held his thumb and forefinger about a half-inch apart. "You're friends with an elf and a dragon and a witch and a Krist. How can you sit there and say those things aren't real when you've been living them for months?"

Arthur's head was spinning. He looked like he was about to cry.

Harpur stifled his amusement. "Look," he began, "I think you're just feeling a bit overwhelmed. I don't blame you. If you want, I can... you know... help you relax." Harpur wiggled his fingers to mime his magic.

Arthur slumped forward and rested his forehead in his hands. He didn't know what he wanted. But oblivion sounded pretty good. Using the heels of his hands, he wiped away the embarrassing tears and nodded as he laid down again. "Knock me out," he said, curling up on his side and closing his eyes.

Harpur stood and leaned over the fire-proof, would-be king. He tapped Arthur's head with his fingers and watched the tension melt out of the Arthur's body. "You'll be fine," he whispered, drawing the blanket up over Arthur's shoulders.

Turning to Hiro, Harpur sighed. "Anayah is safe, right?"

"Oh, yes!" Hiro affirmed. "As long as she stays inside the Sphere, no harm will come to her. Analeetah does have a few witches that are loyal to her stationed there, but they will not breach the protocols of sanctuary. She also has witches at every known Boundary to Thraeh keeping watch in case Anayah should somehow find a way to escape from the Sphere."

"Any thoughts on how we can help her?" Harpur was hoping for a simple solution. He had to grudgingly admire Analeetah's thoroughness.

"Short of persuading Analeetah to forgive Anayah, I'm afraid there isn't anything we can do." Hiro stared forlornly into the flames.

"I'm going to kill her," Harpur announced.

"And risk Anayah hating you? That doesn't sound like a wise course of action."

"If it means that Anayah is free and that she can get her magic back, I can live with her hating me."

"Can you, dragon?" For the first time since Harpur had met Hiro, there was contempt in his voice. "You once spurned her love for you. Now you say you can live with her hatred? I don't believe you."

"I'm a dragon. I don't feel love that way," Harpur growled defensively.

"I know what being in human form does to your kind," Hiro said. "You cannot convince me that you have no feelings for Anayah. You are willing to kill Analeetah to set her free, but you cannot live with her hating you for it. It would be your undoing, Harpur. You know this as well as I do."

Harpur growled. "I'm going to Skull's Keep."

Leaving the Krist to watch over Arthur, Harpur left the cottage and made his way through the rain to the public house. He wanted to leave the city and fly in his true form through the night. But he couldn't do that anymore. His wing was badly misshapen and prevented him from flying more than a few miles at a time. He feared being seen flopping through the sky like a fledgling dragon just out of the egg. He missed the gracefully majestic landings after a flight as well. Now he had to tuck his damaged wing in and crash and roll when he came out of the sky. Every time he did transform, he worried that another dragon would sense his weakness. It was only a matter of time before he would be challenged. And he would lose.

Now that he knew what his blood had done to Arthur, there was a chance that Arthur's powers could heal him completely. Unless it was just too late. It *was* too soon to tell. Arthur needed time to adjust and to learn the full extent of his abilities. He had to get through the trial and be crowned first. *Sok better have done what I asked.*

THE FIRE OF ORHOWYN

When Harpur entered Skull's Keep, he was in a foul mood indeed. He shook off his cloak and stamped the mud off his boots with such force, cups and plates bounced on the tables nearby. Instinctively, patrons shied away from him and averted their eyes. Across the room, he saw Sok sitting at a table with a skinny blonde man with a lyre. On his way over to them, Harpur barked at a barmaid to bring him some ale.

"We're almost done," Sok said as Harpur pulled out a chair and sat down next to the skinny blonde man. The skinny blonde man was instantly frozen by the energy that Harpur was exuding.

"Hurry it up," Harpur snapped. He reached across the table, snatched up Sok's tankard of ale and downed what was left.

Sok, more familiar with Harpur's idiosyncrasies than the appalled skinny blonde minstrel was at seeing someone steal someone else's ale, recognized the black mood for what it was. Something had reminded Harpur of his waning dragonhood. "I'll get more ale."

The minstrel was horrified to see the elf walk away and leave him alone with the cranky giant. He wanted to scuttle off, but was afraid to move.

"When will you be ready to sing?" Harpur growled.

"Now?" the minstrel squeaked.

"Then do it." Harpur ordered. The minstrel couldn't get up fast enough. "And do it right!"

Sok returned with three tankards of ale. "I had to start a tab," he said pushing two of the tankards toward Harpur and keeping one for himself.

Harpur's eyes glowed orange, but he withdrew a handful of coins from his pocket and gave them to Sok.

"Thank you," Sok said. "What did you do to Olly?"

Harpur turned his head toward the huge open fire place where the minstrel, Olly, was tuning his lyre and preparing to sing for the crowd. The bard looked shaken and nervous. Harpur didn't bother to reply.

Sok smiled. "You're going to like this," he said.

As the minstrel strummed the first few chords, the crowd quieted to listen. Songs about the prophecy had become quite popular in the weeks since Bloomregaard's failed coup and Olly's melodic rendition of it was favoured among the Skull's Keep patrons for its vivid lyrics and upbeat rhythm. Like most bards, Olly delivered his song of the prophecy with a measure of theatre, telling his audience that it was an ancient tune written by the elves and passed down through untold generations. In the absence of a king, the prophecy had been quickly adopted and the song instantly *remembered* from childhoods. Olly didn't need the credit for the composition; he only needed the coins people dropped into his hat while he sang it.

That night, as Olly softly strummed his lyre, he looked out across the tavern and regaled his fans with a new twist to the tale.

"I was walking in Braydon Wood the other day," Olly began, "and I happened across an elf of great age. He asked me if I knew of the prophecy of the king of Epoh and I assured him that I did indeed. 'How will we know the king we are promised?' I asked the elf, and he gave me a scroll as ancient as himself." Olly paused for effect, strumming a mysterious strain of chords on his lyre.

"What did the scroll say!" someone in the crowd shouted.

Sok watched as the whole room seemed to lean closer to Olly, eager to know what was on the scroll.

Olly smiled and enigmatic smile. "The scroll was written in the elven language. I couldn't read it myself, but when I turned to ask the old elf what it said..." he paused again. "...the elf was gone."

Disappointed groans filled the room.

"Fear not!" Olly shouted. "I have friends among the elves. I took that scroll to one of them and asked him to tell me what it said. He told me..." Olly strummed his lyre dramatically. "...it was the song of the prophecy."

"Sing it for us!" another patron shouted.

"But..." Olly ramped up the dramatic strumming and the crowd held its collective breath. "...but it was different than the one you all know."

"How was it different?"

"Tell us!"

Olly smiled again. "There was another verse. A verse that has been missing for over a century!"

The crowd oohed.

"Listen now and I will sing for you the complete prophecy of the king..."

THE FIRE OF ORHOWYN

In elder days when stars were young,
And shadows cloaked the land,
A dragon rose with silver tongue,
And flame at his command.
His wings could blot the morning sun,
His roar could crack the stone—
Xzynthyrius the Dreamfinder,
On mountain made his throne.
The kings they pled, the mages fled,
No army dared to stand.
He scorched the fields with dragonfire
And ruled with molten hand.
But one there was who dared the flame,
A knight with heart of steel—
Orhowyn Bravvenshyn,
With blade and burning will.
At dusk they met on crimson ridge,
'Neath skies of ashen gold.
Steel rang on scale, blood scorched the earth,
As battle fierce took hold.
The dragon roared, the knight struck true,
The mountains shook with cries—
And when the dawn at last arose,
The Dreamfinder had died.
But death was not the end that day—
The fire would not be slain.
It seeped into the roots below
And whispered through the rain.
Where dragon's breath had kissed the soil,
A silver sapling grew,
And every fall, its leaves ignite—
The flame is born anew.
So, raise your cup and honor both—
The dragon and the man.
One burned the world to test its soul,

The other shaped its plan.
But hush, good folk, and listen well—
The tale is not yet done.
The fire sleeps, but dreams again,
Beneath a second sun.
A silver leaf, a sacred coin,
A well beneath the moon—
A voice that sings through mists of green,
Foretells a rising soon.
A child is lost beyond the veil,
A king not yet aware—
He bears the fire within his blood,
But does not know it's there.
And one shall come to light the way,
An elven heart made true,
To bind the fates with ancient thread
And see the questing through.
When silver fox is held aloft,
And coin is passed with care,
The flame shall bloom, the crown be claimed,
And dragon's soul laid bare.
So, mark the leaves, and heed the signs,
And watch the burning tree—
From its flames a king shall rise
To shape what is to be.

While Olly's rich tenor crooned to the rapt audience, Harpur drank his ale. "What did you tell him to add?"

Sok leaned across the table to whisper so that no one nearby could hear him. "Just what you told me to tell him, that one of the elders gave me a copy of the prophecy that said the king would be known when a drifter walks into the dragonfoil fire and lives."

Harpur nodded. As the song progressed, he watched the crowd. Several people had little silver fox figurines. When the bards had first started singing the song of the prophecy, the small icons started to appear in the market. People bought them, hoping they would be the one to receive the coin and become the new king. One by one, as they learned how the king would be recognized, the figurines disappeared into pockets. Harpur shook his head in bemusement. *We're going to have to guard every dragonfoil around Colwygshire. At least one idiot is going to try to walk into the flames.*

Arthur awoke early the next morning to find Hiro sleeping in the hover gilly. The events of the previous day came back to him slowly as he lay on his cot and tried to orient himself to his new life with a superpower. Still in his clothes from the day before, he felt sticky and uncomfortable. A shower and clean clothes were in order. He stood up and stretched, and then began undressing. The chill in the cottage drew his attention to the fireplace where embers from the logs Harpur had used to stoke the fire with the night before glowed red in the grate. It wouldn't take much to get it going again.

Using the poker that hung beside the fireplace, Arthur pushed the embers around to open them up and expose the unburnt portions of the logs. Small flames erupted, eager to consume the remaining wood. He squatted down and stared into the dainty flames that danced across the logs like tiny orange ghosts. He could feel their warmth, but there was no threat, no warning, in it. Slowly, he reached out to the fire. As his hand drew closer, he expected the heat to hurt him and was ready to pull it back the second he felt any pain. But the pain didn't come. All there was, was a sense of comforting warmth. Taking a deep breath, he reached into the flames and picked up a piece of log that had broken free. Amazement replaced the cautious trepidation he had always employed around open flames. He held it in his palm for several seconds waiting for his flesh to burn. When nothing happened, he tossed it back onto the grate and added a few pieces of kindling and three logs to the dying fire.

He watched, mesmerized, until they caught and started to burn. *Maybe Harpur's plan isn't so insane after all.*

In the shower, Arthur thought about... Well, everything! But his mind kept coming back to what Harpur had said the night before. *'You're friends with an elf and a dragon.'* Harpur considered him a friend. It's not like the word hadn't been tossed around between them before, but there had been meaning in what Harpur had said and Arthur felt honoured. He also felt guilty about the way he so often treated Harpur. And Sok. And with the difficulties Harpur was facing on a personal level with his unhealed wounds and the toll being in human form was taking, Arthur needed to step up his game as a friend. No more flying off the handle. Sok and Harpur were on his team...

Team Fireman... No! Team Blazeboy... Um, hell no! Team Inferno-man... That isn't too bad. No! This isn't all about me!

Arthur finished his shower and got dressed. He'd given up shaving; that straight razor scared the bejesus out of him. And his hair had long since lost all any style. He'd taken to wearing a cap most of the time to keep the longer locks in check. He was about to head to the market to get something to eat when Sok burst through the door, followed by Harpur.

"Good morning!" Arthur greeted them.

"Good morning," Sok returned the greeting.

"You're in a good mood," Harpur observed.

"I am," Arthur concurred. "What's on the agenda for today?"

Hiro stirred on the hover gilly and sat up.

"Not a lot," Harpur said, sitting down at the table and motioning Sok to bring the basket of food they'd brought with them. "Sok had a minstrel add some new verses to the song last night at Skull's Keep. The city is buzzing with the news. We are going to have to put our plan into action soon."

"How soon?" Arthur poured himself some jamba and took a sip.

"As soon as possible," Harpur said.

Arthur felt a jolt of excitement that he hadn't expected. Part of him was terrified of what Harpur wanted him to do, but another part, a part deep inside him, was bursting with the thrill of it. He pushed the thoughts aside, afraid that if he thought about it too much, the terrified part would win.

"Who's watching the Boundary these days?" Arthur asked. He needed to change the subject.

"There's not been a lot of activity lately. People are more concerned about not having a king. I have a patrol check it regularly." Harpur said. "Why?"

"I was just wondering. It seemed to be a big deal when I first met you... Not letting folks Bound to earth, that is. It just struck me as odd that you're not on Whyte Avenue anymore."

"I was on Whyte Avenue to keep an eye on you, Arthur." Harpur wondered where Arthur was going with this.

"Oh! I didn't realize that was the only reason you were there."

"It wasn't. I was there to catch Bounders and return them here for prosecution."

"So, Bounding isn't as illegal as you made it out to be?"

"No. It's illegal. We don't want humans from Earth coming here. What is this about?"

"So, it's just the Boundaries to Earth that are the problem."

"More or less."

"How many Boundaries to Earth are there in Epoh?"

"Just in Epoh?"

Arthur nodded.

"Just the one, as far as I know."

"Well, why don't we build a keep around it and enchant the entrance so that no one can Bound without permission?"

"That's brilliant!" Sok exclaimed.

Harpur could have pointed out all the problems with that idea. It was all he could do not to scowl at Sok. If anyone sitting at the table should know that the elves would not so openly embrace a structure being built in the forest, he should have. But this is the kind of thing a king should be thinking about. And it would be an excellent way at some future date for Arthur to learn how diplomacy worked on Thraeh. For now, though, he just nodded and affirmed his support.

Arthur wasn't convinced that Harpur was behind this idea one hundred percent. "I just thought that it would be nice if you didn't have to be on Whyte Avenue anymore and were here to help me... and Sok... while I'm learning the ropes." This friendship thing was trickier than he thought.

"You don't think I'm good enough to be your senior advisor?" Sok's offence meter was rising.

"I just think I'm going to need all the help I can get." Arthur pushed an olive branch in the form of a scone toward the elf.

"We can work all the details of that out later," Harpur said, reaching for a scone of his own. *I wonder how long I will be able to help him...*

Arthur spent the day wandering around Colwygshire. The sky was still overcast, but the rain stayed at bay as he made his way through the streets to the market. People were talking about the king. Or rather the lack of a king. There was much speculation about the drifter who would walk into the dragonfoil flames. They wondered where it would happen, when it would happen and hoped they would be there to see it. Some folks said that it was impossible for anyone to survive a burning and that the prophecy was symbolic. Symbolic of what, they did not know.

Arthur wondered how they would react to him as their king. *Will they like me? Will they even accept me?* Harpur's plan was pretty spectacular, but was a bit of theatre enough? If this was a political campaign and his wearing a crown came down to a matter votes, would he win? *Not likely.*

But this was a different world. A different culture than he was used to. This was a world where influence was swayed by magic. Once that crown was placed on his head, it would be there until he died. And that was not necessarily a good thing. He was glad he would have Sok and Harpur looking out for him.

He made his way to the castle gardens and found a bench to sit on where he could watch the masons working on the tower. Davynn had insisted that they use as many stones from the old tower as possible to keep expenses down. Arthur admired his foresight and efficiency and he hoped that Davynn would be among his advisers. The charismatic young captain's leadership abilities were so natural and he had the admiration and respect he so deserved. Arthur wanted to find a way to reward him for all he was doing. *A knighthood? How cool will it be to make men knights?*

Arthur's attention turned to a mound of rubble at the far end of the garden. The stones from the tower that were too damaged to be reused had been piled up out of the way into an unsightly reminder of what Bloomregaard had conspired to do. He wasn't sure what, yet, but he thought he could do something with those broken bits of the old tower... *A monument to those who had died when the tower exploded, perhaps?*

It was all a bit premature Arthur knew. First, he had to be crowned. Then he could make decisions.

He was about to leave and return to his cottage when Sok and Harpur came out of the castle. They descended the wide steps and crossed the circular, cobblestone plaza at the head of the main road leading down to the city gates. Neither of them noticed Arthur in the gardens as they walked purposefully down the road, so he made his way to an arched opening in the hedge that bordered the gardens and joined them on the road.

"Hey! Wait up," Arthur called out.

Sok and Harpur stopped and turned to wait for him. "There you are," Sok said. "We were just on our way to the cottage to see you."

They fell into step together and continued down the road. "How are things going in there?" Arthur asked.

"Oh, you know," Harpur said. "Lots of bickering. Not a lot of common sense. Davynn will be happy to see you *not* burn."

"So will I!" Arthur said.

"Why don't we head over to Skull's Keep for some supper? I'd like to hear the gossip about the prophecy." Harpur suggested.

"Where's Hiro?" Sok asked. "We should find him?"

"He said he had to return to Mysturna and he left right after breakfast." Arthur said. "I tried to convince him to wait until after the... you know... but he said he would gone for a while."

Hiro's jaunts to his home world were common. Harpur didn't think that either Sok or Arthur would be too suspicious about this one. The Krist was on a mission.

Arthur had hoped to spend some time with the Krist figuring out how to make his cell phone work. But they'd had hardly any time alone over the past days of training and when Hiro had announced his intentions that morning, Arthur was annoyed. "I will help you with the device," Hiro had said. "But there's something I need to do." No amount of cajoling would change Hiro's mind.

As usual, Skull's Keep was bustling with trade. It was standing room only in the tavern and Olly was in his spot next to the fireplace, singing about the prophecy. *Soon,* Harpur thought, *he'll have another new verse to add.*

The trio made their way to the bar and ordered stew and ale from the harried barmaid. "Make sure Olly is well taken care of tonight," Harpur said, dropping extra coins on the wood to cover the minstrel's tab as well as their own. Sok noticed a group of men about to leave their table in the far corner and put his elven skills to use wending his way through the crowd to claim it, barely beating out three other men with the same intention. "Sorry, mates," he said, sliding onto a chair and smiling at them.

Arthur and Harpur waited for their food and drink and carried it to the table Sok had procured. All around them, people were indeed gossiping about the prophecy. It seemed that it was all anyone could talk about. Harpur tuned his keen dragon hearing into the chatter and was satisfied that people knew what to expect. Wagers were being made as to when and where the big event might take place. Plans were being made to camp out at different dragonfoil trees near the city. There was a noticeable absence of silver fox figurines.

"So, when are we doing this?" Arthur asked, feeling the trepidation creeping back in.

"Give it a few days. Let the first wave of anticipation run its course. People will soon move on to something else." Harpur said. "People are already tying Gnik's untimely death to the prophecy, so they are expecting something soon. But we don't want to make it seem too easy."

"Yeah, well, you're not the one who has to..."

Arthur was interrupted by a shout and a loud crash coming from across the pub. A fight had broken out between two men, both a little too far into their cups, who were staggering about and swinging wildly at each other. Others, not wanting to be on the receiving end of a poorly aimed fist, were giving the pugilists space and the publican was already shouting an eviction notice at the two brawlers.

"What is that all about?" Arthur wondered aloud as scooped up some succulent stew from his bowl.

"If I had to guess, they are at odds about the prophecy." Harpur didn't have to guess. His keen dragon hearing had picked up parts of the exchange between the two men before the fighting started. They had been discussing which of the two of them were more likely the subject of the prophecy.

Within minutes, the two men had been muscled out of the tavern and pushed into the street with a warning not to return until they had sobered up and could conduct themselves properly. Harpur, Sok and Arthur, like everyone else in the room, continued to eat and drink. Olly continued to sing about a new king on fire.

Arthur turned his attention to the song Olly was singing. About him. It was strange to think that he was the subject of such bizarre events. He listened to the words and tapped his toes to the melody.

A man carrying a flagon of ale came toward the table. As he passed, he dropped a coin and it bounced and landed next to Arthur's foot. He picked it up and went after the man to return it.

"Excuse me," Arthur shouted over the noise of the crowd. "You dropped this."

The man deposited his ale on a table and turned around to see who was talking to him. He took the proffered coin from Arthur. "Thank you, friend," he said, extending his free hand to shake Arthur's hand and introduce himself. "Marc Reaver."

Arthur's mouth fell open. He shook the man's hand and returned to Harpur and Sok.

"You look like you've just seen a ghost," Sok observed.

"Just a Reaver." Arthur shook off the shock and smiled.

The first snow of the winter season fell over night and Arthur woke up to a world covered in icy whiteness. It was the perfect distraction as people busied themselves clearing the wet slush from the streets, piling it into carts and dragging it out beyond the city walls to dump it. Children filled the squares and common greens, building snow castles and pelting each other with snowballs before the adults could clear their playgrounds and assign other, more productive chores. Like shovelling sand from the sand carts onto the icy streets and walkways. Arthur quickly learned that a skating gait was safer than walking wherever there was no sand. He took a crude drawing he had sketched out to one of the blacksmiths and paid him to make six small bars with spikes on one long edge and join three together with a flat bar that ran perpendicular to the three spiked bars. He had the blacksmith attach small loops to either side of the spiked bars.

While the blacksmith made the strange contraptions, Arthur went to a nearby cobbler and purchased six long, leather straps. When the blacksmith was done his work, Arthur took the odd-looking things and laced the leather straps through the loops. He then tied them to his feet and walked safely back and forth on the ice outside the forge to demonstrate his *new invention*.

The blacksmith was impressed and started calculating the money he could make providing Arthur with the traction bars, as he called them. He assumed Arthur would be going into business.

"Tell you what," Arthur said. "If you don't charge me for these ice walkers, you can make them and sell them yourself."

The blacksmith, liking Arthur's name for them better than his own, shook on it before Arthur could see the folly of his ways and dispatched one of his apprentices to go and buy as many leather straps as he could from the cobbler. He could hear the jingling of coins filling his purse already.

It took Arthur twice as long to get back to the cottage. Everyone who noticed Arthur's feet, stopped him to ask where he'd got the ice walkers. By the time he got home, a long line had formed outside the blacksmith's forge. Orders were being made and measurements were being taken. Within days, the other blacksmiths in town would get in on the action, but by then, the blacksmith Arthur had make his own traction devices was imagining a comfortable retirement.

Arthur was finally sitting in the warmth of the cabin, unstrapping his improvised ice walkers when Sok burst through the door. "It's time," he announced. "What are those?"

"Now?" Arthur groaned. "I just got in. They are ice walkers."

"Interesting," Sok said with something less than interest. "Let's go. Harpur is waiting for us down by the gate."

Arthur re-tied the straps, grabbed his cloak and looked longingly at the freshly stoked fire in his hearth. He followed Sok through the labyrinth of streets from the cottage to the main city gate. It was annoying how the ice didn't seem to bother the elf as he walked across it as if it wasn't there.

"How do you do that?" Arthur asked.

"Do what?"

"Walk on the ice without slipping?"

"I'm an elf." As if that explained everything. "Why do humans fall down on it all the time?"

"Because it's slippery." Arthur thought that should be obvious.

"Bah," Sok scoffed. "If you were better connected to the earth, it wouldn't be a problem."

Arthur decided not to pursue that. They continued to the gate and found Harpur standing among a group of guards. A burning was expected and a throng of people were making their way out onto the road to go and watch it. The guards were supposed to be there to keep anyone from attempting to get close to the fire when the dragonfoil burned. Harpur was re-assigning them to another expected burning, assuring them that he would keep the onlookers safe at the this one. It was that time of year and the guards were used to a change of plans. Harpur's authority wasn't even questioned when he informed them that Davynn himself had asked Harpur to do this. Davynn was already making his way to the burning and would be there to assist Harpur if things got out of hand.

They watched the guards walk northward toward their new assignment.

"What in Orhowyn's name are on your feet?" Harpur asked, looking at the ice walkers strapped to Arthur's boots. "Never mind. I don't want to know. Let's get going."

They followed the small crowd of people making their way out to the road and south to where the dragonfoil was quickly shedding its leaves. "Do you know what you have to do?" Harpur asked Arthur.

"From its flames a king shall rise to shape what is to be," he quoted from the Olly's song.

"You have to time it right," Harpur instructed. "You can't go in too soon or someone might try to stop you."

"I know. I know," Arthur snapped. He was nervous and didn't care if Harpur knew it.

"How are you going to keep anyone from stopping him," Sok asked.

"I've got a plan." Harpur didn't elaborate.

"I might not mind so much if someone did stop me. This is insane," Arthur said.

"You'll be fine," Sok and Harpur said together, taking Arthur by the arms in case he bolted at the last minute.

The dragonfoil was situated at the edge of the forest, not far from the footpath that led to the Boundary. The crowd was gathering on the road, keeping a safe distance from the nearly-leafless tree. Davynn was, indeed, already there, directing people to stay back. When he saw Harpur, Sok and Arthur approach, he made a bit of a show of announcing to the crowd that they were going to assist him that day. He wanted the people to know that they needed to respect his deputized helpers.

Harpur and Arthur were sent to the south end of the crowd and told to stand on the forest side of the road. Sok and Davynn would remain at the north end. The crowd was informed that they would need to move off the road and stay on the far side away from the dragonfoil. There was some moaning as they reluctantly moved back, but no one defied the orders Davynn delivered in a firm and decisive tone.

The dragonfoil was hanging on to a dozen or so leaves when the crowd finally settled into a safe position across the road. One by one the leaves dropped. With all eyes glued to the tree, Harpur and Arthur inched farther away from the edge of the road, shortening the gap between them and dragonfoil. They couldn't go too far. They had to look like they were guarding the crowd.

Finally, the last leaf dropped.

The crowd started to surge forward and Davynn and Sok moved quickly out onto the road in front of them to wave them back. Harpur and Arthur kept their eyes on the dragonfoil, but moved in front of the crowd as if they were backing up Sok and Davynn in keeping the crowd away.

The dragonfoil started to glow orange.

"Not yet," Harpur hissed.

"I know!" Arthur hissed back.

Then the sparks from the leaves started to rise.

"Not yet."

"I know!"

When the purple-blue flames engulfed the tree, Arthur turned completely away from the crowd. He saw the dragon beckoning him into the flames and he knew he would, indeed be fine.

"Now!" Harpur shouted.

But Arthur was already running toward the fire.

Screams and shouts followed him as he sprinted forward against the wall of heat. He heard Davynn yelling at him to get back, but knew it was all for show. The dragon in the fire reached out as Arthur drew closer. Slowing down, Arthur took Orhowyn's outstretched hand and walked into the flames.

He could no longer hear the panicking, horrified crowd. Surrounded by flames, there was only the roar of the fire, a deafening rumble like thunder, that he felt as much as heard. Next to him, the image of Orhowyn loomed up and he saw the ancient dragon's wings wrap protectively around him. He stood there, feeling the flames, but not the heat. They seemed to fill him, energizing him, changing him, though he couldn't tell how. Then suddenly it ended. The flames died and Orhowyn vanished.

Arthur looked over at the crowd not sure what he was supposed to do.

The crowd stared back at him, disbelief and shock on every single face.

Several moments passed as everyone gathered tried to process what had just happened.

"The prophecy," Sok finally said. "This is our king!"

"Mama?" a small voice spoke up. "Why is that man naked?"

Chapter 22

"So, Arthur, how does it feel to be king of Epoh at last?" Davynn Willhart leaned forward to see the newly-crowned king sitting two places to this left.

"I'd feel a lot better about it if someone had bothered to warn me that my clothes were not impervious to fire." Arthur glared at Harpur, sitting on his left. He still blamed the dragon-wizard for this oversight. The embarrassing end to what was supposed to have been an epic fulfillment of the prophecy was not the climax he had imagined.

"Are you still going on about that?" Harpur rolled his eyes. "Let it go, Arthur."

"In your defence," Sok, sitting between Arthur and Davynn, said, "it was really, really cold out."

Harpur and Davynn burst into laughter.

"To warmer days ahead!" Harpur toasted.

Everyone, but Arthur raised a cup.

The truth was, Arthur didn't know how he felt. The past few weeks since the prophecy debacle were nothing but a blur. When he had returned to the city on the shoulders of the cheering witnesses at the burning, wearing nothing but Harpur's cloak, he was afraid they were going to slap a crown on his head right there. Harpur and Davynn had had to intervene and finally managed to wrestle him out of the hands of his new-found admirers and spirit him into the castle. It had been touch and go. Literally!

After that, it had been non-stop speeches and fittings and dance lessons and coronation rehearsals and more speeches and more fittings and a parade of noblemen and merchants currying favour by promising to pledge allegiance to him. Suddenly, he was surrounded by food tasters and servants and everyone was calling him M' Lord. By the time someone... Arthur had no idea who... had plopped the crown on his head, Arthur was a walking zombie. The coronation feast he now found himself at was the first chance he'd had in weeks to just sit and relax.

If only this stupid crown fit properly. Arthur removed it from his head and hooked it on one of the spindles on the back of his chair.

A collective gasp rose up from the revelers attending the feast. Arthur put the crown back on his head. The revelers returned to reveling.

"What?" he said. "It doesn't fit properly. And it's heavy."

Sok snapped his fingers and a footman sprung to his side. He whispered something to the footman, who bowed away and disappeared to return a few minutes later with a smaller, lighter circlet, which he handed to the elf. The heavy crown was replaced and three guards stepped forward to take the offending diadem to the royal vault.

"Feel better?" Harpur asked, suppressing a smile.

"I will when I can go to bed. How much longer is this going to last?"

"The rest of your life, I'm afraid," Harpur said. "Drink up. The entertainment is about to begin."

Arthur groaned.

Servants began clearing away dishes and rearranging food so the king could continue to snack at his leisure. Cups were filled with wine and music began to play.

"Your majesty," Sok said, nodding his head toward the floor.

"I really don't feel like dancing," Arthur protested.

"It's tradition," Sok said. Protocol forbade the elf from standing up before the king, but nothing prevented him from poking Arthur in the ribs to get him moving.

"Ow!" Arthur hollered, raising eyebrows throughout the great hall. "Fine! I'll go. Who am I supposed to dance with anyway?"

As if on cue, the doors to the hall opened and every head turned to see who was crashing the party. The coronation feast was by invitation only and no one should have been granted entrance after it had begun.

All Arthur could see at first, was the silhouette of a woman backlit by the torches that burned in the outer hall. But as she walked slowly into the room, Arthur's mouth dropped open. He couldn't believe what he was seeing.

"Alex." He could barely breathe.

Alex walked slowly forward, letting everyone in the room take in her elegant, midnight-blue gown. Her normally unruly curls were pinned up with sapphire combs and a simple sapphire pendant shone from a silver chain around her neck. She stopped when she reached the middle of the open space in front of the head table and smiled up at King Arthur.

"How?" Arthur looked at Harpur for the answer.

"Go get her, tiger," Harpur said. There would be time for explanations later.

The footman rushed to pull Arthur's chair away so he wouldn't knock it over in his attempt to get to the vision waiting for him on the dance floor. Amid curious murmuring and craning necks, Arthur ran to Alex and kissed her. He couldn't speak through the tears of joy.

"Just dance," she whispered, placing a hand on Arthur's shoulder and letting her own tears fall.

The music changed to a slow waltz and the two of them started to dance.

"How did you get here?" Arthur asked when he finally was able to compose himself.

"The same way you did, I suspect." Alex smiled. "You look amazing by the way."

"Oh, Alex. You are so beautiful. I'd almost forgotten how cute you are."

When the music ended, Alex took Arthur's arm and allowed him to lead her back to the head table. The chairs had been rearranged so that Alex was now seated between Arthur and Harpur, whom Arthur kept looking questioningly at. Harpur just smiled as he and the others stood to politely welcome Alex.

Arthur turned to Sok. "Can you get some food for Alex, please?"

"I've already eaten," she said. "But a cup of that wine might help take the edge off." She nodded to the pitcher on the table.

Sok snapped his fingers again and a serving girl appeared to pour the wine for Alex.

"Are you okay?" Alex asked the girl, whose eyes were red and puffy from crying.

"I'm fine, M' Lady," the girl said, shooting a scathing look at Alex and Arthur before leaving.

"I think you may have just broken a few hearts," Harpur said, passing the wine cup to a taster before Alex could drink from it.

"I think I'll pass after all," Alex said through a fake smile.

"I know it's weird," Arthur said to Alex, "but we'll probably get used to it." Then he looked at Alex with alarm. "You are staying here, aren't you?"

"I think so." Alex looked at Harpur. "Hiro and Harpur kept saying that I had to be sure. I don't think they want me Bounding back and forth."

"Hiro? What's he got to do with it?" The Krist's absence over the past weeks had not gone unnoticed. Nor had it been explained. Arthur had assumed he was on Mysturna.

Harpur leaned back and Hiro, now seated on his right, leaned forward and wiggled his fingers at the king.

"Hiro! You're back. Where have you been?" Arthur was relieved to see him again.

"Hello, Sire," Hiro said, giggling loudly.

"This is crazy!" Arthur was giddy with joy. And wine and fatigue. But mostly with joy. "I don't understand. How did you guys...? What made you...? Where did you...?"

"Relax, Arthur." Alex was much more poised than the king. "We'll explain everything in time."

Arthur looked at Alex and smiled. He took her hand and kissed it.

As the evening wore on, bards and jesters and dancers and more bards and more jesters and more dancers sang and recited and juggled and jiggled while Davynn, Sok, Harpur, Alex and Hiro told Arthur how Alex and Hiro had come to be at the feast.

Harpur hadn't wiped Alex's memory that night on Whyte Avenue when she sent Arthur to Thraeh alone. When they found out about Arthur's powers and had a solid plan to fulfil the prophecy, Harpur had sent Hiro to Whyte Avenue to find Alex. She had regretted not going with Arthur and agreed to come to Thraeh with Hiro. She had been living in another council house waiting until the coronation feast to surprise Arthur. She had even been at the dragonfoil burning when Arthur fulfilled the prophecy.

"Oh, my god! You saw that?" Arthur was horrified.

"It's not like I haven't seen it before," Alex said.

Arthur waggled his eyebrows at her. "Would you like to see it again?"

Everyone agreed that Arthur had fulfilled his duty and told them to go. Between a bard and a juggler, Arthur stood up and announced that he would be retiring for the night. "It's been a long, amazing day," he said. "Please feel free to party as long as you like."

The revelers cheered. The servants groaned.

And Alex and Arthur left under escort to retire for the night.

"I guess now we have to plan a wedding," Sok said.

Alex and Arthur spent the night together the way that lovers who have been apart for a while do. In each other's arms, renewing their connection. It wasn't about the sex. Though that was part of it. It was about rediscovering each other and erasing the time they had spent apart.

Entering the king's private chambers as the king for the first time and with Alex on his arm, was about the biggest rush he'd ever felt. He thought he really could pull this off with Alex by his side. He couldn't wait to touch her, but he hungered just as much to hear about what she had been doing since he'd left. They made love. Then they talked. Then they made love again. Then they talked. They laughed. They cried. They laid quietly holding each other. Arthur didn't know how he managed, but the sun was coming up before he finally fell asleep.

A few hours later, Arthur was woken up by the sound of the door banging against the wall. He sat up, groggy and bleary-eyed, to see who had dared to disturb him and Alex. It was the indomitable Finch, carrying a tray with food and a pitcher of steaming jamba. As usual she was talking non-stop, not caring if anyone was listening.

"...not right for a king to still be abed at this hour. First day on the job and already you're slacking off. Just because you didn't burn up in that dragonfoil fire doesn't mean you get to lay about all day. There's things to be done. A kingdom in need of ruling. And whatever tart you got in that bed with you better not be expecting any special treatment. Best be sending her on her way back to the kitchens where she belongs."

Finch put the tray down on the table and drew back the curtains.

"Your valet's been standing out in the hall for two hours waiting for you to rise. Poor man's afraid to come in here. Thinks he'll get himself tossed over the balcony if he disturbs you or some such nonsense."

She poured a cup of jamba.

"I'll be sending Rupert in to do what you're paying him to do. Maid's on her way up to make up the bed and tidy this place up, so you best be putting on a dressing gown. No need to go showing off your royal sceptre and giving her ideas. It's hard enough to keep those girls from tearing each other apart over you. I expect she'll get her turn soon enough. Though the way they were carrying on down there after the feast..." Still muttering away, Finch took her leave.

"What was that?" Alex had woken up.

"Castle icon."

A timid looking man with a large nose, no chin and a humongous Adam's apple peeked into the room.

"Can I help you?" Arthur asked.

"I... I... I'm so s...s...sorry, Sire," the man said. "F-f-f-inch told me you were r-r-r-ready to be d-d-dressed."

"I can dress myself... Rupert, is it?"

Rupert nodded. So did his Adam's apple.

"Thanks anyway, Rupert. You can go now."

"Wow!" Alex giggled. "You sound like a king."

"I... I... I'm sorry, sire, but it's m-m-my j-j-job."

"Yes. Well, I'm sure Sok can find something else for you to do. I'll speak to him later. I really don't need anyone to dress me." Arthur really just wanted the man to leave.

"Oh, come on!" Alex thumped Arthur's arm. "Let the man do his job. Rupert, would you mind tossing me that robe?" She pointed at a purple dressing gown hanging from a peg next to a wardrobe on the other side of the room.

"That is the royal robe, miss." Rupert seemed to be gaining some confidence.

"It's okay, Rupert. Give the lady the robe," Arthur said impatiently.

"But, Sire..."

"Rupert," Arthur said between clenched teeth, "the lady asked you to give her the robe."

"Very well, Sire. But..."

"And then get out."

Rupert took the royal robe off its hook and brought it over to the bed.

"Thank you, Rupert," Alex chirped. "I could get used to this," she said to Arthur as she somehow managed to wrap her cute hippie girl self in the luxurious robe without giving Rupert any ideas.

"Sire, I really must pro..."

"Rupert, leave!"

The offended valet, turned on his heels and marched out the door, pulling it closed behind him.

"Arthur, you shouldn't be so mean to your servants," Alex said, taking a bite of a pastry meant for Arthur.

"What I really should do is talk to Sok and make him make this crap stop." Arthur threw back the covers and got out of bed.

He walked over to the wardrobe and opened its doors, hoping to find a pair of pants. All he could find were velvet breeches and frilly shirts. "I'm going to kill that elf!"

"Here," Alex said slipping out of the royal robe and handing it to Arthur. She pulled one of the frilly shirts out of the wardrobe and was about to pull it on when the door opened and a young girl walked in.

All three of them yelped in surprise.

The young girl covered her eyes and turned her head away. Arthur and Alex scrambled into the robe and the frilly shirt.

"What are you doing here?" Arthur demanded.

"Forgive me, sire. Finch sent me up to make the bed. I saw Rupert coming out and I thought you were dressed." She peeked between her fingers in time to see the royal sceptre before Arthur covered it with the robe.

"Well, that's just great. I thought it was a capitol offence to enter the king's private chambers without permission. And yet you are the third person today to waltz in here uninvited." Arthur was furious.

"Arthur," Alex warned. "Be nice."

"No!" Arthur yelled. "I will not be nice. I am the king. This is my room. I don't want a valet to dress me. And if I want my bed made for me, I'll ask someone to do it."

Alex sighed and made a face at him.

The young girl curtsied. "Forgive me, sire. I'll let Finch know." She left and as she did, she nearly bumped into Sok coming in.

"Oh, good, you are up. I was told you weren't awake yet." Sok walked past Arthur and Alex and helped himself to the only other pastry on the tray. Also intended for Arthur. "Why aren't you dressed? Council meets soon."

"Find me some normal clothes to put on and I'll get dressed," Arthur said, crossing his arms and glaring at his senior advisor.

"I told the tailors that you have conservative tastes, but you know how it is." Sok turned his attention to Alex. "Good morning, Alex! How was your first night as consort to the king?"

"Pretty good," Alex said. "I think I will like it here."

"Sok! I need some proper clothes."

"Good morning!" Hiro floated into the room on his hover gilly and helped himself to a sausage from the tray. "Arthur, you look upset."

"He is upset. He can't find anything to wear," Alex teased and explained at the same time.

Hiro looked at the open wardrobe. There were plenty of outfits in it. "I don't understand."

"He doesn't like the clothes the tailors made for him," Sok said.

"Oh! Well, I can fix that." He opened his satchel and pulled out pair of grey trousers, a navy vest with subtle embroidery and a simple, but classy cream shirt. Then he produced a pair of soft, leather shoes.

"That's much better," Arthur ducked behind a screen and swapped the royal robe for the clothes Hiro had given him. "Thank you," he said when he re- emerged.

"Ooh! Very handsome! Good job, Hiro." Alex clapped her hands. "Can you do me now?"

Hiro and Alex drifted off into a corner to discuss Alex's wardrobe for the day.

"Sok," Arthur said, "we need to talk."

"We need to get moving," a new voice called from the doorway.

Harpur walked in looking around the private chambers of the king. He took the remaining four sausages from the tray. "What happened to the maid? She was supposed to have come up to make the bed a while ago."

"She was here. I nearly bumped into her on my way in. But I don't know why she didn't make the bed." Sok pulled out a notebook and made a note to talk to Finch about the maid.

"I sent her away," Arthur said.

Behind him, Alex squealed with delight. "I love it!"

Arthur turned around to see what it was she loved. She was dressed in a pale-yellow gown with orange flowers on it. A brown leather corset encircled her torso. She was twirling like a five-year-old girl.

"...never heard of such a thing! What king refuses to let his servants do their jobs. I've not got time for this nonsense. Valets and maids crying all over the place and the king's very own bed still a mess. I see you've dressed yourself! Well, aren't you the clever one? But I'll not have this. Good valets are not easy to come by. Maids on the other hand... Get busy girl. That bed isn't going to make itself. I've half a mind to file a grievance..."

Finch had returned. With the maid, who avoided making eye-contact with Arthur as she curtsied her way over to make the bed.

"...not that it will help. Filed plenty of grievances in my day." Finch picked up the tray from the table. "You've barely touched your breakfast. Such a waste of food. I suppose the pigs will thank you, but don't expect me to be grateful. Walking up and down all those steps and you can't even be bothered to finish the food I prepared. Giving tarts pretty dresses isn't going to make their lives any easier. Can't wash floors in fancy gowns, now can you? You better not be on the rotation for this morning. I'll have you flogged if I find out you were supposed to..."

"That one's a real firecracker," Harpur said, waving the last sausage toward Finch's retreating back. "Ready to go, Arthur?"

"Will that be all, sire?" The maid curtsied next to the bed.

"Arthur, is there anything else you want added to the agenda for the council meeting today? Davynn will be sitting with you court after the meeting to help out with..."

"Enough!" Arthur yelled. "Everybody, get out!"

The maid scurried away. The others froze where they were and stared at Arthur. The only things moving in the room were eyeballs as they flicked back and forth looking for cues on how to proceed.

"I said, get out." Arthur spoke quietly, but no one mistook the volume of his seriousness.

Hiro whispered something to Alex and the two of them started to leave the room. Alex paused to put a hand on Arthur's arm. "I love you," she said quietly.

Arthur looked at her and then looked away. "I love you too," he mumbled, feeling bad, but needing to stand his ground.

"I'll just go let council know you'll be along soon." Sok followed Hiro and Alex out of the room.

Harpur sat down in a chair next to the table.

"I'm the king. You're supposed to do what I tell you," Arthur said, hands on his hips.

"I'm a dragon. Make me."

Arthur shook his head and chuckled softly. "I've already screwed up, haven't I?"

"Well, you were bound to sooner or later. Might as well get it over with on your first day."

"Gee, thanks."

"Arthur, there are bugs that need to be worked out. You'll get there. But you have to understand that these people have not had a king for months. They've been in limbo, wondering what was going to happen to them. They are just doing what they were trained to do. Finch is a housekeeper; she keeps house. She's a bit daft, but she knows how to run this place. Rupert is a valet; he dresses the king. Would it kill you to let them do their jobs?"

"It's weird."

"Not to them."

"I don't want people looking after me like that. And I don't want people popping in and out of my bedroom whenever they want. Don't I deserve a little privacy?"

"Sure. Again, these are just bugs that need to be worked out. In the meantime, though, you have duties to attend to. Being a king isn't just doing what you want when you want. It's a job. A huge job and today's the first day of that huge job. This is the day you will be making first impressions and those need to be a little more king-like and a lot less petty-tyrant-like. You get me?"

"Yeah," Arthur sighed. "I just don't know if I'm cut out for this."

"Nobody is," Harpur said, standing up and retrieving the circlet Arthur had dropped on the floor the night before. He put it on Arthur's head. "The trick is to cut it out to fit you."

And so, one journey came to an end while another one began.

Arthur would face many challenges in the days and months ahead. He learned how to pick his battles, how to delegate and who to delegate to. He learned to listen and not just to words. He learned to hear what people didn't say out loud. He learned how to negotiate, what to give into and what to hold onto. He learned how to keep the peace.

There were swordsmanship lessons, riding lessons, hunting lessons and endless life lessons. The lesson he learned the best, though, was to laugh at himself.

He was known throughout the land as King Arthur of the Dragon Fire and was lauded in story and song by bards. He was also known as the Naked King. But never to his face. Those songs were reserved for late at night in the public houses after the lights in the king's private chambers went out.

His reign would be filled with joys and sorrows, triumphs and defeats. And it all started that day in the council chambers and the court. With an apology.

"I'm sorry I'm late," Arthur said, striding into the chambers and standing at the head of the table. He pushed the chair that he was meant to sit in back away from the table.

The council members had all stood up and were waiting for their new king to sit before they could take their seats again.

"I know Sok has a long list of things we're supposed to talk about today, but there's something else I want to take care of."

"Sire?" one of the council members said.

"Help me move this table out of our way." He grabbed the edge, preparing to lift. "Go on."

Confused, the council members moved their own chairs back and then lifted the heavy table. Arthur directed them to put it down against the wall and then picked up an extra, plain chair from a line next to the door and hauled it to the centre of the room. Sitting down, he told the council to get chairs and form a circle with them.

"Here we are all equal," he announced. "Sok, please make a note to have a round table made." When Sok finished making the requested note, Arthur continued. "Before we get to the formal agenda, I'd like to take a few minutes for us all to get to know each other. I know you all know each other, but I'm new to this and I'd like to have a better idea of who you all are. We'll start on my left with Davynn and go around the circle. Tell me who you are, how you came to be on this council and what you hope to achieve as a council member."

The nine men all started to squirm in their seats. They looked at Sok as if asking if this was for real. Davynn, however, rose to the occasion. "I'm Davynn Willhart. I was a captain in the resistance against Edlyngton Bloomregaard," he began. "I'm not actually a member of the council. I'm here to assist our new king..."

"Oh, boy!" Alex said as she and Hiro joined Harpur at the back of the council chambers to watch Arthur's first day.

Harpur was leaning against the wall with his arms folded and his legs crossed at his ankles. He shifted to make room for the Krist and the cute hippie girl. "He'll be fine."

Epilogue

Hiro floated into the council chambers on his hover gilly and came to a stop next to the nearly empty circle of chairs where Harpur sat alone reflecting on all that had happened. The voices of those gathered in the court room drifted in as Arthur settled arguments and dispensed justice for the first time as King of Epoh. Harpur listened with his keen hearing whenever the new king spoke, but otherwise ignored the proceedings.

"I'm surprised you are not watching," Hiro said.

Harpur looked over at the Krist. "Do you want something?"

"I do," Hiro pulled Arthur's cell phone out of his satchel and held it up. "I believe that I can use this to rescue Anayah."

Harpur stared at the illegal device. He knew that Hiro had managed to send a message with it to Arthur once, which was the only reason he hadn't confiscated it when Arthur first came to this world. He had hoped that it might prove useful in other ways. "How?" he grunted.

"I believe that if I can find a safe way to amplify the signal from it, that I can use it to build a transporter. I've been consulting with Bon and he agrees."

"So, what do you need from me?"

"Your blessing."

"Arthur is the king now. Get the blessings you need from him." Harpur turned away from Hiro to resume his reflecting.

Hiro maneuvered the hover gilly over the chairs into the center of the circle. "I am not asking for your permission, Harpur. I'm asking for your blessing."

Harpur lifted his violet eyes until they were level with Hiro's grey ones and waited for the Krist to continue.

"Do you want me to try?"

Harpur shifted his gaze again and stared at the floor. Hiro was asking him not to plot to kill Analeetah for what she'd done to Anayah. He was asking Harpur to give him time to find a way to extract her from the Sphere peacefully. It was a concession to Harpur's deteriorating condition, one that would, if it worked, keep both the dragon and the witch safe. "I want Anayah to be free to live as she chooses," Harpur said at last. He would make no promises.

"Very well," Hiro said, taking that as the blessing he sought, "I will begin working on it immediately." He turned the hover gilly and floated toward the door to leave the dragon-wizard to his reflecting.

"Hiro?" Harpur called after him.

Hiro stopped, but did not turn around.

"Thank you."

The Krist's signature giggle wafted back to Harpur through the closing door.

Acknowledgements

This book would not have been possible without the help of some really amazing people.

First, my undying gratitude goes out to my editor Donna Call. Donna helped me find many hidden treasures in the story. Her encouragement and tireless effort kept me going on this adventure. Much love to you, my dear friend.

Finally, many thanks to Al and Deb for taking the time to read The Fire of Orhowyn and share their honest feedback with me.

About the Author

Saoirse Temple is the author of the *Bounders* trilogy—*The Fire of Orhowyn*, *The Amber Chalice*, and *The Power of Averborn*—as well as the *Dear Diary Style Files*, a humorous series on writing craft. An editor and book coach by trade, she delights in helping stories find their sharpest, brightest forms.

When she isn't writing or wrangling words, Saoirse can often be found sketching dragons, dreaming up new worlds, or coaxing inspiration out of a strong cup of tea.

Discover more at: **www.saoirsetemple.com**

The custom scene break symbol used in this book was created by Saoirse Temple. Visit https://www.saoirsetemple.com/category/all-products to purchase scene break symbols for use in your publications. To order your own custom scene break symbol, contact Saoirse directly at: saoirsealtemple@gmail.com

Follow Saoirse on

Facebook: www.facebook.com/saoirsetempe[1]

Instagram: @saoirsealt

---

1. http://www.facebook.com/saoirsetempe

www.ingramcontent.com/pod-product-compliance
Lightning Source LLC
Chambersburg PA
CBHW030744030726
47497CB00001B/122